Entities

The Selected Novels of Eric Frank Russell

Edited by Rick Katze

The NESFA Press
Post Office Box 809
Framingham, MA 01701

FIRST EDITION
Second Printing

International Standard Book Number:
1-886778-33-7
978-1-886778-33-7

For Esta Dorothy Katze,
a loving mother

Acknowledgments

The introductions to the novels by Jack L. Chalker are original to this volume.

Call Him Dead (Three To Conquer)-Astounding Science Fiction August, September, October, 1955.

*Next of Kin-*Dobson 1959.

Sinister Barrier-Unknown March 1939, Fantasy Press 1948.

Sentinels From Space-Startling November 1951, Bouregy, Curl 1953.

*Wasp-*Avalon 1957, Dobson 1958.

"Legwork"*-Astounding Science Fiction* April 1956.

"Mana"*-Astounding Science Fiction* December 1937.

"Mechanical Mice"*-Astounding Science Fiction* January 1941.

Editor's Introduction by Rick Katze is original to this volume.

Contents

Entities

The Selected Novels of
Eric Frank Russell

EDITOR'S INTRODUCTION

Four years ago I started a project to put Eric Frank Russell back into print. Last September *Major Ingredients* which contained 30 stories of the best short fiction of Eric Frank Russell was published by NESFA Press. At that time I indicated that there was still more that should be back in print. I learned a lot doing the first book. Thus it only took one year for this book to be produced.

It contains five novels, an introduction to each novel by Jack L. Chalker, who is also a fan of Russell, and three short stories which I could not squeeze into the first volume. The novels appear in the order that I wanted them to appear, the short stories appear after the novels.

Editors edit the books which you read. Among other things their job is to act as the final check that the story is readable and does not contain superfluous verbiage. Unfortunately once the final version has been produced, commercial decisions sometimes require a further editing or abridgement of the work in a later edition. Being a longtime reader I've always hated reading edited versions of the final work that had previously appeared in print.

Wasp and *Next of Kin* were reprinted in the U.S. in 1986 in their unabridged versions. All other U.S. editions were abridged. They are printed here in their unabridged format.

Jack L. Chalker in his introduction has talked a little about each of them. I think that they speak for themselves. Hopefully you will enjoy them as much as I have and still do.

"Mechanical Mice" was written under the pseudonym of Maurice G. Hugi. If you find other science fiction written by Hugi, please note that it was not written by Russell. Hugi was a real person who also wrote in the 1930s and 1940s.

For those of you who read the introduction to *Major Ingredients*, I noted that there were six pieces of short fiction that I could not put in that book. A number of readers have asked me to name those stories. Three of them appear in this book. "Seeker of Tomorrow," "The Saga of Pelican West" and "Symbiotica" were the other three stories.

Rick Katze
Norwood, MA
July 2001

9

WASP

Introduction by Jack L. Chalker

Wasp is Eric Frank Russell's most famous and most read novel, and you'll soon see why. It's fast, it's extremely clever, and it's the only World War II novel that I know of set in the Sirian Interstellar Empire.

It's a known fact that the last official fatality of World War I was a SF/fantasy/horror writer, William Hope Hodgson by name. By the time World War II came around, governments in both Britain and the U.S. had better uses for such minds, or at least some of them. Russell went to work in the office of naval intelligence as basically a clerk, but a clerk in the infamous XX or double cross intelligence section. His office was headed by a relatively junior British reservist and former attorney named Ewen Montagu, who had a penchant for *thinking obliquely,* as one associate put it. It was Montagu who became a legend by using the body of a pneumonia victim and a lot of skullduggery to convince the Germans that the allies were going to invade Greece, not Sicily, causing large numbers of German troops to be shifted to the wrong spot.

Montagu liked people who *thought obliquely,* too. After the success of "The Man Who Never Was" he had *carte blanche,* and he assigned a number of office personnel to think of all sorts of nasty, dirty, and debilitating tricks that could be played on the Axis to mess them up. One of the junior clerks in the Europe group was Ian Fleming, some of whose ideas were in fact used, and whose other ideas, too expensive or outlandish or impractical to do, found their way later into a series of novels about a certain British agent with a license to kill. Russell was on the Oriental Team, and there was the rub. The team researched and thought up all these wonderful things to do to the Japanese, but since Britain was so threatened and so close to Germany and so far from Japan none of them were ever put into action. Just as well: even Montagu never believed Russell's theory that a single man could, with minimal support, screw up a region so badly that its military potential would be severely diminished, and Russell could never prove the case.

And so, after the war, he put it all together in *Wasp*, a blueprint for wartime terrorism. Set in the far future, when Earth and its colonial empire faces off against the Sirian Empire in a grand interstellar conflict, it doesn't take a lot of detective work to just scratch the Sirian's purple skin and find Imperial Japan underneath. The Japanese secret police, their Gestapo, is right there at the start, only the *Tempeikai* become the *Kaitempei*. Almost nothing the hero uses in the book is futuristic; almost all of it could be done with Forties technology. Once you're on the alien planet, the whole sense of alienness drops away; you're no longer on another world, you're in another country. And in the story Russell gets to use his slick tricks and prove his point of the wasp.

Terrorism is bloodier and more ham-fisted today than Russell would have it. I've been concerned for a long time that the real message of *Wasp* is that if this sort of campaign is substituted for bombing buildings we may have *no* defense.

One comment: *Wasp* was cut by Avalon Books to fit a predetermined length when first published in the U.S. It's a good edit, but it is an *edit*. Subsequent U.S. paperback editions used the Avalon text so that for decades the only complete version was the one printed in Britain. In the late Eighties I convinced Del Rey to do a paperback using the complete text for the first time. That is the version you'll read here, just as Russell wrote it.

Chapter 1

He ambled into the room, sat in the indicated chair and said nothing. The baffled expression had been on his face quite a time and he was getting a bit tired of wearing it.

The big fellow who had brought him all the way from Alaska now departed, silently closing the door and leaving him alone with the man contemplating him from behind the desk. A small plaque informed that this character's name was William Wolf. It was inappropriate: he looked more like a bull moose.

Wolf said in hard, even tones, "Mr. Mowry, you are entitled to an explanation." A pause, followed by, "You will get one." Then he stared unblinkingly at his listener.

For a long-drawn minute James Mowry suffered the intent scrutiny before he asked, "When?"

"Soon."

With that, Wolf went on staring at him. The gaze was unpleasantly piercing, analytical, and the face around it was about as warm and expressive as a lump of hard rock.

"Mind standing up?"

Mowry stood up.

"Turn around."

He rotated, looking bored.

"Walk to and fro across the room."

He walked.

"Tsk-tsk!" grunted Wolf in a way that indicated neither pleasure nor pain. "I assure you, Mr. Mowry, that I am quite serious when I ask you to oblige by walking bow-legged."

Splaying his knees as much as possible, Mowry stumped around as if riding an invisible horse. Then he resumed his chair and said pointedly, "There'd better be money in this. I don't come three thousand miles and make like a clown for nothing."

"There's no money in it, not a cent," informed Wolf. "If lucky, there is life."

"And if out of luck?"

"Death."

"You're damnably frank about it," Mowry commented.

"In this job I have to be." Wolf stared at him again, long and penetratingly. "You'll do. Yes, I'm sure you'll do."

"Do for what?"

"I'll tell you in a moment." Opening a drawer, he extracted some papers, passed them across. "These will enable you better to understand the position. Read them through—they lead up to what follows."

Mowry glanced at them. They were typescript copies of press reports. Settling back in his chair he perused them slowly and with care.

The first told of a prankster in Romania. This fellow had done nothing more than stand in the road gazing fascinatedly at the sky, occasionally uttering ejaculations and loud phrases such as, "Blue flames!" Curious people had joined him and gaped likewise. The groups became a crowd, the crowd became a mob, and the bigger the mob the faster it grew.

Soon the audience blocked the street, overflowed into sidestreets. Police tried to break it up, making matters worse. Some fool summoned the fire squads. Hysterics on the fringes swore they could see or had seen something weird above the clouds. Reporters and cameramen rushed to the scene. Rumors raced around. The government sent up the air force for a closer look. Panic spread over an area of two hundred square miles from which the original cause had judiciously disappeared.

"Amusing if nothing else," remarked Mowry.

"Read on."

The second report concerned a daring escape from jail of two notorious killers. They had stolen a car, made six hundred miles before recapture. Their term of freedom had lasted exactly fourteen hours.

The third detailed an automobile accident. Three killed, one seriously injured, the car a complete wreck. The sole survivor had died nine hours later.

Handing back the papers, Mowry said, "What's all this to me?"

"We'll take those reports in the order as read," began Wolf. "They prove something of which we've long been aware but maybe you haven't realized yourself. For the first one, that Romanian did nothing, positively nothing save stare at the sky and mumble. All the same, he persuaded a government to start jumping around like fleas on a hot griddle. It shows that in given conditions action and reaction can be hopelessly out of proportion. Also that by doing insignificant things in suitable circumstances one can obtain results monstrously in excess of the effort."

"I'll give you that," Mowry conceded.

"Now the lamsters. They didn't do much either; climbed a wall, grabbed a car, drove like mad until the gasoline ran out, got caught." He leaned forward, continued with added emphasis, "But for most of fourteen hours they monopolized the attention of six planes, ten helicopters, one hundred and twenty patrol cars, eighteen telephone exchanges, uncountable phone lines and radio link-ups, not to mention police, deputies, posses of volunteers, hunters, trackers, forest rangers and National Guardsmen to a grand total of twenty-seven thousands scattered over three states."

"Phew!" Mowry raised his eyebrows.

"Finally, let's consider this auto smash. We know the cause; the survivor was able to tell us before he died. He said the driver lost control at speed while swiping at a wasp which had flown in through a window and started buzzing around his face."

"It nearly happened to me once."

Ignoring that, Wolf went on, "The weight of a wasp is under half an ounce. Compared with a human being its size is minute, its strength negligible. Its sole armament is a tiny syringe holding a drop of irritant, formic acid, and in this case it didn't even use it. Nevertheless it killed four big men and converted a large, powerful car into a heap of scrap."

"I see the point," agreed Mowry, "but where do I come in?"

"Right here," said Wolf. "We want you to become a wasp."

Leaning back, Mowry eyed the other contemplatively, then commented, "The muscle-bound lug who brought me here was a Secret Service agent who had satisfied me as to the genuineness of his credentials. This is a government department. You're a high-ranking official. But for those facts I'd say you're crazy."

"Maybe I am," gave back Wolf, blank-faced, "but I don't think so."

"You want me to do something?"

"Yes."

"Something extra-special?"

"Yes."

"At risk of death?"

"I'm afraid so."

"And for no reward?"

"Correct."

Mowry stood up, reached for his hat. "I'm not crazy either."

"You will be," said Wolf, in the same flat tones, "if you rest content to let the Sirians kick us out of existence."

Letting go the hat, Mowry sat down again, "What d'you mean?"

"There's a war on."

"I know. Everybody knows." He made a disparaging gesture. "We've been fighting the Sirian Combine for ten months. The newspapers say so. The radio says so. The video says so. The government says so. I am credulous enough to believe the lot of them."

"Then perhaps you're willing to stretch your credulity a bit further and swallow a few more items," Wolf suggested.

"Such as?"

"The Terran public is complacent because to date nothing has happened in this sector. They know that already the enemy has launched two determined attacks against our solar system and that both have been beaten off. The public has great confidence in Terran defenses. That confidence is justified; no Sirian task force will ever penetrate this far."

"Well, what have we to worry about?"

"Wars must be won or lost and there's no third alternative. We cannot win merely by keeping the foe at arm's length. We can never gain victory solely by postponing defeat." Suddenly and emphatically he slammed a heavy fist on his desk and made a pen leap two feet into the air. "We've got to do more than that. We've *got* to seize the initiative and get the enemy flat on his back while we beat the bejezus out of him."

"But we'll get around to that in due course, won't we?"

"Maybe," said Wolf. "Or maybe not. It depends."

"Depends upon what?"

"Whether we make full and intelligent use of our resources, especially people—meaning people such as you."

"You could be more specific," Mowry suggested.

"Look, in technical matters we are ahead of the Sirian Combine, a little ahead in some respects and far ahead in others. That gives us the advantage of better weapons, more efficient armaments. But what the public does not know—because nobody has seen fit to tell them—is that the Sirians also have an advantage. They outnumber us by twelve to one and outweigh us by material in the same proportion."

"Is that a fact?"

"Unfortunately it is, though our propagandists don't bother to mention it. Our war-potential is superior qualitatively. The Sirians have superiority quantitatively. That's a very serious handicap to us. We've got to counter it in the best way we know how. It won't be done by playing for time while we make the effort to breed like flies."

"I see." Mowry gnawed his bottom lip, looked thoughtful.

"However," Wolf went on, "the problem becomes less formidable than it looks if we bear in mind that one man can shake a government, two men temporarily can put down an army twenty-seven thousand strong, or one small wasp can slay four comparative giants and destroy their huge machine in the bargain." He paused, watching the other for effect, continued, "Which means that by scrawling suitable words upon a wall, the right man in the right place at the right time might immobilize an armored division with the aid of nothing more than a piece of chalk."

"You're concocting a pretty unorthodox form of warfare."

"So much the better."

"I am sufficiently perverse to like such methods. They appeal to me."

"We know," said Wolf. He took a file from his desk, thumbed through it. "Upon your fourteenth birthday you were fined one hundred Sirian guilders for expressing your opinion of an official, upon a wall, in letters twenty inches high. Your father apologized on your behalf and pleaded the impetuosity of youth. The Sirians were annoyed but let the matter drop."

"Razaduth was a scheming, pot-bellied liar and I say it again." Mowry eyed the file. "That my life-story you've got there?"

"Yes."

"Nosey lot, aren't you?"

"We have to be. Regard it as part of the price to be paid for survival." Shoving the file to one side, Wolf informed, "We've a punched card for every Terran in existence. In no time worth mentioning we can sort out electronically all those who have false teeth, or wear size eleven shoes, or had red-haired mothers, or can be relied upon to try to dodge the draft. Without trouble we can extract any specified type of sheep from the general mass of sheep and goats."

"And I am a specified sheep?"

"Speaking metaphorically, of course. No insult is intended." His face gave a craggy twitch that was the nearest it could come to a smile. "We first dug out about sixteen thousand completely fluent speakers of the several Sirian dialects. Eliminating the females and children brought the number down to nine thousand. Then, step by step, we cut out the elderly, the infirm, the weak, the untrustworthy, the temperamentally unsuitable, those too short, too tall, too fat, too thin, too stupid, too rash, too cautious, and so forth. We weren't left with many among whom we seek for wasps."

"What defines a wasp?"

"Several things—but mostly a shorty who can walk slightly bandy-legged with his ears pinned back and his face dyed purple. In other words, one who can play the part of a native-born Sirian and do it well enough to fool the Sirians."

"Never!" exclaimed Mowry. "Never in a month of Sundays! I'm pink, I've got wisdom teeth and my ears stick out."

"The surplus teeth can be pulled. Surgical removal of a sliver of cartilage will fasten your ears back good and tight, leaving no visible evidence of the operation. Painless and easy, with complete healing in two weeks. That is medical evidence, so don't argue it." Again the craggy twitch. "As for the purple complexion, it's nothing startling. There are some Terrans a good deal more purple-faced than any Sirian, they having acquired the color via many gallons of booze. We can fix you up with a dye guaranteed firm for four months, also a retinting kit that will enable you to carry on as much longer as may be necessary."

"But—"

"Listen to me. You were born in Masham, capital city of Diracta which is the Sirian home planet. Your father was a trader there at the time. You lived on Diracta until age seventeen when you returned with your parents to Terra. Luckily you happen to be a half-pint of just about Sirian size and build. You are now twenty-six and still speak perfect Sirian with a decided Mashambi accent which, if anything, is an advantage. It lends plausibility. About fifty million Sirians speak with Mashambi accents. You're a natural for the job we have in mind."

"What if I invite you to thrust the job right up the airshaft?" asked Mowry, with great interest.

"I would regret it," said Wolf, coldly, "because in time of war it is an old, well-founded adage that one volunteer is worth a thousand conscripts."

"Meaning I'd get my call-up papers?" Mowry made a gesture of irritation. "Damn!—I'd rather walk into something of my own accord than be frogmarched into it."

"So it says here," informed Wolf, motioning toward the file. "James Mowry, twenty-six, restless and pigheaded. Can be trusted to do anything at all—provided the alternative is worse."

"Sounds like my father. Did he tell you that?"

"The Service does not reveal its sources of information."

"Humph!" He pondered a little while, asked, "Suppose I volunteer, what follows?"

"We'll send you to a school. It runs a special course that is fast and tough and takes six to eight weeks. You'll be crammed to the gills with everything likely to be useful to you: weapons, explosives, sabotage, propaganda, psychological warfare, map reading, compass reading, camouflage, judo, radio techniques and maybe a dozen other subjects. By the time they've finished with you, you'll be fully qualified to function as a complete and absolute pain-in-the-neck."

"And after that?"

"You will be dropped surreptitiously upon a Sirian-held planet and be left to make yourself as awkward as possible."

There was a lengthy silence at the end of which Mowry gave begrudgingly, "Once when my father was thoroughly aggravated he said, 'Son, you were born a fool and you'll die a fool.' " He let go a long, deep sigh. "The old man was dead right. I hereby volunteer."

"We knew you would," said Wolf, imperturbably.

He saw Wolf again, that being two days after he had finished the arduous course and passed with satisfactory marks. Wolf arrived at the school, visited him in his room.

"What was it like?"

"Sheer sadism," said Mowry, pulling a face. "So almighty tough that I'm beaten up in mind and body. I feel like a half-stunned cripple."

"You'll have plenty of time to get over that. The journey will take long enough. You're leaving Thursday."

"For where?"

"Sorry, I can't tell you. Your pilot carries sealed orders to be opened only on the last lap. In case of accident or successful interception he destroys them unread."

"What's the likelihood of us being grabbed on the way there?"

"Not great. Your ship will be considerably faster than anything the enemy possesses. But even the best of vessels can get into trouble once in a while. We're taking no chances. You know the stinking reputation of the Sirian Security Police, the Kaitempi. They can make a slab of granite grovel and confess its sins. If they snatch you en route and learn your intended destination they'll take counter-measures and try to trap your successor on arrival."

"My successor? That raises a question nobody here seems willing to answer. Maybe you can tell me, huh?"

"What is it?" asked Wolf.

"Will I be entirely on my own? Or will other Terrans be operating on the same planet? If there will be others how shall I make contact?"

"So far as you're concerned you'll be the only Terran for a hundred million miles around," responded Wolf. "You will have no contacts. By the same token, you won't be able to betray anyone to the Kaitempi. Nothing they can do will extract from you information that you don't possess. Maybe you'll sweat and scream and invent stuff to make them lay off, but it won't be genuine information."

"It would sound better if you didn't smack your lips over the horrid prospect," reproved Mowry. "Anyway, it would be some comfort and encouragement to know that other wasps are similarly active even if only one to a planet."

"You didn't go through this course all on your ownsome, did you? The others weren't here merely to provide company for you." Wolf held out a hand. "Good hunting, be a curse to the foe—*and come back.*"

"I shall return," assured Mowry, "though the way be flinty and the road be long."

That, he thought as Wolf departed, was more of a pious hope than a performable promise. To be dropped single-handed upon a hostile planet was to be plunged neck-deep into a genuinely menacing situation. Casualties could be expected sooner or later. Indeed, Wolf's remark about "your successor" showed that losses had been anticipated and steps taken to provide replacements.

It then occurred to him that perhaps his own status was that of somebody else's successor. Maybe on the world to which he was going some unlucky character had been trapped and pulled apart very slowly. If so, it would be a world forewarned and ready for him. Right now the Kaitempi would be watching the skies, licking their chops in anticipation of their next victim, a dope named James Mowry, twenty-six, restless and pigheaded.

Oh, well, he had committed himself and there was no backing out. Looked like he was doomed to become a hero from sheer lack of courage to be a coward. Slowly he developed a philosophic resignation which still possessed him several weeks later when the corvette's captain summoned him to the mid-cabin.

"Sleep well?"

"Not in the last spell," Mowry admitted. "The propulsors were noisier than usual, the whole ship shuddered and creaked. I spent most of the time lying in my bunk and inventing new cuss-words."

The captain gave a wry smile. "You didn't know it, but we were being chased by four Sirian destroyers. We hit up top speed and lost them."

"You sure they aren't still tracking us?"

"They've fallen behind range of our detectors, therefore we're beyond range of theirs."

"Thank heavens for that," said Mowry.

"I've opened the orders. We're due to arrive in forty-eight Earth-hours."

"Where?"

"On a planet called Jaimec. Ever heard of it?"

"Yes, the Sirian news channels used to mention it every once in a while. It's one of their outpost worlds if I remember right, under-populated and not half developed. I never met anyone from there and so don't know much about it." He registered mild annoyance. "This secretiveness is all very well, but it would help a fellow some to let him know where he's going and give him some useful information about the place before he gets there. Ignorance could prove damn dangerous; it might cost me my neck. Maybe I'm finicky but I value my neck."

"You'll land with all the data we've got," soothed the captain. "They've supplied a stack of stuff along with the orders." He put a wad of papers on the table, also several maps and a number of large photographs. Then he pointed to a cabinet standing against a wall. "That's the stereoscopic viewer. Use it to search these pics for a suitable landing place. The choice is wholly yours. My job is to put you down safely wherever you choose and get away undetected."

"How long have I got?"

"You must show me the selected spot not later than forty hours from now."

"And how long can you allow for dumping me and my equipment?"

"Twenty minutes maximum. Positively no more. I'm sorry about that but it can't be helped. If we sit on the ground and take it easy we'll leave unmistakable signs of our landing, a whacking big rut that can soon be spotted by air patrols and will get the hunt after you in full cry. So we'll have to use the antigravs and move fast. The antigravs soak up power. Twenty minutes' output is the most we can afford."

"All right." Mowry gave a shrug of resignation, took up the papers and started reading them as the captain went out.

Jaimec, ninety-fourth planet of the Sirian Empire. Mass seven-eighths that of Terra. Land area about half that of Terra's, the rest being ocean. First settled two and a half centuries ago. Present population estimated at about eighty millions. Jaimec had cities, railroads, spaceports and all the other features of alien civilization. Nevertheless, much of it remained undeveloped, unexplored and in primitive condition.

He spent a good many hours making close, meticulous study of the planet's surface as shown in the stereoscopic viewer, meanwhile wondering how the big photos had been obtained. Evidently someone had taken a considerable risk to play close with an aerial camera. War had a hundred unsung heroes for every one praised and draped with medals.

By the fortieth hour he had made his choice. It had not been easy to reach a decision. Every seemingly suitable dropping-place had some kind of disadvantage, proving yet again that the ideal hideout does not exist. One would be beautifully positioned from the strategic viewpoint but lack adequate cover. Another would have first-class natural concealment but dangerous location.

The captain came in saying, "I hope you've picked a point on the night-side. If it isn't, we'll have to dodge around until dark and that's not good. The best technique is to go in and get out before they've time to take alarm and organize a counter-blow."

"This is it." Mowry indicated the place on a photo. "It's a lot farther from a road than I'd have liked, about twenty miles and all of it through virgin forest. Whenever I need something out of the cache it will take me a day's hard going to reach it, maybe two days. But by the same token it should remain safe from prying eyes and that's the prime consideration."

Sliding the photo into the viewer, the captain switched on the interior lighting and looked into the rubber eyepiece. He frowned with concentration.

"You mean that marked spot on the cliff?"

"No—it's at the cliff's base. See that outcrop of rock? What's a fraction north of it?"

The captain stared again. "It's hard to tell for certain but it looks mighty like a cave formation." He backed off, picked up the intercom phone. "Hame, come here, will you?"

Hamerton, the chief navigator, arrived and studied the photo, found the indicated point. He compared it with a two-hemisphere map of Jaimec, made swift calculations.

"We'll catch it on the night-side but only by the skin of our teeth."

"You sure of that?"

"If we went straight there we'd make it with a couple of hours to spare. But we daren't go straight; their radar network would plot the dropping-point to within half a mile. So we'll have to dodge around below their radar horizon. Evasive action takes time but with luck we can complete the drop half an hour before sunrise."

"Let's go straight there," prompted Mowry. "It will cut your risks and I'm willing to take a chance on being nabbed. I'm taking the chance anyway, aren't I?"

"Nuts to that," retorted the captain. "We're so close that their detectors are tracking us already. We're picking up their identification-calls and we can't answer, not knowing their code. Pretty soon it will sink into their heads that we're hostile. They'll send up a shower of proximity-fused missiles, as usual too late. The moment we dive below their radar horizon they'll start a full-scale aerial search covering five hundred miles around the point where we disappeared." He gave Mowry a warning frown. "And you, chum, would be dead center of that circle."

"Looks like you've done this job a few times before," prompted Mowry, hoping for a revealing response.

Refusing to take the bait, the captain continued. "Once we're running just above tree-top level they can't track us radar-wise. So we'll duck down a couple of thousand miles from your dropping-point and make for there on a cockeyed course. It's my responsibility to dump you where you want to be put without betraying you to the whole lousy world. If I don't succeed the entire trip has been wasted. Leave this to me, will you?"

"Sure," agreed Mowry, abashed. "Anything you say."

They went out, leaving him to brood. Presently the alarm-gong clanged upon the cabin wall, he grabbed handholds and hung on while the ship made a couple of violent swerves, first one way, then the other. He could see nothing, hear nothing save the dull moan of steering-jets, but his imagination pictured a cluster of fifty ominous vapor-trails rising from below, fifty long, explosive cylinders eagerly sniffing around for the scent of alien metal.

Eleven more times the alarm sounded, followed at once by aerial acrobatics. By now the ship resounded to the soft whistle of passing atmosphere which built up to a faint howl as it thickened.

Getting near now.

Mowry gazed absently at his fingers. They were steady but sweaty. There were queer electric thrills running up and down his spine. His knees felt weak and his stomach felt weaker. He prayed for enough resolution to land without spewing in plain sight of everybody. Hell of a hero he'd look if he did that.

Far away across the void was a planet with a fully comprehensive card-system and because of that he was about to have his pointed head shoved into the lion's mouth. Mentally he damned card-systems, those who'd invented them, those who operated them. The cussing relieved his feelings somewhat but did not restore strength to his knees.

With the arrival so close the philosophic resignation that had sustained him had now evaporated. He fidgeted nervily around, occasionally grabbing the hand holds, heartily wishing the whole dirty business were done with and over.

By the time propulsion ceased and the ship stood silently upon its antigravs above the selected spot he had generated the fatalistic impatience of a man facing a major operation that no longer can be avoided. He half-ran, half-slid down the nylon ladder to ground. A dozen of the corvette's crew followed, equally in a hurry but for different reasons. They worked like maniacs, all the time keeping a wary eye upon the sky.

Chapter 2

The cliff was part of an upthrust plateau rising four hundred feet above the forest. At bottom were two caves, one wide and shallow, one narrow but deep. Before the caves stretched a beach of tiny pebbles at the edge of which a small stream swirled and bubbled.

Cylindrical duralumin containers, thirty in all, were lowered from the ship's belly to the beach, seized and carried to the back of the deep cave, stacked so that the code numbers on their lids faced the light. That done, the twelve scrambled monkeylike up the ladder which was promptly reeled in. An officer waved a hand from the open lock, shouted a last word of encouragement.

"Give 'em hell, Sonny."

The corvette's tail snorted and whumped, making trees wave their tops in a mile-long lane of superheated air. That in itself added to the list of possible risks; if the leaves got scalded, withered and changed color, a scouting airplane would view the phenomenon as a gigantic arrow pointing to the cave. But it was a chance that had to be taken. With swiftly increasing speed the big vessel went away, keeping low and turning in the distance to follow the valley northward.

Watching it depart, Mowry knew that it would not yet head straight for home. First the crew would take added chances for his sake by zooming in plain view over a number of cities and military strongholds. With luck this tactic might persuade the enemy to jump to the conclusion that it was engaged in photographic reconnaissance, that no surreptitious landing of personnel had been intended or performed.

The testing time would come during the long hours of daylight and already dawn was breaking to one side. Systematic aerial search in the vicinity would prove that the enemy's suspicions had been aroused in spite of the corvette's misleading antics. Lack of visible search would not prove the contrary because for all he knew the hunt might be up elsewhere, in the wrong place far beyond his sight and hearing.

Full light would be needed for his trek through the forest, the depths of which were dark enough even at midday. While waiting for the sun to rise he sat on a boulder and gazed in the direction in which the ship had gone. He wouldn't have that captain's job, he decided, for a sack of diamonds. And probably the captain wouldn't have his for two sacks.

After an hour he entered the cave, opened a container, drew from it a well-worn leather case of indisputable Sirian manufacture. There'd be no sharp eyes noting something foreign-looking about that piece of luggage; it was his own property purchased in Masham, on Diracta, many years ago.

Making an easy jump across the little stream he went into the forest and headed westward, frequently checking his direction with the aid of a pocket compass. The going proved rough but not difficult. The forest was wholly a forest and not a jungle. Trees grew large and close together, forming a canopy that shut out all but occasional glimpses of the sky. Luckily, undergrowth was sparse. One could walk with ease and at fast pace providing one took care not to fall over projecting roots. Also, as he soon realized, progress was helped quite a piece by the fact that on Jaimec his weight was down by most of twenty pounds while his luggage was reduced in the same proportion.

Two hours before sunset he reached the road, having covered twenty miles with one stop for a meal and many brief pauses to consult the compass. Behind a roadside tree he upended the case, sat on it and enjoyed fifteen minutes' rest before making wary survey of the road. So far he'd heard no planes or scout-ships snooping overhead in frantic search of Terra's one-man task force. Neither was there any abnormal activity upon the road; in fact during his wait nothing passed along it in either direction.

Refreshed by the sit, he tidied himself, brushed dirt and leaves from his shoes and pants, reknotted his typical neckscarf as only a Sirian could knot it. Then he examined himself in a steel mirror. His Earthmade copy of Sirian clothes would pass muster, he had no doubt of that. His purple face, pinned-back ears and Mashambi accent would be equally convincing. But his greatest protection would be the mental block in every Sirian's mind; they'd just naturally not think of an Earthman masquerading as a Sirian because the idea was too ridiculous to contemplate.

Satisfied that he fitted his role a hundred percent, he emerged from the shelter of the trees, walked boldly across the road and from the other side made careful study of his exit from the forest. It was essential that he should be able to remember it speedily and accurately. The forest was the screen of camouflage around his bolthole and there was no telling when he might need to dive into it in a deuce of a hurry.

Fifty yards farther along the road stood an especially tall tree with a peculiarly wrapped growth around its trunk and a very gnarly branch formation. He fixed it firmly in his mind and for good measure lugged a tablet-shaped slab of stone onto the grass verge and stood it upright beneath the tree.

The result resembled a lonely grave. He stared at the stone and with no trouble at all could imagine words inscribed upon it: *James Mowry—Terran. Strangled by the Kaitempi.* Could be an omen, a forecast that already he had signed his own death warrant. There was a compensatory comfort: he did not believe in omens.

Dismissing ugly thoughts about the Kaitempi, he started trudging along the road, his gait suggestive of a slight bow-leggedness. From now on he must be wholly a Sirian, physically and mentally, name of Shir Agavan, a forestry surveyor employed by the Jaimec Ministry of Natural Resources, therefore a government official and exempt from military service. Or he could be anyone else so long as he remained plainly and visibly a Sirian and could produce the papers to prove it.

He moved good and fast while slowly the sun sank toward the horizon. He was going to thumb a lift, wanted one with the minimum of delay but also wanted it as far as possible from the point where he'd left the forest. It would be wise to divert attention from the real scene of his appearance. Like everyone else, Sirians had tongues. They talked. Others listened. Some hard-faced characters had the full-time jobs of listening, putting two and two together and without undue strain arriving at four. His chief peril came not from guns and garroting-cords but from over-active tongues and alert ears.

More than a mile had been covered before two dynocars and one gas-truck passed him in quick succession, all going the opposite way. None of the occupants favored him with more than a perfunctory glance. Another mile went by before anything came in his own direction. This was another gas-truck, a big, dirty, lumbering monstrosity that wheezed and grunted as it rolled along.

Standing by the shoulder, he waved it down, putting on an air of arrogant authority that never failed to impress all Sirians save those with more arrogance and authority. The truck stopped jerkily and with a tailward boost of fumes. It was loaded with about twenty tons of edible roots. Two Sirians looked down at him from the cab. They were unkempt, their clothes baggy and soiled.

"I am of the government," informed Mowry, giving the statement the right degree of importance. "I wish a ride into town."

The nearest one opened the door, moved closer to the driver and made room. Mowry climbed up, squeezed into the benchseat which was a close fit for three. He held his case on his knees. The truck emitted a loud bang and lurched forward while the Sirian in the middle gazed dully at the case.

"You are a Mashamban, I think," ventured the driver, conversationally.

"Correct. Seems we can't open our mouths without betraying the fact."

"I have never been to Masham," continued the driver using the singsong accents peculiar to Jaimec. "I would like to go there someday. It is a great place." He switched to his fellow Sirian. "Isn't it, Snat?"

"Yar," said Snat, still mooning at the case.

"Besides, Masham or anywhere on Diracta should be a lot safer than here. And perhaps I'd have better luck there. It has been a bad day. It has been a stinking bad day. Hasn't it, Snat?"

"Yar," said Snat.

"Why?" asked Mowry.

"This *soko* of a truck has broken down three times since dawn. And it has stuck in the bog twice. The last time we had to empty it to get it out, and then refill it. With the load we've got that is work. Hard work." He spat out the window. "Wasn't it, Snat?"

"Yar," said Snat, still half-dead from the effort.

"Too bad," Mowry sympathized.

"As for the rest, you know of it," said the driver, irefully. "It has been a bad day."

"I know of what?" Mowry prompted.

"The news."

"I have been in the woods since sunup. One does not hear news in the woods."

"The ten-time radio announced an increase in the war-tax. As if we aren't paying enough. Then the twelve-time radio said a Spakum ship had been zooming around. They had to admit it because the ship was fired upon from a number of places. We are not deaf when guns fire, nor blind when the target is visible." He nudged his fellow. "Are we, Snat?"

"Nar," confirmed Snat.

"Just imagine that—a lousy Spakum ship sneaking around over our very rooftops. You know what *that* means: they are seeking targets for bombing. Well, I hope none of them get through. I hope every Spakum that heads this way runs straight into a break-up barrage."

"So do I," said Mowry, squirting pseudo-patriotism out of his ears. He gave his neighbor a dig in the ribs. "Don't you?"

"Yar," said Snat.

For the rest of the journey the driver maintained his paean of anguish about the general lousiness of the day, the iniquity of truck-builders, the menace and expense of war and the blatant impudence of an enemy ship that had surveyed Jaimec in broad daylight. All the time Snat lolled in the middle of the cab, gaped glassy-eyed at Mowry's leather case and responded in monosyllables only when metaphorically beaten over the head.

"This will do," announced Mowry as they trundled through city suburbs and reached a wide crossroad. The truck stopped, he got down. "Live long!"

"Live long!" responded the driver and tooled away.

He stood on the sidewalk and thoughtfully watched the truck until it passed from sight. Well, he'd put himself to the first minor test and got by without suspicion. Neither the driver nor Snat had nursed the vaguest idea that he was what they called a Spakum—literally a bed bug—an abusive term for Terrans to which he'd listened with no resentment whatsoever. Nor should he resent it: until further notice he was Shir Agavan, a Sirian born and bred.

Holding tight to his case, he entered the city.

This was Pertane, capital of Jaimec, population a little more than two million. No other place on the planet approached it in size. It was the center of Jaimecan civil and military administration, the very heart of the foe's planetary stronghold. By the same token it was potentially the most dangerous area in which a lone Terran could wander on the loose.

Reaching the downtown section, Mowry tramped around until twilight, weighed up the location and external appearance of several small hotels. Finally he picked one in a sidestreet off the main stem. Quiet and modest-looking, it would serve for a short time while he sought a better hideout. But having reached a decision he did not go straight in.

First it was necessary to make an up-to-the-minute check of his papers lest anything wrong with them should put a noose around his neck. The documents with which he had been provided were microscopically accurate replicas of those valid within the Sirian Empire nine or ten months ago. They might have changed the format in the interim. To present for examination papers obviously long out of date was to ask to be nabbed on the spot.

He'd be trapped in a hotel, behind doors, with Sirians all around. Better the open street where if it came to the worst he could throw away his case along with his bandy-legged gait and run like the devil in pursuit of a virgin. So he ambled casually past the hotel, explored nearby streets until he found a policeman. Glancing swiftly around, he marked his getaway route and went up to the officer.

"Pardon, I am a newcomer." He said it stupidly, wearing an expression of slight dopiness. "I arrived from Diracta a few days ago."

"You are lost, *hi?*"

"No, officer, I am embarrassed." He fumbled in a pocket, produced his identity-card, offered it for inspection. His leg muscles were tensed in readiness for swift and effective flight as he went on, "A Pertanian friend tells me that my card is wrong because it must now bear a picture of my nude body. This friend is a persistent prankster. I do not know whether he is to be believed."

Frowning, the policeman examined the card's face. He turned it over, studied its back. Then he returned it to Mowry.

"This card is quite in order. Your friend is a liar. There is no such silly regulation. He would be wise to keep his mouth shut." The frown grew deeper. "If he does not he will someday regret it. The Kaitempi are rough with those who spread false rumors."

"Yes, officer," said Mowry, vastly relieved but looking suitably frightened. "I shall warn him not to be a fool. May you live long!"

"Live long!" said the policeman, curtly.

Hurrah! He went back to the hotel, walked in as though he owned it, said to the clerk, "I wish a room with bath for ten days."

"Your instrument of identity?"

He passed the card across.

The clerk wrote down its details, handed it back, reversed the register on the counter and pointed to a line. "Sign here."

On taking the room his first act was to have a welcome wash. Then he reviewed his position. He had reserved the room for ten days but that was mere camouflage since he had no intention of staying that long in a place so well surveyed by official eyes. If Sirian habits held good for Jaimec he could depend upon some snoop examining the hotel register and, perhaps, asking awkward questions before the week was through. He had all the answers ready—but the correct wasp-tactic is not to be asked so long as it can be avoided.

He'd arrived too late in the day to seek and find better sanctuary. Tomorrow would be well-spent hunting and finding a rooming-house, preferably in a district where inhabitants tended to mind their own business. Meanwhile he could put in two or three hours before bedtime by exploring Pertane, studying the lie of the land and estimating future possibilities.

Before starting out he treated himself to a hearty meal. To a native-born Terran the food would have seemed strange and somewhat obnoxious. But he ate it with gusto, its flavors serving only to remind him of his childhood. It wasn't until he had finished that it occurred to him to wonder whether some other less well-equipped wasp had ever betrayed himself by being sick at a Sirian table.

For the rest of the evening his exploration of Pertane was not as haphazard as it looked. He wandered around with seeming aimlessness, memorizing all geographical features that might prove useful to recall later on. But primarily he was seeking to estimate the climate of public opinion with particular reference to minority opinions.

In every war, no matter how great a government's power, its rule is never absolute. In every war, no matter how allegedly righteous the cause, the effort is never total. No campaign has ever or will ever be fought with the leadership united in favor of it and with the rank and file unitedly behind them.

Always there is a disgruntled minority that opposes a war for a multitude of reasons such as reluctance to make necessary sacrifices, fear of personal loss or suffering, philosophical and ethical objection to warfare as a method of settling disputes, lack of confidence in the ability of the leadership, resentment at being called upon to play a subordinate role, pessimistic belief that victory is far from certain and defeat very possible, egoistic satisfaction of refusing to run with the herd, psychological opposition to being yelled at on any and every petty pretext, a thousand and one other reasons.

No political or military dictatorship ever has been one hundred percent successful in identifying and suppressing the malcontents who, typically, conceal themselves behind a veil of silence and bide their time. By sheer law of averages Jaimec must have its share of such as these. And in addition to the pacifists and quasi-pacifists were the criminal classes whose sole concern in life was to snatch an easy profit while dexterously avoiding involvement in anything deemed unpleasant such as mass antics on a barrack square.

A wasp could make good use of all those who would not heed the bugle-call nor follow the beat of the drum. Indeed, even if it proved impossible to trace any of them and employ them individually he could still exploit the fact of their very existence. All that was necessary was first to satisfy himself that there really was such a minority on Jaimec.

By midnight he was back at the hotel confident that in Pertane there lived an adequate supply of scapegoats. On buses and in bars he'd had fragmentary conversations with about forty citizens and had overheard the talk of a hundred more.

Not one had uttered a word definable as unpatriotic, much less treacherous or subversive. Strong, deep-rooted fear of the Kaitempi was more than enough to deter them from condemning themselves out of their own mouths. But at least a tenth of them had spoken with that vague, elusive air of having more on their minds than they cared to state. In some cases two of this type conversed together and when that happened it was done with a sort of conspiratorial understanding that any onlooker could recognize from fifty yards away but could never produce as evidence before a military court.

Yes, these—the objectors, the selfish, the greedy, the resentful, the conceited, the moral cowards and the criminals—could all be utilized for Terran purposes. When it isn't expedient to use one's own strength, then is the time to exploit the enemy's weakness.

While lying in bed and waiting for sleep to come, he mentally enrolled the whole of this secret opposition in a mythical, dreamed-up organization called *Dirac Angestun Gesept,* the Sirian Freedom Party. He then appointed himself the D.A.G.'s president, secretary, treasurer and field-director for the planetary district of Jaimec. The fact that the entire membership was unaware of its status and had no hand in the election did not matter a hoot. It was irrelevant.

Neither did it matter that sooner or later the aggravated Kaitempi would start organizing the collection of members' dues in the form of strangled necks, or that some members might be so lacking in enthusiasm for the cause as to resist payment. If some Sirians could be given the full-time job of hunting down and garroting other Sirians, and if other Sirians could be given the full-time job of dodging or shooting down the garroters, then a distant and different life form would be saved a few unpleasant chores.

With that happy thought James Mowry alias Shir Agavan dozed off. His breathing was suspiciously slow and regular for the purple-faced lifeform he was supposed to be, his snores were abnormally low-pitched and he snoozed flat on his back instead of lying on his belly. But in the privacy of this room there were none to hear and see a Terran with his defenses momentarily down.

When one man is playing the part of an invading army the essential thing is to move fast, make full use of any and every opportunity, waste no effort. Mowry had to traipse around the city to find a better hideout. It was equally necessary to go hither and thither to make the first moves in his game. So he combined the two purposes.

He unlocked his bag, opening it carefully with the aid of a special non-conducting plastic key. Despite that he knew exactly what he was doing a thin trickle of sweat ran down his spine while he did it. The lock was not as innocent as it looked, in fact it was a veritable death-trap. He could never quite get rid of the feeling that one of these days it might forget that a plastic key is not a metal lock-pick. If ever it did so blunder the resulting blast-area would have a radius of one hundred yards.

Apart from the lethal can wired to the lock, the bag held a dozen small parcels, a mass of printed paper and nothing else. The paper was of two kinds: stickers and money. There was plenty of the latter. In terms of Sirian guilders he was a million-aire. Or with the further supply in that distant cave he was a multi-millionaire.

From the bag he took an inch-thick wad of printed stickers. Not too many of them. Just enough for a day's fast work and, at the same time, few enough to toss away unobserved should the necessity arise. That done, he refastened the bag with the same care, the same beading of perspiration.

It was a tricky business, this continual fiddling with a potential explosion, but it had one great advantage. If any official nosey-poke took it into his head to search the room and check the luggage he would destroy the evidence along with him-self. Moreover, proof of what had happened would be widespread enough to give clear warning to the homecomer: Mowry would turn into the street, take one look at the mess and discreetly fade from sight.

Departing, he caught a cross-town bus, planted the first sticker on the front window of its upper deck at a moment when all other seats were vacant. He dis-mounted at the next stop, casually watched a dozen people boarding the bus. Half of them went upstairs.

The sticker said in bold, easily readable print: *War makes wealth for the few, misery for the many. At the right time Dirac Angestun Gesept will punish the former, bring aid and comfort to the latter.*

That would hit the readers much harder than it would have done a month ago. It was sheer luck that he'd arrived coincidentally with a big boost in the war-tax. It was likely they'd feel sufficiently aggrieved not to tear the sticker down in a patriotic fury. Chances were equally good that they'd spread the news about this new, mysterious movement that had emerged to challenge the government, the military caucus and the Kaitempi. The tale would lose nothing in the telling: gos-sip is the same in any part of the mighty cosmos in that it gains compound inter-est as it goes the rounds.

Within five and a half hours he'd got rid of eighty stickers without once being caught in the act of fixing them. He'd taken a few risks, had a few narrow squeaks, but never was seen actually performing the dirty deed. What followed the plant-ing of the fifty-sixth sticker gave him most satisfaction.

A minor collision on the street caused abusive shouts between drivers and drew a mob of onlookers. Taking prompt advantage of the situation, Mowry slapped number fifty-six bang in the middle of a shop window while backed up against it by the crowd all of whom were looking the other way. He then wormed himself forward and got well into the mob before somebody noticed the window's adorn-ment and attracted general attention to it. The audience turned around, Mowry with them, and gaped at the discovery.

The finder, a gaunt, middle-aged Sirian with pop eyes, pointed an incredulous finger and stuttered, "Just l-l-look at that! They must be m-mad in that shop. The Kaitempi will take them all to p-p-prison."

Mowry edged forward for a better look and read the sticker aloud. *"Those who stand upon the platform and openly approve the war will stand upon the scaffold and weepingly regret it. Dirac Angestun Gesept."* He put on a frown. "The people in the shop can't be responsible for this—they wouldn't dare."

"S-somebody's dared," said Pop Eyes, quite reasonably.

"Yar." Mowry gave him the hard eye. "You saw it first. So maybe it was you, *hi?*"

"Me?" Pop Eyes went a very pale mauve, that being the nearest a Sirian could get to sheet-white. *"I* didn't put it there. You think I'm c-crazy?"

"Well, as you said, somebody did."

"It wasn't me," denied Pop Eyes, angry and agitated. "It must have been s-some crockpat."

"Crackpot," Mowry corrected.

"That's what I just s-said."

Another Sirian, younger and shrewder, chipped in with, "That's not a loony's work. There's more to it than that."

"Why?" demanded Pop Eyes.

"A solitary nut would be more likely to scribble things. Silly ones too." He nodded indicatively toward the subject of discussion. "That's a professional print job. It's also a plain, straightforward threat. Somebody risked his neck to plaster it up there but that didn't stop him. I'll bet there's an illegal organization back of that stunt."

"It says so, doesn't it?" interjected a voice. "The Sirian Freedom Party."

"Never heard of it," commented another.

"You've heard of it now," said Mowry.

"S-s-somebody ought to do s-something about it," declared Pop Eyes, waving his arms around.

S-s-somebody did, to wit, a cop. He muscled through the crowd, looked on the pavement for the body, bent down and felt around in case the victim happened to be invisible. Finding nothing, he straightened up, glowered at the audience and growled, "Now, what's all this?"

Pop Eyes pointed again, this time with the proprietary air of one who has been granted a patent on the discovery. "S-see what it s-says on the window."

The cop looked and saw. Being able to read, he perused it twice while his face went several shades more purple. Then he returned attention to the crowd.

"Who did this?"

Nobody knew.

"You've got eyes—don't you use them?"

Apparently they didn't.

"Who saw this first?"

"I did," said Pop Eyes proudly.

"But you didn't see anyone put it up?"

"No."

The cop stuck out his jaw. "You sure of that?"

"Yes, officer," admitted Pop Eyes, becoming nervous. "There was an accident in the s-street. We were all watching the two d-d-d-" He got himself into a vocal tangle and choked.

Waving him away, the cop addressed the crowd with considerable menace. "If anyone knows the identity of the culprit and refuses to reveal it, he will be deemed equally guilty and will suffer equally when caught."

Those in front backed off a yard or two, those in the rear suddenly discovered they had business elsewhere. A hard core of thirty of the incurably curious stayed put, Mowry among them.

Mowry said mildly, "Maybe they could tell you something in the shop."

The cop scowled. "I know my job, Shortass."

With that, he gave a loud snort, marched into the shop and bawled for the manager. In due course that worthy came out, examined his window with horror and swiftly acquired all the symptoms of a nervous wreck.

"We know nothing of this, officer. I assure you that it is no work of ours. It isn't *inside* the window, officer. It is outside, as you can see. Some passer-by must have done it. I cannot imagine why he should have picked on *this* window. Our patriotic devotion is unquestioned and—"

"Won't take the Kaitempi five seconds to question it," said the cop, cynically.

"But I myself am a reserve officer in the—"

"Shut up!" He jerked a heavy thumb toward the offending sticker. "Get it off."

"Yes, officer. Certainly, officer. I shall remove it immediately."

The manager started digging with his nails at the sticker's corners in an attempt to peel it off. He didn't do so good because Terran technical superiority extended even to common adhesives. After several futile efforts he threw the cop an apologetic look, went inside, came out with a knife and tried again. This time he succeeded in tearing a small triangle from each corner, leaving the message intact.

"Get hot water and soak it off," commanded the cop, rapidly losing patience. He turned and shooed the audience. "Beat it. Go on, get moving."

The crowd mooched reluctantly away. Mowry glanced back from the far corner, saw the manager emerge with a steaming bucket and get busy swabbing the notice. He grinned to himself, knowing that hot water was just the thing to release and activate the hydrofluoric base beneath the print.

Continuing on his way, Mowry disposed of two more stickers where they'd best be seen and cause the most annoyance. It would take twenty minutes for water to free number fifty-six and at the end of that time he couldn't resist returning to the scene. Going back on his tracks, he ambled past the shop.

Sure enough the sticker had disappeared while in its place the same message was etched deeply and milky in the glass. The cop and the manager were now arguing heatedly upon the sidewalk with half a dozen citizens gaping alternately at them and the window.

As Mowry loped past the cop bawled, "I don't care if the window *is* valued at two thousand guilders. You've got to board it up or replace the glass. One thing or the other and no half-measures."

"But, officer—"

"Do as you're told. To exhibit subversive propaganda is a major offense whether intentional or not. There's a war on!"

Mowry wandered away, unnoticed, unsuspected, with eighteen stickers yet to be used before the day was through. By dusk he'd disposed of them all without mishap. He had also found himself a suitable hideaway.

Chapter 3

At the hotel he stopped by the desk and spoke to the clerk. "This war, it makes things difficult. One can plan nothing with certainty." He made the hand-splaying gesture that was the Sirian equivalent of a shrug. "I must leave tomorrow and may be away seven days. It is a great nuisance."

"You wish to cancel your room, Mr. Agavan?"

"No. I reserved it for ten days and will pay for ten." Dipping into his pocket he extracted a wad of guilders. "I shall then be able to claim it if I get back in time. If I don't, well, that'll be my hard luck."

"As you wish, Mr. Agavan." Indifferent to the throwing away of good money so long as it was somebody else's, the other scribbled a receipt, handed it over.

"Thanks," said Mowry. "Live long!"

"May you live long." He gave the response in dead tones, not caring if the customer expired on the spot.

Mowry went to the restaurant and ate. Then to his room where he lay full length on the bed and gave his feet a much needed rest while he waited for darkness to become complete. When the last streamers of sunset had faded away he took another pack of stickers from his case, also a piece of crayon, and departed.

The task was lots easier this time. Poor illumination helped cover his actions, he was now familiar with the locality and the places most deserving of his attentions, he was not diverted by the need to find another and safer address. For more than four hours he could concentrate single-mindedly upon the job of defacing walls and making a mess of the largest, most expensive sheets of plate glass that daytimes were prominently in public view.

Between seven-thirty and midnight he slapped exactly one hundred stickers on shops, offices and vehicles of the city transport system, also inscribed swiftly, clearly and in large size the letters D.A.G. upon twenty-four walls.

The latter feat was performed with Terran crayon, a deceitfully chalk-like substance that made full use of the porosity of brick when water was applied. In other words, the more furiously it was washed the more stubbornly it became embedded. There was only one sure way of obliterating the offensive letters—to knock down the entire wall and rebuild it.

In the morning he breakfasted, walked out with his case, ignored a line of waiting dynocars and caught a bus. He changed buses nine times, switching routes one way or the other and heading nowhere in particular. Five times he traveled without his case which reposed awhile in a rented locker. This tedious rigmarole may not have been necessary but there was no way of telling; it was his duty not only to avoid actual perils but also to anticipate hypothetical ones.

Such as this: "Kaitempi check. Let me see the hotel register. H'm!—much the same as last time. Except for this Shir Agavan. Who is he, *hi?*"

"A forestry surveyor."

"Did you get that from his identity-card?"

"Yes, officer. It was quite in order."

"By whom is he employed?"

"By the Ministry of Natural Resources."

"Was his card embossed with the Ministry's stamp?"

"I don't remember. Maybe it was. I can't say for sure."

"You should notice things like that. You know full well that you'll be asked about them when the check is made."

"Sorry, officer, but I can't see and remember every item that comes my way in a week."

"You could try harder. Oh. Well, I suppose this Agavan character is all right. But maybe I'd better get confirmation if only to show I'm on the job. Give me your phone." A call, a few questions, the phone slammed down, then in harsh tones, "The Ministry has no Shir Agavan upon its roll. The fellow is using a fake identity-card. When did he leave the hotel? Did he look agitated when he went? Did he say anything to indicate where he was going? Wake up, you fool, and answer! Give me the key to his room—it must be searched at once. Did he take a dynocar when he departed? Describe him to me as fully as you can. So he was carrying a case? What sort of a case, *hi?*"

That was the kind of chance that must be taken when one holes up in known and regularly checked haunts. The risk was not enormous, in fact it was small— but it was still there. And when tried, sentenced and waiting for death it is no consolation to know that what came off was a hundred to one chance. To keep going and to maintain the one-man battle the enemy had to be outwitted, if possible, all along the line and all the time.

Satisfied that by now the most persistent of snoops could not follow his tortuous trail through the city, Mowry retrieved his case, lugged it up to the third floor of a crummy tenement building, let himself into his suite of two sour-smelling rooms. The rest of the day he spent cleaning the place up and making it fit to live in.

He'd be lots harder to trace here. The shifty-eyed landlord had not asked to see his identity-card, had accepted him without question as Gast Hurkin, a low-grade railroad official, honest, hard-working and stupid enough to pay his rent regularly and on time. To the landlord's way of thinking the unsavory neighbors rated a higher I.Q.—in terms of that environment—being able to get a crust with less effort and remaining tight-mouthed about how they did it.

Housework finished, Mowry bought a paper, sought through it from front to back for some mention of yesterday's activities. There wasn't a word on the subject. At first he felt disappointed, then on further reflection he became heartened.

Opposition to the war and open defiance of the government definitely made news that justified a front-page spread. No reporter, no editor would pass it up if he could help it. Therefore the papers had passed it up because they could not help it. They'd had no choice about the matter. Somebody high in authority had clamped down upon them with the heavy hand of censorship. Somebody with considerable power had been driven into making a weak countermove.

That was a start, anyway. His first wasping buzzing had forced authority to interfere with the press. What's more, the countermove was feeble and ineffective. It wouldn't work. It was doomed to failure, serving only as a stopgap while they sat around and beat their brains for more decisive measures.

The more persistently a government maintains silence on a given subject of discussion, the more the public talks about it, thinks about it. The longer and more stubborn the silence the guiltier it looks to the talkers and thinkers. In time of war the most morale-lowering question that can be asked is, "What are they hiding from us *now?*"

Some hundreds of citizens would be asking themselves that same question tomorrow, the next day or the next week. The potent words *Dirac Angestun Gesept* would be on a multitude of lips, milling around in a like number of minds, merely because the powers-that-be were afraid to talk.

And if a government fears to admit even the pettiest facts of war, how much faith can the common man place in the leadership's claim not to be afraid of anything? *Hi?*

A disease gains in menace when it spreads, popping up in places far apart and taking on the characteristics of an epidemic. For that reason Mowry's first outing from his new abode was to Radine, a town two hundred and forty miles south of Pertane. Population three hundred thousand, hydroelectric power, bauxite mines, aluminum extraction plants.

He caught an early morning train. It was overcrowded with all those people compelled to move around by the various needs of war: sullen workers, bored soldiers, self-satisfied officials, colorless nonentities. The seat facing him was occupied by a heavy-bellied character with bloated, porcine features, a caricaturist's idea of the Jaimec Minister of Food.

The train set off, hit up a fast clip. People piled in and out at intermediate stations. Pigface contemptuously ignored Mowry, watched the passing landscape with lordly disdain, finally fell asleep and let his mouth hang open. He was twice as hoglike in his slumbers and would have attained near-perfection with a lemon between his teeth.

Thirty miles from Radine the door from the coach ahead slammed open, a civilian policeman entered. He was accompanied by two burly, hard-faced characters in plain clothes. This trio halted by the nearest passenger.

"Your ticket," demanded the cop.

The passenger handed it over, his expression scared. The policeman examined it front and back, passed it to his companions who studied it in turn.

"Your identity-card."

That got the same treatment, the cop looking it over as if doing a routine chore, the other two surveying it more critically and with concealed suspicion.

"Your movement permit."

It passed the triple scrutiny, was given back along with the ticket and identity-card. The recipient's face showed vast relief. The cop picked on the passenger sitting next to him.

"Your ticket."

Mowry, seated two-thirds of the way along the coach, observed this performance with much curiosity and a little apprehension. His feelings boosted to alarm when they reached the seventh passenger.

For some reason best known to themselves the tough-looking pair in plain clothes gazed longer and more intently at this one's documents. Meanwhile, the passenger developed visible signs of agitation. They stared at his strained face, weighing him up. Their own features wore the hungry expressions of predatory animals about to tear down a victim.

"Stand up!" barked one of them.

The passenger shot to his feet and stood quivering. He swayed slightly and it was not due to the rocking of the train. While the cop looked on, the two frisked the passenger with speed and professional thoroughness. They took things out of his pockets, pawed them around, shoved them back. They patted his clothes all over, showing no respect for his person.

Finding nothing of significance, one of them muttered an oath, then yelled at the victim, "Well, what's giving you the shakes?"

"I don't feel so good," said the passenger, feebly.

"Is that so? What's the matter with you?"

"Travel sickness. I always get this way in trains."

"It's a story, anyway." He glowered at the other, lost patience and made a careless gesture. "All right, you can sit."

At that the passenger collapsed into his seat and breathed heavily. He had the mottled complexion of one almost sick from fear and relief. The cop eyed him a moment, let go a sniff and turned attention to number eight.

"Ticket."

There were ten more to be chivvied before these inquisitors reached Mowry. He was willing to take a chance on his documents passing muster but he dared not risk a search. The cop was just a plain, ordinary cop. The other two were members of the all-powerful Kaitempi; if *they* dipped into his pockets the balloon would go up once and for all. And in due time, when on Terra it was realized that his silence was the silence of the grave, a cold-blooded specimen named Wolf would give with the sales talk to another sucker.

"Turn around. Walk bow-legged. We want you to become a wasp."

By now most of the passengers were directing their full attention along the aisle, watching what was going on and meanwhile trying to ooze an aura of patriotic rectitude. Mowry slid a surreptitious look at Pigface who was still lolling opposite with head hanging on chest and mouth wide open. Were those sunken little eyes really closed or were they watching him between narrowed lids?

Short of pushing his face right up against the other's unpleasant countenance he couldn't tell for certain. But it made no difference, the trio were edging nearer every moment and he had to take a risk. Furtively he felt behind him, found a tight but deep gap in the upholstery where the bottom of the backrest met the rear of the seat. Keeping his attention riveted upon Pigface, he edged a pack of stickers and two crayons out of his pocket, crammed them into the gap, poking them well out of sight. The sleeper opposite did not stir or blink an eyelid.

Two minutes later the cop gave Pigface an irritable shove on the shoulder and that worthy woke up with a snort. He glared at the cop, then at the pair in plain clothes.

"So! What is this?"

"Your ticket," said the cop.

"A traffic check, *hi?*" responded Pigface, showing sudden understanding. "Oh, well—" Inserting fat fingers in a vest pocket he took out an ornate card embedded in a slice of transparent plastic. This he exhibited to the trio as if it were the equivalent of the keys to the kingdom. The cop stared at it and became servile. The two toughies stiffened like raw recruits caught dozing on parade.

"Your pardon, Major," apologized the cop.

"It is granted," assured Pigface, showing a well-practiced mixture of arrogance and condescension. "You are only doing your duty." He favored the rest of the coach with a beam of triumph born of petty power, openly enjoying the situation and advertising himself as being several grades above the common herd.

Eyeing him with concealed dislike, Mowry became obsessed with the notion that some buttocks have been designed by Nature specifically to be kicked good and hard and that such a target was within foot-reach right now. His right shoe got the fidgets at the thought of it but he kept it firmly on the floor.

Leery and embarrassed, the cop switched to Mowry, said, "Ticket."

Mowry handed it over, striving to look innocent and bored. Pseudo-nonchalance didn't come easy because now he was the focal point of the coach's battery of eyes. Almost all the other passengers were looking his way, Pigface was surveying him speculatively and the two Kaitempi agents were giving him the granite-hard stare.

"Identity-card."

That got passed across.

"Movement permit."

He surrendered it, braced himself for the half-expected command of, "Stand up!"

It did not come. Anxious to get away from the fat Major's cold, official gaze, the three examined the papers, handed them back without comment and moved on. Mowry shoved the documents into his pocket, tried to keep a great relief out of his voice as he spoke to the other.

"I wonder what they're after."

"It is no business of yours," said Pigface, as insultingly as possible.

"No, of course not," agreed Mowry.

There was silence between them. Pigface sat mooning through the window and showed no inclination to resume his slumbers. Damn the fellow, thought Mowry, retrieving the hidden stickers was going to prove difficult with that slob awake and alert.

A door crashed shut as the cop and Kaitempi agents finished with that coach and went through to the following one. A minute later the train pulled up with such suddenness that a couple of passengers were thrown from their seats. Outside the train and farther back toward the rear end voices started shouting.

Heaving himself to his feet, Pigface opened the window's top half, stuck his head out and looked back toward the source of the noise. Then with speed surprising in one so cumbersome he whipped a gun from his pocket, ran along the aisle and through the end door. Outside the bawling grew louder.

Mowry got up and had a look through the window. Near the tail of the train a small bunch of figures were running alongside the track, the cop and the Kaitempi slightly in the lead. As he watched, the latter swung up their right arms and several sharp cracks rang through the morning air. It was impossible to see at whom they were shooting.

Also beside the train, gun in hand, Pigface was pounding heavily along in pursuit of the pursuers. Curious faces popped out of windows all along the line of coaches. Mowry called to the nearest face.

"What happened?"

"Those three came in to check papers. Some fellow saw them, made a wild dash to the opposite door and jumped out. They stopped the train and went after him."

"Was he hurt when he jumped?"

"Not by the looks of it. Last I saw of him he was diminishing in the distance like a champion *meika*. He got a pretty good start. They'll be lucky to catch him."

"Who was he, anyway?"

"No idea. Some wanted criminal, I suppose."

"Well," offered Mowry, "if the Kaitempi came after me I'd hotfoot it like a scared Spakum."

"Who wouldn't?" said the other.

Withdrawing, Mowry took his seat. All the other travelers were at the windows, their full attention directed outside. This was an opportune moment. He dug a hand into the hiding-place, extracted the stickers and crayons, pocketed them.

The train stayed put for half an hour during which there was no more excitement within hearing. Finally it jerked into motion and at the same time Pigface reappeared and dumped himself into his seat. His face was thunderous. He looked sour enough to pickle his own hams.

"Did you catch him?" asked Mowry, lending his manner all the politeness and respect he could muster.

Pigface bestowed a dirty look. "It is no business of yours."

"No, of course not," confirmed Mowry for the second time.

The previous silence came back and remained until the train pulled into Radine. This being the terminus, everybody got out. Mowry padded along with the mob through the station exit but did not make a beeline for punishable windows and walls.

Instead he followed Pigface.

Shadowing presented no great difficulty. Pigface behaved as though the likelihood of being trailed would be the last thing ever to enter his mind. He went his way with the arrogant assurance of one who has the law in his pocket, all ordinary persons being less than the dust beneath his chariot wheel. In this respect his strength was his weakness, a fatal weakness as he had yet to discover.

Immediately outside the station's arched entrance Pigface turned right, plodded a hundred yards along the approach-road to the parking lot at the farther end. Here he stopped by a long, green dynocar, felt in his pocket for keys.

Lingering in the shadow of a projecting buttress, Mowry watched the quarry unlock the door and squeeze inside. He hustled across the road to a taxi-stand, climbed into the leading vehicle. The move was perfectly timed; he sank into the seat just as the green dynocar whined past.

"Where to?" asked the taxi-driver.

"Can't tell you exactly," said Mowry, evasively. "I've been here only once before and that was years ago. But I know the way. Just follow my instructions."

The taxi's dynamo set up a rising hum as the machine sped down the road while its passenger kept attention on the car ahead and gave curt orders from time to time. It would have been lots easier, he knew, to have pointed and said, "Follow that green car." But that would have linked him in the driver's mind with Pigface or at least with Pigface's green dyno. The Kaitempi were experts at ferreting out such links and following them to the bitter end. As it was, the taxi-driver had no idea that he was shadowing anyone.

Swiftly the chaser and the chased threaded their way through the center of Radine until eventually the leader made a sharp turn to the left and rolled down a ramp into the basement of a large apartment building. Mowry let the taxi run a couple of hundred yards farther on before he called a halt.

"This will do me." He got out, felt for money. "Nice to have a good, dependable memory, isn't it?"

"Yar," said the driver. "One guilder six-tenths."

Mowry gave him two guilders, watched him cruise away. Hastening back to the apartment building, he entered, took an inconspicuous seat in its huge foyer, lay back and pretended to be enjoying a semi-doze while waiting for someone. There were several others sitting around none of whom took the slightest notice of him.

Sure enough he'd not been there half a minute when Pigface came into the other end of the foyer from a door leading to the basement garage. Without so much as a glance around he stepped into one of a bank of small automatic elevators. The door slid shut. The illuminated telltale on the lintel winked a succession of numbers, stopped at seven, held it awhile, then winked downward to zero. The door glided open, showing the box now empty.

After another five minutes Mowry yawned, stretched, consulted his watch and went out. He paced along the street until he found a phone booth. From it he called the apartment building, got its switchboard operator.

"I was supposed to meet somebody in your foyer nearly an hour ago," he explained. "I can't make it. If he's still waiting I'd like him to be told I can't get along."

"Who is he?" asked the operator. "A resident?"

"Yes—but I've clean forgotten his name. Nobody is more stupid than me about names. He is plump, got heavy features, lives on the seventh floor. Major . . . major . . . what a *soko* of a memory I've got!"

"That would be Major Sallana," the operator said.

"Correct," agreed Mowry. "Major Sallana—I had it at the back of my mind all the time."

"Hold on. I'll see if he's still waiting." There followed a minute's silence before the operator returned with, "No, he isn't. I've just called his apartment and there's no reply. Do you wish to leave a message for him?"

"It won't be necessary—he must have given me up. It's not of great importance, anyway. Live long!"

"Live long!" said the operator.

So there was no reply from the apartment. Looked as if Pigface had gone straight in and straight out again. Unless he was lying in his bath and not inclined to answer the phone. That didn't seem likely; he'd hardly had time to fill a tub, undress and get into it. If he really was absent from his rooms it meant that opportunity had presented itself so far as Mowry was concerned and it was up to him to grab it while it was there.

Despite an inward sense of urgency, Mowry paused long enough to cope with other work. He looked through the booth's glass, found himself unobserved. Then he slapped a sticker on the facing window exactly where tireless talkers could contemplate it while holding the phone.

It said: *Power lovers started this war. Dirac Angestun Gesept will end it—and them!*

Returning to the apartments he strolled with deceitful confidence across the foyer, stepped into an unoccupied elevator. He turned to face the open front, became conscious of someone hurrying toward the bank, glanced that way and was aghast to find Pigface approaching.

The fellow was wearing a ruminative scowl, hadn't yet seen him but undoubtedly would do so unless he moved fast. At once Mowry slammed the door and prodded the third button on the panel. The elevator glided up to the third floor, stopped. He kept it there, the door still shut, until he heard the whine of an adjoining box passing him and going higher. Then he dropped back to ground-level, left the building. He felt thwarted and short-tempered and cursed his luck in a steady undertone.

Between then and mid-evening he worked off his ire by running around like mad, decorating Radine with one hundred and twenty stickers and fourteen chalked walls. On no occasion did anyone catch him at it though, as usual, he had several narrow escapes.

Deciding to call it a day for that kind of work, he dropped the remaining half-stick of crayon down a grid and thereby increased his safety margin to some degree. If stopped and searched they'd now find nothing on him immediately recognizable as subversive material.

At the ten-time hour he champed through an overdue meal, having eaten nothing since breakfast. That finished, he looked up Sallana's number, called it, got no reply. *Now* was the time. Repeating his earlier tactic, he went to the building, took an elevator to the seventh floor, this time without mishap. He trod silently along the heavy carpet of the corridor, looking at doors until he found one bearing the name he sought.

He knocked.

No answer.

He knocked again, a fraction louder but not loud enough to arouse others nearby. Silence answered him.

This was where his hectic schooling came in. Taking from his pocket a bunch of keys that looked quite ordinary but weren't, he set to work on the lock, had the door open within precisely thirty-five seconds. Speed was essential for that task— if anyone had chosen that time to enter the corridor he'd have been caught red-handed. Nobody did appear. He slipped through the door, carefully closed it behind him.

His first act was to make swift survey of the rooms and assure himself that nobody was lying around asleep or drunk. There were four rooms, all vacant. Definitely Major Pigface Sallana was not at home.

Returning to the first room, Mowry gave it a sharp examination, spotted a gun lying atop a small filing cabinet. He checked it, found it loaded, stuck it in his pocket.

Next, with expert technique he cracked open a big, heavy desk and started raking through its drawers. The way he did it had the sure, superfast touch of the professional criminal but was in fact a tribute to his college training.

The contents of the fourth drawer on the left made his hair stand on end. He had been seeking with the intention of confiscating whatever it was that made cops servile and even persuaded Kaitempi agents to stand to attention. Jerking open the drawer, he found himself gazing at a neat stack of writing paper bearing official print across its head.

This was more than he'd expected, more than he had hoped for in his most optimistic moments. To his mind it proved that despite his college lectures about caution, caution, everlasting caution, it pays to play hunches and take chances. What the paper's caption said was:

DIRAC KAIMINA TEMPITI.
Leshun Radine

In other words: the Sirian Secret Police—District of Radine. No wonder those thugs on the train had made ready to grovel. Pigface was a Kaitempi brasshat and as such outranked an army brigadier or even a space navy fleet leader.

This discovery upped the speed of his activity still further. From the pile of luggage in the back room he seized a small case, forced it open, tossed the clothing it contained onto the floor. He dumped all the Kaitempi writing paper into the case. A little later he found a small embossing machine, tested it, found that it impressed the letters DKT surmounted by a winged sword. That also went into the case.

Finishing with the desk he started on the adjacent filing cabinet, his nostrils twitching with excitement as he worked at its top drawer. A faint sound came to his ears, he stopped, taut and listening. It was the scrape of a key in the doorlock. The key failed to turn at the first attempt, tried again.

Mowry jumped toward the wall, flattened himself against it where he'd be concealed by the opening door. The key grated a second time, the lock responded, the door swung across his field of vision as Pigface lumbered in.

Pigface took four paces into the room before his brain accepted what his eyes could see. He came to a full stop, stared incredulously and with mounting fury at the ransacked desk while behind him the door drifted around and clicked shut. Reaching a decision, he turned to go out and then saw the invader.

"Good evening," greeted Mowry, flat-voiced.

"*You?*" Pigface glowered at him with outraged authority. "What are you doing here? What is the meaning of this?"

"I'm here as a common thief. The meaning is that you've been robbed."

"Then let me tell you—"

"When robbery is done," Mowry went on, "somebody has to be the victim. This time it's your turn. No reason why you should have all the luck all the time, is there?"

Pigface took a step forward.

"Sit down!" ordered Mowry, in sharp tones.

The other stopped but did not sit. He stood firm upon the carpet, his small, crafty eyes taking on a stubborn glint, his complexion dark. He spoke in a manner suggesting that at any moment he might go bang.

"Put down that gun."

"Who?—me?" said Mowry.

"You don't know what you're doing," declared Pigface, conditioned by a lifetime of creating fear. "Because you don't know who I am. But when you do you'll wish—"

"As happens, I do know who you are," Mowry chipped in. "You're one of the Kaitempi's fat rats. A professional torturer, a paid strangler, a conscienceless *soko* who maims and kills for money and for the sadistic pleasure of it. Sit down when I tell you."

Still Pigface refused to sit. On the contrary, he refuted the popular belief that all bullies are cowards. Like many of his ilk he had brute courage. His eyes flared with hate, he took a heavy but swift step to one side while his hand dived into a pocket.

But the eyes that so often had calmly watched the death-throes of others had now betrayed him to his own end. The step had hardly been taken, the hand only just reached the pocket, when Mowry's gun went *br-r-r-rup!*, not loudly but effectively. For five or six seconds Pigface stood wearing a stupid expression, then he teetered, fell backward with a thud that shook the room, rolled onto his side.

Gently opening the door a few inches, Mowry gazed into the corridor, remained listening awhile. There came no rush of feet toward the apartment, nobody raced away yelling for help. If anyone had heard the muffled burst of shots they must have attributed the noise to the flow of traffic far below.

Satisfied that the alarm had not been raised, he shut the door, bent over the body, had a close look at it. Pigface was as dead as he could be, the brief spray from the machine pistol having put seven slugs through his obese frame.

It was a pity, in a way, because Mowry would much have liked to have hammered, kicked or otherwise got out of him the answers to some cogent questions. Whether he could have gained his purpose in this respect was highly doubtful but it would have been worth the trying. There were many things he wanted to know about the Kaitempi, in particular the identities of its current victims, their physical condition and where they were hidden. No wasp could find supporters more loyal and enthusiastic than genuine natives of the planet rescued from the strangler's noose.

But one cannot thump information from a corpse. That was his sole regret. In all other respects he had cause for gratification. For one thing, factual evidence of the methods of the Kaitempi was of such a revolting nature that to remove any one of them from the scheme of things was to do a favor to Sirians and Terrans alike. For another, such a daring killing was an ideal touch in present circumstances: it lent murderous support to stickers and wall-scrawls.

It was a broad hint to the powers-that-be that somebody was willing and able to do more than talk. The wasp had done plenty of buzzing around. Now it had demonstrated its sting.

He searched the body and got what he had coveted from the moment that Pigface had basked in adulation upon the train. The ornate card set in thin plastic. It bore signs, seals and signatures, certified that the bearer held the rank of major in the Secret Police. Better still, it did not give the bearer's name and personal description, contenting itself with using a code-number in lieu. The Secret Police, it seemed, could be warily secret even between themselves, a habit of which others could take full advantage.

Mowry now returned attention to the filing cabinet. Most of the stuff within it proved to be worthless, revealing nothing not already known to Terran Intelligence. But there were three files containing case-histories of persons who had also been made to conform to the Kaitempi habit of hiding identities under code-numbers. Evidently Pigface had abstracted them from local headquarters and taken them home to study at leisure.

He scanned these papers rapidly. It soon became clear that the three un-knowns had earned the enmity of the government by nursing political ambi-tions. They were potential rivals of those already in power. The case-histories said nothing to indicate whether they were now living or dead. The implica-tion was that they were still alive, with their fate yet to be decided, otherwise it seemed hardly likely that Pigface would waste time on such documents. Anyway, the disappearance of these vital papers would aggravate the powers-that-be and possibly scare a few of them.

So he put the files in the case along with the rest of the loot. After that he made a swift hunt around for anything previously overlooked, searched spare suits in the bedroom, discovered nothing more worth taking. The last chore was to re-move from the apartment all clues capable of linking him with the existing situa-tion.

With the case in one hand and the gun in his pocket, he paused in the door-way, looked back at the body.

"Live long!"

Pigface did not deign to reply. He reposed in silence, his pudgy right hand clasping a paper on which was inscribed: *Executed by Dirac Angestun Gesept.*

Whoever found the body would be sure to pass that message on. It would be equally certain to go from hand to hand, up the ascending scale or rank, right to the top brackets. With any luck at all it would give a few of them the galloping gripes.

Chapter 4

Luck held. Mowry did not have to wait long for a train to Pertane. He was more than glad of this because the bored station police tended to become inquisi-tive about travelers who sat around too long. True, if accosted he could show his documents or, strictly as a last resort, arrogantly use the stolen Kaitempi card to browbeat his way out of a possible trap. But it was better and safer not to become an object of attention in this place at this time.

The train came in and he managed to get aboard without having been noticed by one of several restlessly roaming cops. After a short time it pulled out again, rumbled into pitch darkness. The lateness of the hour meant that passengers were few and the coach he had chosen had plenty of vacant seats. It was easy to select a place where he'd not be pestered by a garrulous neighbor or studied for the full length of the journey by someone with sharp eyes and a long memory. He lolled back, tired and heavy-eyed, and hoped to heaven that if there should be another police check en route his papers, or the Kaitempi card, or his gun would get him out of a jam.

One thing was certain: if Pigface's body were found within the next three or four hours the resulting hullabaloo would spread fast enough and far enough to ensure a thorough end-to-end search of the train. The searchers would have no suspect's description to go upon but they'd take a look into all luggage and recognize stolen property when they found it. Anyone of relatively low brain-power would have the sense to grab the owner of said luggage and disregard all protestations of innocence.

He dozed uneasily to the hypnotic thrum-tiddy-thrum of the train. Every time a door slammed or a window rattled he awoke, nerves stretched, body tense. A couple of times he wondered whether a top priority radio-call was beating the train to its destination.

"Halt and search all passengers and luggage on the 11:20 from Radine."

There was no check on the way. The train slowed, clanked through the points and switches of a large grid system, rolled into Pertane. Its passengers dismounted, all of them sleepy and a few looking half-dead as they straggled untidily toward the exit. Mowry timed himself to be in the rear of the bunch, lagging behind with half a dozen bandy-legged moochers. His full attention was directed straight ahead, watching for evidence of a grim-faced bunch waiting at the barrier.

If they were really there, in ambush for him, there'd be only two courses open to him. He could drop the case and with it the valuable loot, shoot first and fastest, make a bolt and hope to get away in the ensuing confusion. As a tactic it would give him the advantage of surprise. But failure meant immediate death and even success might be dearly bought with a couple of bullets in the body.

Alternatively he could try to bluff by marching straight up to the biggest and ugliest of them, shoving the case into his hands and saying with dopey eagerness, "Pardon, officer, but one of those fellows who just went through dropped this in front of me. I can't imagine why he abandoned his luggage." Then somewhere in the resulting chaos should occur the chance for him to amble around a corner and run as if jet-propelled.

He was sweaty with reaction when he found his fears were not confirmed. It had been his first murder and it *was* a murder because they would define it as such. So he'd been paying for it in his own imagination, fancying himself hunted before the hunt was up. Beyond the barrier lounged two station police eyeing the emerging stream with total lack of interest and yawning from time to time. He went past practically under their noses and they could not have cared less about him.

But he wasn't yet out of the bag. Police on the station expected to see people carrying luggage anytime of day or night. Cops in the city streets were different, being more inclined to question the reason at such an indecent hour. They were nasty-minded about burdened walkers in the night.

That problem could be solved by the easy expedient of taking a taxi—only to create another problem. Taxis have to be driven. Drivers have mouths and memories. The most taciturn of them could become positively gabby when questioned by the Kaitempi.

"You take anyone off the 11:20 from Radine?"

"Yar. Young fellow with a case."

"Notice anything suspicious about him? He act tough or behave warily, for instance?"

"Not that I noticed. Seemed all right to me. Wasn't a native Jaimecan though. Spoke with a real Mashambi growl."

"Remember where you took him, *hi?*"

"Yar, I do. I can show you."

There was an escape from this predicament; he took it by dumping the case in a rented locker in the station and walking away free of the betraying burden. In theory the case should be safe enough for one full Jaimecan day. In ominous fact there was a slight chance of it being discovered and used as bait.

On a world where nothing was sacrosanct from their prying fingers the Kaitempi had master-keys to everything. They weren't above opening and searching every bank of lockers within a thousand miles of the scene of the crime if by any quirk of thought they took it into their heads that to do so would be a smart move. So when he returned in daytime to collect the case he'd have to approach the lockers with considerable caution, making sure that a watch was not being kept upon them by a ring of hard characters.

Pacing rapidly home, he was within half a mile of his destination when two cops stepped from a dark doorway on the other side of the street.

"Hey, you!"

Mowry stopped. They came across, stared at him in grim silence. Then one made a gesture to indicate the high-shining stars, the deserted street.

"Wandering around pretty late, aren't you?"

"Nothing wrong with that, is there?" he answered, making his tone slightly apologetic.

"*We* are asking the questions," retorted the cop. "Where've you been to this hour?"

"On a train."

"From where?"

"Khamasta."

"And where're you going now?"

"Home."

"You'd have made it quicker in a taxi, wouldn't you?"

"Sure would," Mowry agreed. "Unfortunately I happened to be last out. Someone always has to be last out. By that time every taxi had been grabbed."

"Well, it's a story."

At this point the other cop chipped in. He adopted technique Number Seven, namely, a narrowing of the eyes, an out-thrusting of the jaw and a harshening of the voice. Once in a while Number Seven would be rewarded with a guilty look or at least a hopelessly exaggerated expression of innocence. He was very good at it, having practiced it assiduously upon his wife and the bedroom mirror.

"You wouldn't perhaps have been nowhere near Khamasta, *hi?* You wouldn't perhaps have been spending the night taking a nice, easy stroll around Pertane and sort of absentmindedly messing around with walls and windows, would you?"

"No, I wouldn't," said Mowry. "For the reason that nobody would pay me a bad guilder for my trouble. Do I look crazy?"

"Not enough to be noticed," admitted the cop. "But somebody's doing it, crazy or not."

"Well, I can't blame you fellows for wanting to nab him. I don't like loonies myself. They give me the creeps." He made an impatient gesture. "If you're going to search me how about getting the job done? I've had a long day, I'm dog-tired and I want to get home."

"I don't think we'll bother," said the cop. "You show us your identity-card."

Mowry dug it out. The cop gave it no more than a perfunctory glance while his companion ignored it altogether.

"All right, on your way. If you insist on walking the streets at this hour you must expect to be stopped and questioned. There's a war on, see?"

"Yes, officer," said Mowry, meekly.

He pushed off at his best pace, thanking heaven he had got rid of his luggage. If he'd been holding that case they'd have regarded it, rightly enough, as probable evidence of evil-doing. To prevent them from opening it and inspecting the contents he'd have had to subdue them with the Kaitempi card. He didn't want to make use of that tactic if he could help it until sometime after Pigface's killing had been discovered and the resulting uproar had died down. Say in at least one month's time.

Reaching his apartment, he undressed but did not go immediately to sleep. He lay in bed and examined the precious card again and again. Now that he had made time to ponder its full significance and obvious potentialities he found himself torn two ways—should he keep it or not?

The sociopolitical system of the Sirian Empire being what it was, a Kaitempi card was the prime scare-device on any Sirian-held planet. The mere sight of this dreaded totem was enough to make ninety-nine percent of civilians get down on their knees and salaam, their faces in the dust. The fact made a Kaitempi card of tremendous value to any wasp. Yet Terra had not provided him with such a weapon. He'd had to grab it for himself. The obvious conclusion was that Terran Intelligence lacked an original copy.

Out there amid the mist of stars, on the green-blue world called Earth, they could duplicate anything save a living entity—and could produce a very close imitation even of that. Maybe they needed this card. Given the chance, maybe they'd arm every wasp in existence with a mock-majorship in the Kaitempi and by the same token give life to some otherwise doomed to death.

For himself, to surrender the card to Terran authority would be like voluntarily sacrificing his queen while playing a hard-fought and bitter game of chess. All the same, before going to sleep he reached his conclusion: on his first return to the cave he would beam a detailed report of what had happened, the prize he had won and what it was worth. Terra could then decide whether or not to deprive him of it in the interest of the greater number.

The wasp buzzed alone, unaided, but was loyal to the swarm.

At noon he made cautious return to the station, hung around for twenty minutes as if waiting to meet an incoming traveler. He kept sharp, careful watch in all directions while appearing bored and interested in nothing save occasional streams of arrivals. Some fifty or sixty other people were idling about in unconscious imitation of himself: among them he could detect nobody maintaining a sly eye upon the lockers. There were about a dozen who looked overmuscled and wore the deadpan hardness of officials but these were solely interested in people coming through the barriers.

Finally he took the chance, ambled casually up to his locker, stuck his key in its door while wishing to God that he had a third eye located in the back of his neck. Opening the door, he took out the case and had a bad moment as he stood with the damning evidence in his hand. If ever it was going to occur, now was the time for a shout of triumph, a sudden grip on his shoulder, a bunch of callous faces all around.

Still nothing happened. He strolled away looking blandly innocent but deep inside as leery as a fox who hears the dim, distant baying of the hounds. Outside the station he jumped a crosstown bus, maintained a wary watch for followers.

Chances were very high that nobody had noticed him, nobody was interested in him, because in Radine the Kaitempi were still running around in circles without the vaguest notion of where to probe first. But he could not take that for granted nor dare he underestimate their craftiness. There was one chance in a thousand that by some item he'd overlooked or hadn't thought of he'd given them a lead straight to the lockers and that they had decided not to nab him on the spot, hoping that if left to run loose he'd take them to the rest of the presumed mob.

So during the ride he peered repeatedly backward, observed passengers getting on and off, tried to see if he could spot a loaded dynocar tagging along somewhere behind. He changed buses five times, lugged the case along two squalid alleys, walked into the fronts and out the backs of three department stores.

Satisfied at last that there was no surreptitious pursuit he made for his apartment, kicked the case under the bed, let go a deep sigh. They'd warned him that this kind of life would prove a continual strain on the nerves. It sure was!

Going out again, he bought a box of envelopes and a cheap typewriter. Then using the Kaitempi paper he spent the rest of the day and part of the next one typing with forceful brevity. He didn't have to bother about leaving his prints all over this correspondence; Terran fingerprint treatment had turned his impressions into vague, unclassifiable blotches.

When he had finished that task he devoted the following day to patient research in the city library. He made copious notes, went home, addressed a stack of envelopes, stamped the lot.

In the early evening he mailed more than two hundred letters to newspaper editors, radio announcers, military leaders, senior civil servants, police chiefs, prominent politicians and key members of the government. Defiantly positioned under the Kaitempi heading and supported by the embossed seal of its winged sword, the message was short but said plenty.

Sallana is the first.

There are plenty more to come.
The list is long.
Dirac Angestun Gesept.

That done, he burned the envelope-box and dropped the typewriter in the river where it ran deep. If he had occasion to write any more letters he'd buy another one and afterward get rid of it the same way. He could well afford to buy and scrap a hundred typewriters if he thought it necessary. The more the merrier. If the Kaitempi analyzed the type on threatening correspondence and found a number of untraceable machines being used, they'd get the idea that a gigantic organization was at work. Furthermore, every purchase helped inflate the Jaimecan economy with worthless paper.

His next step was to visit a drive-yourself agency and rent a dynocar for a week, using the name of Shir Agavan and the address of the hotel where first he'd holed-up. By its means he got rid of five hundred stickers distributed over six small towns and thirty villages. The job was a lot riskier than it had been in Radine or Pertane.

The villages were by far the worst to handle, the smaller in size the more troublesome they proved. In a city of a quarter million to two million population a stranger is an insignificant nonentity; in a dump of less than one thousand inhabitants he is noticed, remarked upon, his every move watched.

On many occasions a bunch of yokels gave him the chance to slap up a sticker by switching attention from him to his car. Twice somebody took down the car's number, just for the ducks of it. It was a good thing he'd given a blind-alley lead when hiring it because police inquiries about the widespread rash of subversive stickers would almost certainly make them relate the phenomenon to the laconic, fast-moving stranger driving dyno XC17978.

He had been on Jaimec exactly four weeks when he disposed of the last of the stickers from his bag and thus reached the end of phase one. It was at this point he began to feel despondent.

In the papers and over the air officialdom still maintained complete silence about traitorous activities. Not a word had been said about the slaughter of Pigface Sallana. All the outward evidence suggested that the government remained blissfully unaware of waspish buzzings and was totally unconcerned about the existence of an imaginary *Dirac Angestun Gesept.*

Thus deprived of visible reactions Mowry had no way of telling what results he had achieved, if any. In retrospect this paper-war looked pretty futile in spite of all Wolf's glib talk about pinning down an army with little more than gestures. He, Mowry, had been lashing out in the dark and the other fellow wasn't even bothering to hit back.

That made it difficult to maintain enthusiasm at the first feverish pitch. Just one public squeal of pain from the opposition or a howl of fury or a tirade of threats would have given him a big boost by showing him that at last he had landed a real wallop on something solid. But they wouldn't give him the petty satisfaction of hearing them breathing hard.

He was paying the psychological penalty of working alone. There was no companion-in-arms with whom to share stimulating speculations about the enemy's hidden countermoves. Nobody to encourage or from whom to receive encouragement. Nobody sharing the conspiracy and the danger and—as is usual among two or more—the laughs. In his waspish role he was thrown wholly upon his own moral resources which needed feeding with factual evidence that so far had not been forthcoming.

Swiftly he built up a blue spell so dismal and depressing that for two days he hung around the apartment and did nothing but mope. On the third day pessimism evaporated and was replaced with a growing sense of alarm. He did not ignore the new feeling. At training college they'd warned him times without number always to heed it.

"The fact that one is hunted in deadly earnest can cause an abnormal sharpening of the mental perceptions almost to the point of developing a sixth sense. That's what makes hardened criminals difficult to catch. They get hunches and play them. Many a badly wanted crook has moved out one jump ahead of the police with such timeliness that they've suspected a tip-off. All that had really happened was that the fellow suddenly got the jitters and took off good and fast. For the sake of your skin you do the same. If ever you feel they're getting close don't hang around and try to check on it—just beat it someplace else!"

Yes, that's what they'd said to him. He remembered now that he had wondered whether this ability to smell danger might be quasi-telepathic. The police rarely pulled a raid without a stakeout or some sort of preliminary observation. A hound hanging around a hole, sharp-eyed, sharp-toothed and unable to avoid thinking of what he was doing, might give the one in hiding his mental scent that would register not in clear thought-forms but rather as the inward shrilling of an alarm-bell.

On the strength of that he grabbed his bags and bolted out the back way. Nobody was loafing around at that moment, nobody saw him go, nobody tracked him as he went.

Four beefy characters stationed themselves within watching and shooting distance of the back a little before midnight. Two carloads of similar specimens drew up at the front, bashed open the door, charged upstairs. They were there three hours and half-killed the landlord before they became convinced of his ignorance.

Mowry knew nothing of this. It was the much-needed boost he was lucky to miss.

His new sanctuary a mile and a half distant was one long, narrow room at the top of a dilapidated building in Pertane's toughest quarter, a district where slatterns kept house by kicking the dirt around until it got lost. Here he'd not been asked for any name or identity-card, it being one of the more delightful customs of the country to mind one's own goddam business. All that proved necessary was to exhibit a fifty guilder note. The money had been snatched, a cheap and well-worn key given in exchange.

Promptly he made the key useless by buying a cruciform multiward lock and fitting it to the door. He also fixed a couple of recessed bolts to the window despite that it was forty feet above ground and well-nigh unreachable. Finally he built a small hidden trap in the roof, this being his intended escape route if ever the stairs became solidly blocked with enemy carcasses.

For the time being, he reckoned, he stood chiefly in danger of the locality's small-time thieves—the big ones wouldn't bother to cut their way into one room in a slum. The locks and bolts should be plenty good enough to keep out the pikers. He trusted his unsavory neighbors as much as they trusted their own mothers which was as far as said mothers could be thrown with one hand against a strong wind.

Again he had to spend some time cleaning the joint and making it fit for Terran habitation. If ever he was caught by the Kaitempi he'd roll in the deep, stinking filth of a deathcell, naked, manacled and half-starved until they led him to the strangling-post. Dirt would then have to be endured because there'd be no choice about it. But so long as he remained free he insisted on his right to be fastidious. By the time he'd finished his housework the room was brighter and sweeter than ever it had been since the builders moved out and the proletariat moved in.

By now he'd recovered from both his depression and his sense of impending disaster. In better spirits he went outdoors, walked along the road until he reached a vacant lot littered with junk. When nobody was looking he dropped Pigface's gun on the lot at a point near the sidewalk where it could easily be seen.

Ambling onward with hands in pockets, his gait a bow-legged slouch, he reached a doorway, lounged in it and assumed the look of bored cunning of one who sows not neither doth he reap. This was the fashionable expression in that area. Mostly his gaze was aimed across the street but all the time he was keeping surreptitious watch upon the gun lying seventy yards away.

What followed proved yet again that not one person in ten uses his eyes. Within a short time thirty people had passed close by the gun without seeing it. Six of these walked within a few inches of it, one actually stepped over it.

Finally someone spotted it. He was a shrivel-chested, spindly-legged youth with splotches of darker purple on his face. Halting by the gun, he stared at it, bent over for a closer look but did not touch it. Then he glanced hurriedly around, failed to see the watching Mowry who had retreated farther into the doorway. Again he bent toward the gun, put out a hand as if to grab it. At the last moment he changed his mind, hastened away. He crossed right in front of Mowry, his face wearing a mixture of frustrated cupidity and fear.

"Wanted it but too scared to take it," Mowry decided.

Twenty more pedestrians passed. Of these, two noticed the gun and pretended they'd not seen it. Neither came back to claim it when nobody was near. Probably they viewed the weapon as dangerous evidence that someone had seen fit to dump—and they weren't going to be chumps enough to be caught with it. The one who eventually confiscated it was an artist in his own right.

This character, a heavily built individual with hanging jowls and a rolling gait, went by the gun and noted its existence without batting an eyelid or changing pace.

Continuing onward, he stopped at the next corner fifty yards away, looked around with the air of a stranger uncertain of his whereabouts, dug a notebook from his pocket and put on a great play of consulting it. All the time his sharp little eyes were darting this way and that but failed to find the watcher in the doorway.

After a while he retraced his steps, crossed the vacant lot, dropped the notebook on top of the gun, scooped up both in one swift snatch and ambled casually onward. The way the book remained prominently in his hand while the gun disappeared was a wonder to behold.

Letting the fellow get a good lead, Mowry emerged from the doorway and followed. He hoped the other had only a short way to go. This, obviously, was a smart customer likely to notice and throw off a shadower if chased too long. He didn't want to lose him after the trouble he'd taken to find a willing gun-grabber.

Floppy Jowls continued along the road, turned right into a narrower and dirtier street, headed over a crossroad, turned left. At no time did he behave suspiciously, take evasive tactics or show any awareness of being followed.

Near the end of the street he entered a cheap restaurant with dusty windows and a cracked, unreadable sign above its door. A few moments later Mowry mooched past, gave the place a swift once-over. It had an ominous look about it, a typical rat-hole where underworld characters took refuge from the sunshine while they waited for the night. But nothing ventured, nothing gained. Boldly he shoved open the door and walked in.

The place stank of unwashed bodies, stale food and drippings of *zith*. Behind the bar a sallow-faced attendant eyed him with the hostile expression reserved for any and every unfamiliar face. A dozen customers sat in the half-light by the stained and paintless wall and glowered at him on general principles. They looked like choice bunch of hoods.

Mowry leaned on the bar and spoke to Sallow Face, making his tones sound tough. "I'll have a mug of coffee."

"Coffee?" The other jumped as if rammed with a needle. "Blood of Jaime, that's a *Spakum* drink."

"Yar," said Mowry. "I want to spit it all over the floor." He let go a harsh, grating laugh. "Wake up and give me a *zith.*"

The attendant scowled, snatched a none too clean glassite mug from a shelf, pumped it full of low-grade *zith* and slid it across. "Six-tenths."

Paying him, Mowry took the drink across to a small table in the darkest corner, a dozen pairs of eyes following his every move. He sat down, looked idly around and ignored the grim silence. His manner was that of one thoroughly at home when slumming. His questing gaze found Floppy Jowls just as that worthy left his seat, came across mug in hand and joined him at the table.

The latter's move in apparently welcoming the newcomer caused a sudden relaxation in the place. Tension disappeared, toughies lost interest in Mowry, the bar attendant lounged back, general conversation was resumed. That showed Floppy Jowls was sufficiently well-known among the hard-faced clientele for them to take on trust anyone known to him.

Meanwhile, he had squatted face to face with Mowry and introduced himself with, "My name is Arhava, Butin Arhava." He paused, waiting for a response that did not come, then went on, "You're a stranger. From Diracta. Specifically from Masham. I can tell by your accent."

"Clever of you," Mowry encouraged.

"One has to be clever to get by. The stupid don't. They choke on a rope." He took a swig of *zith.* "You wouldn't walk into this place unless you were a genuine stranger—or one of the Kaitempi."

"No?"

"No, I don't think so. And the Kaitempi wouldn't dare send just one man in here. They'd send six. Maybe more. The Kaitempi would expect trouble aplenty in the Cafe Susun."

"That," said Mowry, "suits me very well."

"It suits me even better." Butin Arhava showed the snout of Pigface's gun over the edge of the table. It was pointed straight at the other's middle. "I do not like being followed. If this gun went off nobody in here would give a damn. You wouldn't worry either, not for long. So you'd better talk. Why have you been following me, *hi?*"

"You knew I was behind you all the time?"

"I did. What's the big idea?"

"You'll hardly believe it when I tell you." Leaning across the table, Mowry grinned straight into his scowling face. "I want to give you a thousand guilders."

"That's nice," said Arhava, unimpressed. "That's very nice." His eyes narrowed. "And you're all set to reach into your pocket and give it me, *hi?*"

Mowry nodded, still grinning. "Yes—unless you're so lily-livered that you prefer to reach into it yourself."

"You won't bait me that way," retorted Arhava. "I've got control of the situation and I'm keeping it, see? Now get busy dipping—but if what comes out of that pocket is a gun it's *you* and not me who'll be at the wrong end of the bang. Go ahead and dip. I'm watching."

With the weapon steadily aimed at him over the table's rim, Mowry felt in his right-hand pocket, drew out a neat wad of twenty-guilder notes, poked them across. "There you are. They're all yours."

For a moment Arhava gaped with complete incredulity, then he made a swift pass and the notes vanished. The gun also disappeared. He lay back in his seat and studied Mowry with a mixture of bafflement and suspicion. "Now show me the string."

"No string," Mowry assured. "Just a gift from an admirer."

"Meaning who?"

"Me."

"But you don't know me from the Statue of Jaime."

"I hope to," said Mowry. "I hope to know you well enough to convince you of something mightily important."

"And what is that?"

"There's lots more money where that came from."

"Is that so?" Arhava gave a knowing smirk. "Well, where did it come from?"

"I just told you—an admirer."

"Don't give me that."

"All right. The conversation is over. It's been nice knowing you. Now get back to your own seat."

"Don't be silly." Licking his lips, Arhava glanced cautiously around the room, reduced his voice almost to a whisper. "How much?"

"Twenty thousand guilders."

The other fanned his hands as if beating off an annoying fly. "Sh-h-h! Don't say it so loud!" Another leery look around the room. "Did you actually say *twenty thousand?*"

"Yar."

Arhava took a deep breath. "Who d'you want killed?"

"One—for a start."

"Are you serious?"

"I've just given you a thousand guilders and that's not funny. Besides, you can put the matter to the test. Cut a throat and collect—it's as easy as that."

"Just for a start, you said?"

"I did. By that is meant that if I like your work I'll offer further employment. I've got a list of names and will pay twenty thousand per body." Watching him for effect, Mowry put a note of warning into his voice. "The Kaitempi will reward you with ten thousand for delivering me into their hands. That's money for the taking and with no risk attached. But to get it you'll have to sacrifice all chance at a far bigger sum, maybe a million or more." He paused, finished with pointed sarcasm, "One does not flood one's own goldmine, does one?"

"Nar, not unless one is cracked." Arhava became slightly unnerved as his thoughts milled around. "And what makes you think I'm a professional killer?"

"I don't think anything of the sort. But I know you're a shady character, probably with a police record, otherwise you wouldn't have swiped that gun and neither would you dive into a crummy joint like this. That means you're just the type who'll do some dirty work for me or, alternatively, can introduce me to someone who is willing to do it. Personally, I don't care a hoot who performs the task, you or your Uncle Smatsy. I reek of money. You love the scent of it. If you want to go on sniffing it you've got to do something about it."

Arhava nodded slowly, stuck a hand in his pocket and fondled the thousand guilders. There was a queer fire in his eyes. "I don't do that kind of work, it's not quite in my line. And it needs more than one, but—"

"But what?"

"Not saying. I've got to have time to think this over. I want to discuss it with a couple of friends."

Mowry stood up. "I'll give you four days to find them and chew the fat. By then you'd better have made up your mind one way or the other. I'll be here again in four days' time at this hour." Then he gave the other a light but imperative shove in the shoulder. "*I* don't like being followed either. Lay off if you want to grow old and get rich."

With that, he departed. Arhava remained obediently seated and gazed dreamily at the door. After a time he called for another *zith*. His voice was strangely hoarse.

The barman dumped the drink at his elbow, said with no great interest, "Friend of yours, Butin?"

"Yar—Datham Hain."

Datham Hain being the Sirian version of Santa Claus.

Chapter 5

In the early morning Mowry went to another and different agency, rented a dynocar under the name of Morfid Payth with an address in Radine. He couldn't risk using the same agency twice in succession; it was highly likely that already the police had visited the first one and asked pointed questions. There they'd recognize him as the subject of official investigation, detain him on some pretext while they used the telephone.

He drove out of the town carefully, with circumspection, not wanting to draw the attention of any patrol cars lurking around. Eventually he reached the tree with the abnormal branch formation and the mock-tombstone beneath it. For a few minutes he stopped nearby pretending to tinker with the dynamo until the road became completely clear of traffic in both directions. Then swiftly he drove the car over the grass verge and in between the trees for as far as he could get it.

After that he went back on foot and satisfied himself that it could not be seen from the road. With his feet he scuffed the grass and thus concealed the tire tracks entering the forest. That done, he headed for the distant cave, moving as fast as he could make it.

He got there in the late afternoon. When still deep among the trees and eight hundred yards from his destination the ornamental ring on the middle finger of his left hand started tingling. The sensation grew progressively stronger as he neared. This caused him to make a straight and confident approach with no preliminary skirmishing around. The ring would not have tingled if Container-22 had ceased to radiate and that would happen only on the breaking of its beam by the invasion of the cave by something man-sized.

Yes, if accidentally or otherwise the enemy had found the hidden dump and made a trap of it, the quarry would have faded away with a half-mile running start. And they'd have been left to sit on their butts and wait for him who never arrives.

Also in the cave was something more spectacular than an invisible warning system. Probably the discoverers' curiosity would have got the better of them and they'd start prying open the stacked duralumin cylinders including Container-30. When they interfered with that one the resulting bang would be heard and felt in faraway Pertane.

Once in the cave he opened Container-2, got busy while daylight lasted and treated himself to a real Earth meal concocted of real Earth food. He was far from being a guzzle-guts but shared with exiles a delight in the flavors of home. A small can of pineapple seemed like a taste of heaven, he lingered over every drop of juice and made it last twenty minutes. The feed gave quite a lift to his morale, made the growing forces out there among the stars seem not so far away.

Upon the fall of darkness he rolled Container-5 out of the cave's mouth, opened it on the tiny beach. It was now a tall silver-gray cylinder pointed at the stars. From its side he unclipped a small handle, stuck it into a hole in the slight blister near the base, wound vigorously. Something inside began to murmur a smooth and steady *zuum-zuum.*

He now took the top cap off the cylinder, having to stand on tiptoe to get at it. Then he sat on a nearby rock and waited. After the cylinder had warmed up it emitted a sharp click and the *zuum-zuum* struck a deeper note. He knew that it was now shouting into space, using soundless words far stronger and more penetrating than those of any spoken language.

Whirrup-dzzt-pam! Whirrup-dzzt-pam!

"Jaimec calling! Jaimec calling!"

Now he could do nothing more save bide his time in patience. The call was not being directed straight to Terra which was much too far away to permit a conversation with brief time-lags. It was being squirted at a spatial listening-post and field headquarters near enough to be on or perhaps actually within the rim of the Sirian Empire. He did not know its precise location and, as Wolf had remarked, what he didn't know he couldn't tell.

A prompt response was unlikely. Out there in the dark they'd be listening for a hundred calls on a hundred frequencies and be held on some of them while messages passed to and fro. He'd have to wait his turn.

Nearly three hours crawled by while the cylinder stood on the pebble beach and gave forth its scarcely hearable *zuum-zuum.* Then suddenly a tiny red eye glowed bright and winked steadily near its top.

Again he strained on tiptoe, cursing his shortness, felt into the cylinder's open top and took out what looked exactly like an ordinary telephone. Holding it to his ear, he said into the mouthpiece, "JM on Jaimec."

It was a few minutes before the response came back in the shape of a voice that sounded as though speaking through a load of gravel. But it was a Terran voice speaking the welcome-sounding Terran language. It said, "Ready to tape your report. Fire away."

Mowry tried to sit down while he talked but found the connecting cord too short. So he had to stand. In this position he recited as fast as he could. *The Tale of a Wasp* by Samuel Sucker, he thought wryly. He gave it in full detail and again had to wait quite a while for the comeback.

Then the voice rasped, "Good! You're doing fine!"

"Am I? Can't see any signs of it so far. I've been plastering paper all over the planet and nothing is happening."

"Plenty is happening," contradicted the voice. It came through with a rhythmic variation in amplitude as it fooled Sirian detection devices by switching five times per second through a chain of differently positioned transmitters. "You just can't see the full picture from where you're standing."

"How about giving me a glimpse?"

"The pot is coming slowly but surely to the boil. Their fleets are being widely dispersed, there are vast troop movements from their overcrowded home system to the outer planets of their empire. They're gradually being chivvied into a fix. They can't hold what they've got without spreading all over it. The wider they spread the thinner they get. The thinner they get the easier it is to bite lumps out of them. Hold it a bit while I check your planet." He went off, came back after a time. "Yes, position there is that they daren't take any strength away from Jaimec no matter how greatly needed elsewhere. In fact they may yet have to add to it at the expense of Diracta. You're the cause of that."

"Sweet of you to say so," said Mowry. A thought struck him and he said eagerly, "Hey, who gave you that information?"

"Monitoring and Decoding Service. They dig a lot out of enemy broadcasts."

"Oh." He felt disappointed, having hoped for news of a Terran Intelligence agent somewhere on Jaimec. But of course even if there was one they wouldn't tell him. They'd lie about it. They'd give him no information that Kaitempi persuasion might force out of him. "How about this Kaitempi card and embossing machine? Do I leave them here to be collected or do I keep them for myself?"

"Stand by and I'll find out." The voice went away for more than an hour, returned with, "Sorry about the delay. Distance takes time in any terms. You can keep that stuff and use it as you think best. T.I. got a card recently. An agent bought one for them."

"*Bought* one?" He waggled his eyebrows in surprise.

"Yes—with his life. What did yours cost?"

"Major Sallana's life, as I told you."

"Tsk-tsk! Those cards come mighty dear." There was a pause, then, "Closing down. Best of luck!"

"Thanks!"

With some reluctance Mowry replaced the receiver, switched off the *zuum-zuum,* capped the cylinder and rolled it back into the cave. He'd have liked to listen until dawn to anything that maintained the invisible tie between him and that faraway lifeform. "Best of luck!" the voice had said, not knowing how much more it meant than the alien, "Live long!"

From yet another container he took several packets and small parcels, distributed them about his person, put others into a canvas shoulder-bag of the kind favored by the Sirian peasantry. Impatience prevented him from waiting for the full light of day. Being now more familiar with the forest he felt sure he could fumble his way through it even in the dark. The going would be tougher, the journey would take longer, but he could not resist the urge to get back to the car as soon as possible.

Before leaving his last act was to press the hidden button on Container-22 which had ceased to radiate the moment he'd entered the cave and remained dead ever since. After a one-minute delay it would again set up the invisible barrier that could not be passed without betrayal.

He got out of the cave fast, the parcels heavy around him, and had made thirty yards into the trees when his finger-ring started its tingling. Slowly he moved on, feeling his way from time to time. The tingling gradually weakened with distance, faded out after eight hundred yards.

From then on he consulted his luminous compass at least a hundred times. It led him back to the road at a point half a mile from the car, a pardonable margin of error in a twenty-mile journey two-thirds of which had been covered in darkness. At two hours after dawn he arrived with tired eyes and aching feet, clambered thankfully into the car, edged it unseen from the forest and purred along the highroad to the dump called home.

The day of the appointment kicked off with a highly significant start. On the radio and video, through the public address system and in all the newspapers the government came out with the same announcement. Mowry heard the miserably muffled bellowings of a loudspeaker two streets away, the shrill cries of news venders. He bought a paper, read it over his breakfast.

"Under the War Emergency Powers Act, by order of the Jaimec Ministry of Defense: All organizations, societies, parties and other corporate bodies will be registered at the Central Bureau of Records, Pertane, not later than the twentieth of this month. Secretaries will state in full the objects and purposes of their respective organizations, societies, parties or other corporate bodies, give the address of habitual meeting places and provide a complete list of members.

"Under the War Emergency Powers Act, by order of the Jaimec Ministry of Defense: After the twentieth of this month any organization, society, party or other corporate body will be deemed an illegal movement if not registered in accordance with the above order. Membership of an illegal movement or the giving of aid and comfort to any member of an illegal movement will constitute a treacherous offense punishable by death."

So at last they'd made a countermove. *Dirac Angestun Gesept* must kneel at the confessional or at the strangling-post. By a simple, easy legislative trick they'd got D.A.G. where they wanted it, coming and going. It was a kill-or-cure tactic full of psychological menace and well calculated to scare all the weaklings right out of D.A.G.'s ranks.

Weaklings are blabs.

They talk. They betray their fellows, one by one, right through the chain of command to the top. They represent the rot that spreads through a system and brings it to total collapse. In theory, anyway.

Mowry read it again, grinning to himself and enjoying every word. The government was going to have a tough time enticing informers from the D.A.G. Fat lot of talking can be done by a membership completely unaware of its status. There are no traitors in a phantom army.

For instance, Butin Arhava was a fully paid up member in good standing—and didn't know it. Nobody had bothered to tell him. The Kaitempi could trap him and draw out his bowels very, very slowly without gaining one worthwhile word about the Sirian Freedom Party.

Around mid-day Mowry looked in at the Central Bureau of Records. Sure enough a line stretched from the door to the counter where a couple of disdainful officials were dishing out forms. The line slowly edged forward, composed of secretaries or other officers of trade guilds, *zith*-drinking societies, video fan clubs and every other conceivable kind of organization. The skinny oldster moping in the rear was Area Supervisor of the Pan-Sirian Association of Lizard Watchers. The podgy specimen one step ahead of him represented the Pertane Model Rocket Builders Club. There wasn't one in the entire string who looked capable of spitting in a Spakum eye much less overthrowing his own government.

Joining the line, Mowry said conversationally to Skinny, "Nuisance this, isn't it?"

"Yar. Only the Statue of Jaime knows why it is considered necessary."

"Maybe they're trying to round up people with special talents," Mowry offered. "Radio experts, photographers and folk like those. They can use all sorts of technicians in wartime."

"They could have said so in plain words," opined Skinny impatiently. "They could have published a list of them and ordered them to report in."

"Yar, that's right."

"My group watches lizards. Of what special use is a lizardwatcher, *hi?*"

"I can't imagine. Why watch lizards, anyway?"

"Have *you* ever watched them?"

"No," admitted Mowry, without shame.

"Then you don't know the fascination of it."

Podgy turned round and said with a superior air, "My group builds model rockets."

"Kid stuff," defined Skinny.

"That's what you think. I'll have you know every member is a potential rocket-engineer and in time of war a rocket-engineer is a valuable—"

"Move up," said Skinny, nudging him. They shuffled forward, stopped. Skinny said to Mowry, "What's your crowd do?"

"We etch glass."

"Well, that's a high form of art. I have seen some very attractive examples of it myself. They were luxury articles though. A bit beyond the common purse." He let go a loud sniff. "What good are glass-etchers for winning battles?"

"You guess," Mowry invited.

"Now take rockets," put in Podgy. "The rocket is essential to space war and—"

"Move up," ordered Skinny again.

They reached the stack of forms, were each given one off the top. The group dispersed, going their various ways while a long line of later comers edged toward the counter. Mowry went to the main post office, sat at a vacant table, filled up the form carefully and neatly. He got some satisfaction out of doing it with a government pen and government ink.

Title of organization: *Dirac Angestun Gesept.*

Purpose of organization: *Destruction of present government and termination of war against Terra.*

Customary meeting place: *Wherever Kaitempi can't find us.*

Names and addresses of elected officers: *You'll find out when it's too late.*

Attach hereto complete list of members: *Nar.*

Signature: *Jaime Shallapurta.*

That last touch would get someone hopping mad. It was a calculated insult to the much revered Statue of Jaime. Loosely translated it meant James Stoneybottom.

He bought an envelope, was about to mail it back to the Bureau when it occurred to him to hot it up still more. Forthwith he took the form to his room, shoved it into the embossing machine and impressed it with the Kaitempi cartouche. Then he posted it.

This performance pleased him immensely. A month ago it would have been too childish to bother with and the recipients would have dismissed it as the work of someone feeble-minded. But today the circumstances were vastly different. The powers-that-be had revealed themselves as annoyed if not frightened. They were in a poor mood to relish a raspberry. With moderate luck the sardonic registration form would boost their anger and that would be all to the good because a mind filled with fury cannot think in a cool, logical manner.

When one is fighting a paper-war one uses paper-war tactics that in the long run can be just as lethal as high explosive. And the tactics are not limited in scope by use of one material. The said material is very variable in form. Paper can convey a private warning, a public threat, secret temptation, open defiance; wall-bills, window-stickers, leaflets dropped by the thousands from the roof-tops, cards left on seats or slipped into pockets and purses . . . *money.*

Yes, money.

With paper money he could buy a lot of the deeds needed to back up the words. With paper money he could persuade the Sirian foe to kick himself good and hard in the pants and thereby save the Terrans a tedious chore.

At the proper hour he set out for the Cafe Susun.

Not having yet received the D.A.G.'s thumb-on-nose registration the Jaimecan authorities were still able to think in a calculating and menacing way. Their countermoves had not been confined to that morning's new law. They had taken matters further by concocting a dangerous technique, namely, that of the snap-search.

It almost caught Mowry at the first grab. He did not congratulate himself on his escape, realizing that to avoid one trap might be merely to fall into another. The risk was great, the trick being of such a type that none could tell when or where the next blow would fall.

He was heading for his rendezvous when suddenly a line of uniformed police extended itself across the street. A second line simultaneously did likewise four hundred yards farther on. From the dumbfounded mob trapped between the lines appeared a number of plainclothes members of the Kaitempi. These at once commenced a swift and expert search of everyone thus halted in the street. Meanwhile both lines of police kept their full attention inward, watching to see that nobody ducked into a doorway and bolted through a house to escape the mass-frisk.

Thanking his lucky stars that he was outside the trap and being ignored, Mowry faded into the background as inconspicuously as possible and beat it home fast. In his room he burned all documents relating to Shir Agavan, crumbled the ashes into fine dust. That identity was now dead forever and ever, amen. It would never be used again.

From one of his packages he took a new set of papers swearing before all and sundry that he was Krag Wulkin, special correspondent of a leading news agency, with a home address on Diracta. In some ways it was a better camouflage than the former one. It lent added plausibility to his Mashambi accent. Moreover a complete check on it would involve wasting a month referring back to the Sirian home planet.

Thus armed he started out again. Though better fitted to face awkward questions the risk of being asked them had been greatly boosted by this latest technique and he took to the streets with the queasy feeling that somehow or other the hunt at last had picked up the scent.

There was no way of telling exactly what the snap-searchers were seeking. Maybe they were trying to catch people carrying subversive propaganda on their persons. Or perhaps they were looking for treacherous *sokos* with D.A.G. membership cards. Or could be they were haphazardly groping around for a dynocar renter named Shir Agavan. Whatever their reasons, the tactic proved that someone among Jaimec's big shots had become aggravated.

Luckily no more traps opened in his path before he reached the Cafe Susun. He went in, found Arhava and two others seated at the far table where they were half-concealed in dim light and could keep watch on the door.

"You're late," greeted Arhava. "We thought you weren't coming."

"I got delayed by a police raid on the street. The cops looked surly. You fellows just robbed a bank or something?"

"No, we haven't." Arhava made a casual gesture toward his companions. "Meet Gurd and Skriva."

Mowry acknowledged them with a curt nod, looked them over. They were much alike, obviously brothers. Flat-faced, hard-eyed with pinned-back ears that came up to sharp points. Each looked capable of selling the other into slavery provided there was no comeback with a knife.

"We haven't heard *your* name," said Gurd, speaking between long, narrow teeth.

"You aren't going to, either," responded Mowry.

Gurd bristled. "Why not?"

"Because you don't really care what my name is," Mowry told him. "If the thing atop your neck has a steady tick it's a matter of total indifference to you *who* gives you a load of guilders."

"Yar, that's right," chipped in Skriva, his eyes glittering. "Money is money regardless of who hands it over. Shut up, Gurd."

"I only wanted to know," mumbled Gurd, subdued.

Arhava took over with the mouth-watering eagerness of one on the make. "I've given these boys your proposition. They're interested." He turned to them. "Aren't you?"

"Yar," said Skriva. He concentrated attention upon Mowry. "You want someone in his box. That right?"

"I want someone stone cold and I don't give a hoot whether or not he is boxed."

"We can tend to that." He fixed his toughest expression which told all and sundry that he'd kilt him a b'ar when he wuz only three. Then he said, "For fifty thousand."

Emitting a deep sigh, Mowry stood up, ambled toward the door. "Live long!"

"Come back!" Skriva shot to his feet, waved urgently. Arhava had the appalled look of someone suddenly cut out of a rich uncle's will. Gurd sucked his teeth with visible agitation.

Pausing at the door, Mowry held it open. "You stupes ready to talk sense?"

"Sure," pleaded Skriva. "I was only joking. Come back and sit down."

"Bring us four *ziths,*" said Mowry to the attendant who was blearing behind the counter. He returned to the table, resumed his seat. "No more bad jokes. I don't appreciate them."

"Forget it," advised Skriva. "We've got a couple of questions for you."

"You may voice them," agreed Mowry. He accepted a mug of *zith* from the attendant, paid him, took a swig, eyed Skriva with becoming lordliness.

Skriva said, "Who d'you want us to slap down? And how do we know we're going to get our money?"

"For the first, the victim is Colonel Hage-Ridarta." He scribbled rapidly on a piece of paper, gave it to the other. "That is his address."

"I see." Skriva stared at the slip, went on, "And the money?"

"I'll pay you five thousand right now as an act of faith, fifteen thousand when the job is done." He stopped, gave the three of them the cold, forbidding eye. "I don't take your word for the doing. It's got to be squawked on the news channels before I part with another one-tenth guilder."

"You trust us a lot, don't you?" said Skriva, scowling.

"No more than I have to."

"Same applies on this side."

"Look," Mowry urged, "we've *got* to play ball with each other whether we like it or not. Here's how. I've got a list. If you do the first job for me and I renege you're not going to do the others, are you?"

"No."

"What's more, you'll take it out of my hide first chance you get, won't you?"

"You can bet on that," assured Gurd.

"Similarly, if you pull a fast one on me you will cut off the flow of money, big money. You'll deprive yourselves of far more than the Kaitempi would pay for betraying me and a dozen others. I'm outbidding the Kaitempi by a large margin, see? Don't you fellows *want* to get rich?"

"I hate the idea of it," said Skriva. "Let's see that five thousand."

Mowry slipped him the package under the table. The three checked it in their laps. After a while Skriva looked up, his face slightly flushed.

"We're sold. Who is this Hage-Ridarta *soko?*"

"Just a brasshat who has lived too long."

That was a half-truth. Hage-Ridarta was listed in the city directory as officer commanding an outfit of space marines. But his name had been appended to an authoritative letter in Pigface's files. The tone of the latter had been that of a boss to an underling. Hage-Ridarta was an officially disguised occupant of the Kaitempi top bracket and therefore would make a most satisfactory corpse.

"Why d'you want him out of the way?" demanded Gurd, still sullen and suspicious.

Before Mowry could reply, Skriva said fiercely, "I told you before to shut up. I'll handle this. Can't you button your trap even for twenty thousand?"

"We haven't got it yet," persisted Gurd.

"You will get it," Mowry soothed. "And more, lots more. The day the news of Hage-Ridarta's death is given in the papers or on the radio I'll be here at the same time in the evening complete with fifteen thousand guilders and the next name. If by any chance I'm held up and can't make it, I'll be here at the same time the following evening."

"You'd better be!" informed Gurd, glowering.

Arhava had a question of his own. "What's my percentage for introducing the boys?"

"I don't know." Mowry turned to Skriva. "How much do you intend to give him?"

"Who?—me?" Skriva was taken aback.

"Yes, you. The gentleman thirsts for a rakeoff. You don't expect me to pay him, do you? Think I'm made of money?"

"Somebody had better fork out," declared Arhava, making the mistake of his life. "Or—"

Skriva shoved scowling features up against him and breathed over his face. "Or *what?*"

"Nothing," said Arhava, nervously leaning away. "Nothing at all."

"That's better," Skriva approved in grating tones. "That's a whole lot better. Just sit around and be a good boy, Butin, and we'll feed you crumbs from our table. Get fidgety and you'll soon find yourself in no condition to eat them. In fact you won't be able to swallow. It's tough when a fellow can't swallow. You wouldn't like that, would you, Butin?"

Saying nothing, Arhava sat still. His complexion was slightly mottled.

Repeating the face-shoving act, Skriva shouted, "I just asked you a civil question. I said you wouldn't like it, would you?"

"No," admitted Arhava, tilting back his chair to get away from the face.

Mowry decided the time had come to leave this happy scene. He took his daring far enough to say to Skriva, "Don't get tough ideas about *me*—if you want to stay in business."

With that, he went. He did not worry about the possibility of any of them following him. They wouldn't dare, being too afraid of offending the best customer they'd had since crime came to Pertane.

As he walked rapidly along he pondered the evening's work, decided it had been a wise move to insist that money did not grow on trees. They'd have shown no respect whatsoever if he'd been willing to shove it out regardless as, in fact, he could afford to do should the necessity arise. They'd have put on maximum pressure to gain the most in return for the least and that would have produced more arguments than results.

It was also a good thing that he'd refused a cut to Arhava and left them to fight it out between themselves. The reaction had been revealing. A mob, even a small mob, is only as strong as its weakest link. Anyone capable of ratting to the Kaitempi could blow the whole bunch sky-high. It was important to discover a prospective squealer before it was too late and, if one existed, to be warned accordingly. In this respect Butin Arhava hadn't shown up so good.

"Somebody had better fork out or—"

The testing-time would come soon after he'd paid over fifteen thousand guilders for a job well done and those concerned divided the loot. Well, if the situation seemed to justify it, that's when he'd give the Gurd-Skriva brothers the next name—that of Butin Arhava. He felt no compunction about this decision, no qualms of conscience. So far as he was involved, all Sirians were enemies, any one of them being no more or less a foe than any other.

He continued homeward, deep in thought and not looking where he was going while he settled this matter in his mind. He had just reached the final conclusion that Arhava's throat would have to be slit sooner or later when a heavy hand clamped on his shoulder and a voice rasped in his ear.

"Lift them up, Dreamy, and let's see what you've got in your pockets. Come on, you're not deaf, lift 'em I said!"

With a sense of sudden shock he raised his arms, felt fingers start prying into his clothes. Nearby forty or fifty equally surprised walkers were holding the same pose. A line of phlegmatic police stood across the street a hundred yards away. In the opposite direction a second line looked on with the same indifference. Yet again the random trap had sprung.

Chapter 6

A flood of superfast thoughts raced through his startled brain as he stood with arms extended above his head. Thank heavens he'd got rid of that money; they'd have been unpleasantly inquisitive about so large a sum being carried in one lump. If they were looking for Shir Agavan they were dead out of luck. In any case, he wasn't going to let them take him in, even for questioning. Not if he could help it. Most people who survived a Kaitempi interrogation did so as physical wrecks. It would be better at the last resort to break this searcher's neck and run like blazes.

"If the cops shoot me down it'll be a quicker and easier end. When Terra gets no more signals from me, Wolf will choose my successor and feed the poor sap the same—"

"Hi?" The Kaitempi agent broke his train of thought by holding Mowry's wallet open and gazing with surprise at Pigface's card reposing therein. The tough expression faded from his heavy features as if wiped away with a cloth. "One of us? An officer?" He took a closer look at the other. "But I do not recognize *you.*"

"You wouldn't," informed Mowry, showing just the right degree of arrogance. "I arrived only today from H.Q. on Diracta." He pulled a face. "And this is the reception I get."

"It cannot be helped," apologized the agent. "The revolutionary movement must be suppressed at all costs and it's as big a menace here as on any other planet. You know how things are on Diracta—well, they're not one whit better on Jaimec."

"It won't last," Mowry responded, speaking with authority. "On Diracta we expect to make a complete clean-up in the near future. After that you won't have much trouble here. The movement will collapse from sheer lack of leadership. When you cut off the head, the body dies."

"I hope you're right. The Spakum war is enough without an army of traitors sniping in the rear." He closed the wallet, gave it back. His other hand held the Krag Wulkin documents at which he had not yet looked. Waiting for Mowry to pocket the wallet, he returned the remaining material and said jocularly, "Here are your false papers."

"Nothing is false that has been officially issued," said Mowry, frowning disapproval.

"No, I suppose not. I hadn't thought of it in that light." The agent backed off, anxious to end the talk. "Sorry to have troubled you. I suggest you call at local headquarters as soon as possible and have them circulate your photo so that you'll be known to us. Otherwise you may be stopped and searched repeatedly."

"I'll do that," promised Mowry, unable to imagine anything he'd less intention of doing.

"You'll excuse me—I must tend to these others." So saying, the agent attracted the attention of the nearest police, pointed to Mowry. Then he made for a sour-faced civilian who was standing nearby waiting to be searched. Reluctantly the civilian lifted his arms and permitted the agent to dip into his pockets.

Mowry walked toward the line of police which opened and let him pass through. At such moments, he thought, one is supposed to be cool, calm and collected, radiating supreme self-confidence in all directions. He wasn't like that at all. On the contrary he was weak in the knees and had a vague feeling of sickness in the stomach. He had to force himself to continue steadily onward with what appeared to be absolute nonchalance.

He made six hundred yards, reached the next corner before some warning instinct made him look back. Police were still blocking the road but beyond them four of the Kaitempi had clustered together in conversation. One of them, the agent who had released him, pointed his way. The other three shot a glance in the same direction, resumed talking with vehement gestures. There followed what appeared to be ten seconds of heated argument before they reached a decision.

"Stop him!"

The nearest police turned round startled, their eyes seeking a fleeing quarry. Mowry's legs became filled with an almost irresistible urge to get going twenty to the dozen. He forced them by an effort of will to maintain their steady pace.

There were a lot of people in the street, some merely hanging around and gaping at the trap, others walking the same way as himself. Most of the latter wanted no part of what was going on higher up the road and considered it expedient to amble someplace else. Mowry kept with them, showing no great hurry. That baffled the police; for a few valuable seconds they stayed put, hands on weapons, while they sought in vain for visible evidence of guilt.

It proved sufficient delay to enable him to get round the corner and out of sight. At that point the shouting Kaitempi realized that the police were stalled. They lost patience, broke into a furious sprint. Half a dozen clumping cops immediately raced with them, still without knowing who was being chased or why.

Overtaking a youth who was sauntering dozily along, Mowry gave him an urgent shove in the back. "Quick!—they're after you! The Kaitempi!"

"I've done nothing. I—"

"How long will it take to convince them of that? *Run,* you fool!"

The other used up a few moments gaping skeptically before he heard the oncoming rush of heavy feet, the raucous shouts of pursuers nearing the corner. He lost color, tore down the road at velocity that paid tribute to his innocence. He'd have overtaken and passed a bolting jackrabbit with no trouble at all.

Unhurriedly entering an adjacent shop, Mowry threw a swift look around to see what it sold, said casually, "I wish ten of those small cakes with the toasted-nut tops and—"

The arm of the law thundered round the corner fifty strong. The hunt roared past the shop, its leaders baying with triumph as they spotted the distant figure of him who had done nothing. Mowry stared at the window in dumb amazement. The corpulent Sirian behind the counter eyed the window with sad resignation.

"Whatever is happening?" asked Mowry.

"They're after someone," diagnosed Fatty. He sighed, rubbed his protruding belly. "Always they are after someone. What a world! What a war!"

"Makes you tired, *hi?*"

"Aie, yar! Every day, every minute there is something. Last night, according to the news channels, they destroyed the main Spakum space fleet for the tenth time. Today they are pursuing the remnants of what is said to have been destroyed. For months we have been making triumphant retreats before a demoralized enemy who is advancing in utter disorder." He made a sweeping motion with a podgy hand. It indicated disgust. "I am fat, as you can see. That makes me an idiot. You wish—?"

"Ten of those small cakes with the toasted-nut—"

A belated cop pounded past the window. He was two hundred yards behind the pack and breathless but plain stubborn. As he thudded along he let go a couple of shots into the air just for the heck of it.

"See what I mean?" said Fatso. "You wish—?"

"Ten of those small cakes with the toasted-nut tops. I also wish to order a special celebration cake to be supplied five days hence. Perhaps you can show me some examples or help me with suggestions, *hi?*"

He managed to waste twenty minutes within the shop and the time was well worth the few guilders it cost. If he'd wanted he could have stayed longer. Twenty minutes, he estimated, would be just enough to permit local excitement to die down while the pursuit continued elsewhere. But the longer he extended the time the greater the risk of falling into the hands of frustrated huntsmen who'd returned to comb out the area.

Halfway home he was tempted to donate the cakes to a mournful looking cop, but refrained. The time for having fun had gone by and some restraint was called for. The more he had to dodge authority's frantic fly-swattings the harder it was to play like a wasp and get a laugh out of it.

Within his room he flopped fully dressed on the bed and summarized the day's doings. He had escaped a trap but only by the skin of his teeth. It proved that such traps were escapable—but not forever. What had caused them to take after him he did not know, could only guess at. Probably the intervention of an officious character who had noticed him walking through the cordon.

"Who's that you've let go?"

"An officer, Captain."

"What d'you mean, an officer?"

"A Kaitempi officer, Captain. I do not know him but he had a correct card. He said that he had just been drafted from Diracta."

"A card, *hi?* Did you notice its serial number?"

"I had no particular reason to try to remember it, Captain. It was obviously genuine. But let me see . . . yar . . . it was SXB80313. Or perhaps SXB80131. I am not sure which."

"Major Sallana's card was SXB80131. You half-witted *soko,* you may have had his killer in your hands!"

"STOP HIM!"

Now, by virtue of the fact that he had evaded capture, plus the fact that he had failed to turn up at headquarters to gain photographic identification, they'd assume that Sallana's slayer really had been in the net. Previously they had not known where to start looking other than within the ranks of the mysteriously elusive D.A.G. But they had gained three welcome advantages. They knew the killer was in Pertane. They had a description of him. One Kaitempi agent could be relied upon to recognize him on sight.

In other words, the heat was on with every likelihood of getting hotter. Numberless eyes would be keeping watch of anyone bearing close resemblance to himself. The snap-search technique would be intensified, the net spread wider and with greater frequency. In these conditions he'd have to go around daytimes carrying stuff guaranteed to make the Kaitempi lick their chops like hungry tigers.

Some evenings he'd have to go to the Cafe Susun bearing a load of money that no searcher in his right mind would regard as a beggar's alms.

Henceforth, in Pertane at least, the going would be tougher with the pressure-cell and the strangling-post looming ever nearer. He groaned to himself as he thought of it. He had never asked much of life and would have been quite satisfied merely to sprawl on a golden throne and be fawned upon by sycophants. To be dropped down a Sirian-dug hole, dead cold and dyed purple, was to take things too much to the opposite extreme.

But to counterbalance this dismal prospect there was something heartening—a snatch of conversation.

"The revolutionary movement . . . as big a menace here as on any other planet. You know how things are on Diracta—well, they're not one whit better on Jaimec."

That told him plenty; it revealed that *Dirac Angestun Gesept* was not merely a Wolf-concocted nightmare designed to disturb the sleep of Jaimecan politicos. It was empire-wide, covering more than a hundred planets, its strength or rather its pseudo-strength greatest on the home-world of Diracta, the nerve-center and beating heart of the entire Sirian species. It was more than a hundred times greater than had appeared to him in his purely localized endeavors.

To the Sirian powers-that-be it was a major peril hacking down the back door while the Terrans were busily bashing in the front one.

Cheers! Blow the bugle, beat the drum! Other wasps were at work, separated in space but united in purpose. And in this sense he was not alone.

Somebody in the Sirian High Command—a psychologist or a cynic—worked it out that the more one chivvied the civilian population the lower sank its morale. The constant stream of new emergency orders, regulations, restrictions, the constant police and Kaitempi activity, stoppings, searchings, questionings all tended to create that dull, pessimistic resignation demonstrated by Fatty in the cake shop. An antidote was needed. The citizens had bread. They lacked the circus.

Accordingly a show was put on. The radio, video and newspapers combined to strike up the band and draw the crowds.

GREAT VICTORY IN CENTAURI SECTOR.

Yesterday powerful Terran space forces became trapped in the region of A. Centauri and a fierce battle raged as they tried to break out. The Sirian fourth, sixth and seventh fleets, maneuvering in masterly manner, frustrated all their efforts to get free and escape. Many casualties were inflicted upon the enemy. Precise figures are not yet available but the latest report from the area of conflict states that we have lost four battleships and one light cruiser, the crews of which have all been rescued. More than seventy Terran warships have been destroyed.

And so the story went on for minutes of time and columns of print, complete with pictures of the battleship *Hashim,* the heavy cruiser *Jaimec,* some members of their crews when home on leave a year ago, Rear Admiral Pent-Gurhana saluting a prosperous navy contractor, the Statue of Jaime casting its shadow across a carefully positioned Terran banner and—loveliest touch of all—

a five centuries old photograph of a scowling, bedraggled bunch of Mongolian bandits authoritatively described as "Terran space troops whom we snatched from death as their stricken ship plunged sunward."

One columnist, graciously admitting lack of facts and substituting so-called expert knowledge, devoted half a page to a lurid description of how heroic space marines had performed the snatch-from-death *in vacuo.* How fortunate were the lousy Terrans, he proclaimed, in finding themselves opposed by so daring and gallant a foe.

Mowry absorbed all this guff, found himself unable to decide whether casualty figures had been reversed or whether a fight had taken place at all. Dismissing it with a sniff of disdain, he sought through the rest of the paper without really expecting to find anything worthy of note. But there was a small item on the back page.

Colonel Hage-Ridarta, officer commanding 77 Company S.M. was found dead in his car at midnight last night. He had been shot through the head. A gun was lying nearby. Suicide is not suspected and police investigations are continuing.

So the Gurd-Skriva combination worked mighty fast; they'd done the job within a few hours of taking it on. Yar, money was a wonderful thing especially when Terran engravers had presses that could produce it in unlimited supply with little trouble and at small cost. Money was a formidable weapon in its own right, a paper totem that could cause losses in the enemy's ranks millions of miles behind the fighting front.

This unexpected promptitude set him a new problem. To get more such action he'd have to pay up and thereby risk falling into another trap while on the way to the rendezvous. Right now he dare not show Pigface's card in Pertane though it might prove useful elsewhere. His documents for Krag Wulkin, special correspondent, might possibly get him out of a jam provided the trappers didn't search further, find him loaded with guilders and ask difficult questions about so suspiciously large a wad.

Within an hour the High Command solved the problem for him. They put on the circus in the form of a victory parade. To the beat and blare of a dozen bands a great column of troops, tanks, guns, mobile radar units, flame-throwers, rocket-batteries and gas-projectors, tracked recovery vehicles and other paraphernalia crawled into Pertane from the west, tramped and rumbled toward the east.

Helicopters and jet planes swooped at low level, a small number of nimble space-scouts thundered at great altitude. Citizens assembled in their thousands, lined the streets and cheered more from habit than from genuine enthusiasm.

This, Mowry realized, was his heaven-sent opportunity. Snap-searchers might continue down the side streets and in the city's tough quarters but they'd be well-nigh impossible on the east-west artery with all that military traffic passing through. If he could reach the cross-town route he could head clean out of Pertane with safety. After that he could dance around elsewhere until the time was ripe to return attention to the capital.

He paid his miserly landlord two months' rent in advance without creating more than joyful surprise. Then he checked his false identity papers. Hurriedly he packed his bag with guilders, a fresh supply of stickers, a couple of small packages and got out.

No sudden traps opened out between there and the city center; even if they ran around like mad the police could not be everywhere at once. On the east-west road he carried his bag unnoticed, being of less significance than a grain of sand amid the great mob of spectators that had assembled. By the same token progress was difficult and slow. The route was crowded almost to the walls. Time and again he had to shove his way past the backs of an audience which had its full attention on the road.

Many of the shops he passed had boarded-up windows as evidence that they had been favored by his propaganda. Others displayed new glass and on twenty-seven of these he slapped more stickers while a horde of potential witnesses stood on tiptoe, stared over their fellows at the military procession. One sticker he plastered on a policeman's back, the broad, inviting stretch of black cloth proving irresistible. The cop gaped forward along with the crowd, ignored pressure behind him and got decorated from shoulder to shoulder.

Who will pay for this war?
Those who started it will pay.
With their money—and their lives.
Dirac Angestun Gesept.

After three hours of edging, pushing and some surreptitious sticker-planting he arrived at the city's outskirts. Here the tail end of the parade was still trundling noisily along. Standing spectators had thinned out but a straggling group of goon-fanciers were walking in pace with the troops.

Around stood houses of a suburb too snooty to deserve the attentions of the police and Kaitempi. Ahead stretched the open country and the road to Radine. He carried straight on, following the rearmost troops until the procession turned leftward and headed for the great military stronghold of Khamasta. Here the accompanying civilians halted and watched them go before mooching back to Pertane. Bag in hand, Mowry continued along the Radine road.

Moodiness afflicted him as he walked. He became obsessed with the notion that he had been chased out of the city even if only temporarily and he didn't like it. Every step he took seemed like another triumph for the foe, another defeat for himself. Given the free choice he'd have stayed put, accepting increasing risks as they came, glorying in meeting and beating them. He didn't have a free choice, not really.

At the training college they had lectured him again and again to the same effect. "Maybe you *like* having a mulish character. Well, in some circumstances it's called courage, in others it's downright stupidity. You've got to resist the temptation to indulge unprofitable heroics. Never abandon caution merely because you think it looks like cowardice. It required guts to sacrifice one's ego for the sake of the job. Those are the sort of guts we want and must have. A dead hero is of no earthly use to us!"

Humph! Easy for them to talk, hard for those who have to listen and obey. He was still aggrieved when he reached a permasteel plaque standing by the roadside. It said: *Radine—33 den.* He looked in both directions, found nobody in sight. Opening his bag he took out a package and buried it at the base of the plaque.

That evening he checked in at Radine's best and most expensive hotel. If the Jaimecan authorities succeeded in following his tortuous trail around Pertane they'd notice his penchant for hiding out in overcrowded, slummy areas and tend to seek him in the planet's rat-holes. With luck a high-priced hotel would be the last place in which they'd look for him if the search spread wider afield. All the same he'd have to be wary of the routine check of hotel registers which the Kaitempi made every now and again regardless.

Dumping his bag he left the room at once. Time was pressing. He hurried along the road, unworried about snap-searches which for unknown reasons were confined to the capital, and had not yet been applied to other cities. Reaching a bank of public phone booths a mile from the hotel, he made a call to Pertane. A sour voice answered while the booth's tiny screen remained blank.

"Cafe Susun."

"Skriva there?"

"Who wants him?"

"Me."

"That tells me a lot. Why've you got that scanner switched off?"

"Listen who's talking," growled Mowry, eyeing his faceless screen. "You fetch Skriva and let him cope with his own troubles. You aren't his paid secretary, are you?"

There came a loud snort, a long silence, then Skriva's voice sounded. "Who's this?"

"Give me your pic and I'll give you mine."

"I know who it is—I recognize the tones," said Skriva. He switched his scanner, his unpleasing features gradually bloomed into the screen. Mowry switched likewise. Skriva frowned at him with dark suspicion. "Thought you were going to meet us here. Why are you phoning?"

"I've been called out of town and can't get back for a piece."

"Is *that* so?"

"Yar, that *is* so!" snapped Mowry. "And don't get hard with me because I won't stand for it, see?" He paused to let it sink in, went on, "You got a dyno?"

"Maybe," said Skriva, evasively.

"Can you leave right away?"

"Maybe."

"If you want the goods you can cut out the maybes and move fast." Mowry held his phone before the scanner, tapped it suggestively, pointed to his ears to indicate that one never knew who was listening in these days and might perhaps have to be beaten to it. "Get onto the Radine road and look under marker 33-*den*. *Don't* take Arhava with you."

"Hey, when will you—"

He slammed down the phone, cutting off the other's irate query. Next he sought the local Kaitempi H.Q. the address of which had been revealed in Pigface's secret correspondence.

In a short time he passed the building, keeping as far from it as possible on the other side of the street. He did not give close attention to the building itself, his gaze being concentrated above it. For the next hour he wandered around Radine with seeming aimlessness, still studying the areas above the rooftops.

Eventually satisfied he looked for the city hall, found it, repeated the process. More erratic mooching from street to street while apparently admiring the stars. Finally he returned to the hotel.

Next morning he took a small package from his bag, pocketed it, made straight for a large business block noted the previous evening. With a convincing air of self-assurance he entered the building, took the automatic elevator to the top floor. Here he found a dusty, seldom-used passage with a drop-ladder at one end.

There was nobody around. Even if somebody had come along they might not have been unduly curious. Anyway, he had all his answers ready. Pulling down the ladder he climbed it swiftly, got through the trapdoor at the top and onto the roof. From his package he took a tiny inductance coil fitted with clips and attached to a long half-thin cable with plug-in terminals at its other end.

Climbing a short trellis mast, he counted the wires on the telephone junction at its top, checked the direction in which the seventh one ran. To this he carefully fastened the coil. Then he descended, led the cable to the roof's edge, gently paid it out until it was dangling full length into the road below. Its plug-in terminals were now swinging in the air at a point about four feet above the pavement.

Even as he looked down from the roof half a dozen pedestrians passed the hanging cable and showed no interest in it. A couple of them glanced idly upward, saw somebody above and wandered onward without remark. Nobody questions the activities of a man who clambers over roofs or disappears down grids in the street providing he does it openly and with quiet confidence.

He got down and out without mishap. Within an hour he had performed the same feat atop another building and again got away unchallenged. His next move was to purchase another typewriter, paper, envelopes, a small hand-printing set. It was still only midday when he returned to his room and set to work as fast as he could go. The task continued without abate all that day and most of the next day. When he had finished the hand-printer and typewriter slid silently into the lake.

The result was the placing in his case of two hundred and twenty letters for future use and the immediate mailing of another two hundred and twenty to those who had received his first warning. The recipients, he hoped, would be far from charmed by the arrival of a second letter with a third yet to come.

Hage-Ridarta was the second.
The list is long.
Dirac Angestun Gesept.

After lunch he consulted yesterday's and today's newspapers at which he'd been too busy to look before now. The item he sought was not there: not a word about the late lamented Butin Arhava. Momentarily he wondered whether anything had gone wrong, whether the Gurd-Skriva brothers had jibbed at his choice of a victim or whether they were merely being slow on the uptake.

The general news was much as usual. Victory still loomed nearer and nearer. Casualties in the real or mythical A. Centauri battle were now officially confirmed at eleven Sirian warships, ninety-four Terran ones. That data was given a front-page spread and a double column of editorial hallelujahs.

On an inner page, in an inconspicuous corner, it was announced that Sirian forces had abandoned the twin worlds of Fedira and Fedora, the forty-seventh and forty-eighth planets of the empire, "for strategic reasons." It was also hinted that Gooma, the sixty-second planet, might soon be given up also, "in order to enable us to strengthen our positions elsewhere."

So they were admitting something that could no longer be denied, namely, that two planets had gone down the drain with a third soon to follow. Although they had not said so it was pretty certain that what they had given up the Terrans had grabbed. Mowry grinned to himself as words uttered in the cake shop came back to his mind.

"For months we have been making triumphant retreats before a demoralized enemy advancing in utter disorder."

He went along the road, called the Cafe Susun. "Did you collect?"

"We did," said Skriva, "and the next consignment is overdue."

"I've read nothing about it."

"You wouldn't—nothing having been written."

"Well, I told you before that I pay when I've had proof. Until I get it, nothing doing. No proof, no dough."

"We've got the evidence. It's up to you to take a look at it."

Mowry thought swiftly. "Still got the dyno handy?"

"Yar."

"Maybe you'd better meet me. Make it the ten-time hour, same road, Marker *den*-8."

The car arrived dead on time. Mowry stood by the marker, a dim figure in the darkness of night with only fields and trees around. The car rolled up, headlights glaring. Skriva got out, took a small sack from the trunk, opened its top and exhibited its contents in the blaze of the lights.

"God in heaven!" said Mowry, his stomach jumping.

"It's a ragged job," admitted Skriva. "He had a tough neck, the knife was blunt and Gurd was in a hurry. What's the matter? You squeamish or something?"

"I'd have liked it less messy. A bullet would have been neater."

"You're not paying for neatness. If you want it done sweet and clean and tidy say so and jack up the offer."

"I'm not complaining."

"You bet you're not. Butin's the boy who's entitled to gripe." He kicked the sack. "Aren't you, Butin?"

"Get rid of it," ordered Mowry. "It's spoiling my appetite."

Letting go a grim chuckle, Skriva tossed the sack into an adjacent ditch, put out a hand. "The money."

Giving him the package, Mowry waited in silence while the other checked the contents inside the car with the help of Gurd. They thumbed the neat stack of notes lovingly, with much licking of lips and mutual congratulations.

When they had finished Skriva chuckled again. "That was twenty thousand for nothing. We couldn't have got it easier."

"What d'you mean, for nothing?" Mowry asked.

"We'd have done it anyway, whether you'd named him or not. Butin was making ready to talk. You could see it in the slimy *soko*'s eyes. What d'you say, Gurd?"

Gurd contented himself with a neck-wringing gesture.

Leaning on the car's door, Mowry said, "I've got another and different kind of job for you. Feel like taking it on?" Without waiting for response he exhibited another package. "In here are ten small gadgets. They're fitted with clips and have thin lengths of cable attached. I want these contraptions fastened to telephone lines in or near the center of Pertane. They've got to be set in place so that they aren't visible from the street but the cables can be seen hanging down."

"But," objected Skriva, "if the cables can be seen it's only a matter of time before somebody traces them up to the gadgets. Where's the sense of hiding what is sure to be found?"

"Where's the sense of me giving you good money to do it?" Mowry riposted.

"How much?"

"Five thousand guilders apiece. That's fifty thousand for the lot."

Skriva pursed his lips in a silent whistle.

"I can check whether you've actually fixed them," Mowry went on, "so don't try kidding me, see? We're in business together. Better not kiss the partnership goodbye."

Grabbing the package, Skriva rasped, "I think you're crazy—but who am I to complain?"

Headlights brightened, the car set up a shrill whine and rocked away. Mowry watched until it had gone from sight, then he tramped back into Radine, made for the public booths and phoned Kaitempi H.Q. He was careful to keep his scanner switched off and try to give his voice the singsong tones of a native Jaimecan.

"Somebody's been decapitated."

"Hi?"

"There's a head in a sack near Marker 8-*den* on the road to Pertane."

"Who's that talking? Who—"

He cut off, leaving the voice to gargle futilely. They'd follow up the tip, no doubt of that. It was essential to his plans that authority should find the head and identify it. In this respect he was persuading the Kaitempi to help play his game and he got quite a bit of malicious satisfaction out of it. He went to his hotel, came out, mailed two hundred and twenty letters.

Butin Arhava was the third.

The list is long.
Dirac Angestun Gesept.

That done, he enjoyed an hour's stroll before bedtime, pacing the streets and as usual pondering the day's work. It would not be long, he thought, before someone became curious about hanging cables and an electrician or telephone engineer was called in to investigate. The inevitable result would be a hurried examination of Jaimec's entire telephone system and the discovery of several more taps.

Authority would then find itself confronted with three unanswerable questions, all of them ominous: who's been listening, for how long, and how much have they learned?

He did not envy those in precarious power who were being subjected to this mock build-up of treachery while elsewhere the allegedly defeated Terrans were gaining sanctuary by taking over Sirian planets one after another. Uneasy lies the head that wears a crown—but infinitely more so when a wasp crawls into bed with it.

A little before the twelve-time hour he turned into the road where his high-class hideout was located, came to an abrupt halt. Outside the hotel stood a line of official cars, a fire-pump and an ambulance. A number of uniformed cops were meandering around the vehicles. Tough looking characters in plain clothes were all over the scene.

Two of the latter appeared out of nowhere and confronted him hard-eyed.

"What's happened?" asked Mowry, behaving like a Sunday school superintendent.

"Never mind what's happened. Show us your documents. Come on, what are you waiting for?"

Chapter 7

Carefully Mowry slid a hand into his inner pocket. They were tense, fully alert, watching his movement and ready to react if what he produced was not paper. He drew out his identity-card, handed it over knowing that it bore the proper cachet of Diracta and the overstamp of Jaimec. Then he gave them his personal card and movement permit. Inwardly he hoped with all his heart that they would be easily convinced.

They weren't. They displayed the dogged determination of those under strict orders to make someone pay dearly for something or other. Evidently whatever had occurred was serious enough to have stirred up a hornet's nest.

"A special correspondent," said the larger of the two mouthing the words with contempt. He looked up from the identity-card. "What is special about a correspondent?"

"I've been sent here to cover war news specifically from the Jaimec angle. I do not bother with civilian matters. Those are for ordinary reporters."

"I see." He gave Mowry a long, sharp, penetrating look. His eyes had the beady coldness of a sidewinder's. "From where do you get your news about the war?"

"From official handouts—mostly from the Office of War Information in Pertane."

"You have no other sources?"

"Yes, of course. I keep my ears open for gossip and rumors."

"And what do you do with *that* stuff?"

"I try to draw reasonable conclusions from it, write it up and submit the script to the Board of Censorship. If they approve it, I'm lucky. If they kill it, well"—he spread his hands with an air of helplessness—"I just put up with it."

"Therefore," said the Kaitempi agent, cunningly, "you should be well-known to officials of the Office of War Information and the Board of Censorship, *hi?* They will vouch for you if requested to do so, *hi?*"

"Without a doubt," assured Mowry, praying for a break.

"Good! You will name the ones you know best and we will check with them immediately."

"What, at this time of night?"

"Why should you care what time it is? It is your neck—"

That did it. Mowry punched him on the snout, swiftly, fiercely, putting every ounce of weight behind the blow. The recipient went down good and hard and stayed down. The other fellow was no slouch. Wasting no time in dumbfoundment, he took a bow-legged but quick step forward, shoved a gun into Mowry's face.

"Raise them high, you *soko,* or I'll—"

With the speed and recklessness of one who is desperate, Mowry ducked under the gun, seized the other's extended arm, got it over his shoulder and yanked. The agent let out a thin, piercing yelp and flew through the air with the greatest of ease. His gun dropped to the ground. Mowry scooped it up and started the sprint of his life.

Round the corner, along the street and into an alley. This took him by the back of his hotel and as he tore past he noted out of the corner of one eye a window missing and a great ragged hole in the wall. Hurdling a pile of smashed bricks and splintered timber, he reached the alley's end, shot across the next street.

So that was it. Somehow they had smelled him out, possibly as a result of one of those infernal registration checks. They had searched his room and tried to open his bag with a metal master-key. Then had come the big bang. If the room had been crowded at the time the explosion would have enough force to kill at least a dozen of them. It would be a blow sufficient to get their blood up for a month. If ever they laid hands on him . . .

He kept going as fast as he could make it, the gun in his grip, his ears straining for sounds of pursuit. Pretty soon the radio alarm would be going over the air, they'd close every exit from the town, blocking trains, buses, roads, everything. At all costs he must beat them to it by getting outside the cordon before it was formed—if it could be done.

As far as possible he tried to race through lanes and alleys, avoiding main roads on which patrol cars would be running to and fro loaded with guns and eyes. At this late hour there were few people about, no crowds in which to hide. The streets were almost empty with most folk abed and an armed man sprinting through the night was mighty conspicuous. But nothing could be done about that. To mooch with an air of innocence was to give time for the trap to close about him.

Darkness was his only help, not counting his legs. He pounded through alley after alley, bolted across six streets, halted in deep shadow as he was about to jump the seventh. A car bulging with uniformed cops and plainclothes Kaitempi slid past, its windows full of faces trying to look everywhere at once.

For a short time he stood silent and unmoving in the shadow, heart thumping, chest heaving, a trickle of sweat creeping down his spine. Immediately the hunters had gone he was across the street, into the opposite alley and racing onward. Five times he paused in concealment, mentally cursing the delay, while prowl cars snooped around.

The sixth stop was different. He lurked in the alley's corner as headlights came up the street. A mud-spattered dyno rolled into view, stopped within twenty yards of him. The next moment a solitary civilian got out, went to a nearby door and shoved a key into its lock. Mowry came out of the alley like a quick-moving cat.

The door opened just as the car shot away with a shrill scream from its dynamo. Struck with surprise, the civilian wasted a half a minute gaping after his vanishing property. Then he let go an oath, ran indoors and snatched up the telephone.

Luck has got to be mixed, decided Mowry as he gripped the wheel. There must be good to compensate for bad, a turn for the better to balance a change for the worse. Swinging the car into a broad, well-lit avenue, he slowed it to a more sedate pace.

Two overloaded patrol cars passed him going in the opposite direction, another overtook him and rocked ahead. They weren't interested in a dirty dyno trundling home late; they were hunting a breathless fugitive assumed to be still galloping around on two feet. He estimated that it would be no more than another ten minutes before the radio made them change their minds. It might have been better if he had shot the car's owner and thus gained himself extra valuable minutes. But he hadn't. Too late to regret the omission now.

After seven minutes he passed the last houses of Radine and headed into open country along an unfamiliar road. At once he hit up top speed to make maximum distance while the going was good. The car howled along, headlight beams dipping and swaying, the *den*-needle creeping close to its limit.

Twenty more minutes and he shot like a rocket through a long, straggling village buried deep in slumber. One mile farther on he rounded a bend, got a brief glimpse of a white pole across the road, the glitter of buttons and shine of metal helmets grouped at each end. He set his teeth, aimed straight at the middle without reducing speed by a fraction. The car hit the pole, flung the broken halves aside and raced on. Something struck five sharp blows on the back, two neat holes appeared in the rear window, a third where the windshield joined the roof.

That showed the radio alarm had been given, that forces had been alerted over a wide area. His crashing of the roadblock was a giveaway. They now knew in which direction he was fleeing and could concentrate ahead of him. Just where he was going was more than he knew himself. He'd never been on this road before, the locale was strange and he had no map to consult. Worse, he had little money and no documents of any kind. The loss of his case had deprived him of everything save what was upon his person, plus a hot car and a stolen gun.

Soon he reached a crossroad with a marker dimly visible on each corner. Braking violently, he jumped out, peered at the nearest one in the poor light of night. It said *Radine—27 den.* The opposite marker said *Valapan—92 den.* So that's where he'd been heading—to Valapan. Doubtless the police there were out in full strength, a reception committee too well prepared to permit another crash-through.

The marker on the left-hand road read *Pertane—51 den.* He clambered back into the car, turned left. Still no signs of close pursuit were visible but that meant nothing. Somebody with radio contact and a big map would be moving cars around to head him off as reports of his position filtered in.

At the marker indicating *9 den* he found another crossroad which he recognized. The skyglow of Pertane now shone straight ahead while on his right was the road leading to the cave in the forest. He took an added risk of interception by driving the car a couple of miles nearer Pertane before abandoning it. When they found it there they'd probably jump to the conclusion that he'd sought refuge somewhere in the big city. It would be all to the good if they wasted time and manpower scouring Pertane from end to end.

Walking back, he reached the forest and continued along its fringe. It took him two hours to arrive at the tree and the tombstone. During that period he dived into the woods eleven times and watched carloads of hunters whine past. Looked like he'd got a veritable army to chasing around in the night and that was a worthwhile result if Wolf was to be believed.

Entering the forest, he made for the cave.

At the cave he found everything intact, undisturbed. He arrived thankfully, feeling that he was as safe here as he could be anywhere upon a hostile world. It was hardly likely that the hunt would succeed in tracking him through twenty miles of virgin forest even if it occurred to them to try.

For a short time he sat on a container and let his mind indulge a wrestling match between duty and desire. Orders were that on each visit to the cave he must use the transmitter and send an up-to-the-minute report. There was no need to guess what might happen if he were to do so this time. They'd order him to stay put and indulge in no further activities. Later they'd send a ship, pick him up and dump him on some other Sirian planet where he could start all over again. On Jaimec they'd leave his successor.

The idea of it riled him. All very well them talking about the tactical advantages of replacing a known operator with an unknown one. To the man who suffered replacement it smacked of incompetence and defeat. He flatly refused to consider himself either inefficient or beaten. Hell with 'em! Maybe the Kaitempi had gained a smell at his whiskers but that didn't make him as good as theirs.

Besides, he had carried out phase one and part of phase two. There was yet phase three, the build-up of pressure to the point where the foe would be so busy defending the back door that he'd be in no condition to hold the front one.

Phase three involved strategic bombing both by himself and by anyone he could pay to do it. He had the necessary material for the former and the money for the latter. In yet unopened containers lay enough money to buy a dozen battleships and give every man of their crews a large box of cigars. Also forty different kinds of infernal machines, not one of them recognizable for what it was, and all guaranteed to go *whump* in the right place, at the right moment.

He was not supposed to start offensive action of the phase three type until ordered to do so because usually it preceded full-scale attack by Terran space forces. But in the meantime he could work his way up to it by keeping *Dirac Angestun Gesept* in the public eye, arranging a few more executions and in general performing his proper function of being a pain in the neck.

No, he would not signal them just yet. He would play around a bit longer, long enough to establish his right to remain to the bitter end regardless of whether or not the Kaitempi had him taped. He'd been run out of Radine but he wasn't going to be chased right off the planet. That would be too much for his self-esteem.

Opening a couple of containers, he undressed, put on a wide belly-belt that made him corpulent with guilders. Then he donned ill-cut, heavy clothes typical of the Sirian farmer. A couple of cheek-pads widened and rounded his face. He plucked his eyebrows into slight raggedness, trimmed his hair to comply with the current agricultural fashion.

With purple dye he gave his face the peculiar mottling of a bad complexion. The final touch was to give himself an injection alongside his right nostril; within two hours it would create that faint orange-colored blemish occasionally seen on Sirian features.

He was now a middle-aged, coarse-looking and somewhat overfed Sirian farmer and again he had documents to match. This time he was Rathan Gusulkin, a graingrower. His papers showed that he had emigrated from Diracta five years ago. This served to explain his Mashambi accent which was the only thing he could not successfully conceal.

Before setting out in his new role he enjoyed another real Earth meal and four hours of much-needed sleep. When two miles from the outskirts of Pertane he buried a package holding fifty thousand guilders at the base of the southernmost left-hand buttress of the bridge across the river. Not far from that point, beneath deep water, a typewriter lay in the mud.

From the first booth in Pertane he called the Cafe Susun. The answer was prompt, the voice strange and curt, the distant scanner not operating.

"That the Cafe Susun?" Mowry asked.

"Yar."

"Skriva there?"

A brief silence followed by, "He's somewhere around. Upstairs or out back. Who wants him?"

"His mother."

"Don't give me that!" rasped the voice. "I can tell by your—"

"What's it got to do with you?" Mowry shouted. "Is Skriva there or not?"

The voice became suddenly subdued and sounded completely out of character as it cajoled. "Hold on a piece. I'll go find him for you."

"You needn't bother. Is Gurd there?"

"No, he hasn't been in today. Hold on, I tell you. I'll go find Skriva. He's upstairs or—"

"Listen!" ordered Mowry. He stuck his tongue between his lips and blew hard.

Then he dropped the phone, scrambled out of the booth and beat it at the fastest pace that would not attract attention. Nearby a bored shopkeeper lounged in his doorway and idly watched him go. So also did four people gossiping outside the shop. That meant five witnesses, five descriptions of the fellow who had just used the booth.

"Hold on!" the strange voice had urged, striving but failing to conceal its normal note of arrogant authority. It wasn't the voice of the barkeep nor the careless, slangy tones of any frequenter of the Cafe Susun. It had the characteristic bossiness of a plainclothes cop or a Kaitempi agent. Yar, hold on, Stupid, while we trace the call and pick you up.

Three hundred yards along the road he jumped a bus, looked backward, could not discern whether the shopkeeper and the gossips had noticed what he had done. The bus lumbered forward. A police car rocked past it and braked by the booth. The bus turned a corner. Mowry wondered just how close a close shave can be.

The Cafe Susun was staked, no doubt of that. The cops' prompt arrival at the booth proved it. How they had got a line on the place and what had induced them to raid it was a matter of sheer speculation. Perhaps they'd been led to it by their investigations of the bloody head in a sack.

Or perhaps Gurd and Skriva had been nabbed while tramping heavy-footed all over a roof and waving cables across a street. He could readily imagine them fixing a mock telephone-tap with a thumping noisiness fit to arouse the street. On a rooftop, blinded by easy money, they were liable to make themselves as conspicuous as a pair of drunken elephants.

If they had been caught they'd talk, tough as they were. The Kaitempi would *make* them talk. When fingernails are peeled off one by one with a pair of pliers, or when intermittent voltage from a battery is applied to the corners of the eyeballs, the most granite-hard character becomes positively garrulous.

Yes, they'd talk all right—but they couldn't say much. Only a weird tale about a crackpot with a Mashambi accent and an inexhaustible supply of guilders. Not a word about *Dirac Angestun Gesept.* Not a syllable about Terran intervention on Jaimec.

But there were others who could talk and to better effect.

"You see anyone leave this booth just now?"

"Yar. A fat yokel. Seemed in a hurry."

"Where'd he go?"

"Down the road. Got on a 42 bus."

"What did he look like? Describe him as accurately as you can. Come on, be quick about it!"

"Medium height, middle-aged, round-faced, got a bad complexion. Quite a belly on him, too. Had a red *falkin* alongside his nose. Wearing a fur jacket, brown cord pants, heavy brown boots. Looked the farmer type if you get what I mean."

"That's enough for us. Jalek, let's get after the bus. Where's the mike—I'd better broadcast this description. We'll nail him if we move fast."

"He's a cunning one. Didn't take him long to smell a trap when Lathin answered his call. He blew a dirty noise and ran. Bet you the bus-jump is a blind—he's got a car parked someplace."

"Save your breath and catch up with that bus. Two callers have escaped us already. We'll have a lot of explaining to do if we lose a third."

"Yar, I know."

Mowry got off the bus before anyone had time to overtake it. He caught another one running on a transverse route. But he did not play tag all over the city as he had done in the past. Right now things were a lot livelier, the pursuers almost certainly had a description of him and it looked like he'd got most of Jaimec on the hop.

His third change put him on an express bus heading out of town. It dropped him a mile beyond the bridge where he had hidden fifty thousand guilders for the benefit of those who, for all he knew, might not have another fifty hours to live. Once again he was heading back to the forest and the cave.

To retrace his steps to the bridge and try to unearth the money would be stupid and dangerous. Police cars would be heading this way before long. The hunt for a pot-bellied farmer would not be confined to Pertane. Anytime now they'd start probing the rural areas immediately outside the city limits. So long as daylight remained the best thing for him to do was to get out of sight and stay out until such time as he could assume yet another new guise.

Moving fast he reached the edge of the forest without being stopped and questioned. For a short time he continued to use the road, seeking shelter among the trees whenever a car approached. But traffic increased and vehicles appeared with such frequency that eventually he gave up hope of further progress before dark. He was pretty tired too, his eyelids were heavy, his feet had taken a beating.

Penetrating farther into the woods he found a comfortable, well-concealed spot, lay on a thick bed of moss and let go a sigh of satisfaction. For a while he reposed in thoughtful silence while his eyes idly surveyed small patches of sky visible through leafy gaps.

Wolf had asserted that one man could pin down an army. He wondered how large a number he'd fastened and what real good it had done, if any. The most frustrating thing about this solitary wasp-life was that he had no way of obtaining a glimpse behind the scenes, of looking into the enemy's headquarters and measuring his multiple reactions, of seeing for oneself how widespread and crippled they became.

How many precious man-hours had his presence cost the foe? Thousands, tens of thousands, millions? To what forms of war service would those man-hours have been devoted if he had not compelled the enemy to waste them in other directions? Ah, in the answer to that hypothetical question lay the true measure of a wasp's efficiency.

Gradually he gave up these unprofitable musings and drifted into sleep. Night was upon him when he awoke refreshed and energetic. He was also less soured with events. Things could have been worse, lots worse. For example, he could have gone straight to the Cafe Susun and walked into the arms of the trappers like a prize chump. The Kaitempi wouldn't know what they had grabbed but they'd hold him on general principles and in their own effective way they'd squeeze him of every item of information he possessed. Thinking it over, he doubted his ability to hold out once they really got to work on him. About the only captives from whom the Kaitempi had extracted nothing were those who had managed to commit suicide before questioning.

As he trudged steadily through the dark toward the cave he blessed his luck, wisdom or intuition in making a phone call. Then his thoughts became occupied with Gurd and Skriva. If they had been caught, as seemed likely, it meant he'd been deprived of valuable allies and once again was strictly on his own. He'd have to find some way of replacing them and that wouldn't be easy.

But if, like himself, they had escaped the trap, how was he going to find them? The crummy cafe had been their only recognized point of contact. He didn't know where they lived and it would be foolhardy to go around asking. They didn't know his address, either. They'd want to meet him fully as much as he wanted to meet them. Both sides could waste weeks or months fumbling at random for each other in a city as big as Pertane. Somehow the problem had to be solved.

Arriving at the cave as dawn was breaking, he took off his shoes, sat on the pebble beach and soaked his aching feet in the stream. Still his mind chewed unceasingly at the question of how to find Gurd and Skriva, if they were still free. Eventually the Kaitempi would remove the stakeout from the Cafe Susun either because they were satisfied that they had exploited it to the limit, or because their patience had run out, or because of pressure of other business. It would then be possible to visit the place and find someone able to give all the information he needed. But heaven alone knew when that would be; perhaps as far off as a year next Christmas.

In new and radically changed disguise he could mooch around the neighborhood of the cafe until he found one of its regular customers and used him as a lead to Gurd and Skriva. It would be a risky tactic, a highly dangerous one. Chances were high that, for the time being, the Cafe Susun was the focal point of Kaitempi activity over the entire district with plainclothesmen keeping watch for suspicious-looking characters lounging around anywhere within a mile of the place.

After an hour's meditation he decided that there was one possibility of regaining contact with the brothers. It depended not only on them being on the loose but also having their fair share of brains and imagination. It might work. They were crude and ruthless but not stupid and a steady flow of guilders must have greatly stimulated their natural cunning.

He could leave them a message where he'd left one before, hoping they'd have the sense to think of the same thing themselves and go take a look. On the Radine road under Marker 33 *den.* If they had successfully completed their last job they had fifty thousand guilders owing to them. That should be more than enough to sharpen their wits.

The sun came up, spreading its warmth through the trees and into the cave. It was one of those days that beguiles a man into lying around and doing nothing. Succumbing to temptation he gave himself a holiday and postponed further action until the morrow. It was just as well: constant chasing around, uneasy sleeps and much nervous tension had combined to thin him down and tax his resources.

All that day he loafed in or near the cave, enjoying peace and quietness, freedom from pursuit, cooking himself large and succulent Earth meals. No prowlers came sneaking through the forest, no scout-planes snooped low overhead.

Evidently the enemy was obsessed with the notion that the quarry sought sanctuary only in heavily populated places; it just hadn't occurred to them that anyone would take to the wilds. This was logical enough from their viewpoint, their having accepted *Dirac Angestun Gesept* as a large, well-organized opposition too big and widespread to lurk in a cave. The wasp had magnified himself to such elephantine proportions that they weren't going to waste time looking down rabbit-holes for him.

That night he slept like a child, soundly and solidly, right around the clock. He spent the next morning in total idleness, had a bath in the stream during the heat of noon. Toward evening he cropped his hair in military fashion, leaving himself with no more than a stiff bristle covering his skull. Another injection obliterated the *falkin.* He retinted himself all over, making his color a fresher and slightly deeper purple. Dental plates filled the gaps where his wisdom teeth had been and made his face appear wider, heavier, with squarer jaw line.

A complete change of clothing followed. The shoes he donned were of military type, the civilian suit was of expensive cut, the neck-scarf was knotted in space-marine fashion. To this ensemble he added a platinum watch-fob and a platinum wrist-bangle holding an ornamental identity-disc.

He now looked like somebody several cuts above the Sirian average. The new set of documents he pocketed confirmed this impression. They vouched for the fact that he was Colonel Krasna Halopti of the Military Intelligence Service and as such entitled to claim the assistance of all Sirian authorities anytime, anywhere.

They could execute him out of hand for masquerading as a high-ranking officer. But what matter?—they'd strangle him anyway. A man cannot die twice.

Satisfied that he now looked the part one hundred percent and that he bore little resemblance to any of his previous appearances, he sat on a container and wrote a brief letter.

"I tried to get in touch with you at the cafe and found the place full of K-*sokos*. The money had been buried in readiness for you at the base of the southernmost left-hand buttress of the Asako Bridge. If you are free, and if you are able and willing to take on more work, leave a message here saying when and where I can find you."

Leaving it unsigned, he folded it, slipped it into a damp-proof cellophane envelope. Into his pocket he dropped a small, silent automatic. The gun was of Sirian manufacture and he had a fake permit to carry it.

This new role was more daring and dangerous than the others had been, but had its compensations. A check with official records would expose and damn him in double-quick time. Against this was the average Sirian's respect for authority and reluctance to challenge it. Providing he conducted himself with enough self-assurance and sufficient arrogance even the Kaitempi might be tempted to accept him at face value.

Two hours after the fall of darkness he switched on Container-22 and set forth through the forest bearing a new case larger and heavier than before. Yet again he found himself regretting the distance of his hideout from the nearest road. A twenty mile march each way was tedious and tiring. But it was a cheap price to pay for the security of his supplies.

The walk was longer this time because he did not cut straight through to the road and thumb a lift. To beg a ride in his new guise would have been sufficiently out of character to draw unwelcome attention to himself. So he followed the fringe of the forest to the point where two other roads joined on. Here, in the early morning, he waited between the trees until an express bus appeared in the distance. He stepped out onto the road, caught it and was carried into the center of Pertane.

Within half an hour he had acquired a car. This time he did not bother to rent one; it wasn't worth the trouble for the short period he needed it. Ambling around until he found a parked dyno that suited his purpose, he got in and drove away. Nobody ran after him yelling bloody murder. The theft had gone unobserved.

Making it out to the Radine road, he stopped, waited for the artery to clear in both directions, buried his letter under the marker. Then he returned to Pertane and put the car back where he had found it. He had been away a little over an hour and it was probable that the owner had not missed his machine, would never know that it had been borrowed.

Next, he went to the crowded main post office, took half a dozen small but heavy parcels from his case, addressed them and mailed them. Each held an airtight can containing a cheap clock-movement and a piece of paper, nothing else. The clock-movement emitted a sinister tick just loud enough to be heard if a suspicious-minded person listened closely. The paper bore a message short and to the point.

This package could have killed you.

Two different packages brought together at the right time and place could kill a hundred thousand.
End this war before we end you!
Dirac Angestun Gesept.

Paper threats, that was all. But effective enough to eat still further into the enemy's war effort. They'd alarm the recipients and give their forces something more to worry about. Doubtless the military would provide a personal bodyguard for every big wheel on Jaimec and that alone would pin down a regiment.

Mail would be examined and all suspicious parcels would be taken apart in a blast-proof room. There'd be a city-wide search with radiation-detectors for the component parts of a fission-bomb. Civil defense would be alerted in readiness to cope with a mammoth explosion that might or might not take place. Anyone on the streets who walked with a secretive air and wore a slightly mad expression would be arrested and hauled in for questioning.

Yes, after three murders with the promise of more to come authority dare not dismiss D.A.G.'s threats as the idle talk of some crackpot on the loose. For safety's sake they'd have to assume that fake bombs might soon be followed by real ones and act accordingly.

As he strolled along the road he amused himself by picturing the scene when the receiver of a parcel rushed to dump it in a bucket of water while someone else frantically phoned for the bomb squad. He was so engrossed with these thoughts that it was some time before he became conscious of a shrill whistling sound rising and falling over Pertane. He stopped, looked around, gazed at the sky, saw nothing out of the ordinary. Quite a lot of people seemed to have disappeared from the street but a few, like himself, were standing and staring around bewilderedly.

Chapter 8

The next moment a cop shoved him in the shoulder. "Get down, you fool!"

"Down?" Mowry eyed him without understanding. "Down where? What's the matter?"

"Into the cellars," shouted the cop, making waving motions. "Don't you recognize a raid-alarm when you hear it?" Without waiting for a reply he ran forward, bawling at other people, "Get down! Get down!"

Turning, Mowry scrambled after the rest down a long, steep flight of steps and into the basement of a business block. He was surprised to find the place already crowded. Several hundred people had taken refuge without having to be told. They were standing around, or sitting on wooden benches or leaning against the wall. Upending his case, Mowry sat on it.

Nearby an irate oldster looked him over with a rheumy gaze and said, "A raid-alarm. What d'you think of that?"

"Nothing," answered Mowry. "What's the use of thinking? There's nothing we can do about it."

"But the Spakum fleets have been destroyed," shrilled the oldster, making Mowry the focal point of an address to everyone. "They've said so time and again, on the radio and in the papers. The Spakum fleets have been wiped out. So what has set off an alarm, *hi?* What can raid us, *hi?* Tell me that!"

"Maybe it's just a practice alarm," Mowry soothed.

"Practice?" He spluttered with senile fury. "Why do we need practice and who says so? If the Spakum forces are beaten we've no need to hide. There's nothing to hide from. We don't want any practice."

"Don't pick on me," advised Mowry, bored with the other's whines. "I didn't sound the alarm."

"Some stinking idiot sounded it," persisted the oldster. "Some lying *soko* who wants us to believe the war is as good as over when it isn't. How do we know how much truth there is in what they're telling us?" He spat on the floor, doing it viciously. "A great victory in the Centauri sector—then the raid-alarm is sounded. They must think we're a lot of—"

A squat, heavily built character stepped close to him and snapped, "Shut up!"

The oldster was too absorbed in his woes to cower, too pigheaded to recognize the voice of authority. "I won't shut up. I was walking home when somebody pushed me down here just because a whistle blows and—"

The squat man opened his jacket, displayed a badge and repeated in harsher tones, "I said shut up!"

"Who d'you think you are? At my time of life I'm not going to be—"

With a swift movement the squat man whipped out a rubber truncheon, larruped the oldster over the head with all the force he could muster. The victim went down like a shot steer.

A voice at the back of the crowd shouted, "Shame!" Several others murmured, fidgeted but did nothing.

Grinning, the squat man showed what he thought of this disapproval by kicking the oldster in the face and again in the belly. Glancing up, he met Mowry's gaze and promptly challenged, "Well?"

Mowry said evenly, "Are you of the Kaitempi?"

"Yar. What's it to you?"

"Nothing. I was only curious."

"Then don't be. Keep your dirty nose out of this."

The crowd muttered and fidgeted again. Two cops came down from the street, sat on the bottom step and mopped their foreheads. They looked nervous and jumpy. The Kaitempi agent joined them, took a gun out of his pocket and nursed it in his lap. Mowry smiled at him enigmatically. The oldster still lay unconscious on the floor and breathed with bubbling sounds.

Now the silence of the city crept into the cellar. The crowd became peculiarly tense as everyone listened. After half an hour there sounded in the distance a series of hisses that started on a loud, strong note and swiftly faded into the sky.

Tenseness immediately increased with the knowledge that guided missiles weren't being expended for the fun of it. Somewhere overhead and within theoretical range must be a Spakum ship, perhaps bearing a lethal load that might drop at any moment.

Another volley of hisses. The silence returned. The cops and the agent got to their feet, edged farther into the basement and turned to watch the steps. Individual breathing could be heard, some respirating spasmodically as if finding difficulty in using their lungs. All faces betrayed an inward strain and there was an acrid smell of sweat. Mowry's only thought was that to be disintegrated in a bomb-blast from his own side was a hell of a way to die.

Ten minutes later the floor quivered. The walls vibrated. The entire building shook. From the street came the brittle crash of breaking glass as windows fell out. Still there was no other sound, no roar of a great explosion, no dull rumbling of propulsors in the stratosphere. The quietness was eerie in the extreme.

It was three hours before the same whistling on a lower note proclaimed the all-clear. The crowd hurried out, vastly relieved. They stepped over the oldster, left him lying there. The two cops headed together up the street while the Kaitempi agent strode the opposite way. Mowry caught up with the agent, spoke pleasantly.

"Shock damage only. They must have dropped it a good distance away."

The other grunted.

"I wanted to speak to you but couldn't very well do so in front of all those people."

"Yar? Why not?"

For answer, Mowry produced his identity-card and his warrant, showed them to the agent.

"Colonel Halopti, Military Intelligence." Returning the card, the agent lost some of his belligerence, made an effort to be polite. "What did you want to say—something about that garrulous old fool?"

"No. He deserved all he got. You're to be commended for the way you handled him." He noted the other's look of gratification, added, "An ancient gab like him could have made the whole crowd hysterical."

"Yar, that's right. The way to control a mob is to cut out and beat up its spokesmen."

"When the alarm sounded I was on my way to Kaitempi H.Q. to borrow a dependable agent," explained Mowry. "When I saw you in action I felt you'd save me the trouble. You're just the fellow I want: one who's quick on the uptake and will stand no nonsense. What's your name?"

"Sagramatholou."

"Ah, you're from the K17 system, *hi?* They all use compound names there, don't they?"

"Yar. And you're from Diracta. Halopti is a Diractan name and you've got a Mashambi accent."

Mowry laughed. "Can't hide much from each other, can we?"

"Nar." He looked Mowry over with open curiosity, asked, "What d'you want me for?"

"I hope to nab the leader of a D.A.G. cell. It's got to be done quickly and quietly. If the Kaitempi put fifty on the job and make a major operation of it they'll scare away the rest for miles around. One at a time is the best technique. As the Spakums say, 'Softly, softly, catchee monkey.'"

"Yar, that's the best way," agreed Sagramatholou.

"I'm confident that I could take this character single-handed without frightening away the others. But while I'm going in at the front he may beat it out the back. So it needs two of us." He paused to let it sink in, finished, "I want a reliable man to grab him if he bolts; you'll get full credit for the capture."

The other's eyes narrowed and gained an eager light. "I'll be glad to come along if it's all right with H.Q. I'd better phone and ask them."

"Please yourself," said Mowry with a studied carelessness he was far from feeling. "But you know what will happen for sure?"

"What d'you think?"

"They'll take you off it and give me an officer of equivalent rank." Mowry made a disparaging gesture. "Although I shouldn't say it, being a colonel myself, I'd rather have a tough, experienced man of my own choice."

The other swelled his chest. "You may have something. There are officers and officers."

"Precisely! Well, are you in this with me or not?"

"Do you accept full responsibility if my superiors gripe about it?"

"Of course."

"That's good enough for me. When do we start?"

"At once."

"All right," said Sagramatholou, making up his mind. "I'm on duty another three hours anyway."

"Good! You got a civilian-type dyno?"

"All our dynos are ordinary looking ones—they have to be."

"Mine bears military insignia," lied Mowry. "We'd better use yours."

The other accepted this statement without question. He was completely hooked by his own eagerness to get credit for an important capture. Being what they were, the Kaitempi suffered from their own peculiar form of cupidity; the prospect of finding another victim for the strangling-post was something difficult to resist.

Reaching the parking lot around the corner, Sagramatholou took his seat behind the wheel of a big black dyno. Tossing his case into the back, Mowry got in beside him. The car snored onto the street.

"Where to?"

"South end, back of the Rida Engine Plant. I'll show you from there."

Theatrically the agent made a chopping motion with one hand as he said, "This D.A.G. business is sending us crazy. High time we put an end to it. How did you get a lead on them?"

"We picked it up on Diracta. One of them fell into our hands and talked."

"In great pain?" suggested Sagramatholou, chuckling.

"Yar."

"That's the way to handle them." He turned a corner, let go another chuckle. "They all blab when the suffering gets too cruel to endure. After which they die just the same."

"Yar," repeated Mowry with becoming gusto.

"We snatched a dozen from a cafe in the Laksin quarter," informed Sagramatholou. "They're talking, too. But they aren't talking sense—yet. They've admitted every crime in the calendar except membership of D.A.G. About that organization they know nothing, so they say."

"What took you to the cafe?"

"Somebody got his stupid head knocked off. He was a regular frequenter of the joint. We identified him after a lot of trouble, traced him back and grabbed a bunch of his everloving friends. About six of them have confessed to the killing."

"Six?" Mowry frowned.

"Yar. They did it at six different times, in six different places, for six different reasons. The dirty *sokos* are lying to make us ease up. But we'll get the truth out of them yet."

"Sounds like a mere hoodlum squabble to me. Where's the political angle, if any?"

"I don't know. The higher-ups keep things to themselves. They say they know for a fact that it was a D.A.G. execution and therefore whoever did it is a D.A.G. killer."

"Maybe somebody tipped them," offered Mowry.

"Maybe somebody did. And he could be a liar too." He let go a snort of disgust. "This war is enough without traitors and liars making things worse. We're being run ragged, see? It can't go on forever."

"Any luck with the snap-searches?"

"There was at first. Then the luck petered out because everyone became wary. We've stopped making them for ten days. The lull will give the dodgers a sense of false security. When they're ripe for the taking, we'll take them."

"That's a good idea. One has to use one's wits these days, *hi?*"

"Yar."

"Here we are. Turn left and then first right."

The car shot past the rear of the engine plant, entered a narrow, rutted road, switched into another little better than a lane. All around was an unsavory, semi-deserted area full of old buildings, vacant lots and garbage dumps. They stopped, got out.

Gazing about him, the Kaitempi agent remarked, "A typical vermin-run. A couple of years ago we smoked a gang of godworshippers out of an old warehouse in this district."

Mowry put on a look of revulsion. "You mean a bunch infected with Terran religion?"

"Yar, true believers. When the noose tightened their praying tongues stuck out and went black the same as any sinner's." He laughed at the recollection of it, glanced at the other. "Where now?"

"Along this alley."

Mowry led the way into the alley which was long, dirty and had a dead end. They reached the twelve-foot wall that blocked further progress. There was nobody in sight, nothing could be heard save a distant hum of traffic and the nearer squeak of a hanging sign, old and rusty.

Pointing to the door set in the wall, Mowry said, "This is the bolt-hole. It will take me two or three minutes to get round the front and go in. After that you can expect anything." He tried the door. It refused to budge. "Locked."

"Better unlock it so he can make a clear run," suggested Sagramatholou. "If he finds himself balked he's liable to try to shoot it out with you and I'll be in no position to take part. These *sokos* can become dangerous when desperate." He felt in a pocket, produced a bunch of master-keys. Grinning, he added, "The easiest way is to let him rush straight into my arms."

With that, he faced the door, turning his back on Mowry while he meddled with the lock. Mowry looked back along the alley. Still nobody in sight.

Taking out his gun, he said in calm, unhurried tones, "You kicked the old geezer when he was down."

"Sure did," enthused the agent, still trying the lock. "I hope he dies slowly, the half-witted—" His voice broke off as the incongruity of Mowry's remark sank into his mind. He turned round, one hand braced upon the door, and looked straight into the gun's muzzle. "What's this? What are you—"

The gun gave a *phut* no louder than that of an air-pistol. Sagramatholou remained standing, a blue hole in his forehead. His mouth hung open in an idiotic gape. Then his knees gave way and he plunged forward face first.

Pocketing the gun, Mowry bent over the body. Working fast, he searched it, replaced the wallet after a swift look through it but confiscated the official badge. Hastening out the alley, he got into the car, drove it downtown to within a short distance of a used car lot.

Walking the rest of the way he looked over the big assembly of badly beaten-up dynos. A thin, hard-faced Sirian immediately sidled up to him, his crafty eyes noting the well-cut suit, the platinum fob and wrist-band. This, obviously, was harvest time.

"Lucky you!" announced the Sirian, greasily. "You have found the best place on Jaimec for a genuine bargain. Every car a real sacrifice. There's a war on, prices are going to jump and you just can't go wrong. Now take a look at this beauty right here. A gift, a positive gift. It's a—"

"I've got eyes," said Mowry.

"Yar, sure. I'm pointing out—"

"I've got a mind of my own," Mowry informed. "And I wouldn't drive around in any of these relics unless I was in a hurry to be struck dead."

"But—"

"Like everyone else, I know there's a war on. Before long it's going to be mighty tough getting bits and pieces. I'm interested in something I can strip down for parts." He pointed. "That one, for instance. How much?"

"She's a good runner," expostulated the salesman, donning a look of horror. "Purrs along like brand new. Got current plates—"

"I can see it's got current plates."

". . . and is good and solid from front to back. I'm giving it away, just *giving* it."

"How much?"

"Nine-ninety," said the other, again eyeing the suit and the platinum.

"Robbery," said Mowry.

They haggled for half an hour at the end of which Mowry got it for eight-twenty. He paid and drove it away. It creaked, groaned and lurched in a manner that showed he'd still been soaked for at least two hundred, but he wasn't resentful about that.

On a lot littered with scrap-iron a mile away, with nobody watching, he parked the car, smashed its windshield and lamps, removed its wheels and number plates, took all detachable parts from the motor and effectively converted the machine into what any passer-by could see was an abandoned wreck. He walked off, returned in short time with the dead agent's car, loaded the loose parts into it.

Half an hour later he slung the wheels and other items into the river. With them went Sagramatholou's plates. He drove away bearing the plates taken from the wreck; the exchange had cost him eight-twenty in counterfeit money and was cheap at the price. A police patrol or another Kaitempi car could now follow him for miles without spotting the number for which undoubtedly they'd be seeking.

Assured of no more snap-searches for the time being he idled around town until the sky went dark. Dumping the car in an underground garage, he bought a paper and perused it during a meal.

According to this news-sheet, a lone Terran destroyer—described as "a cowardly sneak-raider"—had managed to make a desperate dash through formidable space defenses and drop one bomb upon the great national armaments complex at Shugruma. Little damage had been done. The invader had been blown apart soon afterward.

The story had been written up to give the impression that a sly dog had got in a harmless bite and been shot for its pains. He wondered how many readers believed it. Shugruma was more than three hundred miles away—yet Pertane had shuddered to the shock-waves of the distant explosion. If that was anything to go by, the target area must now be represented by a crater a couple of miles in diameter.

The second page stated that forty-eight members of the traitorous Sirian Freedom Party had been seized by forces of law and order and would be dealt with appropriately. No details offered, no names given, no charges stated.

This was normal among a species with a secret judicial system, on worlds where any suspect could be snatched from the street and never seen again. There were no judges and juries holding public trials anywhere within the Sirian Empire. If lucky, the arrested one eventually was released, physically enfeebled, without apology or compensation. If out of luck, his next of kin did not so much as receive a jar containing his ashes.

The forty-eight were doomed, whoever they were or whoever they were thought to be. Alternatively, the whole yarn could be an officially concocted lie. The powers-that-be were quite capable of venting their fury on half a dozen common crooks and, for public consumption, defining them as D.A.G. members while multiplying their number by eight. Authority is maintained and wars are fought by propaganda, a cover word for cynical perversion of the facts.

One of the back pages devoted a few lines to the modest statement that Sirian forces had now been withdrawn from the planet Gooma "so that they can be deployed more effectively in the actual area of combat." This implied that Gooma was far outside the area of combat, a transparent piece of nonsense to any reader capable of independent thought. But ninety percent of the readership could not endure the awful strain of thinking: they were content to look and listen and swallow whatever guff got dished out.

Far and away the most significant item was the lead writer's contribution. This was a pompous sermon based on the thesis that total war should end only in total victory which could and must be gained only by total effort. There was no room for political division within the Sirian ranks. Everyone without exception must be solidly behind the leadership in its determination to fight the war to a successful conclusion. Doubters and waverers, dodgers and complainers, the lazy and the shiftless were as much traitors to the cause as any spy or saboteur. They should be dealt with swiftly, once and for all. They should be slaughtered without mercy.

Clearly it was a yelp of agony although *Dirac Angestun Gesept* was not mentioned in plain words. Since in time of war all such lectures were officially inspired, it was reasonable to assume that the brasshats were experiencing acute pains in the buttocks. In effect they were shouting out loud that a wasp could sting. Perhaps some of them had received little parcels that ticked and did not approve of this switch from the general to the personal.

Now that night had fallen Mowry lugged his case to his room. He made the approach warily. Any hideout could become a trap at any time, without warning. Apart from the possibility of the police or Kaitempi lying in wait after having got a line on him, there was also the chance of encountering a landlord who'd become curious about the use of the room by another and more prosperous looking character. True, the landlord was a tightmouth typical of slumdom but even he would curry favor with the Kaitempi if he thought it necessary to save his own neck. The landlord was not to be trusted. On a hostile world nobody was to be trusted.

The building wasn't watched, the room was not staked. He managed to sneak in unobserved. Everything proved to be exactly as he left it, showing that nobody yet had found reason to come nosing around. Thankfully he sprawled on the bed and gave his feet a rest while he considered the situation. It was evident that as far as possible he would have to enter and leave the room only during hours of darkness. The alternative was to seek another hideout, preferably in a better-class area more in keeping with his present character. He didn't want to start another time-wasting search for a rat hole unless he was driven to it.

The following day he regretted the destruction of his first case and all its contents in Radine. This loss piled up the work, made it tedious and boring. But it had to be done. As a result he spent all morning in the public library compiling a list of names and addresses to replace the previous one. Then with plain paper, envelopes and a small hand-printer he used another two days preparing a stack of letters. It was a relief when they were finished and mailed.

Sagramatholou was the fourth.
The list is long.
Dirac Angestun Gesept.

Thus he had killed several birds with one stone. He had avenged the oldster, a motive that gave him a good deal of satisfaction. He had struck another blow at the Kaitempi. He'd acquired a car not traceable through renting agencies or usual sales channels. Finally he had given authority further proof of D.A.G.'s willingness to kill, maim or otherwise muscle its way to power.

To boost this situation he mailed at the same time another six parcels. Outwardly these were identical with the former ones. They emitted the same subdued tick. There the resemblance ended. At periods varying between six and twenty hours after sending, or at any moment that someone tried to pry them open, they were due to go off with a bang sufficiently forceful to plaster a body against the wall.

On the fourth day after his return to the room he slipped out unseen, collected the car and visited marker 33-*den* on the Radine road. Several patrol cars passed him on the way but none betrayed the slightest interest in him. Reaching the marker, he dug at its base, found his own cellophane envelope now containing a small card. All it said was: *Asako* 19-1713.

The trick had come off.

Forthwith he drove back to the first booth he could find, switched off its scanner and called the number. A strange voice answered while the visiscreen remained blank. Evidently there was similar caution at the other end.

"19-1713," it said.

"Gurd or Skriva there?" asked Mowry.

"Wait," ordered the voice.

"One moment and no more," retorted Mowry. "After that—goodbye!"

The only answer was a grunt. Mowry hung on, watching the road, ready to drop the phone and beat it immediately. His intuition told him to get away fast. The college had told him times without number never to disregard the strange, indefinable smell of an ambush. There must be something in it seeing he was still alive and fancy free.

He was nearing the point of taking alarm when Skriva's voice came through and growled, "Who's that?"

"Your benefactor."

"Oh, you. I'm not getting your pic."

"I'm not getting yours either. What's the matter—are you windy?"

"This is no place to talk," said Skriva. "We'd better meet. Where are you?"

A swift series of thoughts flashed through Mowry's mind. *Where are you?* Was Skriva allowing himself to be used as bait? If he'd been caught and given a preliminary taste of rough treatment it was just the sort of crafty trick the Kaitempi would play. They'd get Skriva's full cooperation after showing him the consequences of refusal.

On the other hand it wasn't likely in such circumstances that Skriva would bother asking for his location. The Kaitempi would know it already, having traced the call. Moreover they'd want the conversation prolonged as much as possible to hold Mowry there. Skriva was trying to cut it short. Yes, the betting was against a trap.

"You struck dumb?" shouted Skriva, impatient and suspicious.

That settled the matter from Mowry's viewpoint and he replied, "I was thinking. How about meeting me where you left your phone number?"

"That's as good as anywhere."

"By yourself," warned Mowry. "Nobody else with you excepting Gurd. Nobody following and nobody hanging around."

"Who's windy now?" said Skriva. "I'm coming right away."

Driving back to the marker, Mowry parked his car on the shoulder and waited. Twenty minutes afterward Skriva's dyno rolled up, parked behind. Skriva got out, approached him, halted in mid-step, scowled uncertainly, slid a hand into a pocket and looked hurriedly up and down the road. There were no other cars in sight.

Mowry grinned at him. "What's eating you? Got a guilty conscience or something?"

Coming closer, Skriva eyed him with slight incredulity, then commented, "So it *is* you. What have you been doing to yourself?" Without waiting for a reply he walked around the hood, climbed in, took the other seat. "You don't look the same. It was hard to recognize you."

"That's the idea. A change for the better wouldn't do you any harm, either. Make it harder for the cops to get you."

"Maybe." Skriva was silent for a moment, then, "They got Gurd."

Mowry sat up. "How? When was this?"

"The damn fool came down from a roof straight into the arms of two of them. Not satisfied with that he gave them some lip and went for his gun."

"If he'd behaved like he'd every right to be up there he could have talked his way out of it."

"Gurd couldn't talk his way out of an old sack," opined Skriva. "He's not made like that. I spend a lot of time keeping him out of trouble."

"How come you weren't collared too?"

"I was on another roof halfway down the street. They didn't see me. It was all over before I could get down to help Gurd."

"What happened to him?"

"What you'd expect. The cops were already beating him over the head before he got his hand in his pocket. Last I saw of him was when they flung him into the wagon."

"Tough luck!" sympathized Mowry. He meditated a while, asked, "And what happened at the Cafe Susun?"

"Don't know exactly. Gurd and I weren't there at the time and a fellow tipped us to stay clear. All I know is that the Kaitempi rushed the place twenty strong, grabbed everyone in sight and staked it. I've not shown my face near there since. Some *soko* must have talked too much."

"Butin Arhava, for instance?"

"How could he?" scoffed Skriva. "Gurd took his head off before he'd a chance to blab."

"Maybe he talked *after* Gurd had tended to him," Mowry suggested. "Sort of lost his head about it."

Skriva narrowed his eyes. "What d'you mean?"

"Oh, forget it. Did you collect that roll from the bridge?"

"Yar."

"Want any more—or are you now too rich to care?"

Studying him calculatingly, Skriva asked, "How much money have you got altogether?"

"Enough to pay for all the jobs I want done."

"That tells me nothing."

"It isn't intended to," Mowry assured. "What's on your mind?"

"I like money."

"That fact is more than apparent," said Mowry.

"I'm really fond of it," Skriva went on, as if speaking in parables.

"Who isn't?"

"Yar, who isn't? Gurd loves it too. Most everybody does." Skriva stopped, added, "In fact the chump who doesn't love it is either daft or dead."

"If you're leading up to something, say so," Mowry urged. "Cut out the song and dance act. We've not got all day."

"I know a fellow who loves money."

"So what?"

"He's a jailer," said Skriva pointedly.

Twisting sidewise in his seat, Mowry eyed him carefully. "Let's get down to brass tacks. What's he willing to do and how much does he want?"

"He says Gurd's in a cell along with a couple of old pals of ours. So far none of them have been put through the mill though they'll be worked over sooner or later. Fellows in clink usually are given plenty of time to think over what's coming to them and let their imaginations operate. It helps them break down quicker."

"That's the usual technique," Mowry agreed. "Let them become nervous wrecks before making them physical wrecks."

"Yar, the stinking *sokos*." Skriva spat out the window before he continued, "Whenever a prisoner's number comes up the Kaitempi call at the jail, present an official demand for him and take him to their H.Q. for treatment. Sometimes they bring him back several days later, by which time he's a cripple. Sometimes they don't return him at all. In the latter event they file a death warrant to keep the prison records straight."

"Go on."

"This fellow who loves money will give me the number and location of Gurd's cell. Also the timing of Kaitempi visits and full details of the routine they follow. Finally he'll provide a copy of the official form used for demanding release." He let that sink in, finished, "He wants a hundred thousand."

Mowry pursed his lips in a silent whistle. "You think we should try to get Gurd out?"

"Yar."

"Didn't know you were so fond of him."

"He could stay there and rot for all I care," said Skriva. "He's paying the price of his own stupidity. Why should I worry about him, *hi?*"

"All right, let him stay and rot. We'll save a hundred thousand that way."

"Yar," Skriva approved. "But—"

"But what?"

"I could use the dope and the two with him. So could you if you've more work in mind. Furthermore, if Gurd's kept in he'll talk. They'll make him talk—and he knows too much. But if he escapes they won't be able to force him to say anything. And what's a hundred thousand to you?"

"Too much to throw away on a glib story," Mowry told him bluntly. "Prize fool I'd be to hand you a huge wad just because you say Gurd's in the clink."

Skriva's face darkened with anger. "You don't believe me, *hi?*"

"I've got to be shown," said Mowry, undisturbed.

"Maybe you'd like a specially conducted tour through the jail and have Gurd pointed out to you?"

"The sarcasm is wasted. You seem to forget that while Gurd may be able to put the finger on you for fifty or more major crimes, he can do nothing whatsoever about me. He can talk himself black in the face without saying anything worth a hoot so far as I am concerned. No, when I spend money it'll be *my* money and it'll be spent for *my* reasons, not yours."

"So you won't splurge a guilder on Gurd?" demanded Skriva, still thunderous.

"I don't say that. What I do say is that I won't throw money away for nothing. But I'm willing to pay for full value received."

"Meaning what?"

"Tell this greedy screw that we'll give him twenty thousand for a genuine Kaitempi requisition form—*after* he has handed it over. Also that we'll pay him a further eighty thousand *after* Gurd and his two companions have got away."

A mixture of expressions crossed Skriva's unlovely features, surprise, gratification, doubt and puzzlement. "What if he refuses to play on these terms?"

"He stays poor."

"Well, what if he agrees but refuses to believe I can find the money? How am I going to convince him?"

"Don't bother to try," Mowry advised. "He has to speculate in order to accumulate, same as everyone else. If he won't do it let him remain content with grinding poverty."

"Maybe he'd rather stay poor than take the risk."

"He won't. He's running no real risk and he knows it. There's only one chance he could take and he'll avoid it like the plague."

"Such as?"

"Suppose we arrive to make the rescue and are jumped on before we can open our mouths or show the requisition form, what will it prove? It'll show that this fellow fooled you for the sake of the reward. The Kaitempi will pay him five thousand apiece for laying the trap and tipping them off. He'll make an easy and legal ten thousand on top of the twenty thousand we've already paid him. Correct?"

"Yar," said Skriva, uneasily.

"But he'll lose the eighty thousand yet to come. The difference is plenty big enough to ensure his absolute loyalty up to the moment he gets it in his hot little hands."

"Yar," repeated Skriva, brightening considerably.

"After that—*zunk!*" said Mowry. "Immediately after he's got his claws on the lot we'd better run like hell."

"Hell?" Skriva stared at him. "That's a *Spakum* curse word."

Mowry sweated a bit as he replied offhandedly, "Sure it is. One picks up all sorts of bad language in wartime, especially on Diracta."

"Ah, yes, on Diracta," echoed Skriva, mollified. He got out of the car. "I'll go see this jailer. We'll have to move fast. Phone me this time tomorrow, *hi?*"

"All right."

Mowry remained where he was until the other's dyno had gone from sight. Then he jockeyed his own off the verge and drove into Pertane.

Chapter 9

The next day's work was the easiest to date though not devoid of danger. All he had to do was gossip to anyone willing to listen. This was in accordance with the step-by-step technique taught him by the college.

"First of all you must establish the existence of an internal opposition. Doesn't matter whether it is real or imaginary so long as the enemy becomes convinced of its actuality."

He had done that much.

"Secondly, you must create fear of that opposition and provoke the enemy into striking back at it as best he can."

He'd done that too.

"Thirdly, you must answer the enemy's blows with enough defiance to force him into the open, to bring his reaction to public attention and to create the general impression that the opposition has confidence in its own power."

That also had been achieved.

"The fourth move is ours and not yours. We'll take enough military action to make hay of the enemy's claims of invincibility. After that the morale of the public should be shaky."

One bomb on Shugruma had done the shaking.

"You then take the fifth step by sowing rumors. Listeners will be ripe to absorb them and whisper them around—and the stories will lose nothing in the telling. A good rumor well planted and thoroughly disseminated can spread alarm and despondency over a wide area. But be careful in your choice of victims. If you pick on a fanatical patriot it may be the end of you!"

In any city in any part of the cosmos the public park is a natural haunt of idlers and gossips. That is where Mowry went in the morning. The benches were occupied almost entirely by elderly people. Young folk tended to keep clear of such places lest inquisitive cops ask why they were not at work.

Selecting a seat next to a gloomy looking oldster with a perpetual sniff, Mowry contemplated a bed of tattered flowers until the other turned toward him and said conversationally, "Two more gardeners have gone."

"So? Gone where?"

"Into the armed forces. If they draft the rest of them I don't know what will happen to this park. It needs someone to look after it."

"There's a lot of work involved," agreed Mowry. "But I suppose the war comes first."

"Yar. Always the war comes first." Sniffy said it with cautious disapproval. "It should have been over by now. But it drags on and drags on. Sometimes I wonder when it will end."

"That's the big question," responded Mowry, making himself a fellow spirit.

"Things can't be going as well as they're said to be," continued Sniffy, morbidly. "Else the war would be over. It wouldn't drag on the way it does."

"Personally, I think things are darned bad." Mowry hesitated, went on confidingly, "In fact I know they are."

"You do? Why?"

"Maybe I shouldn't tell you—but it's bound to come out sooner or later."

"What is?" insisted Sniffy, consumed with curiosity.

"The terrible state of affairs at Shugruma. My brother came home this morning and told me."

"Go on—what did he say?"

"He tried to go there for business reasons but couldn't get to the place. A ring of troops turned him back forty *den* from the town. Nobody except the military, or salvage and medical services, is being allowed to enter the area."

"That so?" said Sniffy.

"My brother says he met a fellow who'd escaped the disaster with nothing but the clothes he was wearing. This fellow told him that Shugruma was practically wiped off the map. Not one stone left upon another. Three hundred thousand dead. The stench of bodies would turn your stomach. He said the scene is so awful that the newssheets daren't describe it, in fact they refuse to mention it."

Staring straight ahead, Sniffy said nothing but looked appalled.

Mowry added a few more lurid touches, brooded with him for a short time, took his departure. All that he'd said would be repeated, he could be sure of that. Bad news travels fast. A little later and half a mile away he had another on the hook, a beady-eyed, mean-faced character only too willing to hear the worst.

"Even the papers dare not talk about it," Mowry ended.

Beady-eyes swallowed hard. "If a Spakum ship can dive in and drop a big one so can a dozen others."

"Yar, that's right."

"In fact they could have dropped more than one while they were at it. Why didn't they?"

"Maybe they were making a test-run. Now they know how easy it is they'll come along with a *real* load. If that happens there won't be much left of Pertane." He pulled his right ear and made a *tzzk!* sound between his teeth, that being the Sirian equivalent of showing thumbs down.

"Somebody ought to do something about it," declared Beady, unnerved.

"I'm going to do something myself," informed Mowry. "I'm going to dig me a deep hole way out in the fields."

He left the other half-paralyzed with fright, took a short walk, picked on a cadaverous individual who looked like a mortician on vacation.

"Close friend of mine—he's a fleet leader in the space navy—told me confidentially that a Spakum onslaught has made Gooma completely uninhabitable. He thinks the only reason why they've not given Jaimec the same treatment is because they're planning to grab the place and naturally don't want to rob themselves of the fruits of victory."

"Do you believe all that?" demanded the Embalmer.

"One doesn't know what to believe when the government tells you one thing and grim experience tells you another. It's only his personal opinion anyway. But he's in the space navy and knows a few things that we don't."

"It has been stated authoritatively that the Spakum fleets have been destroyed."

"Yar, they were still saying so when that bomb fell on Shugruma," Mowry reminded him.

"True, true—I felt it land. In my own house two windows collapsed and a bottle of *zith* jumped off the table."

By mid-afternoon thirty people had been fed the tale of the Shugruma and Gooma disasters, plus allegedly first-hand warnings of bacteriological warfare and worse horrors to come. They could no more keep it to themselves than a man can keep a tornado to himself. By early evening a thousand would have the depressing news. At midnight ten thousand would be passing it around. In the morning a hundred thousand—and so on until the whole city was discussing it.

At the arranged time he called Skriva. "What luck?"

"I've got the form. Have you got the money?"

"Yar."

"It's to be paid before tomorrow. Shall we meet same place as last time?"

"No," said Mowry. "It's not wise to create a habit. Let's make it someplace else."

"Where?"

"There's a certain bridge where you collected once before. How about the fifth marker past it going south?"

"That's as good as anywhere. Can you go there at once?"

"I've got to pick up my car. It'll take a little time. You be there at the seven-time hour."

He reached the marker on time, found Skriva already waiting. Handing over the money, he took the requisition form and examined it carefully. One good look told him that the thing was well-nigh impossible for him to copy. It was an ornate document as lavishly engraved as a banknote of high denomination They could cope with it on Terra but it was beyond his ability to duplicate even with the help of various instruments of forgery lying in the cave.

The form was a used one dated three weeks ago and obviously had been pur-loined from the jail's filing system. It called for the release to the Kaitempi of one prisoner named Mabin Gurd but had enough blank spaces for ten names. The date, the prisoner's name and number had been typed. The authorizing signature was in ink.

"Now we've got it," prompted Skriva, "what are we going to do with it?"

"We can't imitate it," Mowry informed him. "The job is too tough and will take too long."

"You mean it's no use to us?" He registered angry disappointment.

"I wouldn't say that."

"Well, what do you say? Am I to give this stinker his twenty thousand or do I cram the form down his gullet?"

"You can pay him." Mowry studied the form again. "I think that if I work on it tonight I can erase the date, name and number. The signature can be left intact."

"That's risky. It's easy to spot erasures."

"Not the way I do them. I know how to gloss the surface afterward. The really difficult task will be that of restoring the broken lines of engraving." He pondered a moment, went on, "But that may not be necessary. There's a good chance the new typing will fill in the blanks. It's hardly likely that they'll put the form under a microscope."

"If they were that suspicious they'd grab us first," Skriva pointed out.

"I need a typewriter. I'll have to buy one in the morning."

"I can get you a typewriter for tonight," offered Skriva.

"You can? How soon?"

"By the eight-time hour."

"Is it in good condition?"

"Yar, it's practically new."

Mowry eyed him and said, "I suppose it's no business of mine but I can't help wondering what use a typewriter is to *you.*"

"I can sell it. I sell all sorts of things."

"Things you just happened to find lying in your hands?"

"That's right," agreed Skriva, unabashed.

"Oh well, who am I to quibble? You get it. Meet me here at eight."

Skriva pushed off. When he'd gone from sight Mowry followed into the city. He had a feed, drove back to the marker. Soon afterward Skriva reappeared, gave him the typewriter.

Mowry said, "I want Gurd's full name and those of his two companions. Somehow or other you'll have to discover their prison numbers too. Can you do that?"

"I've got them already." Taking a slip of paper from his pocket, Skriva read them out while the other made a note of them.

"Did you also learn at what times the Kaitempi make their calls to collect?"

"Yar. Always between the three- and four-time hours. Never earlier, rarely later."

"Can you find out about noon tomorrow whether Gurd and the others are still in the jail? We've got to know that—we'll get ourselves in a fix if we arrive and demand prisoners who were taken away this afternoon."

"I can check on it tomorrow," Skriva assured. Then his face tautened. "Are you planning to get them away *tomorrow?*"

"We've got to do it sometime or not at all. The longer we leave it the bigger the risk of the Kaitempi beating us to the draw. What's wrong with tomorrow, *hi?*"

"Nothing except that I wasn't counting on it being so soon."

"Why?"

"I thought it'd take longer to work things out."

"There's little to work out," declared Mowry. "We've swiped a requisition form. We alter it and use it to demand release of three prisoners. Either we get away with it or we don't. If we do, well and good. If we don't, we shoot first and run fast."

"You make it sound too easy," Skriva objected. "All we've got is this form. It isn't enough—"

"It won't be enough, I can tell you that now. Chances are ten to one they'll expect familiar faces and be surprised by strange ones. We'll have to compensate for that somehow."

"How?"

"Don't worry, we'll cope. Can you dig up a couple more helpers? All they need to do is sit in the cars, keep their traps shut and look tough. I'll pay them five thousand apiece just for that."

"Five thousand each? I could recruit a regiment for that money. Yar, I can find two. But I don't know how good they'd be in a fight."

"Doesn't matter so long as they can look like plug-uglies. By that I don't mean the Cafe Susun kind of roughneck, see? They've got to resemble Kaitempi agents." He gave the other an imperative nudge. "The same applies to you. When it's time to start the job I want to see all three of you clean and tidy, with well-pressed suits and neatly knotted neck-scarves. I want to see you looking as if about to attend a wedding. If you let me down in that respect the deal is off so far as I'm concerned. You can count me out and go pull the stunt on your own. I don't intend to try to kid some hard-faced, gimlet-eyed warden with the aid of three scruffy-looking bums."

"Maybe you'd like us decked out in fashionable jewelry," suggested Skriva sarcastically.

"A diamond on the hand is better than a smear of dirt," Mowry retorted. "I'd rather you overdid the dolling-up than mooched along like hoboes. You'd get away with a splurge because some of these agents are flashy types." He waited for comment but the other said nothing, so he continued, "What's more, these two helpers had better be characters you can trust not to talk afterward—else they may take my five thousand and then get another five thousand from the Kaitempi for betraying you."

Skriva was on firm ground here. He gave an ugly grin and promised, "One thing I can guarantee is that neither of them will say a word."

This assurance and the way it was made bore a sinister meaning but Mowry let it pass and said, "Lastly, we'll need a couple of dynos. We can't use our own unless we change the plates. Any ideas on that?"

"Pinching a pair of dynos is as easy as taking a mug of *zith*. The trouble is keeping them for any length of time. The longer we use them the bigger the chance of being picked up by some lousy patrol with nothing better to do."

"We'll have to cut the use of them to the minimum," Mowry told him. "Take them as late as you can. We'll park our own cars on that lot the other side of the Asako Bridge. When we leave the jail we'll beat it straight there and switch over to them."

"Yar, that is best," Skriva agreed.

"All right. I'll be waiting outside the east gate of the municipal park at the two-time hour tomorrow. You come along with two cars and two helpers and pick me up."

At that point Skriva became strangely restless and showed suspicion. He fidgeted around, opened his mouth, shut it.

Watching him curiously, Mowry invited, "Well, what's the matter? You want to call the whole thing off?"

Skriva mustered his thoughts and burst out with, "Look, Gurd means nothing to you. The others mean even less. But you're paying good money and taking a big risk to get them out of the clink. It doesn't make sense."

"A lot of things don't make sense. This war doesn't make sense—but we're in it up to the neck."

"Curses on the war. That is nothing to do with the matter."

"It has everything to do with the matter," Mowry contradicted. "I don't like it. A lot of people don't like it. If we kick the government in the rumps often enough and hard enough, they won't like it either."

"Oh, so that's what you're up to?" Skriva stared at him in frank surprise, thoughts of purely political reasons never having entered his mind. "You're chivvying the authorities?"

"Any objections?"

"I couldn't care less," informed Skriva, and added virtuously, "Politics is a dirty game. Anyone who plays around in it is crazy. All it gets him in the end is a free burial."

"It'll be my burial, not yours."

"Yar, that's why I don't care." Obviously relieved at having got to the bottom of the other's motives, Skriva finished, "Meet you at the park tomorrow."

"On time. If you're late I won't be there."

As before, he waited until the other had gone from sight before driving to town. It was a good thing, he thought, that Skriva had a criminal mentality. The fellow just wasn't interested in politics, ethics, patriotism or anything similar except insofar as it provided opportunity to snatch easy money. It was highly probable that he viewed his recent activities as profitably illegal but not as treacherous. It simply wouldn't occur to him that there are criminals and there are traitors.

Any one of Skriva's bunch would surrender his own mother to the Kaitempi, not as a duty to the nation but solely for five thousand guilders. Similarly, they'd hand Mowry over and pocket the cash with a hearty laugh. All that prevented them from selling him body and soul was the fact they'd freely admitted, namely, that one does not flood one's goldmine.

Providing the cars and helpers could be obtained Skriva would be there on time tomorrow. He felt sure of that.

Exactly at the two-time hour a big, black dyno paused at the east gate, picked up Mowry and whined onward. Another dyno, older and slightly battered, followed a short distance behind.

Sitting four-square at the wheel of the first car, Skriva looked neater and more respectable than he had done for years. He exuded a faint smell of scented lotion and seemed self-conscious about it. With his gaze fixed firmly ahead, he jerked a manicured thumb over his shoulder to indicate a similarly washed and scented character lounging beetle-browed in the back seat.

"Meet Lithar. He's the sharpest *wert* on Jaimec."

Mowry twisted his head round and gave a polite nod. Lithar rewarded him with a blank stare. Returning attention to the windshield, Mowry wondered what on earth a *wert* might be. He'd never heard the word before and dared not ask its meaning. It might be more than an item of local jargon, perhaps a slang word added to the Sirian language during the years he had been away. It wouldn't be wise to admit ignorance of it.

"The fellow in the other car is Brank," informed Skriva. "He's a red-hot *wert* too. Lithar's right-hand man. That so, Lithar?"

The sharpest *wert* on Jaimec responded with a grunt. To give him his due, he fitted the part of an agent of the typically surly type. In that respect Skriva had chosen well.

Threading their way through a series of side streets they reached a main road, found themselves held up by a long, noisy convoy of half-tracked vehicles crammed with troops. Perforce they stopped and waited. The convoy rolled on and on like a never-ending stream. Skriva began to curse under his breath.

"They're gaping around like newcomers," observed Mowry, watching the passing soldiery. "Must have just arrived from somewhere."

"Yar, from Diracta," Skriva told him. "Six shiploads landed this morning. There's a story going the rounds that ten set out but only six got here."

"That so? It doesn't look so good if they're rushing additional forces to Jaimec despite heavy losses en route."

"Nothing looks good except a stack of guilders twice my height," opined Skriva. He scowled at the rumbling half-tracks. "If they delay us long enough we'll still be here when a couple of boobs start bawling about their missing cars. The cops will find us just waiting to be grabbed."

"So what?" said Mowry. "Your conscience is clear, isn't it?"

Skriva answered that with a look of disgust. At last the procession of military vehicles came to an end. The car jolted forward as he rushed it impatiently into the road and built up speed.

"Take it easy," Mowry advised. "We don't want to be nailed for ignoring some petty regulation."

At a point a short distance from the jail Skriva pulled in to the curb and parked. The other dyno stopped close behind. He turned toward Mowry.

"Before we go any farther let's have a look at that form."

Extracting it from a pocket, Mowry gave it to him. He pored over it, seemed satisfied, handed it to Lithar.

"Looks all right to me. What d'you think?"

Lithar eyed it impassively, gave it back. "It's good enough or it isn't. You'll find out pretty soon."

Sensing something sinister in this remark, Skriva became afflicted with new doubts. He said to Mowry, "The idea is that a couple of us walk in, present this form and wait for them to fetch us the prisoners, *hi?*"

"Correct."

"What if this form isn't enough and they ask for proof of our identities?"

"I can prove mine."

"Yar? What sort of proof?"

"Who cares so long as it convinces them?" Mowry evaded. "As for you, fix this inside your jacket and flash it if necessary." He gave the other Sagramatholou's badge.

Fingering it in open surprise, Skriva demanded, "Where'd you get this?"

"An agent gave it to me. I've influence, see?"

"You expect me to believe that? No Kaitempi *soko* would dream of—"

"It so happened that he had expired," Mowry put in. "Dead agents are very cooperative, as perhaps you've noticed."

"You killed him?"

"Don't be nosy."

"Yar, what's it to us?" interjected Lithar from the back seat. "You're wasting time. Put a move on and let's get the whole thing over—or let's throw it up and go back home."

Thus urged Skriva started up and drove forward. Now that he was rapidly coming to the point of committing himself his edginess was obvious. He knew that if the rescue failed and he was caught he'd certainly pay for the attempt with bulging eyes and protruding tongue. If it succeeded there would follow a hue and cry that would make all of them cower in their rat holes for a month and all he'd have gained would be three henchmen who, for the time being, would be more nuisance than asset.

Inwardly he regretted the idea that had made him suggest this stunt in the first place, namely, that there is safety in numbers. Perhaps he'd be better off without Gurd and his fellow jailbirds. Sure, four heads are better than one, four guns are better than one, but he could do without the official hullabaloo that the escapees would drag behind them like the tail of a meteor.

It was too late to retreat. The jail was now in sight, its great steel doors set in high stone walls. Rolling toward the doors, the two cars stopped. Mowry got out. Skriva followed suit, thin-lipped and resigned.

Mowry thumbed the bell-button set in the wall. A small door which formed a section of the bigger one emitted metallic clankings and opened. Through it an armed guard eyed them questioningly.

"Kaitempi call for three prisoners," announced Mowry with becoming arrogance.

With a brief glance at the waiting cars and their *wert* occupants the guard motioned the two inside, closed the door, slid home its locking-bar. "You're a little early today."

"Yar, we've got a lot to do. We're in a hurry."

"This way."

They tramped after the guard in single file, Skriva last with a hand in a pocket. Taking them into the administration building, along a corridor and past a heavily barred sliding gate, the guard led them into a small room in which a burly, grimfaced Sirian was sitting behind a desk. Upon the desk stood a small plaque reading: *Commandant Tornik.*

"Three prisoners are required for immediate interrogation," said Mowry officiously. "Here is the requisition form, Commandant. We are pressed for time and would be obliged if you'd produce them as quickly as possible."

Tornik frowned over the form but did not examine it closely. Dialing an intercom phone he ordered somebody to bring the three to his office. Then he lay back in his chair and regarded the visitors with complete lack of expression.

"You are new to me."

"Of course, Commandant. There is a reason."

"Indeed? What reason?"

"It is believed that these prisoners may be more than ordinary criminals. We have reason to suspect them of being members of a revolutionary army, namely, *Dirac Angestun Gesept.* Therefore they are to be questioned by Military Intelligence as well as by the Kaitempi. I am the M.I. representative."

"Is that so?" said Tornik, still blank-faced. "We have never had the M.I. here before. May I have evidence of your identity?"

Producing his documents, Mowry handed them over. This wasn't going so swiftly and smoothly as hoped for. Mentally he prayed for the prisoners to appear and put a quick end to the matter. It was obvious that Tornik was the type to fill in time so long as everyone was kept waiting.

After a brief scrutiny Tornik returned the papers and commented, "Colonel Halopti, this is somewhat irregular. The requisition form is quite in order but I am supposed to hand prisoners over only to a Kaitempi escort. That is a very strict rule that cannot be disobeyed even for some other branch of the security forces."

"The escort *is* of the Kaitempi," answered Mowry. He threw an expectant look at Skriva who was standing like one in a dream. Skriva came awake, opened his jacket and displayed the badge. Mowry added, "They provided me with three agents saying their attendance was necessary."

"Yar, that is correct." Pulling open a drawer in his desk, Tornik produced a receipt form, filled it in by copying details from the requisition. When he had finished he studied it doubtfully, complained, "I'm afraid I cannot accept your signature, Colonel. Only a Kaitempi official may sign a receipt for prisoners."

"I'll sign it," offered Skriva, sweating over the delay.

"But you have a badge and not a plastic card," Tornik objected. "You are only an agent and not an officer."

Mentally abusing this infernal insistence upon rigmarole, Mowry interjected, "He is of the Kaitempi and temporarily under my command. I am an officer although not of the Kaitempi."

"That is so, but—"

"A receipt for prisoners must be given by the Kaitempi and by an officer. Therefore the proper conditions will be fulfilled if both of us sign."

Tornik considered this, decided that it agreed with the letter of the law. "Yar, the regulations must be observed. You will both sign."

Just then the door opened, Gurd and his companions shuffled in with a rattle of wrist-chains. A guard followed, produced a key, unlocked the manacles and took them away. Gurd, now worn and haggard, kept his gaze on the floor and maintained a surly expression. One of the others, a competent actor, glowered at Tornik, Mowry and Skriva in turn. The third, who was subject to attacks of delight, beamed around in happy surprise until Skriva bared his teeth at him. The smile then vanished. Luckily neither Tornik nor the attendant guard noticed this by-play.

Mowry signed the receipt with a confident flourish; Skriva appended his hurried scrawl beneath. The three prisoners silently stood by, Gurd still moping, the second scowling, the third wearing the grossly exaggerated expression of one in mourning for a rich aunt. Number three, Mowry decided, was definitely a dope who'd ham his way to an early grave.

"Thank you, Commandant." Mowry turned toward the door. "Let's go."

In shocked tones Tornik exclaimed, "What, without wrist-chains, Colonel? Have you brought no manacles with you?"

Gurd stiffened, number two bunched his fists, number three made ready to faint. Skriva stuck his hand back in his pocket and kept full attention on the guard.

Glancing back at the other, Mowry said, "We have steel anklets fixed to the floors of the cars. That is the M.I. way, Commandant." He smiled with the air of one who knows. "A prisoner runs with his feet and not with his hands."

"Yar, that is true," Tornik conceded.

They went out, led by the guard who had brought them there. The prisoners followed with Skriva and Mowry bringing up the rear. Through the corridor, past the barred gate, out the main door and across the yard. Armed guards patrolling the wall top sauntered along and eyed them indifferently. Five pairs of ears strained for a yell of fury and a rush of feet from the administration building, five bodies were tensed in readiness to slug the guide and make a dash for the exit door.

Reaching the wall, the guard grasped the locking-bar in the small door and just then the bell was rung from outside. This sudden, unexpected sound jolted their nerves, Skriva's gun came halfway out of his pocket. Gurd took a step toward the guard, his expression vicious. The actor jumped as if stung. Dopey opened his mouth to emit a yelp of fright, converted it into a gargle as Mowry rammed a heel on his foot.

Only the guard remained undisturbed. With his back to the others and therefore unable to see their reactions he lugged the locking-bar to one side, turned the handle, opened the door. Beyond stood four sour-faced characters in plain clothes.

One of them said curtly, "Kaitempi call for one prisoner."

For some reason best known to himself the guard found nothing extraordinary about two collecting parties turning up in close succession. He motioned the four inside, held the door open while the first arrivals went out. The newcomers did not head straight across the yard toward the administration block. They took a few steps in that direction, stopped as if by common consent, stared at Mowry and the others as they passed into the road. It was the disheveled look of the prisoners and the chronic alarm on the face of Dopey that attracted their attention.

Just as the door shut Mowry, who was last out, heard an agent rasp at the guard, "Who are those, *hi?*"

The reply wasn't audible but the question was more than enough.

"Jump to it!" he urged. *"Run!"*

They sprinted to the cars, spurred on by expectation of immediate trouble. A third machine now stood behind their own two, a big ugly dyno with nobody at the wheel. Lithar and Brank watched them anxiously, opened the doors in readiness.

Scrambling into the leading dyno, Skriva started its motor while Gurd went through the back door and practically flung himself into Lithar's lap. Behind, the other two piled into the rear of Brank's car.

Mowry gasped at Skriva, "Wait a moment while I see if I can grab theirs—it'll delay the chase."

So saying he raced to the third car, frantically tugged at its handle. It refused to budge. Just then the jail's door opened and somebody roared, "Halt! halt or we—" Brank promptly stuck an arm out his open window, flicked four quick shots toward the door gap and missed each time. But it was sufficient to make the shouter dive for cover. Mowry pelted back to the leading dyno and fell in beside Skriva.

"The cursed thing is locked. Let's get out of here."

The car surged forward, tore down the road, Brank accelerated after them. Watching through the rear window, Mowry saw several figures bolt out of the jail and waste precious moments fumbling by their dyno before they got in.

"They're after us," he told Skriva. "And they'll be bawling their heads off over the radio."

"Yar, but they haven't got us yet."

Chapter 10

Gurd said, "Did nobody think to bring a spare gun?"

"Take mine," responded Lithar, handing it over.

Cuddling it in an eager fist, Gurd grinned at him unpleasantly. "Don't want to be caught with it on you, *hi?* Rather it was me than you, *hi?* Typical *wert,* aren't you?"

"Shut up!" snarled Lithar.

"Look who's telling me to shut up," Gurd invited. He was talking thickly, as if something had gone wrong with his palate. "He's making a stack of money out of me else he wouldn't be here at all. He'd be safe at home checking his stocks of illegal *zith* while the Kaitempi belted me over the gullet. And he tells me to shut up." Leaning forward, he tapped Mowry on the shoulder with the barrel of the gun. "How much is he making out of this, Mashambigab? How much are you giving—"

He swayed wildly and clutched for a hold as the car rocked around a corner, raced down a narrower road, turned sharp right and then sharp left. Brank's car took the same corner at the same speed, made the right turn but not the left one. It rushed straight on and vanished from sight. They turned again into a one-way alley, cut through to the next road. There was now no sign of pursuit.

"We've lost Brank," Mowry told Skriva. "Looks like we've dropped the Kaitempi too."

"It's a safe bet they're chasing Brank. They were closer to him and they had to follow someone when we split up. Suits us, doesn't it?"

Mowry said nothing.

"A lousy *wert* tells *me* to shut up," mumbled Gurd.

Swiftly they zigzagged through a dozen side streets, still without encountering a radio alarmed patrol car. As they squealed around the last corner near to where their own cars were parked there sounded a sharp, hard crack in the rear. Mowry looked back expecting to find a loaded cruiser closing up on them. There was no car behind them. Lithar was lying on his side apparently asleep. He had a neat hole above his right ear. A thin trickle of purplish blood was seeping out of it.

Gurd smirked at Mowry and said, "I've shut *him* up, for keeps."

"Now we're carrying a corpse," complained Mowry. "As if we haven't trouble enough. Where's the sense—"

Skriva interrupted with, "Crack shots, the Kaitempi. Pity they got Lithar—he was just the sweetest *wert* on Jaimec."

He braked hard, jumped out, ran across the road and clambered into his own dyno. Gurd followed, the gun openly in his hand and not caring who noticed it. Mowry stopped by the window as the machine started up.

"What about Brank?"

"What about him?" echoed Skriva.

"If we both beat it he'll get here and find no chance to switch over."

"What, in a city crammed with dynos?" He let the car edge forward. "Brank's not here. That's his woe. Let him cope with his own troubles. We're beating it someplace safe while the going is good. You follow us."

With that he drove off. Mowry gave him a four hundred yards lead, droned along behind while the distance between them slowly increased. Should he let Skriva lead him to a hideout or not? There seemed little point in following to yet another rat hole. The jail job had been done and he'd achieved his purpose of stirring up a greater ruckus. There were no *werts* to pay off; Brank had got himself lost and Lithar was dead. If he wanted to regain contact with Gurd and Skriva he could use that telephone number or if, as was likely, it was no longer valid he could employ their secret post-office under the marker.

Other considerations also decided him to drop the brothers for the time being. For one, the Colonel Halopti identity wouldn't be worth a hoot after they'd wasted a few hours checking through official channels to establish its falsity. That would be by nightfall at the latest. Once again Pertane was becoming too hot to hold him. He'd better get out before it was too late.

For another, he was overdue to beam a report and his conscience was pricking him about his refusal to do so last time. If he didn't send one soon he might never be able to transmit one at all. And Terra was entitled to be kept informed.

By this time the other car had shrunk with distance. Tuning off to the right, he circled back into the city. At once he noticed a great change of atmosphere. There were far more police on the streets and now their number had been augmented by fully armed troops. Patrol cars swarmed like flies though none saw fit to stop and question him. On the pavements were less pedestrians than usual and these hurried along looking furtive, fearful, grim or bewildered.

Stopping by the curb outside a business block he lolled in his seat as if waiting for someone while he watched what was taking place on the street. The police, some uniformed and some in plain clothes, were all in pairs. The troops were in groups of six. Their sole occupation appeared to be that of staring accusatively at everyone who passed by, holding up any individual whose looks they didn't like, questioning and searching him. They also took particular note of cars, studying the occupants and eyeing the plate numbers.

In the time that Mowry sat there he and his car were given the sharp lookover at least twenty times. He endured it with an air of complete boredom and evidently passed muster because nobody took it further and questioned him. But that couldn't go on forever. Somebody more officious than the rest would pick on him merely because the others had not done so. He was tempting fate by staying there.

So he moved off, driving carefully to avoid the attention of numerous cruisers. Something had broken loose, no doubt of that. It was written on the moody faces of the public. He wondered whether the government had been driven to admit a series of reverses in the space war. Or perhaps the rumors he'd spread about Shugruma had come close enough to the truth to make authority concede the facts. Or maybe a couple of exceedingly important bureaucrats had tried to open mailed packages and splattered themselves over the ceiling, this creating a tremendous wave of panic among the powers-that-be. One thing was certain: the recent jail-break could not be solely responsible for the present state of affairs though possibly it may have triggered it into existence.

Slowly he made his way into the crummy quarter where his room was located, determined to pick up his belongings and clear out as quickly as possible. The car nosed its way into his street. As always, a bunch of idlers loafed upon the corner and stared at him as he went by. There was something not quite right about them. Their ill-kept clothes and careless postures gave them the superficial appearance of lazy bums but they were a little too well-fed, their gaze a little too haughty.

With hairs itching on the back of his neck and a peculiar thrill down his spine, he kept going, trying to look as if this street were only a part of a tiresome drive and meant nothing to him whatsoever. Against a lamppost leaned two brawny specimens without jackets or scarves. Nearby four more were shoring a wall. Six were gossiping around an ancient, decrepit truck parked right opposite the house in which his room was at the top. Three more were in the doorway of the house. Every one of these gave him the long, hard look as he rolled by with an air of total indifference.

The entire street was staked, though it didn't look as if they had a detailed description of him. He could be wrong in this belief, perhaps fooled by an overactive imagination. But his instinct told him that the street was covered from end to end, that his only chance of escape lay in driving on non-stop and displaying absolute lack of interest. He did not dare look at his house for evidence of a Radine-type explosion. Just that small touch of curiosity might have been enough to bring the whole lot into action.

Altogether he counted more than forty beefy strangers hanging around the road and doing their best to look shiftless. As he neared the street's end four of them came out of a doorway and walked to the curb. Their attention was his way, their manner that of those about to stop him on general principles.

Promptly he braked and pulled in near two others who were squatting on a doorstep. He lowered the window, stuck his head out. One of the sitters got to his feet, came toward him.

"Pardon," said Mowry, apologetically, "I was told first right and second left for Asako Road. It has got me here. I must have gone wrong somewhere."

"Where were you told?"

"Outside the militia barracks."

"Some people don't know one hand from the other," opined this character. "It should have been first right, second left, turn right again after going through the archway."

"Thanks. One can lose a lot of time in a city this size."

"Yar, especially when dopes point with the wrong hand." The informant returned to his doorstep, sat down. He had not nursed even a dim suspicion.

Evidently they were not on the watch for someone easily recognizable, or, at any rate, not for somebody who looked exactly like Colonel Halopti. Could be that they were in ambush for another badly wanted specimen who happened to live in this street. But he dared not put the matter to the test by returning to the house and going up to his room. If wrong, he would be finally and conclusively wrong to the last choke of breath.

Ahead, the four who'd waited at the curb had now resumed their leaning against the wall, lulled by Mowry's open conversation with their fellows. They ignored him as he drove past. Turning right, he thankfully speeded up. However, he did not congratulate himself. He had still a good way to go and the entire city had become one gigantic trap.

When nearing the city's outskirts a patrol car waved him down. For a couple of seconds he debated whether to obey or try to outrace it. He decided in favor of the former. Bluff had worked before, might do so again. Besides, to run for it would be a complete giveaway and every cruiser in the area would take up the chase. So he braked and hoped for the best.

The car drew alongside, the co-driver dropped his window. "Where are you heading for?"

"Palmare," answered Mowry, naming a village twenty *den* south of Pertane.

"That's what you think. Don't you listen to the news?"

"I haven't heard it since early this morning. Been too busy even to get a square meal. What's happened?"

"All exits barred. Nobody allowed out of the city except with a permit from the military. You'd better go back and get yourself informed. Or buy an evening paper."

The window went up, the patrol car whined into top speed. Mowry watched it go with mixed emotions. Yet again he was sharing all the sensations of a hunted animal. Nobody could stop him or even show undue interest in him without giving him a nervy this-is-it feeling. If it kept up long enough a time must inevitably come when this *would* be it.

He stooged around in the car until he found a newsstand carrying the latest editions still damp from the press. Then he parked a few minutes while he scanned the headlines. They were big enough and likely to give the readership a few unpleasant jolts.

PERTANE UNDER MARTIAL LAW.
TRAVEL BAN—MAYOR DECLARES POPULATION WILL STAND FIRM.
DRASTIC ACTION AGAINST DIRAC ANGESTUM GESEPT.
POLICE ON TRAIL OF MAIL BOMBER.
TWO KILLED, TWO CAPTURED IN DARING JAILBREAK.

Rapidly he read the brief report under the last heading. Lithar's body had been found and the Kaitempi had grabbed the credit for the kill. That made Skriva something of a prophet. Dopey had been shot to death, Brank and the other had been taken alive. These two survivors already had confessed to membership in a revolutionary force. There was no mention of any others having got away and not a single word about the mock Colonel Halopti.

Probably authority had clamped down on some items in the hope of giving the escapees a sense of false security. Well, he'd better not fall into that trap; from now on he must not show his documents to any cop or Kaitempi agent. Neither could he substitute any other papers. The only ones near to hand were locked in his case and surrounded by a horde of agents. The only others were in the forest cave with a ring of troops between here and there.

A ring of troops? Yes, that could be the weak point that he might break through if he put a move on. It was highly likely that the numerically strong armed forces were not yet as well-primed as were the police and Kaitempi. And the average trooper is not inclined to argue with a colonel, even one in plain clothes. The chance of being cross-examined and bullied came only from an individual of equal or higher rank. He could not imagine any colonels or major-generals manning the roadblocks. Anyone outranking a junior lieutenant was more likely to be warming an office chair or boozing and boasting in the nearest *zith*-parlor. At once he decided that here lay his best opportunity to break out of the net. It wasn't a decision difficult to reach. He'd little choice about the matter. He must find freedom in the open country or remain in the city until caught.

About sixty routes radiated from the perimeter of Pertane. The main ones—such as the wide, well-used roads to Shugruma and Radine—were likely to be more heavily guarded than the secondary roads or potholed lanes leading to villages or isolated factories. It was also possible that the biggest, most important roadblocks would have a few police or agents in company with the troops.

Many of the lesser and sneakier outlets were quite unknown to him; a random choice might take him out of the frying-pan and into the fire. But not far away lay a little-used sideroad to Palmare with which he was familiar. It twisted and wound in a direction more or less parallel with the big main road but it got there just the same. Once on it he could not get off it for another forty *den.* He'd have to continue all the way to Palmare, turn there onto a rutted cross-country lane that would take him to the Valapan road. At that point he'd be about half an hour's drive from where he usually entered the forest.

Cutting through the suburbs he headed outward toward this lesser road. Houses gradually thinned away and ceased. As he drove through a market-gardening area a police cruiser whined toward him, passed without pause. He let go a sigh of relief as it disappeared. Presumably it had been in too great a hurry to bother with him or perhaps its occupants had taken it for granted that he possessed a military permit.

Five minutes later he rounded a blind corner and found a roadblock awaiting him two hundred yards beyond. A couple of army trucks stood side-on across the road in such a position that a car could pass provided it slowed to less than walking pace. In front of the trucks a dozen soldiers stood in line, coddling their automatic weapons and looking bored. There was no cop or agent anywhere in sight.

Mowry slowed, stopped, but kept his dynomotor rotating. The soldiers eyed him with bovine curiosity. From behind the nearest truck a broad, squat sergeant appeared, marched up to the car.

"Have you got an exit permit?"

"Don't need one," responded Mowry, speaking with the authority of a four-star general. Opening his wallet, he displayed his identity-card and prayed to God that the sight of it would not produce a howl of triumph.

It didn't. The sergeant looked at it, saluted. Noticing this, the nearby troops straightened themselves and assumed expressions of military alertness.

In apologetic tones the sergeant said, "I regret that I must ask you to wait a moment, Colonel. My orders are to report to the officer in charge if anyone claims the right to go through without a permit."

"Even the Military Intelligence?"

"It has been emphasized that this order covers everyone without exception, sir. I have no choice but to obey."

"Of course, Sergeant," agreed Mowry, condescendingly. "I will wait."

Saluting again, the sergeant went at the double behind the trucks. Meanwhile the twelve troopers posed with the rigid self-consciousness of those aware of a brasshat in the vicinity. In short time the sergeant came back bringing with him a very young and worried-looking lieutenant.

This officer marched precisely up to the car, saluted, opened his mouth just as Mowry beat him to the draw by saying, "You may stand easy, Lieutenant."

The other gulped, let his legs relax, fumbled for words, finally got out, "The sergeant tells me you have no exit permit—Colonel."

"That's right. Have *you* got one?"

Taken aback, the lieutenant floundered a bit, said, "No, sir."

"Why not?"

"We are on duty outside the city."

"So am I," informed Mowry.

"Yes, sir." The lieutenant pulled himself together. He seemed unhappy about something. "Will you be good enough to let me see your identity-card, sir? It is just a formality. I'm sure that everything will be all right."

"I know that everything will be all right," said Mowry, as though giving fatherly warning to the young and inexperienced. Again he displayed the card.

The lieutenant gave it no more than a hurried glance. "Thank you, Colonel. Orders are orders, as you will appreciate." Then he curried favor by demonstrating his efficiency. He took one step backward and gave a classy salute which Mowry acknowledged with a vague wave. Jerking himself round like an automaton, the lieutenant brought his right foot down with a hard thump and screamed at the top of his voice, "Pass one!"

Opening out, the troops obediently passed one. Mowry crawled through the block, curving around the tail of the first truck, twisting the opposite way around the second. Once through he hit up maximum speed. It was a temptation to feel gleeful but he didn't. He was sorry for that young lieutenant who, before long, would be taking a prize lambasting. It was easy to picture the scene when a senior officer arrived at the post to check up.

"Anything to report, Lieutenant?"

"Not much, sir. No trouble of any sort. It has been very quiet. I let one through without a permit."

"You did? What was that?"

"He was Colonel Halopti, sir."

"Halopti? That name seems familiar. I'm sure I heard it mentioned as I left the other post."

Helpfully, "He is in the M.I., sir."

"Yar, yar. But that name means something. Why don't they keep us properly informed? Have you a short-wave set?"

"Not here, sir. There is one at the next main road block. We have a field telephone."

"All right, I'll use that." A little later. "You hopeless imbecile! This Halopti is wanted all over the planet! And you let him slip through your hands—you ought to be shot! How long has he been gone? Did he have anyone with him? Will he have passed through Palmare yet? Sharpen your wits, fool, and answer me! Did you note the number of his car? No, you did not—that would be too much to expect."

And so on and so on. Yes, the balloon would go up most anytime. Perhaps in three or four hours, perhaps within ten minutes. The thought of it made Mowry maintain what was a reckless speed on such a twisting and badly surfaced road.

He shot through small and sleepy Palmare half expecting to be fired upon by local vigilantes. Nothing happened except that a few faces glanced out of windows as he went by. Nobody saw him turn off the road a little beyond the village and take the crude track that led to the Pertane-Valapan artery.

Now he was compelled to slow down whether he liked it or not. Over the terrible surface the car bumped and rolled at quarter speed. If anything came the other way he'd be in a jam because there was no room to pull aside or turn. Two jetplanes moaned through the gathering dusk but carried straight on, indifferent to what was taking place below. Soon after a 'copter came low over the horizon, followed it a short distance, dropped back and disappeared. Its course showed that it was circling around Pertane, possibly checking the completeness of military positions.

Eventually he reached the Pertane-Valapan route without having encountered anything on the track. Accelerating, he made for the forest entry-point. A number of army vehicles trundled heavily along but there was no civilian traffic to or from distant Pertane. Those inside the city could not get out, those outside did not want to go in lest they be detained there for weeks.

At the moment he reached the identifying tree and tombstone the road was clear in both directions. Taking full advantage of the opportunity he drove straight over the verge and into the forest as far as the car could go. Jumping out, he went back and repeated his former performance of carefully eliminating all tire tracks where they entered the forest and checking that the car was invisible from the road.

The dark of night now was halfway across the sky. That meant he had to face another badly slowed-down traipse to the cave. Alternatively he could sleep over-night in the car and start his journey with the dawn. The latter was preferable; even a wasp needs rest and slumber. On the other hand the cave was more peace-ful, more comfortable and a good deal safer than the car. There he could enjoy a real Terran breakfast, after which he could lie full length and snooze like a child instead of rolled up with one ear and one eye open. He started for the cave at once, trying to make the most use of the fading light while it lasted.

With the first streaks of morning he came wearily and red-eyed through the last of the trees. His finger-ring had been tingling for fifteen minutes so that he made his approach with confidence. Clumping along the pebble beach he went into the cave, fixed himself a hearty meal. Then he crawled into a sleeping-bag and surrendered consciousness. The transmission of his report could wait. It would have to wait: communication might bring instructions impossible to carry out before he'd had a good spell of slumber.

He must have needed it because he lay without stirring through the entire day. Dusk again was creeping in when he awoke. Setting up another feed, he ate it, felt on top of the world, expressed it by flexing his muscles and whistling badly off-tune.

For a short while he studied the massed containers and nursed a few regrets. In one of them reposed material for repeated changes of appearance plus docu-ments to cover no less than thirty more fake identities. The situation being what it was he'd be darned lucky to get through three of them. Another con-tainer held publicity stuff including the means to print or mail more letters.

Ait Lithar was the fifth.
The list is long.
Dirac Angestun Gesept.

But what was the use? The Kaitempi had claimed that kill. Moreover he needed to know the names of any mail-bomb victims so that D.A.G. could exploit those too. He lacked this information. Anyway, the time for that kind of propaganda had now gone past. The entire world was on the jump, reinforcements had been poured in from Diracta, battle-stations had been taken up against a revolutionary army that did not exist. In such circumstances threatening letters had become mere fleabites.

Dragging out Container-5 he set it up, wound it into action and let it run. For two and a half hours it operated silently.

Whirrup-dzzt-pam! Whirrup-dzzt-pam!
"Jaimec calling! Jaimec calling!"

Contact was established when the gravelly voice said, "Come in. Ready to tape."

Mowry responded, "JM on Jaimec," then babbled on as fast as he could go and to considerable length. He finished, "Pertane isn't tenable until things quiet down and I don't know how long that will take. Personally, I think the panic will spread to other towns. When they can't find what they're seeking in one place they'll start raking systematically through all the others."

There was a long silence before the faraway voice came back with, "We don't want things to quiet down. We want them to spread. Get working at once on phase nine."

"Nine?" he ejaculated, "I'm only on four. What about five, six, seven and eight?"

"Forget them. Time is running short. There's a ship getting near to you with another wasp on board. We sent him to tend phase nine thinking you'd been nabbed. Anyway, we'll beam instructions that he's to stay on the ship while we pick him another planet. Meanwhile you get busy."

"But phase nine is strictly a pre-invasion tactic."

"That's right," said the voice, dryly. "I just told you time is running short."

It cut off. Communication had ended. Mowry stacked the cylinder back in the cave. Then he went outside and gazed at the stars.

Phase nine was designed to bring about a further dispersal of the enemy's over-stretched resources and to place yet another great strain upon his creaking war-machine. It was, so to speak, one of several possible last straws.

The idea was to make panic truly planet-wide by spreading it from land to water. Jaimec was peculiarly susceptible to this kind of blow. On a colonial world populated by only one race of only one species there had been no national or international rivalries, no local wars, no development of navies. The nearest that Jaimec could produce to a sea-going force consisted of a number of fast motor-boats, lightly armed and used solely for coastal patrol work.

Even the merchant fleet was small by Terran standards. Jaimec was underdeveloped and no more than six hundred ships sailed the planet's seas on about twenty well-defined routes. There wasn't a vessel larger than fifteen thousand tons. Nevertheless the local war effort was critically dependent upon the unhampered coming and going of these ships. To delay their journeys or ruin their schedules or bottle them up in port would play considerable hob with the entire Jaimecan economy.

This sudden switch from phase four to nine meant that the oncoming Terran spaceship must be carrying a load of periboobs which it would scatter in the world's oceans before making a quick getaway. Almost certainly the dropping would be done by night and along the known sea-lanes.

At college Mowry had been given full instruction about this tactic and the part he was expected to play. The stunt had a lot in common with his previous activities, being designed to make a thoroughly aggravated foe hit out left and right at what wasn't there.

He'd been shown a sectionalized periboob. This deceitful contraption resembled an ordinary oil-drum with a twenty-foot tube projecting from its top. At the uppermost end of the tube was fixed a flare nozzle. The drum portion held a simple magneto-sensitive mechanism. The whole thing could be mass produced at low cost.

When in the sea a periboob floated so that its nozzle and four to six feet of tube stood above the surface. If a mass of steel or iron approached to within four hundred yards of it, the mechanism operated and the whole gadget sank from sight. If the metal mass receded, the periboob promptly arose until again its tube poked above the waves.

To function efficiently this gadget needed a prepared stage and a spotlight. The former had been arranged at the outbreak of war by permitting the enemy to get hold of top secret plans of a three-man midget submarine small enough and light enough for an entire flotilla to be transported in one spaceship. Mowry now had to provide the spotlight by causing a couple of merchant vessels to sink at sea after a convincing bang.

Jaimecans were as capable as anyone else of adding two and nothing together and making it four. If everything went as planned the mere sight of a periboob would cause any ship to race for safety while filling the ether with yells for help. Other ships, hearing the alarm, would make wide, time-wasting detours or tie up in port. The dockyards would frantically switch from the building and repair of cargo vessels to the construction of useless destroyers. Numberless jetplanes, 'copters and even space scouts would take over the futile task of patrolling the oceans and bombing periboobs wherever they might be found.

The chief beauty of this form of naughtiness was that it did not matter in the least if the enemy discovered he was being kidded. He could trawl a periboob from the depths, take it apart, demonstrate how it worked to every ship's master on the planet and it would make no difference. If two ships had been sunk, two hundred more might go down. A periscope is a periscope, there's no swift way of telling the false from the real and no captain in his right mind will invite a torpedo while trying to find out.

Alapertane (little Pertane) was the biggest and nearest port on Jaimec. It lay forty *den* west of the capital, seventy *den* northwest of the cave. Population a quarter million. It was highly likely that Alapertane had escaped most of the official hysteria pervading elsewhere, that its police and Kaitempi were less suspicious, less active. Mowry had never visited the place and therefore neither had *Dirac Angestun Gesept.* So far as Alapertane was concerned he had little grief to inherit.

Well, Terra knew what it was doing and orders must be carried out. He would have to make a trip to Alapertane and get the job done as soon as possible. On his own, without the dubious help of Gurd and Skriva—who so long as the hunt was on—remained dangerous liabilities.

Opening a container, Mowry took out a thick wad of documents, thumbed through them and carefully considered the thirty identities available. All of them had been devised to suit specific tasks. There were half a dozen that established his right to roam around the docks and peer at shipping. He chose a set of papers that depicted him as a minor official of the Planetary Board of Maritime Affairs.

Next he made himself up for the part. It took him more than an hour. In the end he was an elderly, bookish bureaucrat peering through steel-rimmed spectacles. That done, he amused himself blinking at his image in a metal mirror and talking nonsense in characteristically querulous tones.

Long hair would have perfected his appearance since he still had the short military crop of Halopti. A wig was out of the question; except for spectacles, the strict rule of facial disguise was to wear nothing that could be knocked, blown or taken off. So he shaved a patch of cranium to suggest approaching baldness and left it at that.

Finally he found himself another case, inserted its plastic key and opened it. Despite all the risks he had taken and might again take this was the action he detested most. He could never get rid of the notion that explosive luggage was highly temperamental, that many a wasp had been blown to the nether regions with a phantom key in his hand and that Terran authorities had kept silent about it.

From yet another container he took three limpet mines, two for use and one as a spare. These were hemispherical objects with a heavy magnetic ring projecting from the flat side, a timing-switch on the opposite, curved side. They weighed eleven pounds apiece and together made a load he'd rather have been without. Putting these in the case, he stuffed a pocket with new money, checked his gun. Switching on Container-22 he set forth, again through the dark.

By now he was becoming more than fed up with the long, trying journey from the cave to the road. It hadn't looked much on an aerial photograph when seen through a stereoscopic viewer but the actual doing of it was tough. Especially when trudging through the dark and carrying a load. Repeatedly he cursed his choice of a hideout while reluctantly admitting that his cache had been protected by its very remoteness.

He reached the car in broad daylight, thankfully dumped the case on the back seat, checked the road for passing vehicles. The coast was clear. Racing back to the car he got it out fast, parked it while he scuffed tire tracks from the verge. Then he headed for Alapertane, choosing a route that kept him as far as possible from the angry capital.

Fifteen minutes later he was compelled to pull up. The road was filled with a convoy of army vehicles that were bucking and rocking as they reversed one by one into treeless space. Troops who had dismounted were filtering in ragged lines between the trees on both sides of the road. A dozen glum civilians were sitting in one truck with four soldiers to guard them.

As Mowry sat watching a captain came alongside the car and asked, "Where're you from?"

"Valapan."

"Where d'you live?"

"Kiestra, just outside Valapan."

"Where're you going?"

"Alapertane."

This seemed to satisfy the other. He made to move off.

Mowry called, "What's happening here, Captain?"

"A round-up. We're collecting the windy and taking them back where they belong."

"The windy?" Mowry looked baffled.

"Yar. The night before last a lot of yellow-bellied *sokos* bolted out of Pertane and took to the woods. They were worried about their skins, see? More followed early yesterday morning. By now half the city would be gone if we hadn't pinned them in. Civilians make me sick."

"What got them on the run?"

"Talk." He gave a sniff of contempt. "Just a lot of talk."

"Well, there's no rush from Valapan," offered Mowry.

"Not yet," the captain gave back. He walked away, bawled out a slow-moving squad.

The last trucks got off the road and Mowry forged ahead. Evidently the jailbreak had coincided with strong governmental action against a jittery populace as well as against subversive forces. The city would have been ringed in any event, whether Gurd had been wangled out of the jug or not.

Speculations about the fate of Gurd and Skriva occupied his mind as he drove along. Had they been caught or were they lying low somewhere within the ring? As he passed through a village he was tempted momentarily to stop, call their telephone number and see what response he got. He resisted the notion as profitless but he did pause long enough to buy a morning paper.

The news was little different, the usual mixture of boastings, threats, promises, directives and warnings. One paragraph stated categorically that more than eighty members of *Dirac Angestun Gesept* had been hauled in "including one of their so-called generals." He wondered how this could be and which unfortunate character had been burdened with the status of a revolutionary general. There was nothing about Gurd and Skriva, no mention of Colonel Halopti.

Throwing the paper away, he continued his journey. Shortly before noon he reached the center of Alapertane and asked a pedestrian the way to the docks. Though hungry once more he did not take time off for a meal. Alapertane was not surrounded, no snap searches were taking place, no patrol car had halted and quizzed him. He felt it wise to cash in on a favorable situation that might soon change for the worse. So without bothering about a feed he made straight for the waterfront.

Planting the dyno in the private parking lot of a shipping company, he approached the gates of the first dock on foot, blinked through his spectacles at the policeman standing by the entrance and asked, "Which way to the harbor-master's office?"

The cop pointed. "Right opposite the third set of gates."

Going there, Mowry entered the office, tapped on the counter with the impatience of an oldster in a hurry. A junior pen-pusher responded.

"You wish?"

Showing him his papers, Mowry said, "I wish to know which ships will depart before dawn tomorrow and from which docks they will leave."

Obediently the other dug out a long, narrow book and sought through its pages. It did not occur to him to question the reason for this request. A piece of paper headed *Planetary Board of Maritime Affairs* was more than enough to satisfy him and, as any fool knew, neither Alapertane nor its ships were menaced by the Spakum forces.

"Destinations as well?" asked the youth.

"No, those don't matter. I wish only the names, the times of departure and the dock numbers." Mowry produced a stub of pencil, a sheet of paper and peered fussily over his glasses.

"There are four," informed the other. "The *Kitsi* at eight-time, dock three. The *Anthus* at eight-time, dock one. The *Su-cattra* at nineteen-time, dock seven. The *Su-limane* at nineteen-time, also dock seven." He flipped a page, added informatively, "The *Melami* was due to leave at nineteen-time but is held up with some kind of trouble in the engine room. It is likely to be delayed several days."

"That one doesn't matter."

Leaving, he returned to the car, got out the case and went to dock seven. The policeman on duty took one look at his documents and let him through the gates without argument. Once inside he walked quickly toward the long shed behind which towered a line of cranes and a couple of funnels. Rounding the end of the shed he found himself facing the stern of the *Su-cattra*.

One glance told him that at present time he had not the slightest hope of fixing a limpet mine unseen. The vessel lay against the dockside, its hatches battened down, its winches silent, but many workers were hand-loading late cargo by lugging it up the gangways from waiting trucks and a small mob of officials stood around watching. Across the basin lay the *Su-limane* also taking cargo aboard.

For a short time he debated within himself whether to go after the *Anthus* and *Kitsi*. There was the disadvantage that they were in different docks a fair distance apart. Here, he had two suitable ships within easy reach of each other. And it was probable that the other vessels also were loading, thus being no easier to victimize.

It seemed that in his haste he had arrived too early. The best thing for him to do would be to go away and come back later after workers and officials had gone home. But if the cop on the gate or a waterfront patrol became nosy it would be hard to explain his need to enter the deserted dock area after all work had ceased. A hundred excuses could turn into a hundred self-betrayals.

"I have a personal message for the captain of the *Su-cattra*."

"Yar? What is his name?"

Or, "I have a corrected cargo manifest to deliver to the *Su-limane*."

"Yar? Let me see it. What's the matter—can't you find it? How can you deliver it if you haven't got it? If it's not in your pockets it may be in that bag. Why don't you look in the bag? You afraid to open it, *hi?*"

Leaving the dockside he walked past the end of the huge shed which stretched the entire length of the dock. Its sliding doors stood three feet ajar. He went through without hesitation. The side farthest from the dock was stacked roof-high with packing cases of every conceivable shape and size. The opposite side was part full. Near the main quayside doors halfway up the shed stood an array of cardboard cartons and bulging sacks which workers were taking out to the *Su-cattra.*

Seeing the name *Melami* stenciled all over the nearest stack of cargo, Mowry looked swiftly toward the distant loaders, assured himself that he had not been observed, dodged behind a big crate. Though no longer visible from inside the shed he could easily be seen by anyone passing the sliding doors through which he had entered. Holding his case endwise ahead of him, he inched through the narrow gap between two more crates, climbed over a big coffin-shaped box, squirmed into a dark alcove between the stack and the shed's outer wall.

It was far from comfortable here. He could not sit, neither could he stand erect. He had to remain half-bent until, tired of that, he knelt on his case. But at least he was safe. The *Melami* was held up and nobody was likely to heave its cargo around for the fun of it.

He stayed there for what seemed a full day. The time came when whistles blew and sounds of outside activity ceased. Through the shed's wall sounded a muffled tramp of many feet as workers left for home. Nobody had bothered to close the shed's doors and he couldn't make up his mind whether that was a good thing or not. Locked doors would suggest an abandoned dockside guarded by none save the cop on the gate. Open doors implied the arrival of a night-shift or perhaps the protection of roving patrols.

Edging out of the alcove he sat on a crate and rubbed his aching kneecaps. He waited two more hours to let overtime workers and other eager beavers get clear. When his patience ran out he walked through the deserted shed, stopped behind its quayside doors that were directly opposite the middle of the *Su-cattra.*

From the case he took a limpet mine, set its timing-switch to give a twenty-hour delay, threaded a length of thin cord through the holding loop. He peeped out the door. There was not a soul on the dockside but a few sailors were busy on the ship's top deck.

Boldly he stepped out of the shed, crossed the intervening ten yards and dropped the mine into the narrow stretch of water between ship and dockside. It hit with a dull plop and a big splash, sank rapidly to the limit of its cord. It was now about eight feet below the surface and did not immediately take hold. He waggled the cord to turn the magnetic face toward the ship. The mine promptly attached itself with a clang loud enough to resound all over the big vessel. Quickly he let go one end of the cord, pulled on the other and reeled it in through the holding loop.

High above him a sailor came to the deckrail, leaned on it and looked down. By that time Mowry had his back toward him and was strolling casually toward the shed. The sailor watched him go inside, glanced at the stars, spat in the water and went back to his chore.

Soon afterward he repeated the performance with the *Su-limane,* sticking the mine amidships and eight feet down. That one also had a twenty-hour delay. Again the clang aroused careless attention, bringing three curious sailors to the side. But they took their time about it, saw nobody, shrugged it off and forgot it.

Mowry made for the exit gates. On the way he passed two officers returning to their ship. Engrossed in conversation, they did not so much as glance at him. If only they'd known of the long swim in store, he thought, they'd willingly have beaten out his brains.

A different policeman was on duty by the gates as he went through.

"Live long!"

"Live long!" echoed the cop, and turned his attention elsewhere.

Trudging a long way down the road and rounding the corner near to the gates of dock three, Mowry saw the parking lot and came to a halt. A hundred yards away his car was standing exactly where he had left it but had become the subject of unwelcome interest. Its hood was raised and a couple of uniformed police were prying around the exposed dynomotor.

They must have unlocked the car with a master key in order to operate the hood's release catch. To go to that length meant they were not amusing themselves by being officious. They were on a definite trail.

Retreating behind the corner, Mowry gave swift thought to the matter. Obviously those cops were looking for the dynomotor's serial number. In another minute one of them would be crawling under the car to check the chassis number. This suggested that at last authority had realized that Sagramatholou's car had changed its plates. So the order had gone out to inspect all cars of that particular date and type.

Right in front of him, hidden from the parking lot, stood the unoccupied cruiser belonging to those nosy-pokes. They must have left it there intending to edge it forward a few feet and use it as a watching-post if necessary. Once they'd satisfied themselves that the suspected dyno was indeed a hot one, they'd come back on the run to set a stakeout.

Cautiously he took a peep around the corner. One was talking excitedly while the other scribbled in a notebook. It would be another minute before they returned because they would close the hood and relock the dyno in order to bait the trap.

Certain that no passerby would question something done with casual confidence, he tried the cruiser's door handle. It was locked. He had no key with which to open it, no time to pick it, and that put an end to any thought of taking one car in lieu of the other. Opening his case, he took out the spare limpet mine, set it for a one-hour delay. He lay in the road, rapidly inched himself under the cruiser and stuck the bomb to the center of its steel framework. Wriggling out, he brushed himself down with his hands. Seven people had seen him go under and emerge. Not one viewed his actions as extraordinary.

He snatched up his case and departed at a pace that was little short of a shambling run. At the next corner he looked back. One cop was now sitting in the cruiser and using its short-wave radio. The other was out of sight, presumably concealed where he could watch the dyno. Evidently they were transmitting the news that the missing car had been found and were summoning help to surround it.

Yet again adverse circumstances were chivvying him into a tight corner. He had lost the car on which he had relied so much and which had stood him in such good stead. All that he now possessed were his gun, a set of false documents, a large wad of counterfeit money and a case that was empty save for what was wired to its lock.

The case he got rid of by placing it in the entrance to the main post office. That action would not help to cool things down. Discovery of his dyno had warned Alapertane that Sagramatholou's killer was somewhere within its bounds. While they were squatting around it in readiness to snare him a police cruiser would shower itself all over the scene. Then somebody would dutifully take a lost case to the nearest precinct station, a cop would try to key it open and make an awful mess of that place.

Alapertane already was half-awake. Two big bangs were going to bring it fully awake and on its toes. Somehow he'd have to get out before they copied the Pertane tactic and ringed the town with troops.

Chapter 11

This was a time when he regretted the destruction of Pigface's card in that explosion at Radine. He could do with it now. Equally he was sorry that he'd given Sagramatholou's badge to Skriva. Despite looking as much like a Kaitempi agent as a purple porcupine, either the card or badge would have enabled him to commandeer any civilian car in town simply by ordering its driver to take him wherever he wished to go, shut up and do as you're told.

He had one advantage: the hunters had no real description of Sagramatholou's killer. Possibly they were shooting in the dark by seeking the elusive Colonel Halopti. Or perhaps they were chasing a purely imaginary description which the Kaitempi had tormented out of its captives. It wasn't likely that they'd be eagerly sniffing around for an elderly, slightly befuddled civilian who wore glasses and was too daft to know one end of a gun from the other.

All the same, they would quiz anyone they caught leaving town in a hurry at this particular time, even if he looked the soul of innocence. They might take it further by searching every outward traveler in which event he'd be damned by possession of a gun and a large sum of money. They might also hold any and every suspect pending a thorough check of identities. That also would get the noose round his neck. The Board of Maritime Affairs had never heard of him.

Therefore escape by train was out of the question. The same applied to long-distance buses. They'd all be watched. Ten to one the entire police network was

ready to take up the relentless pursuit of any car reported stolen; they would
assume that the culprit might have dumped one dyno intending to steal another. It was too late in the day to acquire another car by buying it outright.
But . . . hah, he could do what he'd done before. He could rent one.

It took him quite a while to find a hire-and-drive agency. The evening was drawing in, many businesses already had shut for the night, others were near their closing time. In one way that might be a help: maybe the lateness of the hour would
cover his haste and get him prompt service.

"I wish to rent that bullnozed sportster for four days. Is it available at once?"

"Yar."

"How much?"

"Thirty guilders a day. That's one-twenty."

"I'll take it."

"You want it right away?"

"Yar, I do."

"I'll have it made ready for you and get you the bill. Take a seat. Won't keep
you more than a few minutes." The salesman went into a small office at the back.
The door swung slowly and had not quite closed when his voice penetrated the
gap, saying, "A renter in a hurry, Siskra. He looks all right to me. But you'd better
call and tell them."

Mowry was out the front, down the street and around two corners before the
unseen Siskra had time to finish dialing. He'd been out-thought. The hunt was a
move ahead of him. All renting agencies had been warned to report every appli-
cant for a car. Only a narrow door gap had saved him. If it had closed and silenced
the voice he'd still have been sitting there when a carload of agents burst in.

"Why d'you want this dyno, *hi?* Where d'you plan to go with it? Where d'you live?
Who are you, anyway? Hold your arms up while we have a look at your pockets."

His back was sticky with sweat as he put plenty of distance between him and
the dyno-dump. He threw away his glasses and was mighty glad to be rid of them.
A bus came along bearing the sign: *Airport.* Now he remembered that he'd passed
an airport on the road coming in. Wasn't likely that Alapertane had more than
one of them. Undoubtedly the port itself would be staked right, left and center,
but he did not intend to ride that far. This bus would take him to the outer suburbs and in the direction he wanted to go. Without hesitation he jumped aboard.

Although his knowledge of the town was small his inward journey had given
him a shrewd idea of how far he could go without reaching the fringes. A police
check was likeliest immediately outside the town where the road left the built-up
area and took to the country. At that point all those aboard could be regarded as
leaving Alapertane and therefore fit subjects for questioning. He must get off the
bus before then.

Dismounting in good time, he continued walking outward in the hope that on
foot he could avoid the checking-post by sneaking past unobserved, say by taking
to the fields. Day was almost done; the sun was half under the horizon and light
was dimming fast.

He slowed his pace, decided that he'd stand a better chance of getting through in darkness. But he dared not draw attention to himself by mooching up and down the road or sitting on the curb until nightfall. It was essential that he should look like a local citizen homeward bound. Turning off the main road he detoured at set pace through a long series of side roads, circled back, regained the main one when the sky was black.

Continuing outward, he concentrated his attention straight ahead. After a while the road lights ended, the shine from many house windows ceased and in the distance he could see the sky-glow of the airport. It would be anytime now. He had a strong urge to walk through the darkness on tiptoe.

A bus overtook him, hummed into the heavy gloom, stopped with a brief blaze of braking lights. Cautiously Mowry advanced, got to within twenty yards of the bus. It was fully loaded with passengers and luggage. Three policemen were on board, two of them checking faces and documents while the third blocked the exit door.

On the verge and right alongside Mowry stood a cruiser, its doors wide open and its lights extinguished. It would have been almost invisible but for the glow from the nearby bus. But for the present hold-up he might have sneaked to within grabbing distance before seeing it; they'd have sat in silence, listening to the faint scuffle of his feet, and jumped him as he came abreast of them.

Calmly he got into the cruiser, sat behind its wheel, closed the doors and started the dynomotor. On the bus an irate cop was yelling at a frightened passenger while his two fellows looked on with cynical amusement. The click of door locks and the low whine of a motor went unheard during this stream of abuse. Rolling the cruiser off the verge and onto the road, Mowry switched on the powerful head-lights. Twin beams pierced the night, bathed a long stretch of road in shining amber, filled the bus with their glare. He accelerated past the bus, saw the three cops and a dozen passengers staring out at him.

He bulleted ahead feeling that the fates had been kind and compensated for recent ill fortune. It was going to be some time before the alarm went out and the pursuit commenced. By the looks on the faces of those police they had not real-ized that it was their own car shooting past. Perhaps they thought he was a motor-ist who'd taken advantage of their preoccupation to slip by unquestioned.

But it was likely they'd take action to prevent a repetition. Two of them would continue to browbeat the bus passengers while the third went out to catch any more sneakers. In that event the third could hardly fail to notice the absence of the cruiser.

That's when the fun would start. He'd give a lot to see their faces. No cruiser meant no radio either. They'd have to rush the bus to the far-off airport, or stir their lazy legs and run like mad to the nearest house with a telephone. Better still, they'd have to make a humiliating confession over the line and take a verbal beat-ing-up from the other end.

This mental reminder that in seizing the car he had also acquired a police radio caused Mowry to switch it on. At once it came to life.

"Car Ten. Suspect claims he was examining parked cars because he'd completely forgotten where he's left his own. He is unsteady, his speech is slurred and he smells of *zith*—but he may be putting on an act."

"Bring him in, Car Ten," ordered Alapertane H.Q.

Soon afterward Car Nineteen asked for help in ringing a waterfront warehouse, reason not stated. Three cars were ordered to rush there at once.

Mowry turned the two-way switch to get the other channel. It was silent a long time before it said, "K-car. Waltagan calling. A seventh has now entered house."

A voice rasped back, "You'd better wait. The other two may turn up yet."

That sounded as if some unfortunate household was going to suffer a late-night raid by the Kaitempi. The motive was anyone's guess but it did not necessarily have anything to do with the finding of Sagramatholou's dyno. The Kaitempi could and would snatch anyone for reasons known only to themselves; they could draft any citizen into the ranks of D.A.G. merely by declaring him in. The Kaitempi could do anything they pleased—except smack down a wasp, push away a Spakum space fleet or win a war.

He switched back to the police channel because over that would come the howl of fury about a missing cruiser. The radio continued to mutter about suspects, fugitives, this, that or the other car, go here, go there and so forth. Mowry ignored the gab while he gave his full attention to driving at the best speed he could make.

When twenty-five *den* from Alapertane the radio yelped as the big long-range transmitter in Pertane itself let go with a powerful bellow.

"General call. Car Four stolen from Alapertane Police. Last seen racing south on main road to Valapan. May now be passing through area P6-P7."

Replies came promptly from all cruisers within or near the designated area. There were eleven. The Pertane transmitter started moving them around like pieces on a chessboard, using coded map references that meant nothing to the listener.

One thing seemed certain: if he kept to the main Valapan road it wouldn't be long before a cruiser spotted him and caused every car within range to converge upon him. To take to minor roads and tracks wouldn't help any; they'd expect a trick like that and perhaps even now were taking steps to counter it.

He could dump the car on the other side of a field, all of its lights out, and take to foot—in which case they would not find it before daylight tomorrow. But unless he could grab another car he'd be faced with a walk that would last all night and all next day, perhaps longer if he was forced to take cover frequently.

Listening to the calls still coming over the air, and irritated by the mysterious map references, it struck him that this systematic concentration of the search was based on the supposition that if a suspect flees in a given direction at a given average speed he must be within a given area at a given time. This area had a radius plenty large enough to allow for turnoffs and detours. All they needed to do was bottle all the exits and then run along every road within the trap.

Suppose they did just that and found nothing? Ten to one they'd jump to a couple of alternative conclusions: the fugitive had never entered the area because he had reversed direction and now was racing northward, or else he had made far better speed than expected, had got right through the district before the trap closed and now was southward of it. Either way they'd remove the local pressure, switch the chase nearer to Valapan or northward of Alapertane.

He whizzed past a sideroad before he saw it, braked, reversed, went forward into it. A faint glow strengthened above a rise farther along the road he'd just left. Tearing along the badly rutted sideroad while the distant glow sharpened in brilliance, he waited until the last moment before stopping and switching off his own lights.

In total darkness he sat there while a pair of blazing headlamps came over the hill. Automatically his hand opened the door and he made ready to bolt if the lamps should slow down and enter his own road.

The oncomer approached the junction, stopped.

Mowry got out, stood by his car with gun held ready and legs tensed. The next moment the other car surged forward along its own road, dimmed into the distance and was gone. There was no way of telling whether it had been a hesitant civilian or a police patrol on the rampage. If the latter, they must have looked up the gloom-wrapped sideroad and seen nothing to tempt them into it. They'd get round to that in due time. Finding nothing on the major roads they'd eventually take to the minor ones.

Breathing heavily, Mowry got back behind the wheel, switched on his lights, made good pace onward. Before long he reached a farm, paused to look it over. Its yard and outbuildings adjoined the farmhouse in which thin gleams of light showed the occupants to be still awake. Leaving the place, he pushed on.

He checked two more farms before finding one suitable for his purpose. The house stood in complete darkness and its barn was some distance from it. With dimmed lights, moving slowly and quietly, he drove through the muddy yard, along a narrow lane, stopped under the open end of the barn. Leaving the car he climbed atop the hay and lay there.

Over the next four hours the shine of distant headlights swept repeatedly all around. Twice a car rocked and plunged along the sideroad, passed the farm without stopping. Both times he sat up in the hay, took out his gun. Evidently it did not occur to the hunters that he might park within the trap. On Jaimec fugitives from the police or Kaitempi did not behave like that—given a headstart they kept running good and hard.

Gradually surrounding activity died down and ceased. Mowry got back into the cruiser, resumed his run. It was now three hours to dawn. If all went well he'd make it to the rim of the forest before daybreak.

The Pertane transmitter was still broadcasting orders made incomprehensible by use of symbols but responses from various cruisers now came through with much less strength. He couldn't decide whether or not this fading of radio signals was an encouraging sign. It was certain that the transmitting cars were a good distance away but there was no knowing how many might be nearer and maintaining silence. Knowing full well that he was able to listen in to their calls, the enemy was crafty enough to let some cars play possum.

Whether or not some cruisers were hanging around and saying nothing, he managed to get undetected to within nine *den* of his destination before the car gave up. It was tearing through a cutting that led to the last, dangerous stretch of main road when the green telltale light amid the instruments faded and went out. At the same time the headlamps extinguished and the radio died. The car rolled a short distance under its own momentum and stopped.

Examining the switch, he could find nothing wrong with it. The emergency switch on the floorboard didn't work either. After a good deal of fumbling in the dark he managed to detach one of the intake leads and tried shorting it to the ground terminal. This should have produced a thin thread of blue light. It didn't.

It signified only one thing: the power broadcast from the capital had been cut off. Every car within considerable radius of Pertane had been halted, police and Kaitempi cruisers included. Only vehicles within potency range of other, faraway power transmitters could continue running—unless those also had ceased to radiate.

Leaving the car, he started to trudge the rest of the way. He reached the main road, moved along it at a fast pace while keeping his eyes skinned for armed figures waiting ahead to challenge any walker in the night.

After half an hour a string of lights bloomed far behind him and to his ears came the muffled whine of many motors. Scrambling off the road, he fell into an unseen ditch, climbed out of it, sought refuge amid a bunch of low but thick bushes. The lights came nearer, shot past.

It was a military scout-patrol, twelve in number, mounted on dynocycles independently powered by long-term batteries. In his plastic suit, with night-goggles and duralumin helmet, each rider looked more like a deep-sea diver than a soldier. Across the back of every trooper hung a riot-gun with a big pan-shaped magazine.

Those in authority, he decided, must be more than aggravated to stall all cars and let the army take over the hunt for the missing patrol car and its occupant. Still, from their viewpoint they had good reason to go to such lengths. *Dirac Angestun Gesept* had claimed the execution of Sagramatholou and whoever had collared the agent's machine must be a real, genuine member of D.A.G. They wanted a real member in their hands at any cost.

He speeded up, running short stretches, reverting to a fast walk, running again. Once he lay flat on his face in tall fish-scented stuff that passed for grass on Jaimec. A patrol of six went by. Later he got behind a tree to avoid four more. To one side the sky had turned from black to gray and visibility was improving every minute.

The last lap to the forest was the worst. In ten minutes he leaped for cover ten times, each time uncertain whether he had been seen because now it was possible to observe movement over a considerable distance. This sudden increase in local activity suggested that at last the Alapertane patrol car had been found. If so, they'd soon start seeking a fugitive doing it the hard way, namely, on his feet.

Chances were good that they would not concentrate on the immediate neighborhood. Having no means of telling how long the car had been abandoned they'd credit him with being four hours ahead of where he really was and probably they'd look for him farther afield.

Thankfully he entered the forest, made good time in growing daylight. Tired and hungry, he was compelled to rest ten minutes in every hour but got along as fast as he could between times. By midday, when about an hour from the cave, he had to lie down awhile in a leafy glade and snatch a short sleep. Up to that point he had walked a total of thirty-seven Earth-miles helped by desperation, a sense of urgency and Jaimec's lesser gravitation.

Little refreshed, he resumed his journey and had reduced his pace to a listless mooch when he reached the point where his finger-ring invariably began to tingle. This time it gave no response. He halted at once, looked all around, studied the branches of big trees ahead. The forest was a maze of light and shadow. A silent, motionless sentinel could remain high up in a tree for hours and not be seen by anyone approaching.

What he'd been told at college echoed in his mind. "The ring is a warning, a reliable alarm. Heed it!"

All very well them saying that. It's one thing to give advice, something else again to take it. The choice was not the simple one of going ahead or going back; it was that of finding shelter, food, comfort and necessary equipment or abandoning everything that enabled him to operate as a wasp. It was the choice between continuing as a solitary fighter or becoming a useless bum. He hesitated, sorely tempted to sneak near enough at least to get a good, long look at the cave.

Finally he compromised by moving cautiously forward, edging from tree to tree and taking full advantage of all available cover. In this way he advanced another hundred yards. Still no response from the ring. Removing it from his finger he examined its sensitive crystal, cleaned the back of it, put it on again. Not an itch, not a twitch.

Half-hidden behind an enormous tree root, he again considered the position. Had there really been intruders in the cave, and if so, were they in ambush around it? Or had Container-22 ceased to function because of some internal defect?

While he stood there in an agony of indecision a sound came from twenty yards ahead. Low and faint, he would never have heard it had his senses not been primed by peril. It was like a suppressed sneeze or a muffled cough. That was enough for him. *Someone* was hanging around and striving to keep quiet about it. The cave and its contents had been discovered and the finders were lying in wait for the owner to come along.

Trying to keep full attention on the trees, he backed away almost at a crawl. After that it took him an hour to make a mile, he moved so slowly and warily. Considering himself now at a safe distance he broke into a steady walk, not knowing where to go or what to do.

Though speculation was futile he could not help wondering how the cache had been found. Low flying scout-planes fitted with super-sensitive metal detectors could have pinpointed its exact location if they'd had reason to suspect its existence in that area. But they'd had no such cause so far as he was aware.

Most likely the cave had been stumbled upon by some of those who'd fled from Pertane and taken to the woods—they'd certainly curry favor with authority by excitedly reporting the find. Or perhaps the likely-looking hideout had been probed by an army patrol trying to round up refugees.

Anyway, it no longer mattered a hoot. He had lost the cache as well as further contact with Terra. All that he possessed were the clothes in which he stood, a gun and twenty thousand guilders. He was a rich man who owned nothing but his life and that was not worth much.

It was obvious that he must keep going away from the cave for as long as he retained strength to move. Realizing that they had found a Terran war-dump the powers-that-be wouldn't long rest content with a mere ambush around it. Just as soon as they could collect the troops they'd convert a large section of the forest into a gigantic trap. That process would start most anytime.

So with stumbling legs and empty guts he kept going, steering himself by sun and shadow, maintaining his direction steadily southeast. By dusk he'd had as much as he could take. Flopping into a patch of reeds, he closed his eyes and slept.

It was still dark when he awoke. He lay there until sunrise, dozing and waking at intervals. Then he started out with stronger legs, a fresher mind but weaker insides. His belly kept appealing to his gullet but there was nothing he could do about it yet.

Air activity was endless that day. Scout-planes and 'copters zoomed around within hearing distance all the time. The reason for all this display was a mystery since they'd little hope of spotting one man in that immense forest. Perhaps the presence and size of the cache had misled them into thinking that a Spakum taskforce had landed.

It was easy to imagine the state of wild alarm in the capital, with brasshats running to and fro while messages flashed back and forth between Jaimec and Diracta. The two lamsters Wolf had talked about had accomplished nothing like this. They'd tied up twenty-seven thousand people for fourteen hours. By the looks of it he would preoccupy the entire planet for the next fourteen weeks.

At nightfall all that his belly had received was water and his sleep was made restless with hunger. In the morning he continued, still through thick forest that stretched all the way to the equator.

After five hours he struck a narrow lane, followed it to a clearing in which were a small sawmill and a dozen cottages. Before the mill stood two big, powerful trucks. From the shelter of the trees he regarded them enviously. Nobody was near them at the moment, he could jump into either of them and tear away with no trouble at all. But the news of the theft would get the entire hunt on his tail. Right now they'd no idea of where he'd got to or where he was heading. It was better to let their ignorance remain his bliss.

Snooping carefully between the trees, he bided his time, bolted into a nearby garden, hurriedly filled his pockets with vegetables, his arms with fruit. Back among the trees he ate the fruit as he went along. Later, as twilight fell, he risked a small fire, baked the vegetables, ate half of them and saved the rest for the morrow.

Next day he saw not a living soul, had no food except that reserved from yesterday. The day after was worse: just trees, trees and still more trees with not an edible nut or berry among the lot, no sign of habitation, nothing at all to eat. From far to the north still came the faint humming of aircraft and that was the only thing to suggest the presence of life on the planet.

Four days afterward he reached the sideroad to Elvera, a village south of Valapan. Still keeping to the trees he followed it until houses came in sight. The amount of traffic on the road wasn't abnormal and there were no signs of a special watch being kept.

By now he was in a bad way, haggard with lack of food, his clothing dirty and rumpled. It was fortunate, he thought, that he had darkened his complexion, that depilatory treatment had long abolished the need to shave, and that his last hair-cut had been the Halopti crop followed by imitation balding. Otherwise he'd now look like nothing this side of Aldebaran.

He spent some time brushing his clothes with his hands and tidying him-self as best he could. That done, he walked boldly into the village. If the price of a feed was a noose around the neck he was willing to pay it—providing the meal was a good one and that he was given time to lug out his gun.

There were a dozen shops in the village including a cafe-bar of the kind favored by truckers. Entering, he went straight through to the washroom, had a wash and saw himself in a mirror for the first time in many days. He looked sufficiently harassed to make a nosy cop give him the long, hard stare but at least he wasn't an obvious hobo.

Returning to the front, he sat at the counter, found it difficult to stop his mouth from drooling. The only other customers in the place were two ancient Sirians guz-zling at one table and too intent to bother with the newcomer. A burly character in a white coat appeared behind the counter and eyed Mowry with faint curiosity.

"You wish?"

Mowry told him, got it, almost dribbled on it when it arrived. He set to, forc-ing himself to eat slowly because the other was watching. Finishing, he ordered the next item and disposed of it in the same bored manner. This play-acting was sheer hell; he could have bolted two more complete servings and asked the fellow to wrap up another six for him to take out.

As he shoved across the final drink, the burly one said, "Come far?"

"Only from Valapan."

"Walk it, *hi?*"

"Nar, the dyno stalled two *den* back. I'll fix it after."

The other stared at him. "You came in a dyno? How'd you get out of Valapan?"

"What d'you mean?" countered Mowry, not liking the trend of the conversation.

"No cars allowed into or out of Valapan today. A cop told me so himself."

"When was this?"

"Around the nine-time hour."

"I was away before seven," Mowry said, "I'd a lot of calls to make and got out early. Good thing I did, *hi?*"

"Yar," agreed the other, doubtfully. "But how're you going to get in again?"

"I don't know. They've got to lift the ban sometime. They can't maintain it forever." He paid the bill, made for the door. "Live long."

He sensed that he'd got out of there in good time. The burly one was vaguely suspicious but not sufficiently so to bawl for help, being the type who'd hesitate lest he make a fool of himself.

The next call was at a nearby grocery store. He bought enough of the most concentrated foods to make a package not too heavy to carry for miles. Here he was served without especial interest and the conversation was brief.

"Bad about Valapan, isn't it?"

"Yar," said Mowry, yearning to hear the news.

"Hope they nab every stinking Spakum in the place."

"Yar," Mowry repeated.

"Damn the Spakums!" the other finished. "That will be sixteen and six-tenths."

Going out with the package, he glanced along the road. The fellow at the cafe-bar was standing by his door looking at him. Mowry nodded familiarly, ambled from the village, shot another glance back as he passed the last house. Nosy-poke was still standing there watching him.

With careful rationing the food lasted him ten days as he continued through the forest and saw nobody other than occasional lumberjacks whom he avoided. His direction was now a westward circle that should bring him not far south of Radine. Despite any risks entailed, he was keeping to that part of Jaimec of which he had some knowledge.

He'd made up his mind that when he got near to Radine he was going to use his gun to acquire another car and a set of genuine documents at the cost of burying a corpse in the woods. After that he'd check the lay of the land and if things weren't too hot in Radine maybe he could hole up there. Something drastic had to be done because he could not roam the forests forever. If he'd acquired the status of a lone outlaw he might as well become enough of a thug to prosper.

He did not know it but bigger and wider events were overtaking him and he was no longer a pawn in the cosmic game or the master of his destiny.

Two hours after sunset of his last day of wandering he reached the main Radine-Khamasta road, paralleled it through the forest as he continued toward Radine. At precisely the eleven-time hour a tremendous flash of light yellowed the sky in the direction of the stronghold Khamasta. Beneath his feet the ground gave a distinct quiver. The trees creaked while their tops swayed. A bit later a prolonged, faraway growl came over the horizon.

Traffic on the road swiftly thinned out and finally ceased altogether. A thousand crimson serpents hissed up from darkened Radine and hungrily bored into the night sky. Came another great flash from the region of Khamasta. Something long, black and noisy bulleted low over the forest, momentarily blanking out the stars and sending down a blast of heat.

In the distance sounded faint, muffled rumblings, cracklings, thumps and thuds plus a vague, indefinable babble like the shoutings of a multitude. Mowry went into the empty road and stared up at the sky. The stars vanished wholesale as the thrice-wrecked and ten times decimated Terran fleets thundered overhead four thousand strong.

Below, Mowry danced like a maniac in the middle of the road. He shouted at the sky. He yelled and screamed and bawled tuneless songs with meaningless words. He waved his arms around, tossed twenty thousand guilders into the air so that it floated around like confetti.

As the black, snouty warships roared above a veritable torrent of stuff sailed down, seeking ground with the pale, lemon-colored legs of antigrav beams. He stood fascinated while not far away a huge, cumbersome shape with enormous caterpillar tracks fell featherlike atop twenty columnar rays, landed with squeaks of protest from big springs.

Heart pounding, he tore southward along the road, on and on until he bolted full-tilt into a waiting group of forty figures. They were looking his way, ready for him, having been alerted by the frantic clomping of his feet. The entire bunch topped him by head and shoulders, wore dark green uniforms and were holding things that gleamed in the starlight.

"Take it easy, Blowfly," advised a Terran voice.

Mowry panted for breath. He did not resent this rude counterthrust to the Spakum tag. Every Sirian was a blowfly by virtue of his purple backside.

He pawed at the speaker's sleeve. "My name is James Mowry. I'm not what I seem—I'm a Terran."

The other, a big, lean-faced and cynical sergeant, said, "My name's Napoleon. I'm not what I seem—I'm an emperor." He gestured with a hand holding a whop-gun that looked like a cannon. "Take him to the cage, Rogan."

"But I *am* a Terran," yelped Mowry, flapping his hands.

"Yeah, you look it," said the sergeant.

"I'm *speaking* Terran, aren't I?"

"Sure are. A hundred thousand Blowflies can speak it. They think it gives them a certain something." He waved the cannon again. "The cage, Rogan."

Rogan took him.

For twelve days he mooched around the prisoner-of-war compound. The dump was very big, very full and swiftly became fuller. Prisoners were fed regularly, guarded constantly and that was all.

Of his fellows behind the wire at least fifty sly-eyed specimens boasted of their confidence in the future when the sheep would be sorted from the goats and justice would be done. The reason, they asserted, was that for a long time they'd been secret leaders of *Dirac Angestun Gesept* and undoubtedly would be raised to power when Terran conquerors got around to it. Then, they warned, friends would be rewarded as surely as foes would be punished. This bragging ceased only when three of them somehow got strangled in their sleep.

At least a dozen times Mowry seized the chance to attract the attention of a patrolling sentry when no Sirian happened to be nearby. "Psst! My name's Mowry— I'm a Terran."

Ten times he received confessions of faith such as, "You look it!" or "Is zat *so?*"

A lanky character said, "Don't give me that!"

"It's true—I swear it!"

"You really are a Terran—*hi?*"

"Yar," said Mowry, forgetting himself.

"Yar to you, too."

Once he spelled it so there'd be no possibility of misunderstanding. "See here, Buster, I'm a T-E-R-R-A-N."

To which the sentry replied, "Says Y-O-U," and hefted his gun and continued his patrol.

Came the day when prisoners were paraded in serried ranks, a captain stood on a crate, held a loud-hailer before his mouth and roared all over the camp, "Anyone here named James Mowry?"

Mowry galloped eagerly forward, bow-legged from force of habit. "I am." He scratched himself, a performance that the captain viewed with unconcealed disfavor.

Glowering at him, the captain demanded, "Why the heck haven't you said so before now? We've been searching all Jaimec for you. Let me tell you, Mister, we've got better things to do. You struck dumb or something?"

"I—"

"Shut up! Military Intelligence wants you. Follow me."

So saying, he led the other through heavily guarded gates, along a path toward a prefab hut.

Mowry ventured, "Captain, again and again I tried to tell the sentries that—"

"Prisoners are forbidden to talk to sentries," the captain snapped.

"But I wasn't a prisoner."

"Then what the blazes were you doing in there?" Without waiting for a reply he pushed open the door of the prefab hut and introduced him with, "This is the crummy bum."

The Intelligence officer glanced up from a wad of papers. "So you're Mowry, James Mowry?"

"Correct."

"Well now," said the officer, "we've been primed by beam-radio and we know all about you."

"Do you really?" responded Mowry, pleased and gratified. He braced himself for the coming citation, the paean of praise, the ceremonial stroking of a hero's hair.

"Another mug like you was on Artishain, their tenth planet," the officer went on. "Feller named Kingsley. They say he hasn't sent a signal for quite a piece. Looks like he's got himself nabbed. Chances are he's been stepped on and squashed flat."

Mowry said suspiciously, "What's this to me?"

"We're dropping you in his place. You leave tomorrow."

"Hi? Tomorrow?"

"Sure thing. We want you to become a wasp. Nothing wrong with you, is there?"

"No," said Mowry, very feebly. "Only my head."

SENTINELS FROM SPACE
Introduction by Jack L. Chalker

For me, the novel you're about to read was one of the most influential of all the science fiction books I read growing up. It remains one of my favorites, and has always cemented Russell to me and my work. It is also Russell's most complex work, even though it's told in his usual easy, fast, and expertly-paced thriller style.

This is a version of the "closed loop" plot. An open loop is like a murder mystery—you go from the beginning through the middle to the end, where all is explained. In a closed loop tale there's an extra step. These have beginnings, middles, and ends, and then a second ending that often reveals that you've been reading a different book than the one you thought you were. *Vertigo* is a good example of this. A plot that seems like a good man's descent into mental illness all the way to its climax when he recreates his insane vision, only to find out that, even if he's off his noggin, he's still a great detective and at that point the solution to the murder mystery you didn't know you were reading is explained. I can reveal that *Sentinel* is a hidden loop because Russell gives you a taste of that other plot as you go along. You *know* something beyond what you're reading is going on, but it's very unlikely that you'll guess this one, one of the most cosmic double endings in all modern SF and a unique concept in science fiction as far as I know. No peeking or you will *really* ruin a brilliant *tour de force* of writing.

There is also too much else here to ruin by not reading from the start.

The world that is created here is a fascinating one—near future, interplanetary but not interstellar, familiar yet remote. Terraformed Venus and Mars are well colonized and developed, and are now chafing as colonies under a relatively benign but still undemocratic and unresponsive Earth. Effects of radiation or something from lots of space travel has also had the side effect of creating a small but significant number of people with active extrasensory perception abilities and powers, some quite scary, transmitted to their descendants.

Against a well drawn backdrop of colonial rebellion, reminiscent of what was happening to the postwar British empire Russell had grown up taking for granted, is a secondary plot addressing a subject little discussed or thought of back then, particularly in science fiction—racism, based upon fear and prejudice. In many ways this is a complex novel using science fiction to address the revolutionary social and political waves let loose on the western world by and after World War II, and as metaphor it works extremely well. There is also a moral question of involvement here. Do our obviously alien sentinels hiding here in human form get involved? They are no threat to Earth, that's clear, but they dare not expose themselves for various reasons and they have little use for colonial rebellions and local squabbles. The fear and prejudice, and the intended pogrom that's unearthed, are other more moral matters. If they're opening up the extermination camps in that nation over there, and you're out over here with your own important fish to fry, do you risk your own people and plans *just* on moral principles? These are questions, and attitudes, as valid today as a half century ago when they were posed in this book.

This is Russell, and science fiction, doing what it does best, all in the format of one heck of a good thriller.

Chapter 1

The World Council sat solemn and grave as he walked toward them. They numbered twelve, all sharp-eyed, gray or white of hair, their faces lined with many years and much experience. Silently with thin lips, firmed mouths, they studied his oncoming. The thick carpet kept saying *hush-hush* as his feet swept through it. The expectant quietness, the intent gaze, the whispering of the carpet and the laden weight of deep, unvoiced anxieties showed that this was a moment distinct from other minutes that are not moments.

Reaching the great horseshoe table at which the council members were seated, he halted, looked them over, starting with the untidy man on the extreme left and going slowly, deliberately around to the plump one on the far right. It was a peculiarly penetrating examination that enhanced their uneasiness. One or two fidgeted like men who feel some of their own sureness beginning to evaporate. Each showed relief when the soul-seeking stare passed on to his neighbor.

In the end his attention went back to the leonine-maned Oswald Heraty, who presided at the table's center. As he looked at Heraty the pupils of his eyes shone and the irises were flecked with silver and he spoke in slow, measured tones.

He said, "Captain David Raven at your service, sir."

Leaning back in his chair, Heraty sighed, fixed his attention upon the immense crystal chandelier dangling from the ceiling. It was difficult to tell whether he was marshaling his thoughts, or carefully avoiding the other's gaze, or finding it necessary to do the latter in order to achieve the former.

Other members of the council now had their heads turned toward Heraty, partly to give full attention to what he was about to say, partly because to look at Heraty was a handy pretext not to look at Raven. They had all watched the newcomer's entrance but none wanted to examine him close up, none wanted to be examined by him.

Still frowning at the chandelier, Heraty spoke in the manner of one shouldering an unwanted but immovable burden: "We are at war."

The table waited. There was only silence.

137

Heraty went on, "I address you vocally because I have no alternative. Kindly respond in the same manner."

"Yes, sir," was Raven's inadequate return.

"We are at war," Heraty repeated with a slight touch of irritation. "Does that not surprise you?"

"No, sir."

"It ought to," put in another Council member, somewhat aggrieved by the other's refusal to emote. "We have been at war for about eighteen months and have only just discovered the fact."

"Leave this to me," suggested Heraty, waving aside the interruption. For an instant—only an instant—he met Raven's eyes as he asked, "Have you known or suspected that we are actually at war?"

Smiling to himself, Raven said, "That we would be involved sooner or later has been obvious from the start."

"From what start?" inquired the fat man on the right.

"From the moment we crossed interplanetary space and settled upon another world." Raven was disconcertingly imperturbable about it. "War then became inherent to the newly created circumstances."

"Meaning we blundered in some way or other?"

"Not at all. Progress demands payment. Sooner or later the bill is presented."

It did not satisfy them. His line of reasoning ran too swiftly from premise to conclusion and they were unable to follow the logic of it.

Heraty took over again. "Never mind the past. We, as present day individuals had no control over that. It's our task to cope with immediate problems and those of the near future." He rubbed his bluish jowls, added, "Problem number one is this war. Venus and Mars are attacking us and officially we can't do a thing about it. Reason: it's a war that isn't a war."

"A difference of opinion?" asked Raven.

"It began with that. Now it has gone a whole lot further. They have turned from words to deeds. Without any formal declaration of war—indeed, with every outward appearance of friendship and blood-brotherhood—they are implementing their policies in a military manner. If you can call it military. I don't know how else to describe it." His voice sounded more ireful. "They've been at it for something like eighteen months and we've only just discovered that we are being hit, often and hard. That sort of thing can go on too long."

"All wars go on too long," Raven observed.

They viewed this as a profound thought. There was a murmur of agreement, much nodding of heads. Two of them went so far as to glance straight at him, though as briefly as possible.

"The worst of it is," continued Heraty, morbidly, "that they have got us cunningly fixed in a tangle of our own devising and—officially at any rate—there's no way out. What's the answer to that?" Without waiting for suggestions he provided one himself. "We must take action that is unofficial."

"Me being the goat?" put Raven, shrewdly.

"You being the goat," Heraty confirmed.

For a moment the silence returned while Raven waited politely and the Council occupied itself with various thoughts. There was good cause to ponder. There had been wars before in the far past, the very far past; some slow and tortuous, some swift and bloody. But they had all been Earth wars.

A conflict between worlds was something new, something different. It posed unique problems to which bygone lessons could not apply. Moreover, a new style war, conducted with novel weapons, employing previously unheard of techniques posed fresh problems not solvable on the basis of past experiences. There was nothing to go by other than the hard, grim facts of today.

After a while. Heraty said moodily, "Venus and Mars have long been settled by *homo sapiens,* our own kind, our very flesh and blood. They are our children but no longer see it that way. They think they are now grown up and plenty old enough to go where they like, do what they like, come home any time they want. They've been agitating for self-government the last couple of centuries. They've been demanding the key of the house while they're still damp from their christening. We've consistently refused them their desire. We've told them to wait, be patient." He sighed again, long and deeply. "See where it puts us!"

"Where?" invited Raven, smiling again.

"Squarely on the horns of a dilemma—and both of them uncomfortably sharp." He shifted in his seat as if his southern aspect were peculiarly susceptible to suggestion. "Without self-government the Martians and Venusians remain Terrestrials, officially and legally, sharing this world with us, enjoying all our rights as equal citizens."

"And so?"

"That means they can come here as often and for as long as they please, in any numbers." Bending forward, Heraty slapped the table to emphasize his annoyance. "They can walk straight in through the ever-open door while crammed to the top hairs with arson, sabotage and every other imaginable form of malicious intent. And we can't keep them out. We can't refuse entry except by making them precisely what they want to be, namely, aliens. We won't make aliens of them."

"Too bad," sympathized Raven. "I take it you have good reasons?"

"Of course. Dozens of them. We don't put the brakes on somebody else's progress out of sheer perversity. There are times when we must temporarily sacrifice that which is desirable in order to deal with that which is desperately necessary."

"It would be clearer if it were plainer," suggested Raven.

Hesitating a second or two, Heraty went on, "One major reason is known only to a select few. But I'll tell you: we are on the verge of getting to the Outer Planets. That is a jump, a heck of a big jump. To back it up to the limit, get properly established and settle ourselves in strength we'll need all the combined resources of three worlds unhampered by any short view quibbling between them."

"I can well imagine that," agreed Raven, thinking of Mars' strategic position and of the immensely rich fuel deposits on Venus.

"And that's not all, not by a long shot." Heraty lowered his tone to lend significance to his words. "In due time there will be another jump. It will take us to Alpha Centauri or perhaps farther. There is some unpublished but rather convincing evidence that ultimately we may come head on against another highly intelligent life-form, If that should occur we'll have to hang together lest otherwise we hang separately. There will be no room for Martians, Venusians, Terrestrials, Jovians or any other planetary tribes. We'll all be Solarians, sink or swim. That's how it's got to be and that's how it's going to be whether nationalist-minded specimens like it or not."

"So you're impaled on yet another dilemma," remarked Raven. "Peace might be assured by publishing the warning facts behind your policy—and thereby creating general alarm plus considerable opposition to further expansion."

"Precisely. You've put it in a nutshell. There's a conflict of interests which is being carried too far."

"H'm! A pretty set-up. As sweet a mutual animosity as could be contrived. I like it—it smacks of an enticing chess problem."

"That's exactly how Carson sees it," Heraty informed. "He calls it super-chess for reasons you've yet to learn. He says it's time we put a new piece on the board. You'd better go see him right away. Carson's the man who raked the world for someone like you."

"Me?" David Raven registered mild surprise. "What does he think is so special about me?"

"That I wouldn't know." Heraty showed himself far from anxious to discuss the subject. "Such matters are left entirely to Carson and he has his own secrets. You must see him at once."

"Very well, sir. Is there anything else?"

"Only this: you were not brought here merely to satisfy our curiosity but also to let you see for yourself that the World Council is behind you, though unofficially. Your job is to find some way of ending this war. You'll have no badge, no documents, no authority, nothing to show that your personal status is different from that of any other individual. You'll have to get along by benefit of your own abilities and our moral support. No more!"

"You consider that would be sufficient?"

"I don't know," admitted Heraty worriedly. "I'm in poor position to judge. Carson's more capable in that respect." He leaned forward, added with emphasis, "For what little it is worth my own opinion is that very soon your life won't be worth a moment's purchase—and I sincerely hope I'm wrong."

"Me, too," said Raven, blank-faced.

They fidgeted again, suspecting him of secret amusement at their expense. The deep silence came back and their formerly evasive eyes were on him as he bowed and walked away with the same slow, deliberate, confident gait as when he'd entered. Only the carpet whispered and when he went out the big door closed quietly, without a click.

"War," remarked Heraty, "is a two-way game."

Carson masqueraded as a mortician so far as personal appearance went. He was tall, lean, sad-faced, had the perpetual air of one who regrets the necessity and expense of floral offerings. All this was a mask behind which lurked an agile mind.

A mind that could speak without benefit of lips. In other words, he was a Type One Mutant, a true telepath. There's a distinction here: true telepaths differ from sub-telepaths in being able to close their minds at will.

Glancing with glum approval at Raven's equally tall but broader, heavier frame, and noting the lean, muscular features, the dark gray eyes, the black hair, Carson's mind made contact without an instant's hesitation. Invariably a Type One recognizes another Type One at first sense, just as an ordinary man perceives another simply because he is not blind.

His mind inquired, "Did Heraty give forth?"

"He did—dramatically and uninformatively." Seating himself, Raven eyed the metal plate angled on the other's desk. It bore an inscription reading: *Mr. Carson. Director—Terran Security Bureau.* He pointed to it. "Is that to remind you who you are whenever you become too muddled to remember?"

"In a way, yes. The plate is loaded on the neural band and radiates what it says. The technical boys claim that it's anti-hypnotic." A sour grin came and went. "To date there's been no occasion to try it out. I'm in no great hurry to test it either. A hypno who gets this far isn't going to be put off by a mere gadget."

"Still, the fact that someone thinks you could do with it is a bit ominous," Raven commented. "Has everyone got the heebies around here? Even Heraty insinuated that I've already got one foot in the grave."

"An exaggeration, but not without basis. Heraty shares something with me, namely, the dark suspicion that we've at least one fifth columnist on the Council itself. It's no more than a dark thought but if there's anything to it you're a marked man from now on."

"That's pleasant. You dig me up in order to bury me."

"Your appearance before the Council was unavoidable," Carson told him. 'They insisted on having a look at you whether I approved or not. I didn't approve and Heraty knows it. He countered my objection by turning my own arguments against me."

"How?" Raven invited.

"Said that if you were only one-tenth as good as I claimed you ought to be, there was no need for anxiety. The enemy could do all the worrying instead."

"H'm! So I'm expected to live up to an imaginary reputation you've concocted for me in advance. Don't you think I've enough grief?"

"Plunging you into plenty of grief is my idea," declared Carson, displaying unexpected toughness. "We're in a jam. Nothing for it but to flog the willing horse."

"Half an hour ago I was a goat. Now it's a horse—or maybe part of a horse. Any other animal imitations you'd like? How about a few bird calls?"

"You'll have to call some mighty queer birds to keep pace with the opposition, much less get ahead of it." Sliding open a drawer, Carson took out a paper, surveyed it unhappily. "This is as far as we've got with a top secret list of extra-Terrestrial varieties. Nominally and according to law they're all samples of *homo sapiens.* In deadly fact they're *homo-something-else.*" He glanced at his listener. "To date, Venus and Mars have produced at least twelve separate and distinct types of mutants. Type Six, for instance, are Malleables."

Stiffening in his seat, Raven exclaimed. *"What?"*

"Malleables," repeated Carson. smacking his lips as if viewing an especially appetizing corpse. "They are not one hundred percenters. No radical alteration of the general physique. They can do nothing really startling from a surgeon's viewpoint. But they've been born with faces backed with cartilage in lieu of bones, are incredibly rubber-featured and to that extent are good, really good. You would kiss one thinking he was your own mother if it struck his fancy to look like your mother."

"Speak for yourself," Raven said.

"You know what I mean," Carson persisted. "As facial mimics they have to be seen to be believed."

Indicating the highly polished surface of his desk, Carson continued, "Imagine this is a gigantic checkerboard with numberless squares per side. We're using midget chessmen and playing white. There are two thousand five hundred millions of us against thirty-two millions of Venusians and eighteen million Martians. On the face of it that's a huge preponderance. We've got them hopelessly outnumbered." He made a disparaging gesture. "Outnumbered in what? *In pawns!"*

"Obviously," agreed Raven.

"You can see the way our opponents view the situation: what they lose in numbers, they more than make up for in superior pieces. Knights, bishops, rooks, queens and—what is so much the worse for us—new style pieces endowed with eccentric powers peculiar to themselves. They reckon they can produce them until we're dizzy: mutants by the dozens, each one of them worth more than a regiment of pawns."

Raven said meditatively, "Acceleration of evolutionary factors as a direct result of space conquest was so inevitable that I don't know how it got overlooked in the first place. A child should have seen the logical consequence."

"In those days the old-timers were obsessed by atomic power," responded Carson. "To their way of thinking it needed a world-wide holocaust created by radioactive materials to produce mutations on a large scale. It just didn't occur to them that hordes of Venus-bound settlers could not spend five solid, searing months in space, under intense cosmic ray bombardment, their genes being kicked around every hour and every minute, without there being normal working of cause and effect."

"It's occurring to them now."

"Yes, but in bygone days they couldn't see wood for trees. Heck, they went so far as to build double-shelled ships containing ray absorbing blankets of compressed ozone, cutting down intensity to some eighty times that at Earth level—yet failed to realize that eighty times still remains eighty times. The vagaries of chance even themselves up over a long period of time so that we can now say that Venus trips have created about eighty mutants for every one that would have just come naturally."

"Mars is worse," Raven pointed out.

"You bet it is," agreed Carson. "Despite its smaller population Mars has roughly the same number and variety of mutants as Venus. Reason: it takes eleven months to get there. Every Mars settler has to endure hard radiations about twice as long as any Venus settler—and he goes on enduring them because of Mars' thinner atmosphere. Human genes have a pretty wide tolerance of massive particles like cosmic rays. They can be walloped again and again and again—but there are limits." He paused, his fingers tapping the desk while he reflected briefly. "Inasmuch as a mutant has military value, Mars' war potential fully equals that of Venus. In theory—and it's faulty theory, as we must show them—Mars and Venus together can put enough into the field to give us a run for our money. That is precisely what they are trying to do. Up to the present they've got away with it. We've now reached the point where it has ceased to be funny."

"Seems to me," observed Raven, thoughtfully, "that they're making a mistake similar to that made by the original pioneers; in sheer excess of enthusiasm they're overlooking the obvious."

"Meaning that this planet mans the space fleets and therefore can find some mutants of her own?"

"Yes."

"They'll learn in the same way that we've had to learn. And you're going to show them—I hope."

"Hope springs eternal. In what way do you suggest that I show them?"

"That's up to you," said Carson, dexterously passing the buck. Searching through the papers on his desk, he extracted a couple, looked them over. "I'll tell you of one case that illustrates the squabble in which we're involved and the methods by which it's being fought. It was this particular incident that told us for the first time that there is a war on. We'd got suspicious of a long series of apparently disconnected events, laid several camera-traps. Most were put out of action. A few failed for no known reason. But one registered."

"Ah!" Raven bent forward, eyes keen, attentive.

"The camera showed how three men destroyed some extremely important spaceship data that can't be replaced in less than a year. The first of this trio, a Type One Mutant, a true telepath, kept mental watch for interrupters. The second, a Type Two, a floater—"

"Meaning a levitator?" Raven chipped in.

"Yes, a levitator. He got them over two twenty-foot walls with the help of a rope ladder and then took the ladder up to a high window. The third one, a Type Seven Mutant, a hypno, took care of three guards who intervened at different times, stiffened them into immobility, erased the incident from their minds and substituted false memories covering the cogent minutes. The guards knew nothing of the camera-traps and therefore were not able to give them away to the telepath unwittingly. But for a camera we wouldn't know a darned thing except that in some mysterious manner the data had gone up in smoke."

"Humph!" Raven seemed more amused than aghast.

"There have been several big fires of such strategic importance that we're inclined to blame them on pyrotics—though we can't prove it." Carson shook his head mournfully. "What a war! They make their own rules as they go along. Their antics play hob with military logistics and if there were any brass hats these days they'd be ripe for mental treatment."

"Time has marched on," Raven contributed.

"I know, I know. We're living in modern days." He shoved a sheet of paper at his listener. "There's a copy of my list of known Mars-Venus mutations numbered according to type and lettered for military value, if you can call it that." He sniffed as if there were some doubts about calling it that. *"D* means dangerous. *D-plus* more so, while *I* means innocuous—perhaps. And that list may not be correct. It's as far as we've got to date."

Raven glanced rapidly down the list, asked, "So far as you know all these remain true to type? That is to say, the floaters can levitate only themselves and anything they are able to carry at the time but cannot cause levitation of independent objects? The teleports have the reverse aptitude of levitating objects but cannot lift themselves? The telepaths aren't hypnotic and the hypnos aren't telepathic?"

"That is correct. One man, one supernormal ability."

Raven began to study it carefully. It read:

1.	True Telepaths.	D+.
2.	Levitators.	D.
3.	Pyrotics.	D+.
4.	Chameleons.	I.
5.	Nocturnals.	I.
6.	Malleables.	D.
7.	Hypnos.	D+.
8.	Supersonics.	I.
9.	Mini-engineers.	D+.
10.	Radiosensitives.	D.
11.	Insectivocals.	D+.
12.	Teleports.	D+.

"So!" Smiling to himself, Raven stuffed the list into a pocket, got up, went to the door. "And they're all under the delusion that Old Mother Earth ain't what she used to be?"

"You said it," Carson indorsed. "They say she's aged, decrepit, dimwitted and hopelessly out of touch with the facts of life. She's got nothing left but her last dying kick. You go administer said kick—and where it'll best be felt."

"I'll do just that," Raven promised, "provided I can stay in one piece long enough to take aim." He went out, carefully closing the door behind him.

He was on his own.

Chapter 2

The fun started right outside on the street. It could hardly have been more prompt though, naturally, it lacked the finesse that might have been evident had the organizers enjoyed longer warning and greater time for preparation. A little more elbow room and they'd have been in at the kill. As it was, the spur-of-the-moment tactic gained in swiftness what it lost in thoroughness.

Raven walked boldly through the front entrance of the Security Bureau Building, gave the come-hither sign to an aerial taxi prowling overhead. The machine did a falling turn into the lower northbound level of traffic, dropped out of that and into the sitting level, hit the street with a rubbery bounce.

The taxi was a transparent ball mounted on a ring of smaller balls designed to absorb the landing shock. There were no wings, jets or vanes. It was a latest model antigrav cab worth about twelve thousand credits but its driver hadn't bothered taking depilatory treatment costing two fish.

Opening the door, the driver suffused his beefy features with professional hospitality, noted that the customer did not respond and made no attempt to enter. Welcome gradually faded from the mat. He scowled, scratched his blue-stubbled chin with a cracked fingernail and spoke with a cracked voice.

"See here, Mac, unless I'm imagining things you gave me the—"

"Shut up until I'm ready for you," said Raven, still on the sidewalk and some ten feet from the cab. His eyes were watching nothing in particular; his air was that of one whose mind is elsewhere—listening, perhaps, to faraway fairy bells—and resents a disturbance.

The cabbie intensified his scowl, gave the stubble another rake in sonic imitation of a space-mechanic sandpapering the venturis. His right arm was still extended, holding the door open. Something wafted the sleeve of the arm, depressing it slightly as if an unseen breath had blown upon it. He failed to notice it.

Raven returned his attention to the cab, approached it but did not get inside, "Have you got a melter?"

"Sure! Where'd I be without one if a bounce-arm snapped?" The cabbie extracted one from the instrument board pocket. It resembled a tiny hand gun. "What d'you want it for?"

"I'm going to burn your seat," Raven informed, taking it from him.

"Are you now? That's quite an idea, ain't it?" The other's small, sunken eyes went still smaller, more sunken. A smirk broke across his leathery face, revealed two gaps in his molars. "It's your unlucky day, Daffy." His hand dived again into the pocket, came out holding another melter. "I happen to carry them in pairs. So you fix my pants and I'll fix yours. That's fair, ain't it?"

"A pants-fixing performance would interest several scientists more than mightily," assured Raven, "when done with instruments effective only upon metals." He smiled at the other's sudden look of uncertainty, added, "I was referring to the back seat of the cab."

With that he stuck the nozzle of the midget autowelder into the seat's upholstery, squeezed the handle.

Nothing visible came from the melter though the hand holding it gave a slight jolt. A thin spurt of strong-smelling fumes shot out of the plasticoid upholstery as something concealed within it fused at high heat. Calmly Raven climbed into the cab, closed the door.

"All right, on your way, Shaveless." Bending forward, he put the melter back into its pocket.

The cabbie moped confusedly at his controls while the antigrav machine soared to five thousand feet and drifted southward. His heavy brows waggled from time to time with the effort of striving to think it out. His eyes continually shifted from the observation window to the rear view mirror, keeping surreptitious watch on this passenger who might be capable of anything up to and including setting the world on fire.

Taking no notice of the other's attitude, Raven shoved an investigatory hand into the still warm gap in the upholstery, felt hot metal, brought up a badly warped instrument no longer than a cigarette and not as thick. It was gold colored, had stubby wings curled and distorted by heat. Its pointed front end bore a shining lens half the size of a seed pearl. Its flattened rear was pierced with seven needle-fine holes that served as microscopic jets.

He did not have to pull this tiny contraption to pieces to discern what was inside. It was all there and he *knew* it was there: the lilliputian engine, the guiding scanner, the minuscule radio circuit that could yell *pip-pip-pip* for hours, the match-head-sized self-destroying charge—all in a weight of something under three ounces, Yet but for its destruction it could have loaded the cab with an electronic drag-scent that the hounds would follow for endless miles and in three dimensions.

Turning, he had a look through the rear window. So many cabs, tourers, sportsters and official machines were floating around on various levels that it was quite impossible to decide whether he was still being followed visually. No matter. A mess of traffic effectively hiding the hunters could equally well conceal the hunted.

Tossing the winged cylinder into the pocket occupied by the melters, he said to the driver, "You can have that thingumbob all for your very own. It contains items worth some fifty credits—*if* you can find someone capable of picking it apart without wrecking it entirely."

"There's ten owing for that hole in the seat."

"I'll pay you when I get out."

"All right." The other perked up, took the winged cylinder out of the pocket, fingered it curiously, put it back. "Say, how did you know this thing was there?"

"Somebody had it in his mind."

"Huh?"

"People who shoot gadgets through cab doors should not think of what they're doing even if they are a quarter of a mile away in no detectable direction. Thoughts can be overheard sometimes. They can be as effective as a bellowed warning." He eyed the back of the cabbie's neck. "Have you ever been able to do anything without thinking about it at all?"

"Only once." Holding up his left hand he showed the stump of a thumb. "It cost me this."

"Which goes to show," said Raven, and added mostly to himself, "Pity that mini-engineers aren't also true telepaths."

In silence they covered another forty miles still at the same altitude. Sky traffic was thinning out as they got well beyond the city limits.

"Forgot to bring my mittens," hinted the cabbie. "Shouldn't ought to forget my mittens. I'll need them at the South Pole."

"In that case we'll call it a day partway there. I'll let you know when." Raven had another look behind. "Meanwhile you can put in some practice at shaking off any followers we may have. Not that I can tell whether there are any, but it's possible."

"Dropping the procession will cost you fifty." The cabbie studied him via the rear view mirror, speculating as to whether he'd priced the service too high or too low. "And that includes a shut mouth, guaranteed unopenable."

"You're rash with your guarantees—you'll open for them because you won't be able to help it," Raven informed darkly. "They have techniques involving compulsion and no cash." He emitted a sigh of resignation. "Oh, well, by the time you talk it will be too late to matter. The fifty is yours just for delaying things a while." He grabbed the seat-grips as the cab swayed, darted sidewise, shot into a cloud. The world became hidden by thick fog which whirled around and slid past in streaks of yellow and clumps of dirty white. "You'll have to do better than this. You're not radarproof."

"Give me time. I ain't properly started yet."

Two hours later they thumped upon the lawn behind a long, low house. Nothing was visible in the sky except a high flying police patrol heading north. The patrol bulleted steadily onward in complete disregard of the sphere upon the lawn and whined out of sight.

The woman within the house was a little too big, a little too generously proportioned and moved with the deliberation of those weighty above the average. Her eyes were very big, widely spaced and blackly brilliant. Her mouth was large, her ears likewise, and her hair a huge, coal-black mop. Full-busted and heavy-hipped, there was too much of her to suit the tastes of most men. Nevertheless, although physically no sylph, at one time or another twenty suitors had pursued her and had treated her rejections with despair. The reason: what burned within her shone visibly through those great eyes and made her surpassingly beautiful.

Giving Raven a warm, big-fingered hand, she exclaimed, "David! Whatever brings you here?"

"You would already know had I not thought it expedient to keep my mind closed."

"Of course." She switched from vocal to telepathic means of communication solely because it came easier. "What is it?"

He responded in the same manner, mentally, "Two birds." He smiled into the orbs that made her lovely. "The two I hope to kill with one stone."

"Kill? Why do you have to use that dreadful thought *kill?*" A touch of anxiety came into her face. "You have been talked into something. I know it. I can feel it despite your keeping it hidden from me within your mind. You have been persuaded to interfere." Seating herself on a pneumatic lounge, she gazed morbidly at the wall. "It is the unwritten law that we must never be tempted to interfere except with the prime motive of thwarting the Denebs. We might give ourselves away just sufficiently to frighten humankind, and frightened people tend to strike blindly at the source of their fear. Besides, non-interference lulls all suspicions, encourages them to think we are not capable of it."

"That is excellent logic providing your premise is correct and unfortunately it isn't. Circumstances have changed." He took a seat opposite, studied her gravely. "Leina, we've slipped a little in one respect, namely, that they're shrewder than we expected."

"In what way?"

"Entangled in their own contradictions they became desperate enough to search the world on the million-to-one chance of finding someone able to unravel the strings. And they traced me!"

"Traced you?" Her alarm heightened. "How did they manage to do that?"

"In the only possible way, genetically, through the records. They must have classified, dissected and analyzed some ten, fifteen or twenty successive genera-tions, wading through data on endless births, marriages and deaths, knowing nothing of what they might eventually find but hoping for the best. My deter-minedly conventional pseudoancestors legalized all their alliances and left a long series of documentary pointers leading straight to me. So ultimately the line be-came reeled in and I was the fish gasping at the end."

"If they can do that with you they can do it with others," she commented with-out happiness.

"On this particular planet," he reminded, "there are no others. Only we two. And you are exempt."

"Am I? How can you be sure?"

"The sorting out process has already been completed. I've been grabbed, but not you—maybe because you're a female, Or perhaps you are concealed by ben-efit of ancestors allergic to official documents, such as one or two healthy but immoral pirates."

"Thank you," she said, slightly miffed.

"The pleasure's mine," he assured, grinning.

Her eyes keened into his. "David, what do they want you to do? Tell me!"

In full detail he informed her of what had happened. ending, "So far the Mars-Venus combine has been satisfied merely to try crippling us by degrees—the tech-nique of long maintained and gradually increasing pressure—knowing that un-less we can think up some really effective counter-action we're going to crack sooner or later. To put it another way, they are taking a pint of our blood every chance they get. Someday we'll be too feeble to stand, much less make defensive gestures."

"It's no business of ours," she decided. "Let argumentative worlds fight it out between themselves."

"That's exactly how I was tempted to view the situation," he admitted, "until I remembered how history shows that one darned thing leads to another. Look, Leina, it is only a matter of a short time before Earth decides it's had more than enough and must hit back. If Earth can't strike with finesse it will strike without finesse, roughly and toughly. Mars and Venus promptly become more riled than ever, get really hard. Tempers rise, each side's boosted by the other's. Restraints are thrown away one by one, then in bunches. Scruples are poured down the drain until some badly frightened crackpot on one side or the other plants a hydride bomb to show who's boss. Your own imagination can take it from there."

"It can," she agreed without relish.

"Much as I dislike poking a finger into human affairs," he went on, "I have an even stronger distaste for the notion of hiding under a mountain while the atmosphere flames and the world shudders all around and multimillion humans walk clean off the stage of life. Carson overoptimistically thinks I can do something about it, singlehanded. All the same, I'm willing to have a shot at it providing the opposition lets me live long enough. Nothing ventured, nothing gained."

"Oh, dear!" Her fingers toyed together. "Why must these creatures be so stubborn and idiotic?" Without waiting for an answer, she asked, "What do you wish me to do, David?"

"Keep yourself from becoming involved," he said. "I've come back to destroy a few papers, that's all. There's a chance they'll catch up with me before I leave. In that event, you can perform one small service."

"And that is—?"

"Look after my best suit for a little while." He tapped his chest with much significance. "It fits me perfectly and it's the only one I've got. I like it and don't want to lose it."

"David!" Her mental impulse was sharp and immeasurably shocked. "Not that! You can't do *that!* Not without permission. It is a fundamental violation. It isn't ethical."

"Neither is war. Neither is mass-suicide."

"But—"

"Hush!" He raised a warning finger. "They are coming already. It didn't take them long." He glanced at the wall clock. "Not quite three hours since I left the Bureau. That's what I call efficiency." His gaze came back to her. "Do you sense their approach?"

She nodded and sat waiting in silence while Raven hurried away and dealt with his papers. He came back. Presently the door gongs chimed softly. Standing up, Leina hesitated a moment, glanced at the other. Raven responded with a careless shrug. She went to the door, opened it. Her manner was that of one deprived of initiative.

Five men were grouped by a bullet-shaped sportship four hundred yards from the house. Two more waited on her doorstep. All wore the black and silver uniform of security police.

The pair at the door were burly, leather-face specimens alike enough to be brothers. It was no more than type-similarity because inwardly they were different. The mind of one probed at Leina's while the other's did not. One was a telepath; the other something else. The sudden and fierce thrust of the first one's mind temporarily prevented her examining the second one's and thus identifying his peculiar talent, for perforce she countered the telepath by snapping her own mind shut. The other mentality immediately sensed the closure and recoiled.

"Another Tele," he told his companion. "Just as well we came along in a bunch, isn't it?" Not waiting for comment, he spoke to Leina vocally, "You can talk to me of your own free will." He paused to enjoy a harsh chuckle, went on, "Or you can talk to my friend involuntarily, whichever you please. As you can see, we are police."

Tartly she gave back, "You are nothing of the kind. A police officer would refer to another as his fellow officer and not as his friend. Neither would he utter implied threats before so much as stating his business."

The second man, who had remained silent up to that point, now chipped in. "Rather talk to me, eh?" His eyes gained a strange, eerie light, growing like little moons. A hypno.

Ignoring him, she said to the first man, "What do you want?"

"Raven."

"So?"

"He's here," he insisted, trying to peer over her shoulder. "We know he's here."

"So?"

"We're going to take him along for questioning."

Raven's voice sounded from the room at back. "It is most kind and thoughtful of you, Leina, to try to detain the gentlemen. But it is futile. Please show them in."

She shivered slightly. Her face was a mirror of emotions as she stood aside and let them brush past her. They went in eagerly like steers galloping into the slaughterhouse. She knew what was coming. The doorknob in her hand grew colder and colder.

Chapter 3

The invaders slowed up as they had entered the room. Their expressions became wary, they had small bluesteel guns in their hands, and they kept well apart as if suspecting their quarry of the ability to lay both of them at one swipe.

Not bothering to come to his feet, and obviously amused by their alertness, David Raven said as he picked their identities out of their minds, "Ah, Mr. Grayson and Mr. Steen. A telepath and a hypno—with a gang of other skewboys waiting outside. I am greatly honored."

Grayson, the telepath, snapped at his companion, "Listen who's calling us skewboys." Making an impatient motion at Raven, he added, "All right, Brainpicker, on your feet and start walking."

"To where?"

"You find out when you arrive."

"So it seems," agreed Raven drily. "The ultimate destination is not recorded in your mind, from which I conclude that you do not enjoy the confidence of your superiors."

"Neither do you," Grayson retorted. "Take the weight off your tail. We can't stand here all day."

"Oh, well." Coming erect, Raven stretched himself, yawned. His gaze rested on Steen, the hypno, as he inquired, "What's eating you, Squinty? Never found anyone so fascinating before?"

Maintaining the openly curious stare with which he had fixed Raven from the very start, Steen responded, "When there's any fascinating to be done *I'll* do it!" He carried on with, "I'm wondering what all the excitement is about. You haven't got four arms and two heads. What's supposed to make you so marvelous?"

"He isn't so marvelous," Grayson interrupted with impatience. "Seems to me that headquarters has been stirred up by an exaggerated rumor. I know what he's got and it isn't so much."

"You do?" asked Raven, looking at him.

"Yes, you're merely a new breed of telepath. You can still probe other minds even when your own is closed. Unlike the rest of us, you don't have to open your own before you can snoop into others. It's a nice trick and a useful one." He sniffed his disdain. "But as an interesting variation it's not big enough to worry two planets."

"Then what *are* you worrying about?" Raven pressed. "Having learned the worst you've learned the lot. Now leave me to ponder with pleasure over the sins of my youth."

"We've been ordered to bring you in for questioning. That is to say, in one piece. So we're bringing you." Grayson's contempt grew more evident. "We're dragging back the tiger even though it smells to me of kitten."

"And by whom will I be questioned, the Big Chief or some no-account underling?"

"That's no affair of mine," said Grayson. "All you've got to do is come along and provide the answers."

"Leina, please fetch me my hat and bag." Raven threw an open and meaningful wink to where she stood silently in the doorway.

"No you don't," Grayson rasped at her, naturally not liking the wind. "You stay put." He turned to Raven. "Go fetch them yourself." Then to Steen. "You go with him. I'll keep an eye on the large lady. Do your stuff on him if he so much as clicks his teeth."

The pair walked stolidly into the adjoining room, Raven leading and Steen close behind. Steen's eyes already were glowing with power that was better than bullets. Squatting on one arm of a pneumaseat, Grayson rested his gun-hand on a knee, eyed Leina speculatively.

"Another mental oyster, aren't you?" Grayson said. "Anyway, if you're hoping he'll manage to pull a fast one on Steen you can save your brain the strain of thought. He'll never do it between now and Christmas."

Offering no comment, she continued to gaze expressionlessly at the wall, showing no hint of apprehension.

"Any telepath can outwit and outmaneuver any hypno at a distance because he can read intentions and has space in which to get out from under." Grayson gave it with the authority of personal experience. "But close up he hasn't the chance of a celluloid cat. The hypno is the winnah every time. I know! Many's the lousy hypno trick I've had played on me, especially after a session with a few quarts of Venusian mountain dew."

She did not respond. Her generous features were blank, impassive as she strove to listen through and beyond his chatter. Grayson made a swift and vicious thrust at her mind, hoping to catch it unaware, and struck nothing but an impenetrable shield. She had resisted him without effort and continued listening, listening. A faint almost unhearable scuffle sounded in the other room and was followed by the merest whisper of a gasp.

Grayson swiveled round on one heel, looking like one who suspects himself of failing to hear something he should have heard. "Besides, there's me here with this gun and there's a tough bunch waiting outside." He glanced at the other room's door, became restless. "All the same, they're slow in there."

"Not a chance," she murmured, barely loud enough for him to catch. "Close up there's not a chance."

Something about her face, her eyes, or the tone of her voice aroused his suppressed suspicions, created vague alarm. His lips thinned and he motioned to her with his gun.

"Move, Buxom. Walk in there slowly two paces ahead of me. We'll see what's keeping them."

Leina got up, bracing herself a moment on the arm of the pneumaseat. Reluctantly she turned to face the door, her eyes lowered as if to delay the vision of what lay behind the door or at any second might come through it.

Steen came through it, rubbing his chin and grinning with self-satisfaction. He was alone.

"He tried to be funny," announced Steen, addressing Grayson and pointedly ignoring Leina. "I had a notion he was going to do just that. Result: he's stiffer than a tombstone. We'll need a long board to carry him away."

"Hah!" Grayson relaxed, let the gun droop as the other continued toward him. Triumphantly he said to Leina, "What did I tell you? He was a dope to try it close up. Some people will never learn!"

"Yes," agreed Steen, coming nearer, nearer. "He was a dope." He stopped face to face with Grayson, looking straight at him, gaze level with gaze. "Not a chance, close up!" His eyes were brilliant and very large.

Grayson's fingers twitched, loosened. The gun dropped from them, thumped upon the carpet. His mouth opened and shut. Faint words came out, uttered with difficulty.

"Steen . . . what the heck . . . are . . . *doing?*"

The eyes swelled enormously, became monstrous, irresistibly compelling. Their blaze seemed to fill the cosmos and sear the onlooker's brain. A deep, droning voice came with the blaze, at first faintly, but racing nearer over immense distances at immense velocity and building up to a masterful roar.

"Raven's not here."

"Raven's not here," mumbled Grayson in dreamy tones, his mind overwhelmed.

"We have seen nothing of him. We were too late."

Grayson repeated it like an automaton.

"Too late by forty minutes," the mentally paralyzing voice of Steen insisted.

"Too late by forty minutes," indorsed Grayson.

"He took off in a gold colored, twenty-tube racing craft number XB109, the property of the World Council."

Grayson echoed it word for word. He had the rigid pose and inane expression of a waxy one gathering dust in a tailor's window.

"Destination unknown."

That, too, was parroted.

"There is nobody in this villa but a fat woman, a telepath of no consequence."

"There is nobody," mumbled Grayson, glassy-eyed, half blind, half dead and mentally enslaved. "There is nobody . . . nobody . . . but a fat woman of no consequence."

Steen said, "Pick up your gun. Let's go back and tell Haller."

He pushed past the fat woman of no consequence, Grayson following sheeplike. Neither favored Leina with so much as a glance. Her own attention was on Steen, studying his face, reaching for what lay behind the mask, silently talking at him, reproving him, but he took no notice. His disregard was obvious, deliberate and determined.

She closed the door behind them, sighed and wrung her hands in the manner of women since the beginning of time. There were stumbling sounds behind her. Turning, she faced the figure of David Raven swaying uncertainly two yards away.

The figure bent forward, hands over its face, rubbing its features as though not sure on which side of its head they were placed. It was feeling the alien, the unfamiliar, and horrified by its own sense of touch. The hands came away, revealed a tormented countenance and eyes full of fundamental shock.

"Mine," he said in a voice that was neither Raven's nor Steen's but combined some of the characteristic qualities of both. "He snatched away that which is mine and mine alone! He deprived me of myself!"

He paused staring at her in manner not quite sane while his face continued to picture the psychic struggle within him. Then he edged forward, arms outstretched, fingers crooked.

"You knew about this. By the blackest clots in space, you knew about it and helped. You big ungainly schemer, I could kill you for it!" His fingers trembled with sheer emotion as he reached for her neck while she stood unmoving, impassive, an indescribable something shining through her great orbs. The hands touched her neck, closed around. She made no move to resist.

For several seconds he held her like that, hands cupped around her throat, ripping lightly and not contracting, while his features underwent a peculiar series of contortions. Finally he let go, backed away hurriedly with shock added to shock. He found his voice again.

"Heavens above, you *too!*"

"What one can do another can do and that was the bond between us." She watched him sit down and feel the face he did not know. "There is a law as strong and basic as that of physical survival. It says, 'I am Me—I cannot be Not-Me.' "

He remained silent but rocked to and fro and nursed the face.

"So always you will hunger for that which is rightfully yours. You will hunger as one in imminent danger of death yearns tremendously for life. Always you will crave yourself, badly, madly, and never know peace, rest, tranquillity, never know *completeness,* unless—"

"Unless?" His hands came away fast as he looked up startled.

"Unless you play it our way," she informed. "If you do, then what has been done can be undone."

"What do you want of me?" He was upright now, a gleam of hope showing.

"Implicit obedience."

"You shall have it," he promised fervently.

Briefly and inanely she felt relieved of the problem of Raven's suit and the owner-who-wasn't-the-owner.

The boss of the waiting gang was a thin-boned individual named Haller, six feet tall, Martian born and a Type Three Mutant, a pyrotic. Leaning against the tail of his ship, he fiddled with a silver button on the jacket of his phony police uniform and registered disappointment as Steen and Grayson came up.

"Well?"

"No luck," said Steen. "Gone."

"How long has he been gone?"

"Forty minutes," informed Steen.

"He had three hours' start," Haller said, picking at his teeth, "so that means we're catching up. Where's he making for?"

"That," said Steen casually, "is something he omitted to divulge to the generous helping of femme he left in the house. All she knows is that he came in an antigrav cab, snatched some stuff he had planted here and shot off in XB109."

"A female in the house." Haller stared at him. "What's her place in his life?"

"Ha!" said Steen, smirking.

"I see," declared Haller, not seeing at all. His gaze transferred to the silent, dummylike Grayson, lingered there a while. Eventually a frown corrugated his forehead as he asked, "What the devil is afflicting *you?*"

"Eh?" Grayson blinked uncertainly. "Me?"

"You're a telepath and supposed to be able to read my mind although I can't read yours. I've just asked you ten times mentally whether you've got a bellyache or something, and you've reacted as if thought is a strange phenomenon confined to some outlandish place the other side of Jupiter. What's the matter with you? To look at you one would imagine you were suffering from an overdose of hypno."

"An overdose of his own medicine," Steen put in, quickly smothering Haller's awakening suspicions. "He tangled with the lady who happened to be one of his own kind. How'd you like to be nagged to death telepathetically as well as vocally?"

"Heaven forbid!" said Haller soothed. Dismissing the question of Grayson's peculiar lack of zip he added, "Let's take steps. This Raven isn't giving us any time to waste."

He climbed into the ship, the others following. While the lock closed and the propulsion tubes warmed, he dug out his interplanetary register, thumbed its pages, found the item for which he was seeking,

"Here it is, XB109, a berilligilt-coated single-seater with twenty tubes. Earth-mass three hundred tons. Maximum range half a million miles. Described as a World Council courier boat bearing police and customs exemption. H'm! That makes it awkward to intercept openly with any official witnesses around."

"Assuming that we ever find it," Steen qualified. "One world is a big place."

"We'll get our cross hairs dead on it," asserted Haller, with complete confidence. "That half million range is a comfort. It ties him down to Earth or Moon. We know he can't have sneaked away direct to Mars or Venus."

He consulted a coded list of radio channels correlated with times. Three-thirty: channel nine. Pressing the appropriate stub, he spoke into a hand-microphone. What he said went out in pulses, scrambled, and was much too brief to permit detection and unsorting by any eavesdropper. "Combine call: Haller to Dean. Find XB109."

Turning the pilot's seat sidewise, Haller sat in it, lit a black Venusian cheroot fifteen inches long, puffed luxuriously. He put his feet up on the edge of the instrument board, watched the loudspeaker.

It said, "XB109. Not listed in today's departures. Not shown on any of today's police observation reports. Stand by."

"Service!" boasted Haller, sending an appreciative glance along the cheroot and toward Steen.

Five minutes, then, "XB109. Not in Council parks one to twenty-eight. Stand by."

"Queer," remarked Haller, taking a long suck and blowing a lopsided smoke ring. "If it's not on the floor it must be off the floor. But he couldn't lift it today without getting it marked airborne."

"Maybe he took it yesterday or the day before and stashed it here," Steen suggested. Carefully he closed the door of the pilot's cabin, made sure that it was firmly shut. Sitting on the edge of the instrument board alongside Haller's feet, he waited for the next message. It came after ten minutes.

"Dean to Haller. XB109 in charge of Courier Joseph McArd at Dome City, Luna, refueling for return. Closing channel nine."

"Impossible!" Haller ejaculated. "*Im*-possible!" He stood up, bit an inch off his cheroot, spat it on the floor. "Somebody's lying!" His ireful eyes came level with Steen's and promptly he added, "You?"

"Me?" With a pained expression Steen also stood up. He was almost chest to chest with the other.

"Either that or the dame gave you a cockeyed registration number and Grayson was too dopey to detect the deception in her mind." Haller waved the cheroot. "Maybe it was the dame. She pointed down a blind alley and laughed herself silly when you two went yipping into it. If so, Grayson's to blame for that. He was the mind-probe of you two. Send him in to me—I've got to get to the bottom of this."

"How could Grayson penetrate a mind as flat and blank as a mortuary slab?" asked Steen.

"He could have told you he was stymied and let you put her under the influence. After you'd made her play statues he could have dug out her taste in paper sunshades, couldn't he? Where's the point of you going around in pairs if you're too dumb to co-operate?"

"Not dumb," denied Steen, unoffended.

"Somebody's nursing a month-old mackerel," Haller insisted. "I can smell it. Maybe that darned woman stuffed it up Grayson's vest. He's got the stupefied air of someone whose best friends have just told him. That's not like Grayson. You go fetch him—I want to give him a going over."

"I don't think we'll need him," said Steen, very softly. "This is just between us two."

"Is it?" Haller's self-command and lack of surprise revealed him as a hard character. There was a gun on his desk but he made no attempt to grab it as he gently placed his cheroot beside it and turned to face the other. "I'd a notion it was you who lied. I don't know what's come over you but you'd better not let it go too far."

"No?"

"No! You're a hypno but what of it? I can burn away your insides some three or four seconds before you can paralyze mine, and moreover paralysis wears off after a few hours, whereas charring does not. It's decidedly permanent."

"I know, I know. That is power, pyrotic power." Steen gestured and his hand touched Haller's casually, almost accidentally.

The hand stuck. Haller tried to pull his own away, found he couldn't. The two hands adhered at point of contact like flesh united to flesh—and something outrageous was happening at the junction, through the junction.

"This, too, is power," said Steen.

Far beneath the innocuous pile of warehouses nominally belonging to the Transpatial Trading Company there existed a miniature city that to all intents and purposes was not part of Earth though sited upon it. Unknown to and unsuspected by most surface dwellers it had been taken over long since.

Here was the field headquarters of the Mars-Venus underground movement, its very heart. A thousand came and went along its cool, lengthy passages and through a series of great cellars, a hand-picked thousand none of whom were men as others are men.

In one cellar worked a dozen slim-fingered oldsters who moved around slowly, fumblingly, in the manner of those seven-eighths blind. Their eyes were not eyes but something else, something too short-focused to photograph clearly anything more than three or four inches from the tip of the nose. Yet they were quasi-visual organs that within those brief limits could count the angels dancing on the point of a pin.

The oldsters worked as if continually smelling the objects of their tasks, fingers almost to nose, their not-eyes directed at abnormal angles and functioning with supernormal vividness. These were Type Nine Mutants, generally called mini-engineers. They thought nothing of building a seven-year radium chronometer so incredibly minute that it could serve as the center jewel in a diamond ring.

And in an adjacent cellar were beings similar but not the same. Pranksters continually testing their eerie powers on one another.

The two men sat opposite each other. A swift change of facial features, altering them out of all resemblance. "There you are—I'm Peters."

An equally swift and precisely similar facial change on the part of the other. "That's funny—so am I!"

Two hollow laughs. As alike as twins they sit down and play cards, each surreptitiously watching the other for the first moment when a rubber face would forgetfully relax and betray its owner's true identity.

Two more enter with the motive of turning the card game into a foursome. One registers a moment of intense mental strain, floats clean over the table and into a chair on the opposite side. The second glares at a nearer chair which trembles, hesitates, then places itself under him as if shifted by invisible hands. The twins accept these phenomena as normal, everyday occurrences and proceed to redivide the cards.

The second entrant, the chair-mover, makes his share leap straight into his ready fingers, grunts as he studies them, says with much boredom, "If you two dummies feel that you just *have* to be Peters let's have different smells so we'll know who from which." Another grunt. "I pass."

Someone going along the outer passage pauses to have a look through the door then goes on his way grinning. Ten seconds later the first Peters makes to suck his cigarette and discovers that it is now lit at both ends. With a hearty curse he leaves his chair and shuts the door, taking his cards with him lest during his absence they turn over twice of their own accord.

Grayson came into this subterranean menagerie with his mind closed against all possible intrusions, his eyes alert, suspicious, his manner jumpy. He was in a hurry and had the air of one with every reason to fear his own shadow.

At the end of a long passage where it terminated in a heavy steel door, Grayson came face to face with a hypno guard who said, "No further, chum. This is where the boss lives."

"Yes, I know. I want to see Kayder at once." Grayson stared back along the passage, made an impatient gesture. "Tell him he'd better hear me before all this blows up under us."

The guard eyed him calculatingly, then he opened the mike-trap in the door and spoke to it. Seconds later the door opened.

Grayson went through, tramped across the long room to where its sole occupant was seated at a small bureau.

A squat, broad-shouldered man with heavily underslung jaw, Kayder was of Venusian birth and probably the only Type Eleven Mutant located on Earth. He could converse in low, almost unhearable chirrups with nine species of Venusian bugs, seven of them highly poisonous and willing to perform deadly services for friends. Kayder, therefore, enjoyed all the appalling power of one with a nerveless, inhuman army too vast in numbers to destroy.

"What is it this time?" he snapped, removing his attention from a wad of documents. "Make it quick and to the point. I feel low this morning. This world doesn't suit me."

"Me, too," Grayson endorsed. He went on with, "You dug up something on this David Raven and ordered that he be brought in."

"I did. I don't know what's he's got but it's alleged to be good. Where have you put him?"

"Nowhere. He got away."

"Not for long," assured Kayder with confidence, "I know that he is hell-bent for a hideout someplace. It will take a little while to pry him out." He waved a hand in dismissal. "Keep on the trail. We'll get him in due time."

"But," said Grayson, "we did get him. He was flat on his belly with his tongue hanging out and his sides heaving. A fox right at the last lap. And he got away."

Kayder rocked back on the hind legs of his chair. "Mean to say you actually had him? You let him slip? How was that?"

"I don't know." Grayson was badly worried, made no effort to conceal the fact. "I just don't know. I can't make it out. It has got me baffled. That's why I've come to see you."

"Be more specific. What happened?"

"We broke into his hiding place. A woman was with him—true telepaths, both of them. Steen was with me, as good a hypno as any we've got. Raven made a monkey of him."

"Go on, man! Don't stand there enjoying dramatic pauses!"

"Steen gave *me* the treatment," continued Grayson, hurriedly and morbidly. "He caught me on one leg and made me marble-minded. He compelled me to return to the ship and tell Haller that we'd seen nothing of Raven. Then he went into Haller's cabin."

A small, spidery thing scuttled many-legged up one side of Kayder's pants. Lowering a casual hand, he caught it, helped it onto the bureau. It was thin and bright green with eight crimson pinheads for optics.

Distastefully watching this creature, Grayson said, "A few hours later my wits drifted back. By then Haller was crazy and Steen had disappeared."

"You say Haller was crazy?"

"Yes, he was babbling. Seemed as if his brain had been twisted right round and sort of got itself back to front. Kept talking to himself about the infantile futility of Mars-Venus, Terra squabbles, the supreme wondrousness of the universe, the glory of death and so forth. Acted as if for two pins he'd jump straight into the afterlife but needed time to work up the guts."

"Haller's a pyrotic," Kayder observed. "You are a telepath. Did you overlook those simple facts? Or were you too stupefied by events to remember them?"

"I was not. I had a look inside his skull."

"And what did you find?"

"It was mussed up something awful. His think-stuff was like freshly stirred porridge. He was nursing long chains of pseudo-logic and working through them like prayer beads. One said, 'Steen is me is Raven is you is the others is everyone.'

Another said, 'Life is not-life is soon-life is wonder-life but not other-life.' " He screwed a finger above his right ear. "A complete imbecile."

"Bad overdose of hypno," diagnosed Kayder, undisturbed. "Haller must have had hypno-allergy. There's no way of detecting it until a victim goes off the beaten track. Probably it's permanent, too."

"Maybe it was accidental. Steen wouldn't know that Haller was susceptible. I like to think so."

"That's because you hate to believe that a pal of yours could or would turn on his friends and make them squint down their own spines. Whether by accident or not, Steen put paid to Haller, one of his own crowd and his immediate superior to boot. We have a nasty name for that kind of game. It's treachery!"

"I don't think so," insisted Grayson, doggedly. "Raven's got something to do with this. Steen wouldn't do us dirt without good reason."

"Of course he wouldn't," agreed Kayder, his beefy face sardonic. He threw several tiny chirrups at the green spider-thing. It performed a bizarre little dance that might have meant something.

Kayder continued, "Everyone has a reason, good, bad or indifferent. Take me, for instance. Reason why I'm an honest, loyal and absolutely trustworthy citizen of Venus is because nobody's ever offered me enough inducement to be otherwise. My price is too high." He tossed a knowing glance at the other. "I can make a shrewd guess at what's wrong with Steen. He's a low-priced man and Raven found it out."

"Even if he's the sort to be bought over, which I doubt, how could he be? He made no contacts."

"He was alone with Raven, wasn't he?"

"Yes," admitted Grayson. "For less than a couple of minutes and in the adjoining room with me still listening in. Raven's mind remained blank. Steen's mind told that Raven turned to face him as if about to say something. Raven touched him—and Steen promptly went blank too. A hypno can't do that. A hypno can't shut off like a telepath—but he did!"

"Ah!" said Kayder, watching him.

"That hit me immediately. It was mighty queer. I got up to go see what had happened. Then Steen reappeared. I was so relieved that I failed to notice he was still blank. Before I could catch on to that fact he had me where he wanted me." Apologetically Grayson finished, "I was naturally wary of Raven but completely off guard with Steen. You don't expect an ally suddenly to knock you down."

"Of course not." Kayder chirped again at the spider which obediently moved aside while he reached for his desk-mike. "We'll make it a double hunt. Just as easy to look for two as for one. We'll soon have Steen dragged in for examination."

"You're forgetting something," Grayson offered. *"I'm* here." He paused to let it sink in. "Steen knows of this place, too."

"Meaning you think he might rat on us and we're due for a raid?"

"Yes."

"I doubt it." Calmly Kayder pondered the point. "If Terran counter-forces had learned of this center and decided to put it out of business they'd have moved fast. We'd have had our raid hours ago while there was still an element of surprise."

"What's to stop them being craftier and tougher than that? What's to stop them biding their time while they make suitable preparations and then blowing the entire place sky-high?"

"You're jumpy," scoffed Kayder. "We've got too much talent around here—and besides failure could drive us into hiding. Better the devil you know than the devil you don't."

"I suppose so." Grayson was moody, uncertain.

"Anyhow, they've no publicly satisfactory excuse for taking such drastic measures. They can't take active and open part in a war while pretending it doesn't exist. Until they admit what they don't want to admit we've got them where we want them. The initiative is ours and remains ours."

"I hope you're right."

"You bet I'm right." Kayder sniffed his contempt of any other outlook. He switched his mike, activating it. "D727 Hypno Steen has gone bad on us. Get him at all costs and with minimum of delay!"

Muffled by the heavy door an outside loudspeaker repeated, "D727 Hypno Steen." Then another, farther away along the labyrinth of corridors. "D727 Hypno Steen . . . get him . . . with minimum of delay!"

At the other end of the underground maze and nearer the secret entrance a nose-close worker threw an irritable nod at a loudspeaker he could not see, then delicately inserted into its minuscule holder a triode-hexode radio tube the size of a match-head. Next door, an unshaven pyrotic slapped his jack of clubs on a floater's five of hearts.

"Socko! You owe me fifty." He leaned back, rubbed his chin bristles. "Gone bad on us, eh? Never heard of such a thing."

"He'll be sorry," prophesied a kibitzer,

"Nuts!" said the first. "Nobody's sorry after they're dead!"

Chapter 4

Leina sensed him returning, glanced through the window, saw him entering the path. A hint of disapproval showed in her fine eyes. She drew away from the curtains.

"He's back. Something has gone wrong." She opened the door to the adjoining room, "I refuse to stay here to watch your meeting. Wrong is wrong and right is right. I cannot see it any other way even as a matter of expediency."

"Don't leave me alone with him. Don't, I tell you! I won't be able to control myself. I'll try to kill him though he may kill me. I'll—"

"You will do nothing of the sort," she reproved. "Would you foolishly slaughter your own, your very own self?" She paused, hearing a mental voice call, "Leina!" but not answering it. "Remember your promise: absolute obedience. Do as he tells you; it's your only chance."

She went through, closing the door and leaving him to deal with his fate as ordered. Finding a chair, she seated herself primly. Her air was that of a schoolmarm determined not to be involved in a piece of inexcusable vulgarity.

Someone came into the other room, his mind reaching through the wall and nudging her gently. "It's all right, Leina, you can come out in a minute." Then vocally to the other, "You ready to get back?"

Silence.

"Surely you *want* to get back, don't you?"

A whisper, "You damn vampire, you know I do!"

"Here then!"

Leina closed her eyes though there was nothing to see. A few swift, subdued gasps and one small sob came from the next room. They were followed by a deep and thankful breathing. She stood up, taut-faced, and went to the door. She looked at Steen who sat limp and pale on the pneumatic settee, noted the frightened introspection in orbs that at other times could burn with fierce, hypnotic intensity.

Raven said to Steen, "I took possession of your body. Even though you are an enemy I apologize for that. It is not proper to usurp the persons of the living without their willing permission."

"The *living?*" Steen went two shades paler as he put emphasis on that last word. "Is it therefore proper to usurp the persons of the *dead?* His mind was in a turmoil. "You mean—?"

"Jump to no wild conclusions," advised Raven, seeing the other's thoughts as clearly as if they were a page of print. "You might be right. You might be hopelessly wrong. Either way it won't help you one iota."

"David," put in Leina, eyeing the window, "what if they soon come back in greater strength and better prepared?"

"They'll come," he assured, unworried. "But not just yet. I'm gambling on them thinking it would be nonsensical for the prey to return to the trap. It will occur to them sometime and they'll come along to check up, by which time they'll be too late." He resumed with Steen. "They are scouring the planet for me, attributing to me an importance out of all proportion. Somebody must have given them information to make them so excited. Somebody high up in Terran affairs must have betrayed his trust. Do you know who it is?"

"No."

He accepted the denial without hesitation, for it was written indelibly on the other's mind.

"They're hunting for you as well."

"Me?" Still shaken, Steen tried to pull himself together.

"Yes. I made a bitter mistake, I blundered badly by trying to take over the commander of your vessel. He proved to be something more than a standard pyrotic.

He had intuitive perceptiveness, a well developed form of extra-sensory visions. It enabled him to see or sense or estimate things that he is not entitled to know."

He glanced sidewise as Leina drew in a quick breath and put a hand to her throat.

"I did not expect that. There was no evidence of it and it caught me by surprise," Raven went on. "There's the beginning of a Type Thirteen, a pyrotic with e.s.p. He doesn't realize it himself, doesn't know he's slightly out of the ordinary even for a mutant." Studying the floor, he doodled with the toe of one shoe on the nap of the carpet. "The instant that we made contact he knew me as you will never know me—and he found it too much to bear. He made a frantic snatch at what he conceived to be the only form of self-preservation immediately available. He was wrong, of course. but people don't think logically in a crisis. So he made himself useless to me."

"Meaning?" inquired Steen, looking ghastly.

"He's whirly," said Raven. "They blame *you* for that."

"Blame me?" echoed Steen. "My body?" He stood up, felt himself around the chest and face, studied himself in a mirror. He was like a child ensuring the faultlessness of new clothes. "My body," he repeated. Then with heated protest, "But it wasn't *me!*"

"Try convincing them of that."

"They'll put a telepath to work on me. He'll read the truth. I can't feed him a lot of lies—it's impossible."

"Nothing is impossible. The word ought to be expunged from the dictionary. You could tell outrageous lies all the way from here to Aldebaran if you'd first been conditioned by a hypno more powerful than yourself."

"They wouldn't kill me for that," mused Steen, greatly troubled. "But they'd plant me someplace safe and for keeps. That's a worse fate, being put away. I couldn't endure it. I'd rather be dead!"

Raven chuckled. "You may not know it but you've got something there."

"You're in a sweet position to consider it funny," Steen snapped back, missing the point because it was too far out of reach for him to capture. "Who could put *you* in cold storage when within five minutes you could confiscate the person of a guard and walk out on his legs? Why, you could carry on from there, go grab the right official and sign an order for your own release. You could . . . you could—" His voice trailed off as his thoughts roared along in a mighty flood and tried to carry endless possibilities to an utterly fantastic limit.

Tracking his mind, Raven registered a faint smile as he said, "You certainly can extend it fast and far. But even if in the end I did swap places with the secret lord of the Mars-Venus combine I doubt whether I'd seal the peace I'd imposed by marrying Terra's leading beauty. Tsk-tsk! You've been reading too many of those cheap and lurid Martian romances, or watching them on the spectroscreen."

"That may be," conceded Steen, long accustomed to having his inward notions dragged out and criticized. "All the same it looks like someone will have to blow you apart to stop you." His attention shifted to Leina, came back. "Even that wouldn't do much good if there are any more of your type around, ready to fill your place."

"Beginning to think of us as on the winning side, eh?" Raven smiled again, said to Leina, "Seems it's just as well I did take him over."

"I say it's wrong," she responded, firmly. "Always has been, always will be."

"I agree with you in principle," Raven answered. He returned to Steen. "Look, I've not come back here solely for the fun of it. I've a reason and it concerns you."

"In what way?"

"First of all, are you now willing to play on our side or do you insist on sticking to your own?"

"After this experience," explained Steen, fidgeting, "I feel that changing sides should be the safest. But I can't do it." He shook a positive head. "I'm not made that way. The fellow who'll renege on his own kind is a louse."

"So you remain anti-Terran?"

"No!" He shuffled his feet around, avoided the other's steady gaze. "I won't be a traitor. At the same time I feel that all this anti-Terran business is crazy—gaining nothing." His voice drifted off as morbidly as he considered the situation. "All I really want is to get home, sit tight and be neutral."

That was true. It showed in his troubled mind. Steen had been shaken to his psychic roots, was fed up and lacked all original enthusiasm. It is a great shock to lose a limb; greater to be deprived of a body.

"Back home you're likely to have a rough time trying to sit on the fence," Raven suggested. "When parochial hysterics look around for easy marks on whom to vent their spite they usually choose a neutral."

"I'll take my chance on that."

"Have it your own way." Raven nodded toward the door. "There's your road to freedom; the price is one item of information."

"What do you want to know?"

"As I've told you, some high up Terran ratted on me. Someone on our side is a stinker. You've already said you don't know who it is. Who's likely to know?"

"Kayder," said Steen, mostly because he was in no position to refuse the information. The name popped into his mind automatically, could be read by the other as if inscribed in neon lights.

"Who is he? Where does he live?"

That was easier, not too dangerous. Where does he *live?* It enabled him to picture Kayder and his private residence while managing to suppress all thoughts of the underground center. Nor need his conscience bother him. Outside of the secret center Kayder cynically exercised his Terran rights to the full, even ran a small but genuine Venusian import agency. Kayder was fully capable of looking after himself.

"What's his special talent, if any?" Raven asked, having read the answers.

"I'm not certain of that. I've heard it said he's a bug-talker."

"That will do me." He jerked an indicative thumb toward the door. "Out you go. As a neutral you may be lucky."

"I'll need to be," Steen admitted. Pausing on the outer step, he added fervently, "And I hope I never see either of you again." With that he glanced skyward, rapidly walked away.

"Notice that?" Leina became a little edgy. "He looked upward, kept his expression under control, but his mind revealed what his eyes were seeing. A helicopter coming down!" She had a quick and wary look herself. "Yes, it's falling fast. David, you talked too much and stayed here too long. What are you going to do now?"

He eyed her serenely. "It seems a woman remains a woman."

"What do you mean?"

"When you become jumpy you slide right off humanity's neutral band. You think so hard that you forget to listen. Not everyone is an enemy."

Mastering her anxiety, she did listen. Now that her full attention had returned she could detect the overhead jumble of thoughts radiating from the helicopter. There were four personalities in the descending machine, their mental impulses growing stronger every second and making no attempt to blank out. Pawn-minds, all of them.

"House looks quiet. Who's that turning out of the path and into the road?"

"Dunno, but it isn't him. Too short and lumpy." Pause. "Anyway, Carson said there'd be a voluptuous Amazon here. We can talk to her if we can't find Raven."

"Hear that?" invited Raven. "You've got an unsuspected admirer in the shape of Carson."

"Never met him. You must have been telling him things." She watched the window and continued to listen. The eerie mind-voices were now over the roof.

"They ought to have given us a telepath. I've heard that the best of them can pick a mind right out to the horizon."

Another mind commented, "There will never be a brain-picker in the squad this side of the last trump. The public won't stand for it. Ever since that hullaballoo about thought-police two centuries ago the rule has been that no telepath can become a cop."

A third, with open scorn, "The public! They make me sick!"

Urgently this time, "Hey! Zip those vanes another hundred. That garden is made of dirt, not sponge rubber. Can't you talk without closing your eyes?"

"Who's juggling this gadget, you or me? I was landing 'em on a spread handkerchief when you were biting the bars of your playpen." Pause. "Hold tight, here we touch!"

Dangling from twin circles of light the thing lowered past the window, pressed its balloon tires into a bed of marigolds. Four men emerged, one propping himself boredly against the stubby fuselage while the other three headed toward the house. All were in plain clothes.

Meeting them at the door, Raven asked, "What's this? Is it something urgent?"

"I wouldn't know about that." The leader eyed him up and down. "Yes, you're Raven all right. Carson wants to talk to you." He signed toward the waiting machine. "We came in this drifter because it carries a security beam. You can speak to him direct from there."

"All right."

Climbing into the machine, Raven settled in its cubby hole, allowed the other to switch the beam for him.

Presently the screen livened, glowed, and Carson's features showed themselves in it.

"That was quick," he approved. "I've got ten patrols out for you and thought it might take them a week to locate you." Adjusting a control at his end, he made his image sharper. "What has happened, if anything?"

"Not much," Raven informed. "The opposition has made two fast passes at me. I've made two at them. Nobody has won a battle. At the moment we're sitting in our corners, sucking lemons, waiting for the bell and throwing ugly looks at each other."

Carson frowned. "That's your end of the poker. Ours is less comfortable. In fact right now it's white hot."

"How come?"

"The Baxter United plant went sky-high this A.M. The news is being kept off the spectroscreens for as long as we can."

His hands involuntarily tightening, Raven said. "Baxter's is a pretty big place, isn't it?"

"Big?" Carson's face quirked. "The overnight shift, which is their smallest, was just ending. That cut down the casualties to approximately four thousand."

"Great heavens!"

"It has the superficial appearance of an industrial disaster born of some accident," Carson went on, his tones harsh, "which means a heck of a lot because every such incident is an accident so far as we know. We can't tell otherwise unless a few traps are sprung."

"Were there any in this case?"

"Plenty. Dozens of them. The place has immense strategic value and was guarded accordingly. We're leery, see?"

"So—?"

"Ninety-five percent of our traps were blown to kingdom come. The few remaining were too damaged to function or recorded nothing of an incriminating nature. A score of patrols composed partly of telepaths and hypnos soared with the rubbish."

"No survivors?" Raven inquired.

"Not exactly. There were some eyewitnesses. You could hardly call them survivors since the nearest of them was a mile from the plant. They say there was a sharp tremor in the ground, a tremendous whump and the entire outfit rained around. There was plenty of force behind the blast. A two-hundred-ton shunting locomotive was tossed a thousand yards."

Raven said, "According to what you first told me, the enemy's technique has been one of crafty but effective sabotage carried out without spectacular loss of life, in fact with minimum bloodshed. After all, there are ties of common blood."

He studied the screen, went on, "But if in grim fact this is another of their jobs it means a considerable change of sentiment. They've now decided to rush us along by sheer ruthlessness."

"That is precisely what we fear," indorsed Carson. "Drunk on his own successes, some Venusian or Martian fanatic may have decided to run ahead of public opinion on his own world and force the issue by any means to hand. We can't stand for that!"

Nodding agreement, Raven glanced out of his cubby hole. The helicopter's crew were hanging around well out of earshot, talking, smoking, watching the sky. Far to the east something curved high above the horizon and vanished into the blue, leaving a thin vapor trail behind it. A space liner, outward bound.

"Why call me? Is there something special you want me to do?"

"No," said Carson. "Not any more than indirectly. What you do is mostly up to you. I've given you the information, let you see what it may mean." He emitted a sigh, rubbed his forehead wearily. "The Mars-Venus idea is to arrange natural looking misfortunes that gradually sap our power to the point where we've got to give in. But *real* misfortunes do occur from time to time even in the best regulated communities. Without evidence of some convincing sort we've no way of telling a real disaster from a manufactured one."

"Of course not."

"It's a strong temptation to blame the opposition for a major accident at which they may be as aghast as ourselves. On the other hand, if we *knew* they were responsible, and which individuals had done it, we'd hang them in dangling rows. Terran citizenship wouldn't save them. Murder remains murder any place in the cosmos."

"Would you prefer me to drop everything while I look into this?"

Carson's features sharpened. "Not by any means. Ending this senseless dispute somehow—if it can be ended—is more important than coping one at a time with its incidents. I'd rather you went straight ahead with whatever you've planned. But I also want you to make full use of any opportunity to dig up data on this blast. If you find anything, throw it to me as fast as you can." His jaw lumped, his eyes narrowed. "I'll then take action."

"All right. I'll keep my eyes open and my ears perked. You will get anything I happen to find." Regarding the other curiously, Raven asked, "Just what was this Baxter plant doing, anyway?"

"You would ask me that!"

"Something I shouldn't be told?"

"Well . . . well—" He hesitated, went on, "I know of no satisfactory reason why you shouldn't. If Heraty disapproves he'll have to get on with it. I don't see why operatives should wander around only half informed." He stared hard at the screen as if trying to view his listener's background. "Anyone close up or within hearing distance?"

"No."

"Then keep this strictly to yourself. Baxter's was within two months of completing a battery of one dozen new type engines employing an equally new and revolutionary fuel. A small pilot model ship fitted with such an engine, and under auto-control, did a return trip to the Asteroid Belt end of last year. Nothing has been said to the general public—yet."

"Meaning you're getting set for the Big Jump?" inquired Raven, strangely imperturbable about it.

"We *were.*" Carson displayed a touch of bitterness as he employed the past tense. "Four triple-engined jobs were going to be aimed at the Jovian system. Moreover, that was to be a tryout, a mere jaunt, only the beginning. If they made it without trouble—" He let the sentence hang unfinished.

"The farther planets? On to Pluto?"

"A jaunt," he repeated.

"Alpha Centauri?"

"Maybe farther still than there. It's much too early to estimate the limit, but it should be far away, very far." His attention concentrated more on the other. "You don't look particularly excited about it."

Offering no reason for this unnatural phlegmaticism, Raven asked, "This new fuel is highly explosive?"

"Definitely! That is what has got us all tangled up. It could be an accident despite every imaginable precaution."

"H'm!" He let it stew a moment, then said, "There's a skewboy around here, a Venusian named Kayder. He operates the Morning Star Trading Company. I'm going to chase him up."

"Got anything on him?"

"Only that he is reliably said to be on Terra for purposes other than trade. My informant seems to think he is Mister Big in this part of the battlefield."

"Kayder," repeated Carson, making notes on a pad not in view. "I'll check with Intelligence. Even though he's legally Terran they will have him on file as a native-born Venusian." He finished scribbling and looked up. "Okay. Make use of that copter if you need it. Is there anything else you want?"

"One fertile asteroid for my very own."

"When we've taken over a few hundreds of them I will reserve one for you," promised Carson, without smiling. "At the rate we're going it will be ready for occupation a hundred years after you're dead." His hand reached forward, made a twisting motion. The screen went blank.

For a short time Raven sat gazing at it absent-mindedly. Faint amusement lay over his lean, muscular features. A hundred years after you're dead, Carson had said. It was a date completely without meaning. A point in time that did not exist. There are those for whom the dark angel cannot come. There are those impervious to destruction at human hands.

"*Human* hands, David," broke in Leina's thought-stream coming from the house. "Remember that! Always remember that!"

"It is impossible to forget," he gave back.

"Perhaps not—but don't temporarily ignore the memory, either."

"Why not? There are two of us here: one to remember while the other is excusably preoccupied."

She did not respond. There was no weighty answer she could give. She shared with him a mutual function, willingly accepted, willingly faced. It must always be remembered, never mentioned.

Leina feared neither man nor beast, light or dark, life or death. Her anxieties stemmed from only one source: she was afraid of loneliness, the terrible, searing loneliness of one with an entire world to herself.

Struggling out of his cramped space, Raven stamped his feet around to ease his muscles, put Leina out of his mind. One does not attempt to soothe with sympathy a superior intelligence as powerful as one's own. He spoke to the pilot as the waiting four came up.

"Take me to this address. I'd like to get there soon after sundown."

Chapter 5

Kayder came home as twilight surrendered to darkness, dumped his sportster on the rear plot, watched two men stow it in its little hangar. They fastened the sliding door, joined him in walking to the back door of the house.

"Late again," he griped. "The cops are jumpy tonight. They're swarming all over the sky. I was stopped three times. Can I see your license, please? Can I see your pilot ticket? Can I see your certificate of air-worthiness?" He sniffed his contempt. "Wonder why they didn't demand a look at my birthmarks."

"Something must have happened," ventured one. "There's been nothing out of the ordinary on the spectroscreen, though."

"Seldom is," remarked the second. "Three weeks have gone by and still they've not admitted that raid on—"

"Sh-h-h!" Kayder jogged him with a heavy elbow. "How many times do I have to tell you to keep it buttoned?"

He paused on the step, key in hand, searched the rim of the sky in vain hope of glimpsing a white brilliance he rarely saw. It was an aimless habit for he knew it would not appear before early morning. On the opposite side, halfway to the zenith, a pink light shone. He ignored that one. An ally it might be but that was all. Kayder thought of Mars as an opportunist sphere which had had the sense to ride the Venusian bandwagon.

Unlocking the door, he went inside, warmed his hands at a thermic panel. "What's for dinner?"

"Venus duck with roasted tree almonds and—"

The door gongs clanged sonorously. Kayder shot a sharp look at the taller of the two.

"Who's that?"

The other's mind reached toward the front, came back. He said, "Fellow named David Raven."

Kayder sat down. "You sure of that?"

"It's what his mind says."

"What else does it say?"

"Nothing. Only that his name is David Raven. The rest is blank."

"Delay him a while then show him in."

Going to his huge desk, Kayder hurriedly pulled out a drawer, took from it a small ornamented box of Venusian bogwood. He flipped its lid upward. Beneath lay a thick pad of purplish leaves mixed with dry spike-shaped blossoms. Scattered lightly over the center of this pad was what appeared to be the merest pinch of common salt. He chirruped at the box. Promptly the tiny glistening grains moved, swirled around.

"He knows you're keeping him waiting and why," the tall man pointed out. With ill-concealed uneasiness he kept watch on the box. "He knows exactly what you're doing and what you have in mind to do. He can snatch all your thoughts straight out of your head."

"Let him. What can he do about it?" Kayder poked the box across the desk and nearer the facing chair. A few shining specks soared out of it, danced around the room. "You worry too much, Santil. You telepaths are all alike: obsessed by the fancied danger of open thoughts." He chirped again, giving his lips a peculiarly dexterous twist and somehow creating a ripple of nigh inaudible sounds between his front teeth. More living motes ascended, spun into invisibility. "Show him in."

Santil was glad to get out, his companion likewise. So far as they were concerned, when Kayder started playing around with his boxes the best place was elsewhere. All thoughts of Venus duck and roast tree almonds could be abandoned for the time being.

Their attitude gratified Kayder. It enhanced his sense of personal power. Superiority over pawns is a thing worth having, but to rise above those with redoubtable talents of their own is greatness indeed, His self-satisfied gaze swung slowly round the room, traveling from box to case to exotic vase to lacquered casket, some open, some closed, and he did not care who was reading his mind. A little green spider-thing stirred in its sleep in his right-hand pocket. He was the only man on Earth who had a nerveless, courageous, almost invincible army within sweep of his hand.

The professional smile of a trader welcoming big business suffused his heavy features as Raven came in. He pointed to a chair, was silent as he weighed up the black, glossy hair, the wide shoulders, narrow hips. Collar-ad model, he decided, except for those silver-flecked eyes. He did not like the latter feature, not one little bit. There was something about those eyes. They sort of looked too far, penetrated too deeply.

"They do," said Raven, without expression. "Very much so."

In no way disconcerted, Kayder gave back, "I'm not nervous, see? I've had too many mind-pickers around me too long. Sometimes I can't think up a smart crack without six of them snickering all over the place before I've had time to voice it." He favored the other with another swift, calculating once-over. "I've been looking for you."

"So nice of me to come. What's the motive?"

"I wanted to know what you've got." Kayder would much rather have stalled over that and offered something deceptive. But as he'd remarked he was accustomed to telepaths. When your mind is as wide open as a spectroscreen's Sunday colorstrips the only thing you can do is admit what is on it. "I'm led to believe you're extra-special."

Leaning forward, hands on knees, Raven asked, "Who led you?"

Kayder gave a grating laugh. "You want to know that when you can read it in my mind?"

"It isn't in your mind. Perhaps a hypno dutifully eliminates it for you every now and again as a safety measure. If so, something can be done about it. A stamp can be erased but not the impression underneath."

"For somebody extra-special you lag behind in the matter of wits," Kayder opined. He was always pleased to reduce the status of a telepath. "What a hypno can do, another and better hypno can undo. When I want to keep something right out of my skull I can find better and more effective ways."

"Such as?"

"Such as not taking it into my mind in the first place."

"Meaning you get your information from an unknown source?"

"Of course. I asked that it be kept from me. What I don't know I can't tell and nobody can lug it out of me against my will. The best mind-picker this side of Creation can't extract what isn't there,"

"An excellent precaution," approved Raven, peculiarly pleased with it. He swiped at something in mid-air, swiped again.

"Don't do that!" Kayder ordered, registering a deep scowl.

"Why not?"

"Those marsh nudges belong to me."

"That doesn't entitle them to whine around my ears, does it?" He smacked hands together, wiped out a couple of the near-invisible specks. The rest sheered away like a tiny dust cloud. "Besides, there are plenty more where these came from."

Kayder stood up, his face dark.

In harsh, threatening tones he said, "Those midges can do mighty unpleasant things to a man. They can make his legs swell until each one is thicker than his torso. The swelling creeps up. He becomes one immense elephantine bloat utterly incapable of locomotion."

Obviously deriving sadistic satisfaction from the power of his private army, he continued, "The swelling reaches the heart, at which point the victim expires somewhat noisily. But death does not halt the process. It goes on, makes the neck twice as wide as the head. Finally it blows up the head to a ghastly balloon with hairs scattered singly across its overstretched scalp. By that time the button eyes are sunk four to six inches deep." He stopped while he relished his own descriptive ability, then ended, "A midge victim is by far the most repulsive cadaver between here and Sirius."

"Interesting if melodramatic," commented Raven, cool and undisturbed. "How unpleasant to know I'm unlikely to be the subject of their attentions."

"What makes you think that?" Kayder beetled black brows at him.

"Several items. For example, what information are you going to get out of me when I'm bloated and buried?"

"None. But I won't need it when you're dead."

"An excusable error on your part, my friend. You would be surprised by how much vital information you lack but are going to acquire someday."

"What do you mean?"

"Never mind." Raven motioned it aside. "Sit down and compose yourself. Think of the consequences of bloating me. Nobody but a Venusian insectivocal could arrange such an end. So far as we know you're the only one on this planet."

"I am," admitted Kayder with some pride.

"That narrows the suspects, doesn't it? Terran Intelligence takes one look at the corpse and plants a finger straight on you. They call it murder. They've a penalty for that."

Observing the dust cloud, Kayder said meaningly, "*If* there is a body for Intelligence to brood over. What if there is not?"

"There won't be a body. I'll arrange for it to be disintegrated and thus tidy things up a bit."

"You will arrange it? We're talking about your corpse, not mine."

"We are talking about what is neither yours nor mine."

"You're way out in the blue," declared Kayder, feeling a horrible coldness on the back of his neck. "You're alone where the Moon shines." Bending forward, he pressed a button on his desk, meanwhile eyeing the other as one would watch a suspected lunatic.

Santil opened the door, edged partway through. His entry was reluctant and represented the minimum necessary to answer the summons.

"Have you heard anything?" Kayder demanded.

"No."

"Have you been trying?"

"It was no use. I can overhear only your mind. He can talk and think and feel around while his own mind pretends it's a vacuum. That's more than I can do, more than any telepath I ever met could do."

"All right. You may go." Kayder waited until the door closed. "So you're a new kind of mind-probe, a sort of armor plated telepath, One who can pick without being picked. That confirms what Grayson told me."

"Grayson?" echoed Raven. He shrugged. "He who is only half informed is ill informed."

"That goes for you too!"

"Of course it does. I've plenty to learn." Idly he swung a foot to and fro, studying it with a bored air, then said with casual unexpectedness, "I'd like to learn who organized the Baxter blowup."

"Huh?"

"They suffered a big blast this morning. It was bad, really bad."

"Well, what's that to me?"

"Nothing," Raven admitted, deeply disappointed.

There was good cause for his discontent. A rush of thoughts had poured through Kayder's mind in four seconds flat, and he had perceived every one of them.

A big blowup at Baxter's? Where do I come in? What is he getting at? Putting that huge dump out of action would be rather a masterstroke but we haven't got round to it yet. I wonder whether higher-ups back home have started arranging special jobs without reference to me. No, they wouldn't do that. Besides, there's no point in duplicating organizations and keeping one hidden from the other.

But he suspects me of knowing something about this. Why? Has some false clue led him this way? Or could it be that those itchy Martians have begun to pull fast ones of their own in such a way that we get saddled with the blame? I wouldn't put it beyond them. I don't trust the Martians overmuch.

Raven ended his train of thought by opining, "I doubt whether you trust anyone or anything except, perhaps, these bugs of yours." His attention went to the still swirling cloud. He seemed to have no trouble in distinguishing and identifying every microscopic creature within it. The unflinching gaze roamed on, examining boxes, cases, vases, caskets, estimating the relative powers of their contents, sitting in judgment upon each. "And someday even those will let you down if only because bugs must always be bugs."

"When you talk about insects you're talking to an authority," growled Kayder. He glowered straight ahead. "You've read all my thoughts. I can't blank them out like a telepath and therefore they've been wide open to you. So you know that this Baxter affair is no business of mine. I had nothing whatever to do with it."

"I concede it willingly. No hypno wiped it off your mental slate else you wouldn't have been so confused and frankly speculative about it." He pulled thoughtfully at one ear. "An hour ago I'd have betted heavily that you were the guilty party. I'd have lost. Thanks for saving my money."

"You must need it. How much did you pay Steen?"

"Nothing. Not a button."

"Do you expect me to believe that?"

"Like everyone else, Steen can stand only so much," Raven informed. "Time comes when a man is called upon to put up with more than he can stomach. Either he runs out while the going is good or he stands fast until he cracks. You'd better write Steen off as a case of battle fatigue."

"He'll be dealt with in due course," promised Kayder, lending it menace. "What did you do to Haller?"

"Not so much. Trouble with him is that he's overeager and trying to summon up some gumption. He'll be dead pretty soon."

"I'm told his brain is—" Kayder's voice drifted away, came back on a higher note. "Did you say *dead?*"

"Yes." Raven studied him with cold amusement. "What's wrong with that? We all die eventually. You'll be dead someday. Furthermore, it's only a couple of minutes since you yourself were openly gloating over what I'd look like after your bugs had been to work on me. You enjoyed death then!"

"I can enjoy it right now," Kayder retorted, his blood-pressure shooting upward. His thin, mobile lips took on a queer twist.

The telephone yelped on his desk as if in protest of what was in his mind. For a moment he gaped at the instrument in the manner of one who had forgotten its existence. Then he grabbed it.

"Well?"

It chattered metallically against his ear while a series of expressions chased across his features. Finally he racked it, leaned back in his seat, wiped his forehead.

"Haller has done it."

Raven shrugged with a callousness that appalled the other.

"They say," continued Kayder, "that he babbled a lot of crazy stuff about bright-eyed moths flying through the dark. Then he put himself down for keeps."

"Was he married?"

"No."

"Then it's of little consequence." Raven dismissed it like a minor incident unworthy of a moment's regret. "It was to be expected. He was overeager, like I told you."

"What do you mean by that?"

"Never mind. It's too early. You're not yet old enough to be told." Standing up he seemed to tower over the other. His right hand contemptuously brushed the dust cloud away. "All I will tell you is this: in the same circumstances you would sit in front of me and joyfully cut your own throat from ear to ear, laughing as you did it."

"Like heck I would!"

"Yes, like heck you *would!*"

Kayder pointed an authoritative finger. "See here, we've met each other. We kidded ourselves we were going to take each other and we've found it's not worth the bother. You've got nothing out of me, nothing. I've got all I want out of you, which is that as something super-super you bear a strong resemblance to a flat tire. There's the way out."

"Think as you please." Raven's smile was irritating. "What I hoped to get out of you was the identity of a traitor and perhaps, something on this Baxter case. Intelligence can deal with anything else."

"Bah!" Laying a hand palm upward on his desk, Kayder emitted inviting chirrups. Whirling motes descended and settled over his fingers. "Terran Intelligence has mooched behind me for months. I'm so used to their company I'd feel lost without them. They'll have to produce a better hypno than any we have got before they can arrange some effective unblanking." Tipping his hand over the box he watched the midges pour down like powder. "Just to show you how little I care I don't mind telling you they've every reason to try to nail me down. So what? I'm a Terran engaged in legitimate business and nothing can be proved against me."

"Not yet," qualified Raven, going to the door. "But remember those bright-eyed moths that Haller mentioned. They should have an especial interest for you as an insectivocal—even though the laugh is on you!" He went out, glanced through the open door and finished by way of afterthought, "Thanks for all that stuff on your underground base."

"What?" Kayder dropped the box, midges and all.

"Don't reproach yourself or the hypno who expunges it from your mind every time you leave the base. He made a good, thorough job of it. There wasn't a trace." The door swung to, the click of its lock sounding right on top of his concluding remark, "But it made a beautifully detailed picture in friend Santil's mind."

Diving a hand under his desk, Kayder pulled out a mike, switched it on. His hand trembled and his voice was hoarse. Veins of fury stood out on his forehead.

"Get on the jump and shoot this around: an Intelligence raid is due shortly. Number one cover-up plan to operate at once. Number two plan to be prepared in readiness." His angry glare was directed toward the door as he went on, knowing full well that the escapee must still be near enough to pick up every word. "David Raven is now on the run from this address. Trip him up on sight. Put him out of business any way you can. That's top priority—get Raven!"

The door opened and Santil came in saying, "Look, he caught me napping in a way I—"

"Idiot!" interjected Kayder, bristling at the sight of him: "You telepaths kid yourselves you're superior examples of Nature's handiwork. Pfah! Thank the fates I'm not one myself. Of all the mentally gabby dopes you represent the lowest limit!"

"He was blank, see?" protested Santil, flushing. "When you're born and bred a telepath you can't help being conditioned by it. I forgot this fellow could still feel around while mentally deader than a dead dog and accidentally let slip a thought. He snatched it so quickly I didn't realize he had it until he spoke just now."

"You forgot," jibed Kayder. "It's top of the list of famous last words, 'I forgot.'" His irate features became darker. His gaze shifted to a large, mesh-covered box standing in one corner. "If those jungle hornets were able to recognize individuals I'd send them after him. No matter how far he's gone they'd reach him and strip him down to his skeleton before he could utter a squeak."

Keeping his attention away from the box, Santil said nothing.

"You've got a mind or what passes for one," Kayder went on, acid-toned, slightly vicious. "Come on, use it! Tell me where he is now."

"I can't. He's blank like I said."

"So are you—blanker than a stone wall." He picked up the telephone, dialed, waited a while. "You, Dean? Put those emergency pips on the air. Yes, I want to speak to the-man-we-don't-know. If he phones back tell him Raven's likely to put the finger on local base. I want him to use his influence either to postpone or minimize a raid." Racking the instrument, he pondered irefully, meanwhile plucking at his bottom lip and releasing it with little plopping sounds.

"He's got good range. Ten to one he overheard you," Santil pointed out.

"That is taken for granted. Lot of good may it do him when we don't know ourselves whom we're talking to."

The phone shrilled again.

"This is Murray," announced a voice at the other end. "You sent me to dig up stuff on this Raven."

"What have you got?"

"Not so much. I'd say the Terrans are becoming desperate, scouring the planet and making wild guesses."

"Take care not to make a few of your own," Kayder snapped. "Heraty, Carson and the others are no fools even if they have got a ball and chain shackled to each leg. Give me what you've got and leave the guessing to be done at this end of the line."

"His father was a pilot on the Mars run, an exceptionally efficient telepath coming from four telepathic generations. There was no mixing of talents maritally speaking until Raven's parents met."

"Go on."

"The mother was a radiosensitive with an ancestry of radiosensitives plus one supersonic. According to Professor Hartman, the product of such a union would most likely inherit only the dominant talent. It's remotely possible that the off-spring—meaning Raven—might be telepathically receptive across an abnormally wide band."

"He's wrong there. This skewboy can pull others in even while he's holding them off."

"I wouldn't know about that," Murray evaded. "I'm no professional geneticist. I'm only telling you what Hartman says."

"Never mind. Let's have the rest."

"Raven followed in his father's footsteps to a limited extent. He got his Mars-pilot certificate and thus holds the space rank of captain. That's as far as he went. Though fully qualified he hasn't worked at it. He's never taken a ship Marsward. Having acquired his rank he appears to have done little more than mooch aimlessly around this planet until Carson hauled him in."

"H'm! That's strange!" Kayder's brows became corrugated with thought. "Any reason that you could discover?"

"Maybe he feels that his health won't stand for any Mars trips," hazarded Murray. "Not since he was killed."

"Eh?" His back hairs stiffening, Kayder urged, "Say that again."

"He was at the spaceport ten years ago when the old *Rimfire* exploded like a bomb. It wrecked the control tower and did some slaughter. Remember?"

"Yes, I saw it on the spectroscreen."

"Raven was picked up with the other bodies. Definitely he was one of the dear departed. Some young doc played with the corpse just on whim. He lifted splintered ribs, injected adrenaline, shoved the head into an oxygen auto-breather and massaged the heart. He brought him back from wherever he'd gone. It was one of those rare returned-from-the-grave cases. Murray paused, added, "Since then I reckon he's lost his nerve."

"Nothing more?"

"Is all."

Racking the phone. Kayder lay back, stared at Santil. "Lost his nerve. Bunkum! From what I saw of him he never had any to lose in the first place."

"Who says he lost it?" Santil inquired.

"Shut up and let me think." The spider-thing crept out of his pocket, blinked around. Putting it on the desk, he let it play with his finger-tip while he mused aloud.

"Raven had a weirdly inhuman attitude toward death. He guessed Haller would do the dutch about ten minutes before it happened. That's because it takes one nut to recognize another."

"Maybe you're right."

"It suggests that his own extremely narrow escape has left him queer in the head. He regards death as something to be despised rather than feared because he has defied it once and argues that he can do it again and again." His attention transferred from the spider to Santil. "Raven's death data is so unusual that he makes loony computations upon it. You see what it means?"

"What?" asked Santil, uneasily.

"Unlimited, foolhardy, crackpot courage. He's a better-than-average telepath with the mental attitude of a religious fanatic. One taste of death has killed his fear of it. He's likely to try anything that strikes his fancy at any given moment. That makes him totally unpredictable. Doubtless Carson is counting on precisely those factors: a high-grade adept who thinks nothing of rushing in where angels fear to tread—as he did right here."

"I expected he'd be a lot more than that," Santil ventured.

"So did I. Goes to show that the farther a rumor is passed along the more it becomes exaggerated. I have the measure of him now. Give him enough rope and he'll hang himself."

"Meaning—?"

"Meaning it's always the onrushing, headstrong animals that fall into the pit." He tickled the spider-thing under its crinkled belly. "He is the kind that runs out of one trap straight into another. All we need do is bide our time and wait for him to drop down a hole."

Something went *pip-pip-pip* under the floor. Pulling open a drawer he took from it another and smaller telephone.

"Kayder."

"Ardern here. The raid is on."

"How's it going?"

"Hah! It would give you a big laugh. The hypnos are weighing and bagging tree almonds; the mini-engineers are assembling ladies watches; the teleports are printing news-from-Venus sheets and everyone's acting like they're being good at school. The entire place is happy, peaceful, innocent."

"Got the blanking done in time?"

"Most of it. Six weren't treated when Intelligence burst in. We smuggled them out through the chute. They got away all right."

"Good," said Kayder, with satisfaction.

"That's not all. You've put out an urgent call for a smoothie named David Raven? Well, we've pinned him down."

Kayder sucked in his breath with a low hiss that made the spider jump. He soothed it with a finger.

"How did you manage to find him?"

"No trouble at all. Metaphorically speaking, he walked into the cage, locked the door on himself, hung his identity card on the bars and yelled for us to come look at him." His chuckle sounded hearty over the wires. "He has stitched himself up in a sack and consigned himself to us."

"I'm too leery of him to see it that way. There's something funny going on. I'm going to check on it myself. Expect me around in ten minutes."

Hiding the phone and closing its drawer, he ignored Santil and the spider-thing while he stared introspectively at the desk. For some reason he could not identify he felt apprehensive. And for some other reason equally dodgy his mind kept returning to the notion of bright-eyed moths that glide through the dark.

Brilliant, glowing, soaring through the endless dark.

Chapter 6

Kayder made it in seven minutes. The unpretentious house to which he went was the terminal of the secret chute from underground base. This was where the half dozen unblanked escapees from the Intelligence raid had emerged, taken to the streets and gone their several innocent ways.

The man waiting for him was small, thin and had features permanently yellowed by past spells of Venusian valley fever. He was a Type Two Mutant, a floater with a bad limp acquired in his youth when once he overdid the altitude and exhausted his mental power while coming down.

"Well?" demanded Kayder, staring expectantly round the room.

"Raven's aboard the *Fantôme*," informed Ardern.

Kayder's ire started to rise with characteristic ease. "What d'you mean by giving me that stuff about having him caged with his card on the bars?"

"So he is," insisted Ardern, unabashed. "As you well know, the *Fantôme* is a homeward boat about to blow for Venus."

"With a Terran crew. All spaceship crews are Terrans."

"What of it? Neither he nor they can get up to any tricks in mid-space. They've got to land. This Raven will then be on our own planet, among our own millions, and subject to our own local authority. What more could you want?"

"I wanted him to deal with myself." Going to the window, Kayder mooned through the dark at a string of green lights marking the distant spaceport where the *Fantôme* rested.

Ardern limped across, joined him. "I was by the gangway when this fellow came from the copter as if he'd only ten seconds to spare. He gave the checker his name as David Raven and claimed a cabin. I thought to myself, 'That's the guy Kayder's screaming for,' whereupon he turned, grinned at me like an alligator grinning at a naked swimmer and said, 'You're dead right, my boy!' " He shrugged, finished, "So, of course, I made a dash for the nearest phone and told you."

"He's got enough bare-faced impudence to serve a dozen," Kayder growled. "Does he think he's invincible or something?" He paced rapidly to and fro, afflicted with indecision. "I could dump a box of bugs on that boat but what's the use? My little soldiers don't know one individual from another unless one can talk to them."

"And you don't have much chance to get aboard, anyway," Ardern pointed out. "The *Fantôme* is due to lift in the next five minutes."

"Who's on her that we know?"

"It's too late to get a complete passenger list. She carries some three hundred, not counting the crew. Part of them will be Terrans, the rest plain, ordinary Venusians and Martians incapable of doing or thinking anything not connected with trade." Ardern mused it a moment. "Pity we can't search the lot and pick out the few skewboys. The only ones I know are twelve of our own men returning for fourth-year leave."

"What types are they?"

"Ten mini-engineers and two teleports."

"An ideal combination of talent to send a pinhead explorer through his keyhole and smear him across his bed," said Kayder with much sarcasm. "Bah! He'd read their every intention the moment it jelled and be twenty jumps ahead of them all the way."

"He has to sleep," Ardern volunteered.

"How do we know that? Nocturnals never sleep and maybe he doesn't either."

"Tell you what, there's still radio contact so let's get those twelve to search the ship for a homeward-bound telepath. They could then enlist his help."

"No good," scoffed Kayder, waving it aside. "Raven can make his mind feel like a lump of marble. If a telepath made a pass at him through the cabin door and got a complete blank, how could he tell whether Raven was awake or asleep? And how could he tell whether or not his own bumps were being felt?"

"I reckon he couldn't," Ardern admitted, frowning.

"Some mutational aptitudes give me the gripes." Kayder returned his attention to the far-off lights. "Now and again I get fed up with our so-called array of superior talent. Bugs are best. Nobody can pick a bug's mind. Nobody can hypnotize a bug. But bugs obey those they love and that's that. Let me tell you it's plenty."

"I once saw a pyrotic burn a thousand of them."

"Did you now? And what happened afterward?"

"Ten thousand came and ate him."

"There you are," said Kayder, feeding his own ego. "Bugs—you can't beat them!"

He meandered to and fro, pausing now and again to scowl at the lights, then said, "Nothing for it but to pass the buck."

"How d'you mean?" asked Ardern.

"We'll let them handle him at the other end. If an entire world can't cope with one not-so-hot skewboy we might as well give in right now."

"That's what I told you in the first place. He's caged himself."

"Maybe he has and maybe he hasn't. I'm sitting on *his* world and I'm not caged, am I?"

The faraway lights were suddenly outshone by a vivid shaft of intense white fire that crawled upward from ground level and increased speed until eventually it was spearing into the heavens. Soon after came a deep roaring that made the windows rattle. Darkness swamped back and the green lights reappeared, by contrast seeming dimmer than before.

Ardern screwed up his yellowish face, looked bothered. "I had to leave the gangway to go to the phone—"

"And so—?"

"How do we know he's actually on that boat? He's had all the time in the world to walk off it again. That cabin booking could have been an act to send us snuffling along the wrong trail."

"Could be." Kayder didn't like it. "He's artful enough to try something like that. But we can check up. Are those snoops out of the base yet?"

"I'll see." Ardern flipped a tiny wall switch, spoke into the aperture above it. "Those intelligence characters still messing around?"

"They've just gone."

"Swell, Philby. I'm coming along with Kayder to—"

"Don't know what's so fine about it," interrupted Philby. "They took eight of our men with them."

"Eight? What the devil for?"

"Further questioning."

"Were those eight thoroughly blanked?" Kayder chipped in.

"You bet they were!"

"Then why worry? We're coming to use the short-wave transmitter so get it warmed up."

Reversing the wall switch, Ardern said, "First time they've dragged people away for questioning. I don't like it. Do you suppose they've found a way to break mental blocks?"

"Then why didn't they seize the entire bunch and come after you and me as well?" Kayder made a gesture of disdain. "It's a gag designed to show they're earning their keep. Come on, let's deal with a thing at a time and get in touch with the *Fantôme.*"

The receiver's big screen cleared, showed the features of a swarthy individual with a chest-mike hanging from his neck. The *Fantôme's* operator.

"Quick. Ardern, give me that list of names of our men." Kayder took it, licked his lips in readiness to begin.

"Name, please?" requested the operator, looking at him.

"Arthur Kayder. I want to talk to—"

"Kayder?" put in the operator. His face grew momentarily fuzzy as the screen clouded with static. Long streaks whirled diagonally across the fluorescent surface and were followed by other erratic patterns. Then it cleared once more. "We have a passenger waiting to speak to you. He was expecting your call."

"Hah!" commented Ardern, nudging Kayder. "One of our men has got him marked."

Before Kayder could reply, the operator bent forward, adjusted something not in view. His face flashed off the screen and another one replaced it. The newcomer was Raven.

"Could you learn to love me, Louse-ridden?" he inquired.

"You!" Kayder glowered at him.

"Me in person. I guessed you'd check up when the boat lifted but you were slow, very slow. Tsk-tsk!" He shook his head in solemn reproof. "I've been waiting your call. As you can see for yourself I am really and truly on board."

"You'll be sorry," Kayder promised.

"Meaning when I reach the other end? I know that your next move will be to tell them I'm coming. You'll get on the interplanetary beam and warn a world. I can't help but find it most flattering."

"The word will prove to be *flattening,*" said Kayder, with unconcealed menace.

"That remains to be seen. I'd rather live in hope than die in despair."

"The one will be followed by the other whether you like it or not."

"I doubt it, Bugsy, because—"

"Don't call me Bugsy!" Kayder shouted, his broad features dark red.

"Temper, temper!" Raven chided. "If your looks could kill I'd drop dead right now."

"You're going to do it anyway," Kayder bawled, now completely beside himself. "And as soon as it can be arranged. *I'll* see to that!"

"Sweet of you to say so. Public confession is so good for the soul." Raven eyed him calculatingly and added, "Better put your affairs in order as quickly as you can. You may be away quite a spell."

He switched off, giving the furious Kayder no opportunity for further retort. His features vanished from the screen. The operator came back.

"Do you want someone else, Mr. Kayder?"

"No—it doesn't matter now." Immobilizing the transmitter with a savage flip of the thumb, he turned to Ardern. "What did he mean about me being away quite a spell? I don't get it."

"Me neither."

For some time they stood stewing the problem, feeling inwardly bothered, until Philby came along and said, "There's a call waiting from you-don't-know-who."

Kayder took the phone, listened.

The familiar but unknown voice rasped, "I've more than enough on my plate without taking unnecessary risks to cover up loud-mouthed blabs."

"Eh?" Kayder blinked at the instrument.

"It's like getting down on one's knees and begging for a kick in the rear to utter homicidal threats over an open transmission system with half the Intelligence listening in," continued the voice, acid-toned. "Under Terran law the penalty is five to seven years in the jug. They can pin it on you beyond my power to unpin."

"But—"

"You're a choleric character and he knew it. You let him bait you into shouting illegal intentions all over the ether. You brainless cretin!" A pause, then, "I can't cover you without giving myself away. There's nothing you can do but get out fast. Take the boxes and burn them, contents and all. Then bury yourself until somehow we can smuggle you home."

"How am I going to manage that?" asked Kayder, feeling futile.

"It's your worry. Get out of that base—you mustn't be found there. And be careful about visiting your house for those boxes. They may have a guard on the place already. If you can't collect your stuff in the next hour you'll have to abandon it."

"But my army is there. With them I could—"

"You could do nothing," contradicted the voice, sharply. "Because you won't be given the chance. Don't stand there arguing with me. Get out of sight and lie low. We'll try to put you on a boat after the hue and cry has died down."

"I can fight the charge," Kayder pleaded. "I can say it was no more than meaningless abuse."

"Look," came back the voice wearily, "the Intelligence Service *wants* to tie you down. They've been seeking a pretext for months. Nothing can save you now except Raven's own evidence that he knew you were ribbing—and you won't get *that*. Now shut up and make yourself hard to find."

The other went off the line. Lugubriously Kayder cradled the phone, felt lost for suitable comment.

"What's the matter?" asked Ardern, watching him.

"They're going to try to lug me in for five to seven years."

"Why? What for?"

"Threatening murder."

"Holy smoke!" Ardern backed away, limping as he went. "'They can do it too if they set their minds to it." His face became strained with mental effort, his body appeared to lengthen itself slightly, then his feet left the ground and he soared slowly toward a ceiling shaft. "I'm going while there's still time. I don't know you. You're a complete stranger to me." He drifted up the shaft.

Kayder went out, surveyed his house from a vantage point, found it already covered. He walked the streets and back alleys until two in the morning, thought bitterly of those potent boxes lying in the back room of his home. Without them he was no better than any ordinary pawn. How could he reach them undetected? From how far beyond a ring of guards can one throw a stream of unhearable chirrups?

He was slinking cautiously along the darkest side of a square when four men came out of a black archway, barred his path.

One of them, a telepath, spoke with authoritative assurance. "You're Arthur Kayder. We want you!"

It was useless to dispute a mind-probe, useless to battle against odds of four. He went with them surlily but quietly, still thinking of his precious boxes, still convinced that bugs are best.

Chapter 7

The great crawling mists of Venus lay thick and yellow over the forepeak ports when Raven went into the main cabin for a look at the radar screen. A glistening serration across the fluorescent rectangle marked the huge range of the Sawtooth Mountains. Beyond these lay the rain forests that covered shelf after shelf down to the wide, lush plains on which mankind had established its strongest footholds.

A constant shuddering went through the entire length of the *Fantôme* as its great power plants strove to cope with their most difficult task: the relatively slow maneuvering of a giant designed for superfast motion. It was not easy. It was never easy.

Far below, hidden deep in the greenery of the rain forests, lay four crushed cylinders that once had been ships. At this moment the sole purpose of the *Fantôme's* crew was to ensure that the number did not become five.

All passengers likewise recognized that this was the critical stage of their journey. The inveterate card players became tense and still. The chatterers were silent. The *tambar* drinkers sobered up. All eyes were on the radar screen, watching jaws of rock widen and grow larger as all too sluggishly the ship lowered past them.

In a flat, unemotional voice an officer in the pointed forepeak was reciting over the loudspeaker system, "One forty thousand, one thirty-five, one thirty thousand."

Not sharing the general anxiety, Raven studied the screen and bided his time. The mountains passed center, moved toward the screen's base, slid completely off it. Somebody sighed with relief.

Presently the oval edge of the great plain revealed itself, became clearer, more detailed, streaked with broad rivers. Vibration was now violent as the ship fought to hold its tonnage in near-balance with the planet's gravitational field.

"Twenty thousand. Nineteen five hundred."

Raven arose from his seat and left the cabin, several startled glances following his unusual action. Walking rapidly along a metal corridor he reached the fore starboard airlock. This, he decided, was as good a time as any. The crew had their hands full, their minds completely occupied. The passengers were concerned with the safety of their own skins.

Although long accustomed to humanity's absorbed interest in self-preservation he still found the tendency amusing. So far as they were concerned, it was a case of ignorance being woe. Now if only they were better informed . . .

He was smiling to himself as he operated the automatic door, stepped into the lock, closed it behind him. That action would light a crimson telltale in the control room, set an alarm ringing, and someone would hotfoot along to see who was fooling with the exit facilities at this touchy stage. No matter. Any irate official would be at least half a minute too late.

The lock's own little speaker was muttering in sympathy with its fellows scattered throughout the ship. "Fourteen thousand, thirteen five hundred, thirteen, twelve five hundred."

Swiftly he released the seals of the outer door, unwound it, opened it wide. None of the vessel's air poured out but some higher pressure Venusian atmosphere pushed in, bringing with it a warmth, dampness and strong odors of mass vegetation.

Somebody started hammering and kicking upon the airlock's inner door, doing it with the outraged vigor of authority successfully defied. At the same time the loudspeaker clicked, changed voices and bawled with much vehemence.

"You in Airlock Four, close that outer door and open the inner. You are warned that operation of the locks by any unauthorized person is a serious offense punishable by—"

Waving a sardonic goodby to the loudspeaker. Raven leaped out. He plunged headlong into thick, moist air, fell with many twists and turns. At one instant the *Fantôme* was a long, black cylinder flaming high above him; at the next there was a whirling world of trees and rivers rushing up to meet him.

If anyone on the ship were quick enough with binoculars, he would derive much food for thought from the figure's sprawling, tumbling, apparently uncontrolled descent. Conventionally, only two kinds of people jumped out of space-ships: suicides and fugitive floaters. The latter invariably used their supernormal power to drift down at safe and easy pace. Only the suicides fell like stones. Only two kinds of people jump out of spaceships—and it was inconceivable that there could be any who were not exactly people!

The drop took longer than it would have on Earth. One falls with regular acceleration only until effectively braked by mounting air-pressure, and here the cloying atmosphere soon piled up before a moving object.

By the time he was four hundred feet above the treetops the *Fantôme* had reduced to a foreshortened, pencil-sized vessel about to land just over the horizon. It was impossible for anyone aboard to witness his fate. At that point Raven slowed in mid-air.

This braking was a curious phenomenon having nothing in common with the taut-faced, mind-straining deceleration of an accomplished levitator. The sudden reduction of his rate of fall occurred casually, naturally, much in the manner of a dropping spider that changes its mind and pays out its line less rapidly.

At treetop height, still three hundred and fifty feet above ground, he was descending as if dangling from an invisible parachute. Between enormous top branches as thick as the trunks of adult Earth-trees he went down like a drifting leaf, hit ground with enough force to leave heel marks in the coarse turf.

This point was little more than a mile from the rim of the great plain. The gigantic trees were thinned out here, growing widely apart with quiet, cathedral-like glades between them. Fifty or sixty miles westward the real Venusian jungle began, and with it the multitudinous bad-dream forms of ferocity that only lately had learned to keep their distance from the even deadlier form called Man.

He was not at all worried about the possible appearance of a stray member of this planet's thousand and one killers. Neither had he any apprehension about more efficient huntsmen of his own biped shape despite their being after him in full cry soon.

The news of his jump would gall whatever deputation might be waiting for him at the spaceport. But it would not fool them for a moment. Kayder's message—assuming that they had received it—would tag him as a telepathic oddity to whom Terran characters like Heraty and Carson attached greater importance than apparently deserved. From that they'd deduce that whatever warranted this importance had been missed by Kayder and had yet to be discovered.

Now they'd face the fact that he had left the ship in the manner of a levitator but had not gone down like a levitator. Without hesitation they'd now accept the existence of some new and previously unsuspected quasi-levitatory talent and, adding that to what they'd already got, classify him as the first example of a creature often postulated and mightily feared: the multi-talented offspring of mixed mutants.

Sitting on a lump of emerald bark three feet thick, he smiled to himself as if at a secret joke. A multi-talented sample of mutational posterity. No such individual had ever been discovered though humanity kept constant watch on three worlds for such a one. Genetically there was excellent reason to believe that no such a person ever would be found or could exist as a viable strain.

For reasons peculiarly her own, Nature had long ordained that the children of mixed mutant unions inherited only the dominant talent if any at all. The subordinate aptitude invariably disappeared. Often the dominant one would skip a generation, in which case the skipped generation consisted of mere pawns.

The notion of a super-telepathic super-levitator was patently absurd—but the opposition would swallow the absurdity when it came along in the guise of a self-evident fact. There would be considerable boosting of blood pressure in the hidden Venusian hierarchy when they learned that the first act of Earth's new chess piece was to abolish a natural law. They would want him badly and quickly, before he started playing hob with other man-made laws esteemed for making cash profits or personal power.

The thought of this gratified him. To date he had achieved nothing spectacular by the standards of the day and age. That was good because it was highly undesirable to be too spectacular. Such was the gist of Leina's case against interfering, the basis of her disapproval of the part he'd chosen to play: that at all times one should be unobtrusive, unnoticed and not be tempted to interfere.

But at least he'd created considerable uneasiness in the ranks of the formerly over-confident enemy. Indeed, if they had bolted this multi-talent mutant notion and speculated on the dire possibility of still more formidable types yet to come, they would have every reason to feel afraid. And their fears would divert them from the truth, the truth they must never know lest others pick it out of their minds.

It was a pity they could not be told the truth—but there are facts of life not told to the immature.

No natural laws had been or could be abolished.

A supernatural phenomenon is one that accords with laws not yet known or identified.

There were no multi-talented humans.

There were only bright-eyed moths that swoop and soar through endless reaches of the eternal dark.

He sent out a powerful, tight-beamed mind-call far above the normal telepathic band. "Charles!"

"Yes, David?" It came back promptly, showing that the other had been expecting the summons. The incoming mental impulses impinged on twin receiving centers and proved slightly out of phase.

Raven turned to face the sender's direction as instinctively as one pawn would turn to look at another.

"I dived out of the ship. Doubt whether it was necessary but thought I'd play safe."

"Yes, I know," gave back the distant mind. "Mavis got a call from Leina. As usual they gabbled an hour about personal matters before Leina remembered she'd come through to tell us you were in the *Fantôme*. It seems she'd sooner you had kept to your proper job."

"Females remain females throughout the whole of eternity," Raven offered.

"So I went to the spaceport," continued Charles, "and I'm outside it right now. Can't get in because it's barred to the public and heavily guarded. Frustrated pawns who've come to meet the passengers are hanging around in clusters, biting their nails and swapping baseless rumors. The ship is down and a lot of bellicose officials are behaving as if someone's just swiped their pay checks."

"'Fraid I'm to blame for that."

"Why come on a ship, anyway?" asked Charles. "If for some mysterious reason you had to do it the slow way couldn't you have inflated a small balloon and drifted here?"

"Occasionally there are considerations more important than speed," answered Raven, seeing nothing nonsensical in the question. "For instance, I'm wearing a body."

"It's precisely your body they'll be hunting. It's a giveaway."

"Perhaps so, but it's what I want them to seek. Hunting for a nice human-looking body will stop them getting other ideas."

"You know best," Charles conceded. "You're coming to our place I take it?"

"Of course. I called to make sure you'd be there."

"We will. See you shortly, eh?"

"I'm starting right now."

Forthwith he set off through the shadowy glades toward the plain, striding swiftly along and keeping watch more with his mind than with his eyes. It was always possible to hear things lurking unseen. They could not spy on him without radiating even their rudimentary thoughts. Such as that pair of screech owls glowering in a dark hole two hundred feet up a tremendous tree trunk.

"Man-thing below! *Aaaargsh!*"

At the fringe of the trees came first evidence of the hunt. He stood in the darkness close by a mighty bole while a copter floated over the green umbrella of top branches. It was a big machine held up by four multi-bladed rotors and bearing a crew of ten. Their minds could be counted as they tried to probe the maze beneath.

There were a half a dozen telepaths listening, listening, eager to catch any stray mental impulse he might be careless enough to let go loose. Also one insectivocal cuddling a cage of flying tiger-ants to be tipped over any likely spot indicated by a telepath.

The relief pilot was a nocturnal content to do nothing but wait his turn should the search continue after dark. The remaining pair consisted of a hypno steadily cursing Raven for taking him away from a profitable game of jimbo-jimbo, and a flap-eared supersonic straining to catch the thin whistle of the radium chronometer which the quarry was wrongly assumed to possess.

The menagerie of mutants passed right above and zigzagged onward unaware of his existence immediately under them. A similarly composed outfit was scouring a wide path on a roughly parallel course two miles to the south, and yet another two miles northward.

He let them get well behind him before he stepped into the open, followed the outskirts of the trees until he struck a broad dirt road. Once upon the highway he behaved less warily.

These flying search parties might be made up of exceptionally gifted humans far above pawn standard, but they still tended to fall into pawn errors. They took it for granted that anyone boldly strolling in plain sight, along a road, could have nothing to hide. In any event, if one of them did see fit to display excess of zeal and swoop over him for a pry into his cranium, he'd give them a boring selection of dunderhead pawn thoughts. What's for dinner? If I'm given fried slime-fish again I'll go crazy!

There remained the risk, albeit a slight one, that a clear pictorial record of his features might be in circulation and a hunter might drop low enough to identify him visually.

But nobody showed above-average curiosity until he came within short distance of Plain City. At that point a copter drifted overhead and he felt four minds spiking simultaneously into his own. For their pains he rewarded them with pictures of a sordid domestic wrangle in a squalid home. He could almost hear them snort with contempt as they withdrew their mental probes, whirled their rotors faster and sped toward the rain forest.

At the city's edge he stepped off the road and made way for a ponderous tractor dragging a steel-barred trailer. Two hypnos and one teleport were in charge of this belated addition to the chase, chief feature of which consisted of a score of drooling tree-cats in the trailer. These could follow a spoor one week old and literally sprint up the trunk of any forest giant not smothered in spikes.

As became a pawn he chewed a piece of purplish grass and stared with dull-eyed curiosity as this lot creaked and rumbled past. The minds of the whole bunch were like open books. One of the hypnos was nursing a *tambar* hangover, the other missing a night's sleep and frequently pinching himself to keep alert.

Strangely enough, the teleport was worried lest they catch their prey and he be saddled with the blame should Terran authority get to hear of it. In the days of his youth he had been well and truly kicked in the pants for obeying orders and he was determined to resent it to his dying day.

Even the tree-cats broadcast their own feline desires and schemings. Ten glared longingly at Raven from behind their bars, dripped saliva, and promised that one fine day they would sample the flesh of the master race. Six more were weighing their chances of escaping into the forests and remaining beyond reach of mankind for keeps. The other four had decided exactly what they would do should glorious fate ordain that the hunted man's trail be crossed by that of a female tree-cat. Evidently this quartet's notion of private enterprise was to mix business with pleasure.

On they clanked and rattled down the road, a futile cavalcade made doubly absurd by the mock-dopey watch of its very quarry. Probably by fall of dark they would catch and tear to bloody shreds a rare jungle hobo or an illicit *tambar* distiller and return flushed with success.

Continuing into the city, Raven found his way to a small granite house with brilliant orchids behind its windowpanes. He had no trouble in the finding although this was his first visit to Plain City. He made his way straight to his destination as if it were clearly visible from the beginning, or as one heads through encompassing darkness toward a distant light. And when he reached the door he did not have to knock. Those waiting within had measured his every step and *knew* the moment of arrival.

Chapter 8

Mavis, petite, blonde and blue-eyed, curled herself in a deep chair and observed him with the same deep penetration that his own eyes often showed to the considerable discomfort of others. It was as if she had to look right into him to see his real self behind a concealing mask of flesh.

The other one, Charles, was a plump and rather pompous little man blessed with the lackluster optics of a low-grade pawn. Any talented human would take one look at Charles and unhesitatingly classify him as a fat nitwit. A veneer of matching nitwittery lay over his brain and served to confirm the first impressions of any other mind that might choose to probe. More by good luck than good management Charles was an entity exceptionally well concealed and therefore much to be envied.

"Naturally we're pleased to see you," said Mavis, speaking vocally for the pleasure of feeling her tongue wag. "But what has happened to the rule that one stays on one's appointed ball of dirt?"

"Circumstances alter cases," Raven said. "Anyway, Leina is still there. She can handle anything."

"Except being alone, entirely alone," retorted Mavis, taking Leina's part. "No person can handle that!"

"You're right, of course. But nobody remains isolated forever. In the end there's always a reunion." He chuckled with queer humor, added, "If only in the sweet by-and-by."

"Your theology is showing," commented Charles. He took a pneumaseat beside Mavis, squatting comfortably with his pudgy legs stretched out, his paunch supported in linked hands. "According to Leina, you are busily sticking your fingers into other people's affairs. Is that right?"

"About half right. You've not had the full story. Someone on this planet—aided by unknown co-operators on Mars—is having a good time pulling Terra's hair. They are like mischievous children playing with a gun, neither knowing nor caring that it might be loaded. They are out to gain complete independence by a form of coercion amounting to new style war."

"War?" Charles was doubtful.

"That's what I said. The trouble is that wars have a habit of getting hopelessly out of hand. Those who start one usually find themselves quite unable to stop it. If it can be done, this one must be prevented from starting in real earnest, by which I mean becoming bloodier."

"Ugh!" Charles rubbed a pair of smooth chins. "We know there's a strong nationalist movement on this planet but we've ignored it as being of no especial interest from our viewpoint. Even if they go so far as to swap bombs and bullets with Terra, and murder each other wholesale, what does it matter to us? It's all to the merry, isn't it? Their loss is our gain."

"In one way but not in another."

"Why?"

"The Terrans are badly in need of unity because they are heading toward the Denebs."

"They're heading—?" Charles' voice trailed off. For a moment his dull eyes shone with formerly hidden fires. "Are you telling me that Terran authorities actually *know* about the Denebs? How the deuce *can* they know?"

"Because," Raven told him, "they are now at development stage four. A lot is going on that the general public doesn't suspect, much less those here or on Mars. The Terrans have built a better drive and already tried it out. They're about to test it farther and are unable to forecast its limits. For matter-bound folk they're doing pretty well."

"Evidently," endorsed Charles.

"I've not yet been able to discover exactly how far they have gone or what data has been brought back by test pilots, but I know they've found enough to arouse suspicions that sooner or later they may collide with some other unnamed, undescribed life-form. You and I know that can only be the Denebs." He wagged an emphatic finger. "We also know that the Denebs have long been milling around like a pack of hounds with five hundred trails to follow. They don't know which way to go for the best, but their general trend is in this direction."

"That is true," put in Mavis. "But the last prognosis gave them a minimum of two centuries in which to discover this solar system."

"A reasonable conclusion based on the data then available," answered Raven. "Now we have a new and weighty item to include in our computations, namely, that Homer Saps will soon be rushing out to meet them. The flag is being hoisted, the smoke fires lit and everything is being done to attract attention to this neck of the cosmos. That kind of caper is going to cut down the time before the Denebs are in a hurry to look over what is here."

"Have you reported this?" demanded Charles, fidgeting.

"Most certainly."

"And what was the response?"

"Thanks for the information."

"Nothing more than that?" He lifted an eyebrow.

"Nothing," assured Raven. "What else do you expect?"

"Something more emotional and less coldly phlegmatic," Mavis interjected. "You males are all the same, just so many brass buddhas. Why can't you stand on a table and scream?"

"Would it do any good?" asked Charles.

"Don't you get logical with me," she snapped. "It would take some pressure off the glands. I possess a few glands, in case you don't know it."

"That is a subject about which I am passably informed," said Charles, pointedly. "Moreover, I have glands myself. One of them makes me fat and inclined to laziness, but I appear to lack the one that is bothering you at the moment." He pointed a plump digit. "There's the table. Climb up and let go a few shrill bellows. We won't mind."

"I am not in the habit of bellowing," said Mavis.

"There you are!" He threw a glance at Raven and gave careless shrug. "Women for you. Cold and calculating. Can't take the steam off their zip-bits."

Mavis promised, "Someday I'll trim your wings, Porky."

"Fancy me with wings." Charles laughed until his paunch trembled. "Diving and soaring like an obese angel. Or fluttering like a fat moth." He wiped his eyes, laughed again. "What an imagination!"

Producing a tiny, lace-edged handkerchief, Mavis wept into it very softly and quietly.

Charles stared at her aghast. "Well, what have I said wrong now?"

"You voiced a stimulator." Going over to Mavis, Raven patted her shoulder. "There, there! It isn't right to remain here if memories are growing too strong for you. It isn't right to stay if you want out. We can find another pair who—"

She whipped down the handkerchief and spoke fiercely. "I don't want out. I'll go when it's time and not before. What sort of a person do you think I am? Can't a girl have a good cry if she wants to?"

"Sure she can, but—"

"Forget it." She stuffed the handkerchief into a pocket, blinked a couple of times, smiled at him. "I'm all right now."

"Does Leina ever do that?" asked Charles, looking at Raven.

"Not while I'm around."

"Leina was older when . . . when—" Mavis let the sentence go unfinished.

They knew exactly what she meant.

Nobody else could have guessed it, not even the Denebs, but these few knew.

They were silent quite a while, each busy with entirely personal thoughts that remained hidden behind mental shields. Charles was the first one to cease ruminating and become vocal.

"Let's get down to business, David. What are your plans and where do we come in?"

"The plans are elementary enough. I want to find, identify and effectively deal with the opposition's key man on Venus, the one who decides ways and means, settles all disputes, generally rules the nationalistic roost and is indisputably the big boss. Take away the locking-stone and the whole arch falls down."

"Sometimes," qualified Charles.

"Yes, sometimes," Raven agreed. "If their organization is half as good as it ought to be they'll have a deputy leader held ready to replace him if necessary. Maybe more. Then our task will be more complex."

"And after all that there will still be the Martians," Charles suggested.

"Not for certain. It all depends on how they react to whatever happens here. Mars-Venus liaison is to a great extent boosted along by mutual encouragement. Each keeps giving the other the loud hurrah. Take away the applause and the act doesn't seem so good to the remaining partner. I'm hoping they'll pipe down when Venus drops out."

"One thing I don't understand." Charles was thoughtful. "What's to stop Terra paying back the insurgents in their own coin? Sabotage and all that stuff is a game at which two can play."

Raven told him.

"Ah!" He had another rub at his chins. "The local boys can make a mess of what they regard as other people's property while the Terrans can louse up only what they consider their own."

"It's no business of ours," put in Mavis. "If it were we would have been told as much." Her eyes were shrewd as they examined Raven. "Have you been requested to interfere by anyone other than Terrans?"

"No, lady, and it's not likely I shall be asked."

"Why not?"

"Because large as the issue may loom in this minor corner of the galaxy, it is small and pitifully insignificant by comparison with bigger issues elsewhere. Things look different from far, far away." His expression showed that he knew he was telling her nothing with which she was not already familiar. "And the accepted rule for the likes of us is to use our own initiative with regard to small matters. So I am using mine."

"That is good enough for me," approved Charles, sitting up and easing his stomach. "What d'you want us to do?"

"Not very much. This is your bailiwick and you know more about it than anyone. Give me the name of the man you consider likeliest to be the inspiration behind this separatist tomfoolery. Give me what data you've got on his talent and other resources and tell me where I can find him. Cogent information is what I need most. Please yourself about offering any more help."

"I propose to offer more." Charles glanced sidewise. "How about you, Mavis?"

"Count me out. I intend to follow Leina's example and keep watch. After all, that's what we're here for. Somebody has to do it while you mulish males go gallivanting around."

Raven said, "You're dead right. Keeping watch is all-important. I'm thankful for you fair maidens. Us bullheads are left free for pernicious interfering."

She pulled a face at him but offered no comment.

"The setup here is amusing," Charles informed. "We have an orthodox Terran governor who utters strictly orthodox sentiments and remains diplomatically unaware that the illegal underground nationalist movement already is doing ninety percent of the bossing. The big boss in this movement, the figure the rank and file look up to, is a large and handsome rabble-rouser named Wollencott."

"What's he got that others haven't?"

"The face, figure, and personality for the part," explained Charles. "He is a native-born Type Six Mutant, that is to say, a malleable, with an imposing mane of white hair and an equally imposing voice. Can make himself the perfect picture of a tribal joss any time he wants. He can also speak like an oracle—providing that he has first learned the words by heart. He's incapable of thinking out the words for himself."

"All that doesn't sound so formidable," Raven offered.

"Wait a bit. I've not finished. Wollencott is so well-suited to portray the dynamic leader of a patriotic cause that he might have been especially chosen for the part. And he was!"

"By whom?"

"By a hard character named Thorstern, the *real* boss, the power behind the throne, the lurker in the shadows, the boy who will still be around long after Wollencott is hung."

"The puppet master, eh? Anything extra-special about him?"

"Yes and no. The most surprising feature is that he is not a mutant. He hasn't one paranormal aptitude." Charles paused, ruminated a moment, went on. "But he is ruthless, ambitious, cunning, a top-grade psychologist and has a high-powered, quick-moving brain good enough to serve a thousand monkeys."

"A pawn with high I.Q."

"Exactly! And that means plenty when redoubtable talent doesn't necessarily have redoubtable brains. Given first-class wits, even a pawn can pull the strings of a dopey telepath; his mind can move just that fraction faster than the telepath can pick it up and react."

"I know. I've listened in to one or two such cases. It's the easiest thing in the world for a mutant to fall into the error of underestimating an opponent merely because he is ordinary. Besides, power is never sufficient unto itself; there must also be the ability to apply it. That's where the Denebs excel. They make full use of what they've got." Becoming restless, Raven moved toward the door. "But we haven't to cope with the Denebs just yet. leastways, not *here*. The immediate objective is Thorstern."

"I'm coming with you." Heaving himself out of the pneumaseat, Charles hitched his middle, let guileless eyes rest on Mavis. "Hold the fort, Honey. If anyone asks, tell them Papa has gone fishing—but don't say for what."

"See that you come back," she ordered. "In one piece."

"In this strange phase of existence of life in death one can guarantee nothing." He released a wheezy laugh, his belly quivering in sympathy. "But I'll try."

With that parting crumb of comfort he followed Raven out, leaving her to get on with her chosen task of standing guard over things that were of the Earth but not earthly.

And like Leina as she sat alone, watching, watching—listening, listening—her chief consolation was that her solitude was shared by other silent sentinels elsewhere.

Chapter 9

The invariable eventide fog was now creeping into the city, rolling with sluggish purpose along its streets and avenues in thick yellowish swirls that became still denser as the hidden sun went down. By midnight it would be a warm, damp, all-obscuring blanket through which nothing would move with certainty except blind men, restless, sleepless nocturnals and a few whispering supersonics "echo-walking," that is to say, finding their way like bats.

In the rain forests it was different; the trees lay on considerably higher levels while the fog hugged the valleys and the plains. The search in the forests would continue, with copters whirring over the treetops and hunters scouring the glades.

Charles and Raven passed a shop window in which an outsize spectroscreen displayed ballet dancers moving delicately through a scene from *Les Sylphides*. The prima ballerina drifted across the stage with infinite grace, pale and fragile like a blown snowflake.

Yet only a few miles away, deep within the encroaching dark, were monstrous forms and monstrous vegetation marking the frontiers of the half-known and the unknown. It was a contrast of extremes that few noticed, few thought about. When a planet has been settled long enough to have a population mainly native-born, erstwhile dreams become humdrum, the alien becomes the familiar, old-time fantasies are replaced by new and radically different ones.

Stopping outside the window and studying the scene, Charles said, "See the ease and grace with which she pirouettes, the lithe slenderness of her limbs, the calm, impassive, almost ethereal beauty of her face. Note how she pauses, hesitates, flirts and darts away like a rare and wonderful butterfly. She is a good example of a rather unearthly type that has enthralled humanity for centuries: the ballet type. She fascinates because she makes me wonder."

"About what?" Raven inquired,

"Whether her type are paranormals not recognized as such and not suspecting it themselves. It is possible to have a talent far too subtle to be named and classified."

"Make it clearer," Raven suggested.

"I wonder whether people like her have a subconscious form of extra-sensory perception that impels them to strain poetically toward a goal they can neither name nor describe. Such intuitive awareness gives them an intense yearning that they can express in only one way." He pointed to the screen. "Butterfly-like. A butterfly is a day-loving moth."

"You may have something there."

"I'm sure I have, David." He left the window, continued onward at a fast waddle. "As a life-form in their own right human beings have made a good accumulation of knowledge. How immensely greater would it be if they could add to it all the items they've got subconsciously or instinctively but cannot correlate on the conscious level."

Raven said, "Brother Carson, who is no stupe, is with you in that. He showed me a list of known mutants and then warned that it might be far from complete—types hanging around undiscovered by themselves, much less by others. It is difficult to identify oneself as an oddity unless the oddness happens to be self-advertising."

Nodding vigorously, Charles contributed, "Rumor has it that an entirely new type was discovered this week and by pure accident. A young fellow who lost his hand in an argument with a buzz saw is now supposed to be growing another."

"A bio-mechanic," defined Raven. "Can service himself with new parts. Well, it's an innocuous faculty, which is more than can be said for some."

"Yes, sure, but the point is that up to then he didn't know he could do it because he'd never lost a piece of himself before. But for that accident he could have gone through life and to his grave without the vaguest notion that he possessed a super-normal power. So I often wonder how many more folk lack adequate knowledge of themselves."

"Plenty. Look at what *we* know."

"I am looking," assured Charles, quietly. "It is so much that it would shake a thousand worlds if they shared it." His fingers curled around the other's elbow, digging hard. "In fact, it's so much we take it for granted that it's all. David, do you suppose that . . . that—?"

Raven stopped in mid-stride. His silver-flecked eyes were bright as he gazed into other eyes similarly illuminated.

"Finish it, Charles. Finish what you were going to say."

"Do you think maybe *we* don't know half as much as we believe? That what we do know is very far from being the whole story? That there are others who do know more, watching us exactly as we are watching these, sometimes laughing at us, sometimes pitying us?"

"I can't say." He registered a wry grin. "But if there are, we do know one thing— they don't interfere with *us!*"

"Don't they? Can we be sure of it?"

"They don't in any manner that we can recognize."

"We recognize Deneb tactics," Charles retorted. "They do plenty of shoving around that is intended for us but not felt by us. Conversely, others could push us without knowing whom they were pushing, without us knowing we were being pushed."

"Better still, they could adopt our own methods to our own confusion," offered Raven, manifestly skeptical but willing to take it along. "They could appear to you and me pretty much as we appear to these, visibly ordinary." He waved a hand to encompass the local citizenry. "Just like any other Joe. Suppose I told you I'm a Deneb in fleshly disguise—do you dare to call me a liar?"

"I do," said Charles, with no hesitation. "You are an unblushing liar."

"I resent having to admit it." He gave the other a reassuring clap on the shoulder. "See, you *know* what I am. Therefore you must have intuitive awareness. Definitely, you're a paranormal and ought to express yourself by taking up ballet dancing."

"Eh?" Charles gloomed down at his ample front. It stuck out like a Christmas parcel carried under his vest. "That's what I call throwing it back at me."

He went silent as three men in uniform came round the corner ahead and stopped in their path.

The trio were dressed as forest rangers, the only organized body—apart from special squads of police—officially permitted to bear arms on Venus. They grouped close together like friends having a last chat before going home, but their attention was on the pair coming toward them. Their open minds revealed that all three were pyrotics looking for a man named Raven.

The leader kept tab of the oncomers out of the corners of his eyes, waited until they drew level, wheeled swiftly on one heel and snapped with sudden authority, "Your name David Raven?"

Stopping and lifting a surprised eyebrow, Raven said, "However did you guess?"

"Don't be funny," advised the questioner, scowling.

Raven turned to Charles. His tones were pained. "He tells me not to be funny. Do you think I am funny?"

"Yes," responded Charles, with prompt disloyalty. "You've been that way since you fell on your head at age three." His bland but stupid looking eyes shifted to the ranger. "Why do you want this person named . . . er—?"

"Raven," prompted Raven, being helpful.

"Oh, yes, Raven. Why do you want him?"

"There's money on his head. Don't you ever use your spectroscreen!"

"Occasionally," Charles admitted. "Most times it bores me to tears, so I let it stay dead."

The ranger sneered to his companions. "Now you know why some people stay poor. Opportunity knocks at every door but some refuse to listen." Taking no notice of Raven, he continued with Charles who was looking suitably crushed.

"They've put it on the spectroscreen that he's wanted badly and at once."

"For what?"

"For imperiling the lives of crew and passengers of the *Fantôme.* For opening an airlock contrary to regulations, interfering with navigation, refusing to obey the lawful orders of a ship's officer, landing in a forbidden area, evading medical examination on arrival, evading customs search on arrival, refusing to pass through the antibacterial sterilization chambers and—" He paused for breath, asked one of the others, "Was there anything else?"

"Spitting in the main cabin," suggested that worthy who had long been tempted by that crime merely because a large-lettered notice warned him that he must not.

"I never spit," asserted Raven, giving him the cold eye.

"Shut up, you!" ordered the first one, making it clear that he was taking no back chat from anybody. He switched to Charles, preferring that person's respectful dumbness.

"If you happen to come across this David Raven, or hear anything about him, ring Westwood 1717 and tell us where he is. He's dangerous!" He slipped a sly wink at the others as he emphasized the last word, then promised, "We'll see that you get your fair share of the reward."

"Thanks." Charles was humbly grateful. He said to Raven, "Come on. We're late already. Keep a look-out and remember he resembles you."

They walked off, conscious that the three were watching them go. The trio's surreptitious comments reached them in the form of mental impulses loud and clear.

"Took us for rangers, anyway."

"Let's hope some ranger captain does too, if we happen to meet one."

"We're wasting our time just because a guy on the spectroscreen mentioned money. We could spend a few hours at better than this. There's a *tambar* joint two blocks down, so what say—"

"Why don't they distribute his picture?"

"A telepath would help, like I said. All we'd need do is wait for him to point. Then we'd make the smoke and flames. After that we could wear down our fingers counting the dough."

"Now you mention it, I think there's something queer about that reward. They didn't bid anything like as high for Squinty Mason when he busted those banks and shot a dozen people."

"Perhaps Wollencott wants him for personal reasons."

"Look, fellows, there's a *tambar* joint—"

"All right, we'll go there for half an hour. If anyone catches us there we've got a good excuse. We heard a rumor that Raven was meeting someone in the dump." The mental stream started to fade very slowly. "If Wollencott wants him—"

They continued talking about Wollencott until they dimmed beyond hearing. They thought up twenty ways in which Wollencott might have been offended by the fugitive, forty ways in which the latter might be brought to book, a hundred ways in which Wollencott would make an example of the culprit.

It was Wollencott, Wollencott, Wollencott all the time. Not one mentioned Thorstern or so much as gave that name a passing thought.

Which was quite a tribute to the brains of the owner of that name.

Chapter 10

A great black basalt castle was the home of Emmanuel Thorstern. It dated back to the earliest days of settlement when smooth, high walls six feet thick were sure protection against antagonistic jungle beasts of considerable tonnage. Here the little group of first-comers from Earth had clung stubbornly to their alien plot until more shiploads built them up in numbers and strength of arms. Afterward they'd sallied forth, taken more land and held it.

Seven other similar castles elsewhere on the planet had served the same function for a time, then had been abandoned when their need had passed. These others now stood empty and crumbling like dark monuments to this world's darkest days.

But Thorstern had stepped in and restored this one, strengthening its neglected walls, adding battlemented towers and turrets, spending lavishly as though his calculated obscurity in matters of power had to be counterbalanced by blatancy in another direction. The result was a sable and sinister architectural monstrosity that loomed through the thickening fog like the haunt of some feudal maniac who held a countryside in thrall.

Toying thoughtfully with the lobe of an ear, Raven stood amid swirls of fog and examined this edifice. Only the base was clearly visible in the curling, thickening vapor, the rest becoming shadowy with the growing darkness and merging into the higher haze. Yet his gaze lifted and shifted from point to point as if somehow he could see in full details those features hidden from normal sight.

"Quite a fortress," he remarked. "What does he call it?—the Imperial Palace or Magnolia Cottage or what?"

"Originally it was known as Base Four," Charles replied. "Thorstern renamed it Blackstone. Locally it's referred to as the castle." He stared upward in the same manner as the other, apparently having the same ability to see the unseeable. "Well, what now? Do we go after him in our own way or do we wait for him to come out?"

"We'll go in, I don't feel like hanging around all through the night until some unpredictable time tomorrow."

"Neither do I." He pointed at a high angle. "Do we exert ourselves and go over the top? Or shall we take it easy and walk in?"

"We'll enter like gentlemen, in decent and civilized manner," Raven decided. "To wit: through the front gate." He had another look at their objective. "You do the talking while I hold your arm and let my tongue hang out. Then we'll *both* look simple."

"Thank you very much," said Charles, in no way offended. Strutting officiously up to the gate, he thumbed a bell button, waited with Raven by his side.

Four blasphemous minds located nearby immediately radiated four different but equally potent oaths. They were pawn minds, all of them. Not a mutant in the bunch.

It was to be expected. As an individual without talent other than that provided by above-average brains, Thorstern would make full use of those blessed with paranormal aptitudes but not yearn for their company. So it was likely that the majority of those around him—that is to say, within the castle—would be mere pawns chosen for various merits of loyalty, dependability, subservience to the boss.

In these respects the lord of the black castle ran as true to type as the lowliest of his servitors. All ordinary human beings, clever or stupid, were leery of paranormals, liked them better the farther away they got. It was a natural psychological reaction based on the concealed inferiority complex of Homo Today in the presence of what uncomfortably resembled Homo Tomorrow. The Terran forces controlled by Carson and Heraty could have exploited such instinctive antagonisms to the great discomfort of the opposition—but that would have meant further accentuating human divisions in the name of human unity.

In addition, to stir up masses of pawns against a powerful minority of mutants would be to incite type-riots which—like the racial upsets of long, long ago—could get hopelessly out of hand and spread farther than desired. Terra had some mutants of her own!

So it was a blue-jowled and commonplace kind of pawn who opened a door in the thickness of the wall, came out and peered through the heavy bars of the gate. He was squat, thick-shouldered, irritable, but sufficiently disciplined to try to conceal his ire.

"Wanting someone?"

"Thorstern," said Charles airily.

"It's *Mister* Thorstern to you," reproved the other. "You got an appointment?"

"No."

"He won't see anyone without an appointment. He's a busy man."

"We are not anyone," put in Raven. "We are someone."

"Makes no difference. He's a busy man."

Charles said, "Being so busy he will wish to see us with the minimum of delay."

The guard frowned. He was around I.Q. 70 and steered mostly by his liver. He did not want to use the phone and consult a higher-up lest the reward be a bawling out. More than anything else he yearned for a reasonable excuse to give these callers the easy brushoff. That interrupted game of jimbo-jimbo had reached its most enthralling stage now that he had won first sniff at the green bottle.

"Well?" insisted Charles, fatly bellicose. "You going to keep us here come Monday week?"

The other registered the baffled distaste of a slow mind being pushed faster than it wants to move. The plausible excuse he was seeking seemed strangely elusive. He glowered at the pair as though they had shoved him where he didn't wish to go.

Maybe he *had* better do something about this. The manifold ramifications of Thorstern's business brought all sorts of people to the gate at all times, though seldom as darkness fell. Some were admitted, some were not, and now and again it happened that dopes and crackpots were allowed in while important looking persons were kept out. Anyway, it was his duty only to hold the fort, not to sit in judgment on every caller.

Licking his lips, he asked hoarsely, "What are your names?"

"They don't matter," said Charles.

"Well, what is your business?"

"That *does* matter."

"Cripes, I can't tell them just that!"

"Try it and see," Charles advised.

Hesitating, the guard stared from one to the other, absorbed mental comfort from each without knowing it, went back into the wall. Those in the tiny room beyond greeted him with a chorus of remarks that caused not a whisper outside the door but did spike through the basalt in neural waves and came clearly to the pair waiting outside the gate.

"Oh, Lord, how much longer are you going to be? You're holding up the game."

"What's eating someone, coming along at this hour? It'll be blacker than the inside of a cat pretty soon."

"Who is it, Jesmond? Somebody important?"

"They won't say." informed the guard, with glumness. Taking the phone off the wall, he waited for its visiscreen to clear and show who was responding at the other end.

At the end of a minute his neck was beet-red and his tone apologetic.

Racking the phone, he threw the three scowling, impatient faces at the table a pained glance, went into the rapidly gathering gloom. The impulse that had driven him to report with no information was now gone, but he sensed its absence no more than he had sensed its presence. "See here, you two, the—"

He stopped, gaped outward through the gate. Those couple of minutes had hastened the night. Visibility was now down to a mere four or five yards. Within that small radius there was nobody in view, nobody at all.

"Hey!" he called into the wall of fog. No reply. Again, much louder. "Hey!"

Nothing but a dismal drip of water from black walls and a dim, subdued mixture of sounds from the city a couple of miles away.

"Darn!" Giving it up, he returned to the door. A thought struck him just as he reached it, he came back, tried the gate, shaking it, examining its bolts and the main lock. It was securely fastened. He glanced at the top. A quadruple row of spikes three inches from the overhead rock made it completely impassable. "Darn their hides!" he said, inexplicably uneasy, and went indoors.

The green bottle was the chief object of his attention. It did not occur to him that a great gate's strongest point is also its weakest—the lock. Neither did it strike him that the most complicated lock can be turned from either side providing one has a key—or a satisfactory non-material substitute!

Darkness became complete as the last dim fadings of light were swept away much as if a gigantic shutter had been drawn across the concealed Venusian sky. A long, narrow courtyard stood behind the gate. Within this area visibility was down to an arm's length. As usual upon Venus, the fall of night caused the fog to be pervaded by a hundred exotic odors drawn from trees and jungles, with a crushed marigolds perfume predominant.

The two invaders halted their progress through the courtyard. Immediately to their right a large bolt-studded door was set in the wall. Though well hidden in the all-enveloping cloud, they *knew* the door was there without having perceived it visually. They moved closer and inspected it.

Charles murmured, "They fitted that gate with a wonderlock containing four-teen tricky wards. Then they fitted the lock itself with an alarm guaranteed to scream bloody murder the moment anyone tried to tamper with it. Finally, they included a cut-off for the alarm in the attendant's room so that it wouldn't oper-ate while he was dealing with a caller." He gave a loud sniff. "That's what I call ingenuity carried to the point of imbecility."

"Not necessarily," Raven differed. "They designed that layout solely for coping with their own kind, mutant or nonmutant. It is quite adequate for such a limited purpose. Dealing with Denebs—or the likes of you and me—is quite another prob-lem. Thorstern and all his hosts would have a deuce of a time trying to solve it."

"I suppose you're right. That gate comes near to the unbustable according to this world's notions of unbustability." Charles ran deceitfully dull-witted eyes over the big door and the black rock around it. "Do you see what I see?"

"Yes, there's an invisible light beam across the passage just behind the door. Open the door and break the beam and curfew rings tonight."

"Everything to delay us," grumbled Charles, impatient of time-wasting futili-ties. "You would think they'd done it deliberately." He glanced down at his paunch, feeling that frequent inspection never made it any smaller, added in mournful tones, "This is where we're handicapped by our disguise. Without it we could go straight in."

"The same applied a few minutes ago. We're dealing with men and therefore must do things somewhat like men." He eyed Charles with mild humor. "We *are* men, aren't we?"

"No—some of us are women."

"You know what I mean, Gusty. We are men and women."

"Of course. But sometimes I—" His voice trailed off, his plump face quirked, then he said, "That brings back a thought to me, David. I stew it over from time to time."

"What is it?"

"How many horses really are horses? How many dogs really are dogs?"

"Well, that is something to look into after more urgent and important business has been settled," Raven opined. "It will be an interest to divert us through a few millennia to come." He gestured toward the door. "Right now there's this little trap. The beam has to be switched off whenever anyone answers the door from inside. Following the lines back to the switch is going to take a bit of time if it's deep inside the place."

"You trace the lines while I tend to the door," suggested Charles. "One man, one job."

He got on with his part straightaway. It involved no more than standing with hands in pockets and staring intently at the obstacle.

Meanwhile, Raven gazed with equal concentration at the thick rock to one side. On the face of it there was nothing to see worth seeing, nevertheless his pupils shifted slowly, moving rightward, rising and falling occasionally.

Neither made further remark. Each engrossed in his own special task, they stood side by side, unmoving, and stared to the front as if transfixed by a supernatural apparition. invisible to all but themselves. After a short while, Charles relaxed but was careful not to disturb the other.

Half a minute later Raven likewise eased up, said, "The lines go along a corridor then down a passage to the right and into a small anteroom. The switch made a loud click when it snapped up but luckily the room was empty."

Bracing a hand against the door he gave it a shove. It swung inward, heavily, soundlessly. The two stepped through, closed it behind them, walked along a narrow corridor illuminated by sunken ceiling lights. Their manner had the casual confidence of people who purchased the castle last week and plan to furnish it tomorrow.

"All this gives some indication of the psychology of Thorstern," Raven remarked. "The bolts and bars and invisible light beams could be detected by any mutant endowed with first-class extra-sensory perception, though he'd be unable to do anything about them. On the other hand, a teleport could manipulate the lot without any trouble whatsoever, if only he could see them. So the place is wide open to a multi-talented mutant such as a teleport with e.s.p. Thorstern proceeds on the assumption that there is no such creature, or anything resembling such a creature. He'll hate to think he's wrong."

"He isn't wrong so far as multi-talented humans are concerned."

"Not yet. Not today. But someday he may be. That fellow Haller was classified as a pyrotic and no more, yet he realized too much the moment I touched him. He'd got a rudimentary form of e.s.p. and didn't know it himself until that moment. He'd got one and one-tenths mutational talents."

"A freak," said Charles.

"Yes, you could call him that. So Brother Thorstern is going to be anything but amiable when confronted by two freakier freaks such as ourselves. Being a pawn, even though a clever one, his attitude toward mutants is determined by suppressed fear rather than open jealousy."

"That's a handicap considering that our purpose is to persuade him to see reason."

"Your finger is right on the sore spot, Charles. It's not going to be easy to knock sense into a powerful and ruthless individual motivated by fear. And it's so much the harder when you dare not show him why his suppositions are wrong and his fears utterly groundless."

"Have you ever imagined which of a thousand possible reactions this world would favor were we free to tell it a few cogent things?" asked Charles.

"Yes, many a time. But what is the use of speculating about it? Someday the Denebs are sure to get this far. The less they learn, the better."

"The odds are at least a million to one against them finding anything worth the discovery." Charles was very sure of himself on this point. "Look at Tashgar and Lumina and the Bootes group. They explored the lot, treated the life-forms thereon with contempt and beat it elsewhere, searching, searching, always searching and never getting any place. They'd go clean crazy if they knew that a hundred times over they've found what they're looking for but couldn't recognize it when it was right in their hands." He permitted himself a sardonic chuckle. "The Denebs are geniuses who lack the elementary ability to put two and two together and make it four."

"In given circumstances the addition of two and two can be a really tough mathematical problem," Raven pointed out. "Sometimes I feel sorry for the Denebs. If I were in their shoes I'd become boiling mad at frequent intervals and—"

He let the subject drop as they reached the end of the corridor, turned into the right-hand passage and found several men walking toward them.

Before any one of this small bunch had time to react to his suspicions, Raven said brightly and with disarming confidence, "Pardon me, can you tell me the way to Mr. Thorstern's room?"

He was answered by a burly man in the middle who bore himself with a touch of authority. "First turn on the left, second door on the left."

"Thanks."

They stood aside to let Raven and Charles go past, watched in silence as the pair strolled by them. Their expressions said nothing but their minds were shouting their inmost thoughts.

"Any caller for Thorstern is met at the gate and conducted to his room. How come these two are ambling around on their own?"

"Something out of kilter here," pondered a second one. "Not usual for visitors to be left on the loose; in fact, it never happens."

A third was saying to himself, "I don't like this. Why don't I like it? Is it because I haven't enough worries of my own? I've got plenty!" His thoughts veered away. "To heck with them!"

"Second door on the left, eh?" projected a fourth mind, amused and unworried. "Gargan thought fast when he gave them that one. Trust him to play safe. That's why he never gets anywhere, he always plays safe."

The first one, who was Gargan, resumed by deciding, "The moment they get around that next bend I'll give the boss a warning buzz." He commenced edging toward a wall-stud.

Turning the corner, Raven threw Charles a knowing glance, found the second door to the left, paused before it.

I can pick up a hopeless tangle of thought-streams but not one that says it's coming from Thorstern." He nodded toward the door. "And there are no active minds behind that. The room is empty. Not a soul inside it." Studying the blank panels for a moment, he added, "Half a dozen chairs, a table and a screen cabinet for intercommunication. The walls are solid rock. The door can be sealed by remote control, opened only by remote control. H'm!"

"The better mouse-trap," defined Charles. His fat face developed creases around the mouth. It gave him the look of a child about to break somebody's window. "Just the sort of place I like to enter to show how little I care."

"Me too." Raven gave the door a push. It opened without trouble, Going inside, he relaxed in a chair, eyed the blank screen.

Charles took a seat beside him, making the chair squeak under his bulk. He also turned his attention to the screen but his mind—like Raven's—probed carefully in all directions and tried to sort out the incoherent babble coming through surrounding stonework.

"I was holding two aces when, durn me . . . a typical Martian joint with cold air and warm beer . . . went up with a bang that shook the entire town. We ran for a copter while Intelligence was still . . . got blonde hair that reaches down to her knees . . . left the Terran patrols spinning like dizzy . . . so this stinking skewboy reads my thoughts and beats me to the dame and . . . yes, a hypno named Steen. They wanted him badly, I don't know . . . I tell you these skewboys aren't to be . . . *what's that?*"

"Here it comes," remarked Raven, licking his lips.

"This Steen, it is said that he . . . *Where? Two in Room Ten? How did they get inside? . . .* fed up with Mars in short time. Don't know how guys can . . . *All right, Gargan, leave it to me . . .* when you've finished with the green bottle maybe we can . . . dived headlong into the forest and dug himself a hole twenty feet deep."

Click! went the door as relays operated and a dozen heavy bolts slid home. The screen glowed to life, swirled and colored. A face appeared.

"So Gargan was right. What are you two doing there?"

"Sitting and waiting," said Raven. He stretched out his legs, gave a picture of one making himself thoroughly at home.

"I can see that. You've not much choice about it now." The face exposed a toothy and unpleasant smirk. "The guard at the gate swears that nobody has been admitted. Nevertheless, you two are here. There's only one answer to that: you're a pair of hypnos, You took him over and then wiped the marks off his brain." The smirk gave way to a harsh laugh. "Very clever of you. But look where it's got you. See if you can hypnotize a scanner."

"You seem to think it's a crime to be a hypno," said Raven dexterously kicking the sore spot in a typical pawn-mind.

"It's a crime for a hypno to use his power for illegal purposes," the other retorted. "And just in case you don't know, it's a crime to break into a private residence."

Conscious that all this was a waste of time, Raven growled, "In my considered opinion, it's also a crime for a thick-headed underling to amuse himself indulging adolescent triumph and let his own boss go hang." His face hardened. "We've come to talk to Thorstern. Better get him before someone paddles some sense into your tight end."

"Why, you loudmouthed marsh-stink!" began the other, going livid. "I could—"

"You could what, Vinson?" inquired a deep, resonant voice that came clearly from the cabinet's loudspeaker. "It is a great mistake to lose one's temper. One should retain control of it at all times. At all times, Vinson. To whom are you speaking?"

Charles gave Raven a gentle nudge. "That sounds like the almighty Thorstern himself."

The face in the screen had turned sidewise and become submissive. "It's a couple of skewboys, sir. They busted in somehow. We've pinned them down in Room Ten."

"Indeed?" The voice was rich, calm, unhurried. "Have they offered any reason for such precipitate action?"

"They say they want to talk to you."

"Dear me! I know no justification for gratifying their desire. On the contrary, it would establish a precedent. I would be expected to hobnob with any and every eccentric who managed to crawl through the walls. Do they think I'm at everybody's beck and call?"

"Don't know, sir."

The invisible speaker changed his mind. "Oh, well, providing this occasion is not used as a pretext to cover future ones, I might as well hear what they have to say. There's a remote chance I might learn something useful. I can deal with them most effectively, *most* effectively if it proves that they are trifling with me."

Servilely, "Yes, sir."

The face slipped off the screen, was replaced by another, large, muscular, square-jowled. Thorstern was well past middle age, had a thick mop of white hair, deep bags under his eyes, but was still handsome in a virile way. His character was engraved upon these broad features, intelligent, ambitious.

His calculating eyes estimated Charles first, taking in all details from feet to head, then moved to the other.

Without slightest evidence of surprise, he said, "Ah, I know you! Only a couple of minutes ago I received a copy of your picture The name is David Raven."

Chapter 11

Raven gazed back level-eyed. "Now why on earth should you want a picture of *me?*"

"I did not want it," riposted Thorstern, too quick-witted to admit anything even by implication. "It was thrust upon me by our authorities who, on this planet, can lay fair claim to efficiency. Your photograph is being circulated. Apparently our police are most anxious to get hold of you."

"I wonder why?" said Raven, pretending puzzlement.

Harumphing to clear his throat, Thorstern continued, "A person in my position would be gravely embarrassed were he to be found harboring a wanted man. Therefore if you have anything to say you'd better say it quickly, because you haven't got long."

"After which—?"

Thorstern's broad shoulders rose in an expressive shrug. It was done in the manner of a Roman emperor turning thumbs down.

"The police will take you away and my responsibility will cease."

The way in which it was voiced bore irresistible suggestion that there were special, unmentionable reasons why he should then feel free of responsibility. He had the air of one with an entire police force in his pocket.

His mere nod was enough to cause an arrest, his wink sufficient to guarantee that someone would be shot in the back while allegedly attempting to escape. Obviously Thorstern had power and plenty of it.

"You're quite a character," declared Raven, openly admiring him. "Too bad you insist on balling up the works."

"You are impertinent," pronounced Thorstern. "And it is intentional. You hope to disconcert my mind by creating irritation within it. But I am not so childish. Unreasoning emotion is a luxury only fools can afford."

"But you do not deny the accusation."

"I can neither confirm nor deny that which is completely meaningless."

Raven sighed and went on, "If that is your stance, it makes our task so much the harder but no less necessary."

"What task?"

"To persuade you to call off the undeclared war you are waging against Terra."

"Heavens above!" Thorstern widened his eyes in mock astonishment. "Do you really expect me to believe that Terra would send a petty criminal to interview a business man about a purely fanciful war?"

"There is a war and you're running it with the aid of stooges here and on Mars."

"What proof have you?"

"No proof is required," said Raven, flatly.

"Why not?"

"Because you know it to be true even though you don't choose to admit it. Proof would be needed only to convince a third party. There is no third party present. This is wholly between yourself and us two."

"As one whose business and financial interests are large and widespread," informed Thorstern, becoming ponderous, "inevitably I have been the target of all sorts of rumors and insults. I have become hardened to them. They split no atoms with me whatsoever. They represent the price a man must pay for his considerable measure of success. The jealous and the spiteful are always with us, always will be, and I regard them as beneath contempt. But I must admit that this bald and completely unsupported assertion of surreptitious warmongering is by far the most outrageous that has offended my ears to date."

"It is neither fantastic nor unsupported," Raven contradicted. "Unfortunately, it is a grim fact. It doesn't offend you, either. In fact, you take secret pride in it. You are inwardly gratified that someone has proved shrewd enough to recognize you as the big boss. You are tickled to bits because for once your well-publicized dummy Wollencott has failed to grab the limelight."

"Wollencott?" echoed Thorstern, quite unmoved. "I am now beginning to see things a little more clearly. I presume that Wollencott—a melodramatic rabble-rouser if ever there was one—has stamped on somebody's corns. So you've stupidly followed a false trail he has laid and it brought you straight to me."

Charles stirred in his seat and growled at the screen, "I am not in the habit of smelling along false trails."

"No?" Thorstern studied him a second time, saw nothing but an obese individual with plump, amiable face and lackluster eyes. "So *you* claim the honor of identifying me as the prime motive force behind a non-existent war?"

"If it can be called an honor."

"Then, sir, you are not only a crackpot but a dangerous one!" He made a disparaging gesture. "I have no time for crackpots. It would be best to get you off my hands and let the police deal with you." His face was severe as he finished, coldly, "Like a good citizen, I have the utmost confidence in our police."

Giving him a contemptuous sniff, Charles retorted, "You are referring, of course, to the large number who happen to be in your pay. I know of them. They are feared on this planet and with good reason." His lazy face sharpened suddenly so that for the briefest moment he looked neither fat nor futile. "But we don't fear them!"

"You may find cause to change that opinion." Thorstern switched his attention back to Raven. "I deny all your nonsensical accusations and that is that! If Terra thinks there is need to reassert her authority over Venus let her do so in proper manner. Without a doubt Wollencott is the cause of Terra's trouble. How she's going to cope with him is her problem and not mine."

"We aren't fooled by false fronts or human-shaped red herrings, see? If we snatch Wollencott you will laugh most heartily, replace him with the next stooge on your private list and use the snatching for purposes of propaganda."

"Will I?"

"You won't lift a finger to save Wollencott. On the contrary, you'll assign to him the useful role of Venusian nationalism's first martyr. Terra has something better to do than provide a petty god with one or two saints."

"The said deity being me?" inquired Thorstern, grinning.

"Of course." Raven went on, "Our logical move is to get at the man who pulls the strings of the puppets. That is why we've come direct to you. Our only alternative is to accept that you are not amenable to reason and bring you to heel by more drastic methods."

"That is a threat." Thorstern revealed strong, white teeth. "It comes strangely from one so completely at my mercy. To your other delusions must now be added the weird notion that you are independent of your environment and impervious to circumstances. Stone walls do not a prison make. Hah!"

"Enjoy yourself," Raven advised. "It's later than you think."

"I am now beginning to doubt your inherent criminality," Thorstern continued, ignoring that remark. "I think you are a case for a psychiatrist. You are motivated by a powerful obsession that I, Emmanuel Thorstern, a prosperous Venusian trader, am a kind of Goliath to whom you must play the part of David." He glanced down at a desk not visible in the screen, finished with much acidity, "Yes, I see that your name actually is David. Possibly you are conditioned by it."

"No more so than you are by Thor or Emmanuel."

It produced the first noteworthy reaction in the other's features. Momentarily forsaking his determined composure, Thorstern scowled. Even then he managed to lend the grimace a majestic quality.

He chewed at his bottom up and rasped, "I have broken men for less than that! I have smashed them!" His clenched fist struck the desk. "I have made them as if they had never been!"

"Well! I see you *do* know the significance of your names."

"I am not uneducated." He lifted a bushy eyebrow. "But I am only a trader—not a fanatic. It is you who are obsessed, not me. I seek power, true, but only in material things. Your insults are dangerous—not to me, but to yourself."

"Your threats are of no consequence. The point is that you may smash certain men but you will never smash Terra. Call off this war while yet there is time."

"Or—?"

"Or Terra will decide that she's had more than enough and will strike in her own way. Like to know how?"

"I am listening."

"She will remove the opposition's key men one by one, starting with you!"

Thorstern wasn't fazed. Neither was he annoyed. Sweeping back his thick mop of white hair, he consulted papers below the level of the screen, spoke judicially.

"My conscience being clear, I have no reason to apprehend summary removal. Furthermore, we are all Terrans in law, subject to the Terran system of jurisdiction which lays down that a citizen is deemed innocent until conclusive evidence of guilt is forthcoming. Such evidence will be impossible to produce, especially in the absence of certain witnesses, including yourselves."

"A counter-threat," Raven commented.

"Construe it as you please. You do not seem to appreciate your own position."

"We know it. We are trapped—you hope!"

"You are in a room with solid walls and devoid of windows. The only door is multiple-locked by remote control and cannot be unlocked except from here. It is an anteroom reserved for interviews with paranormals of unknown power and unknown purposes. We get them here from time to time."

"So it seems."

"I am not so foolish as to rely exclusively on one iron gate which could be passed as somehow you passed it. You can learn a belated lesson from this: whoever fights me does so in time and place of my own choosing."

"Rather elaborate precautions for the home of an honest trader, aren't they?" Raven asked, pointedly.

"I have elaborate interests to protect. The means I have detailed are not all, by a long shot. You have reached only the second line of defense." He bent nearer the screen, added with triumphant emphasis, "Even in this room from which I am speaking you would find me invulnerable!"

Smiling to himself, Raven said, "It would be nice to put that to the test."

"You will not be given the chance. Get it into your slow thinking minds that ordinary men are not without ability, Some of us—myself especially—know how best to deal with mutants. We think two jumps ahead of them every time."

"You're two behind but you don't know it."

Disregarding that, Thorstern continued, "If you are proud of your teleportatory powers I suggest you try them on the door bolts. Or if you happen to be hypnos, see whether you can fascinate me through a scanner. Or if you are telepaths, try to detect my thoughts. You cannot read my mind, can you? You don't know where I am, in which direction or how far away. I may be within ten yards of you, my thought-stream grounded by a silver-mesh screen. Or I may be speaking to you from the other side of the planet."

"Sounds as if you're scared of someone."

"I fear nobody," said Thorstern, and was speaking truth. He was Thorstern's body without Thorstern's conscience. "But I do recognize the existence of super-normal powers denied to me. Hence I use prudence. On Venus and Mars one can do little else. Our number of mutants is high. It is a factor Terra should take into account before starting something she might not be able to stop."

"Terra has mutants of her own," Raven told him. "More than you suppose. You folk tend to overlook that item, being so bemused by what you've got yourselves. Who lugged the lot of you to new planets in the first place? The Terran space fleet which was and still is manned by Terrans who've spent fifteen to twenty years zooming through the dark and absorbing hard radiations. There has been the same natural results. Many children of space-dogs aren't quite like other people's children."

"I'll take you up on that." Thorstern showed the gratification of one about to make an unanswerable point. "If, as you pretend, there is a war being waged, why doesn't Terra use her own mutants to retaliate in kind?"

"Who said Venus was using mutants for her attacks?" asked Raven.

Thorstern spent one-tenth of a second chiding himself for the obvious blunder, covered up by asking in mock surprise, "Isn't that what is happening?"

"No."

"What then?"

"Something infinitely worse. They're using a new kind of ray to sterilize our womenfolk."

"That's a blatant lie!" Thorstern's voice was loud and ireful, his face flushed.

"Of course it is." Raven displayed no shame. "And you *know* it. You've just said so. *How* do you know it?"

"Nobody would play so lousy a trick." Secretly irked by this second mistake, Thorstern decided that he would make no more. "I have grown tired of this conversation. It is neither entertaining nor informative. I am going to deal with you as I would with any other menacing crazies who break into my home."

"If you can."

"It will be easy. Every skewboy has the same kind of lungs as everyone else. He falls asleep as swiftly and as deeply even though he may be a nocturnal. Despite his powers he is as helpless in his slumbers as any newborn babe. He is no longer what he fancies himself to be, that is, the biological superior of ordinary, talentless people. Asleep, he is no better than a lump of meat. Any village idiot can handle him."

"Meaning you intend to gas us into insensibility?"

"Precisely," agreed Thorstern, pleased with his powers over the powerful. "There are vapor-conduits running into your room for that very purpose. It is part of the defense system. We use our imagination and think ahead of you, see?" Plucking pensively at a bottom lip, he added by way of afterthought, "I like to do things in the simplest way, smoothly, with minimum of trouble."

"But you refuse to do anything about stopping this war?"

"Don't be silly. I really cannot admit that there is a war, much less that I have any part of it. Your mythical conflict fails to interest me. I am treating you as a pair of unsavory characters who have broken into my home. I am going to ensure that the police take you away peacefully, like removing unwanted luggage."

He leaned forward, reaching for something near the edge of the screen.

Already slumped low in his chair, Charles suddenly slid down farther, quietly, undramatically. His plump face was pale, his eyes closing as though for the last time. His legs sprawled at awkward angles.

Raven stood up, removing his attention from the onlooker in the screen. Bending over Charles, he heaved him into sitting position, slid a hand under his vest, gently rubbed him over the heart.

"Quite a diverting little by-play," remarked Thorstern. his lips pursed in sarcasm. He was still reaching toward the screen but with his hand momentarily arrested. "The fat boy plays sick. You massage his chest, looking serious. In a moment or two you will tell me he's having an attack of coronary thrombosis or something like that. He will die unless something is done quickly. I am then supposed to go into a sympathetic panic, withhold the gas, withdraw the bolts and send somebody running to you with a *tambar* bottle."

His back still turned to the other, Raven said nothing. He remained over Charles, holding him in the chair, rubbing near to the heart.

"Well, it won't work!" Thorstern practically spat out the words. "It is too infantile a trick to deceive a half-wit. In fact, I consider it an insult to my intelligence. Moreover, if that fat boy's stroke did happen to be genuine I would be quite content to sit here and watch him die. Who am I to try to thwart the workings of destiny?"

"I am glad you said that." Raven did not bother to turn around. He was splendidly indifferent to what the other intended to do. "People like us frequently are handicapped by ethical considerations. We waste valuable time trying to persuade others not to let us do things that must be done. We tend to postpone the inevitable until it can be held off no longer. It is our characteristic weakness. We are weak where less scrupulous men like you are strong."

"Thank you," said Thorstern.

"So it is much of a relief when prospective victims sweep all our qualms away," added Raven. Sensing that this was the precise instant, the exact moment, he swung round, stared straight at the screen, his eyes silver-flecked and luminous, "Good-by, Emmanuel! Someday we may meet again!"

The other did not reply. He was incapable of it. His formerly strong and aggressive features were now undergoing a series of violent contortions. The eyes bulged, moved jerkily. The mouth opened and closed, emitting no sounds. A thick layer of sweat broke out on his forehead. He was like one being torn apart.

Still gently chafing the flaccid body in the chair, Raven watched all this without emotion or surprise. Thorstern's tormented features dropped below the level of the screen. A hand appeared, grasping spasmodically. The face came back, contorted in manner harrowing to witness. All this had taken no more than twenty seconds.

Then the eerie phenomenon departed as swiftly as it had arrived. The facial muscles relaxed, the countenance tidied itself though still glistening with perspiration. The deep voice spoke again, cool, calm, collected. Thorstern's voice with an almost indistinguishable timbre that did not belong to Thorstern. Thorstern's mouth and larynx and vocal chords being employed as if he were a ventriloquial dummy. It appeared to be addressing a hidden microphone to the left of the screen.

"Jesmond, my visitors are about to leave. See that they are not obstructed."

The dummy that was—or had been—Thorstern reached forward, touched a stud. The door bolts slid back. It was his last deed in this existence for the whole face changed again, the mouth fell open, the features went through several super-swift alterations of amazing flexibility. Then the head vanished from the screen as the body collapsed beneath it. One could almost hear the distant thump.

Charles stirred as Raven shook him with great vigor. Opening his dull eyes, he shivered, felt himself, got slowly to his feet. He teetered a little, breathing heavily.

"We must move fast, David. I thought I had him for keeps, but the cunning devil—"

"1 know. I saw the face. A *new* face. Come on!"

Jumping to the door, he jerked it open, hustled Charles through. The cabinet was silent, its screen glowing but blank, He closed the door on it, turned down the passage. There was nobody in sight.

"The cunning devil!" repeated Charles. He panted a bit, breathless with haste and full of grievance.

"Shut up. Save it till later."

Hurriedly they passed the area covered by the still inoperative invisible light beam, out through the door and into the fog that filled the courtyard. A welter of surrounding thoughts poured into their minds, lent urgency to their feet.

". . . so this cootch dancer comes on like an educated snake . . . Raven is dead, I tell you. He couldn't . . . take more than a Hotsy to set fire to that dump . . . was reaching for the gas-stud when they got him somehow, I don't know how . . . story goes they had a single-seater test-job on Jupiter a couple of years back but I guess that's just another Terran rumor because . . . they must be multi-talented mutants no matter who says there's no such animal. In that case . . . vein of solid silver over the other side of the Sawtooths, so he's packing and . . . can't have got far. Sound the alarm, you dope! No use gaping at a stiff while those skewboys . . . well, next thing this Martian floater goes up to walk on the ceiling and the picture falls right out of his pocket and into his wife's lap. She takes just one . . . hardly at the gate yet. Get that siren going . . . shoot on sight . . . ought to have played that ace. Hey, what's all the excitement? . . . care what they are or what they can do. They can die like anyone else."

Jesmond, surly as ever, was waiting at the gate. Bad visibility prevented him from recognizing them until they were close. Then his eyes popped wide.

"You? How did you get inside?"

"Is it any business of yours?" Raven gestured at the steel barrier. "Obey orders and open up."

"All right, keep your hair on." Muttering under his breath, Jesmond fumbled with the complicated lock. The evening's disturbances had made him mulish.

"Hurry—we're pressed for time."

"Are you now?" He paused, one hand at the lock, while he glowered at them. "Who's doing this job, you or me?"

"Me!" said Raven promptly. He punched Jesmond on the nose, licked his knuckles. "Sorry, Pal!"

There had been plenty of vim and weight behind the blow. Jesmond went down with a resounding wallop and lay making bubbling noises through his nostrils. His eyes were closed, his mind floating somewhere among the stars.

Turning the lock, Raven flung the gate wide open, said to Charles, "You've done enough. Time you went home."

"Not likely!" Charles gave him a knowing look. "The open gate is a gag, otherwise you wouldn't have smacked down that noisy sleeper. You're going back inside." He commenced retracing his steps into the courtyard, doing it at an agitated waddle. "And so am I."

Then the alarm sounded, an electric siren located high above the black battlements. Beginning with a low and ghastly moan it built up to an ear-splitting screech that ripped through the fog, echoed and re-echoed across surrounding countryside.

Chapter 12

The two hastened through enveloping cloud that pressed cold and damp upon their faces, created pearls of moisture in their hair and trailed streakily behind them in thin, cotton-wool wisps. The typical Venusian night-time odor of crushed marigolds was now very strong. But the fog did nothing to impede their progress; they plowed straight ahead as if moving in broad daylight.

At the farther end of the courtyard and well beyond the door they had previously entered was a narrow stone archway with a lantern dangling from its center. Of lacquered brass, fanciful in design, it hung in ornate innocence and cast a thin fan of invisible light upon a row of pinhead-sized cells set in the step beneath the arch.

The siren was still screaming banshee-like as Raven sought to trace the leads governing this deceitful setup. Finally he stepped through the arch, Charles following. A moment later the siren ceased its clamor. It died out with a horrid moan. Ensuing hush was broken by angry voices and a host of equally riled thought-forms.

"Might have taken longer than I liked to bust that beam," Raven remarked. "Its lines run all over the place and back through a large switchboard. However, I was lucky."

"In what way?"

"Breaking the beam vibrates a visible telltale—and nobody was watching it at the moment. There seems to be a major panic inside. Everyone shouting orders at everyone else."

Standing close to the wall, he peered around the corner and through the arch toward the gate. A scuffling of many feet could be heard in the gloom. Several forms rushed from the courtyard door toward the main exit. There sounded a jabber of voices, each trying to outshout the others. It was easier to listen to their minds.

"Too late. Gate's open. Here he is, flat out."

"Well, you three were in the room. What were you doing when he got conked? Playing jimbo, eh? Hear that?—any skewboys can bust in or out while these lazy bums play jimbo!"

"Oh, so you came on the run when the alarm sounded? Bah, you were an hour behind the times!"

"Quit arguing. We aren't here to hold an inquest. They can't be more than a few hundred yards away. Let's go after them."

"How're we going to do that? Feel our way like blind men? Do you think we've all got radar vision?"

"Shut up! It's the same for them, isn't it?"

"Not on your life. I tell you they're skewboys and multi-talented ones at that! Bet they're sprinting through the haze as if they don't know it exists."

Charles whispered, "If I were like them I'd hate the guts of people like us."

"They do. And I don't blame them—not one little bit." Raven gestured for silence. "Listen!"

"Aw, have it your own way but I'm going after them. They can't escape without making noises. I'm going to shoot at noises and ask questions afterward. Coming along, Sweeny?"

"Yes, sure, I'll come too."

Several pairs of feet crunched gravel beyond the gate and advanced cautiously into outer darkness.

"Suppose they're floaters—how will they make noises then?"

"They'll make them. A floater can't hang in mid-air for ever. What I call a *really* talented fellow is one who can digest a lump of lead."

"Button it, Sweeny. How the devil can we hear them if your dental plates keep up a constant clatter?"

They faded as their minds turned solely to the task of listening for fugitive feet. Those remaining by the gate were still swapping recriminations with the jimbo enthusiasts while trying to revive the stricken Jesmond. Another mess of neural waves was radiating from inside the castle.

"Nothing to show what killed him. Seems like his heart just stopped of its own accord. I tell you it was sheer coincidence. No hypno can function through a scanner, much less cause his subject to die."

"No? Then why did he draw the bolts, order the gate open and make the way clear for those two? He was hypnoed good and proper, I tell you, and through a scanner at that! Those two guys have got something nobody human ought to have."

"You did well there," Charles murmured with approval. "When you scowled into the screen at precisely the right moment it put them clean off the track. They're laying all the blame on you, thinking that somehow you did it with your little peepers."

"I'd hate them to get on the right track."

"Yes, so would I." The plump face puckered as Charles went on. "If only there were some satisfactory way of telling them a few startling truths without thereby giving the facts to Deneb for free."

"There isn't. There is no way, no way at all."

"I know—but more's the pity." He went quiet, again listened to the other minds. "You called Plain City yet?"

"Yes, they've a bunch coming along. Couple of telepaths to listen for them mentally, if that'll do any good. Also half a dozen hypnos, a Hotsy, and a guy with a flock of tree-cats. An assorted bunch of circus roustabouts who can walk tight-ropes and all that stuff."

"The boss will have fourteen fits when he gets back and hears about all this. Reckon a bug-talker with a hive of hornets might do more—"

"There you are!" Raven nudged his companion. "What we wanted to know. Thorstern's not here but is expected fairly soon. That fellow in the room looked nothing like Thorstern by the time you were using him. His face had relapsed into normal shape. He was lantern-jawed, gaunt and so flexible that he could wave his nose like a hand. A malleable, eh?"

"I realized it the moment I made contact with him." Charles became disgruntled again. "He was so good that I hadn't suspected it up to that moment. It came like a shock—but it was nothing to the shock I gave him!"

"He'll have got over it now. Death is quite a considerable relief to the feelings." He gave a quiet laugh. "Isn't it?"

Ignoring the question as one to which the answer was obvious, Charles continued, "The room was lined with a grounded silver screen to keep his mind tight against probes from outside. His name was Greatorex. He was one of the only three mutants permitted in the place."

"For special reasons, of course."

"Yes. They have been trained to impersonate Thorstern to such perfection that it comes second nature. That's why he talked about being invulnerable even in the room. He was speaking in one breath about two people; the big boss himself *was* invulnerable simply because he wasn't there." He mused with a touch of morbidity, finished. "Those three take turns doing duty for Hizonner as and when required."

"Where are the surviving pair? Did his mind tell you?"

"Somewhere in the city, taking it easy until they are wanted."

"Humph! You can see what it means: if Thorstern is due back and doesn't know what has taken place, it's likely that he'll come in person. But if somebody has made contact and given him all the lurid details, he may play safe by handing us another malleable, another expert mockup of himself. He'll use one of them to bait a trap knowing we can't refuse to snap at the bait."

"Even so, they won't catch us."

"Neither will we catch him—that's what gripes me." He frowned to himself, suddenly shifted his attention elsewhere. "Listen to this fellow—he's getting ideas!"

It was coming through the wall from somewhere within the black castle. "All right, the gate was open and one of those dopey guards laid out. Does that mean they've taken it on the run? Or does it mean that's the way they want it to look? Maybe they haven't gone at all. Maybe they're still hanging around. If I were a fox I'd wear a hard hat and sit on a horse. I'd live a lot longer. What if they can pick up my thoughts—will it do them any good? They can't stop me thinking. I say we ought to search this dump and the sooner the better."

A thinner, more impatient mind answered, "You're crammed to the ears with ifs, buts and supposings. If I've nothing better to do, I can think up plenty of them myself. For instance, suppose they happen to be super-malleables, what then? You've not only got to find *where* they are but also *who* they are. Heck, one of them might have bloodied his own beak, laid flat on the floor and had a hard time keeping his face fixed while kidding us that he is Jesmond." A brief pause, then, "Come to that, how do *you* know that I am *me?*"

"You won't last long if you're not. They're sending some telepaths from the city and they'll soon find out exactly who you are. I say we should rake this place with a fine-tooth comb. Bet you the boss will tear off a few heads if we don't."

"Oh, have it your own way, Fidgety. I'll order a search. It's trouble for nix, but we'll do it. Tell everyone to carry a gun in his hand and that he'll be excused if found with a strange corpse."

Raven grumbled under his breath, "Some folk lack the ability to leave well alone."

"That comes nicely from you," observed Charles, enjoying a fat smile.

"I asked for it." Raven gazed again into the courtyard, surveyed surrounding walls. "The hunt is on. We've no choice but to try to dodge them until either Thorstern or another spit-image arrives."

The dodging wasn't so difficult. They sat in the thick, all-concealing mist atop a blank, battlemented wall some forty feet high. A tree-cat might have scented them up there. A chirruping supersonic could have got a revealing stream of echoes from them. Even a floater could have found them by obeying his natural instinct to snoop where ordinary pawns could not.

But the hunters were men in the accepted, everyday sense of the term, men without mutational talents. They had their limitations as has every other life-form, great or small—for the great remain within other, different and often inconceivable limits, just as binding, just as restricting albeit in immensely wider sense.

So two of the great sat in the dark upon the wall-top, perched like ruminating owls, while lesser life prowled warily but futilely around the basalt castle, its yards and outbuildings, weapons held ready, trigger-fingers made nervous by the greatest fear of all: fear of the unknown.

To these pawn-minds a mutant was a kind of vaudeville character who had gone too far, developed delusions of grandeur and might at any time unite with ruthless prototypes to make slaves of normal men. A multi-talented mutant would be infinitely worse, a non-human creature disguised in human shape and theoretically capable of anything, anything at all.

The notion of being suddenly confronted by a biological monstrosity which was hypno-telepath-pyrotic-whatever all rolled into one, with no handicaps other than the sole inability to outjump a bullet, was too much for a couple of the searchers.

One sneaked through the archway, pointing a peculiar handlamp on the studs to keep them activated. He sought in vain around the area, eyes wide, back hairs erect, and passed a couple of times right under the feet of the quarry before he gave up and went out.

At the same time another emerged from the courtyard door, detected the sound of secret movement through the arch, stared toward it. Weapons ready, they pussy-footed toward each other and saw a vague form loom up through the fog.

Both barked, "Who's that?" and triggered without waiting for reply.

One was missed by an inch. The other got a slug in his left arm. The sound of shots stirred the edgy castle still further. Somebody in the distance beyond the gate fired vertically at an imaginary floater, plugged a darker patch of fog that was anything but man-shaped. The ether became full of abuse, all of it passionate and most of it coarse.

Leaning forward, Raven looked down past his dangling feet. "If only one-tenth of the ancestral details now being broadcast are true, Thorstern must have raided an orphanage to staff this place."

"I hear something else." Charles glanced upward. "Do you?"

"Yes. Someone's coming. I have a feeling it's the man we want."

The sound was a superswift *whup-whup-whup* as of giant vanes whirling at considerable altitude. The helicopter was coming from the east flying high above the night fog.

A thin orange-colored ray shot from a corner turret of the castle, spiked through overhead cloud, remained gleaming steadily. Noise of vanes grew louder as the oncoming machine gradually lowered toward the beacon. A minute later it was immediately above, at a few hundred feet and making an explosive roar. There was a distinct downdraft from it. Fog coiled and swirled below it, oozing its scents from far-off jungles.

Guided by its own instruments or by radioed instructions from the ground, the copter lowered into the mist, descended through it, landed on the graveled area outside the gate. The orange beam cut off. Several pairs of feet ran through the courtyard and out the gate toward the new arrival.

"Now to join the deputation."

Edging off the stonework, Raven dropped forty feet to the ground. He did not drift down like a levitator. He fell in the same manner with which he had plunged into the forest; a swift and normal plunge followed by last moment deceleration.

Charles followed in exactly the same uncanny way, landing imperturbably and brushing the seat of his pants. Raven pointed through the arch.

"Let's forget that invisible light trap. If somebody does notice the telltale wobbling it will only give him the creeps and add to the fun."

There was a minor uproar of voices and accompanying thought-forms coming from the direction of the shrouded copter. A dozen agitated men all trying to talk at once. Two of the gate guards were lounging outside their post and looking toward the tumult with such intentness that neither took any notice of the vaguely outlined pair who hastened through the gate, passing them within a couple of yards. Whether or not the telltale had operated and been noticed it was impossible to determine. At any rate, the siren did not resume its wild screaming.

The escaping pair went only a little way toward the machine, just far enough for the fog to hide them from the watchers by the gate. At that point they made a half-circle that brought them near to the copter on the side farthest from the castle. None had noticed them, the gloom was so thick, the subject of discussion too all-absorbing.

A man was standing at the top of the copter's landing ladder, listening to the talkers, grim-faced and gimlet-eyed. He looked like the twin brother of the unfortunate Greatorex.

The minds of those addressing him revealed a most curious situation. Not one of them knew with any degree of certainty whether Thorstern himself had died and they were now reporting the fact to one of his dummies, or whether a substitute had suffered and they were telling Thorstern himself—or another substitute.

With masterful cunning the would-be dictator of a world had been frank with them, let them in on his scheme of quadrupling himself, then drilled them to accept any seeming Thorstern as the real Thorstern. So accustomed had they become to their master's in-hiding technique that automatically their minds grouped Thorstern and his three malleables together as one personality many-bodied. It was a tribute to the man; a greater tribute to the others who so ably played his part.

The trick was useful in the extreme. No antagonistic mind-probe could detect a substitution in the screen-protected brain of anyone pretending to be the big boss. He would have to go direct to the mind of Thorstern himself and feel around that—if he could find it.

Neither could any of the leader's rank and file be tempted to take a treacherous crack at him, since they knew the odds were three to one against nailing the right man, and with vengeance surely to follow should they fail. It created within the organizational setup a most discouraging hide-and-seek factor calculated to make any would-be traitor think twice—and then decide discretion to be the better part of valor.

But for once the man atop the ladder was caught napping in spite of all precautions. No silver-mesh screen ensured the privacy of his mind. He was in the open and primarily concerned with getting a clear idea of what had happened in his very hideout and, on the basis of that, decide whether it were safest to stay or depart.

His mind admitted that he was indeed Emmanuel Thorstern and no other, a fact that would have given comfort to the gripers before him had there been a telepath among them. Already he was juggling with the notion of returning to Plain City to give zip to the hunt and sending another impersonator back to the castle to take the full brunt of any second blow that might be made.

"Then this guy glared straight at him as if to say, 'I hope you drop dead!' " continued the frontmost talker. "Whereupon he did just that! I tell you, boss, it isn't natural. It would put a scare into a bunch of skewboys, let alone the likes of us." He spat on the ground. "When a couple of things that aren't human can waltz straight in and—"

"Through the gate, through the alarm system and everything else," chimed in a second. "Just as if they didn't exist. Then they top it by walking out of a triple-locked room."

A third voiced exactly what was in the listening man's mind. "What gives me the willies is the fact that if they can do it in once they can do it again and again and again—maybe more besides!"

Thorstern backed half a step. "You've searched the place? Thoroughly?"

"Every inch, boss. Couldn't find hide nor hair of them. We called for some help from the city. They're sending a herd of pussies and a few skewboys. Fight fire with fire."

As if in confirmation there came evidence of the pussies referred to. From far away sounded the faint, irritable yowling of haltered tree-cats.

"They'll do a fat lot of good," opined the first, too pessimistic to care who knew it. "Not unless they happen to meet Raven and the pot-bellied chump on the way. They've had a long start by now. Sweeny and his boys won't get within a mile of them and neither will the city crowd." He brooded a couple of seconds, added, "Nor me either, if I can help it."

Feeling that he had heard enough, Thorstern came to a decision. "In view of all this I'd better go back to the city. I'll stir up the authorities and get some drastic action." He drew himself up. "I am not without influence."

"Yes, boss, sure."

"I'll return here immediately I'm satisfied everything's being done that can be done. Expect me back in a couple of hours' time or three at most."

He said it straight-faced, knowing full well that he had not the slightest intention of returning so long as it might be at his personal peril. Another would double for him on his next appearance.

"If anyone else comes asking for me, tell them I'm away and you don't know where. If a caller proves to be this Raven again, or looks somewhat like him, talks or acts like him, or gives reason to think he's animated by similar ideas, don't argue or give him a chance. Use a gun on him and use it effectively." His hard eye gave them a final authoritative going over. "I will accept full responsibility should anyone make a mistake."

With that he stepped inside the copter, doing it with an air of self-confident deliberation that concealed his inward desire to get away fast. He was shaken though he took every care not to show it.

Someone had not been fooled by the false front put up by Wollencott even though they'd proved suckers for Greatorex. Someone had painstakingly traced all hidden leads and found them running to Thorstern. Someone had power exceeding his own and at least equal ruthlessness. Someone was determined to remove him from his own tortuously constructed scheme of things and—even in this first failure—had proved ability to succeed with appalling ease.

He growled at the pilot, "Get going," and lay back in his seat. His mood was worriedly introspective.

The vanes whirled, the machine did a brief bounce, rocked slightly and went up. Raven and his companion went up with it by the simple expedient of stepping close and hooking a leg over the landing-wheel braces. Formerly hidden from view of the talkers by the copter's intervening bulk, they became momentarily visible as they soared. A group of startled faces got a good look at them for two or three seconds before they disappeared into overhead cloud. Reaction was angry and confused.

"Quick, give me that gun! Quick, I say! You got ten thumbs?"

"Let go, you fool! What's the use of firing blindly? You can't see them now."

"Easy, Meaghan, you might hit the boss."

"Or the pilot. D'you want a couple tons of metal dropped on your crust?"

"Got to do something. Darn those skewboys! If I had my way I'd slaughter them all on principle. It'd make life easier for most of us."

"Phone the city again. They'll shoot them off the undercarriage as the copter comes down."

"This is where a couple of well-armed floaters would be useful. Why not—?"

"Stick around, Dillworth. The pilot may smell a rat and descend." The speaker perked his ears, caught the steadily rising *whup-whup-whup.* "No, he's carrying on. Stick around all the same."

"Where are you going?"

"Inside. I'll contact the boss on the radio and tell him what's underneath."

"Good idea. A shower of slugs through the floor will blow them off their perch."

The copter came out of the cloud into bright starlight plus the shine from a mock moon called Terra. They had emerged from the haze at two thousand feet.

In parts it thickened to ten thousand while in others—especially the higher shelves of the rain forests—there was none. Daytimes it rose in a complete strata to forty thousand leaving the ground dull but clear.

To one side the Sawtooths spiked against a sable background powdered with stars. Nearby, percolating through the mist, was the glow of Plain City with an orange beam pointing vertically from its westward rim. Far to the south was another almost indiscernible glow coming from Big Mines.

Heading directly for the Plain City beacon, the pilot was content to skim a mere hundred feet above the fog. There was no point in gaining greater altitude for so short a run. He sat hunched over the controls with Thorstern grim and silent at his side, and kept his attention on the orange beam. Subconsciously he sensed that the machine was less lively than it had been an hour ago. Kind of sluggish. But he wasn't worried about it. Nighttimes the atmosphere's oxygen content varied from hour to hour and tended to make his motors seem temperamental.

He was already over the city when the radio beeped and he put out a hand to switch it on. At the same time the door opened and Raven stepped inside.

"Good evening," he said to Thorstern pleasantly.

With his hand still hovering over the switch, the pilot threw an incredulous glance through the windshield to confirm that he really was airborne and flying high, then growled, "How the blue blazes—!"

"Stowaway reporting, sir." Raven grinned at him. "And there is another outside uncomfortably riding the rods. A much bulkier one." He returned his attention to Thorstern, followed that person's intent gaze to a side pocket. "I wouldn't if I were you," he advised. It was said in ordinary tones yet sounded threatening.

Deciding that the radio might as well be answered, the pilot flipped his switch and snapped, "Corry here."

A voice drummed from the tiny loudspeaker. "Tell Mr. Thorstern to grab a gun and send a dozen slugs between his feet. Those two guys are squatting on the undercarriage."

"He knows," said the pilot.

"He knows?"

"That's what I said."

"Good grief!" The voice turned in an aside to someone else. "The boss already knows." Then it came back. "What's he doing about it?"

"Nothing," the pilot reported.

"Nothing? How's that?"

"Don't ask me. I'm only the pilot."

"You don't mean—" The other's rising tones suddenly cutoff. Came a sharp click as the distant transmitter closed down.

"He's jumped to conclusions," observed Raven. "He thinks you and Mr. Corry are tied up in sacks and that he's been talking to *me.*"

"And who may you be?" inquired Mr. Corry, his tone suggesting that only hoboes came aboard in mid-air.

Thorstern spoke for the first time. "Keep out of this—there's nothing you can do."

His bothered brain provided an interesting example of how inconsequential thoughts sometimes come uppermost in times of crisis. He was in a jam. Judging by what had occurred at the castle, it was a very tight one. There was every reason to believe he was in danger of his life and before long might follow the hapless Greatorex into oblivion. Added to which was the quasi-guilty realization that he had asked for trouble and could not justifiably complain about getting it aplenty.

But all he thought of at that moment was, "An antigrav cab has a load-limit of five hundred pounds. A copter can haul more than a ton. If I'd used an antigrav I wouldn't be in this fix. It couldn't have lifted with two inside and two clinging outside. After this, no more copters for me—not unless I have an escort."

"You have an escort—my friend and myself," Raven pointed out. He shoved the door open. "Come on. We're stepping out."

Thorstern stood up slowly. "I'd break my neck."

"You'll be all right. We'll have hold of you."

"What's to stop you letting go?"

"Not a thing."

The pilot chipped in. "If you two are floaters let me tell you it's against the law to leave an air machine while it's flying over an inhabited area."

Taking no notice of this, Raven continued with Thorstern, "You have several alternatives. Firstly, you can make a snatch at that side pocket and see what happens. Or jump out on your own and see how high you bounce. Or crash the copter and be scraped out of the junkpile. But if you prefer you can come with us and get down in one piece."

Thorstern's mental reaction to that was, "He can hypnotize me into doing anything he wishes, anything at all, even to dying against my will, by remote influence, through a scanner. It would be better to do things of my own accord. I can bide my time. It's his hour now—mine later. Other circumstances provide other opportunities."

"That's using hoss-sense," Raven approved. "Stay with us until we blunder. You can then tear out our hearts."

"I know you're a telepath and can treat my mind like an open book." Thorstern moved toward the door. "And more besides. There is nothing I can do about it—yet."

He braced himself as Raven backed out ahead of him, grasped an arm, and Charles reached up to take the other. Just as those able to levitate almost from birth have minds conditioned by their own peculiar ability, so are others conditioned by their limitations.

Thorstern had brains and his full share of animal courage but nevertheless his whole nature rebelled against an unhampered leap into space. With a parachute or an antigrav belt he would not have hesitated for a moment. With no more than other, hostile hands grasping him it wasn't so good.

So he closed his eyes and held his breath as they left the machine. He felt sick in the pit of his stomach when they plummeted down. Thick atmosphere heavy with vapor enshrouded him and streamed upward, making his pants belly out and his hair stand on end. The air stream whistled past his ears.

He was conjuring fearful visions of a rocky wall or tilted roof rocketing from underneath whiteness to smash his legs or break his body when a powerful pull on both arms slowed him down. Still he kept his eyes shut and strove to control his insides. A gable end rose from the mist, brushed his feet, slid upward. He landed in a street.

High above the pilot was gabbling into his transmitter. "Couple of fellows grabbed him at two thousand four hundred feet. I took it for granted they were floaters but they went down like stones. Eh? No, he didn't resist or give me any orders. Near as I can tell they must have hit in Sector Nine, somewhere around Reece Avenue." A pause, followed by, "Not if I know him. There was something mighty queer about the whole business. He went without wanting to—but he went!"

Raven said, "Your pilot Corry is on the police band and screaming for help."

"I don't think it will be of much use." Thorstern looked around, trying to identify his surroundings in the dim light and poor visibility. "But no matter."

"Becoming fatalistic?"

"I accept conditions temporarily beyond my power to change. At my time of life I have learned to wait. No game goes wholly in one's favor all the time." Pulling out a handkerchief he wiped beads of condensation from his lavish mop of hair. "It is the last move that counts."

The statement was devoid of misplaced confidence or braggadocio. It was the voice of experience, the considered opinion of one whose complicated plans frequently had suffered obstructions, delays, setbacks, all of which had been overcome next week, next month or the following year. He could display infinite patience when the need arose, still keeping the main purpose in sight and pushing toward it the instant the way became clear.

He was admitting that this unlucky night he was beaten and might well be finished for keeps, but warning them that so long as he lived there was always tomorrow, another day. It was a form of defiance, a revealing of teeth when cornered. There wasn't much else he could do—just then.

Chapter 13

Mavis opened the door and let them in without being summoned by knock or ring. Expressing neither pleasure nor surprise, she had the matter-of-fact air of one who has kept in constant touch with events and knew what was happening at any given moment.

In the manner of a mother mildly reproving a small and wayward child, she said to Charles, "You are going to regret this. I can feel it coming." With that, she returned to her kitchen.

"Now we've got still another type of mutant," grumbled Charles, unabashed. He flopped into a chair, making its well-worn seat bulge down between the legs. "A prognosticator."

Staring toward the kitchen in open approval, Thorstern remarked, "It's a pleasure to hear somebody talking sense."

"Everyone talks sense according to his or her particular lights. Each man his own oracle." Raven pushed a pneumaseat toward him. "Sit down. You don't have to freeze up stiff just because you're in bad company."

The other sat. Already he was striving to drive away a series of thoughts that insisted on coming into his mind. He was most anxious not to nurse them because they could be seen whenever either of these two saw fit to peer inside his skull and, for all he knew, they were peering without cease.

He could not be certain of constant eavesdropping. A telepath can feel or sense or detect another mind groping within his own. A non-telepath cannot. Thorstern was unordinary rather than extraordinary and that was a handicap of which he was acutely conscious in his present predicament; at other and safer times he would have dismissed the handicap with a lordly wave. So he tried to swat the thoughts as one would swipe at half a dozen annoying flies, but they hung around and kept buzzing.

"This pair of multi-mutants can protect their thoughts. Probably the woman can also. But I can't hide mine and doubt whether they can shield them from others. Already the patrols will be scouring the streets, some concentrating on this neighborhood. They'll include whatever telepaths can be dug up at this late hour. So unless this room has built-in screens to give privacy there's a fair chance that some passing mind-probe will recognize my thought-stream and trace its source. He will then summon the troops and—"

He managed to shoo it away for a few seconds, but again it returned to completion. "Wish I knew whether a spray of thoughts is as individually characteristic as a voice. Maybe they all seem alike. If so, I'll be out of luck unless I can choose the right moment to radiate an unmistakable giveaway. If this pair happen to pick it up too, they may do something drastic. I'll have to take a chance on that."

Giving Raven a surly eye, he said, "I have jumped out in mid-air. I have sat down when told. I have obeyed orders. What next?"

"A talk."

"It's two in the morning. You could have talked tomorrow and at a reasonable hour." He pursed sour lips. "Was there any real need for all this preliminary melodrama?"

"Unfortunately, yes! You've made it hard to gain contact. Moreover, you've chased me around as if I were the dog that snitched the Sunday roast."

"Me?" Thorstern lifted an incredulous eyebrow.

"You and the organization over which you preside."

"Meaning my extensive trading interests? Nonsense! We have something better to do than chivvy people. Seems to me you're animated by a persecution complex."

"Look, we've been through all this before. The turn loses its novelty the second time round. Didn't you get a record of our conversation with your very accomplished impersonator?"

Much as he would have liked to deny all knowledge of any malleables doubling for him, Thorstern was too wise to let his mouth utter something simultaneously contradicted by his mind. He could not hope to deceive with mere words. But he could be evasive, play for time, fight a delaying action.

So he said, truthfully, "I've not had the details of what you told Greatorex. All I do know is that he is dead and that you had a hand in it. I don't like it." His voice gained a touch of toughness. "Eventually you won't like it, either!"

Charles emitted a short laugh and interjected, "That's a nice, vivid, satisfying picture of people hanging by their necks. Your imagination operates in full colors. I like the way you make their tongues stick out, black and swollen. A few of the details are inaccurate. The knots are in the wrong place—and I don't possess two left feet."

"Do I have to endure criticism in addition to mental prying?" Thorstern asked Raven.

"He couldn't resist it. Sadistic pleasures ask for adverse comment." He paced to and fro, the prisoner's gaze following. "Under the delusion that Greatorex was really you, we asked him to stop cutting off Terra's toes. He fed us a phony line, doing it as to the manner born. We gave him fair warning that toe-cutting is a practice the victim has every right to resent. He insisted on playing the tune as before. Superb as his act proved to be, he was hamstrung by his own limitations."

"Why?" asked Thorstern, watching beetle-browed.

"Not being you, it was not within his power to make a major decision on your behalf. Knowing you, he wouldn't dare. He could do no more than play to the best of his ability the part in which he had been so well drilled. By virtue of his peculiar position he was without the initiative that could have saved him." He made a that-is-that gesture. "And so he is dead."

"For which you are now sorry?"

"Sorry?" Raven faced him, eyes bright with silvery motes shining in the irises. "Certainly not! We couldn't care less!"

It sent a most unpleasant sensation down Thorstern's spine. When there was a highly desirable end in view he could be decidedly cold-blooded himself, but never did he display it with such unashamed callousness. An unctuous washing of hands with much solemn deploring was his technique for brushing off a cadaver with decent dignity. If Greatorex—less burdened with guilt than himself—could be dismissed so airily, like a piece of trash . . .

"Seems there are others who enjoy sadistic pleasures," he stabbed, reasonably enough.

"You misunderstand. We are not happy about the matter but neither do we grieve. Call it splendid indifference."

"Practically the same thing." This was an opportune moment to appeal to a telepathic patrol if one happened to be nearby. "I don't know how you did it, but I call it murder!"

Mavis came in with a percolator and cups. She poured for three, set out a plate of cookies, retired without a word.

"You wish to talk about murder?" Raven asked. "That's a subject you're qualified to discuss."

That was an obtuse crack at himself, Thorstern felt. An undeserved one. Whatever else he might be, he was not a bloodthirsty monster. True, he was running what whining Terrans saw fit to call an undeclared war but in reality was a liberation movement. True also that a few lives had been taken despite instructions that blows be struck to exact minimum loss of life and maximum loss of economic power.

A few killings had been inevitable. He had approved only those absolutely necessary to forward his designs. Not one more, not one of any sort. And even those he had dutifully deplored. He was by far the most humane conqueror in history, bidding fair to achieve the biggest and most spectacular results at the least cost to all concerned.

"Would you care to explain that remark? If you are accusing me of wholesale slaughter I'd like you to state one instance, one specific case."

"There are only individual cases in the past. The greater atrocities are located in the future, if you consider them essential—and if you live that long."

"Ye gods, another prognosticator!" commented Charles, this time completely without humor. Indeed, he made it smack of grim foreboding.

Raven continued with Thorstern, "Only you know how true that is, how far you are prepared to go, how great a cost you are willing to pay to boss a world of your own. But it is written in the depths of your mind. It stands out in letters of fire: *no price is too high.*"

Thorstern could find nothing to say. There wasn't an effective answer. He knew what he wanted. He wanted it cheaply, with as little trouble as possible. But if tough opposition should jack the price sky-high in terms of cash or lives it would still be paid, with regrets, but paid.

At the present moment he was helpless in the hands of this bellyaching pair. They could end his stubborn ambitions, but they would have to finish him like Greatorex. He had no doubt they could do it. That they were willing to do it was something that remained to be seen. *He* would have no qualms.

Stealthily, in the hope that none would notice, his attention turned toward the door. But he could not suppress concomitant thoughts no matter how hard he tried. If a patrol had overheard that talk about murder they would not necessarily bust in at once. They might first go for help of a formidable kind. There was a chance, any minute, of a rowdy diversion during which he might break free.

Raven was still talking although the other only half listened. "If your Venusian nationalist movement really were no more than a means of gaining self-government we could find it in us to sympathize despite the violence of its methods. But it isn't what it pretends to be. Your brain reveals that it's your personal instrument of self-glorification. It is designed solely to gain you the power you crave. You poor little crawling, creeping grub!"

"Eh?" Thorstern's attention snapped back.

"I said you're a poor little crawling, creeping grub, hiding from the light, squirming around in the dark and pathetically afraid of a thousand things including anonymity."

"I fear no—"

"So you yearn for petty predominance over a colony of similar grubs during a mere heart-beat in the span of time. After which you will be gone, for ever and ever. Dust into dust. An empty name in a useless book, mouthed by myopic historians and cursed by weary school children. In distant time some naughty moppet may be punished by having to write a tiresome essay about you. The rise and fall of Emperor Emmanuel." Raven's sniff was loud and contemptuous. "I suppose you call that immortality?"

It was too much. Thorstern's thick hide was thin in one spot. He enjoyed insults because they were acknowledgment of his strength and ability. He appreciated enmity because it gratified his ego to know he was feared. Jealousy he viewed as an oblique form of worship. Hatred served only to magnify him. The one thing he could not endure was to be regarded as a no-account, a piker, a comparative seeker of butts on the sidewalk. He could not tolerate being thought small.

His features livid, he came to his feet, thrust a hand in a pocket, extracted three photographs and flung them on the table. His tones were savage.

"You've some good cards and they tickle you pink. But I've seen them. Now take a look at a few of mine. Not all of them, for you'll never see the rest!"

Picking up the top one, Raven studied it imperturbably. A blown-up photograph of himself, rather old, not very good but still good enough to serve for purposes of identification.

"It's being exhibited on the spectroscreen every hour," said Thorstern, with vicious pleasure. "Reproductions are being issued to patrols as fast as they can be turned out. By midday tomorrow everyone will know your face—and the reward will push the search." He was full of ireful triumph as he stared at the other. "The tougher you get with me the tougher I'll make it for you. You pranced easily into this world in spite of all preparations to grab you on arrival. See if you can get out of it." He switched to Charles. "And the same applies to you, Fatman."

"It doesn't. I have no intention of departing." Charles settled himself lower in his chair. "I'm quite comfortable here. Venus suits me as much—or as little—as any other ball of dirt. Besides, my work is here. How can I do it if I don't stay with it?"

"What work?"

"That," said Charles, "is something you wouldn't understand."

"He walks dogs and is ashamed to admit it," Raven chipped in. Tossing the photograph onto the table, he picked up the second, glanced at it. His features went taut. Flourishing it in front of the other, he demanded, "What did you do to him?"

"Me? Nothing."

"You did your dirty work by proxy."

"I gave no specific instructions," denied Thorstern, taken aback by Raven's reaction. "All I told them was to pick up Steen and make him tell what had occurred." He assumed an expression of fastidious revulsion as he glanced at the offending picture. Running in a typical path, his mind dutifully deplored the sight. "So they did it."

"And enjoyed the doing by the looks of it." Raven was annoyed and showed it openly. "They made a gory mess of him. Now Steen is dead through no fault of his own. I don't mind that any more than he minds it."

"Don't you?" Thorstern was surprised by a comment so contradictory of visible reaction.

"No. His end doesn't matter a hoot. It would have come sometime even though he lived to be a hundred. No man's end matters." With a jerk of disgust he flipped the photograph aside. "What I do dislike most intensely is the fact that he was slow to die. He took a long time over it. That is bad. That is unforgivable." The eyes shone with sudden fires. "It will be remembered when your turn comes!"

Again Thorstern felt a cold shiver. He was not afraid, he told himself. It wasn't within him to admit fear. But he conceded himself a certain degree of apprehension. He had played a card hoping it would serve as a dire warning. Perhaps it had been a mistake.

"They exceeded my orders. I administered a most serious reproof."

"He reproved them," said Raven to Charles. "How nice!"

"They pleaded that he was stubborn and made them go farther than they'd intended." Thorstern decided it might pay to enlarge on this subject while yet it was hot. No rescue party had responded to his earlier talk about murder. Maybe somebody would pick up his dissertation on Steen. Any form of hollering would do so long as it brought results.

He went on, "They used a telepath to try to pick his mind, from a safe distance so Steen couldn't make a dummy of him. It was no use. He could catch only what Steen was thinking and he insisted on thinking about other things. So they had to persuade Steen to mull over what had made him pull a fast one on us. He didn't want to. He tried not to. He tried very hard." Thorstern spread hands to emphasize personal helplessness and lack of blame. "By the time he became co-operative they had overdone the persuading."

"Meaning—?"

"His mind turned, same as Haller's did. He babbled a lot of crazy stuff and passed out for keeps."

"And what was the crazy stuff?"

"He said that you were an entirely new, redoubtable and previously unsuspected type of mutant. You've a detachable ego. He said you had swapped bodies with him against his will."

"By heavens!" interjected Charles, popping his eyes in mock astonishment. "Now we've got bio-mechanics, prognosticators, ego-masters and whatever. There's going to be no end to this."

"It was unadulterated blah," continued Thorstern, peevishly. "I checked with several of our leading authorities on paranormal aptitudes. They declared it ludicrous—but they knew why Steen told it."

"What was their diagnosis?"

"That he'd been out-hypnoed by one of his own type far more powerful than himself. They've no case on record of such absolute dominance but theoretically it is possible."

His gaze shifted sidewise, for the first time noticed his cup of coffee now half cold. Licking dry lips, he picked it up, drank it in three or four gulps.

"For a short time you made Steen believe he was *you.* And you made him send Haller off balance, at which point his delusion ran out. Now, ordinary as I am, I can do some mindreading of my own. You're thinking that if I don't play it your way you will put the same sort of bee on me."

"Will I?"

"Either that or dispose of me outright as you did with Greatorex. Whichever course you take will be futile. If you fix me up like Steen it will wear off. Hypnosis always wears off within twenty-four hours at most. Whatever I'm compelled to do during that time I can undo later."

"True," admitted Raven, gravely.

"While if you finish me completely you will have a mere body on your hands. A body can't call off a war. You've told me six times that the dead don't care. Take a bite out of your own philosophy and think how little I'll care about Terra's troubles. Bah, I'll be less concerned than is Greatorex!" A notion struck him and he demanded, "How did you finish Greatorex? Even a super-super-hypno cannot persuade a man to lay flat and expire. What did you *do* to him?"

"The same as we'll be compelled to do to you once we're convinced that there is no alternative." Raven stared significantly at the other. "Get it into your mulish head that we have few compunctions in dealing with an obstacle. We differ from you only in that we make it mercifully swift. We don't let the subject linger. *That* is the real crime: to prolong deliberately the act of dying!" He studied his listener, finished, "Greatorex went so fast he hardly had time to fight it. Steen was denied that fundamental privilege."

"I told you—"

Raven brushed the words aside. "You are not going to make the planet Venus your personal property and, sometime in the future, join with the Martians to hold Terra to ransom in her hour of trial. If humanity ever gets into a tight corner it's going to be humanity that'll fight its way out, not just Terrans. All of us! So you will cease hostile action against Terra and persuade the Martians to follow suit. Alternatively, you will be removed from the scene forever, after which we shall deal similarly with your successors, whoever they may be. We shall destroy them one by one until your entire movement collapses from sheer lack of leadership." He pointed to the tiny radium chronometer in the ring on Thorstern's middle finger. "You've five minutes to make up your mind."

"I've more than that, much more. In fact, I've got just as long as I like." He poked the third photograph across the table. "Take a look at that."

Not bothering to pick it up, Raven bent over and examined it. His expression did not change in the slightest.

"Who is it?" inquired Charles, too lethargic to get up and see for himself or exercise any other visual sense.

"Leina," informed Raven.

Thorstern laughed. It was a grating sound. He was enjoying his own foresight to the full. In particular, he was pleased with his success in keeping his mind away from the subject of Leina until this moment. Not once had a thought of her drifted through his brain. And again a pawn had out-guessed a mutant.

Nothing delighted him more than to be a jump ahead of a paranormal. It was his characteristic weakness which would have greatly interested any ecologist studying the effect of an environment containing superior life-forms.

"Your woman," he mouthed with unconcealed scorn. "We know her habits, movements, aptitudes. We know, for instance, that she's another superior breed of hypno, like yourself. Steen said so. He wasn't lying, not in his condition. Maybe that's the attraction between you and this heavyweight tart. I can't imagine any other unless you're fond of elephants and—"

"Leave her physical proportions out of this. She was not constructed to suit your taste. Get to the point."

"The point is," said Thorstern, unable to resist showing relish, "that the moment I die or go nuts or obviously out of character"—he tapped the picture with a heavy forefinger—"she pays!"

"That's a laugh," said Raven.

"I hope you'll enjoy it when you find her dead."

"I won't weep," Raven assured, carelessly. It was not at all sardonic. He made it true, dreadfully true.

Even Thorstern thought it horrible. He looked uncertainly at Charles, seeking confirmation of his own feelings in that person's revulsion, found him mooning boredly at the ceiling. His attention came back to Raven, his features incredulous.

"She can die slowly."

"Do you think so?"

"I am positive of it. Unless she happens to have a weak heart she can take ten times longer than did Steen. How would you like that?"

"I think it disgusting."

"Eh?"

"The mastermind, the mighty conqueror, hides behind a woman's skirts."

Back came the old fury at belittlement, but Thorstern managed to beat it down and say, "Listen who's talking—somebody willing to let a woman pay for his sins."

"She won't mind," smiled Raven, offering him a completely unexpected angle.

"You're mad!" declared Thorstern, beginning to believe it.

"Greatorex doesn't mind. Neither does Haller. And Steen is coldly indifferent. So why should Leina care? Why, even you—"

"Shut up, you murderous maniac!" Thorstern was on his feet again, both fists clenched until the knuckles showed white. His voice was loud with a mixture of strain, near-relief and triumph. "You've left it too long. You were so cocky you wanted to chew the fat all night. And we've been overheard, see?" He made an ecstatic gesture toward the front door. "Hear those feet? Twenty of them? Fifty! A hundred! The whole city is roused!"

"Too bad," said Raven, watching him blank-faced.

"Take me and see what it buys you," invited Thorstern, full of nerve. "In a few seconds the rush will come after which you'll get what you've earned." Trying to keep a wary eye on Raven and at the same time watch the front, he added with emphasis, "Unless I am in complete possession of myself and order them to hold their hands."

"It appears that we're in a bad fix," commented Charles, blearing in fat reproof, gazing at the door.

Thorstern was now standing with compressed lips while his mind ran its un-trammeled course without regard for who could read his thoughts. They dare not try anything *now*. The cost would be too great. They will postpone designs to a moment that will never come. They will be dealt with according to Terran law. The case will be sewn up good and tight, beyond Heraty's power to unstitch. Or I could arrange an accident. That might be quicker and more effective. Yes, one way or another—

Like Charles, his full attention was on the door beyond which he had heard— or could have sworn he had heard—the cautious scuffling of many feet. A few of the patrol, he decided, might be made jittery by the presence of such formidable characters as Raven and the other. They'd be dangerously touchy. When they broke in he would have to move fast and roar orders faster lest he fall foul of someone too trigger-happy to look where he was throwing it.

He stiffened, noting out the corner of an eye that neither of the others had moved. Hah, they were resigned to a situation from which there was no escape. Teleportatively manipulated, the lock began to turn slowly and apparently of its own accord.

Chapter 14

The door commenced to move, drifting inward inch by inch as if wafted by a gentle breeze or unobtrusively edged by the ultra-cautious hand of someone lurk-ing in the outer dark. A yellowish coil of night fog slithered through the gradually widening gap and brought odors of resin, rotting leaves, warm bark and wet fungi.

No sound came through the opening other than the dull thumping of fuel pumps over at the spaceport and faint strains of music from four or five streets away where restless nocturnals were trying to live the fuller life. There was utter silence within the room, not even the whispering of a drawn breath. This and the door's tedious motion created an immense tension that was as much as Thorstern's overstretched nerves could stand.

His eyes were straining at the gap, his ears shocked by the total lack of antici-pated uproar, his mind trying to operate along ten channels at once. Who was there, waiting outside? Did they have weapons ready? Fingers taut, triggers already partway back? If he made a mad jump for that opening would he leap into a deadly volley and go down for ever and ever and ever?

Or had they a telepath to warn them of his intentions so that they would hold their fire? But, of course, a telepath could not thus warn them because he was still hesitating, had not reached a decision A telepath could read his thoughts and yet be completely unable to forecast a split-second conclusion. There were no prognosticators in any positive sense.

The moments crawled like eons while he watched the door which now had ceased its motion halfway round its arc and remained invitingly ajar. The dark gap to the street tantalized him.

Why the devil were they waiting? Were they fearful of the risk to himself if they charged blindly through? Perhaps they had a plan that required him to take certain synchronized action. In heaven's name, why were they waiting?

More fog rolled in. Noticing it for the first time, he was smitten with a plausible solution—gas! Yes, that was it, that was the idea! Send gas in with the fog. Anyone familiar with the defenses of the castle, and especially of Room Ten, would have thought of it right away. So they wanted him to stay firmly put until he collapsed along with his captors. Then they would enter in safety, revive him, give him the other pair to pull to pieces.

It was possible that Raven and the fat one knew what was coming. It had sparked brightly within his own mind and therefore they must have seen it—unless they had been too busy probing the think-boxes beyond the door. Can a telepath deal with more than one brain at a time? Can he probe several simultaneously? Thorstern was not certain. He lacked data on the point. Anyway, these two would get the same result from other minds—gas! And what could they do about it? Nothing! The mightiest of mutants is as much an animal as any pawn in that he *has* to breathe.

His nostrils tried to detect the insidious approach of the invisible weapon though he knew almost certainly that it would be odorless. There should be other signs. A slowing of the pulse. Slightly more labored breathing. A sudden miasma in the mind. Eagerly he kept watch on himself, alert for symptoms, and waited a mere half-minute that he sensed as half an hour. Then he broke. It was too much. He could endure no more, no more, no more.

With an agonized bellow of, "Don't shoot! Don't shoot!" he sprang into the gap in the doorway. "It's me! It's Thor—" His voice died away.

Staring with stupefaction into the shrouded night, he posed there a short time while his brain broadcast its reactions.

"Nobody here. Nobody, not a soul. They fooled me. They made me hear things, imagine things. They treated me like a rat in a laboratory, stimulated to see which way it turns in its fight for life. Then they released the lock and opened the door. Hypnos and teleports at one and the same time. That's multitalented, no matter what the experts may say. The hell-devils!" His neural impulses suddenly boosted to maximum amplitude. "Run for it, you idiot, run!"

And then the unexpected happened, the sort of thing that upsets the best laid plans of mice and men. Thorstern's tremendous psychic strain had brought it on, invited it.

With one hand braced on the doorpost, the empty street before him, inwardly bolstered by the certitude that armed search-parties must be somewhere in the locality, he lifted a foot for the first swift step in a wild dash for freedom. He never made it.

His body poised for the effort, he stood unmoving while a thoroughly bewildered expression came into his hard face. Slowly he put down the uplifted foot, slowly sank to his knees like one prostrating himself before an unseeable god. His agitated thought-stream had now gone into a violent swirl that flung out odd words and phrases.

"No . . . oh, no *don't!* . . . I can't, I tell you . . . let me alone . . . *Steen* . . . It wasn't my fault . . . oh, let me—"

He toppled forward, writhed around in soundless pain. Already Raven was bending over him, features tight and serious. Charles had come hurriedly out of his chair, manifestly taken by surprise. Mavis appeared in the kitchen doorway, her eyes condemning but her lips saying nothing.

Raven grasped the stricken man's right hand and at once the bodily contortions ceased. Retaining his grip, he twisted his own arm and bent the elbow several times as one does when trying to cling to a wire loaded with excruciating voltage. He seemed to be battling against something, struggling with something. Thorstern opened his mouth, gasped like a landed fish.

"No, no, go away . . . leave me . . . I—"

Lumbering around to the other side, Charles helped lift the heavy body, take it across the room and settle it in a chair. Mavis closed the door but did not bother to reset the lock. Frowning to herself, she returned to the kitchen.

In a little while Thorstern gulped once or twice, opened shocked eyes, heaved himself upright in the chair. There were weird thrills running through his nerves and a highly unpleasant sensation like effervescence in his blood stream. His limbs lacked strength and his insides seemed turned to water. Much as he hated to admit it even to himself he was more shaken than ever he'd been in his life. His face was colorless, like wax. Curiously enough, his mind retained no memory of the words he had uttered in his throes, no knowledge of what had really taken place.

Glowering at Raven, he said in trembling tones, "You squeezed my heart."

"I did not."

"You almost killed me."

"Not guilty."

"Then it was *you.*" He turned his head to glare at Charles.

"Me, neither. The truth is that we saved you—*if* you can call it salvation." Charles smiled at a secret thought. "But for us you would now be one of the late lamented."

"Do you expect me to believe that? One of you two did it."

"How?" inquired Raven, examining him both outwardly and inwardly.

"One of you is a teleport. He unlocked and opened that door without stirring an inch. He squeezed my heart the same way. *That's* what you did to Greatorex!"

"A teleport moves objects by exterior influence," Raven contradicted. "He can't get inside people and rearrange their plumbing."

"I was nearly gone," insisted Thorstern, rocked by his nearness to death. "I could feel my heart being compressed, my body going down. It was as if I were being dragged by main force out of my own body. Somebody did it!"

"Not necessarily. A million die every day without anyone's assistance."

"I can't die like that." He made it childishly complaining.

"Why not?"

"I'm fifty-eight and there's nothing wrong with me." Gingerly he felt himself, gauged the thumping inside his chest. "Nothing wrong."

"So it seems," said Raven, pointedly.

"If I am fated to go naturally, of a heart attack, it is too much of a coincidence for me to drop at this very moment."

He'd made a good point there, he decided. Pinned it on them effectively. Though it would do no good whatever, he was anxious to saddle them with the blame for no other reason than because they were so insistent about refusing it. He could not understand that. Why should they deny bringing him down flat in the doorway when they could boast about it with far more intimidating effect?

But deep, deep down inside himself—thrust into an obscure corner where he wouldn't have to look at it—lurked the dreadful idea that perhaps they were right. Perhaps his time was more limited by destiny than he had assumed. No man is immortal. Maybe he had only a little time to go and the sands were trickling out fast.

Dragging it right into the light and compelling him to survey it, Raven said, "If you were so fated it would most likely come at a moment of considerable nervous strain. So where is the coincidence? Anyway, you did not run and you did not die. Next week you may expire. Or tomorrow. Or before dawn. No man knoweth the day or the hour." He pointed at the other's midget chronometer. "Meanwhile, the five minutes have become fifteen."

"I give up." Finding a large handkerchief, Thorstern wiped his beaded forehead. His breathing was erratic and he remained sheet-white. "I give up."

It was true. More penetrating minds could see the truth inside him, a genuine verity born of half a dozen hastily thought up reasons, some contradictory but all satisfying.

"Can't run in top gear forever. Ease down and live longer. Got to look after myself. Why build for somebody's benefit after I've gone? Wollencott is twelve years younger than me, thinks he'll be the big boss when I'm down the hole. Why should I work and scheme and sweat for his sake? A ham actor. A malleable I raised from the gutter and made into a man. Just a trap-shooting mutant. *Floreat Venusia*—under a stinking mutant! Even Terra does better. Heraty and most of the Council are normals—Gilchist assured me of that."

Raven made a mental note of that last bit: Gilchist, a World Councilor. The traitor in the camp and undoubtedly the character who had betrayed him to the underground movement on Terra. The man whose name Kayder and the others did not know because they didn't want to know it.

"Or if it's not one mutant it'll be another," morbidly continued Thorstern's mind. "One of them will bide his time, take over my empire like taking milk from a kitten. I was safe enough while all attention was focused on Wollencott but now they've gone back of him and found me. The mutants have powers. Someday they will organize themselves against the common run of men. I wouldn't care to be here then!"

His eyes lifted, discovered the others watching. "I've told you I give up. What more do you want?"

"Nothing." Raven nodded toward the wall phone. "Like me to call an antigrav to take you home?"

"No. I'll walk. Besides, I don't trust you."

Arising shakily, he felt his chest again. Within him was suspicion of their ready acceptance of surrender and their casual release. Judging them by himself, he felt sure that another and different trap was waiting somewhere for him to walk into. Had they timed something to happen at the other end of this road, well away from the house? Perhaps another heart-squeeze, to the finish?

"*We* trust *you* because of what is visible in your mind," Raven told him. "It's your hard luck that you lack the ability to see into ours. If you could you would know beyond all shadow of doubt that we play square. You won't be touched by us—unless you renege."

Mooching to the door, Thorstern opened it, looked them over for the last time. His face retained its pallor and had aged a little, but he had recovered a measure of his dignity.

"I have promised to put a stop to all hostile action against Terra," he said. "I shall keep my promise to the letter—that *and no more!*"

Stepping into the dark, he gave his parting shot a touch of absurdity by carefully closing the door behind him. It would have been more fitting had he thrust it wide or slammed it enough to shake the house. But fifty years ago a tall and bitter woman had boxed his ears for slamming doors and, all unknown to him, the ears still tingled.

Following the walls he hurried along the road at the best pace he could muster. Visibility extended to three yards and that made him like a half-blind man.

Now and again he stopped to listen through the mist, then hastened onward. At this unearthly hour there would be few people about other than fidgety nocturnals or roaming patrols. He had covered an unestimable distance before he detected noises to his left.

Cupping hands, he hailed, "Are you there?"

Feet speeded up. The patrol loomed out of the yellow haze, six of them, heavily armed. "What's the matter?"

"I can tell you where to find David Raven!"

Back in the room Charles stopped his careful listening. "He has tried desperately to remember—but he can't. He is muzzy-minded. Doesn't know which way to send them. He'll soon give up and go home."

Crossing heavy legs, he nursed his stomach. "When he flopped in the doorway I thought for a moment that you were taking him for your very own. Then I picked up your mental yelp of surprise."

"And I thought it was you snatching his ego." Raven frowned to himself. "It caught me napping. Good job I reached him so quickly or he'd have been gone."

"Yes, a heart attack." The moon eyes grew bright. "One more stunt like that and the news will be out."

"Somebody was irrationally precipitate," said Raven, looking serious. "Somebody had a one-track mind and couldn't wait to be educated. That's wrong, very wrong. It mustn't happen again!"

"He held out a long time and gave up slowly, which makes an invitation almost too strong to resist," reminded Charles with the air of one explaining everything. "So the would-be emperor of Venus was mighty lucky. If he had gone it would have been relatively quick. Oh, well, he's a tough character with more than his share of fortitude. Nothing less could have scared him into reasonable pacifism. Maybe it was all for the best. His mind holds no notion of what really occurred and that is the main thing."

"Perhaps you're right,. If he had expired we'd have had more of his fooling around, lots more. Wollencott would have to be dealt with and probably the other pair of impersonators likewise. Either of the latter would be sweetly placed to occupy the seat of the mighty and deceive everyone but telepaths. Added to which there may be a hidden list of sharp-witted non-mutant individuals nominated by Thorstern as his successors, one or two of whom might be located on Mars. This surrender has saved us a lot of grief. Without it we'd have had to follow through to the bitter end."

"A surrender with mental reservations," Charles commented. "He couldn't help stewing them while fumbling his way along the road."

"Yes, I heard him."

"He's a sticker if nothing else. Firstly, he reserves the right to feed his promise to the ducks if at any future time he can discover a way to make himself absolutely mutant-proof. He estimates the chance of that as about a million to one against but he insists on covering that remote chance. Secondly, he reserves the right to slap you clean into the next galaxy but can't imagine a satisfactory method just yet."

"That's not all," contributed Raven. "I'm guessing here on the strength of what we know of his character: he'll get into direct touch with the World Council, criticize Wollencott, heartily damn the underground movement, deplore their misdeeds, sympathize with Terra and offer to put a stop to the whole business for a worthwhile consideration. He'll try to sell his surrender to Terra and make a good profit on it."

"He might, at that!"

"Let him. It's no business of ours. The main purpose has been achieved and that's all that counts." He mused a while, went on, "Thorstern won't like destroying his organization. He will call off the hounds but hate to break up the pack. Only thing that would soothe his soul would be to form a bigger and better pack, openly and legally. There's one way he could do that, and that's with the knowledge and approval of the most influential of his recent opponents, including Heraty and several of the World Council."

"For what purpose? They know nothing of the Denebs and therefore—"

"I told Thorstern that humanity will fight its way out of its own fixes. He may remember it. He is ignorant of the Denebs, as you've just remarked, but may decide—and convince others—that the hour of trial is here already. Pawns versus mutants! Being what he is, Thorstern automatically thinks of human beings as solely of his own kind, while mutants are not quite human, or quasi-human."

"Ah!" Charles narrowed his eyes. "Plenty of intolerance exists today. It wouldn't need much boosting."

Raven shrugged. "Who knows it better than we? Look what he gains if he can co-operate with Martian and Terran prototypes in arranging a synchronized three-world extermination of paranormals. It would give him back his private army, this time composed only of his own pawn-kind, gratify his ego, satisfy his hatred of mutants and provide him with the excuse and the means of removing the chief source of peril to himself. I can't see how he can avoid thinking of it sooner or later. He's got brains and courage and is thoroughly stubborn."

"It wouldn't be easy. The mutant minority is a very small one yet plenty large enough to make extermination a major problem."

"Numerical ratios aren't the whole of it," Raven declared, propping himself against a corner of the table. "I can see two obstacles, both big."

"Such as which?"

"One: they can wipe out only the *known* paranormals. How many more remain unknown? How many are beyond identification by ordinary minds and intend to remain that way?"

"It makes the job impossible to complete. Thorstern may not start it at all if he realizes he can't finish it."

"Maybe he will," agreed Raven, with some doubt. "Obstacle number two is the natural consequence of civilizations coexistent on three planets. Suppose Thorstern tries to persuade them to arrange simultaneous pogroms designed to rid humanity of its too-clever boys. Each planet immediately suspects a trap. If it slaughters its own mutants while the others do not—"

"Mutual distrust." Charles nodded in understanding. "No planet will be eager to take a risk that might place it at a grave disadvantage compared with the others." He thought again, continued, "It could be a big risk, too. What if *two* worlds wiped out their own talent and the third did not? Boy, how soon would it gain mastery over the others! In such an event I could give a shrewd guess at which would be the third world and who would be bossing it."

"Three planets will all see the same picture. Terrans and Martians are neither more nor less dopey than Venusians. So whichever way Thorstern turns he'll have a tough proposition on his hands. The trouble is he's the sort who likes tough propositions. He views them as a challenge to his abilities. I don't think we've heard the last of him yet."

"Neither do I. And, David, we're top of his list for a summary removal." A chuckle sounded low in his belly. "*If* he can do it."

"I'm going back to Terra. Thanks for the hospitality." Crossing the room, Raven put his head through the kitchen doorway, said to Mavis, "Goodby, Delicious!"

"And good riddance, Nuisance!" She gave him a false scowl that fooled him not at all.

He pulled an atrocious face at her, went outside, waved a careless hand at Charles. "You have been a pal. See you in the morgue."

"Someday," promised Charles as if looking forward to this treat. He watched the other fade into the fog, closed the door, waddled back to his chair.

With her mind but not her voice, Mavis told him emphatically, "You are going to regret all this."

"I know it, Honey."

Chapter 15

A rare assortment of craft lay scattered across the numerous dispersal points of the spaceport. Antigravs, copters large and small, several ancient autogyros owned by unshaven prospectors, two dapper World Council courier boats, an auxiliary-engined balloon belonging to a party of virus-tracking scientists, a scarred and battered Martian tramp bearing the name of *Phodeimos,* two passenger ships, one awaiting mail and the other under repair and, finally, a rusty contraption, half gyro, half motorcycle, abandoned by some crazy gadgeteer.

Sodium lamps shed a cold, unholy light over this mechanical menagerie. Night mist was still hanging around but had thinned considerably as the huge but invisible sun started to poke its rim over the horizon. In less than an hour the fog would soar and leave the ground clear.

The whole place was heavily but inefficiently guarded, with small groups of men lounging near the fuel tanks and repair shops. Others mooched singly around the perimeter or between the silent ships. Not one was mentally alert. Bored by a long night devoid of incident and within half an hour of being relieved by the daytime shift, each was solely interested in seeing thirty minutes whisk past so that he could pack up and beat it for breakfast and bed.

Raven appreciated this common state of mind; it created psychological conditions in his favor. Timing is a factor important to success in anything and the clock is a greater autocrat than most folks realize. Attempting something difficult, one could be rebuffed when the clock's hands were in one position and scrape through when in another.

He had reached to within a hundred yards of the perimeter and was exercising caution. Undoubtedly these guards had been warned to look out for him. Thorstern's surrender would not have caused that warning to be withdrawn.

Most of these armed watchers were ordinary, untalented men ignorant of power-wranglers on this world or any other. A few of the others might be followers of

Thorstern in fact—or Wollencott in fancy—and these would have additional, unofficial orders what to do should Raven show up. There was no way of telling which was which because one and all were thinking only of the end of their spell of duty and the petty relaxations to follow.

This fellow coming near had a vivid imagination filled with a large plate of bacon and eggs. He was also a roamer and a floater, which made him a most suitable victim.

Watching him for some time, Raven found this guard was one of the few on an irregular beat, free to wander at will among the grounded machines. A couple of times the guard had registered a moment of strain, left the surface and soared over a vessel that he could not be bothered to walk around. The other guards, all apparently earthbound, had observed these occasional floatings with bland indifference. About ten percent of them had special aptitudes of their own, each much superior to all others in his own view.

Drawn by what he felt as a mere impulse and had no cause to suspect as anything more, the guard ambled boredly round the corner of the little tool shed behind which Raven was waiting. On a similar impulse derived from the same source, he held out his chin at a convenient angle. He was most cooperative and Raven genuinely regretted the poorness of his reward. He smacked the chin, caught the body with its bacon and eggs still whirling, lowered it to ground.

Wearing the other's badged cap and official slicker he came from behind the house and traipsed into the field. The victim had less height. The slicker came barely to Raven's knees but it would not be noticed. The nearest guards were two hundred yards away. Trouble would most likely come from a telepath. If one made a distant pass at him and got a complete blank he'd know immediately that this was more than a mere floater—then the band would start to play with a vengeance!

Bending his arm to hold the gun in its crook exactly as the other had carried it, he came to the passenger ship waiting for mail. It was the *Star Wraith,* one of the latest models, fully fueled and ready to blow. There was no one on board. He tensed and soared over it, landing lightly on the other side.

For all the mess of stuff lying around his choice of an escape vehicle was limited. The gyros, copters and antigravs were strictly localized contraptions. There was nothing capable of leaving the planet other than the *Star Wraith* and the pair of courier boats. Either of the latter would do providing they were fueled and serviced. Thank goodness that on this moonless world there was no danger of grabbing a short range Moon-boat by mistake.

The nearer courier boat had full tanks and was all set, but he passed it by for a look at its fellow. That, too, lacked nothing but its pilot. Both vessels were without personnel and neither was locked. He preferred the second solely because a quarter-mile clearance lay behind its tail whereas the other was nicely positioned to make ashes of a time-worn autogyro that someone might love more than his mother. He chose the second.

Just then a mind behind the little tool house returned from its involuntary vacation, forgot former visions of breakfast, tried to co-ordinate itself. Raven detected it at once. He had been expecting it, waiting for it. The blow had been enough to gain him a couple of minutes and that was all he required, he hoped.

"What did I run into?" it mumbled confusedly. A few seconds, then, "I got slugged!" A slightly longer pause followed by a shrill and agitated, "My cap! My gun! Some mangy pup of a tree-cat has—"

With a deceitfully casual air Raven rose as if to float over the selected ship, instead hit the lock twenty feet up and got inside. Closing the circular door, he snapped its fasteners and sealed it, made his way to the pilot's seat.

"Somebody bopped me!" continued the mind. "Jeepers, he must have been ready!" It faded out for a moment, came back with increased strength as he bellowed both mentally and vocally, "Look out, you dreamers! There's a guy up to something! He pinched my—"

Amid the resulting medley of thought-forms that promptly switched from the subject of off-duty to on-duty four stronger ones emerged from nothingness, felt blindly around ship after ship. They reached the courier boat, touched Raven's mental shield, tried in vain to spike through it, recoiled.

"Who are you?"

He did not reply. The ship went *dum-dum-dum* as its pumps and injectors commenced operation.

"Answer! Who are you?"

They were mentalities of quite a different caliber from the host of others milling around. They were sharp, precise, directable, and knew an armor-plated mind the moment they encountered it.

"Another tele. Won't talk. Got his shield up. He's in that courier KM44. Better surround it."

"Surround it? Not likely! If he lets go a blast from those big propulsors he'll incinerate the tail-side of the circle!"

"I doubt it. He daren't risk a jump before the fog lifts."

"If it's that fellow Raven there are going to be some awful ructions because we're supposed to—"

"I tell you we don't know who it is. Might be just some space-crazy kid squatting there and egging himself on to let her blow." As a pious afterthought, "If he does, I hope he breaks his neck!"

"Bet you it's Raven."

The radio dinged inside the pilot-cabin and the cause of all the excitement flipped the switch. A hoarse voice emanating from the control tower burst forth with outraged authority.

"You in KM44—open the lock!"

He did not respond to that, either. Things were still *dum-dumming* halfway back to the tail. Various meters quivered and a red line on an ivory strip had crept to a point marked: READY.

"You in KM44. I warn you—"

Smiling, he glanced in the rear view periscope, saw a line of armed men fanned out a couple of hundred yards behind his pipes. His forefinger scratched a button, depressed it for a fraction of a second. Something went *whop!* And the vessel gave a slight kick and a neat ball of superheated vapor bulleted backward. The advancing foe raced madly from the center of the target.

The enraged speaker in the control tower was now reciting a harrowing list of pains and penalties selected from regulations one to twenty, sub-sections A to Z, and had become so engrossed in this data on what the human frame could be made to suffer that he was blind to everything outside. He was the only person Raven had ever heard who could mention the most trying items in italics.

The stud went down a second time. A terrific blast of orange-white flame spouted from the rear end. The resulting roar deafened everyone for a mile around but inside the ship it sounded as nothing more than a high moan.

Yammering steadily on, the radio continued with sadistic gusto, ". . . but where the said *crime* incorporates *illegal* use of police and customs exemptions the *penalty* on conviction shall be not less than *four times* that prescribed in sub-section D7 without prejudice to any *further* increases given hereunder in sub-sections—"

Switching the radio to reverse the flow of language, Raven snapped back, "Look, chum, nobody can *live* that *long!*"

Cutting both transmitter and receiver, he slid the off-lever forward and shot away on a column of fire.

A million miles out he set the auto-pilot, examined his rear view screens for evidence of pursuit. There were no signs of any. The likelihood of being chased from Venus was small because futile. Ships had yet to be built capable of catching up with the kind he was using.

It was remotely possible but not probable that some vessel already in the void might be ordered to try to intercept him. But the broad gulf between Earth and Venus was not crammed with boats at this particular stage of interplanetary development.

The forward screens and detectors showed nothing noteworthy ahead except one pinpoint of infrared radiation too far away to identify. Probably the *Fantôme* homeward bound. She should be somewhere around that region right now.

Content to let the auto-pilot do the routine work, he sat awhile in the tiny control cabin and surveyed the awesome spread of the cosmos. His air was that of one who has seen it a thousand times and hopes to see it ten thousand more. He could never grow weary of its tremendous splendor.

Nevertheless he left the sparkling view, lay in the tiny bunk and closed his eyes—but not to sleep. He shut them the better to open his mind and listen as he had never done when listening to the secret thoughts of ordinary men. The vessel's steady purring did not distract him in the slightest, neither did the rare *psst!* and momentary flare of colliding particles of cosmic dust. For the time being his receptivity of the audio-band had ceased to exist while his mind stretched higher listening powers to the utmost.

They could just be heard, the sounds he was seeking, if one overcame one's fleshly muffling by straining hard enough and concentrating sufficiently. Eerie mental voices vibrating through the endless dark. Many of these mysterious impulses lacked amplitude, had flattened wave-forms and had become greatly attenuated by travel across illimitable distances. Others were stronger because relatively nearer, but still far, far away.

"Black ship making for Zaxsis. We are letting it run without hindrance."

"They are about to leave for Baldur 9, a red dwarf with four planets, all sterile. They consider this one a dead loss and aren't likely to come back,"

"Spurned the planet but grabbed the largest satellite because it is rich in heliotrope crystals."

"Came down with a squadron of forty and searched the place from pole to pole. Seemed in a great hurry."

". . . off Hero, giant blue-white in sector twelve of Andromeda. One hundred eighty black ships traveling fast in three fan formations of sixty apiece. A real Deneb expedition!"

"This Deneb made an emergency landing with two tubes busted. He waggled his palps until we understood and helped him do repairs. We acted plausibly stupid, of course. He was grateful in a superior way. Gave the kids several strings of rainbow beads and went away without suspecting."

"Black ship of cruiser type was heading straight for Tharre. We muddled its pilots' minds and turned it back."

"Think he got the notion intuitively but had no way of proving it right. He was dangerously close to the truth and didn't know it. But he liked the idea well enough to make it the basis of a new religion. It might have created an explosive situation if the Denebs had picked up some of that theology. So we destroyed it at the very start by translating him to his next stage and mourning with his kind."

"Enormous black battleship holding eight thousand Denebs has taken possession of a lesser moon. Said they'd send a picket-boat to swap trade with us once in a while but they're not enthusiastic. They have seen us—and all they've seen is a gang of backward aborigines."

". . . long string of a dozen in hot pursuit. Funny how they can't resist chasing the uncatchable."

"Well, I'm all right but she is old and gray and wants out. The years go by the same for us as for those over whom we watch. So if some other couple—"

". . . clustered all over this asteroid giving them the hearty come-on and the Denebs fell for it as usual. They came whooping up and blasted the rock to dust and went away happy. We never did like that rock; it had a very eccentric—"

"The convoy streamed straight past making for the Horse's Head, sector seven, but dropped this half wrecked lifeboat containing one ancient and bleary Deneb. He says he'll stick around and prospect for crystals while the others go on looking for what is right under his elastic nose."

"Armada of eight hundred ships setting out from Scoria to avenge that pair that disappeared. They have shielded the pilots' brains with platinum casques and have new type force projectors installed on every ship. Somebody means business!"

"Made up their minds to play safe and char the world all over merely because the wave-lattice creatures inhabiting it are shiny, only semi-visible and suspiciously un-Deneblike. We couldn't allow that! So we tickled the load in their armory. It made a mess!"

Ham radio had nothing on this for it was neither radio nor amateur: it was long-range *beamed* telepathy and decidedly professional.

The babble continued through the whole trip. A black ship here, another there, a hundred hell-bent for somewhere else. Denebs were doing this, Denebs were doing that, landing on some worlds, departing from others, ignoring a good many more, sometimes craftily attracted toward one, sometimes dexterously turned away from another, all the time helped or thwarted by this widespread host of faraway entities according to the unknown rules of an unknown game.

By and large the Denebs seemed to discard most worlds either at first sight or after a brief stay, yet still they kept on searching, poking, probing through an enormous area, methodically or non-methodically combing the cosmos for what they could not find. If one thing could be positively determined about them it was that they were incurable fidgets.

Raven spent all his time either listening to this talk from the great deeps of infinity or gazing through the fore observation port at the unending concourse of stars. Now and again his eyes held an abstract quality and into his face came an expression suggestive of a curious hunger. All thoughts of Thorstern, Wollencott, Carson, Heraty and the rest had been put aside; their ambitions and rivalries were of submicroscopic insignificance when compared with mightier events elsewhere.

"The Denebs picked a hundred thousand minds before they decided the years aren't long enough to permit a search through five hundred millions. So they have gone. They've departed as ignorant as when they arrived."

". . . sat around for three full circumsolars. They clucked with patronizing amusement over our rocketships, even borrowed a couple to play with and handed them back with thanks. But when you crashed that cruiser they'd sent in pursuit of you, they became really hot and took off after you like—"

"There is a distinct trend toward Bootes for some reason best known to themselves. Better be ready for them coming that way!"

"Laethe, Morcin, Elstar, Gnosst, Weltenstile, Vä, Périè, and Klain. Between two and ten thousand Denebs on each, all seeking rare minerals. They treat the local life-forms as tame but useless animals, throw them uneatable tit-bits. All the same, they've been extremely jumpy since—"

"Nine ships coming down, acting like they're full of their usual suspicion."

It went on and on and on, unhearable to all but minds naturally equipped for the purpose. No pawn-mind could detect them. No Deneb mind, either. Atmosphere blanketed the telepathic beams, and the warps around giant suns bent them a little, had to be estimated and taken into consideration. But in free space, transmitting to suitable receivers correctly attuned, almost all of them got through.

They told of lonely suns and scattered planets and gypsy asteroids as familiarly as mere man could mention the commonplace features of his home town. They identified locales, gave precise sector references and named a thousand names— but not once did any of them mention Terra, Venus, Mars or any of the family of King Sol.

There was no need to refer to any of these worlds for their time had not yet come.

A couple of six-seater police boats jumped off the Moon and tried to follow the stolen courier on its way in. They were out of luck. It plunged at Terra as if it had fifty light-years yet to run, shot sidewise when far ahead of the pursuit, vanished over the planet's eastward rim. By the time the others curved round to that hemisphere the boat had landed and become lost in more scenery than twelve pairs of eyes could scrutinize.

It reposed on a rocky moor where another take-off would damage nobody's property. Raven stood by its cooling tail and studied the sky awhile but the police boats did not appear above the horizon. Probably they were zooming disconsolately three or four hundred miles to the east or west.

Crossing thick heather, he reached a dirt road, went to the farmhouse he'd noted when coming down. He used its phone to call an antigrav which arrived in short time from the nearest village. Within an hour he was at the headquarters of Terran Intelligence.

As long-faced and lugubrious as ever, Carson signed to a seat, put hands together as if about to pray, and spoke with his mind.

"You're a prime headache. You've given me more work to do in a week than usually I get in a month."

"How about the work you gave *me?*"

"That wasn't so tough by the looks of it. You walked out of here and you've walked back with your tie straight and your nose blown. In between times you've annoyed important people and scared the wits out of others. You have thumbed your beak at every existing law and now I've got to cover up your misdeeds, somehow, heaven alone knows how."

"I haven't busted every law," Raven denied. "There are some intact. I have yet to distill ten gallons of *tambar* out in the hills. What I'd like to know is this: *are* you covering me up? The Moon patrols took after me on my way in despite my using a courier boat."

"A stolen one." Carson nodded aggrievedly at a thick bunch of papers on his desk. "You create crime faster than I can whitewash it. I am trying to whitewash that courier right now. But don't worry. The worry is all mine. Some folk seem to think it's the sort of thing I'm paid for. So I've got to find a way to turn this barefaced pinch into an officially permitted borrowing." He rubbed his chin, looked rueful. "And don't you dare tell me you smashed it to bits on landing. Where have you stashed it?"

Raven told him, adding, "I'd have brought it straight into the spaceport but for those cops trying to sit on my neck. Their chase made it look as if I was wanted. Lately I've been wanted quite enough to do me for a time."

"I'll have a pilot pick it up and bring it in." Carson poked the papers away from him. "Woe, woe, all I get is woe."

"Running from Venus to here takes quite a while even in a superfast courier boat," Raven pointed out. "So I've lost touch with local affairs. What's happened to provide the woe?"

Carson said, "Last week we killed two characters caught in the act of trying to destroy an important bridge. Both proved to be Mars-born. Next day a power station went sky-high, plunged ten towns into darkness and stopped industry over a hundred square miles. On the Saturday we found an ingenious contraption planted at the foot of a dam and snatched it away in the nick of time. If it had exploded the result would have amounted to a major disaster."

"Then haven't they—?"

"On the other hand," Carson went on, ignoring him, "scientists now report that the Baxter blowup almost certainly was a genuine accident. They say the fuel proves to be highly unstable in certain exceptional and unforeseen conditions. They claim to have found a cure already."

"That's something worth knowing."

Carson made a gesture of impatience. "It's once in a blue moon I get an authoritative report like that and until I do I'm compelled to regard every accident as something possibly and probably deliberate. We have been handicapped all along the line by inability to distinguish human error from sabotage. Why, we can't even get rid of suspects. We are still holding eight of them taken from that underground dump. Mars or Venus-born skewboys, every one of them. If I had my way I'd deport them and prohibit their re-entry, but it can't be done. Legally they are Terrans, see?"

"Yes, that's the trouble." Raven leaned forward over the desk. "Do you mean to tell me that this war is still continuing?"

"No. I won't go so far as to say that. It certainly was continuing up to end of last week but maybe it is now ended." He surveyed the other speculatively. "Day before yesterday Heraty came along to tell me our worries are now finished. Since then there have been no reports of further incidents. I don't quite know what you've done or how you have done it, but it has been effective *if* what Heraty says is true."

"You have heard nothing about a man named Thorstern?"

"I have." He shifted uneasily in his chair but kept command of his thoughts. "For a long time we've had Intelligence operatives hanging around Wollencott, said to be the leader of Venusian insurgents. Eventually two of them sent in reports saying that this Thorstern was the real driving force behind the movement but they weren't able to dig up convincing evidence in support. It seems this Thorstern goes around tastefully attired in several layers of legality and nobody can prove a darned thing unless he strips."

"That all?"

"No." Carson admitted it with reluctance, not wanting to keep on the subject. "Heraty said that Thorstern is dickering with him."

"Is that so? Did he say what about? Did he offer any details?"

"He remarked that he doubted Thorstern's good faith or, for that matter, that he really is what he claims to be, namely, the man who can call a halt to Venusian intransigence. Thorstern offered to prove it."

"How?"

"By removing Wollencott—just like that!" Carson snapped his fingers. He was silent awhile, then sighed and went on, "That was the day before yesterday. This morning we received a message from Venus giving the news that Wollencott had just fallen out of an antigrav and bounced too hard for his health."

"Umph!" Raven could visualize the wallop, almost hear the crunch of bones. "Nice way to dismiss a faithful servant, isn't it?"

"Better not say that openly—it's libelous."

"I can traduce one or two more. World Councilor Gilchist, for example. He is what might fairly be called a louse."

"What makes you say that?" Carson's expression had become alert.

"He is your suspected fly in the ointment. Thorstern himself said so without knowing he was betraying a traitor." He thought a bit, added, "Don't know what a newcomer like Gilchist resembles, but I sniffed around the Council's minds during that interview and I didn't smell a rat. How was that?"

"He wasn't there." Carson scribbled a short note on a slip of paper. "Four members were absent because of sickness or urgent business. Gilchist was one of them. He turned up a few minutes after you left."

"His urgent business was to put a hurried finger on me," Raven informed. "What are you going to do about him?"

"Nothing. There is nothing I can do merely on your say-so. I'll pass this information to Heraty and the rest is up to him and the World Council. It's one thing to state a fact; another to prove it."

"I guess you're right. Anyway, it's of no consequence if they don't take any action concerning him or even if they award him a gold medal for being sly. Basically, few things of this earth are of real consequence." He stood up, moved to the door, paused with a hand on the panel. "But there is one item with fair claim to a little weight insofar as anything is weighty. Thorstern is a normal individual. So is Heraty. You and I are not."

"What of it?" asked Carson, uneasily.

"There are men whose nature won't let a defeat go unavenged. There are men hard enough to sit in an antigrav and watch a loyal supporter dive to destruction. There are men who can become very frightened if properly stimulated. That is the great curse of this world—fear!" He stared hard at the other, pupils wide, irises shining. "Know what makes men sorely afraid?"

"Death," ventured Carson in sepulchral tones.

"*Other* men," Raven contradicted. "Remember that—especially when Heraty tells you only a little and carefully omits to give you the rest!"

The other did not inquire what he meant. He had been long accustomed to the defensive techniques of normal, non-talented people. They interviewed him in person when they had nothing to conceal, wrote him or phoned him from a safe distance when they had something to hide. More often than not they did have something to hide.

He sat silent as Raven went out, watched the door close. He was a mutant and hadn't failed to recognize Raven's subtle warning.

Heraty, he thought, was fond of doing business by phone.

A tawdry little office up four flights of worn and dirty stairs was the haunt of Samuel Glaustraub, a rudimentary hypno barely able to fascinate a sparrow. Somewhere back in his ancestry there had been one mutant whose talent had skipped a few generations and reappeared greatly weakened. From other forebears he had inherited a legalistic mind and wagging tongue, which features he valued far above the tricks of any skewboy.

Entering this office, Raven propped himself against its short, ink-stained counter and said, "Morning, Sam."

Glaustraub looked up, dark eyes querulous behind horn-rimmed glasses. "Should I know you?"

"Not at all."

"Oh, I thought maybe I should." Putting aside some documents he'd been consulting, he left his desk, weighed up the caller cagily. Deep inside, his mind was complaining to itself, "Where's he get the Sam? Does he think I'm his valet?"

"What, in clothes like those?" Bending over the counter, Raven eyed the other's baggy pants.

"A telepath, eh?" said Mr. Glaustraub, showing big yellow teeth. He smoothed the pants self-consciously. "Well, I don't care. Fortunately I have a clear conscience."

"I envy you. Few people can say as much."

The other frowned, sensing implied skepticism. He said, "What can I do for you?"

"You have a client named Arthur Kayder?"

"Yes, his case is due to be heard tomorrow." He shook a sorrowful head. "I shall defend him to the best of my ability but I'm afraid it will be in vain."

"Why?"

"He is charged with public utterance of homicidal threats and, since the plaintiff has not entered suit because of absence, the charge has been made by the public prosecutor. That makes it very tough. The evidence against him is recorded vocally and pictorially, will be produced in court and cannot be denied." He gave Raven an apologetic examination. "You're a friend of his, I presume?"

"His best enemy so far as I know."

"Ha-ha!" Glaustraub gave a forced laugh, making his belly quiver. "You are joking, of course?"

"Wrong first time, Sammy. I'm the boy he yearns to strip down to a skeleton."

"Eh?" His jaw dropped, he hurried to his desk, scrabbled nervously through a mess of papers, then asked, "Your name David Raven?"

"Correct."

It upset the other. He took off his glasses, tapped them worriedly, put them on and went around looking for them.

"They are on your nose," Raven informed.

"Are they?" The confirmatory squint was violent and gave him a villainous appearance. "So they are. How silly of me." He sat down, stood up. sat down again. "Well, well, Mr. Raven! The hostile witness!"

"Who said I'm a witness against him?"

"Well, I assume so. Seeing you have returned in time to appear on behalf of the prosecution I—"

"Supposing I don't appear—what does the prosecution do then?"

"Proceeds just the same. The recorded evidence will be deemed sufficient to secure conviction."

"Yes, but that's only because my supporting testimony can be taken for granted. What if I say I knew Kayder was only kidding?"

"Mr. Raven, you mean—?" Glaustraub's hands started trembling with excitement. "You really think that?"

"Like heck I do! He meant every word of it. Kayder would enjoy nothing more than to lie on purple silk eating grapes while listening to me dying the death of a thousand cuts."

"Then why . . . why—?" The lawyer gaped around, hopelessly confused.

"I'd rather kill a man outright than let him waste years in clink. Anyway, I don't think Kayder ought to suffer long incarceration merely for shooting off his fat trap." Leaning across the woodwork, he nudged Glaustraub who promptly jumped a foot. "Do you?"

"Who, me? Of course not! Decidedly not!" He asked uncomfortably, "Are you willing to appear as witness for the defense?"

"Not if there's an easier way out."

"You could swear an affidavit," the attorney suggested, filled with a curious mixture of doubt, suspicion and hope.

"That'll do me, Samuel. Where do I swear it?"

Glaustraub grabbed a hat, slammed it on back to front, pawed the desk for his glasses, found them on his nose, and took his caller down two flights at a sedate gallop. He ushered him into another office occupied by four men, all overweight. With their aid he concocted a document which Raven read carefully and signed.

"There you are, Sam, old boy."

"This is generous of you, Mr. Raven." His hands loved the affidavit, his eyes gleamed, his mind pictured the coming masterstroke when Glaustraub for the defense arose amid breathless silence and in calm, confident, well-modulated tones proceeded to snitch the prosecution's britches. Here was a rare opportunity for drama. For once Glaustraub was supremely happy. "Exceedingly generous, if I may say so. My client will appreciate it."

"That is the idea," said Raven, darkly.

"I'm sure you can depend—" Glaustraub's voice broke off and he swapped expressions as he became smitten by the horrid thought that the coming drama might have a price on it. A stiff one. "I beg your pardon?"

Raven explained, "I *want* your client to appreciate it. I want him to think of me as Santa Claus, see?" He prodded a forefinger and again the other jumped. "When a bunch of bums comes after one's scalp there's nothing like a little gratitude for creating discord in the ranks."

"Really?" Glaustraub felt that a lot of cogent points were evading him this morning. He fumbled around the region of his ears.

"They're in your pocket this time," said Raven, and went away.

Chapter 16

The house looked pleasingly quiet and peaceful as Raven approached. Leina was within; he knew that as certainly as she knew he was coming. Your woman, Thorstern had called her, making it sound reprehensible. Yet their association, though unconventional, was utterly devoid of immorality. Other places and other people have other standards of decency and make them very high.

Pausing by the gate, he examined the fresh crater in the field outside. The hole was big enough to swallow an antigrav cab. Apart from this queer feature the house and its surroundings were exactly as he had left them. His attention shifted to the sky, watched the far-off white trail of a Mars-bound freighter going toward the stars, the many, many stars.

Reaching the front door, he turned its lock teleportatively, in the same way that Charles had opened the castle gate. It swung wide. Leina was waiting in the lounge, big hands folded in generous lap, her eyes showing gladness.

"I'm a bit late."

He did not offer any warmer greeting. Neither did he kiss her. The warmth was mutually sensed beyond need of futile physical expression. He had never kissed her, never wanted to, never had been expected to.

"I stopped to take the bite off Kayder. Before I went away it was worth putting him someplace safe but now it's no longer necessary. Things have changed."

"Things never change," she observed.

"The little things have changed. I'm not referring to the big ones."

"The big ones are all-important."

"You're right, Brighteyes, but I don't agree with what you imply, namely, that the little things are unimportant." Under her steady gaze he found it needful to justify himself. "We don't want them to fall foul of the Denebs—but neither do we want them to destroy themselves."

"The latter would be the lesser of two evils—regrettable but not disastrous. The Denebs would learn nothing."

"They'll never be any wiser as it is."

"That may be," she conceded. "But you have sown a few seeds of forbidden knowledge. Sooner or later you will be forced to uproot them."

"Womanly intuition, eh?" He grinned like a mischievous boy. "Mavis feels the same way about it."

"With good reason."

"When the time arrives the seeds can be obliterated, every single one of them. *You* know that, don't you?"

"Of course. You'll be ready and I'll be ready. Where you go I shall go." Her brilliant optics were unblinking, unafraid. "Yet I still think your interference wasn't called for and was extremely risky."

"Risks have to be taken sometimes. The war is ended. In theory, humanity is now able to concentrate on getting farther out."

"Why do you say, 'In theory'?"

His face sobered. "There is a slight chance that they may let the opportunity go by in favor of having another and different conflict."

"I see." Moving to the window, she stood with her back toward him while she looked over the landscape. "David, in such an event will you again insist on taking part?"

"No, definitely not. Such a war would be aimed against our own kind and those thought to be of our kind. So I won't be given the chance to chip in. I'll be smacked down without warning." He went across to her, slid a comforting arm around her waist. "They may deal with you at the same time and in the same way. Do you mind?"

"Not in the least so long as everything remains covered."

"It might not happen, anyway." His gaze turned to the window, found the view beyond. Abruptly he changed the subject. "When are you buying the ducks?"

"Ducks?"

He indicated the crater. "For that pond you're making over there." Without waiting for a reply, he insisted, "What happened?"

"I returned from town last Friday afternoon, made to open the door, sensed something inside the lock."

"What was it?"

"A tiny sphere like a blue bead with a white spot on it. I could see it with my mind. It was so positioned that a key inserted in the lock would press on the white spot. So I teleported it out, laid it over there and made a pebble drop on the white spot. The house shook."

"Some mini-engineer undertook a risky job," he commented, evenly. "Not to mention the teleport who placed it in the lock." Once more his strange callousness revealed itself as he ended, "If the trick had worked as planned, nobody would have been more surprised than you, eh?"

"One person may have been," she corrected. "You!"

The night was exceptionally clear, the stars bright and beckoning. To the naked eye the crater walls stood out clear and sharp on the terminator of the three-quarter Moon. From horizon to horizon the vault of space resembled an enormous curtain of black velvet lavishly powdered with sequins, some sparkling steadily, some intermittently, of all colors, white, blue-white, pale yellow, pink and delicate green.

Lying in a tilt-back chair under the roof's glass dome. Raven studied this scene of incomparable majesty, closed his eyes and listened, opened them to look again. Beside him in a similar chair Leina did the same. These were their own personal, intimate nights: in chairs beneath the dome, looking and listening. There were no bedrooms in this house, no beds. They did not need them. Just the chairs and the dome.

Daytimes they also looked and listened but did it with less concentration and more spasmodically, with their attention more on this world than the countless ones outside. Together they had looked and listened by day and by night for years. The task would have been unbearably monotonous but for the fact there were two of them at it. The presence of one broke the solitude of the other. Moreover, the things they "saw" and "heard" had the merit of infinite variety.

On Terra and far, far beyond Terra things always were happening, always, always. And never did incidents come twice the same. This was the task of the eternal watcher, a responsible job and highly essential. Each was like a sentinel in a midnight tower, protecting a sleeping city by watching the forest beyond the walls for any inward creeping foes. Many shared this job, holding themselves ready to sound the alarm should the need arise, Charles and Mavis on Venus, Horst and Karin on Mars, thousands more—aye, tens of thousands—all posted in pairs.

His mind turning to this last couple, he eyed a pink light hanging low in the sky and called, "Horst! Horst!"

It came after a while, slightly dulled by Terra's atmospheric blanket. "Yes, David?"

"Know what your insurgents are doing?"

"Mostly arguing with each other, David. They have split into several groups. One wants to continue against Terra. Another resents what it calls the treachery of Venus and wants to strike at her. Yet another is anti-mutant. The largest group is disgusted with everything and about to break up."

"So they're going through a period of chronic indecision?"

"That's about it."

"Thanks, Horst. Love to Karin."

He redirected his mind. "Charles! Charles!"

This time it came quicker and with a little more strength. "Yes, David?"

"Any news?"

"Thorstern left for Terra yesterday."

"Know the reason?"

"No, but I can make a guess, It's for something deemed advantageous to himself."

"That's a foregone conclusion. Well, I'll watch for him when he gets here. Let you know what I discover."

"Do that. You've heard about Wollencott?"

"I have. Nasty business."

"Clumsy," endorsed Charles. "Wollencott might have landed in some soft place and suffered injuries that meant slow dying. As it happened he didn't, but that was sheer luck." His mental beam cut off a moment, came back. "Here, the organization appears to be reluctantly falling to bits but its potential will remain and it can be rebuilt anytime. I can't help wondering."

"And I know why."

"Why?"

"Mavis keeps reminding you that you've blundered."

"True," admitted Charles, dolefully. "And I know how you've guessed it."

"How?"

"Leina keeps telling you the same."

"Correct." said Raven. "We've agreed not to agree."

"Same here. You would think I was a juvenile delinquent by the way she looks at me sometimes. The main issue will be protected no matter what happens, so why do women get the heebies?"

"Because, my boy, they look at these worlds from a feminine viewpoint and it's a maternal one. You and I have been throwing the baby too high. It makes them nervous to watch us."

"I suppose you're right." Charles' thought-form became sardonic. "But how do *you* know all this? How many babies—?"

"I use my imagination," interrupted Raven. "'By, Charles."

All that came back was a telepathic grunt. He glanced at Leina. She was reposing in her chair, eyes closed, face to the stars. For a little while he studied her fondly and was not looking at the fleshly features visible to ordinary men. The face was no more than a borrowed mask behind which he could see the real Leina. Most times he failed to notice that she had a face—somebody else's face—and saw only what shone forth from the great orbs.

She was quite unconscious of his scrutiny. Her mind was tuned elsewhere and absorbing the never ending chatter of the heavens. Soon he followed her example, listened to messages dimmed by distance and atmosphere but still discernible.

"Scouting warily around Bluefire, a condensing giant. Twenty black ships of destroyer type."

". . . repeatedly, but complete lack of common ground makes it impossible to communicate with these Flutterers. Can't even make them sense that we're trying to speak to them, much less warn them. If the Denebs arrive and become hostile toward them we'll have to take appropriate action and—"

"Calling from Thais. I got in right away without arousing suspicion. Struck it lucky in finding a suitable one on his way out. He had superswift co-ordination and said, 'Yes, by all means.' "

"The Benders have remarkable visual powers despite that they are low in the scale. See us clearly, call us the Shining Ones and insist on worshipping us. It is very embarrassing."

"We swept past Jilderdeen unnoticed and saw that the Denebs are building an immense crystal-growing plant in its temperate zone. The implication is that they're there for keeps."

". . . poor savages have chosen us for their annual sacrifice to the Twin Suns. Just sheer bad luck that they should pick us two out of all the tribe. It won't be long now! Somebody else had better be ready to take over after we're gone."

That last message bit into his being. Poor savages. All watched worlds were so possessed, including this one, because all children can be poor savages by a genuinely adult standard. He stirred, sat up, felt restless. The stars blazed down but the world around him was deep and dark, bitterly dark.

Over the following three weeks he kept close tab on world news distributed by the radio and spectroscreen networks. It was boringly uneventful but he stuck to the task in the dogged manner of one who waits for something that must not be missed although it may never come.

No mention of erstwhile anti-Terran activities came over the air. This was not remarkable for there had been no hint of any sort even when they were at their height.

Neither was anything said about development of spaceships or prospects of plunging farther into unknown deeps. Bureaucratic love of secrecy again was responsible. The autocratic type of mind insists that news of public interest must not be divulged in the public interest.

Patiently he checked not only the news but also the unending flow of twaddle put over in the guise of entertainment, selecting likely items for close personal examination and seeing them through in all their wearisome completeness. From his peculiar viewpoint, he was like an elderly man compelled to endure hours of face-pulling and rattle-shaking designed to amuse a bunch of mewling babies.

At the end of the third week the fully colored three-dimensional spectroscreen commenced a new thriller serial of four parts. Just another of a regular series of emotion-tickles, it featured a telepathic hero who had looked long and ardently into the non-mutant heroine's mind and found it pure and sweet and clean. The villain was depicted as a low-browed, lower-minded insectivocal with a lopsided sneer and a penchant for the sinister fondling of poisonous centipedes.

It was trash of a kind intended to occupy minds that otherwise might find time to think. Nevertheless, Raven followed the whole performance with the avidity of an incurable addict. When the end came, the villain had been foiled, virtue had triumphed amid soft lights and falling rose petals, and a symbolic boot had crushed a symbolic centipede, he sighed like one satiated—then went to see Kayder.

The man who answered his ring was a pawn resembling a broken-down pugilist. He had a smashed nose, ragged ears, wore a gray sweater.

"Kayder in?"

"Don't know," he lied. "I'll see." His small sunken eyes carefully measured the caller. "Who'll I say?"

"David Raven."

It meant nothing to him. He shambled down the passage, his mind reciting the name as though it would slip away if he didn't go into a clinch with it. Presently he returned.

"Says he'll see you."

Legs bowed and arms swinging so that his fists were level with his knees, he conducted the other to the rear of the house, announced in a hoarse voice, "Mr. Raven," and lumbered away.

It was the same room as before, same ornaments, same desk, but the boxes had gone. Kayder stood up as he entered, tried to decide whether or not to offer his hand, finally contented himself with indicating a chair.

Raven sat, stretched legs out front, smiled at him. "So Sammy did it. He had his little hour."

"The case was dismissed on payment of costs. It set me back a hundred credits but was cheap at the price." Kayder's heavy features quirked as he added, "The old buffoon on the bench saw fit to warn me that even evidence like yours wouldn't save me if I abused the public communication channels a second time."

"Perhaps Sammy annoyed him by overdoing the drama," Raven ventured. "Anyway, all's well that ends well."

"It is." Leaning forward, Kayder eyed him expectantly. "And now you've come to collect?"

"An astute assumption rather crudely expressed," opined Raven. "Let's say I've come to put the squeeze on you."

Pulling open a drawer, Kayder looked resigned. "How much?"

"How much what?"

"Money."

"Money?" Raven echoed it incredulously. He eyed the ceiling, his expression pained. "He talks about money!"

Kayder slammed the drawer shut. "Look, I want to know something: why did you get me in bad one minute and lug me out of it the next?"

"They were different minutes."

"Were they? In what way?"

"In the first there was a conflict and you were a menace safer out of the road. In the second the trouble had ceased or was about to cease and the need to pin you down had vanished."

'So you know the war has been called off?'

"Yes. Have you had orders to that effect?"

"I have," said Kayder, with some sourness. "And I don't like it." He made a gesture indicative of impotence. "I am being candid with you. There's no other choice with you reading my mind whenever you feel like it. I don't care for this sudden collapse but there's nothing I can do about it. The entire movement is going rapidly to pot."

"Which is all to the good. You were fighting for self-government—if the secret dictatorship of one man can be called self-government."

"Wollencott was a natural born leader but he hadn't the guts to be a dictator."

"He didn't need the guts," said Raven. "The intestinal items were supplied by Thorstern."

Kayder raised a surprised eyebrow. "Why drag Thorstern into this?"

"You know of him?"

"Every Venusian knows of him. He's one of the planet's seven biggest men."

"He's the biggest," Raven corrected. "In fact, he's so big he thinks Venus ought to be his personal property. He owned Wollencott body and soul until he gave him his freedom recently."

"Gave him his freedom? You mean—?" His mind stimulated into furious thought, Kayder sat erect and let his fingers drum on his desk. From time to time he frowned to himself.

After a while, he growled, "It could be. I have never met Thorstern in person. He is generally thought of as a hard and ambitious character. If Wollencott was picking up steam from someone else, Thorstern is the likeliest source." He frowned again. "I never suspected him. He kept himself well concealed."

"He did."

"Thorstern, ye gods!" Kayder stared at the other. "Then why did he get rid of Wollencott?"

"Thorstern was persuaded to give up his systematic bleeding of Terra and confine himself to more legitimate activities. So Wollencott, a former asset, immediately became an embarrassing liability. Thorstern has a way of ridding himself of unwanted liabilities."

"I hate to believe all this." Kayder showed resentment. "But I've got to. It all adds up."

"Your mind says more," Raven pointed out. "It says the anti-Terran organization has divided into splinter groups and you fear that some may try to curry favor with the authorities by ratting on the others. You think there are now too many people who know too much."

"I'll take my chances along with the rest," said Kayder, grimly. "Ratting's a game that can be played both ways. I have less on my conscience than some."

"Is a hypno named Steen on your conscience?"

"Steen?" He rocked back. "I never got him. He sneaked aboard the *Star Wraith* couple of days after you left on the *Fantôme.*" He gave his listener a significant glance. "I had more than enough to think about just then, remember?"

Raven nodded without sympathy. "I remember."

"So I heard no more about him."

"He died—very slowly."

"So did Haller!" Kayder shot back with sudden vim.

"Wrong on two counts. Haller went more or less of his own volition. Above all, he went quickly."

"What's the difference? One's as dead as the other."

"The difference is not in their ultimate condition," said Raven, seriously and with emphasis, "but in the speed of their transition to it. Once upon a time you evinced a nasty desire to reduce me to my framework. Had you done it with praiseworthy swiftness I could have passed it off with a light laugh." He gave a light laugh by way of illustration. "But if you had made the process unjustifiably prolonged I would have resented it."

Popping his eyes, Kayder exclaimed, 'That's about the craziest piece of talk I've ever heard!"

Raven said, "It's a crazy trinity of worlds we're in."

"I know that, but—"

"Besides," he continued, ignoring the interruption, "you've not yet heard the half of it. I didn't come round merely to pay a social call and indulge an hour's idle gossip."

"You've told me that already. You want something and it isn't money."

"I did you a favor. Now I want you to do one for me."

"Here it comes!" Kayder regarded him with undisguised suspicion. "What's the favor?"

"I want you to kill Thorstern should the necessity arise."

"Aha, you do? Look, you saved me something though I don't know what. The maximum was seven years in clink but I might have got away with six months. Let's say you've saved me six months upward—do you think that is worth a murder?"

"You have overlooked my qualifying words: should the necessity arise. If it does arise it won't be murder—it'll be summary execution."

"Who's going to say when the time has come?" asked Kayder, looking shrewd.

"You."

"In that case I'll never reach a decision."

"I don't recall you being so finicky a few weeks ago."

"I've had enough. I'm going to carry on with my trading business and behave myself providing other folks leave me alone. Moreover, although the authorities insist that I'm a Terran, I still think of myself as a Venusian and I'm not going to slaughter a fellow Venusian merely to show my gratitude to a Terran." Hooking thumbs in vest pockets, he took on a stubborn expression. "I'd be glad to do you a favor but you ask too much."

"I'm asking very little if you only knew it."

"Too much!" Kayder repeated. "And I'll tell you something else: when it comes to killing somebody you are fully capable yourself. Why don't you do your own dirty work?"

"A fair question. There are two excellent reasons."

"Yes?"

"For one, I've already drawn too much attention to myself and am anxious not to attract more. For another, if the need to remove Thorstern should arise there's every likelihood that the first sign of it will be my own departure from this vale of tears."

"You mean—?"

"I'll be dead."

Kayder said, "You know what is in my mind: I'm indebted to you just so much that when you're dead I won't be especially happy. But it's no use pretending I'll be sorry, either."

"You'll be sorry!" Raven contradicted.

"Care to tell me why?"

"Because it may mean that you're next."

"Next? Next for what?"

"For wiping out of this world."

Standing up, Kayder spread hands on his desk and spoke harshly. "You're getting at something. Who is going to wipe me out? Why should he want to? Seeing that you and I have been on opposite sides, why should I now be on the same list as you?"

Waving him down and waiting for him to compose himself, Raven informed, "From the viewpoint of the masses we share one thing in common—neither of us is normal."

"What of it?"

"Ordinary people are leery of paranormals. It can't be said that they love them."

"I'm not love-starved. I'm used to their attitude." He gave a careless shrug. "They recognize those better endowed by nature and are envious of them."

"It is also an instinctive wariness approaching fear. It is a natural and ineradicable part of their defense-mechanism. Some most remarkable things can be done with mass-fears if you can arouse them to sufficient intensity, control them, direct them."

Stewing it moodily, Kayder offered his conclusions, "I can't read another man's mind but that doesn't mean I'm dopey. I can see where you're going. You think Thorstern may try to regain power of a different but equally satisfactory kind by stirring up an anti-mutant crusade?"

"He might. He used the aptitudes of mutants—such as yourself—to further his schemes. Now, the way he may look at it, the same or similar aptitudes thwarted him, denied him victory, even menaced his life. Being normal himself, he'll realize that he might gain ascendancy over his fellows if all of them were normal likewise."

"All this is sheer speculation," Kayder objected, but showing uneasiness.

"Just that and no more," Raven agreed. "Nothing may happen. Thorstern's drive may go in quite innocuous directions. If so, there will be no need to take action against him."

"He'd be playing a mighty dangerous game if he tried it. Mutants may be few in number but once united by a common peril from hordes of—"

"You're thinking along my original lines," Raven chipped in. "I have switched off them since. I've gone on to another track."

"How d'you mean?"

"Thorstern is fifty-eight. These days plenty of people live to a hundred and retain their faculties into the late nineties. So barring accidents or assassination he has a good while to go."

"What difference does that make?"

"He can afford to be patient and take a longer way round to achieve the same result by less arduous means."

Kayder blinked and suggested, "Make it a bit clearer."

"Way back in the past," Raven informed, "some wiseacre remarked that the most effective technique is not to fight a thing but to set its own parts fighting one another."

It registered like a shock.

"Change your way of thinking," Raven invited. "Go from the general to the particular. There is no such creature as a standardized mutant. The word is a collective noun covering a biped menagerie." He watched the other for effect as he continued, "And, being what you are, I'll bet you consider insectivocals to be the cream of the crop."

"An equivalent notion is nursed by telepaths," observed Kayder, pointedly.

"That's a jab at me, but no matter. Each variety of mutant thinks himself superior to the others. Each is as suspicious and jealous as any mere pawn."

"Well?"

"Such a state of mind can he exploited. Type can be set against type. Remember one thing, my bug-ridden friend: superior powers aren't necessarily accompanied by superior brains."

"I know that much."

"There are telepaths of such acute receptivity that they can probe your mind way out to the horizon yet are so inherently dimwitted that they've trouble with any thought more abstruse than c-a-t spells 'cat.' Mutants are humans with all the faults and follies of humans. Brother Thorstern, being an instinctively good psychologist, won't overlook that useful fact!"

By now Kayder's mind had readjusted. He could see the dire possibilities, was compelled to acknowledge their existence. The picture was anything but a happy one.

"If he tries this out, how do you think he'll start?"

"Systematically," said Raven. "First of all he will gain the secret support of Heraty, the World Council and influential pawns on three planets. His next step will be to collect and correlate all data on mutants that can be assembled from every available source, analyze it, reach a positive decision as to which two types exercise the most destructive powers and therefore are the most dangerous. He will choose one of those types to play the part of ye goode and faythfulle knight, the other for the role of baby-eating dragon."

"And then?"

"Let's say he decides the most effective play is to persuade pyrotics to exterminate insectivocals. Forthwith all the propaganda services of three worlds start mentioning insectivocals in a most casual way but invariably in an unflattering context. This continues, building up subconscious prejudice against them, showing them in an increasingly unfavorable light until eventually most humans—by which I mean pawns and other-type mutants alike—think of insectivocals as prize stinkers with no competition."

"Hell in a mist!" rasped Kayder.

"That much having been done, along comes insidious suggestions that insectivocals hate pyrotics because of the latter's bug-killing powers. From time to time the public is given gentle hints that it's a good thing we have pyrotics around to take care of us."

"Like heck it is!" Kayder said, purpling.

"At the proper moment—and don't forget that precise timing is all-important—a well-publicized official speech is made in defense of insectivocals, appealing for unity and tolerance and authoritatively denying an absurd rumor that educated bugs plan to take over the three planets with the aid of treacherous insectivocals. That does a lot of good. It makes the public—again including other-type mutants—jump to the conclusion that there's no smoke without fire."

"They won't swallow all that guff," protested Kayder, inwardly knowing that they might.

"The public will swallow anything, anything at all no matter how crazy, provided it appears to bear the seal of official approval, is sufficiently long sustained, never contradicted, and plays upon their fears," retorted Raven. "Imagine they're now thoroughly aroused—what comes after?"

"You tell me."

"Something to trigger the situation thus deliberately created." He sought for an example, concocted one on the spur of the moment. "A specially placed skeleton is 'found' on its face in the Sawtooths and is given a hundred times more publicity than it deserves. An inspired rumor flies around that an innocent pyrotic has been stripped down by a murderous insectivocal. Further emotion-arousing fairy tales follow immediately after. A picked rabble-rouser sets a mob on the run when by most remarkable coincidence the police are busy elsewhere. The news of *that* whizzes around and loses nothing in the telling."

Bending forward he stared straight at Kayder. His eyes were cold, cold.

"Before you know it, you and every other identifiable insectivocal will be racing for dear life with a howling pack of ordinary people after you, other-type mutants in the lead and pyrotics panting to get at you first!"

"While Thorstern sits back and smiles?" suggested Kayder, showing big teeth.

"You've got the idea, chum. With the aid of scared humanity he roots out the last findable insectivocal and makes the type extinct. Then follows a carefully calculated period of peace and tranquillity before the propaganda services start their new build-up on the next victims, mini-engineers for example."

"He'll never do it," declared Kayder.

"Maybe not—and maybe! Did you see that last serial on the spectroscreen?"

"No, I didn't. I can find better ways of wasting time."

"You missed something worth noting. It featured mutants."

"That's nothing. They've run mutant characters before."

"Yes, of course. So this serial may be without significance. Or it may represent the beginning of an insidious campaign planned to end when nobody lives who has an extraordinary aptitude." He waited a bit, added, "The hero was a telepath and the extremely obnoxious villain was an insectivocal."

"He'll never do it!" repeated Kayder in louder tones. A pulse was beating in his forehead. "I'll kill him first!"

"That's all I ask. I came to you because you owe me a favor. Also because recently you were the boss of a collection of talents and probably can call upon them again. You've death-dealing power and the gumption to use it. Leave Thorstern alone to live in peace but watch to find which way he's going. If you can see that for the second time he intends to create human disunity—"

"He won't live long enough," Kayder promised with savage determination. "And I'll be doing you no favor. I'll be protecting myself. I'll have no scruples if and when the time comes. A man is entitled to defend himself." He eyed Raven calculatingly. "Just as a guess I'd say *you* will need protecting long before me. What action are you going to take?"

Raven stood up and said, "None."

"None?" Kayder's heavy brows arched in surprise. "Why not?"

"Perhaps, unlike you, I'm unable to take suitable action regarding myself." He opened the door. "Or perhaps I enjoy the prospect of becoming a martyr."

"If that's a wisecrack, I don't get it. If it isn't, then I *know* you're crazy!" Kayder wore a worried frown as he watched the other leave.

Chapter 17

Back in the house Raven sprawled in a pneumaseat and said to Leina, "There's going to be more interference if events make it desirable. But not by our kind. Human schemes will be countered by humans. Are you happy about it?"

"I'd have liked it better if that had been arranged in the first place," she gave back a little tartly.

"They're entitled to their tiny fragment of destiny, aren't they?" He threw her a quizzical glance.

She breathed a sigh of resignation. "The trouble with males is that they never grow up. They remain hopeless romantics." Her great eyes looked right into him. "You know perfectly well that these puny bipeds are entitled to nothing but preservation from destruction at the hands of the Denebs."

"Have it your own way," said Raven, giving up the argument. There was no point in pursuing it with her—she was too entirely right.

"And furthermore," she went on, "I have been listening while you were busy with less weighty affairs. Twelve black ships have been reported in the region of Vega."

He stiffened. "Vega! That's the nearest they've come to date."

"They may come nearer. They may arrive here in the end. Or they may shoot off in some other direction and not be seen in this cosmic sector for ten thousand years." She did not add more but he knew what she was leaving unsaid, "This is a bad time to take foolish risks."

"An error in tactics doesn't matter where there is ability to conceal it and recover," he pointed out. "I think I'll go catch up on the news."

Upstairs he reclined and opened his mind and sought to extract from the ethereal babble that portion emanating from the region of Vega. It was not easy. Too many talking at once.

"The tripedal hoppers of Raemis fled into the damp marsh lands and are fearfully declining all contact with the Denebs. The latter seem to think the world unsuitable for any purpose. They are making ready to depart."

". . . twisted the pilots' minds and turned the entire convoy toward Zebulam, a near-nova in sector fifty-one of the Chasm. They are still bulleting along under the delusion that they're on correct course."

"I asked him for it. He'd discarded it so suddenly and violently that he was too confused to give permission. By the time he'd collected his wits it was too late, the opportunity had passed. So now I've got to wait for another. Meanwhile—"

"These Weltenstiles got the fright of their lives when a cruiser came out of the dark and fastened tractor-beams upon them. It didn't take the Denebs one-thousandth of a time-unit to realize that the ship they'd caught was a crude contraption manned by comparative savages. They let it go unharmed."

". . . twelve in fan formation still heading toward Vega, blue-white in sector one-ninety-one, edge of the Long Spray."

He sat up and gazed at the night sky. The Long Spray gleamed across the zenith like a gauzy veil. Terrans called it the Milky Way. Between here and one insignificant pinpoint in the dark were a thousand worlds to divert the attention of oncoming ships. But they might persist on course, ignoring other attractions. When left alone to go their own sweet ways the Denebs were unpredictable.

The end foreseen by Leina arrived after another three weeks. During that time neither radio nor spectroscreen networks made mention of recent interplanetary animosities, while their other offerings revealed no sinister trend in any direction. Mutants had again been featured in various items of entertainment but the everlasting roles of hero, heroine and villain had been distributed with fine impartiality.

Elsewhere twelve long black ships of space had nosed a quarter turn to starboard and now were approaching the eight unoccupied planets of a minor binary system. Temporarily, at least, the drive toward Vega was arrested.

The morning sun shone down, bright and warm. The sky was a clear blue bowl marred only by a streak of low cloud on the eastward horizon and a great curving vapor-trail rising into the stratosphere. Once more the *Fantôme* was Venus-bound.

A four-seater copter gave first indication that errors must be paid for, that the past has an unpleasant way of catching up with the present. It droned out of the west, landed near the crater already beginning to produce a crop of colorful weeds. One man got out.

Leina admitted him to the house. A young, well-built type with frank, eager features, he was a very junior operative of Terran Intelligence, a sub-telepath able to probe minds but without a shield for his own. From the viewpoint of those who had sent him this made him an excellent choice for his special mission. Essentially he was open and disarming, the sort to establish confidence.

"My name is Grant," he introduced himself. Conditioned by his own status, he spoke vocally, knowing that mental communication placed him under a handicap when dealing with a true telepath. "I have come to tell you that Major Lomax of Terran Intelligence would like to see you as soon as may be convenient."

"Is it urgent?" Raven asked.

"I think so, sir. He instructed me to bring you and this lady in the copter if you were ready to leave at once."

"Oh, so he wants *both* of us?"

"Yes, he asked for you and the lady."

"Do you know what it is about?"

"I'm afraid not, sir." Grant's expression was candid and his unprotected mind confirmed his words.

Raven gave Leina an inquiring glance. "Might as well get it over now. What do you say?"

"I am ready." Her voice was low, her eyes brilliant as she studied the visitor.

His face flushing, Grant fidgeted and prayed for some means of closing his mind which insisted on thinking, "She is looking into me, right inside of me, right at where I'm hiding inside of myself. I wish she couldn't do that. Or I wish I could look at her in the same way. She is big and cumbersome—but very beautiful."

Leina smiled but tactfully made no remark, said instead, "I'll get my coat and handbag, David. Then we can go."

When she reappeared they went to the waiting machine which rose smoothly under whirling vanes and drifted westward. Nobody said anything more during the hour's flight. Grant kept strictly to business, handled the controls, maintained his thoughts in polite and disciplined channels.

Leina studied the bright landscape turning below, giving it the undivided attention of one who is seeing it for the first time—or the last. Raven closed his eyes and attuned himself to calls far above the normal telepathic band.

"David! David!"

"Yes, Charles?"

"They are taking us away."

"We, too, Charles."

The copter lost altitude, floated down toward a stark and lonely building standing upon a windswept moor. A squat, heavily built edifice, it resembled an abandoned power station or perhaps a onetime explosives dump.

Touching earth, the machine jounced a couple of times, settled itself. Grant got out, self-consciously helped Leina down. With the others following he went to the armor plate front door, pressed a button set in thick concrete at its side. A tiny trap in the armor plate opened like an iris diaphragm, revealed a scanner peering at them.

Apparently satisfied the trap closed over the eye. From behind the door came a faint, smooth whirr of machinery as huge bolts were drawn aside.

"Like a fortress, this place," remarked Grant, innocently conversational.

The door swung ajar. The summoned pair stepped through and left the other to return to his copter.

Turning on the threshold, Raven said to Grant, "It reminds me of a crematorium."

Then the armor plate cut him off from view and the bolts slid back into place. Grant stood a moment staring at the door, the concrete, the great windowless walls. He shivered.

"It does at that! What a lousy thought!"

Moodily he took the copter up, noticing that somehow the sun had lost much of its warmth.

Behind the door stretched a long passage down which a distant voice came reverberating. "Please continue straight ahead. You will find me in the room at the end. I regret not being there to meet you but know you will forgive me."

It was real enough, that voice, suave, courteous, but curiously impersonal and devoid of warmth. And when they found the speaker his looks matched his tones.

Seated in a chair behind a long, low desk, Major Lomax proved to be a lean individual in his early thirties. He had light blue eyes that gazed fixedly and rarely blinked. His fair hair was cropped to a short bristle. The most noteworthy feature was his extreme pallor; his face was white, almost waxy and had a permanent tautness on one side.

Motioning to a double pneumaseat, the only other resting place in the room, Lomax said, "Kindly sit there. I thank you for coming so promptly." The blue eyes went from Raven to Leina and back again. "I apologize for not escorting you from the door. I am rather handicapped. It is difficult for me to stand, much less walk."

"I am very sorry," said Leina with womanly sympathy.

There was no easy way of detecting the reaction. A swift probe showed that Lomax was a top-grade telepath with an exceptionally efficient shield. His mind was closed as securely as could be done by any human being. Despite that they might have driven through this defense with a simultaneous and irresistible thrust. By mutual consent they refrained from trying. The other must have sensed their first tentative pass at him, but no sign of it showed on his pale, strained countenance.

Positioning a thin wad of typewritten papers in front of him, Lomax continued in the same cool, unemotional voice as before.

"I don't know whether you now suspect the purpose of this interview, neither can I tell what action on your part may be precipitated by it, but before we begin I want you to know that my function is prescribed here." He tapped the papers. "It has been worked out for me in complete detail and all I must do is follow it through as written."

"You make it sound ominous," offered Raven. "Oh, well, carry on."

There was no visible reaction to that either. The sheet-white face remained as fixed and expressionless as that of a mummy. It suggested that its owner could and would play to perfection the part of an intellectual automaton.

Picking up the top sheet, Lomax read from it. "First, I have to give you a personal message from Mr. Carson, head of Terran Intelligence, to the effect that when informed of this interview he strongly disapproved, opposed it by all legitimate means at his command, but was overruled. He wishes me to convey his sincere regards and assure you that no matter what may take place within this building he will always hold both of you in the greatest esteem."

"Dear me!" said Raven. "This is getting worse."

Lomax let it go by with complete impassivity. "This interview will be conducted only on a vocal basis. There is a reason, for it is being recorded for the benefit of those who arranged it."

Putting the top sheet aside, he took the next one and continued in the same robotlike way. "It is essential that you know I have been chosen for my present task because of a rare combination of qualifications. I am a member of Terran Intelligence and a telepath well able to cover his own mind. Last but by no means least, I am very much of a physical wreck."

Glancing up, he met Leina's great optics and for the first time displayed a faint shadow of expression in the form of vague and swiftly suppressed uneasiness. Like Grant and many others, he was disturbed when looked into so deeply.

He hurried on. "I shall not bore you with full details. In brief, I was involved in a crash and badly injured. Everyone did their best for me but my remaining days are not many, the waiting time is increasingly painful and I shall be glad to go."

The blue eyes lifted, stared straight at them with bold and unmistakable defiance. "I want you to keep that in mind because it is most important: I am in the abnormal mental state of a man who will be glad to die. Therefore I cannot be intimidated by the threat of death."

"Neither can we," assured Raven, amiably bland.

It disconcerted Lomax a little. He had expected nothing less than a heated and indignant demand as to who was threatening his life. Concealing his surprise, he returned his attention to the papers.

"Further, although I do not fear my own dissolution, I shall be compelled to react should my existence be endangered. I have undergone a special course of mental conditioning which has created a purely reactive circuit within my mind. It is not part of my normal thinking processes, cannot be detected or controlled by any other mind-probe. This circuit automatically keys-in the instant I am in peril of losing either my life or control of my free personality. It will force me to do something *unthinkingly*, instinctively, the result of which will be the immediate destruction of all three of us."

Raven frowned and commented, "Somewhere back of all this is a badly frightened man."

Ignoring that, Lomax went determinedly on. "What I shall do is not known to me nor will be until the very moment I do it. Therefore you have nothing to gain by combining to beat down my mental shield and search my mind for what is not consciously there. You have nothing to gain by trying to hypnotize me or seize control of me by any other supernormal means. On the contrary, you have everything to lose—your lives!"

The pair on the pneumaseat glanced at each other, did their best to look outwitted and aghast. Lomax had a precisely defined part to play—but so had they.

It was a curious situation without parallel in human annals, for each side was in mental hiding from the other, each was holding a trump card in the form of power over life and death, each *knew* that victory for itself was certain. And each in his own way was right!

Looking at Lomax who refused to meet her eyes, Leina complained with some exasperation, "We came here in good faith thinking perhaps our help was needed. We find ourselves being treated like uncommon criminals guilty of heaven alone knows what. No charge has been made against us and we are denied the proper processes of the law. Just what are we supposed to have done to deserve all this?"

"Exceptional methods must be applied to exceptional cases," remarked Lomax, quite unmoved. "It is not so much what you have done as what you may do eventually."

"Can't you be more explicit?"

"Please be patient. I am coming to it right now." He resumed his sheets. "This is a condensation of facts sufficient to enable you to understand the reason for this meeting. Certain matters brought to the attention of the World Council—"

"By a schemer named Thorstern?" suggested Raven, picturing Emmanuel's scowl when this came over the recording system.

". . . caused them to order a thorough inquiry into the nature of your activities, especially during your recent operations on behalf of Terran Intelligence," continued Lomax, stubbornly. "Which inquiry was later extended to this lady with whom you—reside."

"You make it sound nasty," reproved Leina.

"Data was drawn from a large number of sources considered reliable and the resulting report, which was complete and exhaustive, made President Heraty decide to appoint a special commission to study it and issue a recommendation."

"Somebody must think we're important." Raven slid a glance at Leina who responded with an I-told-you-so look.

"Composed of two World Council members and ten scientists, this commission held that on the basis of the evidence before them you had displayed supernormal powers of eight distinct classifications, six known and two previously unknown. Or, alternatively, that in addition to the telepathic power which you have never tried to conceal you also possess hypnotic power of such redoubtable strength that you have succeeded in compelling witnesses to attribute other aptitudes you don't really have. Either the witnesses are dependable or they have been deluded by you. Either way the result is the same: the evidence suggests that you are a multi-talented mutant." He did a double-take at the paper, murmured with a touch of annoyance, "That's obviously wrong," and changed it to, "You are *both* multi-talented mutants."

"Is that an offense?" inquired Raven, not bothering to contradict.

"I have no personal views regarding this matter." Lomax leaned forward, held his middle a moment while his face went even whiter. Then he recovered, said, "Kindly permit me to continue. If the evidence had favored no more than that, the World Council would have been compelled to accept that multi-talented mutants do exist in spite of so-called natural laws. But the data is equally in support of an alternative theory toward which some members of the commission lean while others reject it as fantastic."

The listening pair stirred on the pneumaseat, showed curiosity and mild interest. No more than that. No apprehension. No fear of being rooted out like surreptitious scuttlers in the dark. At every moment they were living the part they wished to play, as determined as Lomax to see it through to the bitter end.

"You are entitled to know the cogent items," Lomax carried on. He discarded another sheet. "A careful re-examination of your antecedents shows that both of you might well be persons considerably out of the ordinary by our standards of today. It was by substantially the same method that Mr. Carson traced you in the first place and reached the same conclusion."

He paused while his features quirked to a jolt of agony inside him, then said more slowly, "But the ancestry of David Raven should at best have produced no more than a superb telepath, a mind-probe of unusual penetrating power and extremely acute receptivity. It is conceivable—and contrary to no known laws— that his mental strength might be sufficient to make him impervious to hypnotism, thus causing him to be the first hypno-proof telepath on record. But that is all. That is the limit of his hereditable aptitudes." He gave the rest of it extra emphasis as he went on, "He could *not* exercise hypnotic or quasi-hypnotic powers of his own, even as a multi-talented mutant, because there is not one hypno among his forebears."

"That may be—" began Leina.

Lomax chipped in, "The same remarks apply to you. They apply also to your two confreres on Venus, which pair are now having the same kind of interview in similar precautionary conditions."

"With a similar threat hanging over them?" Raven asked.

Lomax took no notice. Perfectly disciplined, he was answering no questions other than those pertinent to the stage reached in his task.

"Item number two: we discovered that David Raven either had died or shown all symptoms of death and then been resuscitated. The doctor who performed this feat can no longer be called upon for evidence, having died himself three years ago. The incident is not remarkable when considered by itself, as an isolated occurrence. Such things *do* happen though rarely. It becomes noteworthy only when examined in conjunction with other facts."

The blue eyes shot a glance at Leina before he continued, "Such as the fact that this lady once went swimming, was caught in a powerful undercurrent, apparently drowned, but revived by artificial respiration. *Plus* the facts that your two prototypes on Venus have had equally hairsbreadth escapes."

"You've had one yourself," Raven riposted. "You told us so at the beginning. You're lucky to be alive—if it is luck!"

Strongly tempted to admit the escape but deny the pleasure of living in his present condition, Lomax hesitated, nursed his middle, then plowed grimly on.

"Item number three has indirect significance. You have been told by Mr. Carson of certain Terran spaceship experiments so there is no harm in adding more. He did not give you the whole of it. To cut it short, our last exploring vessel went farther into the void than you may suspect. Upon its return the pilot reported that he had been chased by unidentifiable objects of unknown origin. All that his instruments could tell him was that these objects were metallic and radiated heat. There were four of them moving in line abreast at distance too great to permit examination with the naked eye. But they changed course when he changed and undoubtedly were in pursuit. They had greater maneuverability and far more speed."

"Nevertheless he escaped?" put in Raven with a skeptical smile.

"The escape is fully as much a mystery as the pursuit," Lomax retorted. "The pilot says the four were overtaking rapidly when a few strange sparkles and gleamings appeared in front of them, whereupon they swung into reverse course and went away. He is convinced that these four were artificial fabrications and his belief is officially endorsed."

"And what does this mean to us?"

Taking a deep breath, Lomax declared with impressive solemnity, "There is other life in the cosmos and not so far from us either. Its forms, powers, techniques and ways of thought remain matters of pure speculation. It may be humanoid enough to pose as veritable humans, gaining plausibility by using the identities of real humans who have died."

He whisked a sheet aside, continued with the next. "Or it might be parasitic by nature, able to seize and animate the bodies of other creatures, masquerading thereafter in guise mighty close to perfection. We have no data to go upon in these respects, but we can think, imagine, and conceive the infinite possibilities."

"Frightened men have bad dreams," observed Raven.

"I think it's all terribly silly," Leina put in. "Are you seriously suggesting that we may be zombies motivated by intelligent parasites from somewhere else?"

"Lady, I am suggesting nothing. I am merely reading papers prepared by my superiors whose conclusions and motives I am not disposed to question. That is my job."

"Where does it get us?"

"To this point: the commission has informed President Heraty that all four of you—the couple on Venus as well as yourselves—are of identically the same type. Secondly, they are quite unable to define the origin of that type with reasonable certainty. In defiance of the rule that only the dominant talent is inherited, you *may* be multi-talented mutants of natural human birth, in which case the so-called laws of genetics will have to be modified. On the other hand, you *may* be a nonhuman form of life, disguised in our shape and form, living among us unsuspected until lately."

"For what purpose?"

It did not faze him in the least. Passing a hand over his bristly hair, he looked physically and mentally weary as he answered, "The purposes of other life-forms are obscure. We know nothing about them—yet. We can, however, make a justifiable assumption."

"And what is that?"

"If its intentions were friendly another life-form would make contact openly, without attempting concealment."

"Meaning that surreptitious contact is proof of hostile designs."

"Exactly!"

Leina said with some morbidity, "I can think of nothing more absurd than to suggest that human beings are not human beings."

"For the second time, lady," said Lomax, displaying frigid politeness, "I am not making suggestions. I am no more than a deputy appointed to inform you of the conclusions of experts. They say that you two are multi-talented mutants or non-human life-forms and more probably the latter."

"I think they're impertinent," opined Leina, becoming femininely inconsequential.

Lomax let it pass. "If it should be the case that some other form of life has dumped scouts upon our three worlds, unknown to us, the logical conclusion is that their ultimate purpose is antagonistic. It's the criminal who climbs in through the back window. The honest man knocks at the front door."

"You have a point there," admitted Raven, undisturbed.

"Therefore if a life-form powerful enough and intelligent enough to conquer space ahead of ourselves has planted a secret advance party among us, well, it means that humanity soon has to face its greatest crisis ever!" He waved a hand to indicate the fortresslike surroundings. "Hence this extraordinary procedure. Alien invaders stand outside our laws, are not entitled to claim the protection of them."

"I see." Rubbing his chin, Raven regarded the other thoughtfully. "What are we supposed to do about all this wild speculation?"

"The onus now rests on you of proving beyond all manner of doubt that you are natural-born humans and not another life-form. The proof must be watertight. The evidence must be incontrovertible."

Chapter 18

Raven growled in pretended anger, "Darn it, can you prove you're not something out of Sirius?"

"I won't argue with you or permit you to disturb my emotions." Lomax jabbed an indicative thumb at the last sheet of paper. "All I'm concerned with is what it says here. It says you will produce undeniable proof that you are human beings, by which is meant the kind of superior life native to Terra."

"Otherwise—?"

"Terra will assume the worst and take steps to protect herself by every means available. For a start she will wipe out all three of us here in this room, simultaneously deal with those on Venus and make ready to repel any later attack launched upon us from outside."

"H'm! All three of us, you say. Tough on you, isn't it?"

"I told you why I was chosen," Lomax reminded. "I am quite ready to go should it prove necessary, especially since I've been assured that the method to be employed will be superswift and painless."

"That is a great comfort," put in Leina, enigmatically.

He eyed them in turn. "I shall go with you solely to deprive you of the last possible way out, your only avenue of escape. There will be no opportunity for one of you to ensure survival by confiscating my person. No other life-form—if such you should happen to be—is going to walk out of this trap in the guise of a man named Lomax. We survive together or die together according to whether or not you produce the evidence my superiors require."

He was slightly pleased about that. For the first time his resented physical condition had given him power of an invincible kind. In given circumstances such as existed here and now, the ability to contemplate one's own death with absolute calmness could be a veritably appalling form of strength.

If one were devoid of fear while one's opponents were filled with it, the conflict could end in only one way: with the defeat of the cravens. In common with those behind him he was taking it for granted that any form of life, human or non-human, would value its own survival too highly to share his own abnormal nonchalance about destruction.

In that respect neither he nor those who had planned this situation could have been more mistaken. The difficult thing was for prospective victims to conceal the fact. Their essential tactic was not to reveal it outwardly and to give the recording apparatus a series of reactions manifestly natural from the human point of view.

So in suitably disturbed tones, Raven remarked, "Many an innocent has been slaughtered by the chronic suspicions and uncontrolled fears of others. This world has never lacked its full quota of witch hunters." He fidgeted as if on edge and asked, "How long do we have to talk ourselves out of this fix? Is there a time limit?"

"Not by the clock. Either you dig up the proof or you don't." Lomax registered tired indifference as to which way it went. "If you can find proof you'll start trying without delay. If you can't, the knowledge that you can't will drive you to desperation sooner or later. You will then have to try a hazardous way out. When that happens I will—" He let his voice trail off.

"You'll react?"

"Effectively!" Resting elbows on the desk, he propped his chin, took on the air of one prepared to wait for the inevitable. "I am very patient and you're free to take full advantage of it. But I advise you not to play for time by trying to sit here for a week."

"That sounds like another threat."

"It is a friendly warning," Lomax corrected. "Although they have given far less cause for suspicion the pair on Venus are classified with you and are receiving precisely the same treatment. All four of you are birds of a feather, will be released or executed together."

"So a coupling exists between here and there?" inquired Raven.

"Correct. Emergency action here causes a signal to be beamed which precipitates the same action there. The same holds good in reverse. That is why we've kept the two pairs apart. The more time one pair wastes, the greater the chance of the issue being settled for them by the other couple."

"Well, it's a neat arrangement," Raven conceded.

"You have *two* chances of bidding this world good-by forever: at my hands should you cause me to react, or at the hands of your allies on Venus." Lomax revealed the shadow of a smile as he added, "You are in the most unhappy position of the man who remarked that he could cope with his enemies but only God could save him from his friends."

Emitting a deep sigh, Raven lay back and closed his eyes as if concentrating on the problem in hand. That Lomax might try to listen to his thoughts did not worry him in the least. He had complete confidence in the inviolability of his own mental shield and in the inability of any Earth-type telepath to tune so high in the neural band.

"Charles! Charles!"

The response took a long time coming because the other's mind was absorbed in his predicament and had to be drawn away.

"Yes, David?"

"How far have you got?"

"We're now being told how four Denebs took after a Terran but were turned away." A mental chuckle, followed by, "I just can't imagine what turned them."

"You are lagging behind us a few minutes. We're near the end here. Who's dealing with you?"

"A very old man. Quick witted but on his last legs."

"We've got a young one," Raven informed. "Rather a sad case. So much so that it wouldn't be thought extraordinary if he had a serious attack and collapsed under the strain of this interview. We could make it look good and sound good on the recorder system. Deplorable but natural. I think we can successfully cover up by taking advantage of his condition."

"What do you propose?"

"We'll feed the microphones a little real life drama. We'll use it to establish a plausible semblance of innocence. Then he'll have his attack, we'll react naturally and he'll also react to that because he can't help it. The result will get you out of your jam because we here will have jumped the gun and thus denied you the chance to say a word in your own defense."

"How long will it be?"

"In a few minutes' time."

Opening his eyes and sitting up like one who has discovered a bright and hopeful solution, Raven said excitedly, "Look, if my life is known in detail it will be obvious that my body could have been confiscated only at the time of my death and resuscitation."

"No comment," said Lomax. "Others will decide that point."

"They'll agree." He asserted it with confidence. "Now if we accept this far-fetched notion that some other life-form could take over the material body of another creature, how could it also confiscate something so immaterial as that creature's memories?"

"Don't ask me—I'm not an expert." Lomax made a brief note on a pad. "But carry on."

"If I can relate a wealth of childhood memories from the age of three upward," continued Raven, with excellent imitation of triumph, "and have most of them confirmed by persons still living, where do I stand then?"

"I don't know," said Lomax. "The suggestion is now being considered elsewhere. A signal will tell me whether or not you may extend the theme."

"What if I show that during my youth I self-consciously suppressed my powers, knowing that I was a freak? What if I show that the alleged coincidence of four similar freaks in a bunch is attributable to no more than that like clings to like?"

"It may suffice or it may not," Lomax evaded. "We shall hear pretty soon." His face suddenly squirmed from some inner torment and beads of perspiration popped out on his forehead. He pulled himself together, displaying an iron will. "If you've anything more to offer now's the time."

Looking around the room Raven *saw* the scanner lens, the recorder leads buried deep in the wall, the tiny pin in the floor near Lomax's right foot, the connections running from it to a machine in the cellars. Without any difficulty whatever he could examine the machine and estimate the efficiency of the lethal ray it was designed to produce.

He and Leina had become aware of all these features at the very first. It would have been easy to detach various leads by remote operation, teleportatively, without moving from the pneumaseat. It would have been easy to jam the pin or break the power supply to the concealed executioner below. Despite Lomax's belief to the contrary, the way out lay wide open and had been from the start—unfortunately a successful break would have been a complete giveaway.

The present situation showed too much had been revealed. At whatever cost suspicions must be lulled in manner carefully calculated to create false conclusions and, at the same time, the sources of forbidden information must be removed, plausibly and forever. The shadowy figures at the other end of the recorder system must be fed soothing data on which they could compute and get the wrong answer every time.

Concealment was the paramount issue. No fragment of truth must lurk in any biped mind lest someday it be extracted by others. Humans lived in protective ignorance and should continue to do so at whatever cost. A little knowledge could be a highly dangerous thing. They must be denied it for ever and ever and ever.

As for the freedom beckoning beyond the armorplate door, it was only a poor, restricted, third-rate kind of liberty. The freedom of a child to play in the street. The freedom of a babe to wet its triangle and shake its rattle, the freedom of a caterpillar to crawl to mock safety around the underside of a leaf.

Casually his hand touched Leina's, making them of one accord. There were scanners to watch what was about to occur, they would require care. Then there was only the blind, idiot recording system, the little pin, the lethal projector.

"There are and always have been unknown mutants in addition to known ones," he said, making it pleadingly persuasive. "It is a fact that makes ancestral data inadequate and misleading. For example, if my maternal grandfather, being an unmitigated scoundrel, took great care to conceal his hypnotic powers which he preserved solely for illegal purposes, it stands to sense that—"

He broke off while Lomax had another spasm of internal agony that bent him forward. Before Lomax could recover, Leina obligingly contributed a startled yelp of, "Oh, David, look!" and right on top of it shouted, *"What's the matter, Lomax?"*

At the same moment both minds thrust with irresistible strength through the other's mental shield. Lomax had no time to inquire what the devil they were talking about, no time to deny that anything was the matter, not even a split-second to recover and wipe the brief pain from his face. He heard Leina's exclamation and Raven's following question, both uttered in tones of shocked surprise, then came the fierce stab at his brain. He faltered farther forward. The reactive circuit sprang into instantaneous operation. Automatically his foot rammed down on the hidden pin.

For a fragmentary moment his mind shrieked aloud, "I've done it! Heavens above, I've—!"

Then the cry cut off.

There followed a period of soul-searing chaos and absolute bewilderment. Lomax did not know, could not tell whether it was long or short, a matter of seconds or eons. He did not not know whether it was now light or dark, cold or warm, whether he was standing up or lying down, moving or still.

What had occurred when he pressed that pin? Had some new and awful device been tested on himself and the other two guinea pigs? Had it hurled him into the past, the future, or some other dimension? Or worse still, oh, infinitely worse, had it added a mutilated mind to his mutilated body?

Then it struck him that he could no longer sense the throbbing agony that had made his life a personal hell these last two years. Sheer surprise and an overwhelming flood of relief stopped his mind's mad whirling. He began to coordinate slowly, uncertainly, like a little child.

It now seemed that he was floating either up or down amid a mighty host of brilliant bubbles, large and small. All around him they drifted lazily along shining in superbly glowing colors while among them pale wisps of smoke wreathed and curled. He was, he thought, like a tiny, rudderless boat on a wide, iridescent and bubbly river.

The pain had gone, unbelievably gone, and now there was only this sleepy, dreamy swaying along the mainstream of blues and greens, crimson and gold, starry sparklings of purest white, fitful gleams of silver, momentary flashings of little rainbows, on, on into the infinitude of peace. He was slumbersome and content to slumber for ever and ever, for as long as time goes on.

But then his mind stirred as a sense became active and prodded it into reluctant attention. It now seemed that with the palely coiling wreaths of smoke amid the bubbles came an immense multitude of voices that somehow were not really voices but could be heard or sensed or understood and all speaking one tongue.

Some talked in quick, staccato phrases from places tremendously afar. Others were nearer and more leisurely. It was strange that while each had a sort of mental audibility he could also tell—somehow, he did not know how—the precise direction from which each one came and the exact distance of its source relative to the others. A few were near him, very near, voicing mysterious things among the curls of smoke, the spheres and the colors.

"Stay with him!"

"He may have no reason to be vengeful but stay with him—we want no more dangerous impulses like Steen's."

"Said he was ready for this so he should be quicker to adapt."

"It's never easy no matter how ready one may be."

"He must learn that no man can be an enemy."

"The flower cannot hate its own seeds nor the bird its eggs."

More senses sprang into operation even while he wondered whether this was the delirium of mental mutilation. In a confused, out-of-focus way he became conscious that the entities he had known as Raven and Leina were still present, sharing his dream environment. They were holding him without actually touching him, drifting with him through the mists and the bubbles. They were not the same yet he knew who they were beyond all doubt. It was as if he could now see what was to be seen if one looked right into them.

All at once this hazy sense of perception that was not sight cleared itself, adjusted, swung into full and complete functioning. The myriad bubbles fled away as if blown by a mighty breath and took up new positions at enormous distances. They were suns and planets, glowing and spinning within the great spaces of eternal dark.

His new vision was non-stereoscopic, devoid of perspective, but had in lieu an automatic and extremely accurate estimation of relative distances. He *knew* merely by looking which bubbles were near, which far, and exactly how much farther.

Still with the other two in attendance, he heard one cry, "Charles! Charles!" and a reply eerily vibrating from far away, "Coming, David!" The names used were not those names but he thought of them as those names because he could not grasp the new ones—though somehow he knew to whom they referred. This phenomenon did not arouse his curiosity or stimulate his mind to speculation, for he was concentrating on the vision of the bubble-filled cosmos and overcome by its incomparable wonder.

The surfaces of many spheres could be "seen" in splendid detail. On a lot of them strange creatures lived and swarmed, hoppers, creepers, crawlers, flutterers, flame-things, wave-form entities, beings of infinite variety and most of them low in the scale of life.

But one widespread form was high. It had a long, thin, sinuous body covered in dark gray hide, a well developed and efficient brain, many dexterous limbs and e.s.p. organs. It enjoyed telepathic power confined to its own special band. Its individuals could compute as individuals or combine mentally to compute as a mass-mind.

These things roamed far and wide in slender, pencil-shaped, jet black space vessels, exploring other worlds, patroling the gulfs and chasms between, mapping, charting, reporting to numerous bases and always ceaselessly searching, searching.

The Denebs!

In their own esteem these were the lords of creation. Absorbing data being fed to him from he knew not where, Lomax understood a lot about the Denebs. They stood right at the top of the life-scale of bubble-bound creatures, had great tolerance of all other life-forms considered lower than themselves. To these they did no harm, regarding them as satisfactory targets for patronizing superiority. But the Denebs had one great shortcoming—they could not abide the notion of sharing the cosmos with a life-form equal to themselves—or higher.

And there was one still higher!

So for countless centuries the Denebs had been feverishly seeking the home world or worlds whence came unbearable competition. They would destroy rivalry at its source—if the source could be found. Their black ships prowled and poked and probed and searched amid the endless multitude of bubbles, disturbing but not destroying the hoppers, creepers, crawlers, and sometimes nosing around the colonies of little white grublike bipeds established on many widely separated spheres.

Lomax felt a peculiarly intense interest in this last type of creature. Poor little grubs, squirming and wriggling around, building or trying to build or hoping ultimately to build rudimentary, ramshackle rocketships that never would touch more than a fringe of creation. Mournful grubs, sorrowing ones, ecstatic ones, ambitious ones, even petty dictator-grubs.

In all probability there were individuals among them slightly better endowed, talented above the grub-norm. These would think themselves superior merely because they could exercise a minute, fragmentary portion of powers entirely normal but said to be supernormal. Some could, perhaps, read other grub-minds to the pitiful limit of a bubble's horizon. Some could, perhaps, fascinate another grub, creating fear of themselves by compelling obedience.

Doubtless every colony of them had developed a grub-culture, a grub-philosophy, a grub-theology. Being unable to conceive anything infinitely higher, some might go so far as to think of themselves as made in the image of a mighty super-grub.

Now and again one more daring than the rest might have sneaked from the hiding place of its own grub-conditioning and peered furtively into the dark and seen a great, bright-eyed moth like a nocturnal butterfly beating gloriously through the endless night. And it would cower down, sorely afraid, totally unable to recognize—itself!

An enormous surge of life filled Lomax's being as the data filed itself and became estimated. The grubs! The nestlings! Alive with tremendous power, he saw Raven and Leina, Charles and Mavis as he had never seen anyone before. They were with him still, helping him, watching him, urging him to adapt to the environment.

The little two-legged grubs, he was crying. Ours! Our nestlings waiting their natural metamorphosis! If the Denebs—long unable to recognize them for what they are—should now learn the truth from one discerning mind in one colony they will systematically destroy the lot. If one grub learns too much, all may be slaughtered from one end of the heavens to the other.

"Never!" assured the one he had known as Raven. "It will never be known to any of them. There are two watchers in every nest, each living inside a grub-body taken with permission of its former owner exactly as I took the body of David Raven with his permission. They are guardians. They enter in pairs. It needs one to watch, but two to break earthbound solitude."

"The place we left, *you* left?"

"Two more already have gone in."

They began to leave him, moving silently into the immense deeps that were their natural playfields. The Denebs were highest of the bubble-bound, but *these,* the higher ones, were bound to nothing once their childhood's grub-existence had ended. They went like wide-eyed, supersensitive, multi-talented creatures of the great spaces.

Those pale, weak two-legged things, wondered Lomax, what had they called themselves? Oh, yes, Homo Sapiens. Some among them were precocious and hence regarded themselves as Homo Superior. It was pitiful in a way. It was pathetic.

As instinctively as a baby moves feet it is not consciously aware of possessing, or a kitten similarly puts forth claws, so did he spread huge, shining, fan-shaped fields of force and swoop in the wake of his fellows.

He was alive as he'd never been alive before. And filled with a fierce exultation.

For he knew what he had become and what the little white grubs had yet to be.

Homo In Excelsis!

Call Him Dead

Introduction by Jack L. Chalker

Call Him Dead, (Three to Conquer) is a thriller; there's no way around that. It doesn't have a lot of the underlying themes present in much of Russell's other work, and the authorities, once roused, are (almost uniquely for Russell) competent. On the other hand, it's one of the great examples of the pure paranoia-inducing tale and in many ways it's kin to *Sinister Barrier* in its theme (only, in this case, "we are property" becomes "we might *become* property.") It's also one heck of a good read.

The novel is very much in line with an entire school of alien takeover tales, ranging from Campbell's classic "Who Goes There?" through the contemporaneous *Puppet Masters* of Heinlein to the body snatchers of Jack Finney. In one sense, it goes back to the earliest paranoid fears of demonic possession.

The alien threat here is certainly partly our fault; we go to their home and we bring them back with us. We're told little about them, except that they're a collective consciousness within each host and are viral in nature, and in at least one case they have a tendency to think like one creature even to swearing on some alien landscape. But of their "life" on Venus before we get there we know nothing; certainly they are not spacefaring, although they are extremely technologically savvy. They don't have the memories of the host, but they seem pretty adept at learning what they need to learn very quickly and being quite convincing imitators to others. The implication is that they are not native to Venus, either, but have been through this many times before, much like the pod people or the slugs. The fact that they are not fleshed out but that little pieces of their background show up now and again adds to their mystique, and keeps them removed from us. Like Campbell's shape shifters, they see no reason for dialog; they only want to keep us ignorant long enough to allow them to replace the entire human race.

Other than pacing, what distinguishes *Call Him Dead* from the ordinairy is its unique narrator/hero. He's got an unusual occupation, but, more, he's got a secret that saves the world but it can also put him at grave risk even among his own kind if they find out about his peculiar ability, and he's always got to be under control. He is, thus, the first one to learn of the invaders and to act in some small way against them, but he's also caught between a rock and a hard place and that makes this a much more interesting thriller than the basic us-vs.-them tale. How do you convince others that that nice young woman over there is an alien bent on taking over your body, without revealing your secret? And when many of those who would fear and then act against the alien menace might also do the same to you should they find out . . . , well, you've got a problem . . . But to do nothing is to let the aliens win.

Too often characterization has been overlooked in Russell's works, but it's often the key to the success of his books. In this case, it's front and center in a wild and fast-paced battle of wits with our very selves at stake. Hold on and have fun.

Chapter 1

He was a squat man with immense breadth of shoulder, hairy hands, bushy eyebrows. He maintained constant, unblinking attention on the road as he drove into trouble at sixty miles an hour.

It was April 1, 1980. All Fools' Day, he thought wryly. They had two or three moving roadways in Los Angeles, Chicago and New York. Also six airtight stations up there on the Moon. But except for rear engines and doped-alcohol fuel, motor-cars were little different from those of thirty years ago. Helicopters remained beyond reach of the average pocket. Taxpayers still skinned themselves month after month—and brooded over it every All Fools' Day.

For the past ten years there had been talk of mass produced helicopters at two thousand dollars apiece. Nothing had ever come of it. Maybe it was just as well considering the likely death-roll when drunks, half-wits and hot-rod enthusiasts took to the skies.

For the same ten years the scientific write-up boys had been forecasting a landing upon Mars within the next five. Nothing had come of that either. Sometimes he doubted whether anything ever would come of it. A minimum of sixty million miles is a terrible distance for a gadget that squirts itself along.

His train of thought snapped when an unknown voice sounded within his peculiar mind saying, *"It hurts! Oh, God, it . . . hurts!"*

The road was wide and straight and thickly wooded on both sides. The only other vehicle in sight was a lumbering tanker mounting a slight slope two miles ahead. A glance in the rear-view mirror confirmed that there was nothing behind. Despite this, the squat man registered no surprise.

"Hurts!" repeated the voice, weakening rapidly. *"Didn't give me a chance. The bastards!"*

The squat man slowed until his speedometer needle trembled under twenty. He made a dexterous U-turn, drove back to a rutted dirt road leading into the woods. He nosed the car up the road, knowing full well that the voice had come from that direction.

In the first five hundred yards there were two sharp bends, one to the right, one to the left. Around the second bend a car stood squarely in the middle of the road, effectively blocking it to all comers. The squat man braked hard, and swerved over the grass verge to avoid a collision.

He got out, leaving his door open. Speculatively he eyed the other car while he stood still and listened with his mind rather than with his ears.

"*Betty . . .*" whispered the eerie voice. "*Three fellows and a pain in the guts. Darkness. Can't get up. Ought to tell Forst. Where are you, Forst?*"

Turning, the squat man ran heavily along the verge, clambered down a short bank, found the man in the ditch. He did not look long, not more than two seconds. Mounting the bank with furious haste, he dug a flask out of his car-pocket, took it down to him.

Raising the other's head he poured a thin trickle of spirit between pale lips. He did not say anything, asked no questions, uttered no words of comfort and encouragement. Cradling the head on his forearm he tried only to maintain the fading spark of life. And while he did it, he listened. Not with his ears.

"*Tall, blond guy,*" murmured the other's mind, coming from a vast distance. "*Blasted at me . . . others got out . . . slung me off the road. Betty, I'm . . .*"

The mental stream cut off. The squat man dropped his flask, lowered the other's head, examined him without touching. Dead beyond doubt. He made note of the number on the badge fixed to the uniform jacket.

Leaving the body in the ditch he went to the stalled car, sat in the driver's seat, found a hand-microphone, held it while he fiddled tentatively with switches. He was far from sure how the thing operated but intended to find out.

"Hello!" he called, working a likely lever. "Hello!"

Immediately a voice responded, "State police barracks, Sergeant Forst."

"My name is Wade Harper. Can you hear me?"

"Barracks," repeated the voice, a trifle impatiently. "Forst speaking."

Evidently he couldn't hear. Harper tried again, got something adjusted. "Hello! Can you hear me?"

"Yes. What goes on there?"

"I'm calling from Car Seventeen. One of your officers is dead in a ditch near by." He gave the badge number.

There sounded a quick intake of breath, then, "That's Bob Alderson. Where are you now?"

Harper gave it in detail, added, "He's been shot twice, once in the belly and once through the neck. It must have happened recently because he was still living when I got to him. He died in my arms."

"Did he tell anything?"

"Yes; a tall, fair-haired fellow did it. There were others with him, no number stated, no descriptions."

"Were they in a car?"

"He didn't say, but you can bet on that."

"Stay where you are, Mr. Harper. We'll be right out."

There sounded a sharp click and a new voice broke in with, "Car Nine, Lee and Bates. We picked that up, Sarge, and are on our way. We're two miles off."

Replacing the microphone, Harper returned to the top of the bank, gazed moodily down upon the body. Somebody named Betty was going to know heartbreak this night.

Within a few minutes heavy tires squealed on the main artery, a car came into the dirt road. Harper raced round the bend, signaled it down lest it hit the block. Two state troopers piled out. They had the bitter air of men who owed somebody plenty and intended to pay it with interest.

They went down into the ditch, came up, said, "He's gone all right. Some son of a bitch is going to be sorry."

"I hope so," said Harper.

The taller of the two surveyed him curiously and asked, "How did you happen to find him way up here?"

Harper was prepared for that. He had practiced the art of concealment since childhood. At the ripe age of nine he had learned that knowledge can be resented, that the means of acquiring it can be feared.

"I wanted to pay dog-respects to a tree. Found this car planted in the road. First thing I thought was that somebody else had the same idea. Then I heard him moan in the ditch."

"Five hundred yards is a heck of a long way to come just for that," observed the tall one, sharp-eyed and shrewd. "Fifty would have been enough, wouldn't it?"

"Maybe."

"How much farther would you have gone if the road hadn't been blocked?"

"Couldn't say." He shrugged indifferently. "A fellow just looks for a spot that strikes his fancy and stops there, doesn't he?"

"I wouldn't know," said the trooper.

"You ought to," said Harper. "Unless you are physically unique."

"What d'you mean by that?" asked the trooper, showing sudden toughness.

The second trooper chipped in with, "Lay off, Bert. Ledsom will be here any minute. Let him handle this. It's what he's paid for."

Bert grunted, went silent. The pair started hunting around for evidence. In short time they found fresh tire-tracks across a soft patch twenty yards higher up the road. Soon afterwards they discovered a shell in the grass. They were examining the shell when three more cars arrived.

A man with a bag got down into the ditch, came up after a while, said wearily, "Two bullets about .32 caliber. Either could have caused death. No burn marks. Fired from range of a few yards. The slugs aren't in him."

Another with captain's chevrons spoke to the two nearest troopers. "Here's the ambulance—lift him out of there." To several others, "You boys look for those slugs. We've *got* to find them." To Lee and Bates he said, "Put a plank over those tracks. We'll make moulage casts of them. See if you can pick up the other shell. Work up the road for the gun as well: the punk may have thrown it away."

He joined Harper, informed, "I'm Captain Ledsom. It was smart of you to use Alderson's radio to get us."

"Seemed the sensible thing to do."

"People don't always do the sensible thing, especially if they're anxious not to be involved." Ledsom surveyed him with cool authority. "How did you find Alderson?"

"I trundled up here to answer the call of nature. And there he was."

"Came up quite a piece, didn't you?"

"You know how it is. On a narrow track like this you tend to look for a spot where you can turn the car to go back."

"Yes, I guess so. You wouldn't want to park on a bend either." He appeared satisfied with the explanation but Harper could see with complete clarity that his mind suspected everyone within fifty miles radius. "Exactly what did Alderson say before he passed out?"

"He mumbled about Betty and—"

"His wife," interjected Ledsom, frowning. "I hate having to tell her about this."

"He mentioned a big, blond fellow blasting at him. Also that there were others who tossed him into the ditch. He gave no more details unfortunately. He was on his last lap and his mind was rambling."

"Too bad." Ledsom shifted attention as a trooper came up. "Well?"

"Cap, the tracks show that a car turned up here with Alderson following. The car stopped by the verge. Alderson pulled up behind but in the middle of the road. He got out, went toward the first car, was shot down. At least two men picked him up and dumped him out of sight." He held out his hand. "Here's the other shell." He pointed. "It was lying right there."

".32 automatic," said Ledsom, studying the small brass cylinders. "Any sign of Alderson's car having been edged off the road and put back again?"

"No."

"Then they must have pushed straight ahead. They couldn't get out this way with that car stuck across the road." He rubbed his chin thoughtfully and went on, "This track meanders seventeen miles through forest, loops back and joins the main artery about ten miles farther along. So by now they've either got back on the road or they've holed up someplace in the woods."

"Seventeen miles would take at least twenty minutes on a route like this one," ventured Harper. "Even if they're driving like crazy they can't be far off it yet."

"Yes, I know. I'll call the boys to put up roadblocks along the main run. We'll search the loop too. It's used almost entirely by loggers. If those bums are familiar with it the chances are they work or once worked for the logging outfits. We'll follow that line later."

Entering his car, Ledsom spoke awhile on the radio. He came back, said, "That's fixed. Blocks will be established pretty soon. Local sheriff is on his way here with four deputies." He gazed moodily at the surrounding woods. "Just as well they're coming. The fugitives may dump that car and take to their feet, in which case we'll need an army to go through this lot."

"Any way I can help?" asked Harper.

Ledsom looked him over for the third time, carefully, calculatingly, while his mind said to itself, *"Some crazy coot might think it incontrovertible proof of inno-cence to stick his head in the lion's mouth. I'd like to know more about this guy. All we've got to go on so far is his story."*

"Well?" encouraged Harper.

"Finding the murder weapon could give us a lead," remarked Ledsom in the manner of one idly musing. "And we can't afford to overlook any possibility, no matter how remote." Then his eyes stared straight into Harper's and his voice be-came sharp, imperative. "Therefore we must search you and your car."

"Naturally," responded Harper with bland indifference.

"Wrong diagnosis," decided Ledsom's mind. *"He's clean. We'll frisk him all the same."*

They raked the car from end to end, ran hands over Harper, extracted a tiny blued automatic from his right-hand pocket. Ledsom grabbed the gun eagerly, ejected the magazine from the hand-grip, examined it, jerked his eyebrows a bit.

"Holy smoke! What sort of a rod is this supposed to be? Twenty in the mag with slugs the size of match-heads. Where did you get it?"

"Made it myself. Up to fifty yards it is very effective."

"I can imagine. You got a permit for it?"

"Yes." Harper produced it, handed it over.

Ledsom glanced at it, registered more surprise. "Are you a Federal agent?"

"No, Captain. The F.B.I. issued that for reasons of their own. If you want the reasons you'll have to ask them."

"No business of mine," said Ledsom, a little baffled. He handed back the per-mit and the gun. "That toy isn't the weapon we want, anyway. Did you see or hear anything suspicious before or after finding Alderson?"

"Not a thing."

"No sound of a car beating it, for instance?"

"No sound whatever."

"You didn't hear the shots before you arrived?"

"No."

"Umph!" Ledsom was dissatisfied. "So they had at least two or three minutes headstart. You're a material witness and we want a statement from you at the of-fice. Sorry to put you to more trouble and delay but—"

"Only too glad to assist," said Harper.

Ledsom directed two crews to explore the loop road then led the way back to barracks. Reaching his office, he slumped behind his desk; sighed deeply.

"It's a lousy business. I've yet to tell his wife. They hadn't been married that long, either. God knows how she'll take it." He sighed again, dug an official form out of a drawer. "Have to do some clerking myself, seeing all the boys are busy. You got a card on you, Mr. Harper?"

Harper slid one across to him.

It read: WADE HARPER—FORGER.

"So help me Mike," said Ledsom, blinking at it. "That's what I call advertising one's sins. Next thing one of them will write me on a business sheet headed *Baldy O'Brien—Heistman.*"

"I'm a microforger."

"What sort of animal is that?"

"I make surgical and manipulatory instruments so tiny they can be used to operate on a bacillus."

"Oh, now, don't give me that!" said Ledsom. "A fellow couldn't see enough to use them."

"He can—under a powerful microscope."

"Every year they think up something new," marveled Ledsom. "You can't keep up with it."

"There's nothing new about this," Harper assured. "It started back in 1899 with a Dutchman named Dr. Schouten. Since then the only considerable improvement on his technique has been gained by de Fonbrune's one-hand pneumatic micro-manipulator. I make variations on that gadget, too."

"You must be kept mad busy," remarked Ledsom, wondering how many or how few people wanted to dissect a germ.

"I get by. There aren't more than a couple of dozen competent microforgers in the world. The demand is just enough to keep pace with the supply."

"So the F.B.I. thinks they can't afford to lose you?"

"You're making guesses," said Harper.

"This bacteriological warfare business, maybe?"

"You're still guessing."

"Okay. I know when to mind my own business."

He got to work on the official form, put down the witness's name, address and occupation, followed it with a dictated account of what had occurred, shoved it across for the other to read and sign.

When Harper had gone, Ledsom grabbed the phone, made a long distance call. He'd just finished talking when Sergeant Forst entered the office, eyed him curiously.

"Something broken, Cap?"

"That Harper guy fed me a line that would do credit to the best con man in the biz. So I just called his hometown to see if he has a record."

"And he has?"

"Yes."

"Jumping Judas!" said Forst, dropping a couple of books on the desk and making for the door. "I'll put out a pickup call for him."

"No." Ledsom looked pensive. "His hometown cops send him love and kisses. He's helped them solve several tough cases and he's shot down three culprits for good measure."

"What is he, a private dick?"

"Nothing like that. They say he has a habit of falling headlong over something everybody else is looking for. They say he's done it time and again and it's uncanny." He sought for a satisfactory theory, found it, ended, "Reckon he suffers from beginner's luck and makes a hobby of exploiting it."

If the subject of conversation had been within half a mile he'd have picked up that notion and smiled.

Driving at fast pace along the main road Harper passed through three successive roadblocks without incident. His mind was working as he tooled along. If, he argued, a chased car switched into a sidetrack the odds would be at least fifty to one on the driver choosing a turn-off on his own side rather than one across the artery and on the far side. The choice would be automatic or instinctive.

Since he was now running with the loop-road somewhere ahead and on his wrong side it was very likely that Alderson and the chased car had come from the opposite direction, or towards him.

He glanced at his watch. It said six-twenty. He had found Alderson at four-ten, a little over two hours ago. That could put the murderers best part of a hundred miles away if they'd kept going nonstop. Probably the police had roadblocks farther out than that. Probably police had been alerted over a huge area by an eight-state alarm.

It wouldn't do much good. There was no adequate description of the fugitives, none at all of their car. A tall, blond fellow just wasn't enough to go upon. About the only chance the police had of making a quick pinch lay in the possibility that the escapees were using a stolen vehicle that some sharp-witted officer might recognize as a wanted number.

He let a few miles go by until he saw a service-station on the opposite side, the side that in his theory Alderson and the killers had used. He crossed, pulled up near the pumps. Two attendants came over.

"Were you fellows on duty around four o'clock?"

Both nodded.

"See anything of a prowl car driven by a trooper named Alderson? Car Seventeen, it was."

"I know Bob Alderson," said one. "He was around a couple of times this morning."

"Not between three and four?"

"No." He thought a bit. "Or if he was I didn't see him."

"Me neither," said the other.

Their minds told that they spoke truth. Harper knew it with absolute sureness. So far as he was concerned they need not have opened their mouths.

"Anyone else here who might have noticed him around that time?"

"Only Satterthwaite. Want me to ask him?"

"I'd appreciate it."

The attendant went out of sight around the back of the building. It made no difference. Harper could hear them mentally though their voices were out of reach.

"Hey, Satty, a fellow here wants to know if you saw anything of Bob Alderson two or three hours back."

"Nary a sign."

He came back. "No luck, Satty didn't see him."

"Anyone now off-duty who was here at that time?"

"No, mister." He showed curiosity. "Like me to tell Bob you're looking for him if he happens to come along?"

"He won't be along—ever," said Harper.

"What d'you mean?"

"Some hoodlum shot him down around four. He's dead."

"Gee!" said the attendant, going pale.

"You'll have the police here asking similar questions sooner or later." Harper gazed up the road. "Know of any place on his patrol where Alderson was in the habit of stopping awhile?"

"He'd often grab a coffee at the Star Café."

"Where's that?"

"Four miles along, on the crossroads."

"Thanks." He pulled out, drove fast. Two miles farther on and halfway to the café stood another filling station, this time on his own side of the road. Turning into there, he put the same questions.

"Sure I saw him," said a laconic, sandy-haired youth. "Didn't notice the time but it must have been about three hours back."

"Was he chasing somebody?"

The other considered this, said, "Yes, now that I come to think of it maybe he was."

"What happened?"

"One of those low-slung green Thunderbugs went past in a hell of a hurry and he came half a mile behind like he'd no time to waste either."

"But you aren't positive that he was pursuing the Thunderbug?"

"I didn't think so at the time. Most of the stuff on this road moves good and fast, but now that you mention it I guess he may have been after that car."

"Did you notice who was in it?"

"Can't say that I did."

"Did anyone else see this too? Was anyone with you at the time?"

"No."

Harper thanked him and pushed on. So far he'd gained one item: a green Thunderbug. He didn't congratulate himself on that. He'd shown no especial cleverness in picking up this datum. Of a surety the police would find it themselves before the night was through. He was one jump ahead of them solely because he was concentrating on one specific line of search while they were coping with a hundred. Harper had great respect for the police.

At the Star Café a pert waitress reported that Alderson had eaten a meal there and left about one-thirty. Yes, he'd been by himself. No, he hadn't shown particular interest in any other customers or departed coincidentally with anyone else. No, she hadn't seen a tall, blond fellow with a green Thunderbug.

She hadn't noticed which direction Car Seventeen had taken but she'd ask the other girls. She went away, came back, said that one named Dorothy had seen Alderson go up the left-hand crossroad.

Harper took that road, kept the accelerator pedal well down. Fifteen minutes later he found a tavern keeper who had seen Car Seventeen rocketing along at sometime after three. This witness said he had been drawn to the window by the noise of a car going hell for leather. The car had shot past before he could get a view of it but he'd been in time to see Alderson racing by. Yes, he had thought at the time that Alderson was after someone, probably a daft kid in a hot-rod.

Seven miles farther on Harper struck oil. It was at another filling station. An elderly man came out, handed him news worth having.

"Shortly after three a Thunderbug hauled up to the pumps for ten gallons of alk. There were three fellows and a girl in it. The girl was sitting in the back with one of the fellows and she kept giving me funny sort of appealing looks through the window while I stood near by with the hose in the gas-tank. I had an idea that she wanted to scream but didn't dare. The whole setup looked decidedly fishy to me."

"What did you do about it?"

"Nothing at that moment. I was by myself and I'm not as young as I used to be. Those three could have bounced me on my head until my brains fell out."

"So what then?"

"They paid and pushed off without realizing that they'd given me the fidgets. I'd been acting natural because I didn't want any trouble. But as soon as they'd got up a bit of speed I skipped into the road for a look at their plates."

"Did you get the number?" asked Harper, hoping to be dealt an ace out of the pack.

"No. I'd left it a mite too late. I hadn't my glasses on and the figures were too fuzzy to read." The oldster frowned, regretting the lost opportunity. "Couple of minutes later a prowl car came along at easy pace. I flagged it down, told the trooper about this girl. He said he'd look into the matter. He went after the Thunderbug at a good clip." His rheumy eyes quested hopefully. "Did he latch on to something?"

"Yes—a coffin. They plugged him in the neck and belly. He didn't take long to die."

"Good God!" The oldster was visibly shaken. He swallowed hard, said with morbid self-reproach, "And I sent him after them."

"It isn't your fault, Pop. You did the best thing in the circumstances." Harper waited a minute for the other to recover, then asked, "Did those fellows say anything to indicate where they'd come from or where they were going?"

"They spoke exactly one word and no more. The big blond only dropped his window and said, 'Ten!' I asked about oil and water but he shook his head impatiently. Nobody else made any remark. The girl looked as if she'd talk plenty once she got started but was too scared to begin."

"What did this bunch look like? Give me as complete and detailed a description as you can manage."

The other licked his lips and said, "The blond one was doing the driving. He was a husky guy in his late twenties, yellow hair, blue eyes, strong chin, clean-shaven, good-looking and intelligent. You'd have called him a nice kind of fellow if his eyes hadn't been meaner than a snake's."

"No facial scars or other identifying marks?"

"Not that I noticed. Tell you what, though—he was pale. So were the other two guys. You know, whitish, like they get when they've been bottled up quite a piece." He gave Harper a significant glance. "Seeing what's happened I can think up a reason for that."

"So can I. They've just come out of clink. They've escaped or been paroled, more likely the former judging by the way they're acting."

"That's how it looks to me."

"Had they been hitting the booze?" inquired Harper, sensing a possible lead at wherever the stuff had been bought.

"Far as I could tell they were cold sober."

"What else can you add?"

"The fellow sitting alongside the driver was another husky about the same age. Black hair, gray eyes, clean-shaven. He was just as pale-faced, just as mean-looking. I never got a proper look at the third one in the back."

"How about the girl?"

"Around twenty or twenty-one, brown eyes, brown hair, a bit on the plump side. Attractive without being a stunner. Wearing a mustard-colored overcoat, yellow blouse and a string of amber beads. Her hand was up by the window and she had a birthday ring with an opal in it."

"Somebody born in October. You're doing top-notch, Pop."

"Like I told you, I noticed that girl," said the oldster.

"How were the fellows dressed?"

"All the same; dark green jackets, gray shirts and collars, dark green ties. Looking almost as if they wore uniform with buttons and insignia removed. Never seen anyone wearing that sort of rig-out. Have you?"

"No," admitted Harper. "It doesn't resemble prison garb either. Maybe it's sporting togs they've swiped from some store." He continued his cross-examination a few more minutes, finished with, "Have you a telephone here?"

"Sure. Come round the back." He led the way, pointed. "There you are—help yourself."

The voice in the earpiece growled, "State police barracks. Captain Ledsom."

"My lucky day," remarked Harper, unconsciously confirming theories at the other end. "You're the very man I want."

"Who's speaking?"

"Harper. Remember me?"

"Ah, so you've thought up something you forgot to tell us?"

"I gave you all I had at that sorry time. I've since dug up a bit more."

"Such as what?"

"The car you want is a recent model green Thunderbug carrying three fellows and a girl. I have descriptions of all but one of the men."

Ledsom exploded, "Where the blazes did you get all this?"

Grinning to himself, Harper told him where and how.

"Why don't you join the cops and have done with it, instead of fooling around with germ-chivvying gadgets?" Ledsom demanded.

"Because I'm a couple of inches too short, six inches too wide, detest discipline and want to go on living."

Giving a deep grunt, Ledsom said, "I'll send a car out there right away. Maybe the boys will pick up something else. Meanwhile you'd better give me the dirt you've collected."

Harper recited it, finished, "Obviously there are now two leads I couldn't follow even if I wanted. They are properly your work because you have the facilities. Firstly, have any three fellows answering these descriptions been let out of prison or climbed the walls recently? Secondly, has any young girl answering this description been reported missing of late?"

A tolerant chuckle sounded before Ledsom replied, "We'll tend to those and about six more angles you've missed."

"For example."

"Where did they get the clothes they're wearing, the money they're spending, the car they're using, the gun they fired?" He was quiet a moment, then continued, "We'll send out a flier that may bring us the answers from some place. With luck we'll learn the tag-numbers on that Thunderbug. Ten to one it's stolen."

"I could push on along this route and perhaps learn more," said Harper. "They may have stopped for beer or a meal and talked out of turn within somebody's hearing. But why should I bother? What do I pay taxes for? I have business of my own to do."

"You're arguing with yourself, not with me," Ledsom pointed out. "Nobody's asking or expecting you to do anything." He hurried on with, "Of course we really do appreciate the part you've played so far. It shows fine public spirit. Things would be easier for us if everyone were as helpful."

Harper removed the phone from his ear, stared at it suspiciously, put it back, said, "Why can't they have visiscreens on these things in rural areas too?"

"What has that to do with anything?"

"One could watch a guy's expression while he's plastering on the butter." He hooked the phone, turned, said to the oldster, "They're coming straight out. You'd better spend the interim stewing the matter and see if you can recall any item you may have overlooked. They'll need everything you can give them."

Returning to his car, he set about his normal affairs confident that so far as he was concerned the episode was finished. He was out of it, no more involved in it, a momentary witness who had paused and passed on.

He could not have been more wrong.

Chapter 2

He stopped at the next town, found a suitable hotel, booked a room for the night, took in a third-rate show during the evening. He listened to the midnight news before going to bed but it made only brief mention of the killing plus the usual soothing statement that the police hoped to make an early arrest.

The stereoscopic video—called by all and sundry "the pane" since the day a famous cynic had defined the self-styled "window on the world" as "a pane in the neck"—gave the murder a little more attention with pics of troopers and deputies searching the loop-road.

Both radio and video were more interested in vagaries of the weather, sports results, the round-the-globe rocket race, and a complicated legal battle between the government and the Lunar Development Company. According to the latter the government was trying to use its Earth-Moon transport monopoly to bludgeon the L.D.C. into handing itself over complete with fat profits. The L.D.C. was fighting back. It was the decades-old struggle of private enterprise against bureaucratic interference.

Harper sat out this last part in the role of a spectator foreseeing his own fate should he grow too big and become too prosperous. In his line of business he'd had a lot to do with officialdom, but fortunately the basis had been cooperative rather than dictatorial. Nevertheless he sympathized with L.D.C.

He had a sound sleep, arose at eight, breakfasted, spent the morning at the Schultz-Masters Research Laboratories where they needed certain special micro-manipulators and displayed the flattering attitude that only he could make them. At one o'clock he left with two tough technical problems solved, two more yet to be considered, and a provisional order in his pocket.

After a meal he started homeward and at three-thirty was halted by a prowl car at a point forty miles from the scene of yesterday's shooting. One of the two troopers in the car got out and came towards him.

He watched the approach with surprised interest and because the oncomer's mind was warily broadcasting *"Maybe and maybe not, but if so he won't get away with it* this *time!"*

"Something wrong?" Harper asked.

"You Wade Harper?"

"Yes."

"A call went out for you half an hour ago. Captain Ledsom wants to see you."

"I saw him yesterday."

"This is today," the trooper reminded.

"Can I talk to him on your short-wave?"

"He wants you in person."

"Any idea why?"

The other shrugged. His mind showed that he did not know the reason but viewed Harper as a major suspect merely because he was wanted. It showed also that he and his companion were ready to cope in effective manner with any refusal.

"Mean to say I've got to take time off and go all the way to the barracks?"

"That's how it is." He made an authoritative gesture with an added touch of impatience. "Turn her around and get going. Make it a steady pace, not too fast, and no monkey tricks. We'll be right behind."

Feeling rather peeved, Harper did as instructed. It wasn't that he was in a great hurry, in fact he had time to spare, but he disliked being given peremptory orders by a wide-open mind devoid of adequate motive.

He had been the same in this respect since he'd worn rompers. Perceptive mind resented dictatorship by non-perceptive mind. To do exactly as he was told smacked of the sighted being led around by the blind.

Occasionally, in introspective moments, he chided himself for his mutinous tendencies lest the fact that he'd been mentally alone, completely without intimate contact with a mind similar to his own, should be giving him a superiority complex born of a sense of uniqueness. He had no desire to be humble, he had less desire to be sat upon. He was a seeker of the middle way.

Tramping unwillingly into Ledsom's office, he thumped himself into a seat that creaked, stared belligerently across the desk and read the other's change of viewpoint as easily as an ordinary person reads a book.

"Well, here I am."

Ledsom said pointedly, "We're having a tape-recording this time." Leaning sidewise, he switched on the apparatus. "Where were you the night before last?"

"At an hotel."

"Which one?"

Harper told him.

"What time did you leave there?" Ledsom inquired.

"At nine-thirty."

"Where did you spend the morning?"

"At the Pest Control Station."

"Until when?"

"Close on one o'clock. I then had dinner."

"Where?"

"At the Cathay, a Chinese restaurant."

"With whom?"

"Nobody. I was by myself. Say, what's behind all this?" The question was pure concealment. He already knew what was behind it because he could watch Ledsom's brains fizzing.

"Never mind, Mr. Harper. Just you answer the questions. You have nothing to fear, have you?"

"Who hasn't? Any minute Gabriel may blow his horn."

"You know what I mean." Ledsom eyed him without the friendliness of yesterday. "At what time did you leave the Cathay?"

"About two o'clock, give or take five minutes."

"And after that?"

"I headed for Hainesboro. I had business to do there today at the Schultz-Masters place."

"You came this way?"

"Of course. It's on the direct route."

"You were passing the loop-road about when?"

"Four o'clock."

"Now tell me exactly what happened from that point onward."

"Oh, Lord! I gave you the whole story yesterday. You've got it in writing."

"I know. And now we want it again." Ledsom's mind added with mistaken secretiveness, *"A liar needs a good memory. This is where we find contradictions in his story, if any."*

Harper went grimly through the account for the second time while the tape-recorder purred on. It was the same in all details. He knew it and also that Ledsom knew it.

"About that trick gun you've got," said Ledsom. "You wouldn't be in the habit of carrying a second one such as a .32, would you?"

"No, I wouldn't."

"There's a large pond of considerable depth in the woods about fifty yards from where Alderson was killed. Did you notice it?"

"I didn't enter the woods."

"Did you know of the pond's existence?"

"No."

"You told us you went up that road for a certain purpose. Presumably you were balked by what you discovered. Did you achieve that purpose?"

"I did."

"When?"

"After I'd called Forst on the radio."

"You found Alderson, called the police and then went into the woods?"

"It wasn't necessary to go into the woods, there being no ladies present."

Ignoring that point, Ledsom went on, "At what time did you leave your hotel yesterday morning?"

"You've asked that one before. Nine-thirty."

"And you were all morning where?"

"At the Pest Control Station. If you're trying to catch me out you're wasting time and breath. We can go on this way for a week."

"All right," said Ledsom, changing tactics. "If you had a deal in prospect with Schultz-Masters why didn't you go there until today?"

Harper gave a resigned sigh and said, "Firstly, because my appointment was for today and not for yesterday. Secondly, I reached Hainesboro too late for any business calls, in fact it was already too late when I left here."

"That's what interests us," informed Ledsom, gazing at him steadily. "You'd been badly delayed by the time we finished with you. All the same, you took time off to hunt up four people in a Thunderbug. Why did you do that?"

"Alderson died in my arms. I didn't like it."

Ledsom winced but kept firmly to the issue. "Is that your only reason?"

"It's the major one."

"What's a minor one?"

"My day was messed up. A couple of hours one way or the other couldn't make any difference."

"No other motives whatsoever?"

"One," admitted Harper reluctantly.

"Name it."

"I got some personal satisfaction out of finding a trace on the killers myself."

"If they *were* the killers," commented Ledsom. He switched off the recorder, meditated a minute, continued, "Up to a couple of hours ago I didn't doubt it. Now I'm not so sure." He kept his full attention on his listener, watching for reactions. "We're pumping out that pond. Maybe we'll find the gun and learn who used it."

"Meaning me?"

"I haven't said so."

"You're hinting at it with every muscle in your face." Harper made a gesture of disparagement. "I can't blame you in the least for suspecting anyone and everyone. I could have killed Alderson. The time, the place and the opportunity all fit in. Only things lacking are the gun and the motive. You're going to have a hell of a time tying a motive on to me. I had never seen Alderson in my life until that moment."

"We had a senseless killing near here four years ago," answered Ledsom. "Two brothers fell out over an incredibly trivial matter, got equally stubborn about it, gradually switched from argument to abuse and from there to mutual challenges. Finally the hotter tempered of the two upped and slugged the other, killed him, made a very clever try at concealing his guilt by distracting attention elsewhere. He almost succeeded—but not quite!"

"So I followed Alderson into a lane, stopped behind him, swapped backchat. One word led to another. Being cracked, I shot him twice, threw the gun into a pond, called you to come take a look." Harper pulled a wry face. "Time I had my head examined."

"I can't afford to overlook any possibilities," Ledsom gave back. "I've just asked you a lot of questions. Are you willing to take them again with a lie-detector?"

"Positively not!"

Ledsom breathed deeply and said, "You realize that we must attach a certain significance to your refusal?"

"You can tie a couple of tin cans on to it for all I care. The polygraph is an outrageous piece of pseudo-scientific bunkum and its needle-wagglings aren't admissible as legal evidence."

"It has helped extract a few confessions," declared Ledsom, on the defensive.

"Yes, from the babes and sucklings. I am a maker of top-grade scientific instruments myself. You drag a polygraph into court and I'll tear it to pieces for all time."

That worried Ledsom. His thoughts revealed that he believed Harper perfectly capable of it and peculiarly competent to do it. He dismissed the lie-detector as a blunder and wished he had never mentioned it.

"How about scopomaline?" suggested Harper, for good measure. "I'll talk that right out of usage if you'll give me half a chance." He leaned forward, knowing that their respective positions were reversed even if only momentarily, that for a few seconds he was the inquisitor and Ledsom the culprit. "From the criminal viewpoint what have I got that those punks in the Thunderbug haven't got? Do you regard them as figments of my imagination and think I've bribed witnesses to support my story?"

"They were real enough. We have proof of that."

"Well, then?"

"Two hours ago we picked up the girl. Her story doesn't jibe with yours. Somebody's a liar."

Lying back in his seat, Harper eyed him meditatively, said, "So you've got the girl. Is her version a trade secret?"

Ledsom thought it over, decided that there was nothing to lose. "She missed her bus, thumbed a lift. Three fellows picked her up in that green Thunderbug. They were in a humorous mood, took her a long, roundabout way, kidded her she was being kidnapped. At that filling station she really was scared, but after a bit more fooling around they dumped her where she wanted to go. It was all a rib."

"And what about Alderson?"

"She saw nothing of him, knows nothing about him."

"But he chased that car."

"I know. The girl says the blond fellow drove like a maniac for no reason other than the hell of it, so maybe Alderson never caught up with them."

"You believe that yarn?"

"I don't believe any story without satisfactory evidence in support. But hers casts grave doubt upon yours."

"All right. I know you're going to check on mine. Check on hers too and see if it stands up."

"We've already made a partial check on both of you and we're going to finish the job as soon as possible. The girl doesn't know the names of the three fellows or anything else about them other than what we've already got. She didn't notice the number of the car. Having suffered nothing, she had no reason to grab that number."

"That's a big help."

"But the rest looks convincing," said Ledsom. "She is a girl of excellent reputation coming from a highly respected family. She left home when she says she did, missed the bus she says she missed, was seen by two witnesses being offered a lift. She arrived at her destination at the time she states and can prove it."

"Those fellows took her a long way round?"

"Yes. They were feeling their oats."

"Nice way of accounting for lost time such as that involved in stopping, shooting, starting and running every mile of seventeen around a loop-road."

"Look, Mr. Harper, it's almost twenty-four hours since Alderson was shot down. All we've got are you and this girl. All I know is that somebody used a gun and somebody's telling lies."

"If that girl is telling the truth, which I beg leave to doubt," ventured Harper, "there's only one solution. A third party is wandering loose, untraced, unsuspected and laughing up his sleeve."

"There's not the slightest evidence of it." Ledsom hesitated, went on, "I wouldn't dream of chewing the fat with you in this manner if it wasn't that your hometown law gave you a very big hand. That sort of thing counts with me."

"I suppose so."

"Therefore I'll tell you something more. The three fellows don't tally with any trio released or escaped from prison this year."

"How about the military prisons? That old bird at the filling station thought they might be wearing altered uniforms."

"There is no military, naval or air force uniform corresponding with that description."

"Not in this country. Maybe they were foreigners."

"The girl says not. They spoke the language as only we can speak it and knew the country like the backs of their hands."

"Have you asked the authorities whether they know of *any* uniform that does correspond?"

"No. The girl agrees that their clothes had a sort of official look and thinks they were wearing army disposal stuff dyed green. If so, we've poor chance of tracing it. Ex-army jackets have been thrown on the market by the thousands."

"How about their car? You thought it might be stolen."

"To date we've pulled in reports of ten missing in various parts of the country. Four of them are green. We have urgent calls out for those four numbers. No luck so far." He gazed morbidly through an adjacent window. "Anyway, they may have resprayed it and changed the tags. Or it may be legitimately owned. Or it may be a rented car. The Thunderbug is a popular make. It would take months to check all sales and rentals from coast to coast."

Harper thought it over and said, "Well, you'll know it if ever you lay hands on it. You have a tire-cast and that's something."

"Doesn't follow it's one of theirs. Anybody could have gone up that lane any time the same day. All we've discovered is that it doesn't belong to any logging vehicle. Neither do those three fellows answer the descriptions of any logging company's employees, past or present."

"No matter what that girl says, I still think they're the boys you want."

"The girl was an unwilling witness in that event. She wasn't a guilty party. So why should she cover up for a bunch of strangers?"

"Maybe they weren't strangers," Harper offered.

"What d'you mean?"

"Doesn't follow that because they gave her a lift they must have been unknown to her."

"She swears she didn't know them from Adam."

"You could bet on her saying that—if one of them happened to be a crazy boyfriend or a shiftless relative."

"H'm!" Ledsom viewed this as remotely possible but rather unlikely. He made a note on a pad. "Her local police gave us a report on her character, home conditions, status of parents and that's all. Might be worth probing more deeply into her background."

"If she's telling lies about a murder she must have a very strong reason. Perhaps she's been intimidated. Perhaps they have convinced her that they'll be back to cut her throat if she dares speak out of turn."

"Wrong guess," snapped Ledsom, positively. "I've been in this game a long time and I can tell when a suspect is secretly afraid. She wasn't. She was frankly bewildered at being dragged into something she didn't know a damn thing about."

"I'm a suspect too. A bigger and better one, to judge by what's happening right now. Think I'm scared?"

"No," admitted Ledsom.

"I ought to be—if I did it. But I didn't."

"Somebody did. We know that much." Ledsom studied him levelly. "I can hold you for twenty-four hours, and I'd do it if I'd a fair chance of pinning something on you by then. But it's going to take that long to empty the pond. So you can go. God help you if we salvage a gun traceable to you."

"I should worry."

Harper departed feeling distinctly surly, made the long drive home in ruminating silence. He passed at least fifty Thunderbugs in those seven hundred miles, saw no persons resembling the missing trio.

Chapter 3

He had a small plant employing six myopic but deft-fingered men. Also an office barely large enough to hold his desk and that of a secretary cum stenographer cum telephone operator. This person, name of Moira, was three inches taller than himself and about half the width. Cupid couldn't lug a ladder into the room and that fact suited Harper top-notch.

Sitting at his desk, he was examining a set of minuscule glass forceps under a powerful magnifier when Riley opened the door and took the two steps necessary to reach the middle. His plainclothes effectively advertised him as a cop in disguise.

"Morning, Lieutenant," greeted Harper, glancing up momentarily before returning attention to the task in hand.

"Morning, Neanderthal." There being no extra chair or space for one, Riley hooked a thick leg over a desk corner, rested himself as best he could. He bent forward to stare through the magnifier. "Beats me how paws so thick and hairy can fiddle with stuff that size."

"Why not? You pick your teeth, don't you?"

"Leave my personal habits out of this." His eyes became accusing. "Let's discuss some of yours."

Harper sighed, fitted the forceps into a velvet-lined case, placed it in a drawer. He shoved the magnifier to one side, looked up.

"Such as what?"

"Being around when things happen."

"Can I help it?"

"I don't know. Sometimes I wonder. It's mighty queer the way you latch on to this and that."

"Be specific," Harper invited.

"We've had a call. Fellow wants to know if you're still around. And if not, why not."

"All right, I'm still around. Go tell him."

"I wanted to know *why* he wanted to know," said Riley pointedly.

"And he told you. He said it isn't in the mud."

"Mud? What mud?"

"At the bottom of the pond." Harper grinned up at him. "He also asked whether I'm known to own a .32."

"You're right. It was Captain Ledsom. He gave me the details from first to last."

"Whereupon you solved the whole case for him," suggested Harper. "Two minds being better than one."

"*You* are going to solve it," said Riley.

"Am I?" Harper rubbed a chin and produced rasping noises. "Moira, throw this bum out."

"Do your own dirty work," ordered Riley. "You aren't paying her to act as bouncer as well, are you?" He turned to Moira. "How much are you making, Sylph?"

Moira giggled and said, "Not enough."

"Disgraceful," opined Riley, "I don't know why you stick with this hirsute cur-mudgeon."

"Such words," put in Harper. "I'll bet you can read too."

"And without moving my lips," Riley boasted. "So let's get down to basics. You're going to let business go to pot while you play Sherlock."

"Why?"

"Firstly because I told Ledsom you could clear up the matter if continuously kicked in the buttocks. So he wants me to kick."

"Secondly?"

"Because there's now a reward for information leading to apprehension and conviction of the killer or killers. Being human and in old shoes and wearing a tie obviously given with a gallon of alk, you could use the dough."

"That all?"

"Not by a long shot. I've saved the best bit to the last." He grinned, revealing big teeth. "An hour ago some hoarse-voiced character phoned Ledsom and said he'd seen Alderson having an argument with a compressed bruiser answering more or less to your description. Know what that makes you?"

"The sacrificial goat," said Harper moodily.

Riley nodded. "We'd pick you up and sweat a confession out of you but for two things. One is that we know you too well to believe you did it. The other is that the witness is not available to identify you."

"Why isn't he?"

"He said his piece and cut off. So Ledsom doesn't know who called."

"That looks fishy."

"Some folk hate to get involved," observed Riley. "More's the pity."

"I'm not surprised. I became too public-spirited myself. See what it's bought me."

"You jumped into it. Get busy and wriggle out of it."

"I can't afford the time," Harper complained.

"You can't afford a spell in clink either," Riley pointed out. "If Ledsom asks us to take you in we'll have to do it."

"Do you think that's likely?"

"God knows. It depends on what they turn up in the way of further evidence."

"If they find any pointing at me it will be purely circumstantial."

"That's a hell of a consolation when you're sitting around awaiting trial," said Riley. "The moment Ledsom believes he's got enough to convince a jury he'll make the pinch. He may then find he's wrong because the jury proves difficult to satisfy. So even if you get away with it you'll have been put through the mill, lost a lot of patience, time and money."

Harper said flatly, "They haven't the chance of a celluloid cat unless they find that witness and he identifies me. Even that won't be proof. It will do no more than suggest a motive. And if the witness does identify me he'll be a liar who knows something about the shooting and aims to divert attention. He can't appear without becoming a suspect himself."

"Could be. A way to find out would be to trace him and beat the truth out of him."

"The state troopers can do that themselves."

"Maybe," said Riley. "And maybe they couldn't."

"Maybe I couldn't either."

"I'm not so sure. You've done some darned funny things these last few years."

"Such as what?"

"That Grace Walterson murder. Twelve years old and unsolved—until you sit on a park bench and hear a boozy tramp muttering about it in his sleep. You tell us. We grab him and he confesses."

"Sheer luck," informed Harper.

"Was it? The Grace Walterson case had been long forgotten and wasn't in our bailiwick anyway. We had to check across country to get details. That guy did it all right. He was drunk like you said. There was only one respect in which his story didn't jibe with yours."

"What was that?"

"He didn't go to sleep and he didn't mutter. He swears he sat there blurry-eyed but wide-awake and wordless while you slid away and brought back a patrolman."

"He wrote his confession on paper and I ate it," said Harper. "I just can't resist paper." He frowned at the other. "You must be nuts. The sot voiced the burden on his conscience and gave himself away."

"All right." Riley stared at him very hard. "But *you* had to be there when he did it. Then there was the Tony Giacomo case. He heists a bank, kills two, and *you* have to be lounging near by two days later when he—"

"Oh, give it a rest," suggested Harper wearily. "I'm thirty-seven years old, have rubbed shoulders with nine wanted men and you pretend it's remarkable. How many have you sat next to in your half century of sin?"

"Plenty, I dare say. Not one of them told me he was wanted and begged me to take him in."

"None begged me, either."

"The entire bunch did the next best thing. They made the mistake of being someplace where you were too. You've upped our score of snatches by quite a piece and the Commissioner thinks you're Jesus. Smacks more of the Devil to me. There's something decidedly odd about it."

"Name it, then."

"I can't," confessed Riley. "I can't so much as imagine an explanation."

"Some folks are always there when accidents happen," Harper pointed out. "They can't help it. It's the way things go. Take my Aunt Matilda—"

"Let somebody else take her—I'm married," said Riley. "Are you going to break this case or do you prefer to squat on your fat tokus until I'm ordered to bring you in?"

"How much is the reward?"

Riley looked prayerfully at the ceiling. "He weakens at the thought of money. Five thousand dollars."

"I'll stew it awhile."

"If the idea is to wait for the reward to be jacked up," warned Riley, "you may wait too long. By the tone of his voice Ledsom's feeling mean enough to put his own mother in the jug."

With that, he bestowed a curt nod on Moira and walked out. They listened to his heavy footsteps parading along the outer passage and fading away in the distance.

"Moira, do you sense anything strange about me?"

"Oh no, Mr. Harper," she assured.

It was true enough. Her mind revealed that she wished he were ten inches taller and ten years younger. It might add a little spice to office work. She asked no more than that because her stronger emotional interests were being satisfied elsewhere.

He did not probe any more deeply into her thinking processes. His life resembled that of one perpetually walking by night through a city of well-lit and wide open bedrooms. He tried not to look, didn't want to look, but often could not avoid seeing. He was guilty of invasion of privacy twenty times per day, and just as frequently regretted it.

"Riley must be talking through his hat."

"Yes, Mr. Harper."

He called Riley on the phone mid-morning of the following day, announced, "You've given me the fidgets."

"That was my intention," said Riley, smirking in the tiny visiscreen.

"Everything is well in hand here, we being better organized than are some police headquarters. I reckon I can leave for a few days without risk of bankruptcy. But I'm not going away blind."

"What d'you mean?"

"For a start, I'll get nowhere if the moment I set foot across the line Ledsom's boys grab me for the hell of it."

"I'll tend to that," Riley promised. "They'll leave you alone—unless they can prove you're ready for cooking."

"I want the addresses of Alderson's widow and of that girl. Also of the fellow who phoned Ledsom—if they've managed to trace him."

"Leave it with me. I'll call you back as soon as I can." Harper pronged the phone, watched its fluorescent dial cloud over and go blank. He did not like the situation. He felt no real concern over entanglement in a murder. That affair would straighten itself out sooner or later. It was the least of his worries.

What bothered him was the hulking but agile-minded Riley's vague suspicions concerning his aptitude for uncovering evil long hidden from everyone else. Though devoid of a satisfactory theory to explain it, Riley had him tagged as a natural born smeller-out of witches.

The trick was easy enough. He had found out long ago that if he stared too long at a man with a guilty conscience the recipient of the stare became wary while the guilt radiated from his mind in vivid details. Nine times in the last ten years he had gazed absently at people who had rung a mental alarm-bell and unknowingly broadcast their reason for doing so. They had literally thought themselves into jail or the chair.

Harper had no difficulty in imagining the reaction should the news ever get out that no individual's mind was truly his own. He would be left without a friend other than some person of his own peculiar type, if such a one existed.

As for the criminal element, they'd see to it that his life wasn't worth a moment's purchase. The world's pleasantness so long preserved by his self-concealment would change to a hell of avoidance by day and menace by night.

While waiting for Riley, he indulged macabre amusement by picturing the manner of his own demise at the hands of the fearful. Obviously they couldn't use the conventional method of the gunman lurking in an alley. Such an assassin could not ready himself without thinking about the task in hand and thus warning the victim of the impending deed. No tactic could be effective that involved the presence of an active mind.

They would have to turn to some delayed or remotely controlled device that could function without radiating its intentions. A time-bomb might be suitable.

So he'd come to the office one morning, give Moira the cheery hiho, sit at his desk, pull open a drawer and—*bam!* Then the smoke would clear away and give him a view of the afterlife, if any.

Possibly he had been followed-up in police thought as a direct result of his foolishness in passing them news so openly and so often. He had been impelled to do it mostly because he detested finding himself in the presence of somebody who had got away with mayhem and any time might try to get away with it again. It irked his sense of justice. And it gratified him to feel that at long last some hapless victim had been avenged.

One fellow he had detected, chased and finally shot down had been seven times guilty of rape and once of murder accompanied by criminal assault. He could not let a louse like that freely run around for the sake of keeping Riley at arm's length.

In future it might be better to pass the word to the police by some indirect method such as, for example, the anonymous telephone call. It was doubtful whether that would serve. He had become too well-known a local character to leave the police puzzling over the source of the tip-offs. Any one of them, from the Commissioner downward, could put two and two together and make it four.

The phone yelped and Riley came on. "I've got those two addresses." He read them out while Harper made a note of them, then said, "The unknown caller hasn't been traced but Ledsom now thinks there's nothing to his message. They've found a fellow roughly corresponding to your description who gave Alderson some lip in the mid-morning. There were several witnesses and the caller in all probability was one of those."

"What was this squabbler doing at 4 p.m.?"

"He's in the clear. He was miles away and can prove it."

"H'm! All right, I'll go take a look around and hope my luck holds out."

"*Is* it luck?" asked Riley pointedly.

"Bad luck, to my way of thinking," said Harper. "If you had fathered ten sets of twins you'd appreciate without being told that some men can be afflicted."

"More likely I'd appreciate that some guys know how," Riley retorted. "And that's the trouble with you—so go to it!"

He faded off the screen. Harper sighed for the third time, tucked the slip of paper with its addresses into a vest pocket, spoke to Moira.

"I'll phone each day to see what's doing. If you can't handle something urgent and important you'll have to nurse it until I ring through."

"Yes, Mr. Harper."

"And if anyone turns up to pinch me tell them they're too late—I'm on the lam."

"Oh, Mr. Harper!"

Ruth Alderson proved to be a pretty blond with sad eyes. Obviously she was still in much of a mental whirl.

Sitting opposite her and idly turning his hat in his hands, Harper said, "I hate to trouble you at such a time, Mrs. Alderson, but it is necessary. I have a special interest in this case. I found your husband and was the last to speak to him."

"Did he—?" She swallowed hard, stared at him pathetically. "Did he . . . suffer much?"

"It was all very quick. He was too dazed to feel pain. He talked of you then kind of faded away. 'Betty,' he said, 'Betty.' Then he was gone." He frowned in puzzlement, added, "But your name is Ruth."

"He always called me Betty. Said it suited me. He made a pet name of it."

She put on a sudden tearfulness, covered her face with her hands, made no sound. He watched her quietly awhile.

When she had recovered, he said, "There's a slight chance you might be able to help find the rat who did it."

"How?"

"Tell me, did Bob have any enemies?"

She considered the question, gathering her thoughts with difficulty. "He arrested a number of people. Some went to jail. I don't suppose they loved him for that."

"Did any of them promise to get him when they came out?"

"If they did, he never mentioned it to me. It isn't the sort of thing he would tell." She paused, went on, "Four years ago he caught a man named Josef Grundoff and Bob said that when he was sentenced Grundoff swore to kill the judge."

"But he did not threaten your husband?"

"Not to my knowledge."

"You cannot recall any occasion on which somebody has menaced your husband specifically?"

"No, I can't."

"Nor any time when extraordinary resentment has been shown as a result of his doing his duty?"

"He had wordy arguments twice a week," she said wearily. "He often came home riled about someone. But as far as I can tell it was the normal give and take between the police and the public. I know of nobody who hated him enough to kill him."

"Only this Grundoff?"

"Grundoff only threatened the judge."

"I don't like pestering you this way, Mrs. Alderson, but can you recall any incident that seemed to worry your husband, even if only temporarily? Any small happening, no matter how insignificant, at any time in the past?"

"Not in connection with his police duties," she replied. A faint smile came into her features. "All his bothers were domestic ones. He was a bag of nerves when my babies were due."

Harper nodded understanding, continued with, "One more angle. It is imperative that I try it. Please forgive me, won't you?"

"What do you mean?" Her eyes widened.

"You are an attractive person, Mrs. Alderson. Did Bob earn anyone's enmity by marrying you?"

She flushed and gave back strongly, "The idea is quite ridiculous."

"Not at all. Such things have happened. They will happen again and again. Jealousy is perhaps the oldest motive for murder. It feeds upon itself, unseen, unsuspected. You might well have been admired and desired without realizing it."

"I don't think so."

"Since your marriage has any male friend or acquaintance shown undue attention toward you or displayed more than average friendship?" He saw the revulsion rising in her mind, knew that he could have expressed himself more tactfully, added with haste, "I do not expect you to be aware of an unconfessed lover. I am asking you to help seek a possible killer."

She cooled down, said dully, "There is nobody."

"When you first met Bob did you leave anybody for his sake?"

"I did not. I was free and unattached."

"Thank you, Mrs. Alderson." He stood up, glad to be at the end of the matter. "I apologize most sincerely for subjecting you to all this. And I really do appreciate your cooperation." He followed her to the front door, paused there, patted her gently on the shoulder. "Nothing anyone can say is adequate. Actions speak louder than words. You have my card. Any time I can help, please call on me to do so. I shall consider it a privilege."

"You are very kind," she murmured.

He got into his car, watched her close the door, said to himself savagely, "Damn! Damn!"

A mile down the road he stopped beside a phone booth and called Ledsom.

"So it's you," said the police captain, not visibly overjoyed. "What d'you want this time?"

"Some information."

"About what?"

"A character named Josef Grundoff."

"You're doing fine, digging up that hoodlum," Ledsom commented. "I wouldn't have thought of him myself."

"Why not?"

"He got twenty years for second degree murder. It will be a long, long time before he's out."

"Is that all?" asked Harper.

"How much more do you want?"

"Official reassurance that he's still inside. Maybe he has escaped."

"We'd have been advised of it. They'd send out fliers within twenty-four hours."

"Do you think it worth checking?" Harper persisted. "Just in case some notice has gone astray?"

"I can do that in five minutes," Ledsom became crabbed and demanded, "How did you get hold of Grundoff's name, anyway?"

"From Mrs. Alderson."

The other registered surprise. "Surely she hasn't told you that Grundoff—?"

"She said only that he'd sworn to get the judge," Harper chipped in. "So it seemed to me possible that he might have had Alderson's name on his list as well."

"He had no list. He was merely making tough talk. The judge said twenty years and Grundoff went nuts. That sort of thing happens often." He was silent a moment then continued, "I'll check all the same. It's one chance in a million but we can't overlook it. Call me back a bit later."

Harper phoned him from a diner twenty miles farther on.

"No luck," Ledsom informed. "Grundoff is still in the jug."

"Did he have any pals who might do his dirty work for him?"

"No. He was a lone wolf."

"Do you think he may have made friends in clink who've been released and started tending his affairs?"

"Not on your life," scoffed Ledsom. "No ex-con is going to shoot up a cop merely to please some con still inside. There would have to be money in it, big money. Grundoff couldn't dig up ten bucks."

"Thanks," said Harper glumly. "So that's another wrong tree up which I've barked. Oh well, press on regardless."

"To where?"

"That girl who was in the Thunderbug. Did you learn any more about her?"

"Yes. Her boy friend is in the armed forces and serving overseas. She has no relative with a police record, no bad egg in the family. Helps us a lot, doesn't it?"

"How about her protecting a girl friend who, perhaps, is afflicted with a trigger-happy lover?"

"How about pigs taking wings? The follow-up has been good and thorough. Her entire circle of relatives, neighbors and friends is in the clear."

"All right, keep your hair on. I'm only a major suspect trying to establish my pristine purity."

Ledsom let go a loud snort and cut off. Evidently lack of progress was trying his patience.

The second address was that of the central house in an old-fashioned but still imposing terrace of substantially built property. The road was wide, quiet, tree-lined and had an air of stuffy respectability. Harper went up six steps, thumbed the bell-stud.

A tall, good-looking youth of about eighteen answered the door, eyed him quizzically.

"Miss Jocelyn Whittingham in?" Harper asked, trying to sound official or at least semi-official.

"No." The other's mind confirmed the truth of that but went on to whisper to itself, *"Joyce doesn't want to see anybody. Who is this muscle-bound ape? Another nosey cop? Or a reporter? Joyce is fed up answering questions. Why don't they leave her alone?"*

"Any idea when she'll be back?"

"No."

That was a lie. The girl had promised to return by six.

"H'm!" Harper glanced up and down the road in the manner of one idly wondering what to do next. In deceptively casual tones he tried to hand the other a mental wallop. "Ever plugged a state trooper?"

No alarm-bell rang in the opposing brain. The youth's thoughts swirled confusedly while he doubted his own ears.

"Have I ever *what?*"

"Sorry," said Harper, knowing his blow had gone wide of the mark. "I was thinking out loud about something else. When do you suppose I could see Miss Whittingham?"

"I don't know." Same lie again.

"Too bad." Harper registered indecision.

"What d'you want to see her about?" inquired the youth.

"A personal matter."

"Well, she isn't in, and I don't know when she'll be in."

"Suppose I call back between six and seven?"

"Please yourself." He showed facial indifference while his mind nursed the notion that the visitor could go jump in the lake.

"All right, I'll try again later."

The youth nodded, shut the door. He was not sufficiently interested even to ask Harper's name. He was devoid of guilt and bored by the affairs of his sister, Miss Jocelyn Whittingham.

Harper spent an hour strolling aimlessly around the town while his car was greased and serviced in a central garage. At twenty to six he returned on foot to the road, stationed himself by a bus stop fifty yards from the house, kept watch for the girl's homecoming.

He had only a rough description of his quarry, but needed no more than that. One question would serve to stimulate self-identification voluntarily or involuntarily. There is no way of preventing the brain from registering its negatives or affirmatives no matter how great the desire to distort it.

Once the girl got inside that house the puzzle then would be how to gain an interview contrary to her wishes. If she flatly refused to see him he had no power to compel her to do so. In such circumstances his only positive tactic would be to cajole the local police into bringing her in for further questioning. They would not do that without excellent reason, and it was distasteful to him to invent a reason.

A face-to-face interview was imperative. If she were indoors he could stand there all night picking up her thoughts and sorting them out from other nearby thoughts with no difficulty whatsoever. He could, if he wished, spy upon her mind for a week.

It would do him not the slightest bit of good so long as her mind and its thinking processes moved only in channels having nothing to do with the case in hand. Questions were necessary to force her brain on to the case and make it reveal any cogent evidence it might be hiding. A vocal stimulus was required. To provide it he must ask her about this and that, drawing useful conclusions from all points where her thoughts contradicted her words.

Twice while he waited a girl walked past and momentarily captured his attention. So long as they did not mount the steps to the house he made no attempt to identify them mentally. He had his code of ethics developed since early childhood; he did not listen to private musings except when circumstances impelled him to do so. Of course, he could not avoid hearing the sudden cry of an alarmed conscience or a loud call for help such as Alderson had broadcast. But the muted voice of a passing mind, lacking the amplitude of defensive untruths, went by him unheard. He merely watched those girls until they had gone beyond the house and departed from sight.

A few minutes later a third girl came from the farther end of the road. She, too, ignored the house, continued straight on and rounded the far corner. A bus pulled up at the stop, discharged four passengers and rolled away. One of them, a tall, sallow man, eyed him curiously.

"It'll be half an hour before there's another."

"Yes, I know."

The other shrugged, crossed the road, entered the house facing the stop. Harper moved some distance down the road where he could keep watch without being snooped upon from the windows by the sallow man.

At five to six a girl entered the road from the end nearest his former post, walked hurriedly along with a sharp click-click of high heels. She was of medium height, fresh-featured, plump and about twenty. Without glancing around or noticing Harper, she climbed the steps to the house, felt in her handbag for a key.

From seventy yards away Harper probed at her, seeking confirmation of her identity. The result was shocking. The precise instant his mind touched hers she became aware of the contact and he, in his turn, knew that she was aware. She dropped the handbag in her flurry, bent and grabbed for it as he started to run toward her.

Getting the bag, she fumbled inside it with frantic haste while his feet pounded heavily along the sidewalk. Her eyes held a luminous glare as she found the key, stabbed it at the door. Perspiration beaded the running Harper's broad features while his right hand pawed under his left arm and his legs continued to race.

The key slid in and turned. Harper stopped at ten yards distance, leveled his gun and squeezed its butt. The thing went *spat-spat-spat* with such swiftness that it sounded like somebody tearing a foot of canvas. The noise was not loud. A stream of matchhead sized steel balls hit the target dead center.

Miss Jocelyn Whittingham let go the key, sank to her knees without a sound, keeled over with her head against the door. Harper stood sweating, watched the blood run out of her hair and listened to her brain packing up for keeps.

He stared around, saw no onlookers, no witnesses. The brief plinking of gunfire had attracted nobody's attention. He left her lying there and paced swiftly up the road. His face was strained and wet as he retrieved his car and got out of town fast.

Chapter 4

The police must have moved fast and skillfully. He had covered a mere three hundred miles before he was advertised on the air and in the news-sheets. He was having supper in a cheap hashery when he got an evening paper carrying the news.

WANTED FOR MURDER, it said. There followed a fairly accurate description of himself and of his car, complete with tag number. He cursed under his breath as he read it. There were twenty customers in the place, most of them long-distance truckers. Half of them had read or were reading the same sheet. Some were unaware of his existence; the others glanced at him casually and without suspecting that the subject of the report was here under their very eyes. He knew their lack of suspicion with absolute certainty and that was about the only advantage he possessed.

Outside, in plain view, stood the car. Its numbers seemed to swell and grow enormous even as he looked at them. Three big men in denims lumbered past its rear end without giving it so much as a second look, got into an adjacent machine and pulled away. His luck might hold out like that for some time but it just couldn't last for ever. Sooner or later the number-plate would be spotted waiting somewhere, by somebody with sharp eyes and a good memory.

He could leave the car where it was and help himself to another. When you're wanted for murder a mere theft can't add to the grief. But to do that would have compensating disadvantages. The number of the stolen car would be broadcast in short time, leaving him no better off than before. Moreover, right now the law did not know whether he was heading for Peking or Pernambuco but a car-swap would give away the direction of his escape and get every hick deputy on the lookout for him ahead. Also it would reveal that he had crossed state lines to evade arrest, a federal offence that might bring in the F.B.I.

The F.B.I. needed bringing in. Of that he was more than positive. But he did not relish the notion of the F.B.I. taking part in a nation-wide hunt for himself, especially since someone over-excitable might copy his recent tactic by shooting first and asking questions afterward. He was in the most peculiar position of wanting to get to the F.B.I. before they could get to him.

The means by which the law had tagged him as the culprit could be guessed quite easily. Ledsom's knowledge that he was visiting the girl. Her brother's description of the caller at the door. The sallow man's evidence about the lounger at the bus stop. Above all, the missiles in the body, like unto bullets from no other gun.

Stewing it over, he could not help wondering whether Ledsom now felt certain that he knew who had killed Alderson. It would be a very natural tendency on that officer's part to assume the same hand in both cases even though different weapons had been used.

What he liked least about this sudden howl for a man named Harper was not that it boosted the official hunt for him, but that it might start an unofficial search. The forces of law and order should not be the only ones to take deep interest in the datum that he had killed Miss Jocelyn Whittingham. Certain others undoubtedly would be after him, anxious to know how it all came about, anxious to deal with him before it was too late. Those three fellows in the Thunderbug, for instance.

Swallowing the rest of his coffee, he got out of the place as quickly as he could without drawing attention to his urgency. He waited nervily by a row of alk-pumps while his tank was filled, then drove at top pace into the twilight that rapidly became night, a dark, moonless night. He had more than five hundred miles yet to go.

At four-forty in the morning, with the pale halo of dawn beginning to show in the east, some wide-awake sharp-eye either read his plates or chased him on general principles.

He reached a half-mile stretch of road under repair, perforce crawled at fifteen over the torn surface. A watchman's hut stood at the end, and beside it a car with side-lamps glowing. He passed the hut, accelerated, gained speed and a mile and a half lead when the parked car came to life, shot out on to the road, went after him with spotlight blinking.

Harper could not hear a siren nor pick up following thoughts. He was too far ahead and too preoccupied with driving. He shoved the pedal down to the floor-boards and let the machine leap ahead. If the pursuers were police, as their spot-light suggested, that alone would be enough to convince them that they were on to something worth running down.

There was no alternative other than letting them chase. If he was going to be taken in it must be by people who were peculiarly well informed and knew how many beans make five. He was pretty certain that no county sheriff, no state, city or town police possessed the information that qualified them to become his captors.

Tires squealed, headlights swung and rocked as he took a couple of bends at breakneck speed. The car was powerful and fast, in tiptop condition, but the one behind might be even better. So far as he could judge from frequent glances at the rear-view mirror, the other machine did have a slight advantage because its wink-ing spotlight seemed to be creeping up on him ever so gradually.

With his needle trembling at over ninety he tore through a crossroads, along a main artery darkened still more by large trees on both sides. The trees whizzed past like huge ghosts, arms out, transfixed by this night-time pursuit.

There was no traffic other than his own car and the one behind. Far ahead and slightly to his right he could see the sky-glow from streetlights of a sizeable city, wondered whether he could make it that distance and, if so, what he'd do when he got there. Maybe if the ones behind came close enough in the next ten miles they'd start shooting. What to do then?

He rocked around another half-bend, momentarily lost the lights in the mirror which by now were less than a mile to the rear. His own beams swung briefly across the end of a track through thick timber. He dived into it so suddenly and recklessly that for a second or two he feared the machine would overturn.

Switching off all lamps he plowed another fifty yards into complete blackness, meanwhile praying that he would not hit an invisible tree or dive into a hidden ditch. Twigs crackled and snapped under rolling wheels but luck remained with him. He braked, dropped a window, watched and listened.

The siren could be heard now. A prowl car, sure enough. By this time it was on top of the bend. Headlights slewed across the night as it came round and the next moment it thundered past, wailing as it went. Its passing was far too swift to en-able Harper to see how many were within or to pick up a random thought.

He sat in darkness until he could see faint, diminished beams racing up a slope four miles away. Then he reversed, got back on to the road, made off in the way he had come. Reaching the crossroads over which he had recently blundered, he turned to the right, continued along this new route.

Without further incident he reached Washington late in the morning, planted the car in a park on the outskirts, took a bus into the city. There he found a phone and called the office.

Either the office visiscreen was out of order or had been switched off, for his own screen remained blank and Moira's response was equally blank.

"Harper plant. Can I help you?"

"Only God can help me," he said. "This is your boss."

She let out a distinct gasp.

"What's so soul-shaking about that?" he demanded. "You have spoken to me many a time before."

"Yes, Mr. Harper. Of course, Mr. Harper." She sought desperately for words. "I didn't expect you just yet."

"Tsk!" He grinned wolfishly at the dead screen. "Why not? I told you I'd call, didn't I?"

"Certainly, Mr. Harper, but—"

"But *what?*"

She hadn't the vaguest idea what. She was tongue-tied and in a tangle.

"You've been reading the papers," he observed grimly. "But no matter. Has anything turned up?"

"Turned up?"

"Look, Moira, pay no attention to those fat-butted dicks sitting on my desk. Listen to me: has anything come along in the mail that requires my personal handling?"

"N-n-no, Mr. Harper."

"Any complications I'm needed to clear up?"

"N-n-no."

"All right. Put one of those guys on the phone."

She got into a worse tangle. "I don't understand, Mr. Harper. There isn't—"

"Now, now, no lies!" he ordered.

At that point she gave up and he heard her say weakly to somebody else, "He knows you're here and insists on speaking to you."

There sounded a deep grunt that somehow conveyed disgust. Harper's screen suddenly cleared and showed a beefy face scowling at him.

Before the other could speak Harper said, "When I can't see a thing in my own office I know somebody doesn't want me to look. I also know Moira's been told to keep me on as long as she can while this call is being traced. Well, you're wasting your time for which suffering taxpayers are paying, of whom I am one. You pack up and get busy on the local sinners. Tell Riley I love him despite all his faults."

The face scowled more deeply. "Now see here, Harper—"

"Listen to me for once," continued Harper impatiently. "It may help persuade you that you're doing no good warming my blotter if I tell you I'm calling from Washington and that I'm making for F.B.I. headquarters to give myself up."

Incredulity expressed itself on the distant features. "You mean that?"

"Check with the F.B.I. in about fifteen minutes' time. They'll tell you they've got me. And don't celebrate by pawing Moira around. She draws her pay from me, not from you!"

He pronged the phone and walked out, joined the crowds on the sidewalk. He had covered two blocks when a tall, dark-haired, neatly dressed young man threw him a brief but penetrating glance in passing, did a swift double-take, continued a few yards beyond then turned and followed.

Harper strolled steadily on, smiling to himself as he filched data out of the shadower's mind. Robert Slade, thirty-two, F.B.I. agent, obsessed by the notion that Harper bore a very close resemblance to Harper. The encounter was purely accidental but the boy intended to stick to the opportunity until he was sure enough to make a pinch.

Turning down a side street, Harper covered three more blocks, became a mite uncertain of his whereabouts. He was not very familiar with Washington. He stopped on a corner, lit a cigarette, gazed furtively over cupped hands, found Slade studiously examining a window full of panes-in-the-neck.

Ambling back he touched Slade's elbow, said, "Pardon me. I'm looking for F.B.I. headquarters. Can you direct me?"

It shook Slade more than if he'd suddenly stuck a gun in his belly.

"Why . . . er . . . yes, of course." His clear gray eyes betrayed uncertainty about his suspicions. His mind was saying, *"Hell of a coincidence!"*

"You're Robert Slade, aren't you?" inquired Harper, pleasantly conversational.

The other rocked back. "I am. You have the advantage of me, though. I don't recall knowing you."

"Would it do you any good to make an arrest?"

"What d'you mean?"

"I'm seeking your H.Q. You can show me the way. If you would like to call it a pinch it's all right with me. I'm Wade Harper."

Slade took in a deep breath. "You're not kidding?"

"Why should I? Don't I look like Harper?"

"You sure do. And maybe you're fed up being mistaken for him. If so, there's little we can do about it."

"That can soon be settled. You have my prints on file." He felt under an arm. "Here's my gun. Don't let the comparison boys in the ballistics department lose it—I hope to get it back someday."

"Thanks." Openly baffled, Slade shoved it into a pocket, pointed down the street. "This way."

They moved along side by side. Slade made no suggestion of using his handcuffs, neither was he particularly wary. Harper's attitude had created within him a condition of chronic skepticism; he was inclined to think this capture would gain him no kudos because the captive was too self-possessed to be other than innocent.

Reaching the big building they went inside. Slade showed Harper into a small room, said, "Wait there a minute," and departed. The exit and the open street were within easy reach. There was no obstacle to an escape other than that provided by a hard-looking character on duty at the door.

Taking his ease in a pneumatic chair Harper amused himself tracking Slade's mind. The agent went along a short corridor, entered an office, spoke to somebody there.

"I've just picked up Wade Harper. He's in room number four."

"By himself?"

"Yes."

"Are you cracked? He can make a dive and—"

"He was on his way here when I found him," interjected Slade, honestly refusing the credit for the grab. *"He* wanted *to come."*

"Holy smoke! There's something mighty funny about this." A pause, then, *"Bring him in here."*

Harper got up, walked along the passage, arrived at the door just as Slade opened it to come and get him. For the third successive time Slade was taken aback. He stood aside, silent and puzzled, while Harper marched boldly in, took a seat and gazed at the lean-faced man behind the desk. The latter returned his gaze and gave himself away without knowing it. William Pritchard, thirty-nine, area supervisor.

"Morning, Mr. Pritchard," said Harper with the cheerful air of one who has not a worry in the world.

Pritchard blinked, marshaled his wits, said, "There's a call out for you. You're wanted for the murder of Jocelyn Whittingham."

"Yes, I know. I read the papers."

"Somebody's blundered," thought Pritchard, impressed by this coolness. *"He's got an alibi."* Clearing his throat, he asked, "Well, do you wish to say anything about it?"

"Plenty—but not to you."

"Why not to me?"

"No personal reason, I assure you. I'd like to talk to Sam Stevens."

"Go see where he is," Pritchard ordered after a little hesitation, deciding that one interlocutor was as good as another.

Slade went away, came back, informed, "Stevens is in Seattle."

The phone called shrilly, Pritchard picked it off his desk, said, "Yes? How did you know? Oh, he told you himself, did he? No, he wasn't fooling. He's here all right. He's in front of me right now." He racked the phone, stared hard at Harper. "You can't see Stevens. He isn't available."

"A pity. He could have got me somebody high up. I want to talk as high as I can get."

"Why?"

"I refuse to say."

Frowning disapproval, Pritchard leaned forward. "Did you or did you not shoot this Whittingham girl?"

"Yes, I did."

"All right. Are you willing to sign a confession to that effect?"

"No."

"You admit shooting her but you refuse to sign a confession?"

"That's right."

"Care to offer a reason?" Pritchard invited, studying him carefully.

"I've a good reason. I didn't kill her."

"But she's dead. She's as dead as mutton. Didn't you know that?"

Harper made two waves of a hand in manner suggesting that this was a minor point of little consequence.

"So you shot her but didn't kill her?" Pritchard persisted. "You put a dozen steel beads through her skull but somehow refrained from committing homicide?"

"Correct."

That did it. Pritchard's and Slade's minds worked in perfect accord, weighed the evidence, reached a simultaneous verdict: not guilty of murder by reason of insanity.

Sighing deeply, Harper said, "Sam Stevens is the only boy I know in this outfit. He made a check on my plant once, about two years ago. He entered it on some sort of national security list which you people keep on file. He gave me a gun permit and a bunch of bureaucratic instructions chief of which says I'm federal property the moment war breaks out. I become confiscated lock, stock and barrel."

"So?" prompted Pritchard, seeing no point in this.

"The Whittingham business has to do more or less with the same issue, namely, national security. Therefore I can talk only to somebody who'll know what I'm talking about."

"That would be Jameson," promptly whispered Pritchard's thoughts.

"Such as Jameson," Harper added.

They reacted as though he had uttered a holy name in the unholy precincts of a cheap saloon.

"Or whoever is *his* boss," said Harper, for good measure.

With a touch of severity, Pritchard demanded, "You just said that Stevens is the only member of the F.B.I. known to you. So how do you know of Jameson? Come to that, how did you know *my* name?"

"He knew mine too," put in Slade, openly itching for a plausible explanation.

"That's a problem I'll solve only in the presence of somebody way up top," said Harper. He smiled at Pritchard and inquired, "How's your body?"

"Eh?"

Out of the other's bafflement Harper extracted a clear and detailed picture of the body, said in helpful tones, "You have a fish-shaped birthmark on the inside of your left thigh."

"That's enough for me!" Pritchard stood up, badly worried. He said to Slade, "You keep an eye on this Houdini while I go see what Jameson says." He departed hurriedly.

Harper asked Slade, "May I have a sheet of paper, please?"

Extracting one from a drawer in the desk Slade slipped it across. He watched Harper take out a fountain-pen and prepare to write. The confession after all, he thought. Definitely a nut who'd refuse a thing one moment and give it the next. Strange how even an intelligent man could go so completely off his rocker. An hereditary weakness, perhaps.

Ignoring these uncomplimentary ideas which assailed him as clearly as if they'd been shouted aloud, Harper waited a few moments then began to write. He scribbled with great rapidity, finished a short time before Pritchard's return.

"He won't see you," announced Pritchard with a that-is-that air.

"I know." Harper gave him the paper.

Glancing over it, Pritchard popped his eyes, ran out full tilt. Slade stared after him, turning a questioning gaze upon Harper.

"That was a complete and accurate transcript of their conversation," Harper informed. "Want to lay any bets against him seeing me now?"

"No," said Slade, developing the willies. "I don't care to throw away good money."

Jameson proved to be a middle-aged bull of a man with a thick mop of curly gray hair. His eyes were blue and cold, his manner that of one long accustomed to the exercising of authority. Sitting erect in his chair he kept one strong forefinger firmly planted on the sheet of paper lying on the desk before him. He wasted no time in getting down to business.

"How did you do it?"

"Easily enough. I took aim, fired and down she slid."

"I'm not asking about that." The finger tapped impatiently. "I am referring to this."

"Oh, the eavesdropping." Harper pretended to gain an understanding that he had not lost in the first place. "I did it in the same way the enemy might be able to do it any time he wants to know what we're up to."

"You may go," Jameson said to Pritchard. "I'll call you when I want you." He waited until the door had closed, fixed full attention on the other. "Are you categorically asserting that agents of other powers are able to read our minds at will?"

"No."

"Then why make such a suggestion?"

"I'm merely putting over the theory that what one can do another can do," said Harper. "It's a notion I've nursed for years. So far I've been unable to find any evidence in support."

"Obviously you are talking about something *you* can do. What can you do?"

"That," said Harper, pointing to the paper.

Jameson was no fool. He had got the idea at the start but found considerable difficulty in absorbing it. The manifest explanation was proving indigestible. He tried again to cope with it, failed, decided to put the issue fairly and squarely.

"It would take a telepath to play these sort of tricks."

"Nothing else but," agreed Harper.

"Whoever heard of one?" asked Jameson, baffling his own incredulity.

Harper merely shrugged.

Switching his little intercom board, Jameson spoke into its mike. "Is Miss Keyes there? Put her on. Miss Keyes, I want you to type a column of twenty-eight-digit numbers chosen at random. Bring it to me immediately you have finished." He switched off, gave Harper a challenging look, poked the paper toward him and said, "See what you can do with that."

"Now I've got to search through the general mess for somebody concocting meaningless numbers," Harper complained. "I may miss the first one or two while I'm feeling around."

"Never mind. Do the best you can. If you get only a quarter of them it will convince me that the age of miracles has not passed."

Harper wrote down eighteen of them plus the last two digits of the nineteenth. Taking the paper without comment, Jameson waited for Miss Keyes. She arrived shortly, gave him her list, departed with no visible surprise. If she'd been ordered to wear her machine's dust-cover as a hat she would have done it without question. Jameson compared the two columns.

Finally he said, "This is worse than a bomb in the Pentagon. Nothing is private property any more."

"I know."

"How did it happen?"

"Can a man with a hare-lip tell you how it happened? All I know is that I was born that way. For a few years I assumed that everyone else was precisely like myself. Being a child it took quite a time to learn that it was not so, to learn that I was a one-eyed man in the kingdom of the blind, to learn that I could be feared and that the feared are hated."

"There must be a reason for it," said Jameson.

"Does it matter?"

"It matters a hell of a lot. You are a freak created by some very special arrangement of circumstances. If we could detail those circumstances fully and completely we could estimate the likelihood of them being duplicated elsewhere. That in turn would give us a fair idea of whether there are any more like you and, if so, who's got them."

Harper said quietly and soberly, "I don't think that matters a damn either. Not any more."

"Why doesn't it?"

"Because I made mental contact with Jocelyn Whittingham and she promptly called me an insulting name. So I shot her."

"You considered that adequate motive for murder?" prompted Jameson.

"In view of the name, yes!"

"What did she call you?"

"A terrestrial bastard," informed Harper, hard-eyed.

Chapter 5

For a full two minutes Jameson sat there like one paralyzed. His thoughts milled wildly around and he was momentarily oblivious of the fact that the other could read them as easily as if they shone in neons.

Then he asked, "Are you sure of that?"

"The only person in the world who can be positive about someone else's mind is a telepath," assured Harper. "I'll tell you something else: I shot her because I knew I couldn't kill her. It was a physical impossibility."

"How d'you make that out?"

"No living man could harm Jocelyn Whittingham—because she was already dead."

"Now see here, we have a detailed police report—"

"I killed something else," said Harper, with devastating effect. "The thing that had already slaughtered her."

Jameson promptly went into another whirl. He had a cool, incisive mind used to dealing with highly complicated but essentially normal problems. This was the first time within his considerable experience that he had been slapped in the face by a sample of the supernormal. Even now he strove to cope with it in rational, everyday terms. It was about as easy as trying to use a yardstick to measure the distance to the Moon.

One thing surprised the observing Harper, namely, that much of the other's confusion stemmed from the fact that he lacked certain information he could reasonably be expected to possess. High up in the bureaucratic hierarchy Jameson might be, evidently he was not high enough. All the same, he had enough pull to take the matter further and get some action.

Harper said, "You've got the bald account from police sources. It isn't enough. I'd like to give you my side of the story."

"Go ahead," invited Jameson, glad to concentrate on something that might clear up the muddle.

Commencing with his pick-up of the dying Alderson's broadcast, Harper took it through to the end.

Then he said, "No ordinary human being is ever aware of his mind being read. He gains no sense of physical contact that might serve to warn him. He remains completely unconscious of being pried into. I have been absorbing your thoughts the whole time we've been here together; your senses have not registered the probe in any way whatever, have they?"

"No," Jameson admitted.

"And if I had not told you that I'm a telepath, and satisfied you as to the truth of it, you'd have found no cause to suspect that your mind is wide open to me, would you?"

"No,"

"Well," went on Harper reminiscently, "the instant I touched the mind inside Jocelyn Whittingham it felt the contact, knew whence it came, took wild alarm and hated me with a most appalling ferocity. In the same instant I detected all its reactions and recognized it as non-human. The contact did not last a fiftieth of a second but it was enough. I knew it as nothing born of woman. I knew it as surely as your own eyes can tell you that a rattlesnake is not a mewling babe."

"If it wasn't human," inquired Jameson, with much skepticism, "what was it?"

"That I don't know."

"Of what shape or form?"

"The shape and form of the Whittingham girl. It *had* to be that. It was using her body."

Disbelief suddenly swamped Jameson's brain. "I will concede that you are either a genuine telepath or the practitioner of some new and superb trick that makes you look like one. But that doesn't mean I have to swallow this murder story. What your defense boils down to is that you shot a corpse animated by God knows what. No jury on earth will give such an incredible plea a moment's consideration."

"I'll never face a jury," Harper told him.

"I think you will—unless you drop dead beforehand. The law must take its course."

"For the first time in my naughty life I'm above the law," said Harper, impressively confident. "What's more, the law itself is going to say so."

"How do you reach that remarkable conclusion?"

"The law isn't interested only in the death of Jocelyn Whittingham. It is even more concerned about the slaying of Trooper Alderson, he having been a police officer. And you can't pin *that* one on me if you try from now to Christmas. Reason why you can't is because I didn't do it."

"Then who did?" Jameson challenged.

"A-a-ah!" Harper eyed him meaningfully. "Now you're getting right down to the heart of the matter. Who killed Alderson and why?"

"Well?"

"Three men in a Thunderbug. Three men who, in all probability, resented Alderson's intrusion at a critical moment when the Whittingham girl was being taken over."

"Taken over?"

"Don't stare at me like that. How do I know precisely what occurred? All I do know is that something must have happened, something did happen to produce the result I discovered."

Jameson looked baffled.

"Three men," continued Harper, giving it emphasis. "In green suits, matching green ties, gray shirts and collars. Three men wearing uniforms with which nobody is familiar. Why haven't those uniforms been recognized?"

"Because they were not uniforms at all," Jameson hazarded. "They merely looked that way, having a sort of official cut, let us say."

"Or because they were uniforms that nobody knows about," suggested Harper. "Because the government has said nothing to anybody. Because officialdom hasn't breathed a word to a soul. Is the taxpayer always told where his money is going?"

"What the devil are you getting at?"

"We're pulling the Moon to pieces and nobody thinks anything of it. It's been going on long enough to have become commonplace. A moon-boat is now about as remarkable as a Cunarder used to be. We're so sophisticated about such matters that we've lost the capacity for surprise."

"I'm aware of all this, since I live in the present," said Jameson, a trifle impatiently. "What of it?"

"Who's cooked up notions of exploiting Venus or Mars? Have you sent anyone there to take a look and, if so, when was it? Are they due back by now? Were they three men in green uniforms with gray shirts?"

"My God!" ejaculated Jameson, becoming visibly strained.

"Three men went somewhere, got more than they bargained for, involuntarily brought it back to spread around. That's my theory. Try it for size."

"If I approach the proper quarter with such a fantasy they'll think I'm cracked."

"I know why you fear that; I can read your mind, remember? Firstly, you personally know of no space-expedition, have heard not the slightest hint of one. Secondly, you cannot credit my diagnosis. Right?"

"Fat lot of use denying it."

"Then look at it this way: I know even if you don't that for a fragmentary moment I touched a genuinely alien mind in possession of a human body. That entity could not have solidified out of sheer nothingness. It must have arrived in some concealed manner. Somebody must have brought it. The only possible suspects are those three men."

"Go on," encouraged Jameson.

"We have not the vaguest notion how long those three have been gallivanting around. Maybe for a week, maybe for a year." He fixed his listener with an accusative stare. "Therefore the Whittingham girl may not be the first or by any means the last. That trio may have given the treatment to a hundred and be busily tending to a hundred more while we're sitting here making useless noises. If we continue to flatten our fannies long enough they'll enslave half the world before we wake up."

Jameson fidgeted and gloomed hesitantly at the phone.

"Brockman of Special Services," said Harper. "He's the guy you've got in mind right now." He made an urgent gesture. "All right, get through to him. What is there to lose? Perhaps he'll tell you what he wouldn't dream of telling me. Ask him if an expedition is out in space and when it's due back."

"Ten to one he'll ignore the question and want to know why I'm asking," Jameson protested. "I can hardly offer him your notions, and second hand at that."

"He'll try to pull down your pants only if there's no such expedition," Harper asserted. "But if in fact there is one, and it's a top secret, your query will make his mustache drop off, if he has a mustache. He'll hotfoot over to find how the news got out. Try him and let's hear what he says."

Doubtfully, Jameson picked up the phone, said in resigned tones, "Get me Special Services Department, Mr. Brockman."

When the call went through Jameson spoke in the reluctant manner of one compelled to announce the arrest of Snow White and all the seven dwarfs.

"We're on to something peculiar here. I won't take up your time with the full details. It would help considerably if you can tell me whether a new space-venture has been made in secret." He listened a bit while his expression gradually went flat. "Yes, it's highly important that we should know one way or the other. Will you? Thanks a lot!" He planted the phone.

"He doesn't know?" said Harper.

"Correct."

"*Should* he know?"

"I assumed that he would. I could be wrong. The more highly confidential a piece of knowledge, the fewer entrusted with it and the further we'll have to seek for an answer, if there is a satisfactory answer." Taking a large blue hand-kerchief from his breast pocket he mopped his brow although he was not per-spiring. "Brockman will call back as soon as he can make it."

"It would save valuable time to ring the White House and ask the President. Don't tell me *he* won't know what's going on."

Jameson was shocked. "Look, leave me to handle this in my own way, will you?"

"Sure. But the longer we take over this the sooner you may start handling things in some unearthly way." Harper registered a sour grin. "Not having my gun I'd then be forced to strangle you with my own hands—if I could do so without *you* taking *me* over."

"Shut up!" ordered Jameson, looking slightly sick. He scowled at the phone which promptly emitted a yelp. The unexpectedness of it made him jerk in his chair. He snatched it up, said, "Well?" and let half a dozen expressions run over his face. Then he racked the phone, came to his feet, said, "They want us over there immediately."

"And we know why, don't we?"

Offering no response, Jameson led the way down, got into a car driven by an agent who resembled a cross between a haberdashery salesman and a wrestling champ. They rolled ten blocks, went up to the twentieth floor of a glass and con-crete building, entered an office in which waited four serious men.

These four glanced briefly at Harper without recognizing him despite all the recent publicity. Apparently they rarely got around to reading the newspapers or watching the video.

The oldest of the quartet, a lean-faced individual with sharp eyes and fine white hair, snapped at Jameson, "What's all this about a space-expedition? Where did you pick up such a story?"

Seeing nothing for it but to pass the buck, Jameson indicated his companion. "This is Wade Harper. State police have him tagged as a murderer. He came to us an hour or so ago. My query arose from his story."

Four pairs of eyes shifted to Harper. "What story?"

These men were edgy and Harper could see it. He could also see why they had the willies: they were deeply concerned about reserved data becoming public prop-erty. And he could see, too, that for the moment Jameson had forgotten his spe-cial aptitude. It isn't easy for people to become accustomed to an almost mythical abnormality in the thoroughly normal-looking.

Addressing the white-haired man, he filched his name and said. "Mr. King, I know for a fact that eighteen months ago we sent a ship to Venus, the nearest planet. That ship was the result of twenty years of governmental experimentation. It bore a crew of three hand-picked men. Its return has two alternative dates. If the crew found conditions unbearable the ship should have been back last November. If conditions permit them to exist and indulge a little exploration they're due in mid June, about five weeks hence. The fact that they are not known to have re-turned is officially considered encouraging. The government awaits their arrival before giving the news to the world."

King heard all this with facial impassivity that he fondly imagined concealed his boiling thoughts. He asked with forced calmness, "And how did you obtain this information?"

It was too much for Jameson who had listened with amazement to the recital and been awakened by it. "This man is telepathic, Mr. King. He has proved it to my satisfaction. He has picked the facts out of your mind."

"Indeed?" King was openly skeptical. "Then how do you account for the nature of your call to Brockman twenty minutes ago?"

"I suspected it then," Harper chipped in. "But now I *know.*" He studied King levelly, added, "At the moment you're thinking that if the world is to be afflicted with such creatures as telepaths it might be a good thing to put them out of harm's way, and fast."

"You know too much," said King. "No government could function with any degree of security with people like you hanging around."

"I've been hanging around enough years to make me wish they were fewer. We haven't had a bloody revolution yet."

"But we have a suspected murderer dragged into a government office by a departmental director of the F.B.I.," said King, making it sound like a legitimate grievance. "It is certainly a new and previously unheard-of practice. I hope they had the forethought to search you for concealed weapons."

By Harper's side Jameson reddened and interjected, "Pardon me, Mr. King, but there is far more to this issue than the aspect that seems to irritate you."

"Such as what?"

"The ship is back," Harper put in.

All four jerked as though stabbed with needles.

King demanded, "When did it return? Where did it land?"

"I don't know."

They relaxed, suddenly confident that Harper was talking through the rear of his neck.

"Then how do you know it is back?"

"He found a trace of the crew," informed Jameson. "Or that's how it looks."

Harper contradicted carefully, "No, I don't think I did. I think the crew is dead."

"So the crew died and you've not the faintest notion of where their ship is planted?" inquired King, by this time toying with the theory that Harper was off his nut but puzzled to find a plausible reason why so shrewd an individual as Jameson had become equally cracked. "Nevertheless you *know* that the ship has returned?"

"I'd bet a million dollars on it."

"It made the trip all on its ownsome? A unique spatial convulsion flung it thirty million miles or more across the void and dumped it someplace unknown to all and unsuspected by anyone but you?"

"Your sarcasm is pointless, doesn't help any and furthermore it gives me a pain in the seat," snapped Harper, becoming tough. "The ship was brought here by a bunch of Venusians. How d'you like that, eh?"

King didn't like it at all. His mind unhesitatingly rejected the bald state-ment, started sorting out a dozen objections and deciding which to voice first.

The bespectacled man on his right took advantage of the pause to chip in and speak to Harper as one would do a wayward child.

"Piloting a space-ship is not an easy matter."

"No, Mr. Smedley, I guess it isn't."

"It's highly technical. It requires a great deal of know-how."

"That," said Harper, "is precisely the hell of it."

"What do you mean?"

"Anyone who can hijack a ship and run it forthwith, without any tuition, can take over anything else we've got with as little trouble." He gave them a few sec-onds to stew the point, then added for good measure, "Bit by bit, piece by piece, until they have everything and we have nothing—not even our souls."

"That idea is detestable," said King, beginning to feel cold.

"It should be," agreed Harper. "And further, you'd do well to abandon this lat-est notion you're concocting."

"What notion?"

"That I'm the agent of a scheming gang across the ocean who, in some myste-rious way, are trying to pull a fast one. All that feuding is over as from today. They're in the same mess along with the rest of humanity and the sooner that's realized the better. They're going to become just as scared as I am right now."

"I doubt it. They'll be equally suspicious. They'll blame us for trying to disturb the world with a better and bigger bogey."

"It won't matter a cuss who blames whom when we're no longer human. Come to that, we won't be mentally capable of apportioning blame."

King argued stubbornly, "It seems to me that you're taking a devil of a lot for granted on the basis of very little evidence. That evidence may be real enough to you. To us it comes secondhand. Even if we accept Jameson's statement that you are a genuine telepath, even if we take at face value the symptoms of it which you have displayed in this room, the fact remains that you're just as capable as anyone else of imagining things. I can conceive no logical reason for supposing that a telepath is impervious to delusions. Do you seriously expect us to alert the entire defenses of this country on the strength of an unproven story?"

"No, I don't," admitted Harper. "I'm not that daft."

"Then what do you expect of us?"

"Firstly, I wanted official confirmation of my suspicion that a ship really has been sent somewhere beyond the Moon. That is why I came all the way here and avoided being picked up by local police who know too little and bark too much. Somehow or other I *had* to learn about that ship."

"Secondly?"

"I now expect action within reasonable limits. If it produces the proof you re-quire I expect further action on a national scale."

"It is far easier to talk about getting proof than to go out and dig it up. If proof exists why didn't you find it yourself and bring it with you? Surely your own commonsense should tell you that the wilder a story the more proof it requires to make convincing?"

"I know," said Harper. "And I reckon I could have got enough to make you leap out of your shirt if only I'd possessed an item hidden in your top-secret files."

"To what are you referring?"

"The photographs of those three spacemen." He eyed King and his confreres with the sorrowful reproof of one surprised by their inability to perceive the obvious. "We have a witness who got a good, close look at two of those three and made careful note of them. Show him your pictures. If he says they're the boys, that settles it. The balloon goes up next minute."

Jameson waggled his eyebrows and put in, "Yes, that is the logical move. It should decide the matter one way or the other. We can do better than that, too. We can remove any element of doubt."

"How?" inquired King.

"That Thunderbug must have come from somewhere. It may have traveled hundreds of miles before reaching the fateful spot. A dozen, twenty or forty people may have noticed it and the three men with it. I can put agents on the job of tracing that back-track and finding the witnesses. If all of them say the same thing, namely, that those three men are your missing pilots—" He let it die out, thereby making it sound highly sinister.

"To enable you to do that," King pointed out, "we would have to get those photographs released from secret files and provide you with a large number of copies."

"Of course."

"But that means the general dissemination of reserved data."

Harper emitted a loud groan, rubbed his jaw and recited the names of the twelve apostles.

Staring at him distastefully, King said, "I'll see what the appropriate department decides."

"While you're at it," Harper suggested, "you can persuade some other appropriate department to seize the body of Jocelyn Whittingham and subject it to an expert autopsy. I don't know whether that will tell us anything, but it might. The bet is worth taking, anyway."

"I'll see what they decide," repeated King. He went out with visible unwillingness. The remaining three fidgeted and registered the discomfort of men compelled to hold a buck that cannot be passed.

"Have you got a gun?" Harper asked Jameson.

"Yes."

"Better hold on to it good and tight."

"Why?"

"Because if he gets nowhere with the higher-ups I'm going to run amok."

"You'd better not!" warned Jameson.

"I'd rather die quickly in a fracas here than slowly someplace else," said Harper fervently.

The three watched him with open apprehension.

King was gone a long time. Eventually he returned with a heavily built, military-looking man named Benfield. The latter grasped three large photographs which he exhibited to Harper as he spoke.

"Know these fellows?"

"No."

"Sure of that?"

"I'm positive. They're complete strangers to me."

"Humph! Can you say that they answer to the descriptions of the trio you have in mind?"

"Fairly well. I could be more definite if those pics were in color. The uniforms convey nothing in black and white."

'They are dark green uniforms with silver buttons, gray shirts, green ties."

"Apart from the silver buttons the details match up."

"All right. We'll make an immediate check. Who's this witness?"

Harper told him about the oldster at the filling station while Benfield made note of it on a scratch-pad.

Benfield said to Jameson, "We'll try this one first. If the check proves confirmatory we'll run off enough clear copies to enable your men to follow the back trail. Meanwhile, we'll radio a set to your office out there. Won't take them long to determine whether or not this is a gag, will it?"

"A couple of hours," said Jameson.

"A couple of minutes would be better," observed Harper. "And how about taking the heat off me while you're at it?"

"We'll think about that when the report comes in. If it makes hay of your story we'd better have you examined by a mental specialist."

"That would be fun," Harper assured. "He'd play all the kings and I'd play all the aces. In the end you'd have to put *him* away."

Benfield let it pass. He was taking this tale of telepathic power and all the rest of the story with a sizeable dose of salt. The sole feature that impressed him was that somehow or other a wanted felon had succeeded in talking his way into the higher echelons of Washington. That suggested either a modicum of incredible truth or a superb gift of the gab. But he was just. He was willing to pursue the matter for the sake of finding any factual grain that might be lying around.

"Put him somewhere safe," Benfield ordered Jameson, "and hold him until we get our reply."

Harper protested, "D'you think I'm going to run off after coming all the way here?"

"No, I don't think so—because you're not going to be given the chance." He threw Jameson a look of warning, departed with the photographs in his hand.

"We'll phone you at your H.Q. immediately we hear," promised King. He stared Harper out of face in effort to reassert authority, continued to stare at the other's broad back as he went out. But his thoughts skittered wildly around and were not free from fear.

Sitting boredly in Jameson's office Harper said, "Thanks for the lunch. Before long you can buy me dinner as well." He glanced at his wrist-watch. "It's three-forty. Why don't they report direct to you? They're your men, aren't they?"

"They have their orders."

"Yes, I know. Orders from somebody else. At this moment you're pondering the fact that this business isn't properly within your bailiwick. The F.B.I. has been called upon to hunt most everything but prodigal space-pilots. That's how you look at it. And you can't decide whether anything is likely to come of it."

"We'll know in due course."

"They're taking long enough to find out." Harper brooded silently for a couple of minutes, then showed alarm. "What if that oldster is dead and no longer able to identify anything?"

"Any particular reason why he might be?" inquired Jameson, surveying him keenly.

"Yes. Those three may have figured things out for themselves and returned to shut his mouth."

"Why should they do that? Miss Whittingham's evidence cleared them of suspicion. To involve themselves afresh would be a singularly stupid move; it would redirect attention their way after they've succeeded in averting it."

"You're examining it from the wrong angle," declared Harper, "and you err on two counts."

"Name them."

"For one, you're assuming that if guilty they will behave like any other Earthborn thugs who've killed a cop. But why should they? The crime doesn't mean the same to them. For all I know to the contrary they thought as little of it as does some thick-headed farmer who sees a strange bird in the woods, points his gun and shoots it. Maybe it was the rarest bird in the world, now made extinct. Does he give a damn?"

"That's pretty good reason why they should not come back to shut up the witness," Jameson pointed out. "They don't care enough to bother."

"It's nothing of the sort. It's an argument against your supposition that Alderson's death should be their primary concern. I reckon they've a worry far bigger."

"Such as what?"

"Fear of being identified too soon. They're not anxious to be recognized as spacemen and never mind the criminal angle. To be spotted as the missing space-crew would start up a transcontinental hunt. At this stage they don't want to be recognized and pursued. They need time to do whatever they've come here to do."

"Since you're so well-informed," commented Jameson, a trifle sardonically, "perhaps you can reveal their purpose in coming."

"God alone knows. But it's a dirty one. Why else should they try do it on the sly? An honest motive warrants an open approach. The skulker in the shadows is up to no good."

"You may be making the very same mistake that you've just tied on to me," said Jameson. "You're weighing them up in human terms. That's not a good way of judging alien purposes, is it?"

Harper sniffed his contempt. "In so far as their actions affect us we must look at them from our own viewpoint. It may well be that they are justifiably rated as the greatest adventurers and biggest patriots in Venusian history. But if their loyal shenanigans are going to cost me a toenail they're a trio of prize stinkers so far as I'm concerned."

"I agree with you there."

"All right. Now that old geezer at the filling station cannot possibly finger them for the murder of Alderson. The most he can do with respect to that is point suspiciously. His evidence wouldn't hang them in a month of Sundays." He leaned forward, gaze intent. "But what he *can* do is exactly what they're trying to get him to do right now. He can look at three pictures, give the nod and start the hunt. There's only one sure way to prevent him and that is by closing his trap for keeps before it's too late."

"That's clear enough reasoning," said Jameson, "but it has one major flaw."

"What is it?"

"All the news channels have publicized details of both the Alderson and Whittingham killings. Everyone from coast to coast knows that you're wanted for the latter and suspected of the former. The three fugitives know that they don't fit in this picture and that, in any event, your witness's description of them would fit a thousand others. There's nothing whatever in the news to suggest the remotest likelihood of a witness being shown photographs dug out of confidential files in Washington. So why should they deduce that possibility?"

"Because I shot down the Whittingham girl."

"I don't understand," confessed Jameson, frowning.

"Look, I've given you the facts as I saw them. They picked up that girl for some reason or other, probably because the opportunity presented itself and they wanted to try their technique. Maybe they're missionaries making converts and pass up no chances on the general principle of the more the merrier. Anyway, they turned her into another of their own kind. She ceased to be Jocelyn Whittingham but continued to masquerade as such. Don't ask me how it was done because I don't know and can't guess."

"Well?"

"The big question now is: were they able to learn and remember that girl's Earth-identity? Or was it something they failed to record either because they viewed it as of no consequence or because it was incomprehensible to them?"

"Go on," Jameson encouraged.

"If they don't know her identity the news of her death will mean nothing to them. It will look just like any other sordid murder and they won't realize they're linked with it in any way. But if they *do* know her identity—"

"For crime's sake, don't keep me in suspense," pleaded Jameson.

"The killing will get them on to their roller-skates and going at top speed. They'll want to know why she was killed. They'll want to know whether she died because a Venusian can be recognized and, if so, how and by whom. They can see with half an eye that real knowledge of their presence will inevitably be linked with that space-expedition and they'll be eager to find out whether there's time to break the linkage by cutting a couple of throats."

"Including yours."

"Yes. I'm the sacrificial goat. The news-channels have shouted my name and address all over the shop and invited them to come and get me—if they can. It won't be a quick death, either. They'll do me in slowly, very slowly."

"What makes you say that?"

"So far as I can guess they've one weapon and one only. But it's a formidable one. They can double as human beings without possibility of detection except by some freak like myself. It's of the greatest importance to them to find out how I did it. Without that knowledge they can't take steps to prevent it happening again. They can't counter a menace without knowing the nature of it. They will have to get the truth out of me in any way it can be done, no matter how bloody and no matter at what risk. Otherwise there's no telling how many more folk can tag them or when the next moment will be their last. Their lives wouldn't be worth living."

"Telepaths aren't ten a penny," Jameson pointed out. "You've said so yourself."

"But *they* don't know that. They're left guessing in circumstances where no guess is too far-fetched. To them, it might well be that every red-haired human can smell them—and there are a deuce of a lot of redheads around. They've *got* to know how it's done."

"You're no carrot-top," said Jameson, "but if someday we find you lying around without your scalp we'll consider it fair evidence of your veracity."

"Thanks," conceded Harper. "You boys have a good time over my body. Enjoy a few hearty laughs while there remains something to snicker about. Won't be long before you'll wish you were me!"

"You know I was only ribbing. I—"

He grabbed the phone before it had time to give a proper whirr, held it to his ear. Harper came to his feet, looking anticipatory.

"Same as before," Jameson told him, replacing the instrument and reaching for his hat. "They want us over at once. We might as well have stayed there in the first place."

"Something has broken," declared Harper as they hustled outside and clambered into the car. "If those pics had proved to be duds they'd have said so, with acid for sauce. They wouldn't drag us ten blocks merely to tell us the check proved a flop. Or would they? After all, it's the taxpayers' gas we're using."

Jameson sat tight-faced and offered no comment.

Chapter 6

There were only two men waiting this time. One had stern, leathery features famous throughout the world: General Conway, tall, gray-haired, distinguished. The other one was Benfield, now decidedly grim.

"So!" rumbled General Conway, fixing Harper with a cold eye. "You are the mind-reader?"

"Putting it that way makes me seem like a vaudeville act," said Harper, far from overawed.

"Quite probably," agreed the general, thinking it wasn't so far removed either. He examined the other carefully from the shoes up, letting his gaze linger longest on a pair of thick and exceedingly hairy wrists. His mental diagnosis was not flattering: it determined the subject to be a powerful and presumably intelligent man who would have the misfortune to look like an ape when in officer's uniform. Too broad, squat and hirsute to fit the part of a captain or colonel.

Harper said informatively, "That's nothing. You ought to see me naked. I resemble a curly rug. Hence the word rugged."

The general stiffened authoritatively. Jameson looked appalled. Benfield was too preoccupied to have any reaction.

"If you know what is in my mind there's little need to speak," declared General Conway, annoyed at the loss of his privacy. "What does it tell you?"

"An awful ruckus has started," replied Harper without hesitation. "And I'm certified sane."

The other nodded. "Your witness has confirmed that the men in that car were the same three who set out for Venus about eighteen months ago. The F.B.I. is following their trail forward and backward and already has found two more witnesses who say the same." He rested on a table-edge, folded his arms, gazed steadily at his listener. "This is a most serious business."

"It'll get worse," Harper promised. "If that is any consolation."

"This is a poor time for levity," reproved the general. "We are treating the matter with the importance it deserves. All forces of law and order in the west are combining in effort to trace that Thunderbug back to its starting-point in the hope that the ship may be located in that area. A forward trace is also being made despite that it's likely to prove futile, the machine having been abandoned by this time."

"Neither the ship nor the car matter very much. It's those three rampaging—"

"We are after those as well," Conway interrupted. "All police, military and ancillary organizations have been or soon will be alerted. Photographs, fingerprint formulae and other necessary information is being distributed as fast as we can produce. The capture is being given top priority, all other criminological investigations to be dropped pending its achievement. Unfortunately, at this stage we cannot warn the public as a whole without creating widespread alarm and consequences that may get out of control."

"Good enough," approved Harper. "So this is where I go out."

"On the contrary, this is where you stay in. We have got you and intend to keep you. There's a war on and you're drafted."

"Then I apply for indeterminate leave forthwith."

"Permission denied," snapped Conway, too concerned even to smile. He walked around the table, sat behind it, let his fingers tap restlessly on its surface. "The air forces are out in full strength scouting for that ship. Every civilian plane that can be mustered is under orders to assist. We have confiscated the bodies of that girl and the trooper, handed them over to scientists for special examination. Everything that can be done has been or soon will be done. The issue of the moment is that of how to deal with you."

"Me?"

"Yes. There are a lot of questions that must be answered. Firstly, have you any explanation of your telepathic power? Can you say how it originated?"

"No."

"It just happened?"

"So far as I can recall I was born that way."

"H'm!" Conway was dissatisfied, went on. "We are making exhaustive search into the backgrounds of your parents and grandparents. If possible, we must discover the reason why you are what you are."

"Personally," remarked Harper, "I couldn't care less about the reason. It has never interested me."

"It interests us. We must determine as soon as we can whether any more of your kind may be hanging around and, if so, in what number. Also whether there is any positive method of finding them and conscripting them until this crisis is over."

"After which they in turn will be treated from the crisis viewpoint," thrust Harper. "And your big problem will be how to put them out of harm's way until such time as they may be needed again."

"Now see here—"

"I know what you're thinking and you cannot conceal it from me. I know that authority is squatting on the horns of a large and sharp-pointed dilemma. A telepath is a menace to those in power but a protection against foes such as we are facing right now. You cannot destroy the menace without thereby depriving yourselves of the protection. You cannot ensure mental privacy except at the prospective price of mental slavery. You're in a first-class jam that doesn't really exist because it's purely imaginary and born of the conditioning of non-telepathic minds."

Conway made no attempt to dispute this vigorous revealing of his thoughts. He sat in silence, his cold attention on Harper, spoke only when he had finished.

"And what makes you say that there is no such quandary?"

"Because all the irrational bigots swarming on this cockeyed world invariably jump to the conclusion that anyone radically different from themselves must be bad. It inflates badly shriveled egos to look at things that way. Every man his own paragon of virtue and goodness." He glowered at General Conway and said with ire, "A telepath has a code of ethics fully as good as anyone else's and perhaps a damn sight better because he has to beat off more temptation. I don't listen unless circumstances make it necessary. I don't hear unless I'm shouted at."

The other was blunt enough to appreciate straight talk. He was openly impressed. Leaning back in his chair he surveyed Harper afresh.

"We've done a deal of checking on you already. You heard Trooper Alderson from a distance of approximately six hundred yards. Without listening, I presume?"

"I heard his death-cry. On the neural band it's as effective as a scream. I couldn't help hearing."

"You have helped nail a number of wanted criminals and it is now obvious how you did it. But you never listen?"

"Guilt yells across the street. Fear bellows like an angry bull."

"Is there *anything* that broadcasts on a level sufficiently muted to escape your attention?"

"Yes—ordinary, everyday, innocent thoughts."

"You do not listen to those?"

"Why on earth should I bother? Do you try to sort out every spoken word from the continual hum of conversation around you in a restaurant? Does a busy telephone operator take time off to absorb the babble going through her switchboard? If I went around trying to pick up everything that's going I'd have qualified for a strait jacket ten years ago. Continual, ceaseless yap can torture a telepath unless he closes his mind to it."

By now Conway was three-quarters convinced. His mind had made considerable readjustment. He resumed his table-tapping, cast an inquiring glance at Benfield and Jameson. They immediately put on the blank expressions of impartial onlookers not qualified to make decisions.

"I understand," continued Conway, "that to date you have not encountered another telepath?"

"No," agreed Harper regretfully.

"But if two of you passed by without listening, neither of you would become aware of the other's existence?"

"I suppose so. But I couldn't swear to it. If we radiate more powerfully than the average human—"

"Yes, but your lack of contact is no proof of your uniqueness? For all we know to the contrary there may be fifty or a hundred telepaths in this very city?"

"I think it most unlikely but wouldn't define it as impossible."

"What is your effective range?" asked Conway.

"About eight hundred yards. It varies from time to time. On rare occasions I have received at three times that distance. Other times it drops to a hundred or less."

"Do you know the cause of such variation? Is it due to the nature of surroundings, blanking by big buildings or anything similar?"

"I could not say for sure, not having subjected the matter to systematic test. Surroundings make no difference and that's all I'm certain about."

"But you have a theory?" Conway pressed.

"Yes," admitted Harper. "I suspect that on any given occasion my range is determined by the amplitude of the other person's radiations. The more powerfully he broadcasts the greater the distance over which I can pick him up. The weaker, the less a distance. As I've said, it would require scientific tests to establish the truth or falsity of that notion."

"Are you willing to undergo such tests?"

"I am not," declared Harper, showing pugnacity.

"Why not?"

"The immediate problem is not that of what to do about telepaths. It's that of what to do about invading Venusians. Nobody is going to use me for a guinea-pig. Go pick on the quarry you're already hunting. They've done plenty and aim to do a lot more. My only crime is that of performing a public service."

"Don't view it in that light, Mr. Harper," Conway soothed. "We appreciate to the full the excellent part you have played. The trouble is that we're not satisfied. We want more of you. We want all you can give. In fact we need it so badly that we demand it as of right."

"What do you require of me?"

"All the information we can get out of you now and perhaps some action later."

"Go ahead. Let no man say Wade Harper was unable to suffer."

Conway signed to Benfield. "Switch on that tape-recorder." He returned his attention to Harper. "This one is of the utmost importance. I want you to answer it with the greatest clarity you can command. What impelled you to shoot Jocelyn Whittingham?"

"That's a tough question," Harper replied. "I cannot translate it in terms you can understand; it's like trying to describe a rose to a man blind from birth."

"Never mind. Do your best."

"All right. It was somewhat like this: you're in your wife's bedroom. You notice a new and pretty jewel-box on her dressing-table. Full of curiosity, you open it. The thing contains a live whip-snake. The snake sees you the same instant. It leaps out. Despite the shock you act fast. You swipe it in mid air, knock it to the floor, crush it under heel. That's how it was."

"I see." Conway stared at him thoughtfully, then asked, "Can't you express it in manner more in keeping with what actually happened?"

"She started up the steps. I knew she might be the girl I was seeking. I made a stab at her mind for the sole purpose of identifying her. The moment I touched I realized what I had touched. At the same moment—"

"*What* did you touch?" inquired Conway.

"Something not human. I cannot describe it more accurately. I planted a tele-pathic hand fairly and squarely on the slimy mental field of a non-human entity. At the same instant it felt my touch. That was additional confirmation if any were needed, because no normal human being can sense a telepathic probe. I realized several things in that split-second. Firstly, she didn't know whence the probe had come. She had no directional sense such as I possess. But she correctly assumed that it came from me because I was in plain sight and already racing toward her."

"She did not *know* it was you?" repeated Conway. "You mean she was in no way telepathic herself?"

"I hadn't any evidence of it. There was only that abnormal sensitivity which, I suppose, has been developed as a defense-mechanism some place else. She did know beyond all doubt that suddenly and without warning a strange and dangerous mind had lifted her mask and seen beneath. She gave out a panicky thought that she must get away, she must warn the others that they're not as well-hidden as they think, that they *can* be exposed."

"A—a—ah!" Conway displayed hopefulness. "So she knew the precise location of these others? She knew how to get into touch with them?"

"If so," said Harper, "her mind did not admit it. Things were moving fast. We were both thunderstruck by the encounter. Her mind was yelling, *'Escape, escape, escape!'* while mine ordered imperatively, *'Stop her, stop, stop . . . kill, kill!'* I shot her down without any compunctions whatsoever. I'd quite forgotten that she was a girl or had been a girl. For the moment she was something else, something that had to be laid good and cold. I gave her the magazine right through the bean. I heard the alien mentality cease sizzling and fade to nothingness. That showed it could die just the same as anybody else."

"Then you went away without making further examination?"

"I did. I went fast. I'd no time for further horsing around. I didn't dare risk being picked up anywhere but here. To tell this story in any police barracks or sheriff's office, where they didn't know the score, would eventually land me in an asylum."

"Couldn't you have saved time, trouble and anxiety by calling us long distance?"

"How far would I have got that way? Some underling would have listened, smirked knowingly and sent police to the booth to pick up a loony. I've had a tough enough job reaching the right people in person. At that I reckon I'm lucky. I hope to make it to the Pearly Gates with less trouble."

None of the listeners relished that remark but were unable to deny the truth of it. A formidable guard of minor officials stood between the high executive and a besieging force of malcontents, theorists, halfwits and world-doomers. Perforce they also held at bay the rare individual with something genuinely worth hearing.

General Conway harrumphed, decided that there were no satisfactory methods of overcoming this difficulty, went on to say, "You have made contact with an alien life-form. So far as we know you're the only one who has done so and remained able and willing to talk about it. Can you add anything that may help us to determine the true nature of the foe?"

"I didn't see it with my own two eyes. Therefore I cannot assist you with an accurate description."

"Quite so. But you must have gained some kind of an impression."

Thinking it over, Harper conceded, "Yes, that's true."

"Let us have it. No matter how vague or fleeting, we need every datum we can get on this subject."

"For no apparent reason I felt that alien ownership of another body is a natural phenomenon. That is to say, I knew more or less instinctively that the thing occupying the body of Jocelyn Whittingham was functionally designed for such a purpose, was perfectly at home and knew how to use what it had gained. The girl was a human being from toes to hair in all respects but one: another and different life-spark had been substituted."

"Which suggests that its nature is wholly parasitic?" asked Conway. "It normally exists in possession of some other life-form?"

"Yes. It's an old hand at that game."

"And that in turn suggests that when it acquires another body it also gains the data within the brain, all the knowledge, the memory and so forth?"

"Undoubtedly. It could not survive without doing so. Otherwise its own incompetence would betray it at once."

Turning his attention to Benfield, the general remarked, "The inevitable deduction is that Venus harbors various life-forms, some of which are the natural prey of a possessive parasite. Also that this parasite is capable of taking over a form higher than any in its own habitat. It can adapt right out of its own environment and, if I may put it that way, it can raise itself by its own bootstraps."

Benfield nodded agreement.

"Also," continued Conway, "it is probably microscopic or germlike. That's my guess. I'll have to leave that angle to others more expert. They'll be able to make shrewder estimates of its characteristics."

"It would help more than somewhat if we could discover how that girl was mastered," Harper pointed out. "Her body might tell the story."

"That is being looked into. We have confiscated her corpse despite violent objections from her relatives."

Harper looked at him, eyes glowing. "Which of them raised the biggest outcry?"

About to add something more, Conway paused, closed his mouth, opened it, registered momentary bafflement.

"Why?"

"We Venusians must stick together."

"You mean—?"

"Yes, I mean what you're now thinking."

Firming his lips, Conway reached for the phone, ordered, "Take the entire Whittingham family into safe keeping at once. No, it is not an arrest. There are no charges. Tell them it's for their own protection. Eh? If their lawyer chips in, refer him directly to me."

"That will do a fat lot of good," remarked Harper. "If one or more of the Whittinghams is no longer of this world you're helping him create a bunch of Venusian cops out west."

"It's a risk we'll have to take."

"Not necessarily. You could put them in animal cages and feed them with long tongs. Anything, anything so long as they can't get near enough to help themselves to their own guards."

"That would be gross violation of their constitutional rights. We could get away with such tactics only by justifying them before the public. To do that we must release information that we wish to preserve, at least for the time being." His eyes questioned Harper as if to say, "What's the answer to that?"

Harper took it up promptly. "Tell them the truth. Tell the Whittinghams that Jocelyn died of a new, malignant and highly contagious disease. They must be isolated until found free from it. The black plague again."

"What, when they know she was shot?"

"*I* had the disease. I was raving mad with it. I touched her, contaminated her. She's lucky to be dead. You've got to give a clean bill of health to whoever handled her afterward. Scare them with a yarn like that. Some clause in the health laws can be finagled to cover their incarceration. No protectors of civil liberties are going to bawl about the freedom of suspected lepers. And the story will be substantially true, won't it?"

"You may have something there." Conway used the phone again, gave instructions, finished, "Consult Professor Holzberger about the technical description of a suitable pretext. What is needed is something strong enough to convince but not strong enough to cause a panic." He ended, said to Harper, "And now what?"

"When there's a chance, let me go out there to look them over. If I find them all clean, give them a mock check-up by some worried-looking medico, then let them go. They'll be too relieved to gripe."

"But if one of them is possessed?"

"I'll smell him at first sniff. He'll know it, too. Keep him at all costs. When the others have gone, pull him apart and see if you can find the pea in his whistle. You could do that without a qualm. So far as humanity is concerned he's already dead. You'll be carving an animated corpse. With luck you might be able to isolate whatever is combing his hair."

Conway frowned. Jameson looked slightly sick. Benfield didn't enjoy it either; he was visualizing his hands shaving himself at another's behest.

"We'll take that up shortly," said Conway. "There is one more cogent point yet to be considered. You say that the instant you recognized the Whittingham girl her immediate thought was of escape?"

"Yes."

"But not to a specific place?"

"No."

"Therefore her impulse to flee was instinctive and no more?"

"Not entirely. She experienced the shock of somebody deprived without warning of a long-established and greatly valued truth, namely, that recognition is impossible. She was confronted with an irrefutable datum contrary to all experience. She felt the dire need to get away from me and tell the others."

"Which others? *Where?*"

"I don't know."

"You know only that *she* didn't know?"

Harper fidgeted around, brooded at the floor. "Frankly, I'm unable to give a satisfactory answer. Possibly she didn't have the remotest notion of where the others might be and in that respect had been made irrational by the crisis. Or she may have known but succeeded in suppressing the knowledge, which I doubt. Or—"

"Or what?"

"She may have possessed some alien sense which enables her kind to contact each other. A sense we haven't got and cannot understand. Something like the homing instinct of pigeons or dogs, but on a species basis."

"But you are convinced that she was not telepathic?"

"Not in the way that I am."

"In some other way, perhaps?"

"Nothing is impossible," said Harper flatly. "It is beyond my power to list the attributes of things native to some place umpteen millions of miles away after a one-second glance. Catch me another dozen. I'll take a longer look and tell you more."

Responding to Conway's gesture, Benfield switched off the tape-recorder.

"Catch you another dozen," echoed Conway. "How the devil are we going to do that? We know of three, and it's not beyond our resources to find and seize them sooner or later. Getting any others who may be around is a different matter. We have nothing to go upon, no details concerning them, no way of identifying them." His gaze came up, leveled on Harper. "Excepting through you. That's why you're drafted. We require your services to test every suspect we can lay hands on."

"So I'm expected to stay put, wait for your lineups, look them over and say yes or no?"

"Exactly. There is no other way."

"There is," Harper contradicted.

"For instance?"

"You could use me for bait."

"Eh?"

"They want my matted corpus as badly as you want theirs. They need to learn what makes me a nuisance fully as much as you need to learn about them. In that respect they have an advantage. You must try to grab an unknown number of unknown pseudo-people. They have to snatch one man whose name, address and car tag number have been shouted all over the country. I'm the most desirable subject for vivisection they ever heard about since their last picnic on Saturn. Give them half a chance and they'll swarm around me drooling. All you need do is step in and pinch everyone holding a scalpel."

Conway breathed heavily and objected, "It's a risk, a grave risk."

"Think I'm tickled pink about it?"

"If anything should go wrong we'll have lost our most effective counter-weapon and be without means to replace it."

"The beauty of that will be," said Harper cheerfully, "that I will no longer care one-tenth of a damn. The dead are splendidly indifferent about who wins a war or gains a world."

"Perhaps not. But we'll still be living."

"That won't concern me either. My great-grandmother doesn't give a hoot about the hole in my sock."

"And *you* may still be living," retorted Conway. "Even though dead."

"I'll be a goner either way," Harper gave back with ghoulish philosophy. "What if some midget alien *is* wearing me like mink?"

He grinned at them, enjoying the repulsion in their minds.

The general was like a chess-player trying to decide whether mate could be ensured by sacrificing his queen. He was far from positive about it but could think up no satisfactory alternative. To his military mind, telepaths were expendable providing the supply of them was unending. Unfortunately they were neither shells nor guns. They could not be manufactured to order. So far as could be determined he had one and only one telepathic weapon in his armory. If that one went there'd be no more.

Even if people with supernormal faculties existed in sufficient number to dispose of this extra-terrestrial menace once and for all, the situation would remain critical. There would come the aftermath. What of them? Could they be trusted to let the world go by? Or would experience of recent events waken them to their own power, tempt them to unite and confiscate the planet? They'd have a good excuse for doing so, an excuse convincing enough to sway the masses: only we could save you last time, only we can save you next time.

Conway was still stewing it over when again his phone called for attention. He took it meditatively, listened, abruptly came to full attention.

"Who? When did this happen? Yes, yes, you'd better." He cradled it, scowled forward.

"Something wrong?" asked Harper.

"You know what's wrong. You must have heard the details being recorded in my mind."

"I wasn't listening. I was full of my own thoughts. I can't make noises at myself and at the same time take note of other people's cerebral trumpetings."

"One of the witnesses is dead; the old man at the filling station."

"Murdered?"

"Yes. It happened a couple of hours ago but they found him only within the last fifteen minutes. Whoever did it has a good head start." Conway cocked an inquiring eye at Jameson. "I don't know what to think of it. You've far more experience in such matters. Do you suppose this may be mere coincidence?"

"How was he killed?" Jameson asked.

"They discovered him lying by his pumps, his skull crushed by a single blow from a heavy instrument. They say it looks as if he filled somebody's tank and was struck down when he tried to collect."

"Any evidence of robbery? Had his pockets been emptied or the cash register cleaned out?"

"No."

"H'm. That doesn't indicate that robbery wasn't the motive," Jameson opined. "The culprits may have been scared off before they could complete the job. Or maybe they were joyriders who slugged him for a free tank of alk, overdid it and made it murder." He pursed his lips while he mused a bit, finished, "These isolated filling stations get more than their fair share of rough stuff and have done for years. I think it's quite likely that this is a genuine coincidence. To treat it as of special significance may cause us to lose time chasing up the wrong alley."

Conway turned attention to Harper. "The police out there feel hamstrung because they're under strict orders to abandon everything in favor of the hunt for missing pilots. Yet one investigation may be part of the other and I don't want it to be temporarily ignored if there is a connection. On the other hand, I'd rather not countermand orders unless such a connection exists. What is your opinion?"

"If Venusians did it to shut the old fellow's trap, they arrived too late. He saw their photos and set the fireworks going before they could stop him. But *they* wouldn't know that."

"You think they did it and therefore this is not a coincidence?"

"No," said Harper carefully. "Jameson has given his viewpoint and I'm trying to consider its opposite. I'm telling you that if those three are aware of the identity of the girl they converted, her death will give them the shakes. Two and two make four on any planet. They'll add up the news, make it the correct total, decide she'd been found out somehow, God knows how."

"And so—?"

"They know a nation-wide hunt will be after them unless they can cover up. Even that will do no more than delay matters, but delay is all they need. If they can postpone capture long enough it will come too late. Many people spotted them in that Thunderbug but only two saw them actually with the girl, took a close look at them at the time. Those were Alderson and the oldster. The former is too dead to study pictures. It would help them some to have the latter in the same condition. That's how they'd look at it. The basic requirements of survival can be seen by any type of mind no matter where it's from."

"Then why were they so slow to get at him?" commented Conway. "They dealt with him three to four hours behind time."

"I killed that girl and came here as fast as I could go and have been hanging around all day. The news didn't break until some time after I'd left. If when they saw the news they had to rush back as far, or perhaps farther, they must have moved as swiftly as they dared. It takes time to cover territory even in these days."

"I suppose so." Doubtfully, Conway shifted gaze to Benfield. "Have you any ideas?"

"Yes, General. I think it best to pursue this matter in the principle of overlooking nothing."

"That's the boy," approved Harper. "With all the troops and police littering this country we should be able to spare a couple of dozen to chase a possibility. The grave loss of manpower won't make us topple any quicker."

Conway did not approve the humor, which smacked to him of unwarranted sarcasm. But it served its purpose of stinging him into immediate action. He handled the phone with the air of being fed up holding it, made his call.

"Williams, about that filling station murder. I want it looked into. Make it quick and thorough. Yes, orders are suspended with respect to this case only. It may be linked with the search. If so, one of the wanted men has been in that area today. Call me and report directly you make progress." He ended, gave a challenging look at the others. "That settles that. There's little more we can do until we make our first capture—and it's to be hoped we get him alive."

"It's also to be hoped that one will lead to the others," put in Benfield.

"And it's further to be hoped that some time before Christmas somebody will make up their mind about accepting or rejecting my offer to dangle on the hook," said Harper.

"Your first job is to check the Whittingham family," Conway shot back. "After that we'll consider what to do with you next."

"Then let's go." Harper waved a familiar good-bye to General Conway, performing it in the manner of a rookie too raw to know better. Conway involuntarily bristled at him, a fact he found most pleasing.

"There's no sense in going out of your way to irritate the old boy," reproved Jameson when they had exited and reached the car. "He has troubles enough."

"I was reasserting the freedom of the individual at the moment when it's likeliest to become disputed," snapped Harper. "And furthermore, a cat may look at a king. That holds good though the heavens fall."

Jameson did not choose to argue the point.

Back at headquarters Jameson said, "The sooner you get out there and do your stuff, the better. We'll send you by plane or copter. Sit down and wait—I'll find out what can be done."

"You can restore my good character while you're at it," Harper suggested. "Cancel that call for me. I don't like it even if it is being ignored. Priority of pilot-search won't prevent some sharp-eyed cuss grabbing me if he notices me right under his nose."

"We'll tend to that eventually. Meanwhile I'll send a couple of agents with you, to be on the safe side."

"Think I can't look after myself?"

"It's Conway's order."

"Oh, all right." As the other went through the door, Harper called, "And I want my gun back. It's my property, isn't it?"

Jameson returned in two minutes, tossed him the weapon and a large brown envelope. "Study that while I get things moving—all planes are busy and you'll have to use a copter." He departed again.

Tucking the gun under his left arm, Harper extracted the envelope's flap, slid out three full-plate glossy photographs. Each had a typed slip of data attached to its back. He examined them closely.

The first was of William Gould, twenty-eight, test-pilot-in-chief, a frank-faced, blond-haired, husky individual who weighed one-eighty pounds and had a half-moon scar on the left brow. The thinner, dark-haired face smiling from the second picture was that of Cory McDonald, twenty-four, test-pilot and computer, a wiry type of one-fifty-five pounds, no identifying marks on body. Picture number three showed the thoughtful, serious features of Earl James Langley, twenty-seven, test-pilot and astronavigator, dark-haired, one-sixty-two pounds, small mole on right thigh, white scars on both kneecaps.

"Gould, McDonald and Langley," recited Harper to himself as he shuffled the photos to and fro and memorized the faces. "Gould, McDonald and Langley. Three good boys who went away full of hope and came back full of hell. God rest their souls!"

He felt vengeful as he looked at them. Didn't seem right that humanity's outward growth should be paid for by such as these. The salt of the earth thrown away for Earth's sake. And the payment they had made was not in full. They had given their lives. When their own kind found them and destroyed them they would also have given their bodies. Payment would then be complete.

Not for one moment did he doubt that should he come face to face with one of these three he would shoot him down like a rabid dog, as unhesitatingly as he had shot Jocelyn Whittingham. It was easier for him than for others to perform such cold-blooded execution; mentally he could *see* the terrible emptiness of the human shell and the thing squirming within.

Three fine young men.

Three rotten apples.

"Damn!" he said loudly. "Damn!"

"What are you cussing over?" inquired Jameson, coming through the door.

"Somebody's sons—and what's been done to them."

"Don't bother your head about them. We've a bigger worry, namely, that of what they're doing to others."

"I know. But it's in my nature to deplore the deplorable." He returned the photographs to the envelope, handed it over. "If I can have copies will you see they're put in my car? They're too large to fold into my pocket."

"We're printing thousands of smaller ones, wallet-size. You'll get a set in due course." Jameson gazed expectantly toward the door. Two men entered. They were young, lean, well-dressed, had an air of quiet competence. Jameson introduced them. "Meet Dan Morris and Bill Rausch. Try getting away from them."

"These are the escort?"

"Yes."

"Hope I won't bore you, boys," said Harper. "Are we ready to go?"

"Right away," Jameson informed. "An army copter is on the roof."

Accompanied by the two silent agents, Harper rode an elevator to its limit, gained the waiting machine, which proved to be a big thirty-seater with port and starboard rotors.

Engines whined into the high note, rotors spun into circles of light. The copter made one small bounce then soared rapidly. At five thousand feet the tail jet spurted flame and sped them westward.

Three and a half hours later they landed in the ornate grounds of a state isolation hospital. An agent met them as they stepped to ground, identified himself as Vern Pritchard.

"You're holding the Whittinghams here?" Harper asked.

"Yes. There are five in the family. They swallowed our story of possible contagion and came without protest. They fear they may be incubating something and can hardly wait to find out."

"None of them have tried to escape?"

"No," said Pritchard.

"Or communicate with somebody at a distance?"

"No."

"Whereabouts are they?"

Pritchard pointed. "In that annex over there."

Gazing meditatively at the place indicated, which was about four hundred yards away, Harper said after a while, "They're okay. You can let them go."

Incredulity came into Pritchard's features as he protested, "But you haven't *seen* them!"

"I don't need to."

"Well, my orders are to be governed entirely by what you say. I take it that you do know what you're saying?"

"I do. I say they're clean. You can release them."

"All right." Hopelessly baffled, Pritchard covered himself against a possible blunder by saying to his fellow agents, "You two are witnesses to this."

They signified agreement, followed Harper back into the copter as Pritchard walked toward the annex. The copter rose, started the return trip.

"Thank the Lord not everyone knows what's wrong with me," remarked Harper, thereby stimulating companion minds into revealing channels.

Mental reactions showed that they didn't know either. Jameson had told them no more than was strictly necessary. The powers-that-be were trying to hide two menaces from the public, not just one.

Authority was trying to conceal a human pryer as well as an inhuman enslaver. The idea was to use the former to destroy the latter—and then decide the fate of the former.

Chapter 7

Moira stood like one paralyzed when he marched surlily into the office, planted himself behind his desk and commenced rummaging through delayed correspondence.

After a while he glanced up and growled, "Well, what's eating you? Have I turned into a purple opprobrium around here?"

"No, Mr. Harper." She sat down weakly, still looking at him wide-eyed. Her ears were perked for sound of oncoming sirens while she wondered how to duck the resulting fracas.

"Don't let your mouth hang open that way. It makes you resemble a half-starved carp. Where's the Pest Control progress-report? They're bellyaching already."

She flew to a cabinet, jerked open a drawer, riffled its cards, extracted one and gave it to him. Her mind was whirly with the belief that she was alone with public enemy number one and somebody ought to do something about it.

"Mr. Riley has been around several times," she informed, making it sound like a warning and hoping he'd take the hint. "He said he'd call again today."

"He would, the big ugly bum." He studied the card, his expression sour. "Umph! When I say six weeks I mean six weeks and not six days. Dear sirs, in reply to your query of yesterday's date—"

Grabbing her pencil, she scribbled with frantic haste. He spouted another forty words, knew she was making a hopeless mess of her script. He ceased dictating, spoke with a judicious mixture of sorrow and severity.

"See here, Lanky, I am not a convicted criminal. During my absence I have disemboweled none save the few hundred who deserved it. I am not wanted by cops, wardens, army recruiters or the Christian ministry. I am loved only as I have been loved since days of yore. Now pull yourself together and apply your mind to the job. Dear sirs, in reply to your query—"

This time she managed to take it down without error. She slipped paper into her machine, adjusted it, paused expectantly as heavy footsteps approached the office door.

"Here he is," announced Harper, with mock tenseness. "Dive under the desk when the shooting starts."

Moira sat frozen, one finger poised over a key. She dared not look round lest what she saw proved him to be deadly serious. She listened for the faint rustle of clothes indicating that he was drawing his gun.

Next moment Riley bashed open the door in his usual elephantine manner, took the usual two steps to reach the desk. If his scowl had forced his eyebrows an inch lower they'd have served as a mustache. He splayed both hands on the desk while he leaned across it to stare into the other's eyes. Behind him, Moira felt faint with relief, gave the key a tentative tap.

"Now," said Riley hoarsely, "you're going to tell me what the flaming hell is happening right and left. Why are you wanted for murder one moment and not wanted the next? Why do they list you at top one day and remove you from the bottom another day? Why can't they make up their minds whether you're a hirsute hoodlum or not?"

"Life is just a bowl of cherries. I—"

"Shut up! I haven't finished yet. Why has the F.B.I. emigrated wholesale into this area and calmly confiscated my four best squads? Why have they staked this crummy joint from the roof, the cellars, across the street, up the street, down the street, at both ends of the street and in half a dozen adjoining streets? Why—"

"Why do you turn Moira into a nervous wreck the minute my back is turned?" Harper demanded.

"Me?" Riley fumed a bit. "I never touched her. I'm not that kind. I'm married and happy at it. If she told you I touched her she's a liar. I don't believe she did tell you. You're inventing things in effort to change the subject. But it won't work, see? Why—"

"You looked at her and *thought* things," asserted Harper.

Riley crimsoned and bawled, "All right. I get it. You refuse to talk. You know I can't make you talk. And you're enjoying the situation. It gratifies your simian ego." He let his voice drop a couple of decibels, went on, "Would your lordship grant me the favor of one question? Just one little question, eh?"

"You may voice it," said Harper, trying to be lordly.

"To whom must I go to get the answers?"

"General Conway."

"Jumping Jehoshaphat!" ejaculated Riley. He hitched his pants lest they fall down. "Is it *that* important?"

"Unfortunately, yes. And if they haven't seen fit to give you the details I mustn't do so either. If I told you all I'd usurp authority, and I'm given to understand it's a dreadful thing to usurp authority. It's the unforgivable sin. It breeds anarchy with all its attending features of godlessness, promiscuousness and every form of untaxable naughtiness. Compile your own list—you know more about the wicked." He reached for another letter from the waiting pile. "Close the door gently as you go out. The glass won't hold under more than another two of your assaults."

"I could assault somebody right now," Riley informed, showing big teeth. "Two burglaries, one hold-up and one case of arson last night. I'm supposed to dismiss them with a light laugh. I'm supposed to concentrate exclusively on looking for three guys named McDonald, Langley and Gould, and do it while robbed of four prowl cars. Nothing else matters but finding a trio of toughies against whom no criminal charge has been entered."

"Nothing else matters," Harper agreed.

Riley leaned closer and whispered, "Be a pal and tell me—what have they done?"

"Ask Conway."

"Thanks for nothing." Riley rattled the glass as he departed.

"Director of Research, Swain Laboratories, Trenton, N.J.," Harper recited while Moira snatched at her pencil. "In response to your inquiry for slow-motion pneumatic micromanipulators suitable for use with type-Z electron microscopes, we have pleasure in quoting for our—" He glanced at the door which had opened. "Well?"

Agent Norris said, "We heard the conversation through the mike. What's that police officer to you?"

"A friend. He thinks he's entitled to my confidence." He sniffed, rubbed his nose, added, "I think so too."

"Why do you say that?"

"I know him of old. He's to be trusted."

"Make note of Harper's friends and intimates," droned Norris's mind, repeating orders in mistaken secrecy. *"They are to be thoroughly checked."* Vocally, he informed, "We let him through to you, being who he is. But we were wondering why he should come out with such peremptory demands for an explanation. What is good enough for the Commissioner ought to be plenty good enough for him, shouldn't it?"

"He's in a privileged position so far as I'm concerned."

"Are you sure he did not have an ulterior motive in cross-examining you?"

"I did not look to see. I don't peer into everybody's nut, regardless. Besides, I'm busy trying to rescue myself from imminent bankruptcy. What motive could he have?"

"You can guess as well as anyone else—except that you don't have to guess," said Norris. "In a situation such as this it's wise to suspect everyone, including your own mother."

He went out, joined Rausch in the machine-shop. Harper continued with his mail. When lunch-time arrived and Moira had gone out to eat, Harper summoned

Norris to the office.

"Moira is a nice girl. She tops me by three inches because I've pulled both her legs so often that they've stretched. But we get along all right."

"What's this to me?" Norris asked.

"I wouldn't like her to get hurt if she was around when a hatchet-man broke in. She's another worm on the same hook and I'm not paying her for taking those risks."

"You're the one who's supposed to warn us of an attack," Norris pointed out. "Without you we're working blind."

"I know. But I'm not holding her hand twenty-four hours per day. Do you suppose it might be best to get rid of her for a while? How about me sending her on paid leave until this affair is over?"

"No. You can play your part only by sticking to normal routine. Make enough changes and a trap starts looking like a trap."

"They might jump her outside, hoping to use her to get at me. It wouldn't work, thank God. I'd know what was coming before it got here. Yet I'd hate to turn the guns on her because she'd ceased to be Moira any more. What's done can't be undone. I'd like to prevent the doing in the first place."

"She must take her chances the same as everybody else," said Norris impassively. "It's no worse for one than for another."

"It is worse," Harper contradicted, "because one's more likely to be picked on than another. I'd be happier if she had a guard, day and night."

"She has. We tied a couple of men on to her at the start. Same applies to your other employees. We've covered all your regular contacts as well. If anyone tries the tactic of approaching you in familiar form they're going to have a hard time finding one suitable and fancy free."

"I could find one any minute," Harper declared.

Norris jerked an eyebrow. "Somebody not under continual observation?"

"Yes."

"Then it's your duty to tell me."

"An agent," said Harper. "Any agent. Who is watching the watchers?"

"That problem is beyond solution. Our men are working in pairs already. We could group them in threes, fours, tens or twenties and find it not enough. The line has to be drawn somewhere between the desirable and the performable. They're operating in pairs, and that makes it impossible for one man to be taken by himself."

"So they must be confiscated two at a time?"

"If that can be done."

"The enemy can do anything that human beings can do. For all I know to the contrary they can also do one or two things that we can't."

"We'll see about that," promised Norris.

The fourth successive day of ordinary, uneventful business routine found Harper bored with playing bait for fish that apparently had ceased to exist. His chosen role didn't seem such a bright idea after all. Perhaps he had based it on a grossly exaggerated sense of his own importance. Perhaps Venusian plans already had developed far enough to remove fear of premature detection. Perhaps they'd become sufficiently well established no longer to care a damn for Harper or any of his ilk.

Meanwhile he had become fed up with being followed wherever he went, finding G-men lounging at every street corner, occupying nearby tables in restaurants, standing beside him in comfort stations, breathing down his neck at the theater, mooching outside his bedroom night-times. The price of human liberty was to sacrifice his own.

Monotony was broken and faith in his purpose restored when he arrived at the office early, spread the morning paper across his desk and found a news item tucked away at bottom of a column inside.

Savannah, GA. A brief but bloody gun-battle took place near here at midnight when F.B.I. agents raided the Rankovic farm. Two men were killed, four taken into custody. Two more are believed to have escaped. Declining to reveal the purpose of the raid, Area Director Stephen Maddox states that the F.B.I. acted upon direct orders from Washington.

It was a most unusual report in several respects. For one, it had been played down. For another, the precise location was not stated and no names were mentioned other than that of Maddox. Lastly, this fight had occurred when all forces of law and order were engaged in one task and one only. Obviously, therefore, the incident had some bearing on the main issue.

This was confirmed ten minutes later when Jameson phoned long distance. "Seen the news?"

"I've just been reading it."

"It should have been on the dawn radiocast but we kept it off. We're having a heck of a time persuading news services to minimize such items. Naturally they want to know why and we can't tell them."

"What happened?" asked Harper, watching the other's face in the visiscreen.

"I can't say too much even on an officially cleared line. In brief, one of our men picked up Langley's trail, followed it to the Rankovic farm. Langley must have moved out during the short lapse of time between our man's report and the raid. Anyway, we didn't get him. The fox had bolted, leaving the hole still warm."

"More's the pity."

"Two are dead. Their bodies are being shipped out for examination," Jameson went on. "Of the four we captured three emphatically deny that they took any active part in the battle. They say they merely happened to be in the house when the shooting started and took cover until it ended. We've given them the paraffin test and the result is negative."

"What about the fourth?"

"He's brother of one of the casualties. Says he was in bed, woke up when the ruckus started. Pulled on his pants and ran downstairs, joined his brother and another guy in slinging slugs out the windows. He swears that none of them knew they were firing upon the law."

"Sounds plausible," commented Harper.

"He gave up when tear-gas got him. By that time the other two were going cold. All four captives recognize Langley's picture, know nothing about him except that he'd been rooming there a couple of days and left at ten-forty or not much more than an hour before the raid."

"Almost seems as if he'd been tipped off."

"He couldn't possibly have been. He was just plain lucky. Anyhow, I've not called merely to tell you the story. There's more to it than that. When we made the raid we surrounded the place, knocked and demanded entry. Somebody fired back through the door. Therefore, although Langley wasn't present, it made little difference—the house still concealed someone anxious not to be grabbed. What does that suggest to you?"

"Langley had made himself a pal."

"Yes, and he may have made himself more than one. Some fellow named Waggoner pulled out same time as Langley. We know nothing about him except that he and Langley are teamed up. We have a good description and, of course, the search is continuing for both."

"You learned nothing about the other two?" Harper asked.

"McDonald and Gould? No, not in that locality. They appear to have split up. They're trying to make it harder for us by keeping apart." He paused while the screen showed him to be consulting a document below the level of the distant scanner. "I want these four captives put to the test without delay. They may not be what they appear to be."

"Want me to come there?"

"No. It would spoil that set-up at your end. We're flying the four to you. Give them the penetrating eye and say whether they are or they aren't."

"I'll do that."

"Thanks a lot. There's something else too. So far nobody has taken a bite at your buttocks. As you said yourself, it all depends on whether they knew the identity of that girl and whether or not the filling station murder was a coincidence. To date we have no evidence to show that they actually know they're being sought or that they know we have learned of the ship's return. So it's—"

"Has the ship been found yet?" interjected Harper.

"Not a sign of it. It couldn't have been destroyed beyond recognition; a professional breaking-up yard with gas-cutters and furnaces would take a month to get rid of that mass of metal. Latest theory is that it's concealed somewhere in sub-Arctic wastes or has been dumped in the ocean. The latter seems the more likely. In that case the crew must have got ashore by using their rubber raft. We're raking the coasts in effort to discover it."

"Well, it's an idea. What were you saying about nobody biting me?"

"I was pointing out that up to last night they may not have known for sure that the hunt is already in full cry. But the newspaper yap specifically mentioning the Rankovic farm could be a giveaway if Langley reads it. We tried to persuade the press to leave it alone or at least suppress the name of the farm. For our pains we got a bleat about freedom of speech and liberty of publication. There's now a fair chance that the fugitives are no longer basking in a sense of false security. They may look into the question of what ended it and belatedly trace the cause to you. You'd do well to be extra-wary from now on."

"I'll tell Norris," said Harper. "He's my nursemaid."

"There's no need to. If he isn't actually listening-in he'll soon be informed by somebody who is listening. All your calls are being monitored."

"Solely as a measure of protection?" inquired Harper.

"Yes," said Jameson, without hesitation. He cut off. The visiscreen clouded, went blank.

"Lousy liar!" Harper glowered at the wall. "They are more bothered about my big ears than my whole skin."

The suspected quartet arrived a few minutes before the office was due to close. Norris lined them up in the machine-shop where they stood manacled together, staring around, openly puzzled by their presence in such a place as this. Half a dozen agents shared their company and watched them narrow-eyed.

Norris went into the office and said, "They're here. How about it?"

"No luck," Harper told him. "They are normal enough to be downright dull."

"Okay." He went out, came back. "I've had three of them taken away. Jameson wants your report on the remaining guy. He admits taking part in the shooting, claims that he didn't realize what he was doing. Is he telling the truth?"

Shoving aside the papers with which he'd been dealing. Harper appeared to lay back while he pondered the question. He listened, picked up a worry that nagged like toothache but failed to provide an answer. So he probed, drove the mind in the other room away from its present anxiety and on to the recent cause.

"It's true enough. He got a scare that sent him into a panic."

"That's all we want to know."

Harper watched him depart, sighed deeply, slid the papers into a drawer and looked at his watch. It was time to call it a day.

At three o'clock the following afternoon the elusive foe put in its first appearance. Harper was taking it easy just then, his chair tilted on its back legs, his feet on the rim of the desk, his mind wide open as idly he watched Moira sorting invoices.

His mental faculty had two distinct methods of functioning which he liked to symbolize as radio and radar. When he was playing at radio he merely listened and put up with whatever programs were being broadcast in the vicinity. If he switched to radar he transmitted a pulse of his own which stimulated some other mind into producing a required response.

When he listened he took pot luck, accepted what was being offered whether informative or not, and ninety-nine times out of a hundred it was stuff not worthy of a moment's attention. But when he probed he got what he wanted by nudging the other mind into thinking of it. So far as ordinary human beings were concerned it made not the slightest difference which method he adopted because they were blissfully unconscious of both.

With a Venusian mind it wasn't the same; that had been his first lesson learned when he contacted the entity owning the Whittingham girl. In some subtle way

the Venusians differed. He could listen to one, radio-fashion, without it realizing that it was being overheard. But if, radar-like, he prodded one to compel
release of a wanted datum, it felt the prod and took immediate alarm.

Telepathic power had its limitations. None knew that better than he did. Even
with normal humans it became frequently necessary to conceal probing under a
cloak of speech, to hold conversations spiced with leading questions that would
stimulate desired responses. The alternative was to pick up a useless mess of stuff
cerebrated at the others' whims.

To deal with a Venusian mind was not as easy. It became doubly difficult when
squatting in the middle of an ambush. He could listen in the hope that the prey
would betray its own coming but had to be extremely careful about administering
a mental jab. To probe too early might result in the other's escape with the news
that one or more minds could detect things hidden from a million eyes. To probe
too late might bring about a last minute struggle and the death of something they
wanted to catch alive.

Right now he was slowly and rhythmically rocking the chair and straining its
hind legs which gave forth protesting squeaks. Over the last few days he had not
listened continuously. It was impossible to do that and give attention to other
matters. Besides, there was no need to do so. It was sufficient for his mind to
make a two-seconds sweep around the neighborhood every couple of minutes,
much like a lighthouse beam circling across dark and stormy seas.

He rocked and made his umpteen hundredth or thousandth sweep, ceased pun-
ishing the chair, sat erect. Moira glanced at him expectantly, saw that his attention
was not on her, resumed her sorting. He listened again to something far away,
maybe a thousand yards or more, half-hidden in the general hubbub. It drew nearer,
slowly but steadily, at a rate corresponding with walking pace. It was an inhuman
mind gaggling like an angry gander.

"Norris!" he yelled.

Moira gave a jerk, dropped a bunch of papers, scrabbled for them on the floor.
The door whisked open and the agent looked in. "What's the matter?"

"I think this is it."

"You mean—?"

"It's coming on two feet. No car. On the sidewalk taking a stroll."

"Stay where you are!" ordered Norris. He bolted from sight.

Going to the window, Harper looked on to the road ten feet below. He opened
the casement, leaned out to get a better view. That this made him an excellent
target did not worry him in the least; there was no point in them coming after
him except to learn his technique—and secrets cannot be extracted from the dead.

If there was one pedestrian in sight there must have been a thousand. The mind
he sought had to be among that cluster on the left-hand side of the road between
four and five hundred yards to the north. His directional sense assured him of that
much but it could not detach one individual from a distant bunch of nondescripts.

Still leaning out and watching, he waited for the weird mind to draw closer.
Three hundred yards, two hundred, one fifty. By now he had narrowed the possibility down to three people; a smart housewife tripping along perkily; a plump

and prosperous-looking business man in his early forties; a lanky, lantern-jawed individual who slunk along close to the wall.

Behind him, Norris reappeared and said, "All set. Now can you—?"

Ignoring him, Harper made a vicious mental stab along the receiving-line. The result came back in a split second: intense shock, wild alarm, frantic desire to escape and bear warning elsewhere.

The housewife kept going without faltering or changing pace. The lanky slinker maintained gait and manner. The plump man stopped in his tracks, glared wildly around, swung on one heel and hurried back whence he had come. He moved at a rapid walk, about as fast as he could go without attracting unwelcome attention.

Harper jumped out the window. He heard a gasp from Norris, an exclamation from Moira before he landed heavily. His gun was already in his right fist as he regained balance and plunged forward in the wake of the escapee.

Something in the expressions of passers-by told the quarry that things had begun to happen behind him and now was the time to hustle. He did not bother to look backward for confirmation. Lifting arms to sides he broke into a headlong run. For one of his portly build he showed a remarkable turn of speed.

A bewildered clerk carrying a large box danced in front of the charging Harper who snarled, "Out of my way, Stupid!" then brushed him aside and pounded on. Back of him someone was shouting indistinguishable words in authoritative tones. On the corner six hundred yards ahead someone else blew a shrill whistle. A police car siren started wailing. Two agents stepped out of a doorway ahead of the fugitive, weapons in hands, and bawled an order to halt. Two more came racing down the opposite side of the road.

The plump man wasn't finished yet. Taking as little notice of the guns as one would of peashooters, he dived through the main door of an office building. Harper went in five seconds later, red-faced and breathing hard. Two agents followed close upon his heels. A car squealed into the curb, unloaded four more.

One of a bank of self-operated elevators was going up fast, taking the fugitive with it. Stopping at its folding gate, Harper scowled upward, watched the other's feet disappear from sight. One pair of agents raced up nearby stairs. Two more jumped into an adjoining elevator and boosted it skyward.

Putting the muzzle of his weapon to the gate's lock, Harper fired, busted it, hauled the gate open and halted the elevator at third floor level. He had hoped to get the quarry stuck between floors but the apparatus proved to be of automatic-leveling type and responded to sudden loss of power by letting its box sink into adjustment.

Listening to the minds above he detected the fugitive's break-out on the third floor, the nearness to him of the agents on the stairs, and knew what was going to happen before he could prevent it.

He galloped up the stairs with sweat beading his brow. He had covered the first flight and half the second, taking steps three at a time, when overhead there sounded a terrific blast, a tinkle of falling glass, a brief pause followed by a hammering burst of explosions. His speed upped itself another twenty per cent while his lungs heaved.

While taking the turn from second to third he heard the yowl of an alien spark becoming extinguished in a useless body, also the wild, despairing cry of something more human on its way out. He slowed, mounting the remaining stairs at normal pace, sadly knowing that he was too late.

The third floor corridor was a shambles. Three agents stood in a little group looking over the scene. One was holding a heavy riot-gun still warm in the muzzle. Another was mopping blood that dripped steadily from his left ear. The third was gazing gloomily at the body of a fourth sprawled near the top of the stairs, crimson splotches on chest and face.

Ten yards from the elevator lay the corpse of the plump man. He was not a pleasant sight. The riot-gun had tried to cut him in half and nearly succeeded. Glass from two broken doors and shattered ceiling lights lay in glittering shards along with flakes of paint and fragments of plaster. One or two scared faces began peeking furtively from doorways farther along. The plump man showed them his ample backside and lay content to bleed.

Chapter 8

The man with the dripping ear bent over the agent supine by the stairs, slid a hand under his vest, felt around and rasped, "He's dead." He stood up, patted a crimson-spotted handkerchief to the side of his head. "If he hadn't beaten me to the top he mightn't have got it. And if I hadn't been four steps lower I'd have got it all over and right through."

"We soared past him in that other box," explained the one with the riot-gun to Harper. "When he stopped so suddenly we overshot him and had to back down. It was just then that he got out and tossed an egg at the other pair. A splinter went right through the floor and between my feet. We jerked open the gate, saw him running down there and gave him a burst before he could throw any more."

A horde came charging up the stairs, Norris and Rausch in the lead. Loud murmurings came from the street far below. Harper realized that he was still gripping his gun, tucked it away.

Norris glanced around, thinned his lips, examined the agent lying by the stairs. "He looks gone to me. Rush him down to the ambulance, just in case." He turned to the others. "What happened?"

They told him, finishing, "Fat lot of chance we had of taking him alive."

One of the onlookers opened a penknife, picked at the wall, dug out a ragged piece of metal. He studied it closely and said, "Army grenade by the looks of it." He gave the fragment to Norris. "What do you think?"

"Yes, you may be right. We'll have to start checking the armories. Frisk him and let's see what else he's got."

They made thorough search of the plump man's clothes. No more weapons, not even a vest-pocket gun. The grenade was all he had carried in the way of lethal objects. He had an expensive watch, a diamond stickpin and a well-filled wallet. His clothes were of top quality and his hand-made shoes had cost him plenty. It was pretty obvious that instead of walking down the street he could well have afforded to come along in a private copter and dump himself on Harper's roof.

They laid him flat on his back, revealing a double-chinned and amiable face closely shaven and well cared for. Even now his features wore the expression of one who would not harm a fly—unless it tried to make off with the stickpin. His hands were clean and soft with pink, almond-shaped nails expertly manicured.

Apart from the watch, pin, wallet and two fine linen handkerchiefs he hadn't another thing in his pockets. That was singular: not a driving permit, business card or identity card; no pen, cigarette case, lighter or bunch of keys. His clothes were devoid of a tailor's label; his shoes bore no maker's mark other than that indicating the size. There wasn't a thing by means of which he could be identified quickly.

"More delay," remarked Norris, with bitterness. "It's going to use up valuable time finding out who he is." Again he pawed through the wallet and still found nothing but money, of which there was a sizeable wad. "We must nail him down before we can start the job of tracing all his contacts. He must have been in touch sometime and somewhere—otherwise he wouldn't have run off the rails." He became momentarily hopeful. "I don't suppose *you* can tell us anything about him?"

"Sorry," said Harper, genuinely regretful. It was beyond his power to dig data out of a dead brain. Although he had not had a chance to put it to the test he suspected that a probe might not have forced self-identification from the plump man's living brain. A Venusian involuntarily identifies himself as a Venusian and not as the entity he has usurped. That was the cause of all the trouble, the reason why one exceptional man could recognize them.

"We'll have to do the best we can and do it quickly, too." Norris handed the wallet to an agent. "Make a list of those numbers and have them circulated to the banks fifty miles around. See if anyone has them recorded as paid out and, if so, to whom."

Rausch had opened the watch and examined its insides. He snapped it shut, gave it to another of his men. "This ought to tell us something. It's one of those new-fangled jobs drawing power from variations in barometric pressure. There shouldn't be a million of them around considering what they cost. Find the local distributor. He'll have the movement number on his books and be able to say where it went. Follow it through until you learn who bought it."

The agent took the watch, hastened downstairs.

Studying the stickpin, Rausch said to Norris, "It's a poorer bet but we'll have to take it." He beckoned another agent. "Show it to the leading jewelers. Phone us at once if you trace a sale."

"If his prints are on record we'll know him in a few hours' time," commented Norris, inwardly doubting that they were recorded. "We'll roll a copy and let

Washington have a look. Let's hope they've got him on their files. Somebody had better tote those shoes around town. Any good shoeshop should be able to tell us who makes jobs like those."

"May I see them?" asked Harper. He took them, turned them over and over, doubled them toe to heel and felt their softness and pliability. He handed them back. "Made to measure for him."

Norris nodded, let go a yell of, "Where's the cameraman?"

That worthy appeared, his apparatus dangling from one shoulder. He glanced at the corpse with the professional air of one who had yet to see a stiff with a new shape, size, expression or attitude.

"Tidy his pan and make him look sweet," Norris ordered. "I want a good head and shoulders stereo study to put through the pane. Some gawker might recognize him mooning out of the screen. Give me the pic just as soon as you can have it ready." He turned to Harper. "That's all we can do for the moment. We'll escort you back to your office."

Harper rubbed his chin, looked hesitant, said, "I'm so overawed by surrounding talent that I'm reluctant to offer a suggestion."

"Let's have it," urged Norris.

"You don't mind me amateuring right under your nose?"

"Of course not."

"Well, then," said Harper, "how many grown men go round without even a solitary key in their pockets?"

"That's right. He hasn't a key of any sort. I think he stripped himself of anything he thought likely to give us a lead but he made a sloppy job of it. Or maybe he knew that if anything happened to him it would be enough for him to cause a little delay."

"I also noticed that his right shoe is worn in the center of the sole," Harper went on. "More worn than is the left shoe." He paused thoughtfully, continued, "And he has the general appearance of a man who had enjoyed prosperity for many years. If he's ever been without a thick wad it was a long, long time ago. Yet he *walked* down the street."

"What are you getting at?"

"Fatty has a car and uses it. His type almost invariably goes in for a big, powerful car the size of an ocean liner. But he didn't employ it this time. Why? Answer: for reasons best known to himself he parked it some place and did the rest on foot. But he did not leave it locked, otherwise he'd have the keys. Why didn't he lock it? Because somebody's sitting in it waiting for him, with the missing keys dangling from the instrument-board. Is that someone still sitting and waiting? Answer: unless he has parked near enough to have seen or heard the ruckus he'll be blissfully ignorant of it."

"Let's go down to the cruiser and put out a radio call. I have enough prowlers to rake the whole area and—"

"Now, now!" Harper chided. "More space, less heed. There are hundreds of parked cars standing around and dozens have people sitting in them. Unless Fatty's playmate happens to be Langley, McDonald or Gould how are you going to spot him?"

"He *may* be one of those three," said Norris, bursting to start the search. "Probably that's why this dead boy walked part of the way. None of those three would risk exhibiting himself near your place in case it was well-covered and he was recognized. He would have to squat out of sight and let a stooge do his dirty work."

"All right. Then I suggest you have all cars search for Langley and company, paying special attention to parked jobs with waiting occupants. If the accomplice is not one of those three then he's Mr. Anonymous and your men are out of luck. They wouldn't be able to tell him from Joe Soap even if he were cavorting in his naked pelt."

"But *you* could identify him?"

"Providing I manage to get near enough. You'd better take me on a personal tour of all the parking places within, say, half an hour's walk. Within two miles radius. Fatty wasn't running merely for exercise. He scooted in hope of losing himself a short while until he could make a fast getaway. Ten to one that means he had a car stalled some place."

"I think you may be right," agreed Norris. "Let's go!"

They piled into one of the several cruisers now lined up outside the building. Norris took the wheel, Rausch sat by his side, Harper slumped in the back with another agent. About to start, Norris was struck with a thought, looked over his shoulder at the agent in rear.

"We don't know this area too well. You'd better get out and make room for a local cop who can show us around."

"I can direct you to all the likeliest places," said Harper. "Get going. Take the second turn on the right."

At once they moved off, made the turn, reached a park holding some two hundred cars. The machines stood in neat rows like a parade of hardback beetles. Seven had people sitting inside or lounging near by. Harper made a mental dig at each, picked up no vicious reactions.

"Turn left," he ordered. "There are a couple of small dumps on that road and a big one about a mile up on our nearside."

They trundled along at moderate pace while examining all machines *en route*. Nothing was seen to arouse suspicion and no alarm was sprung.

A mile farther on they reached an underground hiding-place holding more than a thousand cars. Rolling down one of the half-dozen wide entrance-ramps they entered a brightly lit cavern in which concrete pillars soared at intervals from a mass of silent vehicles. An attendant came toward them, his curiosity aroused by sight of a police prowler. Norris dropped his window and stuck a head out to speak.

"Quick!" yelped Harper, sitting up and staring ahead. "There he goes—out the middle exit!"

Norris jumped the car forward, narrowly escaped knocking down the attendant. The car roared along the mainway between packed ranks of its fellows. Overhead lights flashed by faster and faster, receded into the rear distance. Supporting pillars zipped past with enough speed to make them resemble a paled fence. The car's hood lifted as they hit the exit ramp. The last light fled by, they shot into daylight and the street.

From the left Harper could still pick up the rapidly fading gobble-gobble-gobble of an agitated brain intent on escaping with what it had learned, namely, that gobblings can be heard.

The siren commenced wailing as they spun off the ramp and started down the middle of the broad street. Traffic scattered, fled to the sides and left a clear road far along which a big black car was hurtling as if driven by a maniac. Holding grimly to the wheel, Norris pressed the accelerator to the floorboard. Rausch felt around under a panel, took out a handmike, held it near to his mouth.

"Black Roadking escaping southward on Bailey Avenue. All cars in region of Bailey Avenue South, Greer Avenue South and Mason Turnpike intercept black Roadking."

"If this loaded heap catches a Roadking it'll be a miracle," Harper observed.

They took no notice. The agent beside him leaned over, tugged a gun from a pocket, held it on his knees.

"Car Forty-One making for Bailey Avenue South," said an impassive cop, speaking out of the instrument board.

Harper squinted ahead, decided they'd lost a couple of hundred yards in less than a mile. He held on as they rocked around a halted bus.

"Car Eleven on Mason," announced another voice.

"Car Four on Mason at Perkins Corner," said a third.

The fleeing Roadking, now visibly diminished by its increased lead, made a sudden swerve as if about to dive up a side road, but at the last moment swerved back, cut the corner and continued down Bailey.

A moment later the reason became evident when a cruiser rocked out of the side road, set after it in hot pursuit. The newcomer was about half-way between Harper's car and the Roadking, made better pace because of its lesser load but still could not gain an inch on the excessively high-powered fugitive.

"What did I tell you?" griped Harper. "Fat men with fat wallets buy fat engines that guzzle a gallon of alk to the mile." He sniffed in disgust, added by way of comfort, "You can't bust his balloons either. Those Roadkings run on sorbo-centered solids."

"Car Twenty-eight at junction of Mason and Bailey."

"That's the spot," gritted Norris. "They'll stop him."

"They'll have to crash him and it'll be a hell of a wallop by the way he's going," said Rausch, holding his mike to one side as he gazed anxiously ahead. "There's no safe way to halt him unless we follow until—"

Taking advantage of the other's preoccupation, Harper leaned forward and bawled into the conveniently held mike, "No half measures! Shoot the bastard!"

"Hey, you!" Rausch snatched the mike away, turned his head to throw a scowl.

In that instant the listening Car Twenty-eight opened fire. The cruiser ahead of Harper's car promptly swung in to the curb, crawled cautiously forward and gave full view of the second cruiser parked half a mile farther along.

The Roadking whizzed hell for leather past Car Twenty-eight, covered a hundred and fifty yards, yawed wildly twice, made a violent turn that took it over the sidewalk and into a shopfront. The sound of the crash was like an explosion. Haberdashery sprayed outward. An inflated shirt tried to soar across the avenue on flapping arms. Two police officers scrambled out of Car Twenty-eight, raced toward the wreckage.

"That's done it," growled Norris, easing pressure on the pedal and reducing pace. He snapped over his shoulder at Harper, "Who's running this show?"

"I am. And if you didn't know it before you know it now."

"Our orders are—"

"To blue blazes with your orders," said Harper toughly. "I appreciate your cooperation and sometime or other you're going to appreciate mine."

He opened the door as the car stopped, got out, made for the Roadking knowing in advance that yet again an alien spark had become extinguished within a broken body. But at least no normal human being had been killed—that was one consolation.

In the rear of the shopfront a busted show-robot sprawled over the Roadking's hood and leered inanely at the dead driver. The robot wore a tartan hat tilted drunkenly over one eye and the force of the impact had filled its pants with broken parts. The driver sat bowed forward, his face rammed into the wheel, a pair of lurid socks complete with pricetag draped across his neck.

Two police officers waded through smashed glass, torn handkerchiefs and tattered pajamas, dragged at the car's door. They knocked display-stands out of the way the better to get at it.

Harper was about to join them when a slender individual pranced out of the shop, picked on him with much gesturing of white hands and indignant fluttering of long eyelashes.

"Look at that!" shrilly insisted this apparition. "Just *look* at it! What am I going to do *now?*"

"I could make a suggestion," said Harper, surveying him. "But I don't care to be suggestive."

"This is too bad," insisted the other. "Simply too *too* bad. Somebody will have to pay for it. Somebody—"

"Sue the stiff in the car," Harper told him. "He did it." Joining the police, he helped lug out the body.

The protestor shifted attention to Norris who was following close upon Harper's heels. "Only last night I dressed that window. It's really *sickening*. It makes me so mad I could *spit*. I don't know what—" He broke off and his large eyes went next size larger as they saw the corpse being carried past and laid on the sidewalk. "Why, Mr. Baum!"

"You know this porker?" demanded Norris swiftly.

"Yes, indeed. He's Mr. Baum. Mr. Philip Baum. Only last week I sold him a most fetching line in—"

Staring down at the plump and slightly familiar features, Harper interjected, "Has he a brother?"

"Yes," said the slender man, working his eyelashes and gazing fascinatedly at the dead face. "Mr. Ambrose Baum. A little older. Three or four years, perhaps. Isn't this *awful?* Mr. Baum! My window! Just *look* at it! It makes my stomach turn right over!"

"Where do the Baums live?" asked Norris.

"In Reevesboro. I'd—" He stopped, let his mouth hang open while he looked with horror at the shattered show-robot which slowly slid down from the hood and on to its knees, belched loudly, emitted a whirr and two clicks then went cross-eyed. He shuddered at the sight. "Alexander is ruined, completely *ruined.* I'd like to know who's going to compensate for all this."

"Pick on your insurance company," said Norris. "Where in Reevesboro is the Baum house?"

"Somewhere on Pinewalk Avenue, I believe. I can't recall the number. It should be in the phone book."

"Bring out your phone book and let's have a look at it."

"There's no need," put in one of the police officers, searching the body. He straightened up, holding a card. "He's carrying identification. It says he is Philip Kalman Baum of 408 Pinewalk Avenue, Reevesboro. The car is registered in name of Ambrose Baum of same address."

The other officer added, "This one is deader than a mackerel. His chest is shoved right in. The wheel did it."

Norris turned to the agent who had accompanied them from the beginning. "You take charge here. You know how to handle it. Tell the pressmen nothing. Let 'em yawp—and refer them to our field office." He beckoned to Harper. "We need you along."

Entering the cruiser the three hustled away from the scene around which pedestrians had gathered in a murmuring semicircle.

"We may want more help than we've got," remarked Norris, driving at high speed. "You'd better cancel that Roadking call and see who's still on the turnpike. Tell them to follow us into Reevesboro."

Rausch found the mike, sent out the message and a voice came back saying, "Car Four on Mason Turnpike at Perkins Corner."

"Pick us up and tail us to Reevesboro," Rausch ordered.

They reached the big twelve-track artery, gained top pace. A green Thunderbug was running ahead of them. They overhauled it slowly, passed, moved ahead. The Thunderbug was being driven by a matronly blonde. Harper stared at her thoughtfully, picked his teeth and said nothing. He was tired of feeling around inside green Thunderbugs.

After four miles a prowl-car shot off the verge and raced behind them. Another six miles and they side-tracked from the turnpike, ran into Reevesboro, found the address they were seeking. It was a small but attractive house standing in a half-acre plot.

Driving a short distance past, Norris stopped, signaled the following car to close up behind. He got out, went to the other car in which were two police and two agents.

He said to the police, "You fellows stay here in case some escapee takes a fancy to an official auto." Then to the agents, "You two get around to the back of that house. If anyone beats it that way as we go in through the front, he's your meat."

"You're wasting time," advised Harper, near enough to the house to know that nothing alien lurked within.

"I'm the judge of that," Norris retorted. He waited for the two agents to make their way round the back, then started toward the front door. "Come on!"

A gray-haired, motherly woman answered the bell. She was in her late fifties or early sixties, had toil-worn hands and meek features.

"This is the Baum house," said Norris, making it a statement rather than a question.

"That's right," she agreed. "But Mr. Philip and Mr. Ambrose aren't here just now. I don't know when they'll be back."

"They'll never be back," Norris told her.

Her wrinkled hand went to her mouth while she gazed at him in thoroughly startled manner. "Has . . . something happened?"

"Unfortunately, yes. Are you a relative?"

"I'm Mrs. Clague, their housekeeper," she informed a little dazedly. "Are they—?"

"Any relatives living here?" interrupted Norris.

"Oh, no. They're confirmed bachelors and have nobody related to them near by. In this house there's only the maid and myself." She swallowed hard. "Are they hurt?—badly?"

"They're dead. We're law officers. We'd like to have a look around."

"Dead?" She whispered it as she stepped backward and let Norris enter with Harper and Rausch following. Her mind had some difficulty in grasping the full import of the news. "Not *both* of them surely?"

"Both, Mrs. Clague. I'm sorry." Norris extracted three photographs from his wallet, showed them to her. "Do you recognize any of these men?"

She blew her nose, wiped her eyes, studied the pictures bemusedly. "No, I don't."

"Sure you haven't seen any of them recently?"

"I'm positive."

"Where's this maid you mentioned?"

"In the kitchen. Do you wish to speak with her?"

"Yes."

She called, "Winnie! Winnie!"

Winnie slouched in, a plump, ungainly girl with the placid eyes of a ruminating cow.

"Know these?" demanded Norris.

She ogled the photographs. "No, sir."

"If any of them had visited recently would you or Mrs. Clague have been sure to have seen them?"

"Uhu. I guess so."

The housekeeper put in, "Mr. Ambrose and Mr. Philip seldom had visitors. They used this house only for relaxation and sleep. And they kept late hours. Two or three o'clock in the morning they'd come home sometimes. But always sober, I'll say that for them. I—"

"What did they do for a living?" Norris asked.

"They have three jewelry shops somewhere or other. And a small wholesale ware-house in town. Their father started the business, I believe. He's been gone a good many years. They were two nice gentlemen and it's terrible to think they're—"

Norris cut the garrulity with an impatient gesture. "We want to look over any papers they've left lying around. Where did they keep their correspondence?"

"All their business files will be at the office," said Mrs. Clague. "But their personal letters will be in that desk or perhaps upstairs in their rooms."

"All right, Mrs. Clague. We're sorry to trouble you but these things happen. If you're not too busy how about fixing some coffee?"

Still somewhat bewildered, she agreed, retreated to the kitchen as if glad to escape their questions. Winnie slopped along behind her, turned twice to look back with a bovine smile before she too disappeared. Norris frowned after her.

"What was that slut smirking at?" he asked.

"You," Harper informed. "She's about I.Q. 70 but that doesn't spoil her appetite for a tasty hunk of man. It's what comes of being a handsome Fed."

"Nuts!" growled Norris, looking sour. He spoke to Rausch. "We've no time for search-warrant formalities and by the looks of it there's nobody around to bawl about the matter. I'll rake through this desk. You give the bedrooms a going-over. When we've finished we'll run into town and frisk the office. We must compile a list of all contacts they've made these last few weeks."

Rausch tramped upstairs, Norris spent five minutes trying to open the desk, failed, called in one of the two agents stationed at back.

"Finagle this lock for me, Yensen."

Examining it, Yensen went out to the garage, returned with a length of wire. "Another Roadking is stashed in there. Same model and one number higher. They must have bought them together." He fiddled with the wire, turned the lock, rolled up the lid which automatically released the drawers.

Avidly Norris pounced on the contents, pulling documents from pigeon-holes, scanning them rapidly, putting them aside. He lugged out the drawers one by one, found a dull black gun concealed in a camera carton, handed it to Yensen.

"Hang on to that. The ballistics boys may be able to dig some data out of it."

After a while he finished reading the last of a bunch of letters, shoved them back, grunted discontentedly. "Go ask Mrs. Clague when the Baums were last here."

Yensen departed, came back. "She says they had breakfast this morning."

"That's peculiar." He turned to Harper. "All this stuff is chitchat, mostly from friends in the trade. It averages a letter a day. But there's nothing filed for the last five days. If the average was maintained there are five letters missing."

"They may be at the office," Harper suggested. "Or—"

"Or what?"

"Maybe they destroyed them on receipt."

"Why should they do that?"

"Because the messages were devoid of interest, they having become alien to the readers."

"We'll check at their office before we jump to any conclusions," Norris decided. "Either they kept them or they didn't."

"If a search elsewhere fails to produce them we can bet on two things," said Harper. "Firstly, that the Baums were taken over about five days ago. Secondly, that the enemy is no longer so desperate to get established in number and is starting to be choosy."

"How d'you make that out?"

"The Baums have been in daily contact with Mrs. Clague and Winnie. We know that much. But neither of the women were touched. They've been left alone despite that they're easy prey. They've lived with the Devil but retained their souls. Aren't they the luckiest people?"

"You give me the creeps," Norris complained. He turned to Yensen. "Make a list of names and addresses from this correspondence and bring it to H.Q. We'll have to follow up every one of them."

Rausch reappeared saying, "Nothing of any significance up there except a couple of telephone numbers scribbled on a pad by the phone in Ambrose's room."

"We'll look into those later." Norris had a final, dissatisfied glance around, saw nothing of fresh interest. "If the fate of the Baums isn't yet known to those we're seeking you can see what's likely to happen. Somebody's going to come along wanting to know how the brothers made out. If all of us go to their office there will be nobody here to make a grab. We'll have to stake this place until the news gets out and warns off possible visitors."

"I'll stay with Yensen," Rausch volunteered. "If anybody—"

Something went *whirr-whirr* above.

"The phone!" yelped Norris.

He charged upstairs, taking steps two at a time. The others crowded behind him. Entering Ambrose's room he eyed its bedside phone warily.

"Notice any other telephone here?"

They shook their heads.

"Too bad. No chance of holding the caller while we trace him." Extracting his pocket handkerchief he draped it over the tiny scanner then lifted the earpiece. The small visiscreen at once lit up but revealed no picture. That meant a similarly obscured scanner at the other end. "Hello!" he said.

"Var silvin, Wend?" demanded a voice bearing the sharpness of deep suspicion.

"Baum residence," said Norris, frowning. "Can I help you?"

Click! The line went dead. Norris rattled the instrument, raised the operator, identified himself. "Where did that call originate? Let me know quickly—it's urgent!" He hung on for most of a minute, listened again, snorted, racked the phone and told the others, "The Baum warehouse. Evidently they had a rendezvous there with somebody who got worried and called after they'd failed to turn up. We missed a trick by not finding out the place and going there first."

"Get along right now," urged Rausch. "I'll stay with Yensen, just in case."

Norris nodded, signed to Harper and they hastened to the car. Ordering one of the waiting police to join them, he drove away at top pace.

"You might as well take it easy," advised Harper, with unconcealed pessimism. "There'll be nobody at the place. Whoever hangs up on a call isn't going to sit around."

"That's what I think," agreed Norris, maintaining speed. "But if we fail to catch somebody it won't be for lack of trying." He used a hand to indicate the microphone under the dashboard. "Put out a call. Any cars near the warehouse to go there at once. Detain anyone found on the premises."

Harper did as told. Two voices answered, said they'd be there within a couple of minutes.

"A couple of minutes too late," he commented, replacing the mike.

Chapter 9

The warehouse proved to be an ancient but solid redbrick building with six heavily barred and shuttered windows and a cumbersome steel door. It had the appearance of property once designed to hold merchandise regarded as a chronic temptation to the backward neighborhood. Two cars were lined up outside and three police were standing defeatedly near by.

"We've three men waiting around the back," one of them told Norris. "The place is locked. Nobody answers the bell. No sounds inside. Looks like it's empty."

"Then we'll break through the door."

It took some time to do that but they managed without overmuch damage. Not a soul lurked within. The first floor held a number of flat glass showcases exhibiting costume jewelry arrayed on black velvet. The floor above was littered with light crates and cardboard cartons, some full, some empty. A small office of clapboard and plastiglass stood in a corner.

Entering the office, Norris moved carefully around, said to one of the police, "Fetch the fingerprint man. Given enough luck we may be able to discover who was waiting here." To Harper he added, "It takes a professional criminal to wipe a place clean of prints—and the characters we're after don't fall into that category."

He went to the desk, slid out its drawers. The contents were not enlighten-ing, mostly billheads, invoices and other business items. A metal filing cabinet proved no more informative.

"Tell you one thing," remarked Harper, sniffing the air. "The Baums and their associates seem fond of cold-cure."

"What makes you say that?" asked Norris.

"Ambrose had a faint odor. So did Philip. And I can smell it again here."

Norris twitched his nostrils a couple of times. "Your sense of smell must be a great deal sharper than mine."

"People vary that way. So do dogs. I can detect it all right. And I know what it is."

"What is it?"

"Eucalyptus."

"Well, that's mighty useful," commented Norris sardonically. "Now all we need do is track down somebody stinking of eucalyptus."

"You could do worse," Harper opined. "Three smellers in a row, and in one day, means something. Like tobacco. If I'm in a deep forest and smell burning tobacco I know a man is somewhere near."

"So—?"

"Maybe somebody *likes* eucalyptus."

"You come up with the damnedest ideas," said Norris.

"They've got to come from somewhere if we're going to make any progress at all." Harper shoved hands deep in pockets, gazed moodily around. "Anyway, why shouldn't certain people have a craving for the stuff? Koala bears dote on it, so I'm told."

"They eat the leaves," Norris informed. "Besides, we're not trying to cope with koala bears. We're in pursuit of things with bigger teeth and claws."

"So what? Even tigers have fads."

Norris frowned at him, reached for the telephone, handling it delicately so as not to spoil any latent prints. He dialed, spoke to someone.

"This is no more than a wild guess but you'd better note it: check all suspects for an odor of eucalyptus." He racked the instrument, admitted, "It would sound silly to me if this entire business wasn't so crazy."

"Not being a full-time Sherlock," said Harper, "I tend to miss things that are obvious to you but spot others that you may overlook. For instance, what's the scientific conclusion to be drawn from a liking for eucalyptus?"

"I don't know."

"That elsewhere the natural prey is vegetarian and feeds on aromatic shrubs, its favorite food being something akin to eucalyptus. So here the host feels a need born of centuries of conditioning. In other words, they've found a local drug that reminds them of home, sweet home."

"What the devil are you talking about?"

"Sorry, I forgot you've been told only part of the story," said Harper. "You've got to know the whole of it to guess the way I'm guessing."

"Eucalyptus isn't a drug," declared Norris, baffled.

"Not to us, it isn't. God knows what it is to some other guppies."

"Look, did you sniff the stuff when you shot that girl?"

"No, I didn't go near enough or hang around long enough. Her case being the first, I was in a jam, had to get out fast, had no time or inclination to look for what I suspect only now."

"Humph!" Norris thought a bit, resorted to the phone again, called the Baum house, spoke to Rausch. "We're out of luck here. The bird had flown." He listened to some comment from the other end, then continued, "Harper smells eucalyptus, says the Baums smelled of it too. I didn't notice it. Did you?"

Rausch said, "Yes. But I thought nothing of it."

Cutting off, Norris observed, "I should have my nasal passages irrigated."

"This is important," Harper pointed out. "Ambrose and Philip carried the odor. Whoever was here reeked of it. Maybe they stumbled across the stuff with the same glee as a bunch of hopheads discovering a field of Mexican hemp. If so, they'll pass the news one to another."

"Well?"

"The habit will hand humanity a small advantage. If you can't tell what's going on in a suspect's mind you can at least smell his breath." He thought again, added, "By 'you' I mean the forces of law and order in general. *You* couldn't smell an overheated goat under your own bed."

"Thanks for the criticism," grunted Norris. He lapsed into silence as the fingerprint man arrived and set about his business. The newcomer raised prints all over the place, most of them undoubtedly being those of the Baum brothers. When he had finished, Norris ordered, "Get them checked as quickly as possible and let me know the results." He turned to Harper. "Momentarily we're stalled. Let's get back to your office."

"And put the worm on the hook once more, eh?"

Norris glanced at his wrist-watch. "I don't think so. It's a bit too late to expect further action there. You'll be just in time to lock up and go home. If anyone else comes after your blood before tomorrow it's likeliest to be while you're in bed."

"That idea makes for peaceful sleep."

"Don't worry. You're well guarded around the clock."

"I know. Too well for my liking. By the looks of it I'm going to have official company for the rest of my natural life."

"Oh, I wouldn't say that," opined Norris. "This rigmarole is only for the duration of the emergency."

"So it is alleged," Harper grumbled. "But higher up are a few authoritative coots who resent the unalterable facts of life. They're not above replacing one emergency with another so long as it suits their power-game to do so."

He got into the car, sat alongside Norris and returned to the office in silence. He was grouchily aware that when the present crisis ended—if ever it were ended—he would then have the problem of how to get authority off his neck and for keeps.

It wasn't going to be easy.

Morning brought news. Norris poked a head into the office, beckoned him away from Moira's hearing.

"Things are beginning to break," he announced. "Firstly, there were two calls to the Baum house during the night. The caller hung up immediately Rausch answered. Both calls emanated from public booths. That means the Baums' contact man is still in town someplace."

"Assuming there's only one of them," said Harper. "For all we know, there may be a dozen."

"Perhaps. Anyway, we got identifiable prints out of that warehouse office. They are McDonald's."

"Ah! So *he* was waiting there?"

Norris nodded. "We missed him by minutes. Further, we've found that he was with the Baums in an hotel one evening. He left with them in Ambrose's car and hasn't been seen since. Two waiters and a barkeep have identified his picture."

"When did he pick them up?"

"Six days ago."

"Just the time we estimated," Harper remarked.

"We're searching the locality for him right now," Norris continued. "If he's still here today we'll find him."

"That may prove more difficult than you expect."

"Why?"

"He doesn't have to stay at an hotel or rooming house. So you'll gain little making the rounds of those. He doesn't have to rent a flat. He doesn't have to sleep out in the open."

"Then what does he do?"

"He lives in a private house, as one of the family—having *made* himself one of the family." Harper eyed him skeptically. "How are you going to search several thousand private homes?"

"We won't try. There are quicker ways of picking up leads."

"How?"

"Every street has its gossip, its incurable snoop. We have enough photos of McDonald to check with every busybody for miles around. What's more, he can't operate while sitting in a back room behind drawn curtains. He has to emerge sometime. If it was he who called Rausch, he went outside his hole-up to do it. He took a risk and was mighty lucky not to be recognized."

"How about sounding the drugstores for abnormal sales of eucalyptus?"

"We've thought of that. Four agents are on the job."

The phone shrilled in the office. Moira picked it up, called to them, "It's for Mr. Norris or Mr. Rausch."

Norris went inside, listened for a while, came back and said to Harper, "That was Jameson."

"Anything new?"

"Yes. Langley's dead."

"So they caught up with him?"

"He was spotted in a stolen car at dawn. Two men were with him, Waggoner and a fellow now known to be a certain Joe Scaife. They ran up against a roadblock, abandoned the car and took to the woods. Police, agents and national guardsmen dived in after them. Jameson says they put up such a desperate fight it proved impossible to take them alive. Langley and Scaife were shot dead. Waggoner used his last bullet on himself. That was about an hour ago. Their big problem now is what to tell the newshawks."

"This looks bad to me," Harper admitted.

"Bad isn't the word for it," said Norris seriously. "Waggoner's deed speaks for itself. If these reactions are any criterion we're up against a crazy crowd who'd far rather be killed than caught."

"The Baums behaved the same way," Harper reminded. "The death-before-dis-honor touch."

"It's inhuman."

"Of course it is! Get it into your head that we are fighting against mentalities with standards far different from yours and mine. To them, capture may seem a fate considerably worse than death. If so, it wouldn't be enough for us to try to win a battle. More is needed. We must also prevent a last-minute suicide to get one of them alive."

"Our orders are to take them alive at all costs."

"Easier said than done."

"Well, you're supposed to be an ace in the pack," Norris pointed out. "How would you go about it if you happened to find one of them, McDonald for in-stance?"

Harper mulled the problem, then said, "The all-important thing would be not to let him realize or suspect that he'd been tagged. I don't see anything else for it but to sit around in patience and wait a chance to knock him unconscious or pin him down before he could make a move."

"That comes well from the man who got Ambrose Baum on the run."

"I had to make him react to find out who was which. Up to that point there was no telling with such a crowd in the road. We knew nothing about him until then. McDonald's different. We do know what he looks like. We don't have to kick his breeches to make him betray himself. His face is sufficient giveaway."

"True enough."

"If it comes to that," Harper went on, "and I could organize things my own way—which unfortunately I can't—I would not try to take McDonald alive or dead. I'd let him run free."

"Why?"

"So that he could lead me to others."

"He wouldn't play sucker for long," Norris scoffed. "If you think you could exploit him for months, you're mistaken."

"For what reason?"

"Because it's no darned use him leading you to others unless you profit by it. Therefore you'd have to grab them sooner or later. And directly his contacts start disappearing he'll take alarm, scoot out of sight or blow his head off." Sniffing his disdain of amateur tactics, he finished, "If we can capture him unscratched and intact he'll do all the leading we require and whether he likes it or not. We'll see to that!"

"Have it your own way." Harper returned to his office, saying, "I'm going to carry on with business, otherwise it will never get done." He squatted behind his desk, spent half an hour considering a large blueprint, then gave ten minutes to the long letter that had come with it. "All right, Moira, wet your pencil and be careful with the big words. I—"

Norris looked in and commanded, "Put your hat on. You're wanted again."

"Oh, not now, surely?" growled Harper. "I've important work to do."

"You bet you have," agreed Norris. "But you can't do it there. Hoist your buttocks and come along."

Throwing him an ugly look, Harper said to Moira, "Much more of this and you can have the business as a gift, you being the only one left to cope with it unchivvied."

"Hurry up!" urged Norris. "Never mind the gripes."

Harper did as bidden, went out, followed him down to the car, clambered in.

"They think they know where McDonald has hidden himself," Norris explained.

After a brief run the car halted at one end of a long, tree-lined road sided by tidy bungalows. No other official cruisers were in sight as Norris pointed through the windshield and spoke.

"It's a pink-washed house half-way down on the left. The boys are keeping clear of it so as not to raise an alarm. We'll roll casually past. Take a look as we go by and tell me what you think."

He shifted into gear and let the car move forward at modest pace. They trundled by the pink house which had a close-clipped lawn in front, a locked garage at one side. Nobody could be seen about the place, nobody maintaining a lookout from a window. Reaching the end of the road, Norris parked by the curb.

"What's the verdict?"

"Nothing doing."

Norris registered acute disappointment. "Are you sure of that?"

"We'll circle around and try again if you're not satisfied."

They circled.

"Nothing doing," repeated Harper. "For all I can tell the house is empty." He glanced at the other. "How did you get a line on this address?"

"One of our agents went the rounds of the taxi companies on the theory that if it was McDonald who made those calls to the Baum house he did not walk to or from the booths. The agent found a driver who recognized McDonald's picture, claimed to have picked him up after midnight and run him to this place."

"After which McDonald walked around the corner and made for wherever his sanctuary really is," Harper suggested.

"The driver saw him use a key and go in. That's likely enough. After all, McDonald isn't a hardened crook, wise in the ways of the underworld. He would be naive enough not to think of a taxi-trace."

"That's so. Anyway, all I can tell you is that he isn't there at this moment. Maybe he's in my office making preparations for my return. Moira wouldn't like that. Let's go back."

"Bide your time," Norris ordered. "Your correspondence can wait. It'll have to wait. It'll wait a hell of a while when you're dead, won't it?"

"I'll worry none at that stage. I don't have to eat when down the hole."

Taking no notice, Norris pondered a moment, decided, "I'll take a chance on setting off the alarm." Turning the car round, he drove to the house standing next to the pink one. A middle-aged woman was at the door watching him. He beckoned to her and she crossed her lawn, examined him with beady-eyed curiosity. "Can you tell me who lives next door?" he asked, pointing.

"Mr. and Mrs. Reed," she informed.

"Nobody else?"

"No. They have no family. They're not the kind who would, I reckon." She thought again, added, "They've a nephew staying with them just now. He's from someplace out west, so I've heard."

"Would this be the nephew?" inquired Norris, showing her McDonald's photograph.

"Yes. Only he looks a bit older than that."

Norris took in a deep breath. "How long has he been rooming there?"

"About a week." She reconsidered, went on, "Yes, I first saw him last Thursday." Her sharp eyes studied his plain clothes, had a look at the car. Her mind showed her to be impressed by Norris's official tones. "Are you police?"

"If we were we'd have said so," Norris evaded. "We just want to make sure of the Reeds' address."

"That's their house all right," she confirmed. "But you won't find anyone in. They took their car out this morning and haven't come back."

"About what time did they leave?"

"Eight o'clock. And they were in a real hurry, I can tell you that."

"Don't happen to know where they've gone, do you?" put Norris, with faint hope.

"Oh, no. They said nothing to me, and I didn't ask. I mind my own affairs and leave other people to mind theirs."

"Quite proper of you," said Norris. "I suppose there's nothing for it but to come back later when they're in."

"Heaven knows when that will be," she volunteered. "They took a lot of luggage with them. It gave me the idea that they were going for quite a piece. Not that it's any business of mine, of course. But sometimes one just can't help noticing things."

Norris considered this evidence of her ability to mind her own affairs, then asked, "Have they any friends locally who might put us in touch with them?"

"Not that I know of," she answered. "Those Reeds aren't overly sociable and became even less so after that nephew arrived. In fact if you ask me, they've been downright surly these last few days. Wouldn't speak unless spoken to and then said no more than they could help. Acted as if I were a complete stranger to them, me who's lived next door for twelve years. It made me wonder what on earth had come over them. That nephew had something to do with it, I'm sure."

Harper put in, "Who told you that he was their nephew?"

"Mrs. Reed," she informed. "I said to her, 'Who's the young man?' and she gave me a sharp look and snapped, 'Just a nephew.' You'd have thought I'd asked her for the loan of a hundred dollars from the way she spoke. Naturally I didn't mention him again. I know when to keep my mouth shut."

"Thanks for the information," said Norris. He got the car going while she remained on the lawn and showed deep disappointment at giving so much and learning so little.

"If that female minds her own business," remarked Harper as they rounded the end corner, "how much might we get out of someone who doesn't?"

Norris grunted and offered no comment.

"What do you propose to do about McDonald?" Harper pursued. "Are you going to stake this place as thoroughly as you've staked mine?"

"It has been watched continually since nine o'clock, but evidently we started an hour too late. And although you saw no sign of the fact, it's still under observation." He weaved the car through traffic, went on, "First thing is to get the tag-number of the Reed car from the vehicle registration bureau and put out a general call for it. The second step is to have that house searched on some pretext or other. The third is to find how and where McDonald picked up the Reeds and, more importantly, whether he's had contact with anyone else beside the Reeds and the Baums. Lastly, I want to know how he's managed to smuggle himself out of this area seeing that all routes are sealed."

"Maybe he isn't out of the area. Maybe he is hidden somewhere nearby."

"We'll soon learn." He drove another mile, asked, "Well, what are you thinking about?"

"Langley's dead. McDonald's not too far away and now being sought."

"What of it?"

"Strange that there's not been a whisper about the third fellow, Gould."

"No, there hasn't," Norris admitted. "He appears to have vanished into thin air. That proves nothing except that luck runs better with some than with others."

"If it is luck."

"What do you mean?"

"It doesn't have to be luck. Perhaps he is the cleverest of the three, a really crafty character. If so, he is also the most dangerous."

"He'll fall over his own feet eventually," Norris assured. "They always do!"

"I've been the subject of a nationwide hunt myself," Harper pointed out. "Admittedly it wasn't so urgent and intensive. But I had to jump around plenty to stay free. I know what it means to be on the run, which is more than you do, always having been the chaser and never the chased. The man who can disappear like Gould is good. He's too good for comfort."

"That won't save him forever."

"We haven't got forever. Time is running short. Every day, every hour counts against us." He shoved open the door as they halted at their destination. "You know only as much as they've seen fit to tell you. I'll tell you something more."

"What's that?"

"If progress proves too slow for success, if we're compelled to face defeat, you'll have another bird's egg in your mental nest before the new year. You'll be really cuckoo in a new and novel sense of the term. Just like everyone else. At least you'll be in the fashion—when it's the latest thing to be one of the walking dead!"

Chapter 10

Business was stalled yet again first thing the next morning, and before he had time even to look through the mail. He arrived at the office, having been tailed by his escort all the way from home, removed his hat and made ready to sling it on to a hook.

"Don't let go," advised Norris. "Haul it back and stick it on your head. You're departing right away."

"Where to?"

"I don't know. They haven't seen fit to confide in me." That was true enough. Norris's mind held no more information than that an official car had arrived to take Harper some place else, that he would be away the full day and that the guard was commanded to maintain its watch on the plant during his absence.

Harper did not argue the matter this time. Reluctantly he was becoming resigned to the situation. Replacing the hat, he went outside, entered the car in which sat only a driver.

As they moved off a second machine bearing four men followed close behind. Harper waved a satirical goodbye to Norris, who was standing on the sidewalk trying to puzzle out the reason for this peremptory removal of the bait from the trap. Around the corner a third car suddenly pulled out from the curb and took the lead. This one also held a hard-looking quartet.

"Quite a cavalcade," Harper remarked. "Somebody is according me the importance I've long deserved."

The driver made no response, concentrated solely on following the car ahead. He was a beetle-browed individual of the type that doesn't know the meaning of fear—or any other words. To the rear the third vehicle kept a careful twenty yards distant.

"A hundred dollars if you step on it and lose the entire bunch."

No reply. Not so much as a smile.

Giving it up, Harper slumped in his seat, half-closed his eyes while his mind felt around like invisible fingers. His own driver, he found, knew nothing except that he must keep on the tail of the leading machine, be prepared for trouble and on no account face it if he could run out of it.

The fingers explored farther.

Those in the leading car knew where the procession was heading. And from that moment, so did Harper. He mulled the new-found knowledge a minute or two, dismissed the purpose as something he would learn in due course, gazed idly through the door-glass at passing shops and pedestrians. With habit born of the last few days he made a mental sweep of the neighborhood every now and again.

They had passed through two sets of traffic lights and over a dozen cross-streets when alien impulses reached him, weak with distance but discernible. Something high up that side-road, six, eight or maybe ten hundred yards away.

Something that flashed pseudo-human thoughts in spasms with gigglings and gobblings between.

He sat up red-faced and snapped, "Quick! Turn up there."

Beetle-brows firmed his thick lips, gave a warning toot on his horn and speeded up. Two faces peered through the rear window of the car ahead which likewise increased its pace. They whizzed across the road without turning and continued straight on.

"You're too slow to keep up with your own boots," commented Harper, sharp-eyed and still listening. "Take this next turn. Make it fast. We can buzz round the block and get him before he fades out."

The car plunged on. It ignored the turn and the next and the next. The faraway squirming mind thinned into nothingness and was lost.

"You bladderhead!" swore Harper. "You've missed a prize chance."

No retort.

He gave it up, lapsed into ireful silence, wondered whether the brief emanations he'd picked up had come from McDonald himself or from yet another of his unsuspected dupes. There was no way of telling. Such minds do not reveal themselves in terms of human identity. All that could be said for certain was that a mortal enemy wandered loose despite that the whole town was beginning to resemble an armed camp.

Surliness remained with him two hours later when the cars rolled through a strongly guarded gateway in a heavily fenced area, went over a small hill and stopped before a cluster of buildings hidden from sight of the main road. A painted board stood beside the main entrance.

Department Of Defense
Biological Research Laboratories

The four from the pilot car escorted him through the doors in the wary manner of men convinced that given half a chance he would take wings and fly. More people given only part of the story and exaggerating the rest, he decided.

He took a chair in the waiting-room and sat, watched by three of them while the fourth went in search of someone else. In due time the latter returned with a white-coated, gray-haired individual who registered prompt surprise.

"Wade Harper! Well I'm blessed!"

"What's dumbfounding about it?" growled Harper. "You weren't soul-shaken last time we met, four years back."

One of the escort chipped in, saying, "If you and Doctor Leeming already know each other you don't need an introduction. So we'll get along." He went out, taking the others with him.

Leeming explained, "My instructions are to make a check with the help of a specialist who would be brought here this morning. I am given to understand that what he says must be treated as decisive. The specialist's identity wasn't revealed." He backed off a short way, looked the other up and down. "And it's you. Four years haven't done you any good. You look older and uglier."

"So would you if you were in my breeches." Harper gave a sniff of discontent, went on, "I came like royalty, under strong protection. Toughies to the front of me, toughies to the back of me, and for all I know there was a fleet of helicopters parading overhead. All that rigmarole wasn't so you could hand me another problem about how to shave the whiskers off a bacillus. Moreover, my mercenary instinct tells me you aren't aiming to give me a repeat order for twelve thousand dollars' worth of apparatus. So what's this all about?"

"I'll show you." Doctor Leeming beckoned. "Come along."

Taking him through a series of corridors, Leeming conducted him into a long room cluttered with scientific glassware, stainless steel instruments and, Harper swiftly noted, a few silk-lined cases of his own especial products. A young man, white-coated, bespectacled and serious, glanced up nervously as they entered.

"My assistant, Doctor Balir," introduced Leeming. "Meet Wade Harper." He gestured toward a nearby micromanipulator and its array of accessories. "He's the fellow who makes this stuff."

Balir looked suitably impressed, said, "Glad to know you."

"Then you may number yourself among a select few," Harper responded.

"Take no notice," Leeming advised Balir. "He says the first thing that pops into his head."

"Hence the general ruckus," commented Harper, "seeing what's been popping of late." He stared around. "Well, why am I here?"

Leeming went to a large cabinet, took from it a photograph blown up to full-plate size, handed it over for inspection. It showed a fuzzy white sphere with a band of slight discoloration across its middle.

"A picture of the planet Jupiter," Harper hazarded, momentarily too preoccupied to check his guess by mental probing.

"On the contrary," informed Leeming, "it is something far smaller, though massive enough as such things go. That's an electron-microscope's view of a protein molecule."

"If you want to dissect it you're right out of luck. I can't get down to any method of handling things *that* tiny."

"More's the pity," said Leeming. "But that's not what we're after."

Returning the photo to the cabinet, he turned to a heavy steel safe set in the wall. Opening it carefully, he took out a transparent plastic sealed container in which was a wadded test-tube one quarter filled with a clear-colorless liquid.

"This," he announced, "is the same thing multiplied a millionfold. Does it mean anything to you?"

Harper peered at the fluid. "Not a thing."

"Consider carefully," Leeming advised. "Because to the best of our belief this is still alive."

"Alive?"

"By that, I mean potent. It is a virus extracted from the brainpans and spinal cords of certain bodies."

"A recognizable virus?"

"No."

"Filterable?"

"We did not attempt to filter it. We isolated it by a new centrifugal process."

"Then if it's not dead it's still dizzy from being whirled," said Harper. "Let me try again when it has come to its senses."

"Ah! That's precisely what we want to know. *Has* it any senses? My information is that you, and you alone, can tell us." He frowned and continued, "I have my orders which say that it is for you to pronounce the verdict. If you say that this virus is innocuous, it means either that it has been rendered so by processing and isolation or, alternatively, that we're on the wrong track and must start all over again."

Harper said, "Anyway, you don't have to stand there holding it out at arm's length like a man who's just dug up a dead cat. Put it back in its coffin and screw down the lid. It will make not the slightest difference to my ability to weigh it up. If that stuff were willing and able to advertise its suspected nature I could have told you about it in the waiting-room without bothering to come this near."

Doing as bidden, Leeming fastened the steel safe, spread expressive hands. "So we're no farther than at the beginning?"

"Not necessarily," Harper replied. Leaning against a lab bench, he put on a musing expression while he picked the minds of both Leeming and Balir. Then he said, "You've been told that three space-explorers have returned from Venus afflicted with a possessive disease which is spreading. They have sent you bodies of known victims, starting with a girl named Joyce Whittingham. Your job is to isolate what's doing it, learn its nature and, if possible, devise a cure."

"Correct," admitted Leeming. "It's top secret information. Evidently you've been given it too."

"Given it? I took it with both hands. And it was like pulling teeth." Harper leaned forward, eyed him intently. "Are you positive that you have extracted the real cause in the form of that virus?"

"I was fairly certain—until your arrival. Now I'm not."

"What made you so sure?"

"No words of mine can tell you how thoroughly we've dealt with those corpses. The task was made doubly difficult by virtue of everything having to be handled remotely, with every possible precaution against direct contact and contamination. We've had our leading experts on the job twenty-four hours per day and they've done it down to the last fragment of flesh, blood, bone, skin and hair. All we've got to show for it is a formerly unknown virus. That could be it. That should be it." He paused, finished, "But, according to you, it isn't."

"I haven't said so."

"You said it meant nothing to you."

"Neither does it—in its present state." Harper hesitated, continued, "I have the peculiar power to recognize persons afflicted with this disease. If they've not told you how I can do it, I cannot either. Call it another top-secret. The damn world's getting crammed with top-secrets. However, I can tell you one thing."

"What's that?"

"I recognize the symptoms. You're asking me to put a finger on the cause. It's not the same thing, not by a long shot. So far as I'm concerned it's a quite different problem."

"Well, can you help with any suggestions?" asked Leeming.

"I can give you my ideas. It's up to you to decide whether they make sense or nonsense."

"Let's have them. We need every angle we can get."

"All right. Understand that I'm not criticizing you people in any way when I say that I think the authorities rushed me here because they'd jumped to a silly conclusion."

"What conclusion?"

"That you can undress when you're stark naked. That you can swim without water. That you can pedal down the road without a bicycle between your legs."

"Be more explicit," Leeming suggested.

"You can't be a disease when you've nothing to work upon. You can't run without legs, talk without a mouth, think without brains. If that stuff is what you believe it to be, and what for all I know it really may be, it's hamstrung, tied up, fastened down, gagged and slugged. It is therefore no more than what it appears to be, namely, a dollop of goo. Its power, if any, has ceased to be actual and become only potential. I can detect an actuality. But I can't sit in judgment upon potentiality any more than I can read the future."

"I see what you mean." Leeming put on a slow smile. "You don't give us credit for overmuch intelligence, do you?"

"I haven't defined you as stupid. I'm merely theorizing about my own ability to help."

"All right." Leeming waved a hand toward the steel safe. "That's not all we've got. It's only half of it. We used the rest for a time-honored purpose: we tried it on the dog."

"You mean you've actually squirted it into someone?"

"Yes, a dog, as I've just said."

Harper gazed at him defeatedly. In all his life he had never picked up a thought radiating from any of the lower animals. Telepathically, the dogs and cats, the birds and bees just did not exist. They cerebrated somewhere above or below the human waveband. He could no more listen to their minds working than he could see beyond the ultraviolet.

"What's happened to it?"

"It lived. It's still living. Like to see it?"

"Yes, I would."

The dog proved to be a black Labrador retriever imprisoned in a heavy cage apparently commandeered from a circus or from some nearby zoo. The cage had a steel floor, heavy steel bars on all sides and across the top, also a sliding mid-gate by means of which the animal could be pinned in one half of its quarters while the other half was being cleaned, its food and water bowls replenished. The Labrador looked incongruous and not a little pathetic in surroundings formidable enough to hold an irate rhinoceros.

Noticing the approaching pair, the dog turned to face them, pawed at the bars, wagged its tail vigorously and emitted a pleading whine. A perfect picture of canine friendliness, it concentrated its attention particularly upon Harper, subjecting him to all the appeal of a pet-shop pup begging to be bought.

"Any comments?" inquired Leeming.

"If appearance is anything to go by, you injected it with nothing more dangerous than dill-water."

"Within the limits of that condition, I agree. But can we place faith in appearances? You've said that you can recognize an actuality. Well, this dog is actual enough. So what is your diagnosis?"

"I can't give one," said Harper. "It's no use me trying to smell out witches among the canine species. My power functions only with respect to a two-legged creature very much like myself but less hairy."

"H'm!" Leeming eyed the Labrador which now was standing on its hind legs, forepaws against bars, and openly inviting Harper to take it out for a walk. He frowned deeply, said, "Notice how all its attention is on you and how it is ignoring me?"

"That's natural. I'd prefer me to you if I were a dog."

"I'm not joking," Leeming assured. "I'm deadly serious."

"Why?"

"We shot a dose of virus into that animal at noon yesterday. We did it in that cage, got out fast and watched results from this side of the bars."

"And what happened?"

"It behaved normally at first, licked the spot where we'd inserted the needle, wandered aimlessly around and threw us those looks of bewildered reproof which some dogs give when they think they've been kicked for nothing. After four minutes it collapsed, had a violent fit during which its body jerked spasmodically, it foamed at the mouth and gave muffled yelps."

"After that?"

"It recovered with surprising swiftness," Leeming detailed. "It went ten times around the cage, examining every part of it, and obviously seeking a means of escape. Finding none, it snarled at Balir, who happened to be standing nearest. It gave a display of ferocious hatred that had to be seen to be believed. Dill-water or not, it certainly wasn't the same dog as before."

"It seems mild enough now," Harper pointed out.

"I know. And that is highly significant, I believe. It raged against Balir. Then it turned its fury upon me. For a couple of hours it gave a display of maniac enmity toward anyone and everyone who came in sight. The emotional reaction to entrapment, see?"

"Could be."

"But after those couple of hours it changed character with the swift dexterity of an actor changing costumes between acts. The hatred vanished. The dog did its darnedest to ingratiate itself with Balir and put on so good a performance that he began to pity it. Knowing or sensing the effect, it redoubled its efforts to gain his friendship. However, Balir is a scientist. He refused to let himself be influenced by irrational sentiment. Therefore he did not respond."

"What did it do next?"

"It transferred its cajolings to me. I'll admit without shame that I had moments of feeling sorry for it—until I remembered that my sympathy could be expressed in only two ways, namely, to get within reach and fondle it, which might be most dangerous, or to release it, which could well be downright disastrous. So I remained hard."

"Is that all?"

"No. Early this morning it tried all its best tricks on Jim Calthorpe, who tends to its feeding. Calthorpe had been warned to use the slide-gate and keep out of the dog's reach no matter what. He refused to respond to its overtures. Now it is picking on you in your turn." Leeming glanced at the other and asked, "What do you deduce from such behavior?"

"Constructive thought," Harper replied. "It has satisfied itself that escape is impossible without help. Its only chance is to find a weakling who'll cooperate. So it is testing the various candidates in order of arrival."

"That's what I suspect. But if we are correct, if it is being purposefully selective in its appeals, isn't that just a bit too clever for the average dog?"

"I don't know. I really don't know. As I told you before, I am no expert on canines. All I do know is that some dogs are alleged to be mighty smart and quite capable of coping with moderately complicated problems. Almost human is the conventional description for them."

"Yes, but the exceptionally intelligent dog has developed its mental status almost from birth. It hasn't acquired it all of a sudden, like being fitted with a new collar."

"Well?"

"This particular animal was as average a specimen as you could find in a long day's march. Now it's better than average. It has jumped from Dog I.Q. 70 to Dog I.Q. 100 or more. That is somewhat alarming in view of the circumstances. It points to a conclusion we hoped you could confirm. We are going to have a difficult time proving it without your help."

"There's a satisfactory way out," Harper suggested, "if anyone has the guts to take it."

"And what may that be?"

"Knock off that hound, recover the hell-juice from it, resquirt it into a human being. Or if you can spare the stuff you showed me in the lab, use that and save yourself time and trouble."

"Impossible!" declared Leeming.

"Show me an injected human being and I can tell you positively whether or not you have tracked down and isolated the real cause of all the trouble."

"Unthinkable!" Leeming said.

"Don't talk silly," Harper reproved. "How can it be unthinkable, seeing that I've thought of it?"

"You know what I mean. We cannot subject a fellow being to such a drastic test."

"It's a bit late for science to start taking count of moral considerations. The time for that was fifty years ago. Today, one more dirty trick will pass unnoticed. The public has got used to the idea that we've all degenerated to a bunch of guinea-pigs."

Leeming let that pass with no more than a disapproving frown, then said, "It might be all right if we could get a volunteer. Where are we going to find one? Would *you* offer your body for this?"

"I would not. And even if I were daft enough to submit, I would not be permitted to do so. Uncle Sam thinks me too precious to lose." He tapped Leeming's chest with a heavy forefinger. "And that fact alone suggests where you may get your experimental carcass, namely, from among those who aren't precious, those whose loss won't matter a hoot to anyone, even to themselves."

"What do you mean?"

"There are thugs in the death-house waiting to be hung, electrocuted or gassed. Offer any of them the one-in-a-thousand chance to gain release and watch him jump at it. Tell him that you want him to take a squirt. If he goes under, well, he's facing that as it is. But if you can cure him he'll be given a pardon and freed. Maybe Old Whiskers will find him a government job as a reward for public service."

"I have no authority to make such an extra-judicial bargain."

"Somebody has. Find him and keep kicking his pants until he wakes up."

"I doubt whether anyone less than the President could do it and even he'd have to stretch his powers to the limit."

"All right. Then chivvy the President. If you don't go after him somebody else will—and for a more formidable purpose."

"Look, Wade, talk comes cheap. Performance is a different matter altogether. Have you ever tried moving the top brass?"

"Yes."

"How far did you get?" Leeming asked with interest.

"I reached General Conway and got him on the hop good and proper. Come to think of it, he's the boy to ask for a hunk of forked meat. Tell him exactly what's happened here, what I've said to you, what you want to do about it. Tell him your test-subject has got to be a man and nothing less than a man. Dump the problem right in his lap and tell him that so far as you're concerned he's stuck with it. He won't nurse it any longer than he can help, you can bet on that!"

Harper studied the dog again while letting Leeming think it over. The Labrador whined, made pawing motions between the bars. It looked every inch a dog and nothing else save a dog. But that was no proof for or against. Elsewhere slunk creatures who bore equally close resemblance to people but were not people. The number one question: was this animal still a mere dog or had it become in effect a weredog?

He tried to listen to its mind as it begged his attention, and he heard precisely nothing. A blank, a complete blank. His natural range of reception just wasn't wide enough to pick up emanations from other than his own species. He switched from listening and probed at it sharply, fiercely, in manner that had brought immediate reaction from hiders in human shape. It had no effect upon the dog, which continued its fawning with obvious unconsciousness of his mental stabbing.

The silent experiment served only to confirm what he had already known: that the canine brain functions solely with respect to its own kind and that the so-called ability of dogs to read thoughts is no more than an expert appraisal of gestures, expressions, mannerisms and vocal tones. Because of that the Labrador represented a sterile line of research upon which Leeming had entered in good faith but little chance of satisfactory conclusion. Having got this far, it could be taken no farther. Another and more progressive line must involve a higher form of life.

Leeming broke into his meditation by saying, "I don't like it and I don't think I'll get away with it. Nevertheless I am willing to bait Conway providing you're standing by to back me up. He might listen to you when he won't to me."

"You don't know until you've tried."

"I do know that I am a scientist while he is a military figurehead. We don't talk the same language. The academic voice reasons while the voice of authority barks. If he can't or won't understand what I'm trying to explain and needs some cussing to make head or tail of it, you take the phone and use the necessary swear-words."

"Conway isn't that dopey," Harper answered. "High rank doesn't create a hollow head despite certain exceptions that prove the rule."

"Let's go to my office," suggested Leeming. "You get hold of him then I'll see what can be done."

Harper called Jameson first, said, "I'm at the Biological Research Laboratories as probably you are aware, you having had something to do with bringing me here. I'm going to put through a call to General Conway. Doctor Leeming wants a brief talk with him."

"Then why get on to me?" Jameson asked.

"Because I've tried to reach Conway before, remember? It's like seeking to hold the hand of God. And neither Leeming nor I have the time or patience to be messed around by every underling in Washington. It's up to you to tell them to shove my call straight through."

"See here, Harper—"

"Shut up!" Harper ordered. "You've used me plenty. Now I'm using you. Get busy and do as you're told."

He slammed the instrument on to its rack, sat in a handy chair, scowled at the phone and snorted.

Leeming said apprehensively, "Who is this Jameson?"

"A big cheese in the F.B.I."

"And *you* tell *him* where *he* gets off?"

"It's the first time," said Harper. "And from what I know of him it'll also be the last." He brooded a bit, darkened in color and snapped, "Anyway, why should one bunch of guys do all the order-giving and another all the order-taking? Time we reversed roles once in a while, isn't it? Is this a democracy or am I deluded?"

"Now, now," protested Leeming. "Don't pick on me. I just accept things as they are."

"Like hell you do. If some of you scientists had been more content to leave well alone we'd all—" He let rest go unsaid, chewed his bottom lip a piece, finished, "Take no notice. Once a month I have to give forth or go bang. Jameson's had long enough to ensure some action. If he hasn't taken steps by now he doesn't intend to."

"My bet is that he's done nothing."

"The odds are greatly in your favor, much as I hate to admit it." Harper regained the phone. "Anyway, we'll see."

His call went through, a youthful face appeared in his instrument's visiscreen.

"My name is Wade Harper," he told the face. "I want to speak to General Conway and it's urgent."

"Just a moment, please." The face went away, was replaced by another, older, more officious.

"About what do you wish to talk to the General?" inquired the newcomer.

"What's it to do with you?" demanded Harper toughly. "Go straight to Connie and find out once and for all whether or not he will condescend to have a word with me."

"I'm afraid I cannot do that unless I can first brief him on the subject matter of your—" The face ceased talking, glanced sidewise, said hurriedly, "Pardon me a moment," and disappeared. A few seconds later it returned wearing a startled expression. "Hold on, Mr. Harper. We're switching you through as speedily as possible."

Harper grinned at the now empty screen and said to Leeming, "Looks like you've lost your bet. Jameson got into motion although a bit slow at it."

"That surprises me."

"It surprises me, too. And it goes to show something or other if I had time to think it out."

The visiscreen registered eccentric patterns as the line was switched through intercom-boards, then cleared and held General Conway's austere features.

"What is it, Mr. Harper?"

Giving a short, succinct explanation, Harper handed the phone to Leeming who detailed the current state of affairs, ended by expressing his need for a human subject and the hope that Conway could do something about it.

"I disapprove such a tactic," declared Conway flatly.

Leeming reddened and said, "In that case, General, we can make no more progress. We are balked."

"Nonsense, man! I appreciate your desire and the ingenuity of what you suggest. But I cannot spend valuable hours seeking some legal means of making use of a condemned felon when such a move is superfluous and unnecessary."

"I make the request only because I deem it necessary," Leeming pointed out.

"You are wrong. You have been sent four bodies of known victims. Two more have become available today and you will receive them shortly. With the spread of this peril and the increase in number of people affected it becomes inevitable that before long we shall succeed in capturing one alive. What more could you want than that?"

Leeming sighed and persisted patiently, "A live victim would help but not conclusively. The most incontrovertible proof of a cause is a demonstration that it creates the characteristic effect. I cannot demonstrate contagion with the aid of a subject already riddled with it."

"Perhaps not," agreed Conway. "But such a subject, being more communicative than a dog, can be compelled to identify the cause himself. It should not be beyond your wit to devise a suitable technique for enforcing what might be termed self-betrayal."

"Offhand I can think of only one way to achieve that," Leeming said. "And the trouble with it is that it's likely to be long and tedious and it will mean considerable working in the dark."

"What method?"

"Assuming that this virus is the true cause—which is still a matter of doubt—we must seek an effective antigen. Our proof will then rest upon our ability to cure the live specimen. If we fail—"

"A cure has *got* to be found," asserted Conway, in manner making it final and beyond all dispute. "Somehow, anyhow. The only alternative is longterm, systematic extermination of all victims on an eventual scale that none dare contemplate. Indeed, we could well be faced by a majority problem far too large for a minority to overcome, in which case the minority is doomed and humanity along with it."

"And you think that the life of one hardened criminal is too high a price to pay for freedom from that fate?" asked Leeming shrewdly.

"I think nothing of the sort," Conway contradicted. "I would unhesitatingly sacrifice the entire population of our prisons had I the power to do so and were I convinced that it was our only hope. But I have not the power and I am not convinced of the necessity."

"Let me speak to him," urged Harper, seeing Leeming's look of despair. He got the phone, gazed belligerently at the face in the screen knowing that it was now looking at his own. "General Conway, you say you lack the power and you're not persuaded?"

"That is correct," Conway agreed.

"The President, if consulted, might think differently. He has the necessary authority or, if not, can obtain it. Aren't you usurping his right to make a decision about this?"

"Usurping?" Conway repeated the word as if it were the ultimate in insults. He gathered himself together with visible effort, spoke in tones of restraint, "The President cannot work more than twenty-four hours per day. Therefore he deputes certain of his powers and responsibilities. I am now exercising some of the authority so assigned."

"By virtue of which you have his ear while others have not," Harper riposted. "So how about putting the matter to him?"

"No."

"All right. I am no longer asking you to do so. I am telling you to do so."

"Telling me?" The other registered incredulity.

"That's what I said: I am telling you. Refusal to cooperate is a game at which two can play. You can take Leeming's proposition to the President or count me out of this fracas as from now."

"You cannot do that."

"I can."

"You know full well that we're dependent upon you to make positive identification where opportunity arises. You cannot possibly stand idly by knowing what's happening, watching it happen and doing nothing."

"I can. And what's more, I shall. You aren't the only one who can make like a mule."

"This is outrageous!" General Conway exploded.

"It's mutinous, too," endorsed Harper, showing indecent relish. "It's barefaced treachery. You could have me shot for it. Try it and see what good it does you. I'd be even less useful dead than dumb."

Conway breathed heavily while his face showed exasperation, then he said, "Against my better judgment I will take this up with the President and do my best to persuade him. I promise to try to get the required action with minimum of delay but I offer no guarantee of success."

"Your word is plenty good enough for me," said Harper. "You're an officer and a gentleman. And in our antagonistic ways we're both working for the same end, aren't we?"

He got a grunt of irritation for that, put down the phone, eyed Leeming. "He'll do it. He's the sort who sticks to a promise like grim death once it's been forced out of him."

"You've got a nerve," offered Leeming, showing a touch of envy. "You've got so much nerve I wonder you've any friends. Someday you'll push it too far and somebody will slap your skull into its underlying mess."

"What are you talking about? Conway's a man and I'm a man. We both get haircuts, both wear pants. Once upon a time we both bawled and had our diapers changed. And we'll both smell as bad a month after we're dead. Am I supposed to kiss his feet in between times?"

"No, I suppose not."

"Then we're in sweet agreement." He consulted his wristwatch. "Before I go there's one thing I'd like to know, if you can tell me."

"What's that?"

"How does this progressive disease become epidemic? How is it passed from one to another?"

"The same way as the dog got it," Leeming informed. "That girl Joyce Whittingham had received an injection in the upper arm, presumably with the blood of a victim."

"We can't say for certain that the dog has got it."

"No, but we do know the Whittingham girl had it. And we know she'd received an injection. So had two others. The fourth corpse had a plaster-covered cut that told the same story. My guess is that their reactions were the same as the dog's, a few minutes' confusion, collapse into a brief fit, rapid recovery."

"Well, the fact that contact alone evidently is not sufficient helps a little," mused Harper. "It means a prospect can't be taken just by sneezing in his direction. He has to be grabbed and held long enough to receive and get over a shot, eh?"

Leeming nodded and went on, "If this virus is not the actual cause it's a definite by-product, and if it's not the cause, well"—he spread hands expressively—"we're at a complete loss for any other."

"Anything else you can tell me about it?"

"Yes. It locates itself in the brain and spinal column. That is its natural habitat. The rest is theory and you can have it for what it's worth. I believe that the virus increases until it overflows into the bloodstream and thereby creates an urge to transmit the surplus, to seek another circulatory system leading to another brain and spinal column. You can think of it as the non-human equivalent of sexual desire, the actual transference being a substitute for copulation. It's the irresistible response to the universal law: Be fruitful and multiply."

"Humph!" Harper stewed that a while. He was curious about how transmission from creature to creature was accomplished on the world of origin. Did the preferred hosts on Venus take the shape of a lifeform high enough to manufacture and manipulate hypodermic needles? Or were they something lower in the scale of life, something peculiarly fanged and able to transmit impregnated blood with a single bite?

He suspected the latter. No matter how alien from the terrestrial viewpoint, this plague was born of Nature, designed to exist in masterful symbiosis with a similarly evolved partner. Therefore the mode of increase was likely to be natural rather than artificial and the injection-technique used on Earth was nothing but a substitute justified by proving satisfactory.

If all these bald assumptions happened to be correct, that imprisoned dog might well be capable of creating its own rescuer and much-wanted ally by getting in one good snap at an unwary leg or by licking a hand on which was a minute cut. The presence of virus in its saliva could open the gates to freedom and a wholesale conversion of human forms. Theoretically the animal was more dangerous than a cobalt bomb.

"If you want my advice," he said to Leeming, "you'd do well to put an end to that dog before it puts an end to you."

"Don't worry. We're used to coping with such matters here. Nobody goes near enough to be spat upon, much less touched."

"You know your own business. And it's high time I resumed tending to mine. I am going home, back to the trap that Conway hopes will catch a live one." Harper let go a harsh chuckle. "If I'm dead out of luck they may bring you a struggling zombie that will prove to be me."

"What d'you mean?" inquired Leeming, wide-eyed.

"Never mind. Let's find the escort. If I return without them there'll be the deuce to pay." He glanced at the ceiling as if appealing to heaven. "What a world!"

Chapter 11

Rausch was hanging around the office when Harper arrived in the morning. He said, "We stayed put until eight last evening thinking you'd be sure to return here. If your guard hadn't advised us that they'd delivered you safely home we'd have been stuck in this dump all night."

"What with one thing and other, including three stops *en route,* I got back too late." Hanging his hat, Harper sat at his desk, reached for the mail. "Where's Norris? How come you're here? I thought you were making an ambush of the Baum place?"

"We've abandoned hope of catching anyone there. The news about the Baums appeared in yesterday's last editions and got reported as an automobile smash. A pic on the wrecked car being towed away was shown in the pane's midnight summary. Despite the cover-up it's more than enough to warn off the Baums' play-mates. We'll grab nobody there if we try for a year."

"Well, all I can say is that some people appear pretty good at thwarting the Feds." Harper tore open a couple of envelopes, rapidly scanned their contents. "They're much too sharp for my liking. And they're playing hob with my pet theory that basically all criminals are dopes." Then he glanced up from a letter, added thoughtfully, "If this bunch can properly be called criminals."

"How else can you describe them?"

"As a menace. A red-hot menace. Like a gang of dogs with rabies. Or a group of smallpox carriers hiding from the health authorities. But worse than that, infinitely worse." He reread the letter, dumped it into a wire basket. "Where did you say Norris has gone?"

"I didn't say. If it's any satisfaction to you he has dashed out on what is probably another fruitless trip."

"What do you mean by 'another'?"

"Yesterday, while you were absent," explained Rausch, "the boys picked up no less than eight alleged McDonalds. It would have been a top notch performance if any of them had turned out to be McDonald. But none were. Half an hour ago Norris rushed away for a look at number nine."

"How's he checking?"

"Easily enough. He has mug-shots, prints and so forth. He's got sufficient to pin down the right one beyond all shadow of doubt. We've not yet laid hands on the right one."

"I'd give much to know how he's keeping out of reach," Harper observed. "The technique might be extremely useful to me some day."

Rausch stared at him. "What's on your mind?"

"Embezzlement." Then he gave a false laugh. "But of course. How silly of me. If I abscond with this outfit's money I'm merely taking my own. Which proves yet again that an employer can do no wrong. Think it over."

"I am thinking," informed Rausch suspiciously. "And I think you're kidding me. I also think it isn't funny."

"It wasn't intended to be." He grabbed more mail, ripped off the covers. "Anything else happened that I ought to know about?"

"Your police friend Riley called in the afternoon, became nosey about where you'd gone."

"Did you tell him?"

"How could we? We didn't know ourselves. And even if we'd possessed the information we wouldn't have given it. He is not entitled to be told."

"Did he state the purpose of his visit?"

"No. I got the impression that it was just a casual drop-in for a gab. He said he'd call again today. He fooled around trying to make your secretary, then went."

Harper dropped the letter he was holding, eyed Rausch sharply. "Say that again, the bit about my secretary."

"Riley horsed about with her a bit, then departed."

"Never! Never in a month of Sundays! He wouldn't make a pass at Moira if she begged him to eat her. That's why I kid him about it. He's so solidly married that it's boring."

"He did," asserted Rausch. "Maybe the solidity is becoming slightly undermined. You wouldn't know about that. You don't sleep with him."

Harper relaxed, said, "You've made a point there. Moira is due to arrive in about ten minutes. I'll ask her about this."

"I don't see the need. Not unless you've a lien on her love-life."

"The bond between us is firmly based upon a mutual affection for hard cash," Harper informed. "That and no more."

"Have it your own way," said Rausch, shrugging. He mooched into the workshop, amused himself watching micromanipulators being assembled, came back when Moira appeared.

Waiting until she had settled herself behind her typewriter, Harper asked, "What is this about you and Riley?"

She was taken aback. "I don't understand, Mr. Harper."

"I'm told the lumbering elephant made a play for you."

"Oh no, not really." She gained a slight flush. "He only joshed me a bit. I knew he meant nothing by it."

"But he's never done that before, has he?"

"No, Mr. Harper. I think he was just filling in time, not finding you here."

Harper leaned forward, gazing at her but not picking her mind. "Did he try to date you?"

She was shocked and a little indignant. "Certainly not. He did offer me a theater ticket someone had given him. He said he wasn't able to use it and I could have it."

"Did you accept it?"

"No. It was for last night. I had a date already and couldn't go."

"Was he disappointed when you refused the ticket?"

"Not that I noticed." Her attention shifted to the listening Rausch, then back to Harper, her features expressing bafflement. "What is all this, anyway?"

"Nothing much, Lanky. I am trying to determine whether Riley was drunk or sober yesterday afternoon. It's an interesting speculation because never in my life have I known him to get stinko."

"A person doesn't have to be drunk to notice my existence," she gave back more than pointedly.

"That's the baby!" approved Rausch, coming in on her side. "You landed that one right on the button."

"Keep your beak out of my domestic affairs," ordered Harper. He picked up a letter. "Forget it, Moira. Let's get down to business. Take this reply to the Vester Clinic. Replacement titanium-alloy needles for Model Fourteen are immediately available in sets of six. We quote you—"

He had finished dictating and was presiding in the workshop when Norris returned sour-faced and said, "You wouldn't think so many people could have a superficial but passable resemblance to one wanted man."

"Meaning they'd grabbed another dud?"

"Yes. A paint salesman sufficiently like McDonald to make the pinch excusable. Moreover, he was in a devil of a hurry, lost his temper, tried to crash a roadblock. That was his undoing."

"Look," said Harper, "McDonald escaped loaded with luggage and had at least an hour's start. Do you really suppose that he is still in this town?"

"No, I don't. I reckon the chances are a hundred to one against it. Not only have we found no trace of him but none of the Reeds or their car either. I think they slipped through the cordon and are now way out in the wilds. But we're passing up no chances no matter how remote."

"All right. Then I'll tell you something: if those three have escaped they've left at least one contact here."

"How do you know that?" Norris demanded.

"Because we whizzed past one yesterday. I tried to get the cavalcade to go after him but they refused to stop. They had their orders and they stuck to them. It shows how blind obedience can make a hash of initiative."

Norris did not like that last remark but let it go by and inquired, "Did you get any clue to his identity?"

"Not a one. If I had I'd have told you last night and saved your time. He might be anybody, anybody at all. The best I can do is guess."

"Go ahead and do some guessing. You've made a few lucky shots so far."

"This is a wild one fired entirely at random," Harper told him, almost apologetically. "I can't get rid of the idea that about the safest place in the world for a

hunted man is a town where every man jack is hunting for some other character. He benefits from the general distraction, see? His safety factor is increased
more than somewhat by virtue of the obvious fact that you can concentrate on
one thing only by ignoring other things."

"Go on," urged Norris, interested.

"So if the presence of my carcass makes this town an area of irresistible attraction to the opposition, and everyone here is chasing around in search of McDonald—"

"Finish it, man, finish it!"

"What a wonderful set-up for William Gould." Harper regarded the other levelly. "Who's looking for *him?*"

"The entire country. You know that."

"I'm not considering the entire country. I'm thinking only of this town. Unlike
the rest of the country, it's obsessed by McDonald to such an extent that Gould
could step in and baby-sit for you and you'd pay him two dollars with thanks." He
drummed restless fingers on the desk while that sank in, then added for good
measure, "After which it would never be the same baby again."

Rausch chipped in, "Whether that guess is on or off the mark makes no difference. Gould is wanted as badly as McDonald. It would do no harm to distribute
a local reminder of that fact."

"It wouldn't at that," agreed Norris. "You go out and see to it right now." Norris
watched Rausch hurry out then returned attention to Harper. "Where do you dig
up these notions?"

"The onlooker sees the most of the game. And as I told you before, I've been on
the run myself while you have not. It helps a lot when one tries to put oneself in
the other fellow's shoes. That's why the first and perhaps one of the best detectives
in history was an ex-con with a long record."

"Who was that?"

"Eugene Francoise Vidocq."

"I'll look him up some day," Norris promised. "If by then I'm not in the jug
busily completing my education."

"You'll never look him up. He died long before you were born. All the same,
I—"

He shut up as his mental searchlight made one of its periodic circlings and
found something in the surrounding ocean of emanations. He was quiet while his
mind listened.

It was coming again.

Gobble-gobble.

Failing to notice this sudden preoccupation, Norris prompted, "You were about
to say?"

"Nothing of consequence. Let it pass."

Harper made a disparaging gesture, returned to his office and sat erect in
his chair. He felt under one arm to make sure the gun was readily available.

"Moira," he said quietly, "there's a packet for Schultz-Masters ready in the shop. It's urgent. I'd like you to take it to the post office at once. See that it goes by the midday mail. You need not hurry back. It'll do if you return after lunch."

"What about this correspondence, Mr. Harper?"

"You'll have all afternoon to cope with it. Put a move on and get rid of that consignment so that I'll have an answer ready if Schultz-Masters start bawling over the phone."

"Very well." She adjusted her hat on her head, picked up her handbag, went into the workshop and collected the package.

Going to the window, he watched her hurrying along the street in the direction opposite to that from which danger was coming. Well, that got her away from the scene of prospective trouble.

A couple of burly characters walked ten yards behind her rapidly clicking heels. They knew where she was going because the mike planted in the office had informed Norris or whoever happened to be listening-in. But they weren't going to let her out of their sight and hadn't done from the start of fixing the trap. It was just as well.

He did not open the window as he had done at the approach of Ambrose Baum. Leaving it fastened, he stood behind it surveying as much of the street as could be seen while stretching his receptive power to the utmost.

This time he was not going to make the mistake of transmitting a mental stab and getting the foe to flee with the knowledge so ardently sought. He was going to do no more than listen and thus leave the other mind blissfully unconscious of its open state. True, that meant he dare not stimulate desired information and had to rest content with whatever the hidden thinker saw fit to offer, regardless of whether said offerings made sense or nonsense.

Leaving the window he flopped into his chair, stared unseeingly at Moira's desk while he listened and waited. It was a unique and most curious experience despite previous brief encounters.

Judging by the chronically slow increase in amplitude of the distant impulses the oncoming entity was progressing at little more than a crawl; probably walking warily with frequent pauses for pretended examinations of shop windows. It was not hesitant in the manner of one fearful and on edge. On the contrary, it was cold-bloodedly aware of many dangers and trying to side-step any that became apparent.

The mind did not identify itself in human terms because at the moment it was not thinking in human terms. Cogitatively, it was bilingual. The queer ganderlike gobble-gobble was another-world sound track synchronized with another-world thought-forms. It was obedient to a habit born of countless centuries of possession by doing its thinking in the mental terms of its faraway hosts. Occupation of a completely human-type brain in no way handicapped this function. All brains utilize the data filed therein and this one was armed with knowledge of two worlds and at least two distinct species.

Even though directing his attention elsewhere, Harper was able to do some thinking of his own. What if this gradually nearing sneaker were none other than William Gould? How could he hope to walk in on Harper and get away with whatever he schemed to do?

It was hardly likely that his purpose was to kill, even at cost of his own life, because the foe would gain little enough from that. The prize they wanted and must secure at all costs was accurate knowledge of the means by which they could be identified. To slay the only one able to reveal this secret would leave them as perilously ignorant as before.

Their sole rational tactic was to capture and hold Harper for long enough to force the truth out of him. Once successfully grabbed, the technique of compulsion would be simple and effective. They'd take possession of him exactly as others had become possessed, after which they would find the wanted datum recorded in his mind, and it would be theirs, entirely theirs to use as they wished.

Nothing less than that would tell them what they had to combat and enable them to devise means of mastering any similar threats from any other source. Therefore the oncomer must be at least a scout tentatively tasting local defenses or at most a would-be kidnapper hoping to pull the job single-handed somehow, heaven alone knew how.

In the latter event there must be more to the present situation than was yet evident to the eyes. The enemy was far from stupid. No delegate of theirs would try to snatch Harper in these circumstances unless playing a part that offered at least a moderate chance of success.

The alien thought-stream had grown much stronger now and was replete with brief, unrecognizable scenes like glimpses of some nightmarish landscape. Harper removed attention from it for a moment while he scoured the area for minds like it. Perhaps there were a dozen or twenty converging by prearrangement upon his address, hoping to take him by sheer weight of numbers.

There were not. He failed to detect any others. Only one was approaching and if any more of them were around they must be lurking beyond detectable range. If so, had they chosen their concealing distance by pure accident or had they started to make some very shrewd guesses?

Still he did not probe. Neither did he warn Norris as he was supposed to do. He sat tight, determined for the time being to play things his own way. Regulation tactics had gained nothing but several corpses and a picture of a fuzzy ball. A little irregularity might prove more profitable. He did not bother to consider the risk involved or the possible cost to his own skin. His lack in this respect was more the measure of his impatience than his courage.

The other mind was now passing beneath his window but he did not try to take a look that, if noticed, might create premature alarm. If it continued onward along the sidewalk, ignoring his front door, he was going to get out fast and nail it. But if it came in he was going to sit right there and meet it as man to mock-man.

It turned in at the front door and immediately the thought-stream switched to human terms with all the brilliant clarity of the pane when it is suddenly adjusted after being mistily off-focus. There was a reason for that. The arrival had come into contact with a couple of agents on guard and immediately adapted itself to cope with a human situation. It was done with speed and polished perfection possible only to a lifeform that had never worn anything but fleshy masks because it had no face of its own.

And in that pregnant moment Harper learned whom to expect. He read it in the minds of the agents even as they swapped a few words with the newcomer.

"Is the orangoutang here? Or has he gone out chasing a percentage?"

"He's warming his office chair."

"Mind if I bust in?"

"Go help yourself."

Harper smiled grimly. He picked up the agents' mental images as they let the enemy walk through. He changed attention to Norris, outside sitting on a bench in the workshop, almost saw through his eyes as idly he watched the other reach the door.

Then the gobbler entered and Harper said in the manner of one completely fooled, "Hello, Riley. What brings you here?"

Helping himself to the absent Moira's chair, Riley seated himself carefully, looking at Harper and all unwittingly gave him a piece of his mind.

"He is supposed to know us on sight in some mysterious way. Everything adds up to that fact. But he does not react in this case. That is strange. Something's wrong somewhere."

Vocally, Riley responded, "I'm keeping my finger on your pulse."

"Why?"

"There's a five thousand dollar reward in the bag for whoever finds Alderson's killer. Captain Ledsom hasn't forgotten it despite all the hullabaloo about three fellows who've done nobody knows what. I haven't forgotten it either. It's a lot of money."

"So you're hoping to sell me for that sum eventually?"

"No, I'm not. I don't believe you did it. But I think you know more than you've told. And I'm betting that when all this ruckus is over you'll get busy on it."

"And then?"

"You may need my help. Or I may need yours. Between the two of us we might lay hands on that sack of gold."

"You're becoming mercenary in your old age, and sloppy to boot."

"What do you mean, sloppy?"

Carefully steering the conversation into mentally revealing channels, Harper said, "Fooling with Moira while I'm away."

"Bunk!"

"Cajoling her with a theater ticket."

That did it.

The responding flash of secret thought lasted no more than two or three seconds but was detailed enough to present the picture. Moira innocently enjoying the show in seat U.17. William Gould apparently doing likewise in U.18. Conversation between acts, a planned pick-up and stroll home—with Moira finishing up no longer human.

Gould was young, attractive, had enough glamour to make the plot workable. Only a previous date had spoiled it. In any case, Moira's unshakable escort would have proved troublesome unless Gould escaped them by persuading her to invite him into her home. Perhaps that was what he had planned. The brief stream from Riley's brain lacked data on this point.

"I couldn't use it," said Riley. "What should I have done with it? Masticate it?"

"You could have given it to your wife."

Another picture came in response to that and confirmed what Harper had reluctantly taken for granted. Riley's wife was no longer a wife. She was a living colony of fuzzy balls that had the urge to spread but were utterly indifferent to the sex of the host. By implication, that added one more datum to knowledge of the foe, namely, that a person could not be confiscated by means of sexual union with one of the possessed. The virus could not or preferred not to penetrate by osmosis; it needed direct entry from the suffused bloodstream to the new bloodstream.

"She doesn't like to go by herself," said Riley. "What are you griping about, anyway? Why should you care where Moira goes or what she does of an evening?"

And then, *"There's something significant in this sudden concern for Moira. It smacks of deep suspicion. I don't see how he can be suspicious. Either he actually knows or he doesn't, and by the looks of it he does not know."*

"According to the Feds I'm in some sort of danger," informed Harper. "If so, Moira shares it simply by working with me and being closest to me. I don't want her to suffer for my sake."

That had its calculated effect by lulling the other mind. It was much like playing a conversational version of chess, Harper thought. Move and countermove, deceitfulness and entrapment, prompt seizure of any advantage or opening likely to lead toward checkmate.

The next moment Riley emphasized the simile by making a dangerous move. "That may be so. But I am not Gould, McDonald or Langley. So why pick on me?"

There was nothing for it but to accept the challenge by making a bold advance.

Eyeing him steadily, Harper said, "I am not yawping about you personally. I am uneasy because I don't know who gave you that ticket."

The mental answer came at once: Gould.

"What does it matter?" Riley evaded. "How was he to know I wouldn't use it myself or that I'd offer it to Moira?"

"Oh, let's drop the subject," Harper suggested, with pretended weariness. "This chase after three men has got me jumpy enough to question the motives of my own mother."

Soothing lotion again. The opposing brain mopped it up solely because it was plausible.

"The sooner they're picked up the better I'll like it," continued Harper, offering fresh bait. "Take McDonald, for instance. He was around these parts quite recently. A smart copper like you ought to be able to find him."

Eureka! Out came the reaction as clearly as if written upon paper. Gould, McDonald, the Reeds and two others previously unknown were clustered together in Riley's own house, waiting, waiting for Harper to come along on the strength of whatever pretext Riley could think up.

So here was the real purpose of the visit. Riley had not yet got around to the enticement but would do so before leaving. Come into my parlor, said the spider to the fly.

And in due course—it was hoped—Harper would drop in upon the Rileys while his bunch of shadows politely hung around outside. He would go in like a lamb to the slaughter and, after a while, emerge visibly no different. The shadowers would then escort him home and leave him to weird dreams of a far-off land where blind bugs serviced themselves from portions of their own dead and poison-spiked cacti tottered around on writhing roots and few agile creatures had souls to call their own.

The foreign intelligence now animating Riley proved itself sharp enough to bait the baiter. "What makes you think that I should succeed where a regiment of agents has failed?"

Harper had to react fast to that one. "Only because you're a local boy. They're out-of-towners. You've sources of information not available to them. You know the ropes, or ought to after all these years."

It was not quite enough to halt the probe.

"Then why didn't they rely on the police instead of pushing themselves in by the dozens?"

"Ask me another," Harper said, shrugging. "Probably someone's decided that the more men on the job, the better."

"It has bought them nothing so far, has it?" asked Riley, seemingly a little sarcastic.

But it was not sarcasm. It was temptation hidden under a cloak of mild acidity. It was an invitation to make mention of the Baums, to come out with a reply indicating how they'd been recognized for what they were.

The mind of Riley was working fast, driven on by the urgency of the slime that commanded it. But seek as he might, he could not find a satisfactory explanation of the contrast between his own immunity and the speedy downfall of others of his type.

Temporarily, the only theory that fitted the circumstances was an unsatisfactory one, namely, that Harper's menacing ability functioned haphazardly or under certain specific conditions not present at this moment. However, no theory served to explain how it was done. On the contrary, the existing situation complicated the puzzle. What could be the nature of positive detection that operated only in spasms?

In the few seconds that Riley spent mulling these problems, Harper strove to cope satisfactorily with some of his own. By dexterous use of leading comments how much could he get out of Riley without giving himself away? How best to frame questions and remarks that would draw essential information from the other's mind? How to find out the means by which Riley himself had been taken over, how many others had become possessed, their names, their hiding-places, their plans and so forth?

"No," agreed Harper, thwarting him. "It hasn't gained them a cent so far."

Refusing to be stalled, Riley took it further. "Except that they've wiped out a couple of boys named Baum. We got a routine report from a patrolman about that. It wasn't an auto accident, no matter what the official version says. It was the result of a fracas in which you were involved."

Harper offered no remark.

"Maybe it's no business of mine," Riley went on with just the right mixture of resentment and persuasiveness, "but if I knew how and why the Baums were finished it might give me a lead to this McDonald."

"Why?" asked Harper, looking straight at him. "Is there any connection?"

"You know there is. It's all part of the same crazy business."

"Who says so?"

The other's mind had a moment of confusion born of sudden need to cast doubt on what it knew to be true.

"Well, isn't it?"

"Maybe and maybe not," said Harper, keeping a perfectly expressionless face.

"Damn it, if you don't know what's going on, who does?"

That was another dexterously dug pitfall, a call to produce an evasive answer that might reveal plenty by its various implications.

Harper side-stepped the trap, feeling cold down his back as he did it.

"All I can tell you is that they were known to have become pally with McDonald. Therefore they were wanted for questioning. Immediately they were spotted they fled for dear life and one thing led to another." He paused, fought cunning with cunning by adding as a mystified afterthought, "It beats me completely. They weren't accused of a major crime, so why did they flee?"

Turmoil grew strong in the opposing brain. It had been asked the very question to which it desired the answer, as a matter of life or death. The assumed holder of the secret was seeking the solution himself.

Why did they flee?

Why did they flee?

Round and round whirled the problem and persistently threw out the only answer, namely, that the Baums had run because they'd become known and had realized *how* they'd become known. Therefore the mode of identification must be self-revealing. The possessed could not be fingered without sensing the touch.

Yet now that it was put to actual test there was no recognition, no dramatic exposure, no feelable contact, no touch, nothing.

What's the answer to that?

"As a guess, divide this world's bipeds into types A and B. The former is vulnerable because identifiable by some method yet to be discovered. Joyce Whittingham was of that type. So were the Baums. So might others be. But for unknown reasons type B is impervious to the power of Harper and any more who may share it. By sheer good fortune this body called Riley happens to be of that kind."

So the alien thought-stream ruminated while Harper listened, mentally thanking God that it had retained its pseudo-human role and not switched to transspatial double-talk.

It went on, *"If this notion should be correct, then salvation lies around the corner. We must learn the critical factor that protects type B and how to distinguish one type from another. Henceforth we must take over only type B. The vulnerable ones can be dealt with afterwards."*

We! The plural! Momentarily, in his concentration, Riley was thinking of himself as a mob!

Deep down inside himself Harper was sickened by this first-hand reminder of the ugly facts. The invader was a horde multi-millions strong. Each capture of a human body was victory for a complete army corps represented by a few drops of potent goo in which the individual warrior was—what?

A tiny sphere of hazy outline.

A fuzzy ball.

My brother's keeper!

Determined to make the most of his opportunity while it lasted, Harper went on, "Someone once remarked that the only difference between those in prison and those outside is that the latter have never been found out. Possibly the Baum brothers had something on their consciences and wrongly supposed it had been discovered. So they ran like jackrabbits."

"Could be," admitted Riley, while his thoughts said, *"It doesn't fit the facts. They had no cause for flight other than realization of betrayal. Harper knew them for what they were but refuses to admit it. That is at least consistent of him. He always did keep a tight mouth about his power."* A pause, followed by, *"Yet at the moment he lacks that power. Why? The reason must be found!"*

"Anyway, what's the use of gabbing?" Harper continued, craftily spurring the other on. "Talk gets us nowhere and I have work to do."

"You can't give me one useful hint concerning McDonald?"

"No. Go look for him yourself. You'll get plenty of kudos if you nail him. Besides, he may lead you to Gould, who is wanted just as badly."

"Gould?" He stared across, thinking, *"Do they know or suspect that he is in this town?"*

"And his contacts," added Harper, panning for paydirt. "Every one of them for the past three months."

The result was disappointing. He got fleeting, fragmentary pictures of a score of people without any means of determining who they were or where they lived, of what parts they were playing in this struggle for a world.

"When Gould and McDonald have been fastened down good and tight," he went on, "we may then have time to seek afresh for Alderson's killer and try for that five thousand you covet."

He was doing fine. The reference to Alderson brought the hoped-for reaction: a fragment of memory radiated with vividness. McDonald holding Joyce Whittingham while Gould sank a needle into her arm. Joyce struggling and screaming. A police cruiser suddenly halting right behind. Alderson jumping out and making for the Thunderbug. Langley pulling a gun and dropping him before he could intervene. So Langley had done it.

Hah! That brought up something else of considerable significance. The country's entire forces of law and order, Riley included, had been alerted to capture three men, not two. Yet Riley had shown no curiosity about Langley. He had asked about McDonald. He had accepted without question the reminder concerning Gould. Any normal individual would have brought up the subject of the third quarry—unless he knew that he was dead. Did Riley know that? If so, how had he learned it? How to find out?

Daringly, he rushed the issue. "As for Langley, nobody need worry about him any more."

Riley said nothing vocally but did utter a mental, *"Of course not. He's finished."*

"Who told you?" asked Harper.

"Told me what?"

"About Langley?"

"I don't know what you mean. Nobody has said anything to me concerning him."

"I've just mentioned that Langley is out of the running," Harper reminded. "You made no remark, showed no surprise. So I took it for granted that it was old news to you though I can't imagine how you got hold of it."

"You're wrong," contradicted Riley, hastening to cover up a minor blunder. "It's the first I've heard of it. The information failed to sink in."

He was too late. His mind had lagged seconds behind Harper's wits and his tongue had come last in the field. Despite intervening hundreds of miles, Riley had known of Langley's end the moment it occurred. He had sensed it as surely as one may gaze across a valley at night and see a distant light become suddenly extinguished.

It was a wholly alien faculty having nothing in common with any human sense. The possessed enjoyed a peculiar awareness of the existence of their own kind, could follow it blindly until they had gravitated together. By the same token, loss of awareness with respect to one particular focal point meant death far away over the horizon. Just the bare fact of death, without any details.

The same sense could detect a dreadful urgency radiated by another, the equivalent of a cry for help. It was strictly non-telepathic. A psi-factor. In effect, Riley could look afar, see the life-light emanating from one of his own kind, see it winking a summons for assistance, see it go dark. No more than that.

Perhaps it was the ultimate form of what Earth called the herd instinct. An alien protective device evolved on another world where survival sometimes demanded a rapid gathering of the clans and the lone individual went under.

Therefore, elsewhere they must have a natural enemy, a constant antagonist not strong enough to keep them in total subjection, much less eliminate them, but sufficiently redoubtable to restrict their spread and help maintain a distant world's balance of competing life-forms.

What could it be? Some strong-stomached animal that craved and consumed a potent virus with all the avidity of a cat lapping cream? A creature capable of devouring a possessed body without harm to itself? Or something smaller which came like warrior ants in hordes of its own and lived by ingesting armies of the vicious?

The datum was precious enough to be worth discovering if it could be gotten. But how to get it? How could he entice it from a hostile and wary mind without giving himself away? How can one question a Venusian concerning the fauna and flora of Venus while successfully managing to uphold the pretense of regarding him as a natural born native of Earth?

Another expedition might pick up the information some day—providing it did not succumb to the same fate as the first. But if urgent problems were not solved here and now there would never be another expedition, or not one that was truly human.

Knowledge of a deadly enemy's own especial foe was there, right there across the desk, buried within a mastered brain. If only it could be extracted, the scientists could search Earth for a local counterpart fully as capable of handling this alien menace. It was a glittering prize worth far more in the long run than capture of all this world's afflicted. It meant ability to deal with the root cause instead of fooling around with the symptoms.

Harper sought frantically for a method of making a highly dangerous move appear disarmingly innocent. He looked into Riley's questioning eyes which all along had seemed entirely normal and gave no hint of what was lurking behind.

Wetting his lips, he said, "Langley and some other fellow were trapped. They shot it out like madmen. It proved impossible to take them alive."

Riley raised an eyebrow in false surprise. "Everybody knew he was wanted but nobody's been told what for. Judging by that reaction the reason must have been mighty serious. So where's the sense in all the secrecy?"

"Don't ask me. I have no say in government policy." He made a gesture of bafflement. "You know how the top boys sometimes love to be mysterious."

The other grunted in disdain.

Now then, this was it, the critical play. It had to be done delicately, like handling dynamite. One slip and there'd be an explosion of wild action with Norris and the others caught by surprise. Thank goodness Moira was out of it.

With a deceitfully reminiscent air, Harper went on, "It's possible that Langley really was cracked in the head. If so, I don't like it. Everyone has pet fears and I've got mine."

"Such as what?"

"When I was a small child I was afraid of big black dogs. Now I'm older I have a violent revulsion toward mental disease. I fear loonies." He pulled a face, nerved himself and made the move. "What scares *you* the most?"

By God, he got it! He got it as clearly and vividly as only a lifelong terror can be pictured. What's more, he felt sure that he recognized it, not by its form but by its brutal nature. And it was here, on Earth, waiting around and ready for use. He had to tighten his mouth to prevent himself from shouting aloud.

Standing up, Riley frowned at him and asked in taut tones, "What makes you ask me that?" And his mind followed on with, *"A while ago he said that talk was of no avail, that he was busy and had work to do. Yet he's been maintaining the conversation ever since. He has been prompting me repeatedly and I've had to keep avoiding his leads. Nevertheless he appears satisfied with answers that I've been careful not to give. How can that be?"*

The enemy mentality was searching with swiftly mounting alarm. Telepathy was completely outside its experience, nothing like it having been encountered in its native habitat. But when an astute mind fails to solve a problem on the basis of recorded data and steps right outside of experience to seek a solution within the imagination, anything is possible.

At any moment Riley was going to conceive the formerly inconceivable.

Then would come the eruption.

Chapter 12

Casually scratching under one arm in order to have fingers near the gun, Harper said, "I don't know why I asked you. I'm not in the least interested. If you feel touchy on the subject you can attribute my question to mere yap. I've been doing too much of that considering the jobs waiting to be done. Go away and let me tend to my business."

He failed in his attempt to divert the thoughtstream into another direction.

"He has a weapon there," it flowed on. *"I have seen him carrying it many a time. He has his hand on it and cannot conceal his tenseness. He would not be like that if he knew nothing. Therefore he knows something in spite of all my attempts to hide it."* A puzzled pause, then, *"I came in the role of an old friend. Yet he makes ready to deal with. me for what I am."*

Grinning at him, Harper withdrew the hand, used it scratch his head instead. It was a mistake.

"By the Great Black Rock of Karsim, he can hear my thoughts!"

The desk went over with a crash that shook the floor as Harper dived headlong across it and grabbed the hand which Riley was digging into a pocket. Something small, oval and metallic lay in the pocket but did not come out.

Voicing a loud oath in no known language, Riley used his free hand to try to haul Harper from the pinioned one. He was a heavy, powerful man with a huge grip that had clamped itself unbreakably on many a struggling felon. Hauling with irresistible strength, he was caught unaware when Harper went willingly with the pull and helped it farther. The unexpected co-operation sent him teetering on his heels, at which point Harper shoved with all his might.

Together they fell to the floor, with Harper partly on top. Riley's eyes were aflame, his features crimson as he fought to beat off his opponent long enough to get at the object in his pocket. Pinning him down was like trying to fasten an enraged tiger to the earth.

A thick-knuckled fist landed squarely on Harper's mouth and brought a spurt of blood from split lips. The sight of it created a horrible eagerness in Riley's features. He redoubled his efforts to throw the other off, heaving tremendously and keeping his gaze on the blood.

Panting as he strove to maintain his position of vantage, Harper caught a knee-thrust in the stomach, whooshed expelled breath, spat crimson drops and hoarsed, "No you don't, you—!" He released his hold on Riley's right wrist, got a two-handed grip on his neck and dug thumbs into his windpipe.

At that point Norris jumped through the doorway, gun in hand, and bawled, "Break it up! Break it up, I tell you!"

Riley heaved with maniac force, tossed Harper off his middle, kicked at his head as he rolled aside and missed. He shot upright, glaring at Norris and showing complete disregard of the gun. He made a motion toward his pocket, came down flat before he could touch it as Harper twisted on the floor and snatched the feet from under him.

Clutching each other afresh, the two threshed around with bodies squirming and legs flailing right and left. A tall filing cabinet shuddered under their impact, rocked forward, toppled and flung a shower of business papers across the office. The telephone leaped from its rack, two bottles of ink and one of paste added themselves to the mess. The combatants continued to fight fiercely amid the litter.

Rausch and two more agents appeared just as Norris firmed his lips and stepped forward determined to end the battle. The four made a concerted rush that swept Harper aside and got Riley good and tight. They dragged him upright.

Sweating profusely, Riley stood in their grip, forced righteous indignation into his face and declaimed with plausible resentfulness, "The man's gone completely mad. He attacked me without warning and for no reason at all. There must be something wrong with him."

It was said with such a natural air that Norris had a nervy moment of wondering whether Harper had gone bad right under his nose and despite all their precautions.

"Feel in his pocket and see what he's got," suggested Harper. Sitting on the edge of the upended desk, he dabbed his bleeding lips with a handkerchief.

Norris did that, produced a grenade, examined it. "Army model, same as Baum used." He gazed hard-eyed at Riley. "Funny sort of thing for a police officer to carry around, isn't it?"

"He's not a police officer any more," Harper put in. "And he isn't Riley either. Rush him down to the Biological Research Laboratory. They need him there at once."

These words created a sudden frenzy in the prisoner. His arms were held but his legs were not. He kicked Norris in the middle, tore loose, tried to snatch the grenade. Norris bent forward doubled with agony, but held on to it. Riley pulled at him, gobbling and foaming, making strange whining noises and working his features almost out of recognition.

An agent sapped him. Riley rocked dazedly, let his hands hang. The agent slogged him again, a vicious crack devoid of mercy. Riley collapsed like an empty sack. He lay with eyes closed, lips shut and breathed with eerie bubbling sounds.

"I've no time for belly-kickers," said the agent.

Norris straightened himself painfully, his face white and strained. He held out the grenade. "Take it away some place where it can do no harm."

"Same applies to the owner," Harper reminded. "Tie him up so he can't choke himself with his own fingers and get him to the Bio. Lab."

"Is he—?"

"Yes, he is. And it's my fault. He had entry to this office and it's cost him his soul."

"I thought you were supposed to be able to smell them coming," Norris complained. "What's the use of us guarding you for half a mile around if they can walk in like this and—"

"I knew he was coming."

"Then why didn't you tell us? I was listening-in to your conversation and thought it decidedly fishy. You were needling him for some reason or other. But seeing that you had sounded no alarm we—"

"Look," said Harper firmly, "this is no time for explanations or post-mortems. Rush him to Doctor Leeming at the Bio. Lab. as fast as you can make it. And don't give him the slightest opportunity to finish himself on the way there. I'm giving you fair warning that if he can't escape he'll kill himself by any means to hand. He must be delivered alive and in one piece."

"All right."

Norris signed to the others. They lifted Riley, who now had steel cuffs on wrists and ankles and was still unconscious. They carried him out.

Mopping his lips again, Harper stared moodily at the wreckage of his office. He was not really seeing it, though. He was physically and spiritually shaken and striving to overcome it. Crazy circumstances had turned an old law topsy-turvy and made the reversal equally true: greater love hath no man than this, that he lay down a friend's life for himself.

Horrible, horrible!

Moira came in, saying, "I left all my money behind, so I couldn't—" She halted, went wide-eyed, let go a gasp. "Why, Mr. Harper, what on earth has happened?"

"I had a fit of sneezing."

Dragging his desk upright and restoring his chair to its legs, he sat and continued to ruminate while Moira scrabbled for loose papers. Then suddenly he smacked a hand to his forehead and ejaculated, "I go dafter as I get older!"

He dashed out while Moira knelt in the middle of the floor and gaped after him.

On the sidewalk Norris and Rausch were standing with hands in pockets while watching two cruisers speed along the street.

Norris greeted him with, "He's gone. They'll hand him over to Leeming in no time." Then a mite doubtfully, "And I hope you know what you're doing.

There'll be plenty of trouble if we've blundered in this case."

"You've not dealt with the half of it yet," informed Harper hurriedly. "There's a gang of them hiding in his home. What's more, I've reason to think they knew of his capture the moment he was slapped to sleep. Ten to one it got them on the run forthwith. You'll have to move fast to nab them."

"We can do no more than our best," said Norris unimpressed and making no move.

"McDonald's there and several others," Harper urged. He scowled impatiently at the other. "Well, are you going to take action or do I have to go myself?"

Easy now," Norris advised. He gave a slow smile. "We know exactly where Riley lives. He's been followed time and again."

"What of it?"

"When we carted him out a raid on his house became the next logical step. Five cars with twenty men have gone there. They'll grab everyone they can lay hands on. Afterwards, and if necessary, we'll use you to tell us who is which."

"So you've been thinking ahead of me, eh?"

"It happens sometimes," assured Norris, smiling again. "You can't lead the field all the way. Nobody can do that, no matter what his mental speed."

"Thanks for the reminder. Send a man round the garbage cans to get a few ashes, will you? I wish to put them upon my head while work proceeds."

He returned to the office. Moira had already succeeded in restoring some semblance of order. She filed the last of the scattered papers in the cabinet, closed it with an emphatic slam, surveyed him much as a long-suffering mother would regard an irresponsible child. That did nothing for his ego, either.

"Thank you, Angel. Now go get your lunch."

He waited until she had departed, picked up the phone, made a long-distance call to Leeming.

"A live one is on the way to you right now and, with luck, there'll be several more to come. Don't tell me what you propose to do to the first arrival. I don't want to know."

"Why not?" Leeming asked, exhibiting curiosity through the visiscreen. "Is it somebody close to you?"

"Yes. A big, lumbering, good-natured cop I've known for years. I hate to think of you carving him up."

"He won't be carved. We've done all we need of that on dead bodies. Living victims will be used as test-subjects for likely vaccines."

"What's the chance of developing a satisfactory cure?" Harper asked.

"There's another problem far more important," Leeming gave back. "Namely, whether we can find one in adequate time. We can succeed and yet fail because success comes too late."

"That doesn't answer my question."

"I refuse to commit myself at this stage. We aren't the only ones on the job. In a crisis of this sort, the government turns to anyone and everyone who can lend a hand, private laboratories included. Somebody else may strike lucky and come up with a solution while we're still seeking it. All we can do here is work like hell and pray."

"If producible, an effective vaccine should be innocuous, shouldn't it?" Harper pursued.

"What do you mean?"

"The cure shouldn't be little better than the disease?"

"What the devil are you getting at?"

Harper hesitated, continued carefully, "I'll tell you something. That virus cannot think by itself any more than you can drive a non-existent car. But it can think when in possession of a brain. And I know one thing it thinks about. It is scared to death of meningococci."

"What?" yelled Leeming, thunderstruck.

"I'm giving you a genuine, basic fact. That alien nightmare has a nightmare of its own. No living thing can be afflicted by it and have cerebro-spinal meningitis at one and the same time. Something has to go under and it's the virus that does the going."

"Where did you learn all this?"

"From a victim. The one they're taking down to you at this moment."

"How did you find out?"

"He told me without realizing it. He named his alien obsession and I'm giving it you for what it's worth."

Leeming breathed heavily, excitement showing in his eyes.

"It could be, too. It really could be. Areas of local infection are identical. Brain and spinal column. You can see what that means—a fight for living space."

"Suppose you squirt someone full of meningococci," Harper went on, "and he becomes cured with respect to the foreign disease. What'll he be like with respect to the cure itself?"

"That's something we've yet to discover," said Leeming, grim and determined.

"Well, I've no choice but to leave it with you. All I ask is for you to remember that your first test-subject is my friend."

He cut off, racked the phone, sat twisting his fingers and staring at them. After a while he held his face in his hands and murmured, "It had to be Riley and his wife. Poor devils!"

In the late afternoon Norris beckoned him out of Moira's hearing, said, "They got Mrs. Riley, Mrs. Reed and two men named Farley and Moore. We've discovered that the women are sisters. Farley and Moore were friends of the Reeds. Moore was a close business associate of the Baum brothers. You can see the link-up and how trouble has spread from one to another."

"Did they put up a fight?"

"You bet they did. When the boys got there the house was empty and the front door still swinging. The rats had run for it but hadn't time to escape from sight. Mrs. Riley, Farley and Moore were nabbed on the street half a mile away. They needed three men apiece to hold them."

"And what of the others?" Harper asked.

"Mrs. Reed was picked up in a store pretending to be one of the crowd. She reacted like a wildcat. Reed himself stepped off a roof rather than be taken. McDonald was trapped in a parking lot while trying to steal a car. He was armed. He shot it out to the finish."

"He is dead?"

"Yes. Same as Langley and for the same reason. It was impossible to take him alive."

"How about Gould?"

Norris rocked back. "What d'you mean, how about Gould?"

"He was there at Riley's house."

"Are you sure of that?"

"I'm positive."

Accepting that without argument, Norris affirmed, "There was no sign of him. But he'll be found." He mused a bit, went on, "We're now tracing all contacts of the entire bunch and pulling them in as fast as we find them. The total number may come to hundreds. Anyone known to have stood within a yard of any one of them is liable to be taken for questioning. You'd better hold yourself in readiness to look them over as we line them up."

"All right."

"It may go on for weeks, perhaps months."

"I'll suffer it." Harper eyed him speculatively. "You say that Riley's house was deserted when your men arrived?"

"Yes."

"Who tipped them to leave in a hurry?"

"Nobody," said Norris. "When Riley didn't return on time they took alarm and fled."

"It was more positive than that," Harper informed. "They were tipped."

"By whom?"

"By Riley himself. He couldn't help it. He lost consciousness and that was enough for them. They got out fast the moment one of your boys clouted Riley on the head. They *knew* he'd been caught."

"I don't see how," Norris protested.

"Never mind how. I'm telling you that each one of them knows when another has been put out of action."

"What of it, anyway?"

"At the Bio. Lab. they're holding an afflicted dog. I've a feeling that sooner or later that animal may be able to summon help. It's a guess and nothing more. How about persuading Jameson to put a guard on the place?"

"It's already protected. You ought to know that. You've been there."

"The guard is a military one. It isn't prepared for the sort of trouble we're having here."

"You're doing the identification for us at this end," said Norris. "Who'll do it for them down there?"

"Me."

"What, over such a distance?"

"I'm going there. I'm a constant center of interest to the foe no matter where I may be. That dog is a focal point for them. So is each and every live victim we hold. Get them all in one place and we thereby create a cumulative attraction that may prove irresistible. Desire for revenge, rescue and continued concealment should be more than enough to draw the enemy's full strength to the one spot. Their best bet lies in making a concerted effort. It would be about the only chance we'd ever get of settling them with a single blow."

"I'll put it to Jameson and ask him to consult General Conway," said Norris. "The plan is worth considering."

"While you're at it you can tell Jameson that I'm on my way, no matter what is decided."

"You can't do that."

"I can. Try giving me contrary orders and see where it gets you." He grinned at Norris. "I'm a free individual and intend to remain one with or without the kind permission of Conway or any other character."

"But Rausch and I have to stay with you," Norris objected. "And we're supposed to work this trap. It's operating all right. Look at today's catch."

"The bait is transferring itself to a bigger and better rat-run," Harper gave back. "Please yourself whether you come along."

He tramped into the office, found his week-end case, checked its contents, said to Moira, "Hold the fort, rush out the products, make excuses for me and bank the profits. Papa's taking another trip."

Norris and Rausch piled into his car as he was about to start, and the former said, "We've got to hang on to your coat-tails, no matter what you do. Your plant remains under guard. But if someone cockeyed walks into it there'll be nobody to give warning."

"Same applies at the Bio. Lab., which is now a more enticing target." Harper pulled out from the curb and took the center of the street. "And I cannot be in two places at once."

He drove fast with another burdened car following close behind. His mind reached out and felt around as he went through the town. This time, he decided, a faint threnody of alien thoughts would not be ignored. He was at the wheel and he'd go after it.

But it did not come. They cleared the town and roared into the country without being drawn into hectic pursuit of a lone masquerader among the multitude. That did not mean that Gould or any fellow conspirators had fled the place; only that if still there they were lurking out of receptive range.

The car swung into its fenced and patrolled destination an hour after darkness had fallen. Norris immediately put through a call to Jameson, briefed him on latest events. Some time later Jameson called back.

"You're getting your own way," Norris informed Harper. "Conway has ordered special measures to protect this place."

"Unless I've gravely miscalculated, we'll need 'em."

They did.

The attack came four days afterwards, by which time the delay had given some the secret belief that nothing would ever happen. It employed a technique characteristic of alien-controlled minds filled with two-world data and trying to combine the tactics of both. The plan represented a compromise between sneakiness and direct assault.

At midday a large, official-looking car slid up to the gates barring the main entrance. Its driver was attired as a sergeant of military police and its sole passenger was a gray-haired, autocratic man in the uniform of a four-star general. The sergeant showed the sentry an imposing pass, stamped, signed and ornamented with a large seal. The sentry scanned it slowly, making no attempt to open the gates. He smelled eucalyptus.

"Hurry up, Mister!" urged the sergeant authoritatively, while the general gazed forth with an air of stern reproof.

Though made nervous by the presence of high rank, the sentry took his time. He had been well-trained these last few days and understood that the gates were barred to God himself unless a bell in a nearby hut clanged permission to enter.

The bell did not sound. In the hut, at back of the fence, a watching agent pressed a stud. And in a building a quarter of a mile away a buzzer drew Harper's attention to the gate. He heard the whirr, ceased conversation with Rausch, listened, pressed another stud. A shrill peep sounded from the hut and an alarm siren started wailing over the main building.

Startled, the sentry dropped the pass, leveled his gun at the sergeant. Four agents leaped from the hut, weapons in hands. A dozen more appeared in the roadway behind the car.

Once more the possessed displayed their inhuman contempt for bullets and sudden death. Without slightest change of expression the sergeant let the car charge forward. The sentry fired two seconds before the hood struck his chest. The car hit the gate squarely in the middle and exploded.

The gate, the entire front of the hut, the car, its occupants, the sentry and six agents flew to pieces. Four more agents lay mauled and dead. Six groaned by the fence, injured but alive.

Two heavily loaded cars screamed along the road and rocked through the gap. The wounded agents fired into them as they passed, without visible result.

Neither vehicle got more than twenty yards beyond the wrecked gateway despite the lunatic speed with which they had arrived. The alarm had sounded too promptly, the preparations for it were too good, the drill too well-organized.

The leading car found its route blocked by an eighty-ton tank which lumbered forward spewing fire from three loopholes, riddling the target at the rate of two thousand bullets per minute. Shedding glass, metal splinters and blood, it slewed-on to grass and overturned. Nothing stirred within it.

Its follower halted just inside the fence, disgorged eight men who spread fanwise and raced inward at an angle outside the arc of fire. Ignoring them, the tank busily wrecked their machine.

Something farther back gave a low, dull *whoompwhoomp* and spurts of heavy vapor sprang from the ground one jump ahead of the invading eight. It did not halt them or give them to pause. They pelted headlong through the curtain of mist, made another twenty yards, collapsed one by one.

A pair of them dropped clutching grenades in hands that lost grip as vapor compelled their minds to swirl into unconsciousness. Released plungers walloped detonators, there came two brief eruptions of turf, dirt and flesh.

Masked men picked up the remaining six as the tank crunched forward on noisy caterpillars and filled the torn gateway. Shots and shouts sounded far away at the other side of the area where six men had picked off two patrolling guards, climbed the fence and been trapped. It was a foolhardy tactic depending for success in sufficient diversion at the front gate.

Five minutes after the battle had ended a convoy of armored cars toured the countryside for fifty miles around, Harper being a passenger in the first one. It was two hours before he picked up the only trace.

"There!" he said, pointing to an abandoned farmhouse.

They kept him out of reach while they made the attack. It produced three corpses and two badly wounded captives.

No more were findable before dawn, when the search became complete. Harper arrived back red-eyed, tousle-haired and fed up.

"Gould was in that first car," Norris informed.

"Dead?"

"All of them, nine in number. That tank made a job of it." He shrugged, added, "Now we've the task of discovering the identities of all those involved, including those whose bodies got scattered around. After that, we must trace all their contacts and bring them in for clearance by you. I can see this lasting my lifetime."

Leeming entered the room. He was pale and drawn from lack of sleep. He said to Harper, "I'd like you to come take a look."

Leading the other through a series of corridors in which an armed guard stood at every corner, he reached a row of strongly barred cells, pointed into one.

"What can you tell me?" he asked in strained and anxious tones.

Harper looked. Inside, clad only in socks and pants, Riley sat aimlessly on the edge of a bed. His eyes were lackluster but his beefy face held an expression of childish amusement.

"Well?" pressed Leeming. "Is the virus conquered?"

"Yes." He voiced it without triumph and the other heard it without joy.

"You can say positively that it is no longer active within his system?"

"Yes."

Leeming hesitated, spoke solemnly. "I gave him what you said he feared the most. We had to try it. We just can't wait for a vaccine. First things come first—and humanity comes before the individual. So I called in Gottlieb and Mathers of the Bacteriological Warfare Station and we tried it."

Harper made no remark.

"It has proved a cure," Leeming went on. "Physically there are no ill effects. He shows no symptoms of meningitis from that viewpoint. Nevertheless, he has paid a price. I know it but I want your confirmation." He looked at Harper as if hoping for the one chance in a thousand that he would be pronounced wrong. "What is the price?"

"Insanity," said Harper.

"I hate to hear you say it." Leeming stood silently awhile and tasted the bitter ashes of victory, then said with faint hope, "There's another one in the next cell. A fellow named Moore."

Harper went there, gazed in and declared, "The same." Then something inside him gave way and he growled, "They're better off dead. Do you hear me? They have minds like porridge, all messed up to hell, and they're better off dead."

"They are dead," informed Leeming, on the defense. "They were dead when first brought to me. I cannot restore a human spirit already lost, I cannot recall an expelled soul. Science has its limits. When it can get that far it will have ceased to be science. The best we can manage is to defend the community by destroying a source of infection. And that we have achieved."

"I know, I know. Don't think I'm blaming you or anyone else." He patted Leeming's shoulder by way of comfort. "And don't reproach yourself, either. It's my illogical habit to regret the dirtier facts of life even when they're unalterable."

"Everything that can be done will be done," assured Leeming, perking up slightly. "We're treating all of them in the same way because at least it's swift and sure. After that, some of the country's best mental specialists will take them over. That's right out of my field but I wouldn't say they're beyond help. Maybe others can restore them to normality."

"Never," asserted Harper. "A battlefield is a torn and sterile area pock-marked with craters, littered with rubble and stinking of decomposition. That's what their brains are like."

He walked away, twitching fingers as he went. The war for a world had been won because, as usual, the few had sacrificed themselves for the many. The few who were humanity's best. Always it had been so, always would be.

It was two years before the last echoes of combat died away. That was when they called upon him to inspect and pass judgment on a small group of frightened people finally run down in faraway places. These were the only remaining contacts with any of the possessed. None proved subject to otherworld mastery.

During that long time he had looked over more than eight thousand suspects, many of them shipped back from overseas by co-operation of warned and wary governments. In the first week he had discovered four men who were not men, and in the second week one woman who was not a woman. After that there had been no more. The world had cleared itself of mental sepsis.

The missing space-vessel had been discovered lying in a hundred fathoms beyond Puget Sound, and salvage outfits were still toiling to raise it piecemeal. Scientists were busily devising positive means of protection for a second Venusian expedition and seeking an effective weapon with which to free the Wends, an agile, intelligent, lemur-like creature that could speak.

"Var silvin, Wend?"

The Lunar Development Company had won its suit and the powers-that-be had received a legalistic rap across the knuckles. A reward of five thousand dollars had been used to start a fund for the dependents of spacemen and already the total sum had passed the million mark. From Harper's viewpoint, these were by far the two most pleasing items to date.

But no heavy hand bashed open his door, nobody brushed his papers aside to make seating room on his desk, nobody claimed some of his time for an exchange of insults. Riley was away in a big house in the country, helping with the gardening, doing petty chores, smiling at chirping sparrows, being gently led to his bedroom when sleepy time came. Like all the others, a little child. He would never be any different. Never, never, never.

So far as Harper personally was concerned, the aftereffects of the fracas would remain with him all his life. Not only in memory but also in immediate circumstances.

For instance, business had grown as he expanded into ancillary products. Forty men now worked in the plant. One of them, Weiss, was not only a highly skilled instrument maker, but also a government stooge. Conway's eye. He could blind it by firing the man—only to be watched by another. There was no way of getting rid of constant observation.

His mail was watched. There were many times when he suspected a tap on his telephone line. Whenever he made a swift move by car or plane he was followed. Norris or Rausch called once a month for an idle chat designed to remind him that the memory of authority is long and unforgiving.

What they were after was continued proof of his genuine uniqueness to the end of his days or, alternatively, evidence that birds of a feather were beginning to flock together. One Harper was enough. Two would be dangerous. Ten would represent a major crisis.

Despite rapidly increasing prosperity he was irritable, frustrated and desperately lonely. He experienced all the soul-searing solitude of a rare animal in the zoo constantly stared at by numberless curious eyes. Sometimes he felt that they'd willingly shoot him and stuff him but for the remote possibility of a recurrence of past events. They might need him again.

Yes, they feared him, but feared other things more.

There was no escape from the situation other than that of burying himself in business, of concentrating on one thing to the exclusion of everything else. That he had done to the best of his ability. So the plant had grown and micromanipulators become only a minor part of his output. He was heading for the role of a wealthy man locked in a worldwide jail.

Another thirty months crawled by, making four and a half years in all. Then the miracle happened. It was unbelievable. But it was true.

He was about to take his car from a parking lot when he caught a brief flicker of alien thought. It struck him like a physical blow. The direction and range were sensed automatically: from the south, about four miles away. A distance far beyond his normal receptivity.

With sweating hand on the car's door he stood and listened again, seeking it directively. There it came. It was not alien. It had only seemed to be so because new and strange, like nothing previously encountered. It had power and clarity as different from other thought-streams as champagne differs from water.

He probed at it and immediately it came back with shock equal to his own. Getting into his car, he sat there shakily. His mind fizzed with excitement and there were butterflies in his stomach while he remained staring through the windshield and apparently day-dreaming. Finally, he drove to a large restaurant, ordered dinner.

She had a table to herself far away at the opposite end of the room. A strawberry blonde, small, plump, in her middle thirties. Her face was pleasantly freckled and she had a tip-tilted nose. At no time did she glance his way. Neither did he pay any attention to her when he departed.

After that they met frequently without ever coming near each other or exchanging one vocal word. Sometimes he ate in one place while she sipped coffee in another half a mile away. Other times he mused absently in the office while she became thoughtful in a distant store. They took in the same show, he in one part of the theater and she in another, and neither saw much of the performance.

They were waiting, waiting for circumstances to change with enough naturalness and inevitability to fool the watchers. The opportunity was coming, they both knew that. Moira was wearing a diamond ring.

In due course Moira departed with congratulations and a wedding gift. Twenty girls answered the call for her successor. Harper interviewed them all, according the same courtesy, putting the same questions, displaying no visible favoritism one way or the other.

He chose Frances, a strawberry blonde with plump figure and pert nose.

Ten days later Norris arrived on his periodic visit, looked over the newcomer, favored her with a pleasant smile, mentally defined her as nice and nothing more. He started the chit-chat while Harper listened and gazed dreamily at a point behind the other's back.

"For the fiftieth time, will you marry me?"

"For the fiftieth time, yes. But you must be patient. We'll fall into it gradually."

"So this fellow showed the manager a bunch of documents certifying him to be a bank manager from head office," droned Norris. "The manager fell for it and—" He paused, added in louder tones, "Hey! Are you paying attention?"

"Of course. Carry on. I can hardly wait for the climax."

"I don't want to be patient. I don't want to be gradual. I want to fall into it fast."

"You know better than that. We must be careful."

"I want children just like us."

"Wait!"

She slipped paper into her typewriter, adjusted it, pink-faced and smiling.

"That was his downfall," finished Norris, completely innocent of the by-play. "So he tied himself up for life."

"Don't we all?" said Harper, hiding his bliss.

NEXT OF KIN

Introduction by Jack L. Chalker

Next of Kin is one of those rare science fiction novels that is sheer fun. Oh, it has much of Russell's cynicism and his opinions of authority and bureaucracy, and, as with many of his classic shorter fiction tales, its hero is somebody who is so off-kilter his superiors are *happy* to send him off on what is probably a suicide mission. What our hero discovers is that the reason we're so totally at war with the opposing galactic empire isn't because of two different political systems or social systems or whatever, but, rather, because the enemy's so much like us we can't stand them.

If you have previously read some of Russell's short fiction, though, and particularly if you've read *Major Ingredients*, NESFA Press's collection of some of the best of Russell's shorter works, you might have a sense of *deja vu* even if you've never heard of *Next of Kin* before. That's because you probably read it—or, rather, *some* of it.

You see, *Next of Kin* was written not once, not twice, but three times.

As the novel *Next of Kin*, it was submitted, as much of Russell's work always was, to John W. Campbell's *Astounding Science Fiction*. This wasn't because the British Russell was so in love with the United States, but rather it was because, from the start, Campbell paid more than anybody else in the field and had the largest audience. In a day when independent science fiction novels as books were just emerging as viable, having a three part serial in *Astounding* at three cents a world in 1950s dollars while retaining the option to then sell the book rights was irresistible. Campbell, however, for that very reason, was always up to his armpits in good novels to serialize, and *Next of Kin* wasn't *Sinister Barrier*—that is, it wasn't a novel with something new and different no matter how much fun it was. He did, however, see in the core of the novel a novelette that could be pulled from it retaining the entire main story. With Campbell's markups, Russell then rewrote the story as a novelette and it was published in *Astounding* as "Plus X," and may be found in *Major Ingredients*.

Russell had little trouble selling the book in Britain as written, but his U.S. agent could get no takers from the hardcover or emerging paperback markets. The only nibble came from Ace, which at that time was publishing only Ace Double Novels—twin books of about 40,000 words each that were put together back to back and bound as one. Many of these pairings made no sense at all, combining authors that had far different appeal or very different sorts of books, but for some authors Ace would do a twin by the same popular name. If Russell could trim *Next of Kin* to around, say, 40,000 words, then, they'd publish it as one-half a double novel. They also then said that he could pick short stories of his that hadn't been previously collected and make a similarly length collection for the other half. Russell agreed, and thus an in-between version, titled *The Space Willies*, appeared together with a collection of Russell shorts, *Six Worlds Yonder*. From that point, the only way to read the complete novel was in the U.K. Dobson hardcover or subsequent British paperbacks. It wasn't until my project to get some of Russell's best novels back in print in the U.S. via Del Rey in the late 1980s that *Next of Kin* finally appeared in the U.S., and then only in a one printing paperback.

Many people say that they can't sense the extra length one way or the other from "Plus X". Either way, it's a fun exercise in Russell's twisted logic and some reverse paranoia. In the end, Mayor Snorkum still lays a cake, we still don't know if it's a torpid mouse or a tepid moose, and the Sirians still have the Willies.

Chapter 1

He knew he'd stuck his neck out and it was too late to withdraw. It had been the same since early childhood when he'd accepted dares and been sorry immediately afterward. They say that one learns from experience; if that were true the human race would now be devoid of folly. He'd learned plenty in his time and forgotten most of it within a week. So yet again he'd wangled himself into a predicament and undoubtedly would be left to wangle himself out of it as best he could.

Once more he knocked at the door, a little harder but not imperatively. Behind the panels a chair scraped and a harsh voice responded with hearable impatience.

"Come in!"

Marching inside, he stood at attention before the desk, head erect, thumbs in line with the seams of the pants, feet at an angle of forty-five degrees. A robot, he thought, just a damned robot.

Fleet-Admiral Markham surveyed him from beneath bushy brows, his cold gaze slowly rising from feet to head then descending from head to feet.

"Who are you?"

"Scout-Officer John Leeming, sir."

"Oh, yes." Markham maintained the stare then suddenly barked, "Button your fly."

Leeming jerked and showed embarrassment. "I can't, sir. It has a defective zipper."

"Then why haven't you visited the tailor? That's what the base tailor-shop is for, isn't it? Does your commanding officer approve of his men appearing before me sloppily dressed? I doubt it! What the devil do you mean by it?"

"I haven't had time to tend to it, sir. The zipper packed up only a few minutes ago," explained Leeming.

"Is that so?" Fleet-Admiral Markham lay back in his chair and scowled at nothing. "There's a war on, a galactic war. To fight it successfully and to win it we are wholly dependent upon our space-navies. It's a hell of a thing when the navy goes into battle with defective zippers."

Since he seemed to expect a reply to that one, Leeming gave it. "With all respect, sir, I don't see that it matters. During a battle a man doesn't care what happens to his pants so long as he survives intact."

"I agree," said Markham. "But what worries me is the question of how much other and more important material may prove to be substandard. If civilian contractors fail on little things they'll certainly fail on big ones. Such failures can cost lives."

"Yes, sir," said Leeming, wondering what the other was getting at.

"A new and untried ship, for instance," Markham went on. "If it operates as planned, well and good. If it doesn't—" He let the sentence peter out, thought awhile, continued, "We asked for volunteers for special long-range reconnaissance patrols. You were the first to hand in your name. I want to know why."

"If the job has to be done somebody must do it," answered Leeming evasively.

"I am fully aware of the fact. But I want to know exactly why you volunteered." He waited a bit, urged, "Come on, speak up! I won't penalize a risk-taker for giving his reasons."

Thus encouraged, Leeming said, "I like action. I like working on my own. I don't like the time-wasting discipline they go in for around the base. It gives me a pain in the seat. Stand here, stand there, put your chest out, pull your belly in, polish your shoes, get a haircut, take that silly look off your face, who'd you think you're speaking to? I'm a fully trained scout pilot and not a dressed-up dummy for uniformed loudmouths to bark at. I want to get on with the work for which I am suited and that's all there is to it."

Markham showed no ire. On the contrary, he nodded understandingly. "So do most of us. Terrans always were an impatient bunch. Do you think I'm not frustrated sitting behind a desk while a major war is being fought?" Without waiting for a response he added, "I've no time for a man who volunteers because he's been crossed in love or wants to do some heavy bragging or anything like that. I want a competent pilot who is an individualist afflicted with the fidgets."

"Yes, sir."

"You seem to fit the part all right. Your technical record is first-class. Your disciplinary record stinks to high heaven." He eyed his listener blank-faced. "Two charges of refusing to obey a lawful order. Four for insolence and insubordination. One for parading with your cap on back to front. What on earth made you do that?"

"I had a bad attack of what-the-hell, sir," explained Leeming.

"Did you? Well, it's obvious that you're a confounded nuisance. The spacebase would be better off without you."

"Yes, sir."

"As you know, we and a few allies are fighting a big combine led by the Lathians. The size of the opposition doesn't worry us. What we lack in numbers we more than make up for in competence and efficiency. Our war-potential is great and rapidly growing greater. We'll skin the Lathians alive before we're through."

Leeming offered no comment, having become tired of yessing.

"We've one serious weakness," Markham informed. "We lack adequate information about the enemy's cosmic hinterland. We know how wide the Combine spreads but not how deep into the starfield it goes. It's true that the enemy is no wiser with regard to us, but that's his worry."

Again Leeming made no remark.

"Ordinary warships haven't flight-duration sufficiently prolonged to dig deep behind the Combine's spatial front. That difficulty will be overcome when we capture one or more of their outpost worlds with repair and refueling facilities. However, we can't afford to wait until then. Our Intelligence Service wants some essential data just as soon as it can be got. Do you understand?"

"Yes, sir."

"Good! We have developed a new kind of superfast scout-ship. I can't tell you how it functions except that it does not use the normal cesium-ion form of propulsion. Its type of power-unit is a top secret. For that reason it must not fall into the enemy's hands. At the last resort the pilot must destroy it even if it means also destroying himself."

"Completely wrecking a ship, though a small one, is much more difficult than it seems."

"Not this ship," Markham retorted. "She carries an effective charge in her engine-room. The pilot need but press a button to scatter the power-units piecemeal over a wide area."

"I see."

"That charge is the sole explosive aboard. The ship has not a gun, not a guided missile, no armament of any sort. It's a stripped-down vessel with everything sacrificed for the sake of speed and its only defense is to scoot good and fast. That, I assure you, it can do. Nothing in the galaxy can catch it providing it is squirting from all twenty propulsors."

"Sounds good to me, sir," approved Leeming, licking his lips.

"It is good. It's got to be good. The unanswered question is that of whether it is good enough to take the beating of a long, long trip. The tubes are the weakest part of any spaceship. Sooner or later they burn out. That's what bothers me. The tubes on this ship have very special linings. In theory they should last for months. In practice they might not. You know what that means?"

"No repairs and no replacements in enemy territory, no means of getting back," Leeming offered.

"Correct. And the vessel would have to be destroyed. From that moment the pilot, if still surviving, has isolated himself somewhere within the mists of Creation. His chance of seeing humankind again is remote enough to verge on the impossible."

"There could be worse situations. I'd rather be alive someplace else than stone-dead here. While there's life there's hope."

"You still wish to go through with this?"

"Sure thing, sir."

"Then upon your own head be it," said Markham with grim humor. "Go along the corridor, seventh door on the right, and report to Colonel Farmer. Tell him I sent you."

"Yes, sir."

"And before you go try that damned zipper again."

Obediently, Leeming tried it. The thing slid all the way as smoothly as if oiled. He stared at the other with a mixture of astonishment and injured innocence.

"I started in the ranks and I haven't forgotten it," said Markham, pointedly. "You can't fool me."

Colonel Farmer, of Military Intelligence, was a beefy, florid-faced character who looked slightly dumb but had a sharp mind. He was examining a huge star-map hung upon one wall when Leeming walked in. Farmer swung around as if expecting to be stabbed in the back.

"Haven't you been taught to knock before you enter?"

"Yes, sir."

"Then why didn't you?"

"I forgot, sir. My mind was occupied with the interview I've just had with Fleet-Admiral Markham."

"Did he send you to me?"

"Yes, sir."

"Oh, so you're the long-range reconnaissance pilot, eh? I don't suppose Commodore Keen will be sorry to see you go. You've been somewhat of a thorn in his side, haven't you?"

"No, sir," denied Leeming. "I have been a pain in his seat—every time he's tried to sit on me."

"In the armed forces one must get used to that sort of thing."

"Sorry, sir, but I don't agree. One joins the forces to help win a war and for no other purpose. I am not a juvenile delinquent called up for reformation by the Commodore or by anyone else."

"He'd differ from you there. He's a stickler for discipline." Farmer let go a chuckle at some secret joke, added, "Keen by name and keen by nature." He contemplated the other a short while, went on more soberly, "You've picked yourself a tough job."

"That doesn't worry me," Leeming assured. "Birth, marriage and death are tough jobs."

"You might never come back."

"Makes little difference. Eventually we'll all take a ride from which we'll never come back."

"Well, you needn't mention it with such ghoulish satisfaction," Farmer complained. "Are you married?"

"No, sir. Whenever I get the urge I just lie down quietly until the feeling passes off."

Farmer eyed the ceiling and said, "God!"

"What else do you expect?" asked Leeming, displaying slight aggressiveness. "A scout-pilot operates single-handed. He's like a bug in a metal can and has to learn to dispense with a lot of things, especially companionship. It's surprising how much one can do without if one really tries."

"I'm sure," soothed Farmer. He gestured toward the star-map. "On that, the nearest points of light are arrayed across the enemy's front. The mist of stars behind them are unknown territory. The Combine may be far weaker than we think because its front is wafer-thin. Or it may be more powerful because its authority stretches far to the rear. The only way to find out exactly what we're up against is to effect a deep penetration through the enemy's spatial lines."

Leeming said nothing.

"We propose to send a special scout-ship through this area where occupied worlds lie far apart, the Combine's defenses are somewhat scattered and their detector devices are relatively sparse." Farmer put his finger on a dark patch on the map. "With the speed your vessel possesses, the enemy will have hardly enough time to identify you as hostile before they lose trace of you. We have every reason to believe that you'll be able to slip through into their rear without trouble."

"I hope so," contributed Leeming, seeing that a response was expected.

"The only danger point is here." Shifting his finger an inch, Farmer placed it on a bright star. "A Lathian-held solar system containing at least four large space-navy stations. If those fleets happen to be zooming around the bolt-hole they might intercept you more by accident than good judgment. So you'll be accompanied that far by a strong escort."

"That's nice."

"If the escort should become involved in a fight you will not attempt to take part. It would be futile to do so, anyway, because your vessel carries no offensive armament. You will take full advantage of the diversion to race out of range and dive through the Combine's front. Is that understood?"

"Yes, sir."

"After you get through you must use your initiative. Bear in mind that we don't want to know how far beyond there are worlds holding intelligent life—you would never reach the end of those even if you continued to the crack of doom. We want to know only how far back there are such worlds in regular communication with various members of the Combine. Whenever you come across an organized planet playing ball with the Combine you will at once transmit all the details you can offer."

"I will."

"Immediately you are satisfied that you have gained the measure of the enemy's depth you will return as quickly as possible. You must get the ship back here if it can be done. If for any reason you cannot return, the ship must be converted into scrap. No abandoning it in free space, no dumping it into an ocean or anything like that. The ship *must* be destroyed. Markham has emphasized this, hasn't he?"

"Yes, sir."

"All right. We're giving you forty-eight hours in which to clear up your personal affairs. After that, you will report to Number Ten Spaceport." Farmer held out his hand. "I wish you all the luck you can get."

"Thinking I'll need it?" Leeming grinned and went on, "You're laying very heavy odds against ever seeing me again. It's written across your face. I'll be back—want to bet on it?"

"No," said Farmer. "I never gamble because I'm a bad loser. But if and when you do return I'll tuck you into bed with my own two hands."

"That's a promise," warned Leeming.

He went to his tiny room, found another fellow already in occupation. This character eyed him with faint embarrassment.

"You Leeming?"

"That's right."

"I'm Davies, Jack Davies."

"Glad to know you." Grabbing his bags, Leeming started packing them, stuffing away with careless haste shirts, collars and handkerchiefs.

Sitting on the bed, Davies informed, "They told me to take over your room. They said you'd be leaving today."

"Correct."

"Going far?"

"Don't know for certain. It might be too far."

"Are you pleased to go?"

"Sure am," Leeming enthused.

"Can't say I blame you." Davies ruminated a moment in glum silence, went on, "I arrived a couple of hours ago and reported to the Base C.O. An autocratic type if ever I saw one." He gave a brief, unflattering description of Commodore Keen. "I don't know his name."

"Mallarqui," Leeming informed.

"That so? Uncommon, isn't it?"

"No." Closing the case, Leeming kneeled on its lid while he locked it, started on the next one. "It's as old as the hills. You've heard of a lot of Mallarqui, haven't you?"

"Yes, I have."

"Well, in this dump there's too much of it."

"I think you're right. Mallarqui took one look at me and yelled, 'Haircut!' " Ruefully, Davies rubbed the short bristle covering his pate. "So I went and got one. What a Space Navy! Immediately you show your face they scalp you. And what d'you suppose happened next?"

"They issued you with a brush and comb."

"They did just that." He massaged the bristle again. "What for?"

"Same reason as they do everything else," explained Leeming. "B.B.B."

"B.B.B.? What d'you mean?"

"It's a motto adopted by the boys on inactive service. You'll find yourself reciting it about twenty times per day. Baloney Baffles Brains."

"I see," said Davies, taking on a worried look.

"The only way to escape is to fall foul of Keen. He'll get rid of you—after he's broken your heart."

"Keen? Who's he?"

"Mallarqui," corrected Leeming, hurriedly. "The fellows call him Keen behind his back. If you want to stay out of the pokey don't *ever* call him Commodore Keen to his face. He likes to be addressed as Mr. Mallarqui."

"Thanks for the tip," said Davies, innocently grateful.

"You're quite welcome. Take your butt off the bed—I want my pajamas."

"Sorry." Davies stood up, sat down again.

Cramming the pajamas into the case, Leeming closed it, took a long look around.

"That's about all, I guess. Victory has been postponed by sheer lack of efficient zippers. I got that information straight from the top. So they're rushing me out to win the war. From now on all you need do is sit around and count the days." He made for the door, a bag in each hand.

Coming to his feet again, Davies said awkwardly, "Happy landings."

"Thanks."

In the corridor the first person Leeming encountered was Commodore Keen. Being too burdened to salute, he threw the other a regulation eyes-left which Keen acknowledged with a curt nod. Keen brushed past and entered the room. His loud, harsh voice boosted out the open door.

"Ah, Davies, so you have settled in. Since you won't be required today you can clean up this hog-pen in readiness for my inspection this evening."

"Yes, Mr. Mallarqui."

"WHAT?"

Outside, Leeming took a firmer grip on his bags and ran like hell.

The ship was a beauty, the same diameter as an ordinary scout-vessel but over twice the length. These proportions made it look less like a one-man snoop-boat than a miniature cruiser. Standing on its tail, it towered so high that its nose seemed to reach halfway towards the clouds.

Studying it appreciatively, Leeming asked, "Any more like this?"

"Three," responded Montecelli, the spaceport's chief engineer. "All hidden elsewhere with a tight security ring around them. Strict orders from above say that this type of vessel may be used only one at a time. A second must not be sent out until after yours has returned."

"So I'm first on the list, eh? What if I don't come back? What if this ship is destroyed and you've no way of knowing?"

The other shrugged. "That's the War Staff's worry, not mine. I only obey directives from above and those can be trouble enough."

"H'm! Probably they've set a time limit for my safe return. If I'm not back by then they'll assume that I'm a gone goose."

"They haven't said anything to you about it?"

"No."

"Then don't you worry either. Life's too short. In time of war it gets shortened for many." Montecelli scowled at the sky. "Whenever a boat boosts upward on a column of flame I never know whether that'll be the last I'll ever see of it."

"That's right, cheer me on my way," said Leeming. "The life and soul of the party."

"Sorry, I clean forgot you're going." He pointed to an adjacent building. "In there we've set up a duplicate nose-cabin for training purposes. It will take you most of a week to become accustomed to the new-type controls, to learn to handle the transspatial radio and generally get the feel of things. You can start your education as soon as you like."

"All I'm bothered about is the autopilot," Leeming told him. "It had better be a good one. A fellow can't travel for days and weeks without sleep and he can't snooze with the ship running wild. A really reliable autopilot is his fairy godmother."

"Listen, son, if this one could do more than hold you on course while jerking you away from dangers, if it could see and think and transmit reports, we'd send it away without you." Montecelli gave his listener a reassuring slap on the shoulder. "It's the best ever. It'd take care of you even if you were on your honeymoon and temporarily unconscious of the cosmos."

"The only resemblance is that I'll need my strength," said Leeming. He entered the building and more or less stayed in it for the prescribed week.

The take-off came at one hour after sunset. There was a cloudless sky, velvet black and spangled with stars. Strange to think that far, far out there, concealed by sheer distance, were countless populated worlds with Combine warships parading warily between some of them while the allied fleets of Terrans, Sirians, Rigellians and others were on the prowl across an enormous front.

Below, long chains of arc-lights dithered as a gentle breeze swept across the spaceport. Beyond the safety barriers that defined the coming blast-area a group of people were waiting to witness the ascent. If the ship toppled instead of going up, thought Leeming wryly, the whole lot of them would race for sanctuary with burning backsides. It did not occur to him that in such an event he would be in poor position to enjoy the sight.

A voice came out of the tiny loudspeaker set in the cabin wall. "Warm up, Pilot."

He pressed a button. Something went *whump,* then the ship groaned and shuddered while a great circular cloud of dust and vapor rolled across the concrete and concealed the safety barriers. The low groaning and trembling continued while he sat in silence, his full attention upon the instrument bank. The needles of twenty meters crawled to the right, quivered awhile, became still. That meant steady and equal pressure in the twenty stern tubes.

"Everything all right, Pilot?"

"Yes."

"Take off at will." A pause, followed by, "Lots of luck!"

"Thanks!"

He let the tubes blow for another half minute before gradually he moved the tiny boost-lever toward him. Shuddering increased, the groan raised its pitch until it became a howl, the cabin windows misted over and the sky was obscured.

For a nerve-racking second the vessel rocked on its tail-fins. Then it began to creep upward, a foot, a yard, ten yards. The howl was now a shriek. The chronically slow rate of climb suddenly changed as something seemed to give the vessel a hearty shove in the rear. Up it went, a hundred feet, a thousand, ten thousand. Through the clouds and into the deep of the night. The cabin windows were clear, the sky was full of stars and the Moon looked huge.

The loudspeaker said in faint, squeaky tones, "Nice work, Pilot."

"All my work is nice," retorted Leeming. "See you in the asylum."

There was no answer to that. They knew that he'd become afflicted with an exaggerated sense of freedom referred to as take-off intoxication. Most pilots suffered from it as soon as a planet lay behind their tail and only the stars could be seen ahead. The symptoms consisted of sardonic comments and abuse raining down from the sky.

"Go get a haircut," bawled Leeming into his microphone. He jiggled around in his seat while the ship boomed onward. "And clean up that hog-pen. Haven't you been taught how to salute? Baloney baffles brains!"

They didn't answer that, either.

But down in the spaceport control-tower the duty officer pulled a face and said to Montecelli, "You know, I think that Einstein never worked out the whole of it."

"What d'you mean?"

"I have a theory that as one approaches the velocity of light one's inhibitions shrink to zero."

"You may have something there," Montecelli conceded.

"Pork and beans, pork and beans, Holy God, pork and beans," squawked the control-tower speaker with swiftly fading strength. "Get undressed because I want to test your eyes. Now inhale. Keen by name and keen by—"

The duty officer switched it off.

Chapter 2

He picked up the escort in the Sirian sector, the first encounter being made when he was fast asleep. Activated by a challenging signal on a pre-set frequency, the alarm sounded just above his ear and caused him to dive out of the bunk while no more than half awake. For a moment he gazed stupidly around while the ship vibrated and the autopilot went tick-tick.

"Zern kaid-whit?" rasped the loudspeaker. *"Zern kaid-whit?"*

That was code and meant, "Identify yourself—friend or foe?"

Taking the pilot's seat, he turned a key that caused his transmitter to squirt forth a short and ultra-rapid series of numbers. Then he rubbed his eyes and looked into the forward starfield. Apart from the majestic haze of suns shining in the dark there was nothing to be seen with the naked eye.

So he switched on his thermosensitive detector screens and was rewarded with a line of brilliant dots paralleling his course to starboard while a second group, in arrow formation, was about to cut across far ahead of his nose. He was not seeing the ships, of course, but only the visible evidence of their white-hot propulsion tubes and flaming tails.

"*Keefa!*" said the loudspeaker, meaning, "All correct!"

Crawling back into the bunk, Leeming hauled a blanket over his face, closed his eyes and left the autopilot to carry on. After ten minutes his mind began to drift into a pleasant, soothing dream about sleeping in free space with nobody to bother him.

Dropping its code-talk, the loudspeaker yelped in plain language. "Cut speed before we lose you."

He sat up as if stung, stared blearily across the cabin. Somebody had spoken, somebody with a parade-ground voice. Or had he imagined it? He waited a bit but nothing happened and so he lay down again.

The loudspeaker bawled impatiently. "You deaf? Cut speed before we lose you!"

Leeming clambered irefully from the bunk, sat at the controls, adjusted them slowly. A thin braking-jet in the bow let go a double plume of vapor that swept back on either side as the ship overtook and passed by. The stern tubes meanwhile decreased their thrust. He watched his meters until he thought their needles had dropped far enough to make the others happy. Then he returned to bed and hid himself under the blanket.

It seemed to him that he was swinging in a celestial hammock and enjoying a wonderful idleness when the loudspeaker roared, "Cut more! Cut more!"

He shot out from under the blanket, scrambled to the controls and cut more. Then he switched on his transmitter and made a speech distinguished by its passion. It was partly a seditious outburst and partly a lecture upon the basic functions of the human body. For all he knew the astonished listeners might include two rear-admirals and a dozen commodores. If so, he was educating them.

In return he received no heated retorts, no angry voice of authority. If he had broadcast the same words from a heavily manned battleship they'd have plastered him with forty charges and set the date for his court-martial. But it was space-navy convention that a lone scout's job created an unavoidable craziness among all those who performed it and that ninety per cent of them were overdue for psychiatric treatment. A scout on active service could and often did say things that nobody else in the space-navy dared utter. It is a wonderful thing to be recognized as dotty.

For three weeks they accompanied him in the glum silence with which a family takes around an imbecile relation. He chafed impatiently during this period because their top speed was far, far below his maximum velocity and the need to keep pace with them gave him the feeling of an urgent motorist trapped behind a funeral procession.

The Sirian battleship *Wassoon* was the chief culprit, a great, clumsy contraption that wallowed along like a bloated hippopotamus while a shoal of faster cruisers and destroyers were compelled to amble with it. He did not know its name but he did know that it was a battleship because on his detector screens it resembled a glowing pea amid an array of fiery pinheads. Every time he looked at the pea he cursed it something awful. He was again venting his ire upon it when the loud-speaker chipped in and spoke for the first time in many days.

"*Ponk!*"

Ponk? What the devil was ponk? The word meant something mighty important, he could remember that much. Hastily he scrabbled through the code-book and found it: *Enemy in sight.*

No sign of the foe was visible on his screens. Evidently they were beyond detector range and had been spotted only by the escort's advance-guard of four destroyers running far ahead.

"Dial F," ordered the loudspeaker.

So they were changing frequency in readiness for battle. Leeming turned the dial of his multiband receiver from T back to F. Laconic interfleet messages came through the speaker in a steady stream.

"Offside group port twenty, rising inclination twelve."

"Check!"

"Break off."

"Check!"

On the screens five glowing dots swiftly angled away from the main body of the escort. Four were mere pinheads, the fifth and middle one about half the size of the pea. A cruiser and four destroyers were escaping the combat area for the time-honored purpose of getting between the enemy and his nearest base.

In a three-dimensional medium where speeds were tremendous and space was vast this tactic never worked. It did not stop both sides from trying to make it work whenever the opportunity came along. This could be viewed as eternal optimism or persistent stupidity, according to the state of one's liver.

The small group of would-be ambushers scooted as fast as they could make it, hoping to become lost within the confusing welter of starlights before the enemy came near enough to detect the move. Meanwhile the *Wassoon* and its attendant cohort plugged steadily onward. Ahead, almost at the limit of the fleet's detector range, the four destroyers continued to advance without attempting to disperse or change course.

"Two groups of ten converging from forty-five degrees rightward, descending inclination fifteen," reported the forward destroyers.

"Classification?" demanded the *Wassoon.*

"Not possible yet."

Silence for six hours, then, "Two groups still maintaining same course; each appears to consist of two heavy cruisers and eight monitors."

That was sheer guesswork based upon the theory that the greater the detectable heat the bigger the ship. Leeming watched his screens knowing full well that the enemy's vessels might prove to be warships as the observers supposed or might equally well turn out to be escorted convoys of merchantmen. Since the spatial war first broke out many a lumbering tramp had been mistaken for a monitor.

Slowly, ever so slowly, twenty faintly discernible dots bloomed into his screens. This was the time when he and his escort should be discovered by the enemy's detection devices. The foe must have spotted the leading destroyers hours ago;

either they weren't worried about a mere four ships or, more likely, had taken it for granted that they were friendly. It would be interesting to watch their reaction when they found the strong force farther behind.

He did not get the chance to observe this pleasing phenomenon. The loudspeaker let go a squawk of, "Ware zenith!" and automatically his gaze jerked upward to the screens above his head. They were poxed with a host of rapidly enlarging dots. He estimated that sixty to eighty ships were diving in fast at ninety degrees to the plane of the escort, but he didn't stop to count them. One glance was sufficient to tell him that he was in a definite hot-spot.

Forthwith he lifted his slender vessel's nose and switched to full boost. The result pinned him in his seat while his intestines tried to wrap themselves around his spine. It was easy to imagine the effect upon the enemy's screens; they would see one mysterious, unidentifiable ship break loose from the target area and swoop around them at a speed previously thought impossible.

With luck, they might assume that what one ship could do all the others could do likewise. If there is anything a spaceship captain detests it is to have another and faster ship sneaking up on his tail. The fiery end of a spaceship is its weak spot for there can be no effective armament in an area filled with propulsors.

Stubbornly, Leeming stuck to the upward curve which, if maintained long enough, would take him well to one side of the approaching attackers and round to the back of them. He kept full attention upon his screens. The oncomers held course in a tight, vengeful knot for four hours, by which time they were almost within shooting range of the escort. At that point their nerve failed. The fact that the escort still kept impassive formation while one ship headed like a shooting star for their rear made them suspect a trap. One thing the Combine never lacked was suspicion of the Allies' motives and unshakable faith in their cunning.

So they curved out at right-angles and spread in all directions like the petals of a blown flower, their detectors probing for another and bigger fleet that might be lurking just beyond visibility.

Belting along at top pace, one Lathian light cruiser realized that its new course would bring it within range of the missiles with which Leeming's strange, superfast ship presumably was armed. It tried to play safe by changing course again and thereby delivered itself into the hands of the *Wassoon's* electronic predictors. The *Wassoon* fired, its missiles met the cruiser at the precise point where it came within range. Cruiser and missiles tried to occupy the same space at the same time. The result was a soundless explosion of great magnitude and a flare of heat that temporarily obliterated every detector screen within reach.

Another blast shone briefly high in the starfield and far beyond reach of the escort's armaments. A few minutes later a thin, reedy voice, distorted by static, reported that a straggling enemy destroyer had fallen foul of the distant ambushing party. This sudden loss, right outside the scene of action, seemed to confirm the enemy's belief that the *Wassoon* and its attendant fleet might be mere bait in a trap loaded with something formidable. They continued to radiate fast from their common center in an effort to locate the hidden menace and, at the same time, avoid being caught in a bunch.

Seeing them thus darting away like a shoal of frightened fish, Leeming muttered steadily to himself. A dispersed fleet should be easy prey to a superfast ship capable of overhauling and dealing with its units one by one. He had to face the fact that his vessel could do nothing more than scare them individually while he lavished futile curses upon them. Without a single effective weapon he was impotent to take advantage of an opportunity that might never occur again. For the moment he had quite forgotten his role, not to mention his strict orders to avoid a space-fight at all costs.

The *Wassoon* soon reminded him with a sharp call of, "Scout-pilot, where the hell d'you think you're going?"

"Up and around," replied Leeming sourly.

"You're more of a liability than an asset," retorted the *Wassoon,* unappreciative of his efforts. "Get out while the going is good."

Leeming yelled into the microphone, "I know when I'm not wanted, see? Spitting on parade is a punishable offense, see? Remember man, you must *always* salute a commodore. Stand properly to attention when you speak to me! We're being sabotaged by defective zippers. Come on, lift those feet Dopey—one, two, three, *hup!*"

As before, the listeners took no notice whatsoever. Leeming turned his ship on to a new course with plane parallel to that of the escort and high above them. They now became visible on his underbelly screens and showed themselves in the same unbroken formation but sweeping in a wide circle to get on the reverse course. That meant they were leaving him and heading homeward. The enemy, still scattered beyond shooting range, must have viewed this move as wicked temptation for although in superior strength they continued to refrain from direct attack.

Quickly the escort's array of shining dots slid off the screens as Leeming's vessel shot away from them. Ahead and well to starboard the detectors showed the two enemy groups that had first appeared. They had not dispersed in the same manner that their main force had done but their course showed that they were fleeing the area at the best pace they could muster. This fact suggested that they really were two convoys of merchantmen hugging close to their protecting cruisers. With deep regret Leeming watched them go. Given the weapons he could have swooped upon the bloated parade and slaughtered a couple of heavily-laden ships before the cruisers had time to wake up.

At full pelt he dived into the Combine's front and headed toward the unknown back areas. Just before his detectors lost range his tailward screen flared up twice in quick succession. Far behind him two ships had ceased to exist and there was no way of telling whether these losses had been suffered by the escort or the enemy.

He tried to find out by calling on the interfleet frequency, "What goes? What goes?"

No answer.

A third flash covered the screen. It was weak with distance and swiftly fading sensitivity.

Keying the transmitter to give his identifying code-number, he called again.

No reply.

If the battle had joined far to his rear they'd be much too busy to bother with his queries. He'd have given a lot to turn back and see for himself what was happening, to join the hooley and help litter the cosmos with wreckage. But without a major or minor weapon he was precisely what the *Wassoon* had declared him to be, namely, an unmitigated nuisance.

Chewing his bottom lip with annoyance, he squatted four-square in the pilot's seat and scowled straight ahead while the ship arrowed toward a dark gap in the hostile starfield. In due time he got beyond the full limit of Allied warships' non-stop range. At that point he also got beyond help.

The first world was easy meat. Believing it impossible for any Allied ship to penetrate this far without refueling and changing tubes, the enemy assumed that any ship detected in local space must be friendly or, at least, neutral. Therefore when picked up by their detectors they did not bother to radio a challenge and identify him as hostile by his inability to give a correct reply. They let him zoom around unhampered by official nosiness.

So he found the first occupied world by the simple process of shadowing a small convoy heading inward from the spatial front, following them long enough to make an accurate plot of their course. Then, because he could not afford to waste days and weeks crawling along at their relatively slow pace, he arced over them and raced ahead until he reached the inhabited planet for which they were bound.

Checking the planet was equally easy. He went twice around its equator at altitude sufficiently low to permit swift visual observation. Complete coverage of the sphere was not necessary to gain a shrewd idea of its status, development and potentialities. What he could see in a narrow strip around its belly was enough of a sampling for the purposes of the Terran Intelligence Service.

In short time he spotted three spaceports, two empty, the third holding eight merchant ships of unknown origin and three Combine war vessels. Other evidence showed the world to be heavily populated and well-advanced. He could safely mark it as a pro-Combine planet of considerable military value.

Shooting back into free space, he dialed X, the special long-range frequency, and beamed this information together with the planet's approximate diameter, mass and spatial coordinates.

"I dived in and circumnavigated the dump," he said, and let go a snigger. He couldn't help it because he was recalling his careless response to a similar situation set as a test piece in his first examination.

He had written, "I made cautious approach to the strange planet and then quickly circumcised it."

The paper had come back marked, "Why?"

He'd replied, "I could get around better by taking shortcuts."

It had cost him ten marks and the dead-pan comment, "This information lacks either accuracy or wit." But he had passed all the same.

There was no reply to his signal and he did not expect one. He could beam signals outward with impunity but they could not beam back into enemy territory without awakening hostile listening-posts to the fact that someone must be operating in their back areas. Beamed signals were highly directional and the enemy was always on the alert to pick up and decipher anything emanating from the Allied front while ignoring all broadcasts from the rear.

The next twelve worlds were found in substantially the same manner as the first one: by plotting interplanetary and interstellar shipping routes and following them to their termini. He signaled details of each one and each time was rewarded with silence. By this time he found himself deploring the necessary lack of response because he had been going long enough to yearn for the sound of a human voice.

After weeks that stretched to months, enclosed in a thundering metal bottle, he was becoming afflicted with an appalling loneliness. Amid this vast stretch of stars, with seemingly endless planets on which lived not a soul to call him Joe, he could have really enjoyed the arrival from faraway of an irate human voice bawling him out good and proper for some error, real or fancied. He'd have sat there and bathed his mind in the stream of abuse. Constant, never-ending silence was the worst of all, the hardest to bear.

Occasionally he tried to break the hex by singing at the top of his voice or by holding heated arguments with himself while the ship howled onward. It was a poor and ineffectual substitute because he was less musical than a tumescent tomcat and he couldn't win an argument without also losing it.

His sleeps were lousy, too. Sometimes he dreamed that the autopilot had gone haywire and that the ship was heading full-tilt into a blazing sun. Then he'd wake up with his belly jumping and make quick, anxious check of the apparatus before returning to slumber. Other times he awoke heavy-eyed and dry-mouthed feeling that he'd had no sleep at all, but had been lying supine through hours of constant trembling and a long, sustained roar.

Several times he had pursuit-dreams in which he was being chased through dark, metallic corridors that bellowed and quivered all around while close behind him sounded the rapid, vengeful tread of feet that were not feet. Invariably he woke up just as he was about to be grabbed by hands that were not hands.

In theory there was no need for him to suffer the wear and tear of long-range reconnaissance. A case full of wonder-drugs had been provided to cope with every conceivable condition of mind or body. The trouble was that they were effective or they were not. If ineffective, the taking of them proved sheer waste of time. If effective, they tended to shove things to the opposite extreme.

Before one sleep-period he had experimented by taking a so-called normalizing capsule positively guaranteed to get rid of nightmares and ensure happy, interesting dreams. The result had been ten completely uninhibited hours in a harem. They had been hours so utterly interesting that they'd left him flat out. He never took another capsule.

It was while he was nosing after a merchant convoy, in expectation of tracing a thirteenth planet, that he got some vocal sounds that at least broke the monotony. He was following far behind and high above the group of ships and they, feeling secure in their own backyard, were keeping no detector-watch and were unaware of his presence. Fiddling idly with the controls of his receiver he suddenly hit upon an enemy interfleet frequency and picked up a conversation between ships.

The unknown lifeform manning the vessels had loud, somewhat bellicose voices but spoke a language with sound-forms curiously akin to Terran speech. To Leeming's ears it came as a stream of cross-talk that his mind instinctively framed in Terran words. It went like this:

First voice: "Mayor Snorkum will lay the cake."

Second voice: "What for the cake be laid by Snorkum?"

First voice: "He will starch his mustache."

Second voice: "That is night-gab. How can he starch a tepid mouse?"

They spent the next ten minutes in what sounded like an acrimonious argument about what one repeatedly called a tepid mouse while the other insisted that it was a torpid moose. Leeming found that trying to follow the point and counterpoint of this debate put quite a strain upon the cerebellum. He suffered it until something snapped.

Tuning his transmitter to the same frequency, he bawled, "Mouse or moose, make up your goddam minds!"

This produced a moment of dumbfounded silence before the first voice harshed, "Gnof, can you lap a pie-chain?"

"No, he can't," shouted Leeming, giving the unfortunate Gnof no chance to brag of his ability as a pie-chain lapper.

There came another pause, then Gnof resentfully told all and sundry, "I shall lambast my mother."

"Dirty dog!" said Leeming. "Shame on you!"

The other voice now informed, mysteriously, "Mine is a fat one."

"I can imagine," Leeming agreed.

"Clam-shack?" demanded Gnof in tones clearly translatable as, "Who is that?"

"Mayor Snorkum," Leeming told him.

For some weird reason known only to alien minds this information caused the argument to start all over again. They commenced by debating Mayor Snorkum's antecedents and future prospects (or so it sounded) and gradually and enthusiastically worked their way along to the tepid mouse (or torpid moose).

There were moments when they became mutually heated about something or other, possibly Snorkum's habit of keeping his moose on a pie-chain. Finally they dropped the subject by common consent and switched to the abstruse question of how to paddle a puddle (according to one) or how to peddle a poodle (according to the other).

"Holy cow!" said Leeming fervently.

It must have borne close resemblance to something pretty potent in the hearers' language because they broke off and again Gnof challenged, "Clam-shack?"

"Go jump, Buster!" Leeming invited.

"Bosta? My ham-plank is Bosta, *enk?*" His tones suggested considerable passion about the matter as he repeated, "Bosta, *enk?*"

"Yeah," confirmed Leeming. *"Enk!"*

Apparently this was regarded as the last straw for their voices went off and even the faint hum of the carrier-wave disappeared. It looked as though he had managed to utter something extremely vulgar without having the vaguest notion of what he had said.

Soon afterward the carrier-wave came on and another and different voice called in guttural but fluent Cosmoglotta, "What ship? What ship?"

Leeming did not answer.

A long wait before again the voice demanded, "What ship?"

Still Leeming took no notice. The mere fact that they had not broadcast a challenge in war-code showed that they did not believe it possible for a hostile vessel to be in the vicinity. Indeed, this was suggested by the stolid way in which the convoy continued to plug along without changing course or showing visible sign of alarm.

It was highly likely that they could not so much as see his ship, not being equipped with sufficiently sensitive detectors. The call of, "What ship?" had been nothing more than a random feel in the dark, an effort to check up before seeking a practical joker somewhere within the convoy itself.

Having obtained adequate data on the enemy's course, Leeming bulleted ahead of them and in due time came across the thirteenth planet. He beamed the information homeward, went in search of the next. It was found quickly, being in an adjacent solar system

Time rolled by as his probes took him across a broad stretch of Combine-controlled space and measured its precise depth. After discovering the fiftieth planet he was tempted to return to base for overhaul and further orders. One can have a surfeit of exploration and he was sorely in need of a taste of Terra, its fresh air, green fields, and human companionship.

What kept him going were the facts that the ship was running well, his fuel supply was only a quarter expended, and he could not resist the notion that the more thoroughly he did this job the greater the triumph upon his return and the better the prospect of quick promotion.

So on he went and piled up the total to seventy-two planets before he reached a preselected point where he was deep in the enemy hinterland at a part facing the Allied outposts around Rigel. From here he was expected to send a coded signal to which they would respond, this being the only message they'd risk sending him.

He beamed the one word, "Awa!" repeated at intervals for a couple of hours. It meant, "Able to proceed—awaiting instructions." To that they should give a reply too brief for enemy interceptors to catch; either the word, "Reeter!" meaning "We have sufficient information—return at once," or else the word, "Buzz" meaning "We need more information—continue your reconnaissance."

What he did get back was a short-short squirt of sound that he recognized as an ultra-rapid series of numbers. They came in so fast that it was impossible to note them aurally. Perforce he taped them as they were repeated, then reached for his code-book as he played them off slowly.

The result was, "47926 Scout-Pilot John Leeming promoted Lieutenant as from date of receipt."

He stared at this a long time before he resumed sending, *"Awa! Awa!"* For his pains he got back the word, "Foit!" He tried again and once more was rewarded with *"Foit!"* It looked vaguely blasphemous to him, like the favorite curse of some rubbery creature that had no palate.

Irritated by this piece of nonsense, he stewed it over in his mind, decided that some intervening Combine station was playing his own game by chipping in with confusing comments. In theory the enemy shouldn't be able to do it because he was using a frequency far higher than those favored by the Lathians and others, while both his and the Allied messages were scrambled. All the same, *somebody* was doing it.

To the faraway listeners near Rigel he beamed the interesting biological statement that Mayor Snorkum would lay the moose and left them to sort it out for themselves. Maybe it would teach some nuthead that he was now dealing with a full lieutenant and not a mere scout-pilot. Or, if the enemy intercepted it, they could drop their war-effort while they argued their way around to a final and satisfactory peddling of the poodle.

Concluding that no recall meant the same thing as not being recalled, he resumed his search for hostile planets. It was four days later that he happened to be looking idly through his code-book and found the word *"Foit"* defined as "Use your own judgment."

He thought it over, decided that to go home with a record of seventy-two planets discovered and identified would be a wonderful thing, but to be credited with a nice, round, imposing number such as one hundred would be wonderful enough to verge upon the miraculous. They'd make him a Space Admiral at least. He'd be able to tell Colonel Farmer to get a haircut and order Commodore Keen to polish his buttons. He could strut around clanking with medals and be a saint to all the privates and spacecadets, a swine to all the brasshats.

This absurd picture was so appealing that he at once settled for a score of one hundred planets as his target-figure before returning to base. As if to give him the flavor of coming glory, four enemy-held worlds were found close together in the next solar system and these boosted his total to seventy-six.

He shoved the score up to eighty. Then to eighty-one.

The first hint of impending disaster showed itself as he approached number eighty-two.

Chapter 3

Two dots glowed in his detector-screens. They were fat but slow-moving and it was impossible to decide whether they were warships or cargo-boats. But they were traveling in line abreast and obviously headed someplace to which he'd not yet been. Using his always successful tactics of shadowing them until he had obtained a plot, he followed them awhile, made sure of the star toward which they were heading and then bolted onward.

He had got so far in advance that the two ships had faded right out of his screens when suddenly a propulsor-tube blew its desiccated lining forty miles back along the jet-track. The first he knew of it was when the alarm-bell shrilled on the instrument-board, the needle of the pressure meter dropped halfway back, the needle of its companion heat meter crawled toward the red dot that indicated melting-point.

Swiftly he cut off the feed to that propulsor. Its pressure meter immediately fell to zero, its heat meter climbed a few more degrees, hesitated, stayed put a short while then reluctantly slid back.

The ship's tail fin was filled with twenty huge propulsors around which were splayed eight steering jets of comparatively small diameter. If any one propulsor ceased to function the effect was not serious. It meant no more than a five per cent loss in power output and a corresponding loss in the ship's functional efficiency. On Earth they had told him that he could sacrifice as many as eight propulsors—providing that they were symmetrically positioned—before his speed and maneuverability were reduced to those of a Combine destroyer.

From the viewpoint of his technical advantage over the foe he had nothing to worry about—yet. He could still move fast enough to make them look like spatial sluggards. What *was* worrying was the fact that the sudden breakdown of the refractory lining of one main driver might be forewarning of the general condition of the rest. For all he knew, another propulsor might go haywire any minute and be followed by the remainder in rapid succession.

Deep inside him was the feeling that now was the time to turn back and make for home while the going was good. Equally deep was the hunch that he'd never get there because already he had traveled too long and too far. The ship was doomed never to see Earth again; inwardly he was as sure of that as one can be sure of anything.

But the end of the ship need not mean the end of its pilot even though he be wandering like a lost soul through strange areas of a hostile starfield. The precognition that told Leeming his ship was heading for its grave also assured him that he was not. He felt it in his bones that the day was yet to come when, figuratively speaking, he would blow his nose in Colonel Farmer's handkerchief.

Rejecting the impulse to reverse course and run for Rigel, he kept stubbornly on toward planet number eighty-two, reached it, surveyed it and beamed the information. Then he detected a shipping route between here and a nearby solar system, started along it in the hope of finding planet number eighty-three and adding it to his score. A second propulsor shed its lining when halfway there, a third just before arrival.

All the same, he circumnavigated the world at reduced speed, headed for free space with the intention of transmitting the data but never did so. Five more propulsors blew their linings simultaneously. He had to move mighty fast to cut off the feed before their unhampered blasts could melt his entire tail away.

The defective drivers must have been bunched together off-center for the ship now refused to run straight. Instead it started to describe a wide curve that eventually would bring it back in a great circle to the planet it had just left. To make matters worse, it also commenced a slow, regular rotation around its longitudinal axis with the result that the entire starfield seemed to revolve before Leeming's eyes.

Desperately he tried to straighten the ship's course by means of the steering jets but this only produced an eerie swaying which, combined with the rotation, caused his fire-trail to shape itself into an elongated spiral. The curve continued until planet eighty-three slid into one side of his observation port and spun slowly around it. Two more propulsors blew long, thin clouds of ceramic dust far backward. The planet swelled enormously in the armorglass. Yet another propulsor gave up the ghost.

The vessel was now beyond all hope of salvation as a cosmos-traversing vehicle and the best he could hope to do with it was to get it down in one piece for the sake of his own skin. He concentrated solely upon achieving this end. Though in serious condition the ship was not wholly beyond control because the steering jets could function perfectly when not countered by a lopsided drive, while the braking jets were capable of roaring with full-throated power.

As the planet filled the forward view and its crinkled surface expanded into hills and valleys, he cut off all remaining tail propulsors, used his steering jets to hold the ship straight and blew his braking jets repeatedly. The longitudinal rotation ceased and speed of descent slowed while his hands sweated at the controls.

It was dead certain that he could not land in the orthodox manner by standing the ship on its tail-fins. He lacked enough power-output to come down atop a carefully-controlled column of fire. The ship was suffering from a much-dreaded condition known to the space service as weak-arse and that meant he'd have to make a belly landing at just enough speed to retain control up to the last moment.

His eyes strained at the observation port while the oncoming hills widened, the valleys lengthened and the planet's surface fuzz changed to a pattern of massed treetops. Then the whole picture appeared to leap at him as if suddenly brought into focus under a powerful microscope. He fired four propulsors and the lower steering jets in an effort to level-off.

The nose lifted as the vessel shot across a valley and cleared the opposite hill by a few hundred feet. In the next two minutes he saw five miles of tree-tops, a clearing from which arose an army of trellis masts bearing radio antennas, a large village standing beside a river, another great expanse of trees followed by a gently rolling stretch of moorland.

This was the place! Mentally offering a quick prayer to God, he swooped in a shallow curve with all braking jets going full blast. Despite this dexterous handling the first contact slung him clean out of his seat and threw him against the metal wall beneath his bunk. Bruised and shaken but otherwise unhurt, he scrambled from under the bunk while still the ship slid forward to the accompaniment of scraping, knocking sounds from under its belly.

Gaining the control-board, he stopped the braking jets, cut off all power. A moment later the vessel expended the last of its forward momentum and came to a halt. The resulting silence was like nothing he had experienced in many months.

It seemed almost to bang against his ears. Each breath he took became a loud hiss, each step a noisy, metallic clank.

Going to the lock, he examined the atmospheric analyzer. It registered exterior air pressure at fifteen pounds and said that it was much like Terra's except that it was slightly richer in oxygen. At once he went through the air-lock, stood in the rim of its outer door and found himself fourteen feet above ground-level.

The automatic ladder was of no use in this predicament since it was constructed to extend itself from airlock to tail, a direction that now was horizontal. He could hang by his hands from the rim and let himself drop without risk of injury but he could not jump fourteen feet to get back in. The one thing he lacked was a length of rope.

"They think of everything," he complained, talking out loud because a justifiable gripe deserves to be uttered. "They think of everything imaginable. Therefore twenty feet of rope is not imaginable. Therefore I can imagine the unimaginable. Therefore I am cracked. Anyone who talks to himself is cracked. It's legitimate for a loony to say what he likes. When I get back I'll say what I like and it'll be plenty!"

Feeling a bit better for that he returned to the cabin, hunted in vain for something that would serve in lieu of rope. He was about to rip his blankets into suitable strips when he remembered the power cables snaking from control-board to engine-room. It took him a hurried half hour to detach a suitable length from its terminals and tear it from its wall fastenings.

During the whole of this time his nerves were tense and his ears were continually perked for outside sounds indicating the approach of the enemy. If they should arrive in time to trap him within the ship he'd have no choice but to set off the explosive charge and blow himself apart along with the vessel. It was of major importance that the ship should not fall intact into alien hands and his own life was a secondary consideration.

Naturally he was most reluctant to spread himself in bloody shreds over the landscape and therefore moved fast with jumpy nerves, taut mind and stretched ears. Silence was still supreme when he tied one end of the cable inside the lock, tossed the rest outside and slid down it to ground.

He landed in thick, cushiony vegetation bearing slight resemblance to heather. Racing to the ship's tail, he had a look at the array of propulsors, realized that he was lucky to have survived. Eleven of the great tubes were completely without their essential linings, the remaining nine were in poor condition and obviously could not have withstood more than another two or three days of steady blasting.

It was out of the question to effect any repairs or even to take the ship up again for a short hop to somewhere more secluded. The long, sleek boat had set up an all-time record by bearing him safely through a good slice of the galaxy, past strange suns and around unknown worlds, and now it was finished. He could not help feeling mournful about it. To destroy such a ship would be like cold-blooded murder—but it had to be done.

Now he took a quick look at what was visible of the world on which he stood. The sky was a deep, dark blue verging obscurely to purple, with a faint, cloudlike haze on the eastern horizon. The sun, now past its zenith, looked a fraction larger than Sol, had a redder color, and its rays produced a slight and not unpleasant stinging sensation.

Underfoot the heather-like growth covered a gently undulating landscape running to the eastward horizon where the first ranks of trees stood guard. Through it, an immense scar ran the long, deep rut caused by the ship's belly-skid. To the west the undergrowth again gave way to great trees, the edge of the forest being half a mile away.

Leeming now found himself in another quandary of the kind not foreseen by those unable to imagine a need for rope. If he blew the ship to pieces he would destroy with it a lot of stuff he needed now or might need later on, in particular a large stock of concentrated food. To save the latter he would have to remove it from the ship, take it a safe distance from the coming explosion and hide it someplace where enemy patrols would not find it.

The nearby forest was the ideal place for a cache. But to salvage everything worth having he'd have to make several trips into the forest and risk the enemy putting in an appearance when he was too far from the ship to regain it ahead of them and set off the big bang.

If he became a wandering fugitive, as he intended, it was possible that he'd have no trouble finding enough food to keep him going for years. But he could not be sure of that. He knew nothing about this world except that it held intelligent life and was part of or in cahoots with the Combine. He couldn't so much as guess what its native lifeform looked like though it was a pretty safe bet that—like every other known sentient form—it was more or less humanoid.

Sense of urgency prevented him from pondering the situation very long. This was a time for action rather than thought. He started working like a maniac, grabbing packages and cans from the ship's store and throwing them out of the airlock. This went on until the entire food stock had been cleared. Still the enemy was conspicuous by his absence.

Now he took up armloads from the waiting pile and bore them into the edge of the forest. Sheer anxiety made him waste a lot of effort for at each trip he tried to take more than he could hold. His route into the forest was marked back by dropped cans that had to be picked up at each return to the ship. These returns he made at the run, pausing only to snatch up the fallen stuff, and arriving breathless and already half-loaded.

By dint of haste and perspiration he transferred all the foodstuffs into the forest, climbed aboard the ship, had a last look around for anything worth saving. Making a roll of his blankets, he tied a waterproof sheet over them to form a compact bundle.

Regretfully he eyed the radio transmitter. It would be easy to send out a signal saying that he was marooned on planet number eighty-three and giving its coordinates. But it would not do him any good. No Allied vessel other than a special scout-ship could hope to get this far without refueling and having its tubes relined. Even if a ship did manage to cover the distance non-stop it stood little chance of finding and picking up one lone Terran hiding on a hostile world.

Satisfied that nothing remained worth taking, he put on his storm-coat, tucked the bundle under his arm and pressed the red button at one side of the control-board. There was supposed to be a delay of two minutes between activation and the resulting wallop. It wasn't much time. Bolting through the air-lock, he jumped straight out, landed heavily in the cushion of vegetation and dashed at top speed toward the forest. Nothing had happened by the time he reached the trees. Standing behind the protective thickness of a great trunk, he waited for the bang.

Seconds ticked by without results. Something must have gone wrong. Perhaps those who could not imagine rope could not think of a fuse or detonator either. He peeked cautiously around the rim of the trunk, debating within himself whether to go back and examine the connections to the explosive charge. At that point the ship blew up.

It flew apart with a tremendous, ear-splitting roar that bent the trees and shook the skies. A great column of smoke, dirt and shapeless lumps soared to a considerable height. Gobs of distorted metal screamed through the treetops and brought branches crashing down. A blast of hot wind rushed either side of the trunk behind which Leeming was sheltering, for a moment created a partial vacuum that made him gasp for breath.

Then followed a pattering sound like that of heavy rain, also many loud thumps as soil and scrap metal fell back to earth. Somewhat awed by the unexpected violence of the explosion, he sneaked another look around the tree-trunk, saw a smoking crater surrounded by two or three acres of torn vegetation. It was a sobering thought that for countless millions of miles he had been sitting on top of a bang that size.

When tardily the foe arrived it was pretty certain that they would start a hunt for the missing crew. Leeming's preliminary survey of the world, though consisting only of one quick sweep around its equator, had found evidence of some sort of organized civilization and included one space-port holding five merchant ships and one Combine light cruiser, all of antiquated pattern. This showed that the local lifeform was at least of normal intelligence and as capable as anyone else of adding two and two together.

The relative shallowness of the crater and the wide scattering of remnants was clear evidence that the mystery ship had not plunged to destruction but rather had blown apart after making a successful landing. Natives in the nearest village could confirm that there had been quite a long delay between the ship's plunge over their rooftops and the subsequent explosion. The foe would know that none of his own ships were missing in that area. Examination of fragments would reveal non-Combine material. Their inevitable conclusion: that the vessel had been a hostile one and that its crew had got away unscathed.

It would be wise, he decided, to put more distance between himself and the crater before the enemy arrived and started sniffing around the vicinity. Perhaps he was fated to be caught eventually but it was up to him to postpone the evil day as long as possible.

The basic necessities of life are food, drink and shelter, with the main emphasis on the first of these. This fact delayed his departure a little while. He had food enough to last for several months. It was one thing to have it, another to keep it safe from harm. At all costs he must find a better hiding place to which he could return from time to time with the assurance that the supply would still be there.

He pressed farther into the forest, moving in a wide zigzag as he cast about for a suitable dump. Visibility was good because the sun remained high and the trees did not entirely obscure the overhead view. He sought here and there, muttering angrily to himself and making vulgar remarks about officials who decided what equipment a scout-ship should carry. If he'd had a spade he could have dug a neat hole and buried the stuff. But he did not have a spade and it would take too long to scrabble a hideout with his bare hands.

Finally he found a cave-like opening between the great arched roots of an immense tree. It was far from ideal but it did have the virtue of being deep within the woods and providing a certain amount of concealment. Casting around, he picked up a smooth, heavy pebble, flung it through the opening with all the force he could muster. There came no answering yelp, howl or squeal, no sudden rush of some outlandish creature intent on mayhem. The cave was unoccupied.

It took him more than an hour to shift the food-pile for the third time and stack it neatly within the hole, leaving out a small quantity representing seven days' rations. When this task had been completed he built up part of the opening with clumps of earth, used twigs and branches to fill in the rest. He now felt that if a regiment of enemy troops explored the locality, as they were likely to do, there was small chance of them discovering and either confiscating or destroying the cache on which his continued liberty might depend.

Stuffing the seven days' rations into a small rucksack and tying the bundled blankets thereto, he set off at fast pace along the fringe of the forest and headed southward. Right now he had no plan in mind, no especial purpose other than that of evading capture by making distance before the foe found the crater and searched the vicinity. He doubted whether the enemy would maintain such a local hunt for more than a couple of days after which they'd decide that there were no survivors or, alternatively, that it was high time that they started seeking them farther afield. Therefore it should be reasonably safe for him to return for food in about one week's time.

He had been going three hours and had covered eleven miles before the enemy showed the first signs of activity. With the moorland on his right and the forest on his left, he was trudging along when a black dot soared above the horizon, swelled in size, shot silently overhead and was followed some seconds later by a shrill scream.

Going at that height and at that speed the jet plane's pilot could not possibly have seen him. Unperturbed, he stepped into the shadow of a tree, turned to watch the machine as it diminished northward. It was again a mere dot when suddenly it swept around in a wide circle, spiraled upward and continued circling. As nearly as Leeming could judge it was turning high above the crater.

It was an easy guess that the jet plane had come in response to a telephone or radio call telling about a spaceship in distress and a following explosion. Having found the scene of disaster it was zooming above the spot while summoning help.

No doubt there'd be great activity at the base from which it had come; receiving confirmation that a ship had indeed been lost, the authorities would assume it to be one of their own and start checking by radio to find which one was missing. With luck it might be quite a time before they accepted the fact that a vessel of unknown origin, probably hostile, had reached this far.

In any case, from now on they'd keep a sharp watch for survivors. Leeming decided that this was the time to leave the forest's fringe and progress under cover. His rate of movement would be slowed but at least he'd travel unobserved. There were two dangers in taking to the woods but they'd have to be accepted as lesser evils.

For one, unless he was mighty careful he could lose his sense of direction and wander in a huge curve that eventually would take him back to the crater and straight into the arms of whoever was waiting there. For another, he ran the risk of encountering unknown forms of wild life possessed of unimaginable weapons and unthinkable appetites.

Against the latter peril he had a defense that was extremely effective but hateful to use, namely a powerful compressed-air pistol that fired breakable pellets filled with a stench so foul that one whiff would make anything that lived and breathed vomit for hours—including, as often as not, the user.

Some Terran genius had worked it out that the real king of the wilds is not the lion nor the grizzly bear but a kittenish creature named Joe Skunk whose every battle was a victorious rearguard action, so to speak. Some other genius had synthesized a horrible liquid seventy-seven times more revolting than Joe's—with the result that an endangered spaceman could never make up his mind whether to run like hell and chance being caught or whether to stand firm, shoot and subsequently puke himself to death.

Freedom is worth a host of risks, so he plunged deep into the forest and kept going. After about an hour's steady progress he heard the *whup-whup* of many helicopters passing overhead and traveling toward the north. By the sound of it there were quite a lot of them but none could be seen crossing the few patches of sky visible between the tree-tops.

He made a guess that they were a squadron of troop carriers transporting a search party to the region of the crater. Sometime later a solitary machine crept above with a loud humming noise while a downward blast of air made the trees rustle and wave their topmost branches. It was low and slow-moving and sounded like a buoyant fan that probably was carrying one observer. He stopped close by a gnarly trunk until it had passed.

Soon afterward he began to feel tired and decided to rest awhile upon a mossy bank. Reposing at ease, he pondered this exhaustion, realized that although his survey had shown this world to be approximately the same size as Terra it must in fact be a little bigger or had slightly greater mass. His own weight was up perhaps by as much as ten per cent, though he had no way of checking it.

True, after a long period of incarceration in a ship he must be out of condition but he was making full allowance for that fact. He was undoubtedly heavier than he'd been since birth, the rucksack was heavier, so were the blankets, so were his feet. Therefore his ability to cover mileage would be cut down in proportion and, in any emergency, so would his ability to run.

It then struck him that the day must be considerably longer than Earth's. The sinking sun was now about forty degrees above the horizon. In the time since he'd landed the arc it had covered showed that the day was somewhere between thirty and thirty-two hours in length. He'd have to accommodate himself to that with extended walks and prolonged sleeps and it wouldn't be easy. Wherever they may be, Terrans have a natural tendency to retain their own time-habits.

Isolation in space is a hell of a thing, he thought, as idly he toyed with the flat, oblong-shaped lump under the left-hand pocket of his jacket. The lump had been there so long that he was only dimly conscious of its existence and, even when reminded of it, tended to suppose that all jackets were made lumpy for some perverse reason known only to members of the International Garment Workers' Union. Now it struck him with what approximated to a flash of pure genius that in the long, long ago someone had once mentioned his lump and described it as "the built-in emergency-pack."

Taking out his pocket-knife, he used its point to unpick the lining of his jacket. This produced a flat, shallow box of brown plastic. A hair-thin line ran around its rim but there was no button, keyhole, grip or any other visible means of opening it. Pulling and pushing it in a dozen different ways had no effect whatever. He tried to insert the knife-blade in the hairline and pry the whole thing open; that failed and the knife slipped and he nicked his thumb. Sucking the thumb, he shoved his other hand through the slit lining and felt all around his jacket in the hope of discovering written instructions of some sort. All he got for his pains was fluff in his fingernails.

Reciting several of the nine million names of God, he kicked the box with aggravated vim. Either the kick was the officially approved method of dealing with it or some of the names were potent, for the box snapped open. At once he commenced examining the contents which, in theory, should assist him toward ultimate salvation.

The first was a tiny, bead-sized vial of transparent plastic ornamented with an embossed skull and containing an oily, yellowish liquid. Presumably this was the death-pill to be taken as a last extreme. Apart from the skull there was nothing to distinguish it from a love-potion.

Next came a long, thin bottle filled with what looked like diluted mud and marked with a long, imposing list of vitamins, proteins and trace elements. What one took it for, how much was supposed to be taken at a time, and how often, were left to the judgment of the beneficiary—or the victim.

After this came a small sealed can bearing no identifying markings and devoid of a can-opener to go with it. For all he knew it might be full of boot polish, sockeye salmon or putty. He wouldn't put it past them to thoughtfully provide some putty in case he wanted to fix a window someplace and thus save his life by ingratiating himself with his captors. If, back home, some genius got it into his head that no lifeform known or unknown could possibly murder a window-fixer, a can of putty automatically became a must.

Dumping it at one side, he took up the next can. This was longer, narrower and had a rotatable cap. He twisted the cap and uncovered a sprinkler. Shaking it over his open palm he got a puff of fine powder resembling pepper. Well, that would come in very useful for coping with a pack of bloodhounds, assuming that there were bloodhounds in these here parts. Cautiously he sniffed at his palm. The stuff smelled exactly like pepper.

He let go a violent sneeze, wiped his dusty hand on a handkerchief, closed the can and concocted some heated remarks about the people at the space-base. This had immediate effect for the handkerchief burst into flames in his pocket. He tore it out, flung it down and danced on it. Opening the can again, he let a few grains of pepper fall upon a dry piece of rotten wood. A minute later the wood spat sparks and started blazing. This sent a betraying column of smoke skyward, so he danced on the wood until it ceased.

Exhibit number five really did explain itself—providing that its owner had the power of long-range clairvoyance. It was a tiny bottle of colorless liquid around which was wrapped a paper that said, "Administer two drops per hundred pounds bulk only in a non-carbonated beverage." A skull complete with crossbones added a sinister touch to this mysterious injunction.

After studying it for some time Leeming decided that the liquid was either a poison or the knock-out additive favored by Mr. Michael Finn. Apparently, if one were to encounter a twenty-ton rhinoceros the correct technique was to weigh it upon the nearest weighing-machine, calculate the appropriate dosage and administer it to the unfortunate animal in a non-carbonated beverage. One would then be safe because the creature would drop dead or fall asleep and lie with its legs in the air.

Number six was a miniature camera small enough to be concealed in the palm of the hand. As an aid to survival its value was nil. It must have been included in the kit with some other intention. Perhaps Terran Intelligence had insisted that it be provided in the hope that anyone who made successful escape from a hostile world could bring a lot of photographic data home with him. Well, it was nice to think that someone could be *that* optimistic. He pocketed the camera, not with any expectation of using it, but solely because it was a beautiful piece of microscopic workmanship too good to be thrown away.

The seventh and last was the most welcome and, so far as he was concerned, the only item worth a hoot; a luminous compass. He put it carefully into a vest pocket. After some consideration he decided to keep the pepper-pot but discarded the remaining cans and bottles. The death-pill he flicked into an adjacent bush. The bottles he shied between the trees. Finally he took the can of boot polish, sockeye, putty or whatever and hurled it as far as he could.

The result was a tremendous crash, a roar of flame and a large tree leaped twenty feet into the air with dirt showering from its roots. The blast knocked him full length on the moss; he picked himself up in time to see a great spurt of smoke sticking out of the tree-tops like a beckoning finger. Obviously visible for miles, it could not have been more effective if he'd sent up a balloon-borne banner bearing the words, "Here I am!"

Only one thing could be done and that was to get out fast. Grabbing up his load he scooted southward at the best pace he could make between the trees. He had covered about two miles when the buoyant fan hummed low down and slightly to his rear. A little later he heard the distant, muted *whup-whup* of a helicopter descending upon the scene of the crime. There'd be plenty of room for it to drop into the forest because the explosive can of something-or-other had cleared a wide gap. He tried to increase his speed, dodging around bushes, clambering up sharply sloping banks, jumping across deep, ditchlike depressions and all the time moving on leaden feet that felt as if he was wearing size twenty boots.

As the sun sank low and shadows lengthened he was again forced to rest through sheer exhaustion. By now he had no idea of the total distance covered; it had been impossible to travel in a dead, straight line and the constant zigzagging between the trees made mileage impossible to estimate. However, there were now no sounds of aerial activity either near or far away and, for all the evidence of the presence of other life, he might have the entire cosmos to himself.

Recovering, he pushed on until darkness was relieved only by the sparkle of countless stars and the shine of two small moons. Then he had a meal and bedded down in a secluded glade, rolling the blankets tightly around him and keeping his stink-gun near to hand. What kind of dangerous animal might stalk through the night he did not know and was long past caring. A man must have sleep come what may, even at the risk of waking up in somebody's belly.

Chapter 4

Lulled by the silence and his own tiredness, he slept for twelve hours. It was not an undisturbed slumber. Twice he awoke with the vague feeling that something had slunk past him in the dark. He lay completely still, nerves tense, gun in hand, his eyes straining to probe the surrounding gloom until at last sleep claimed him again, the eyelids fluttered and closed, he let go a subdued snore. Another time he awakened to see five moons in the sky, including a tiny, fast-moving one that arced across the vault of the heavens with a faint but hearable hiss. The vision was so brief and abnormal that for some time he was not sure whether he had actually witnessed it or merely dreamed it.

Despite the long and satisfying snooze he was only partway through the alien night. There were many hours to go before sunrise. Feeling refreshed and becoming bored by waiting, he gave way to his fidgets, rolled his blankets, consulted the compass and tried to continue his southward march. In short time he had tripped headlong over unseeable roots, stumbled knee-deep into a hidden stream.

Progress in open country was possible in the combined light of stars and moons, but not within the forest. Reluctantly he gave up the attempt. There was no point in wearing himself out blundering around in barely visible patches that alternated with areas of stygian darkness. Somehow he managed to find the glade again. There he lay in the blankets and waited with some impatience for the delayed dawn.

As the first faint glow appeared at one side of the sky something passed between the trees a hundred yards away. He got to his feet, gun pointing in that direction, watching and listening. Bushes rustled, dead leaves crackled and twigs snapped over a distance stretching from his left to far to his right.

The rate of motion was slow, laborious and the sounds suggested that the cause was sluggish and very heavy. Seeing nothing, he was unable to determine whether the noise was created by a troop of things crawling one behind the other or by one monstrous lifeform resembling a colossal worm, the grandpappy of all anacondas. Whatever it was, it did not come near to him and gradually the sounds died away.

Immediately daylight had become sufficiently strong to permit progress he resumed his southward trek and kept it up until mid-day. At that point he found a big rocky hollow that looked very much like an abandoned quarry. Trees grew thickly around its rim, bushes and lesser growths covered its floor, various kinds of creepers straggled down its walls. A tiny spring fed a midget stream that meandered across the floor until it disappeared down a hole in the base-rock. At least six caves were half-hidden in the walls, these varying from a narrow cleft to an opening the size of a large room.

Surveying the place, he realized that here was an ideal hideout. He had no thought of settling there for the rest of his natural life even if the availability of food permitted him to do so. He'd get nowhere by sitting on his quoit until he was old and rheumy. Besides, he'd had enough of a hermit's life in space without suffering more of it on firm land. But at least this locale would serve as a hiding-place until the hue and cry died down and he'd had time to think out his future plan of action.

Climbing down the steep, almost vertical sides to the floor of the place proved a tough task. From his viewpoint this was so much the better; whatever was difficult for him would be equally difficult for others and might deter any searching patrols that came snooping around. With that complete absence of logic that afflicts one at times, it didn't occur to him that a helicopter could come down upon him with no trouble at all. He soon found a suitable cave and settled himself in by dumping his load on the dry, sandy ground. The next job was that of preparing a meal. Building a smokeless fire of wood chips, he filled his dixie with water and converted part of his rations into a thick soup. This, with some enriched wholemeal flatcakes, served to fill his belly and bring on a sense of peaceful well-being.

For a while he mooched around his sunken domain which covered four acres. The surrounding walls were eighty feet high while the crest of trees towered another two hundred feet higher. A scout-ship could have landed tail-first in this area and remained concealed for years from all eyes save those directly above. He found himself regretting that he had not known of this place and attempted an orthodox landing within it. Even if the ship toppled over through lack of adequate power, and he survived uninjured, he'd have the use of it as a permanent home and, if necessary, a fortress. Wouldn't be easy for the foe to winkle a man out of a heavy metal shell particularly when the said shell has fore and aft jets as effective as several batteries of guns.

Here and there were small holes in the ground. Similar holes were in evidence at the base of the walls. They reminded him of rabbit burrows. If whatever had made them was the alien equivalent of the rabbit it would be a welcome addition to his larder.

Getting down in crawling position, he peered into several of these apertures but could see nothing. He found a long, thin stick and poked it down some of them, without result. Finally he sat silent and motionless outside an array of holes for nearly two hours. At the end of that time a creature came out, saw him immediately and bolted back in. It resembled a fat and furry spider. Perhaps it was edible but the thought of eating it turned his stomach.

It then struck him that despite this planet's profuse supply of trees he had not seen or heard anything resembling a bird. If any arboreal creatures existed they must be in small number, or not native to this locality, or wholly nocturnal. There was also a noteworthy lack of insects and for this he was thankful. On any alien world the insect type of life could be and often was a major menace to any wandering Terran. That weird world of Hypatia, for instance, held streamlined whizz-bugs capable of traveling at six hundred miles per hour. A whizz-bug could drill a hole through a human being, space-suit and all, as neatly and effectively as a .45 slug.

At one end of the area grew a thick patch of feathery plants somewhat like giant ferns. They exuded a pleasantly aromatic scent. He gathered a good supply of these, laid them at the back of the cave, spread his blankets over them and thus made himself a bed more springy and comfortable than any he had enjoyed since childhood.

Although he had done everything in the most lackadaisical, time-wasting manner of which he was capable he still found it well-nigh impossible to cope with the lengthy day. He'd explored the pseudo-quarry from side to side, from one end to the other, had two meals, tidied the cave, done various chores necessary and unnecessary, and still the sun was far from setting. As nearly as he could calculate it would be another six hours before darkness fell. There was nothing to stop him from going to bed at the first yawn but if he did he'd surely wake up and face an equally long night. Adjustment to alien time did not come easy.

So he sat at the entrance to his cave and amused himself working out what best to do in the future. For a start, he could spend a couple of weeks transferring his foodstock from its place of concealment near the crater to this cave. Then, using his present headquarters as a strategic center, he could make systematic exploration in all directions and get to know as much as possible about the potentialities of this world.

If investigation proved it possible to live off the land he could then travel farther afield, scout warily around inhabited areas until eventually he found a spaceport. Sooner or later the opportunity might come to sneak aboard a fully fueled enemy scout-ship after dark and take it up with a triumphant bang. It was only one chance in a thousand, perhaps one in ten thousand, but it might come off. Yes, he'd go seeking such a chance and *make* it come off.

Even if he did manage to blast free in a Combine scout his problem would not be solved. No vessel could reach the Rigellian sector non-stop from here without at least one refueling and one overhaul of propulsor tubes. To reach the Allied front he'd have to break his journey partway there and repeat his present performance by dumping the ship and stealing another. What can be done once can be done twice. All the same, the odds against him ever seeing Terra were so tremendous that he did not care to think of them. He concentrated solely upon the ages-old thesis that while there's life there's hope.

Shortly before dusk a jet plane screamed across the sky as if to remind him that this world really was inhabited by superior life. Up to then the perpetual silence and total lack of birds or bees had made his situation seem like a crazy dream. Standing outside the cave, he watched the high dot shoot across the heavens and disappear to the south. A little later he went to bed.

Early in the morning eight helicopters went over, moving in line abreast. Spread out a hundred yards apart from each other, they floated fifty feet above the tree-tops. What they hoped to see beneath the concealing mass of vegetation was a mystery but it was obvious that they were searching all the same.

Going through the motions, thought Leeming as he watched them drift beyond his hiding-place. They had been ordered to look around, therefore they were looking around even though there was nothing to be seen. The pilots were enjoying a pleasant ride on the pretext that orders must be obeyed. In all probability the brass hat who had issued the command had never looked down into a forest in his life but, by virtue of his rank, was a self-styled authority upon the subject of how to find a flea in a dog's home. Baloney baffles brains in any part of the cosmos. Leeming had long nursed a private theory that wars do not end with victory for the side with the most brains: they are terminated by the defeat of the side with the most dopes. Also, that wars are prolonged because there is stiff competition in general imbecility.

By the end of the fourth day he was bored to tears. Squatting in a cave was not his idea of the full life and he could no longer resist the urge to get busy. He'd have to bestir himself before long in order to replenish his food supplies. The time had come, he felt, to make a start on the tedious chore of shifting the hidden dump southward and installing it in the cave.

Accordingly he set forth at dawn and pushed to the north as fast as he could go. This activity boosted his spirits considerably and he had to suppress the desire to whistle as he went along. In his haste he was making noise enough and there was no sense in further advertising his coming to any patrols that might be prowling through the woods.

As he neared the scene of his landing his pace slowed to the minimum. Here, if anywhere, caution was imperative since there was no knowing how many of the foe might still be lurking in the area. By the time he came within easy reach of his cache he was slinking from tree to tree, pausing frequently to look ahead and listen.

It was a great relief to find that the food-dump had not been disturbed. The supply was intact, exactly as he had left it. There was no sign that the enemy had been anywhere near it or, for the matter of that, was within fifty miles of it at the present moment. Emboldened by this, he decided to go to the edge of the forest and have another look at the crater. It would be interesting to learn whether the local lifeform had shown enough intelligence to take away the ship's shattered remnants with the idea of establishing its origin. The knowledge that they had done so would not help him one little bit—but he was curious and temporarily afflicted with a sense of false security.

As quietly and carefully as a cat stalking a bird, he sneaked the short distance to the forest's rim, gained it a couple of hundred yards from where he'd expected to view the crater. Walking farther along the edge of the trees, he stopped and stared at the graveyard of his ship, his attention concentrated upon it to the exclusion of all else. Many distorted hunks of metal still lay around and it was impossible to tell whether any of the junk had been removed.

Swinging his gaze to take in the total blast area, he was dumbfounded to discover three helicopters parked in line close to the trees. They were a quarter mile away, apparently unoccupied and with nobody hanging around. That meant their crews must be somewhere nearby. At once he started to back into the forest, his hairs tickling with alarm. He had taken only two steps when fallen leaves crunched behind him, something hard rammed into the middle of his back and a voice spoke in harsh, guttural tones.

"Smooge!" it said.

Bitterness at his own folly surged through Leeming's soul as he turned around to face the speaker. He found himself confronted by a humanoid six inches shorter than himself but almost twice as broad; a squat, powerful creature wearing dun-colored uniform, a metal helmet and grasping a lethal instrument recognizable as some kind of gun. This character had a scaly, lizardlike skin, horn-covered eyes and no eyelids. He watched Leeming with the cold, unwinking stare of a rattlesnake.

"Smooge!" he repeated, giving a prod with the gun.

Raising his hands, Leeming offered a deceitful smile and said in fluent Cosmoglotta, "There is no need for this. I am a friend, an ally."

It was a waste of breath. Either the other did not understand Cosmoglotta or he could recognize a thundering lie when it was offered. His reptilian face showed not the slightest change of expression, his eyes retained their blank stare as he emitted a shrill whistle. Leeming noticed that his captor performed this feat without pursing his lips, the sound apparently coming straight from the throat.

Twenty more of the enemy responded by emerging from the forest at a point near where the helicopters were stationed. Their feet made distinct thuds as they ran with the stubby, clumping gait of very heavy men. Surrounding Leeming, they examined him with the same expressionless state that lacked surprise, curiosity or any other human trait. Next they gabbled together in a language slightly reminiscent of the crazy talk he had interrupted in space.

"Let me elucidate the goose."

"Dry up—the bostaniks all have six feet."

"I am a friend, an ally," informed Leeming, with suitable dignity.

This statement caused them to shut up with one accord. They gave him a mutual snake-look and then the biggest of them asked, "Snapnose?"

"I'm a Combine scout from far, far away," asserted Leeming, swearing it upon an invisible Bible. "As such I demand to be released."

It meant nothing whatever. Nobody smiled, nobody kissed him and it was obvious that none knew a word of Cosmoglotta. They were ill-educated types with not an officer among the lot.

"Now look here," he began, lowering his arms.

"Smooge!" shouted his captor, making a menacing gesture with the gun.

Leeming raised his arms again and glowered at them. Now they held a brief conversation containing frequent mention of cheese and spark-plugs. It ended to their common satisfaction after which they searched him. This was done by the simple method of confiscation, taking everything in his possession including his braces.

That done, they chivvied him toward the helicopters. Perforce he went, trudging surlily along while holding up his pants with his hands. The pants were supposed to be self-supporting, the braces having been worn out of sheer pessimism, but he had lost a good deal of weight during his space trip, his middle was somewhat reduced in circumference and he had no desire to exhibit his posterior to alien eyes.

At command he climbed into a helicopter, turned quickly to slam the door in the hope that he might be able to lock them out long enough to take to the air without getting shot. They did not give him a chance. One was following close upon his heels and was halfway through the door even as he turned. Four more piled in. The pilot took his seat, started the motor. Overhead vanes jerked, rotated slowly, speeded up.

The 'copter bounced a couple of times, left the ground, soared into the purplish sky. It did not travel far. Crossing the wide expanse of moorland and the woods beyond, it descended upon the large village that Leeming had roared over only a few days ago. Gently it landed upon a concrete square at the back of a grim-looking building that, to Leeming's mind, resembled a military barracks or an asylum for the insane.

Here, they entered the building, hustled him along a corridor and into a stone-walled cell. They slammed and locked the heavy door in which was a small barred grille. A moment later one of them peered between the bars.

"We shall bend Murgatroyd's socks," announced the face reassuringly.

"Thanks," said Leeming. "Damned decent of you."

The face went away. Leeming walked ten times around the cell before sitting on a bare wooden plank that presumably was intended to serve as both seat and bed. There was no window through which to look upon the outside world, no opening other than the door. Resting his elbows on his knees, he held his face in his hands.

God, what a chump he'd been. If only he had remained content to take from the cache all the food he could carry and get away fast. If only he had accepted the good fortune of finding the food-dump intact and been satisfied to grab and run. But no, he had to be nosey and walk right into a trap. Perhaps the nervous strain of his long journey or something peculiar about the atmosphere of this planet had made him weak-minded. Whatever the reason, he was caught and ready for the chop.

As for his future prospects, he did not care to guess at them. It was known that the Combine had taken several hundreds of prisoners, mostly settlers on outpost worlds who'd been attacked without warning. Their fate was a mystery. Rumor insisted that the various lifeforms belonging to the Combine had widely different notions of how to handle the prisoner-of-war problem and that some were less humane than others. Since nothing whatever was known about the lifeform inhabiting this particular world the tactics they favored were a matter for speculation or, in his own case, grim experience.

It was said—with what truth nobody knew—that the Lathians, for instance, treated as bona fide prisoners-of-war only those who happened to be captured unarmed and that anyone taken while bearing a weapon was slaughtered out of hand. Also that possession of a knife was regarded as justification for immediate murder providing that the said knife came within their definition of a weapon by having a blade longer than its owner's middle finger. This story might be ten miles wide of the facts. The space service always had been a happy hunting ground for incurable crap-mongers.

How long he sat there he did not know. They had deprived him of his watch, he could not observe the progress of the sun and had no means of estimating the time. But after a long while a guard opened the door, made an unmistakable gesture that he was to come out. He exited, found a second guard waiting in the corridor. With one in the lead and the other following, he was conducted through the building and into a large office.

The sole occupant was an autocratic specimen seated behind a desk on which was arrayed the contents of the prisoner's pockets. Leeming came to a halt before the desk, still holding up his pants. The guards positioned themselves either side of the door and managed to assume expressions of blank servility.

In fluent Cosmoglotta, the one behind the desk said, "I am Major Klavith. You will address me respectfully as becomes my rank. Do you understand?"

"Yes."

"What is your name, rank and number?"

"John Leeming, Lieutenant, 47926."

"Your species?"

"Terran. Haven't you ever seen a Terran before?"

"I am asking the questions," retorted Klavith, "and you will provide the answers." He paused to let that sink in, then continued. "You arrived here in a ship of Terran origin, did you not?"

"Sure did," agreed Leeming, with relish.

Bending forward, Klavith demanded with great emphasis, "On which planet was your vessel refueled?"

There was silence as Leeming's thoughts moved fast. Obviously they could not credit that he had reached here non-stop because such a feat was far beyond their own technical ability. Therefore they believed that he had been assisted by some world within the Combine's ranks. He was being ordered to name the traitors. It was a wonderful opportunity to create dissension but unfortunately he was unable to make good use of it. He'd done no more than scout around hostile worlds, landing on none of them, and for the life of him he could not name or describe a Combine species anywhere on his route.

"Are you going to tell me you don't know?" prompted Klavith sarcastically.

"I do and I don't," Leeming responded. "The world was named to me only as XB 173. I haven't the faintest notion of what you call it or what it calls itself."

"In the morning we shall produce comprehensive star-maps and you will mark thereon the exact location of this world. Between now and then you had better make sure that your memory will be accurate." Another long pause accompanied by the cold, lizardlike stare of his kind. "You have given us a lot of trouble. I have been flown here because I am the only person on this planet who speaks Cosmoglotta."

"The Lathians speak it."

"We are not Lathians as you well know. We are Zangastans. We do not slavishly imitate our allies in everything. The Combine is an association of free peoples."

"That may be your opinion. There are others."

"I am not in the least bit interested in other opinions. And I am not here to bandy words with you on the subject of interstellar politics." Surveying the stuff that littered his desk, Klavith poked forward the pepper-pot. "When you were caught you were carrying this container of incendiary powder. We know what it is because we have tested it. Why were you supplied with it?"

"It was part of my emergency kit."

"Why should you need incendiary powder in an emergency kit?"

"To start a fire to cook food or to warm myself," said Leeming, mentally damning the unknown inventor of emergency kits.

"I do not believe you. See where I am pointing: an automatic lighter. Is that not sufficient?"

"Those lighters wear out or become exhausted."

"Neither does the powder last forever. You are lying to me. You brought this stuff for purposes of sabotage."

"Fat lot of good I'd do starting a few blazes umpteen millions of miles from home. When we hit the Combine we do it harder and more effectively."

"That may be so," Klavith conceded. "But I am far from satisfied with your explanation."

"If I gave you the true one you wouldn't believe it."

"Let me be the judge of that."

"All right. The powder was included in my kit merely because some high-ranking official thought it a wonderful idea."

"And why should he think so?" Klavith urged.

"Because any idea thought up by him must be wonderful."

"I don't see it."

"Neither do I. But *he* does and his opinion counts."

"Not with me it doesn't," Klavith denied. "Anyway, we intend to analyze this powder. Obviously it does not burst into flame when air reaches it, otherwise it would be too risky to carry. It must be in direct contact with an inflammable substance before it will function. A ship bearing a heavy load of this stuff could destroy a lot of crops. Enough systematic burning would starve an entire species into submission, would it not?"

Leeming did not answer.

"I suggest that one of your motives in coming here was to test the military effectiveness of this powder."

"What, when we could try it on our own wastelands without the bother of transporting it partway across a galaxy?"

"That is not the same as inflicting it upon an enemy."

"If I'd toted it all the way here just to do some wholesale burning," Leeming pointed out, "I'd have brought a hundred tons and not a couple of ounces."

Klavith could not find a satisfactory answer to that so he changed the subject by poking another object on his desk. "I have identified this thing as a midget camera. It is a remarkable instrument and cleverly made. But since aerial photography is far easier, quicker, wider in scope and more efficient than anything you could achieve with this gadget, I see no point in you being equipped with it."

"Neither do I," agreed Leeming.

"Then why did you continue to carry it?"

"Because it seemed a darned shame to throw it away."

This reason was accepted without dispute. Grabbing the camera, Klavith put it in his pocket.

"I can understand that. It is as beautiful as a jewel. Henceforth it is my personal property." He showed his teeth in what was supposed to be a triumphant grin. "The spoils of conquest." With contemptuous generosity he picked up the braces and tossed them at Leeming. "You may have these back. Put them on at once—a prisoner should be here properly dressed while in my presence." He watched in silence as the other secured his pants, then said, "You were also in possession of a luminous compass. That I can understand. It is about the only item that makes sense."

Leeming offered no comment.

"Except perhaps for this." Klavith took up the stink-gun. "Either it is a mock weapon or it is real." He pulled the trigger a couple of times and nothing happened. "Which is it?"

"Real."

"Then how does it work?"

"'To prime it you must press the barrel inward."

"That must be done every time you are about to use it?"

"Yes."

"In that case it is nothing better than a compressed-air gun?"

"Correct."

"I find it hard to credit that your authorities would arm you with anything so primitive," opined Klavith, showing concealed suspicion.

"Such a gun is not to be despised," offered Leeming. "It has its advantages. It needs no explosive ammunition. It will fire any missile that fits its barrel and it is comparatively silent. Moreover, it is just as intimidating as any other kind of gun."

"You argue very plausibly," Klavith admitted, "but I doubt whether you are telling me the whole truth."

"There's nothing to stop you trying it and seeing for yourself," Leeming invited. His stomach started jumping at the mere thought of it.

"I intend to do just that." Switching to his own language, Klavith let go a flood of words at one of the guards.

Showing some reluctance, the guard propped his rifle the wall, crossed the room and took the gun. Under Klavith's instructions, he put the muzzle to the floor and shoved. The barrel sank back, popped forward when the pressure was released. Pointing the gun at the wall he squeezed the trigger.

The weapon went *phut!* A tiny pellet burst on the wall and its contents immediately gasified. For a moment Klavith sat gazing in puzzlement at the damp spot. Then the awful stench hit him. His face took on a peculiar mottling, he leaned forward and spewed with such violence that he fell off his chair.

Holding his nose with his left hand, Leeming snatched the compass from the desk with his right and raced for the door. The guard who had fired the gun was now rolling on the carpet and trying to turn himself inside-out with such single-minded concentration that he neither knew nor cared what anyone else was doing. By the door the other guard had dropped his rifle while he leaned against the wall and emitted a rapid succession of violent whoops. Not one of the three was in any condition to pull up his own socks much less get in the way of an escapee.

Still gripping his nostrils, Leeming jerked open the door, dashed along the passage and out of the building. Hearing the clatter of his boots, three more guards rushed out of a room, pulled up as if held back by an invisible hand and threw their dinners over each other.

Outside, Leeming let go his nose. His straining lungs took in great gasps of fresh air as he sprinted toward the helicopter that had brought him here. This machine provided his only chance of freedom since the barracks and the entire village would be aroused at any moment and he could not hope to outrun the lot on foot.

Reaching the helicopter, he clambered into it, locked its door. The alien controls did not baffle him because he had made careful note of them during his previous ride. Still breathing hard while his nerves twanged with excitement, he started the motor. The vanes began to turn.

Nobody had yet emerged from the stench-ridden exit he had used but somebody did come out of another door farther along the building. This character was unarmed and apparently unaware that anything extraordinary had taken place. But he did know that the humming helicopter was in wrong possession. He yelled and waved his arms as the vanes speeded up. Then he dived back into the building, came out holding a rifle.

The 'copter made its usual preliminary bumps, then soared. Below and a hundred yards away the rifle went off like a fire-cracker. Four holes appeared in the machine's plastic dome, something nicked the lobe of Leeming's left ear and drew blood, the tachometer flew to pieces on the instrument-board. A couple of fierce, hammerlike clunks sounded on the engine but it continued to run without falter and the 'copter gained height.

Bending sidewise, Leeming looked out and down through the perforated dome. His assailant was frantically shoving another magazine into the gun. A second burst of fire came when the 'copter was five hundred feet up and scooting fast. There came a sharp ping as a sliver of metal flew off the tail-fan but that was the only hit.

Leeming took another look below. The marksman had been joined by half a dozen others, all gazing skyward. None were attempting to shoot because the fugitive was now out of range. Even as he watched, the whole bunch of them ran into the building, still using the smell-free door. He could give a guess where they were heading for, namely, the radio-room.

The sight killed any elation he might have enjoyed. He had the sky to himself but it wasn't going to be forever. Now the moot question was whether he could keep it to himself long enough to make distance before he landed in the wilds and took to his heels again.

Chapter 5

Definitely he was not escaping the easy way. In many respects he was worse off than he'd been before. Afoot in the forest he'd been able to trudge around in concealment, feed himself, get some sleep. Now the whole world knew—or soon would know—that a Terran was on the loose. To keep watch while flying he needed eyes in the back of his head and even those wouldn't save him if something superfast such as a jetplane appeared. And if he succeeded in dumping his machine unseen he'd have to roam the world without a weapon of any kind.

Mentally he cursed the extreme haste with which he had dashed out of that room. The guard who'd fired the stink-gun had promptly collapsed upon it, hiding it with his body, but there might have been time to roll the fellow out of the way and snatch it up. And by the door had been two rifles either of which he could have grabbed and taken with him. He awarded himself the Idiot's Medal for passing up these opportunities despite the knowledge that at the time his only concern had been to hold his breath long enough to reach uncontaminated air.

Yes, his sole object had been to race clear of a paralyzing nausea—but that needn't have stopped him from swiping a gun if he'd been quicker on the uptake. Perhaps there was a gun aboard the 'copter. Flying at two thousand feet, he was trying to

keep full attention six ways at once, before, behind, to either side, above and below. He couldn't do that and examine the machine's interior as well. The search
would have to wait until after he had landed.

By now he was some distance over the forest in which he'd been wandering. It
struck him that when he'd been captured and taken away two helicopters had remained parked in this area. Possibly they had since departed for an unknown base.
Or perhaps they were still there and about to rise in response to a radioed alarm.

His alertness increased, he kept throwing swift glances around in all directions
while the machine hummed onward. After twenty minutes a tiny dot arose from
the far horizon. At that distance it was impossible to tell whether it was a 'copter,
a jetplane, or what. His motor chose this moment to splutter and squirt a thin
stream of smoke. The whirling vanes hesitated, resumed their steady *whup-whup*.

Leeming sweated with anxiety and watched the faraway dot. Again the motor
lost rhythm and spurted more smoke. The dot grew a little larger but was moving
at an angle that showed it was not heading straight for him. Probably it was the
herald of an aerial hunt that would find him in short time.

The motor now became asthmatic, the vanes slowed, the 'copter lost height.
Greasy smoke shot from its casing in a series of forceful puffs, a fishy smell came
with them. If a bullet had broken an oil-line, thought Leeming, he couldn't keep
up much longer. It would be best to descend while he still retained some control.

As the machine lowered he swung its tail-fan in an effort to zigzag and find a
suitable clearing amid the mass of trees. Down he went to one thousand feet, to
five hundred, and nowhere could he see a gap. There was nothing for it but to use
a tree as a cushion and hope for the best.

Reversing the tail-fan to arrest his forward motion, he sank into an enormous
tree that looked capable of supporting a house. Appearances proved deceptive for
the huge branches were very brittle and easily gave way under the weight imposed
upon them. To the accompaniment of repeated cracks the 'copter fell through the
foliage in a rapid series of halts and jolts that made its occupant feel as though
locked in a barrel that was bumping down a steep flight of stairs.

The last drop was the longest but ended in thick bushes and heavy undergrowth
that served to absorb the shock. Leeming crawled out with bruised cheekbone
and shaken frame. Blood slowly oozed from the ear-lobe that had been grazed by
a bullet. He gazed upward. There was now a wide hole in the overhead vegetation
but he doubted whether it would be noticed by any aerial observer unless flying
very low.

The 'copter lay tilted to one side, its bent and twisted vanes forced to a sharp
angle with the drive-shaft, bits of twig and bark still clinging to their edges. Hurriedly he searched the big six-seater cabin for anything that might prove useful.
Of weapons there were none. In the tool-box he did find a twenty-inch spanner of
metal resembling bronze and this he confiscated thinking it better than nothing.

Under the two seats at the rear he discovered neat compartments filled with
alien food. It was peculiar stuff and not particularly appetizing in appearance but
right now he was hungry enough to gnaw a long-dead goat covered with flies. So
he tried a circular sandwich made of what looked and tasted like two flat disks of

unleavened bread with a thin layer of white grease between them. It went down, stayed down and made him feel better. For all he knew the grease might have been derived from a pregnant lizard. He was long past caring. His belly demanded more and he ate another two sandwiches.

There was quite a stack of these sandwiches plus a goodly number of blue-green cubes of what seemed to be some highly compressed vegetable. Also a can of sawdust that smelled like chopped peanuts and tasted like a weird mixture of minced beef and seaweed. And finally a plastic bottle filled with mysterious white tablets.

Taking no chances on the tablets, he slung them into the undergrowth but retained the bottle which would serve for carrying water. The can holding the dehydrated stuff was equally valuable; it was strong, well-made and would do duty as a cooking utensil. He now had food and a primitive weapon but lacked the means of transporting the lot. There was far too much to go into his pockets.

While he pondered this problem something howled across the sky about half a mile to the east. The sound had only just died away in the distance when something else whined on a parallel course half a mile to the west. Evidently the hunt was on.

Checking his impulse to run to some place better hidden from above, he took a saw-toothed instrument out of the tool-kit, used it to remove the canvas covering from a seat. This formed an excellent bag, clumsy in shape, without straps or handles, but of just the right size. Filling it with his supplies, he made a last inspection of the wrecked helicopter and noticed that its tiny altimeter-dial was fronted with a magnifying lens. The rim holding the lens was strong and stubborn, he had to work carefully to extract the lens without breaking it.

Under the engine-casing he found the reservoir of a wind-shield water-spray. It took the form of a light metal bottle holding about one quart. Detaching it, he emptied it, filled it with fuel from the 'copter's tank. These final acquisitions gave him the means of making a quick fire. Klavith could keep the automatic lighter and the pepper-pot and burn down the barracks with them. He, Leeming, had got something better. A lens does not exhaust itself or wear out. He was so gratified with his loot he forgot that a lens was somewhat useless night-times.

The unseen jet planes screamed back, still a mile apart and on parallel courses. This showed that the hunt was being conducted systematically with more machines probing the air in other directions. Having failed to find the missing 'copter anywhere within the maximum distance it could travel since it was stolen, they'd soon realize that it had landed and start looking for it from lower altitude. That meant a painstaking survey from little more than tree-top height.

Now that he was all set to go he wasn't worried about how soon the searchers spotted the tree-gap and the 'copter. In the time it would take them to drop troops on the spot he could flee beyond sight or sound, becoming lost within the maze of trees. The only thing that bothered him was the possibility that they might have some species of trained animal capable of tracking him wherever he went.

He didn't relish the idea of a Zangastan land-octopus, or whatever it might be, snuffling up to him in the middle of the night and embracing him with rubbery tentacles while he was asleep. There were several people back home for whom such a fate would be more suitable, professional loud-shouters who'd be shut up for keeps. However, chances had to be taken. Shouldering his canvas bag he left the scene.

By nightfall he'd put about four miles between himself and the abandoned helicopter. He could not have done more even if he'd wished; the stars and three tiny moons did not provide enough light to permit further progress. Aerial activity continued without abate during the whole of this time but ceased when the sun went down.

The best sanctuary he could find for the night was a depression between huge tree-roots. With rocks and sods he built a screen at one end of it, making it sufficiently high to conceal a fire from anyone stalking him at ground level. That done, he gathered a good supply of dry twigs, wood chips and leaves. With everything ready he suddenly discovered himself lacking the means to start a blaze. The lens was useless in the dark; it was strictly for day-time only, beneath an unobscured sun.

This started him on a long spell of inspired cussing after which he hunted around until he found a stick with a sharply splintered point. This he rubbed hard and vigorously in the crack of a dead log. Powdered wood accumulated in the channel as he kept on rubbing with all his weight behind the stick. It took twenty-seven minutes of continuous effort before the wood-powder glowed and gave forth a thin wisp of smoke. Quickly he stuck a splinter wetted with 'copter fuel into the middle of the faint glow and at once it burst into flame. The sight made him feel as triumphant as if he'd won the war single-handed.

Now he got the fire going properly. The crackle and spit of it was a great comfort in his loneliness. Emptying the beef-seaweed compound onto a glossy leaf half the size of a blanket, he three-quarters filled the can with water, stood it on the fire. To the water he added a small quantity of the stuff on the leaf, also a vegetable cube and hoped that the result would be a hot and nourishing soup. While waiting for this alien mixture to cook he gathered more fuel, stacked it nearby, sat close to the flames and ate a grease sandwich.

After the soup had simmered for some time he put it aside to cool sufficiently to be sipped straight from the can. When eventually he tried it the stuff tasted much better than expected, thick, heavy and now containing a faint flavor of mushrooms. He absorbed the lot, washed the can in an adjacent stream, dried it by the fire and carefully refilled it with the compound on the leaf. Choosing the biggest lumps of wood from his supply, he arranged them on the flames to last as long as possible, and lay down within warming distance.

It was his intention to spend an hour or two considering his present situation and working out his future plans. But the soothing heat and the satisfying sensation of a full paunch lulled him to sleep within five minutes. He sprawled in the jungle with the great tree towering overhead, its roots rising on either side, the fire glowing near his feet while he emitted gentle snores and enjoyed one of the longest, deepest sleeps he had ever known.

The snooze lasted ten hours so that when he awoke he was only partway through the lengthy night. His eyes opened to see stars glimmering through the tree-gaps and for a moody moment they seemed impossibly far away. Rested but cold, he sat up and looked beyond his feet. Nothing could be seen of the fire. It must have burned itself out. He wished most heartily that he had awakened a couple of times and added more wood. But he had slept solidly, almost as if drugged. Perhaps some portion of that alien fodder was a drug in its effect upon the Terran digestive system.

Edging toward where the fire had been he felt around it. The ground was warm. His exploring hand went farther, plunged into hot ash. Three or four sparks gleamed fitfully and he burned a finger. Grabbing a twig he dunked it in the fuel-bottle and then used it to stir the embers. It flamed like a torch. Soon he had the fire going again and the coldness crept away.

Chewing a sandwich, he let his mind toy with current problems. The first thought that struck him was that he'd missed another chance when looting the helicopter. He had taken one seat-cover to function as a bag; if he'd had the horse sense to rob all the other seats and cut their covers wide open he'd have provided himself with bedclothes. Night-times he was going to miss his blankets unless somehow he could keep a fire going continuously. The seat-covers would have served to keep him wrapped and warm.

Damning himself for his stupidity he played with the idea of returning to the 'copter and making good the deficiency. Then he decided that the risk was too great. He'd been caught once by his own insistence upon returning to the scene of the crime and he'd be a prize fool to let himself be trapped the same way again.

For the time being he'd have to cope as best he could without blankets or anything in lieu thereof. If he shivered it was nobody's fault but his own. A wise, far-seeing Providence had created the dull-witted especially to do all the suffering. It was right and proper that he should pay for his blunders with his fair quota of discomfort.

Of course, even the sharpest brain could find itself ensnared by sheer hard luck or by misfortunes impossible to foresee. Chance operates for and against the individual with complete haphazardness. All the same, the bigger the blow the greater the need to use one's wits in countering it. Obstacles were made to be surmounted and not to be wept over.

Employing his wits to the best of his ability, he came to several conclusions. Firstly, that it was not enough merely to remain free because he had no desire to spend the rest of his natural life hiding upon an alien world. Somehow he must get off the planet and metaphorically kiss it goodbye forever.

Secondly, that there was no way of leaving except by spaceship, no way of returning to Earth except by spaceship. Therefore he must concentrate upon the formidable task of stealing a suitable ship. Any ship would not do. Making off with a war vessel or a cargo-boat or a passenger liner was far beyond his ability since all needed a complete crew to handle them. It would have to be a one-man or two-man scout-boat, fully fueled and ready for long-range fight. Such ships existed in large numbers. But finding one and getting away with it was something else again.

Thirdly, even if by a near-miracle he could seize a scout-boat and vanish into space he'd have solved one major problem only to be faced by another identically the same. The ship could not reach Rigel, much less Earth, without at least one overhaul and refueling on the way. No Combine group could be expected to perform this service for him unless he had the incredible luck to drop upon a species not in their right minds. His only answer to this predicament would be to land upon a planet with hiding-places, abandon his worn-out vessel and steal another. If either of these two ships failed to come up to scratch he might have to make yet another landing and grab a third one.

It was a grim prospect. The odds were of the order of a million to one against him. All the same, there had been times when the millionth chance came off and there should be times when it would do so again.

There was another alternative that he dismissed as not worthy of consideration, namely, to stay put in the hope that the war would end reasonably soon and he'd be permitted to go home in peace. But the termination of the conflict had no fixed date. For all he knew, it might end when he was old and grey-bearded or fifty years after he was dead. All wars are the same in that there are times when they seem to have settled down forever lasting and lack of strife becomes almost unthinkable.

His ponderings ceased abruptly when something let go a deep-bellied cough and four green eyes stared at him out of the dark. Leaping to the fire, he snatched a flaming branch and hurled it in that direction. It described a blazing arc and fell into a bush.

The eyes blinked out, blinked on, then disappeared. There came the scuffling, slithering sounds of a cumbersome creature backing away fast. Gradually the noise died out in the distance. Leeming found himself unable to decide whether it had been one animal or two, whether it walked or crawled, whether it was the Zangastan equivalent of a prowling tiger or no more than a curious cow. At any rate, it had gone.

Sitting by the tree-trunk, he kept the fire going and maintained a waxy watch until the dawn.

With the sunrise he breakfasted on a can of soup and a sandwich. Stamping out the fire, he picked up his belongings and headed to the south. This direction would take him farther from the center of the search and, to his inward regret, would also put mileage between him and the concealed dump of real Terran food. On the other hand, a southward trek would bring him nearer to the equatorial belt in which he had seen three spaceports during his circumnavigation. Where there are ports there are ships.

Dawn had not lasted an hour before a jet plane shot overhead. A little later four helicopters came, all going slow and skimming the trees. Leeming squatted under a bush until they had passed, resumed his journey and was nearly spotted by a buoyant fan following close behind the 'copters. He heard the whoosh of it in the nick of time, flung himself flat beside a rotting log and did his best to look like a shapeless patch of earth. The thing's downward air-blast sprayed across his back as it floated above him. Nearby trees rustled their branches, dead leaves fluttered to ground. It required all his self-control to remain perfectly motionless while a pair of expressionless, snakelike eyes stared down.

The fan drifted away, its pilot fooled. Leeming got to his feet, glanced at his compass and pressed on. Energetically he cussed all fans, those who made them and those who rode them. They were slow, had short range and carried only one man. But they were dangerously silent. If a fugitive became preoccupied with his own thoughts, ceasing to be on the alert, he could amble along unaware of the presence of such a machine until he felt the air-blast.

Judging by this early activity the search was being pursued in manner sufficient to show that some high-ranking brasshat had been infuriated by his escape. It would not be Klavith, he thought. A major did not stand high enough in the military caste system. Somebody bigger and more influential had swung into action. Such a character would make an example of the unfortunate Klavith and every guard in the barrack-block. While warily he trudged onward he couldn't help wondering what Klavith's fate had been; quite likely anything from being boiled in oil to demotion to private, fourth class. On an alien world one cannot define disciplinary measures in Terran terms.

But it was a safe bet that if he, John Leeming, were to be caught again they'd take lots better care of him—such as by binding him in mummy-wrappings or amputating his feet or something equally unpleasant. He'd had one chance of freedom and had grabbed it with both hands; they wouldn't give him another opportunity. Among any species the escaper is regarded as a determined troublemaker deserving of special treatment.

All that day he continued to plod southward. Half a dozen times he sought brief shelter while air machines of one sort or another scouted overhead. At dusk he was still within the forest and the aerial snooping ceased. The night was a repetition of the previous one with the same regrets over the loss of his blankets, the same difficulty in making a fire. Sitting by the soothing blaze, his insides filled and his legs enjoying a welcome rest, he felt vaguely surprised that the foe had not thought to maintain the search through the night. Although he had shielded his fire from ground-level observation it could easily be spotted by a night-flying plane; it was a complete giveaway that he could not hope to extinguish before it was seen from above.

The next day was uneventful. Aerial activity appeared to have ceased. At any rate, no machines came his way. Perhaps for some reason known only to themselves they were concentrating the search elsewhere. He made good progress without interruption or molestation and, when the sun stood highest, used the lens to create a smokeless fire and give himself another meal. Again he ate well, since the insipid but satisfying alien food was having no adverse effect upon his system. A check on how much he had left showed that there was sufficient for another five or six days.

In the mid-afternoon of the second day afterward he reached the southern limit of the forest and found himself facing a broad road. Beyond it stretched cultivated flatlands containing several sprawling buildings that he assumed to be farms. About four miles away there arose from the plain a cluster of stone-built structures around which ran a high wall. At that distance he could not determine whether the place was a fortress, a prison, a hospital, a lunatic asylum, a factory protected by a top security barrier, or something unthinkable that Zangastans preferred to screen from public gaze. Whatever it was, it had a menacing appearance. His intuition told him to keep his distance from it.

Retreating a couple of hundred yards into the forest, he found a heavily wooded hollow, sat on a log and readjusted his plans. Faced with an open plain that stretched as far as the eye could see, with habitations scattered around and with towns and villages probably just over the horizon, it was obvious that he could no longer make progress in broad daylight. On a planet populated by broad, squat, lizard-skinned people a lighter-built and pink-faced Terran would stand out as conspicuously as a giant panda at a bishops' convention. He'd be grabbed on sight, especially if the radio and video had broadcast his description with the information that he was wanted.

The Combine included about twenty species, half of whom the majority of Zangastans had never seen. But they had a rough idea of what their copartners looked like and they'd know a fugitive Terran when they found him. His chance of kidding his captors that he was an unfamiliar ally was mighty small; even if he could talk a bunch of peasants into half-believing him they'd hold him pending a check by authority.

Up to this moment he'd been bored by the forest with its long parade of trees, its primitiveness, its silence, its lack of visible life. Now he viewed it as a sanctuary about to withdraw its protection. Henceforth he'd have to march by night and sleep by day—providing that he could find suitable hiding places in which to hold up. It was a grim prospect.

But the issue was clear-cut. If he wanted to reach a spaceport and steal a scout-boat he must press forward no matter what the terrain and regardless of risks. Alternatively, he must play safe by remaining in the forest, perpetually foraging for food around its outskirts, living the life of a hermit until ready for burial.

The extended day had several hours yet to go; he decided to have a meal and get some sleep before the fall of darkness. Accordingly he started a small fire with the lens, made himself a can of hot soup and had two sandwiches. Then he curled himself up in a wad of huge leaves and closed his eyes. The sun gave a pleasant warmth, sleep seemed to come easy. He slipped into a quick doze. Half a dozen vehicles buzzed and rattled along the nearby road. Brought wide awake, he cussed them with fervor, shut his eyes and tried again. It wasn't long before more passing traffic disturbed him.

This continued until the stars came out and two of the five small moons shed an eerie light over the landscape. He stood in the shadow of a tree, overlooking the road and waited for the natives to go to bed—if they did go to bed rather than hang bat-like by their heels from the rafters.

A few small trucks went past during this time. They had orange-colored headlights and emitted puffs of white smoke or vapor. They sounded somewhat like model locomotives. Leeming got the notion that each one was steam-powered, probably with a flash-boiler fired with wood. There was no way of checking on this.

Ordinarily he wouldn't have cared a hoot how Zangastan trucks operated. Right now it was a matter of some importance. The opportunity might come to steal a vehicle and thus help himself on his way to wherever he was going. But as a fully qualified space-pilot he had not the vaguest idea of how to drive a steam-engine. Indeed, if threatened with the death of a thousand cuts he'd have been compelled to admit that he could not ride a bike.

While mulling his educational handicaps it occurred to him that he'd be dimwitted to sneak furtively through the night hoping for a chance to swipe a car or truck. The man of initiative *makes* his chances and does not sit around praying for them to be placed in his lap.

Upbraiding himself, he sought around in the gloom until he found a nice, smooth, fist-sized rock. Then he waited for a victim to come along. The first vehicle to appear was traveling in the wrong direction, using the farther side of the road. Most of an hour crawled by before two more came together, also on the farther side, one close behind the other.

Across the road were no trees, bushes or other means of concealment; he'd no choice but to keep to his own side and wait in patience for his luck to turn. After what seemed an interminable period a pair of orange lamps gleamed in the distance, sped toward him. As the lights grew larger and more brilliant he tensed in readiness.

At exactly the right moment he sprang from beside the tree, hurled the rock and leaped back into darkness. In his haste and excitement, he missed. The rock shot within an inch of the windshield's rim and clattered on the road. Having had no more than a brief glimpse of a vague, gesticulating shadow, the driver continued blithely on, unaware that he'd escaped a taste of thuggery.

Making a few remarks more emphatic than cogent, Leeming recovered the rock and resumed his vigil. The next truck showed up the same time as another one coming in the opposite direction. He shifted to behind the tree-trunk. The two vehicles passed each other at a point almost level with his hiding-place. Scowling after their diminishing beams he took up position again.

Traffic had thinned with the lateness of the hour and it was a good while before more headlights came beaming in the dark and running on the road's near side. This time he reacted with greater care and took better aim. A swift jump, he heaved the rock, jumped back.

The result was the dull *whup* of a hole being bashed through transparent plastic. A guttural voice shouted something about a turkey-leg, this being an oath in local dialect. The truck rolled another twenty yards, pulled up. A broad, squat figure scrambled out of the cab and ran toward the rear in evident belief that he'd hit something.

Leeming, who had anticipated this move, met him with raised spanner. The driver didn't even see him; he bolted round the truck's tail and the spanner whanged on his pate and he went down without a sound. For a horrid moment Leeming thought that he had killed the fellow. Not that one Zangastan mattered more or less in the general scheme of things. But he had his own peculiar status to consider. Even the Terrans showed scant mercy to prisoners who killed while escaping.

However, the victim emitted bubbling snorts like a hog in childbirth and had plenty of life left in him. Dragging him onto the verge and under a tree, Leeming searched him, found nothing worth taking. The wad of paper money was devoid of value to a Terran who'd have no opportunity to spend it.

Just then a long, low tanker rumbled into view. Taking a tight grip on the spanner, Leeming watched its approach and prepared to fight or run as circumstances dictated. It went straight past, showing no interest in the halted truck.

Climbing into the cab, he had a look around, found that the truck was not steam-powered as he had thought. The engine was still running but there was no fire-box or anything resembling one. The only clue to power-source was a strong scent like that of alcohol mixed with a highly aromatic oil.

Tentatively he pressed a button and the headlights went out. He pressed it again and they came on. The next button produced a shrill, catlike yowl out front. The third had no effect whatever: he assumed that it controlled the self-starter. After some fiddling around he found that the solitary pedal was the footbrake and that a lever on the steering-wheel caused the machine to move forward or backward at speed proportionate to the degree of its shift. There was no sign of an ignition-switch, gear-change lever, headlight dipper or parking brake. The whole layout was a curious mixture of the ultra-modem and the antiquated.

Satisfied that he could drive it, he advanced the lever. The truck rolled forward, accelerated to a moderate pace and kept going at that. He moved the lever farther and the speed increased. The forest slid past on his left, the flatlands on his right and the road was a yellow ribbon streaming under the bonnet. Man, this was the life! Relaxing in his seat and feeling pretty good, he broke into ribald song.

The road split. Without hesitation he chose the arm that tended southward. It took him through a straggling village in which very few lights were visible. Reaching the country beyond he got onto a road running in a dead straight line across the plain. Now all five moons were in the sky, the landscape looked ghostly and forbidding. Shoving the lever a few more degrees, he raced onward.

After an estimated eighty miles he by-passed a city, met desultory traffic on the road but continued in peace and unchallenged. Next he drove past a high stone wall surrounding a cluster of buildings resembling those seen earlier. Peering upward as he swept by, he tried to see whether there were any guards patrolling the wall-top but it was impossible to tell without stopping the truck and getting out. That he did not wish to do, preferring to travel as fast and as far as possible while the going was good.

He'd been driving non-stop at high speed for several hours when a fire-trail bloomed in the sky and moved like a tiny crimson feather across the stars. As he watched, the feather floated round in a deep curve, grew bigger and brighter as it descended. A ship was coming in. Slightly to his left and far over the horizon there must be a spaceport.

Maybe within easy reach of him there was a scout-boat fully fueled and just begging to be taken up. He licked his lips at the thought of it.

With its engine still running smoothly the truck passed through the limb of another large forest. He made mental note of the place lest within a short time he should be compelled to abandon the vehicle and take to his heels once more. After recent experiences he found himself developing a strong affection for forests; on a hostile world they were the only places offering anonymity and liberty.

Gradually the road tended leftward, leading him nearer and nearer toward where the hidden spaceport was presumed to be. The truck rushed through four small villages in rapid succession, all dark, silent and in deep slumber. Again the road split and this time he found himself in a quandary. Which arm would take him to the place of ships?

Nearby stood a signpost but its alien script meant nothing to him. Stopping the truck, he got out and examined his choice of routes as best he could in the poor light. The right arm seemed to be the more heavily used to judge by the condition of its surface. Picking the right side, he drove ahead.

Time went on so long without evidence of a spaceport that he was commencing to think he'd made a mistake when a faint glow appeared low in the forward sky. It came from somewhere behind a rise in the terrain, strengthened as he neared. He tooled up the hill, came over the crest and saw in a shallow valley a big array of floodlights illuminating buildings, concrete emplacements, blast-pits and four snouty ships standing on their tailfins.

Chapter 6

He should have felt overjoyed. Instead he became filled with a sense of wariness and foreboding. A complete getaway just couldn't be as easy as he'd planned: there had to be a snag somewhere.

Edging the truck onto the verge, he braked and switched off his lights. Then he surveyed the scene more carefully. From this distance the four vessels looked too big and fat to be scout-boats, too small and out-of-date to be warships. It was very likely that they were cargo-carriers, probably of the trampship type.

Assuming that they were in good condition and fully prepared for flight, it was not impossible for an experienced, determined pilot to take one up single-handed. And if it was fitted with an autopilot he could keep it going for days and weeks. Without such assistance he was liable to drop dead through sheer exhaustion long before he was due to arrive anywhere worth reaching. The same problem did not apply to a genuine scout-boat because a one-man ship *had* to be filled with robotic aids. He estimated that these small merchantmen normally carried a crew of at least twelve apiece, perhaps as many as twenty.

Furthermore, he had seen a vessel coming in to land—so at least one of these four had not yet been serviced and was unfit for flight. There was no way of telling which one was the latest arrival. But a ship in the hand is worth ten someplace else. To one of his profession the sight of waiting vessels was irresistible.

Reluctance to part company with the truck until the last moment, plus his natural audacity, made him decide that there was no point in trying to sneak across the well-lit spaceport and reach a ship on foot. He'd do better to take the enemy by surprise, boldly drive into the place, park alongside a vessel and scoot up its ladder before they had time to collect their wits.

Once inside a ship with the airlock closed he'd be comparatively safe. It would take them far longer to get him out than it would to take him to master the strange controls and make ready to boost. He'd have shut himself inside a metal fortress and the first blast of its propulsors would clear the area for a couple of hundred yards around. Their only means of thwarting him would be to bring up heavy artillery and hole or topple the ship. By the time they'd dragged big guns to the scene he should be crossing the orbit of the nearest moon.

He consoled himself with these thoughts as he chivvied the truck onto the road and let it surge forward, but all the time he knew deep within his mind that this was to be a crazy gamble. There was a good chance that he'd grab himself a cold-dead rocket short of fuel and incapable of taking off. In that event all the irate Zangastans need do was sit around until he'd surrendered or starved to death. That they'd be so slow to react as to give him time to swap ships was a possibility almost non-existent.

Thundering down the valley road, the truck took a wide bend, raced for the spaceport's main gates. These were partly closed, leaving a yard-wide gap in the middle. An armed sentry stood at one side, behind him a hut containing others of the guard.

As the truck shot into view and roared toward him the sentry gaped at it in dumb amazement, showed the typical reaction of one far from the area of combat. Instead of pointing his automatic weapon in readiness to challenge he jumped into the road and tugged frantically to open the gates. The half at which he was pulling swung wide just in time for the truck to bullet through with a few inches to spare on either side. Now the sentry resented the driver's failure to say "Good morning!" or "Drop dead!" or anything equally courteous. Brandishing his gun, he performed a clumsy war-dance and screamed vitriolic remarks.

Concentrating on his driving to the exclusion of all else, Leeming went full tilt around the spaceport's concrete perimeter toward where the ships were parked. A bunch of lizard-skinned characters strolling along his path scattered and ran for their lives. Farther on a long, low motorized trolley loaded with fuel cylinders slid out of a shed, stopped in the middle of the road. Its driver threw himself off his seat and tried to dig himself out of sight as the truck wildly swerved around him and threatened to overturn.

Picking the most distant ship as the one it would take the foe longest to reach, Leeming braked by its tail-fins, jumped out of the cab, looked up. No ladder.

Sprinting around the base, he found the ladder on the other side, went up it like a frightened monkey.

It was like climbing the side of a factory chimney. Halfway up he paused for breath, looked around. Diminished by distance and depth, a hundred figures were racing toward him. So also were four trucks and a thing resembling an armored car. He resumed his climb, going as fast as he could but using great care because he was now so high that one slip would be fatal.

Anxiety increased as he neared the airlock at top. A few more seconds and he'd be out of shooting range. But they'd know that, too, and were liable to start popping at him while yet there was time. As he tried to make more speed his belly quirked at the thought of a last-moment bullet plowing through him. His hands grabbed half a dozen rungs in quick succession, reached the airlock rim at which point he rammed his head against an unexpected metal rod. Surprised, he raised his gaze, found himself looking into the muzzle of a gun not as big as a cannon.

"Shatsi!" ordered the owner of the gun, making a downward motion with it. "Amash!"

For a mad moment Leeming thought of holding on with one hand while he snatched his opponent's feet with the other. He raised himself in readiness to grab. Either the fellow was impatient or read his intention because he hammered Lemming's fingers with the gun-barrel.

"Amash! Shatsi—amash!"

Leeming went slowly and reluctantly down the ladder. Black despair grew blacker with every step he descended. To be caught at the start of a chase was one thing; to be grabbed near the end of it, within reach of success, was something else. Hell's bells, he'd almost got away with it and that's what made the situation so bitter.

Hereafter they'd fasten him up twice as tightly and keep a doubly close watch upon him. Even if in spite of these precautions he broke free a second time, his chance of total escape would be too small to be worth considering; with an armed guard aboard every ship he'd be sticking his head in the trap whenever he shoved it into an airlock. By the looks of it he was stuck with this stinking world until such time as a Terran task-force captured it or the war ended, either of which events might take place a couple of centuries hence.

Reaching the bottom, he stepped onto concrete and turned around expecting to be given a kick in the stomach or a bust on the nose. Instead he found himself faced by a muttering but blank-faced group containing an officer whose attitude suggested that he was more baffled than enraged. Favoring Leeming with an unwinking stare, the officer let go a stream of incomprehensible gabble that ended on a note of query. Leeming spread his hands and shrugged.

The officer tried again. Leeming responded with another shrug and did his best to look contrite. Accepting this lack of understanding as something that proved nothing one way or the other, the officer bawled at the crowd. Four armed guards emerged from the mob, hustled the prisoner into the armored car, slammed and locked the door and took him away.

At the end of the ride they shoved him into the back room of a rock house with two guards as company, the other two outside the door. Sitting on a low, hard chair, he sighed, gazed blankly at the wall for two hours. The guards also squatted, watched him as expressionlessly as a pair of snakes and said not a word.

At the end of that time a trooper brought food and water. Leeming gulped it down in silence, studied the wall for another two hours. Meanwhile his thoughts milled around. It seemed pretty obvious, he decided, that the local gang had not realized that they'd caught a Terran. All their reactions showed that they were far from certain what they'd got.

To a certain extent this was excusable. On the Allied side of the battle was a federation of thirteen lifeforms, four of them human and three more very human-like. The Combine consisted of an uneasy, precarious union of at least twenty lifeforms, three of which also were rather humanlike. Pending getting the answers from higher authority, this particular bunch of quasi-reptilians couldn't tell enemy from ally.

All the same, they were taking no chances and he could imagine what was going on while they kept him sitting on his butt. The officer would grab the telephone—or whatever they used in lieu—and call the nearest garrison town. The highest ranker there would promptly transfer responsibility to military headquarters. There, Klavith's alarm would have been filed and forgotten and a ten-star panjandrum would pass the query to the main beamstation. An operator would transmit a message asking the three humanlike allies whether they had lost track of a scout in this region.

When back came a signal saying, "No!" the local gang would realize that a rare bird had been caught deep within the spatial empire. They wouldn't like it. Holding-troops far behind the lines share all the glory and none of the grief and they're happy to let things stay that way. A sudden intrusion of the enemy where he's no right to be is an event disturbing to the even tenor of life and not to be greeted with cries of martial joy. Besides, from their viewpoint where one can sneak in, an army can follow, and it is disconcerting to be taken in force from the rear.

Then when the news got around Klavith would arrive at full gallop to remind everyone that this was not the first time Leeming had been captured, but the second. What would they do to him eventually? He was far from sure because previously he hadn't given them time to settle down to the job. It was most unlikely that they'd shoot him out of hand. If sufficiently civilized they'd cross-examine him and then imprison him for the duration. If uncivilized they'd dig up Klavith or maybe an ally able to talk Terran and milk the prisoner of every item of information he possessed by methods ruthless and bloody.

Back toward the dawn of history when conflict had been confined to one planet there had existed a protective device known as the Geneva Convention. It had organized neutral inspection of prison camps, brought occasional letters from home, provided food parcels that had kept alive many a captive who otherwise might have died.

There was nothing like that today. A prisoner had only two forms of protection, those being his own resources and the power of his side to retaliate against the prisoners they'd got. And the latter was a threat more potential than real. There cannot be retaliation without actual knowledge of maltreatment.

The day dragged on. The guards were changed twice. More food and water came. Eventually the one window showed that darkness was approaching. Eyeing the window furtively, Leeming decided that it would be suicidal to take a running jump at it under two guns. It was small and high, difficult to scramble through in a hurry. How he wished he had his own stink-gun now!

A prisoner's first duty is to escape. That means biding one's time with appalling patience until occurs an opportunity that may be seized and exploited to the utmost. He'd done it once and he must do it again. If no way of total escape existed he'd have to invent one.

The prospect before him was tough indeed; before long it was likely to become a good deal tougher. If only he'd been able to talk the local language, or any Combine language, he might have been able to convince even the linguistic Klavith that black was white. Sheer impudence can pay dividends. Maybe he could have landed his ship, persuaded them with smooth words, unlimited self-assurance and just the right touch of arrogance to repair and reline his propulsors and cheer him on his way never suspecting that they had been talked into providing aid and comfort for the enemy.

It was a beautiful dream but an idle one. Lack of ability to communicate in any Combine tongue had balled up such a scheme at the start. You can't chivvy a sucker into donating his pants merely by making noises at him. Some other chance must now be watched for and grabbed, swiftly and with both hands—providing that they were fools enough to permit a chance.

Weighing up his guards in the same way as he had estimated the officer, his earlier captors and Klavith, he didn't think that this species was numbered among the Combine's brightest brains. All the same they were broad in the back, sour in the puss and plenty good enough to put someone in the pokey and keep him there for a long, long time.

In fact they were naturals as prison wardens.

He remained in the house four days, eating and drinking at regular intervals, sleeping halfway through the lengthy nights, cogitating for hours and often glowering at his impassive guards. Mentally he concocted, examined and rejected a thousand ways of regaining his liberty, most of them spectacular, fantastic and impossible.

At one time he went so far as to try to stare the guards into a hypnotic trance, gazing intently at them until his own eyeballs felt locked for keeps. It did not bother them in the least. They had the reptilian ability to remain motionless and outstare him until kingdom come.

Mid-morning of the fourth day the officer strutted in, yelled, "Amash! Amash!" and gestured toward the door. His tone and manner were decidedly unfriendly. Evidently someone had identified the prisoner as an Allied space louse.

Getting off his seat, Leeming walked out, two guards ahead, two behind, the officer in the rear. A box-bodied car sheathed in steel waited on the road. They urged him into it, locked it. A pair of guards stood on the rear platform hard against the doors and clung to the handrails. A third joined the driver at the front.

The journey took thirteen hours, the whole of which the inmate spent jouncing around in complete darkness.

By the time the car halted Leeming had invented one new and exceedingly repulsive word. He used it immediately the rear doors opened.

"Quilpole—enk?" he growled. *"Enk?"*

"Amash!" bawled the guard, unappreciative of alien contributions to the vocabulary of invective. He gave the other a powerful shove.

With poor grace Leeming amashed. He glimpsed great walls rearing against the night and a zone of brilliant light high up before he was pushed through a metal portal and into a large room. Here a reception committee of six thuglike samples awaited him. One of the six signed a paper presented by the escort. The guards withdrew, the door closed, the six eyed the arrival with complete lack of amiability.

One of them said something in an authoritative voice and made motions indicative of undressing.

Leeming called him a smelly quilpole conceived in an alien marsh.

It did him no good. The six grabbed him, stripped him naked, searched every vestige of his clothing, paying special attention to seams and linings. They displayed the expert technique of ones who'd done this job countless times already, knew exactly where to look and what to look for. None showed the slightest interest in his alien physique despite that he was posing fully revealed in the raw.

Everything he possessed was put on one side and his clothes shied back at him. He dressed himself while they pawed through the loot and gabbled together. Satisfied that the captive now owned nothing more than was necessary to hide his shame, they led him through the farther door, up a flight of thick stone stairs, along a stone corridor and into a cell. The door slammed with a sound like that of the crack of doom.

In the dark of night eight small stars and one tiny moon shone through a heavily barred opening high up in one wall. Along the bottom of the gap shone a faint yellow glow from some outside illumination.

Fumbling around in the gloom he found a wooden bench against one wall. It moved when he lugged it. Dragging it beneath the opening he stood upon it but found himself a couple of feet too low to get a view outside. Though heavy, he struggled with it until he had it propped at an angle against the wall, then he crawled carefully up it and had a look between the bars.

Forty feet below lay a bare stone-floored space fifty yards wide and extending to the limited distance he could see rightward and leftward. Beyond the space a smooth-surfaced stone wall rising to his own level. The top of the wall angled at about sixty degrees to form a sharp apex ten inches above which ran a single line of taut wire, without barbs.

From unseeable sources to right and left poured powerful beams of light that flooded the entire area between cell-block and outer wall as well as a similarly wide space beyond the wall. There was no sign of life. There was only the wall, the flares of light, the overhanging night and the distant stars.

"So I'm in the jug," he said. "That's torn it!"

He jumped to the invisible floor and the slight thrust made the bench fall with a resounding crash. It sounded as if he had produced a rocket and let himself be whisked through the roof. Feet raced along the outside passage, light poured through a suddenly opened spyhole in the heavy metal door. An eye appeared in the hole.

"Sach invigia, faplap!" shouted the guard.

Leeming called him a flatfooted, duck-assed quilpole and added six more words, older, time-worn but still potent. The spyhole slammed shut. He lay on the hard bench and tried to sleep.

An hour later he kicked hell out of the door and when the spyhole opened he said, "Faplap yourself!"

After that he did sleep.

Breakfast consisted of one lukewarm bowl of stewed grain resembling millet and a mug of water. Both were served with disdain and eaten with disgust. It wasn't as good as the alien muck on which he had lived in the forest. But of course he hadn't been on convict's rations then; he'd been eating the meals of some unlucky helicopter crew.

Sometime later a thin-lipped specimen arrived in company with two guards. With a long series of complicated gestures this character explained that the prisoner was to learn a civilized language and, what was more, would learn it fast—by order. Education would commence forthwith.

Puzzled by the necessity, Leeming asked, "What about Major Klavith?"

"Snapnose?"

"Why can't Klavith do the talking? Has he been struck dumb or something?"

A light dawned upon the other. Making stabbing motions with his forefinger, he said, "Klavith—fat, fat, fat!"

"Huh?"

"Klavith—fat, fat, fat!" He tapped his chest several times, pretended to crumple to the floor, and succeeded in conveying that Klavith had expired with official assistance.

"Holy cow!" said Leeming.

In businesslike manner the tutor produced a stack of juvenile picture books and started the imparting process while the guards lounged against the wall and looked bored. Leeming cooperated as one does with the enemy, namely, by misunderstanding everything, mispronouncing everything and overlooking nothing that would prove him a linguistic moron.

The lesson ended at noon and was celebrated by the arrival of another bowl of gruel containing a hunk of stringy, rubbery substance resembling the hind end of a rat. He drank the gruel, sucked the portion of animal, shoved the bowl aside.

Then he pondered the significance of their decision to teach him how to talk. In bumping off the unfortunate Klavith they had become the victims of their own ruthlessness. They'd deprived themselves of the world's only speaker of Cosmoglotta. Probably they had a few others who could speak it stationed on allied worlds, but it would take time and trouble to bring one of those back here.

Someone had blundered by ordering Klavith's execution; he was going to cover up the mistake by teaching the prisoner to squeal.

Evidently they'd got nothing resembling Earth's electronic brain-pryers and could extract information only by question-and-answer methods aided by unknown forms of persuasion. They wanted to know things and intended to learn them if possible. The slower he was to gain fluency the longer it would be before they put him on the rack, if that was their intention.

His speculations ended when the guards opened the door and ordered him out. Leading him along the corridor, down the stairs, they released him into a great yard filled with figures mooching aimlessly around under a bright sun. He halted in surprise.

Rigellians! About two thousand of them. These were allies, fighting friends of Terra. He looked them over with mounting excitement, seeking a few more familiar shapes amid the mob. Perhaps an Earthman or two. Or even a few humanlike Centaurians.

But there were none. Only rubber-limbed, pop-eyed Rigellians shuffling around in the dreary manner of those confronted with many wasted years and no perceivable future.

Even as he gazed at them he sensed something peculiar. They could see him as clearly as he could see them and, being the only Earthman, he was a legitimate object of attention, a friend from another star. They should have been crowding up to him, full of talk, seeking the latest news of the war, asking questions and offering information.

It wasn't like that at all. They took no notice of him, behaved as if the arrival of a Terran were of no consequence whatever. Slowly and deliberately he walked across the yard, inviting some sort of fraternal reaction. They got out of his way. A few eyed him furtively, the majority pretended to be unaware of his existence. Nobody offered a word of comfort. Obviously they were giving him the conspicuous brush-off.

He trapped a small group of them in a corner of the yard and demanded with ill-concealed irritation, "Any of you speak Terran?"

They looked at the sky, the wall, the ground, or at each other, and remained silent. "Anyone know Centaurian?"

No answer.

"Well, how about Cosmoglotta?"

No reply.

Riled, he walked away and tried another bunch. No luck. Within an hour he had fired questions at two or three hundred without getting a single response. It puzzled him completely. Their manner was not contemptuous or hostile but something else. He tried to analyze it, came to the conclusion that for an unknown reason they were wary, they were afraid to speak to him.

Sitting on a stone step he watched them until a shrill whistle signaled that exercise time was over. The Rigellians formed up in long lines in readiness to march back to their quarters. Leeming's guards gave him a kick in the pants and chivvied him to his cell.

Temporarily he dismissed the problem of unsociable allies. After dark was the time for thinking because then there was nothing else to do. He wanted to spend the remaining hours of daylight in studying the picture-books and getting well ahead with the local lingo while appearing to lay far behind. Fluency might prove an advantage some day. Too bad that he had never learned Rigellian, for instance.

So he applied himself fully to the task until print and pictures ceased to be visible. He ate his evening portion of mush, after which he lay on the bench, closed his eyes, set his mind to work.

In all of his hectic life he'd met no more than about twenty Rigellians. Never once had he visited their three closely bunched solar systems. What little he knew of them was hearsay evidence. It was said that their standard of intelligence was good, they were technologically efficient, they had been consistently friendly toward men of Earth since first contact nearly a thousand years ago. Fifty percent of them spoke Cosmoglotta, about one per cent knew the Terran tongue.

Therefore if the average held up, several hundreds of those met in the yard should have been able to converse with him in one language or another. Why had they steered clear of him and maintained silence? And why had they been mighty unanimous about it?

Determined to solve this puzzle he invented, examined and discarded a dozen theories, all with sufficient flaws to strain the credulity. It was about two hours before he hit upon the obvious solution.

These Rigellians were prisoners deprived of liberty for an unknown number of years to come. Some of them must have seen an Earthman at one time or another. But all of them knew that in the Combine's ranks were a few species superficially humanlike. They couldn't swear to it that a Terran really was a Terran and they were taking no chances on him being a spy, an ear of the enemy planted among them to listen for plots.

That in turn meant something else: when a big mob of prisoners become excessively suspicious of a possible traitor in their midst it's because they have something to hide. Yes, that was it! He slapped his knee in delight. The Rigellians had an escape scheme in process of hatching and meanwhile were taking no chances.

They had been here plenty long enough to become at least bored, at most desperate, and seek the means to make a break. Having found a way out, or being in process of making one, they were refusing to take the risk of letting the plot be messed up by a stranger of doubtful origin. Now his problem was that of how to overcome their suspicions, gain their confidence and get himself included in whatever was afoot. To this he gave considerable thought.

Next day, at the end of exercise time, a guard swung a heavy leg and administered the usual kick. Leeming promptly hauled off and punched him clean on the snout. Four guards jumped in and gave the culprit a thorough going over. They did it good and proper, with zest and effectiveness that no onlooking Rigellian could possibly mistake for a piece of dramatic play-acting. It was an object lesson and intended as such. The limp body was taken out of the yard and lugged upstairs, its face a mess of blood.

Chapter 7

It was a week before Leeming was fit enough to reappear in the yard. The price of confidence had proved rough, tough and heavy and his features were still an ugly sight. He strolled through the crowd, ignored as before, chose a soft spot in the sun and sat.

Soon afterward a prisoner sprawled tiredly on the ground a couple of yards away, watched distant guards and spoke in little more than a whisper.

"Where d'you come from?"

"Terra."

"How'd you get here?"

Leeming told him briefly.

"How's the war going?"

"We're pushing them back slowly but surely. But it'll take a long time to finish the job."

"How long do you suppose?"

"I don't know. It's anyone's guess." Leeming eyed him curiously. "What brought your bunch here?"

"We're not combatants but civilian colonists. Our government placed advance parties, all male, on four new planets that were ours by right of discovery. Twelve thousand of us altogether." The Rigellian paused while he looked carefully around, noted the positions of various guards. "The Combine descended on us in force. That was two years ago. It was easy. We weren't prepared for trouble, weren't adequately armed, didn't even know that a war was on."

"They grabbed your four planets?"

"You bet they did. And laughed in our faces."

Leeming nodded understanding. Cynical and ruthless claim-jumping had been the original cause of the fracas now extended across a great slice of the galaxy. On one planet a colony had put up an heroic resistance and died to the last man. The sacrifice had fired a blaze of fury, the Allies had struck back and were still striking good and hard.

"Twelve thousand, you said. Where are the others?"

"Scattered around in prisons like this one. You certainly picked a choice dump on which to sit out the war. The Combine has made this its chief penal planet. It's far from the fighting front, unlikely ever to be discovered. The local lifeform isn't much good for space-battles but plenty good enough to hold what its allies have captured. They're throwing up big jails all over the world. If the war goes on long enough this cosmic dump will become solid with prisoners."

"So your crowd has been here about two years?"

"Sure have—and it seems more like ten."

"And done nothing about it?"

"Nothing much," agreed the Rigellian. "Just enough to get forty of us shot for trying."

"Sorry," said Leeming sincerely.

"Don't let it bother you. I know exactly how you feel. The first few weeks are the worst. The idea of being pinned down for keeps can drive you crazy unless you learn to be philosophical about it." He mused awhile, indicated a heavily built guard patrolling by the farther wall. "A few days ago that lying swine boasted that already there are two hundred thousand Allied prisoners on this planet and added that by this time next year there would be two million. I hope he never lives to see it."

"I'm getting out of here," said Leeming.

"How?"

"I don't know yet. But I'm getting out. I'm not going to stay here and rot." He waited in the hope of some comment about others feeling the same way, perhaps evasive mention of a coming break, a hint that he might be invited to join in.

Standing up, the Rigellian murmured, "Well, I wish you luck. You'll need all you can get."

He ambled away, having betrayed nothing. A whistle blew, the guards shouted, "Merse, faplaps! Amash!" And that was that.

Over the next four weeks he had frequent conversations with the same Rigellian and about twenty others, picking up odd items of information but finding them peculiarly evasive whenever the subject of freedom came up. They were friendly, in fact cordial, but remained determinedly tightmouthed.

One day he was having a surreptitious chat and asked, "Why does everyone insist on talking to me secretively and in whispers? The guards don't seem to care how much you gab to one another."

"You haven't yet been cross-examined. If in the mean-time they notice that we've had plenty to say to you they will try to force out of you everything we've said—with particular reference to ideas on escape."

Leeming immediately pounced upon the lovely word.

"Ah, escape, that's all there is to live for right now. If anyone is thinking of making a bid maybe I can help them and they can help me. I'm a competent space-pilot and that fact is worth something."

The other cooled at once. "Nothing doing."

"Why not?"

"We've been behind walls a long time and have been taught many things that you've yet to learn."

"Such as?"

"We've discovered at bitter cost that escape attempts fail when too many know what is going on. Some planted spy betrays us. Or some selfish fool messes things up by pushing in at the wrong moment."

"I am neither a spy nor a fool. I'm certainly not enough of an imbecile to spoil my own chance of breaking free."

"That may be," the Regillian conceded. "But imprisonment creates its own special conventions. One firm rule we have established here is that an escape-plot is the exclusive property of those who concocted it and only they can make the attempt by that method. Nobody else is told about it. Nobody else knows until the resulting hullabaloo starts going. Secrecy is a protective screen that would-be escapers must maintain at all costs. They'll give nobody a momentary peek through it, not even a Terran and not even a qualified space-pilot."

"So I'm strictly on my own?"

"Afraid so. You're on your own in any case. We sleep in dormitories, fifty to a room. You're in a cell all by yourself. You're in no position to help with anything."

"I can damned well help myself," Leeming retorted angrily.

And it was his turn to walk away.

He'd been in the pokey just thirteen weeks when the tutor handed him a meta-phorical firecracker. Finishing a session distinguished only by Leeming's dopiness and slowness to learn, the tutor scowled at him and gave forth to some point.

"You are pleased to wear the cloak of idiocy. But am I an idiot too? I do not think so! I am not deceived—you are far more fluent that you pretend. In seven days time I shall report to the Commandant that you are ready for examination."

"How's that again," asked Leeming, putting on a baffled frown.

"You will be questioned by the Commandant seven days hence."

"I have already been questioned by Major Klavith."

"That was verbal, Klavith is dead and we have no record of what you told him."

Slam went the door. Came the gruel and a jaundiced lump of something unchewable. The local catering department seemed to be obsessed by the edibility of a rat's buttocks. Exercise time followed.

"I've been told they're going to put me through the mill a week from now."

"Don't let that scare you," advised the Rigellian. "They would as soon kill you as spit in the sink. But one thing keeps them in check."

"What's that?"

"The Allies are holding a stack of prisoners, too."

"Yes, but what they don't know they can't grieve over."

"There'll be more grief for the entire Zangastan species if the victor finds him-self expected to exchange very live prisoners for very dead corpses."

"You've made a point there," agreed Leeming. "Maybe it would help if I had nine feet of rope to dangle suggestively in front of the Commandant."

"It would help if I had a very large bottle of *virx* and a shapely female to stroke my hair," sighed the Rigellian.

"If you can feel that way after two years of semi-starvation, what are you like on a full diet?"

"It's all in the mind," the Rigellian said. "I like to think of what might have been."

The whistle again. More intensive study while daylight lasted. Another bowl of ersatz porridge. Darkness and a few small stars peeping through the barred slot high up. Time seemed to stand still, as it does with a high wall around it.

He lay on the bench and produced thoughts like bubbles from a fountain. No place, positively no place is absolutely impregnable. Given brawn and brains, time and patience, there's always a way in or out. Escapees shot down as they bolted had chosen the wrong time and wrong place, or the right time but the wrong place, or the right place but the wrong time. Or they had neglected brawn in favor of brains, a common fault of the overcautious. Or they'd neglected brains in favor of brawn, a fault of the reckless.

With eyes closed he carefully reviewed the situation. He was in a cell with rock walls of granite hardness at least four feet thick. The only openings were a narrow gap blocked by five massive steel bars, also an armor-plated door in constant view of patrolling guards.

On his person he had no hacksaw, no lock-pick, no implement of any sort, nothing but the bedraggled clothes in which he reposed. If he pulled the bench to pieces and somehow succeeded in doing it unheard he'd acquire several large lumps of wood, a dozen six-inch nails and a couple of steel bolts. None of that junk would serve to open the door or cut the window-bars. And there was no other material available.

Outside stretched a brilliantly illuminated gap fifty yards wide that must be crossed to gain freedom. Then a smooth stone wall forty feet high, devoid of handholds. Atop the wall an apex much too sharp to give grip to the feet while stepping over an alarm-wire that would set the sirens going if either touched or cut.

The great wall completely encircled the entire prison. It was octagonal in shape and topped at each angle by a watch-tower containing guards, floodlights and guns. To get out, the wall would have to be surmounted right under the nose of itchy-fingered watchers, in bright light, without touching the wire. That wouldn't be the end of it either; beyond the wall was another illuminated area also to be crossed. An unlucky last-lapper could get over the wall by some kind of miracle, only to be shot to bloody shreds during his subsequent dash for darkness.

Yes, the whole set-up had the professional touch of those who knew what to do to keep prisoners in prison. Escape over the wall was well-nigh impossible though not completely so. If somebody got out of his cell or dormitory armed with a rope and grapnel, and if he had a daring confederate who'd break into the power-room and switch off everything at exactly the right moment, he might make it. Up the wall and over the dead, unresponsive alarm-wire in total darkness.

In a solitary cell there is no rope, no grapnel, nothing capable of being adapted as either. There is no desperate and trustworthy confederate. Even if these things had been available he'd have considered such a project as near-suicidal.

If he pondered once the most remote possibilities and took stock of the minimum resources needed, he pondered them a hundred times. By long after midnight he'd been beating his brains sufficiently hard to make them come up with anything, including ideas that were slightly mad.

For example: he could pull a plastic button from his jacket, swallow it and hope that the result would get him a transfer to hospital. True, the hospital was within the prison's confines but it might offer better opportunity to escape. Then he thought a second time, decided that an intestinal blockage would not guarantee his removal elsewhere. They might do no more than force a powerful purgative down his neck and thus add to his present discomforts.

As dawn broke he arrived at a final conclusion. Thirty, forty or fifty Rigellians working in a patient, determined group might tunnel under the wall and both illuminated areas and get away. But he had one resource and one only. That was guile. There was nothing else he could employ.

He let go a loud groan and complained to himself, "So I'll have to use both my heads!"

This inane remark percolated through the innermost recesses of his mind and began to ferment like yeast. After a while he sat up startled, gazed at what little he could see of the brightening sky and said in a tone approaching a yelp, "Yes, sure, that's it—*both* heads!"

Stewing the idea over and over again, Leeming decided by exercise time that it was essential to have a gadget. A crucifix or a crystal ball provides psychological advantages too good to miss. His gadget could be of any shape, size or design, made of any material so long as it was visibly and undeniably a contraption. Moreover, its potency would be greater if not made from items obtainable within his cell such as parts of his clothing or pieces of the bench. Preferably it should be constructed of stuff from somewhere else and should convey the irresistible suggestion of a strange, unknown technology.

He doubted whether the Rigellians could help. Twelve hours per day they slaved in the prison's workshops, a fate that he would share after he'd been questioned and his aptitudes defined. The Rigellians made military pants and jackets, harness and boots, a small range of light engineering and electrical components. They detested producing for the enemy but their choice was a simple one: work or starve.

According to what he'd been told they hadn't the remotest chance of smuggling out of the workshops anything really useful such as a knife, chisel, hammer or hacksaw blade. At the end of each work period the slaves were paraded and none allowed to break ranks until every machine had been checked, every loose tool accounted for and locked away.

The first fifteen minutes of the mid-day break he spent searching the yard for any loose item that might somehow be turned to advantage. He wandered around with his gaze fixed on the ground like a worried kid seeking a lost coin. The only things he found were a couple of pieces of wood four inches square by one inch thick, and these he slipped into his pocket without having the vaguest notion of what he intended to do with them.

Finishing the hunt, he squatted by the wall, had a whispered chat with a couple of Rigellians. His mind wasn't on the conversation and the pair mooched off when a curious guard came near. Later another Rigellian edged up to him.

"Earthman, are you still going to get out of here?"

"You bet I am."

The other chuckled and scratched an ear, an action that his species used to express polite skepticism. "I think we've a better chance than you're ever likely to get."

Leeming shot him a sharp glance. "Why?"

"There are more of us and we're together," evaded the Rigellian, as though re-alizing that he'd been on the point of saying too much. "What can one do on one's own?"

"Bust out and run like blazes first chance," said Leeming.

Just then he noticed the ring on the other's ear-scratching finger and became fascinated with it. He'd seen the modest ornament before. A number of Rigellians were wearing similar objects. So were some of the guards. These rings were neat affairs consisting of four or five turns of thin wire with the ends shaped and sol-dered to form the owner's initials.

"Where'd you dig up the jewelry?" he asked.

"Where did I get what?"

"The ring."

"Oh, that." Lowering his hand, the Rigellian studied the ring with satisfaction. "We make them ourselves in the workshops. It breaks the monotony."

"Mean to say the guards don't stop you?"

"They don't interfere. There's no harm in it. Besides, we've made quite a few for the guards themselves. We've made them some automatic lighters as well and could have turned out a lot for ourselves if we'd had any use for them." He paused, looked thoughtful and added, "We think the guards have been selling rings and lighters outside. At least, we hope so."

"Why?"

"Maybe they'll build up a nice, steady trade. Then when they are comfortably settled in it we'll cut supplies and demand a rake-off in the form of extra rations and a few unofficial privileges."

"That's a smart idea," approved Leeming. "It would help all concerned to have a high-pressure salesman pushing the goods in the big towns. How about putting me down for that job?"

Giving a faint smile, the Rigellian continued, "Handmade junk doesn't matter. But let the guards find that one small screwdriver is missing and there's hell to pay. Everyone is stripped naked on the spot and the culprit suffers."

"They wouldn't care about losing a small coil of that wire, would they?"

"I doubt it. There's plenty of it, they don't bother to check the stock. What can anyone do with a piece of wire?"

"Heaven alone knows," Leeming admitted. "But I want some all the same."

"You'll never pick a lock with it in a million moons," warned the other. "It's too soft and thin."

"I want enough to make a set of Zulu bangles. I sort of fancy myself in Zulu bangles."

"And what are those?"

"Never mind. Get me some of that wire—that's all I ask."

"You can steal it yourself in the near future. After you've been questioned they'll send you to the workshops."

"I want it before then. I want it just as soon as I can get it. The more the better and the sooner the better."

Going silent, the Rigellian thought it over, finally said, "If you've a plan in your mind keep it to yourself. Don't let slip a hint of it to anyone. Open your mouth once too often and somebody will beat you to it."

"Thanks for the good advice, friend," said Leeming. "Now how about a supply of wire?"

"See you this time tomorrow."

With that, the Rigellian left him, wandered into the crowd.

At the appointed hour the other was there, passed him the loot. "Nobody gave this to you, see? You found it lying in the yard. Or you found it hidden in your cell. Or you conjured it out of thin air. But nobody gave it to you."

"Don't worry. I won't involve you in any way. And thanks a million."

The wire was a thick, pocket-sized coil of tinned copper. When unrolled in the darkness of his cell it measured a little more than his own length, or about seven feet.

Leeming doubled it, waggled it to and fro until it broke, hid one half under the bottom of the bench. Then he spent a couple of hours worrying a nail out of the bench's end. It was hard going and it played hob with his fingers, but he persisted until the nail was free.

Finding one of the small, squares of wood, he approximated its center, stamped the nail-point into it with the heel of his boot. Footsteps sounded along the corridor, he shoved the stuff out of sight beneath the bench, lay down just in time before the spyhole opened. The light flashed on, a cold, reptilian eye looked in, somebody grunted. The light cut off, the spyhole shut.

Resuming his task, Leeming twisted the nail one way and then the other, stamping on it with his boot from time to time. The task was tedious but at least it gave him something to do. He persevered until he had drilled a neat hole two-thirds of the way through the wood.

Next, he took his half-length of wire, broke it into two unequal parts, shaped the shorter piece to form a neat loop with two legs each three or four inches long. He tried to make the loop as near to a perfect circle as possible. The longer piece he wound tightly around the loop so that it formed a close-fitting coil with legs matching the others.

Propping his bench against the wall, he climbed it to the window and examined his handiwork in the glow from outside floodlights, made a few minor adjustments and felt satisfied. He replaced the bench and used the nail to make on its edge two small nicks representing the exact diameter of the loop. Lastly he counted the number of turns to the coil. There were twenty-seven.

It was important to remember these details because in all likelihood he would have to make a second gadget as nearly identical as possible. That very similarity would help to bother the enemy. When a plotter makes two mysterious objects to all intents and purposes the same, it is hard to resist the notion that he knows what he is doing and has a sinister purpose.

To complete his preparations he coaxed the nail back into the place where it belonged. Some time he'd need it again as a valuable tool. They'd never find it and deprive him of it because, to the searcher's mind, anything visibly not disturbed is not suspect.

Carefully he forced the four legs of the coiled loop into the hole that he'd drilled, thus making the square wood function as a supporting base. He now had a gadget, a thingamabob, a means to an end. He was the original inventor and sole proprietor of the Leeming-Finagle something-or-other.

Certain chemical reactions take place only in the presence of a catalyst, like marriages legalized by the presence of an official. Some equations can be solved only by the inclusion of an unknown quantity called X. If you haven't enough to obtain a desired result you've got to add what's needed. If you require outside help that doesn't exist you must invent it.

Whenever Man had found himself unable to master his environment with his bare hands, thought Leeming, the said environment had been coerced or bullied into submission by Man plus X. That had been so since the beginning of time: Man plus a tool or a weapon.

But X did not have to be anything concrete or solid, it did not have to be lethal or even visible. It could be as intangible and unprovable as the threat of hellfire or the promise of heaven. It could be a dream, an illusion, a whacking great thundering lie—just *anything*.

There was only one positive test: whether it worked.

If it did, it was efficient.

Now to see.

There was no sense in using the Terran language except perhaps as an incantation when one was necessary. Nobody here understood Terran, to them it was just an alien gabble. Besides, his delaying tactic of pretending to be slow to learn the local tongue was no longer effective. They knew that he could speak it almost as well as they could themselves.

Holding the loop assembly in his left hand, he went to the door, applied his ear to the closed spyhole, listened for the sound of patrolling feet. It was twenty minutes before heavy boots came clumping toward him.

"Are you there?" he called, not too loudly but enough to be heard. "Are you there?"

Backing off fast, he lay on his belly on the floor and stood the loop six inches in front of his face.

"Are you there?"

The spyhole clicked open, the light came on, a sour eye looked through.

Completely ignoring the watcher and behaving with the air of one far too absorbed in his task to notice that he was being observed, Leeming spoke through the coiled loop.

"Are you there?"

"What are you doing?" demanded the guard.

Recognizing the other's voice, Leeming decided that for once luck must be turning his way. This character, a chump named Marsin, knew enough to point a gun and fire it, or, if unable to do so, yell for help. In all other matters he was not of the elite. In fact Marsin would have to think twice to pass muster as a half-wit.

"What are you doing?" insisted Marsin, raising his voice.

"Calling," said Leeming, apparently just waking up to the other's existence.

"Calling? Calling what or where?"

"Mind your own quilpole business," Leeming ordered, giving a nice display of impatience. Concentrating attention upon the loop, he turned it round a couple of degrees. "Are you there?"

"It is forbidden," insisted Marsin.

Letting go the loud sigh of one compelled to bear fools gladly, Leeming said, "What is forbidden?"

"To call."

"Don't display your ignorance. My species is *always* allowed to call. Where would we be if we couldn't, *enk?*"

That got Marsin badly tangled. He knew nothing about Earthmen or what peculiar privileges they considered essential to life. Neither could he give a guess as to where they'd be without them.

Moreover, he dared not enter the cell and put a stop to whatever was going on. An armed guard was strictly prohibited from going into a cell by himself and that rule had been rigid ever since a fed-up Rigellian had slugged one, snatched his gun and killed six while trying to make a break.

If he wanted to interfere he'd have to go and see the sergeant of the guard and demand that something be done to stop pink-skinned aliens making noises through loops. The sergeant was an unlovely character with a tendency to shout the most intimate details of personal histories all over the landscape. It was the witching hour between midnight and dawn, a time when the sergeant's liver malfunctioned most audibly. And lastly he, Marsin, had proved himself a misbegotten faplap far too often.

"You will cease calling and go to sleep," ordered Marsin with a touch of desperation, "or in the morning I shall report your insubordination to the officer of the day."

"Go ride a camel," Leeming invited. He rotated the loop in manner of one making careful adjustment. "Are you there?"

"I have warned you," Marsin persisted, his only visible eye popping at the loop.

"Fibble off!" roared Leeming.

Marsin shut the spyhole and fibbled off.

As was inevitable after being up most of the night, Leeming overslept. His awakening was abrupt and rude.

The door burst open with a loud crash, three guards plunged in followed by an officer.

Without ceremony the prisoner was jerked off the bench, stripped and shoved into the corridor stark naked. The guards then searched through the clothing while the officer minced around watching them. He was, decided Leeming, definitely a fairy.

Finding nothing in the clothes, they started examining the cell. Right off one of them discovered the loop-assembly and gave it to the officer, who held it gingerly as if it were a bouquet suspected of being a bomb.

Another guard trod on the second piece of wood, kicked it aside and ignored it. They tapped the floor and walls, seeking hollow sounds. Dragging the bench away from the wall, they looked over the other side of it but failed to turn it upside-down and see anything underneath. However, they handled the bench so much that it got on Leeming's nerves and he decided that now was the time to take a walk. He started along the corridor, a picture of nonchalant nudity.

The officer let go a howl of rage and pointed. The guard erupted from the cell, bawled orders to halt. A fourth guard, attracted by the noise, came round the bend of the corridor, aimed his gun threateningly. Leeming turned round and ambled back.

He stopped as he reached the officer, who was now outside the cell and fuming with temper. Striking a modest pose, he said, "Look—*September Morn.*"

It meant nothing to the other, who flourished the loop, did a little dance of rage and yelled, "What is this thing?"

"My property," declared Leeming with naked dignity.

"You are not entitled to possess it. As a prisoner of war you are not allowed to have anything."

"Who says so?"

"*I* say so!" informed the fairy somewhat violently.

"Who're you?" asked Leeming, showing no more than academic interest.

"By the Great Blue Sun, I'll show you who I am! Guards, take him inside and—"

"You're not the boss," interrupted Leeming, impressively cocksure. "The Commandant is the boss here. I say so and he says so. If you want to dispute it, let's go ask him."

The guards hesitated, assumed expressions of chronic uncertainty. They were unanimous in passing the buck to the officer. That worthy was taken aback. Staring incredulously at the prisoner, he became wary.

"Are you asserting that the Commandant has given permission for you to have this object?"

"I'm telling you that he hasn't refused permission. Also that it is not for you to give it or refuse it. You roll in your own hog-pen and don't try usurp the position of your betters."

"Hog-pen? What is that?"

"You wouldn't know."

"I shall consult the Commandant about this." Deflated and unsure of himself, the officer turned to the guards. "Put him back in his cell and give him his breakfast as usual."

"How about returning my property, *enk?*" Leeming prompted.

"Not until I have seen the Commandant."

They hustled him into the cell. He got dressed. Breakfast came, the inevitable bowl of slop. He cussed the guards for not making it bacon and eggs. That was deliberate and of malice aforethought. A display of self-assurance and some aggressiveness was necessary to push the game along.

For some reason the tutor did not appear, so he spent the morning furbishing his fluency with the aid of the books. At mid-day they let him into the yard and he could detect no evidence of a special watch being kept upon him while he mingled with the crowd.

The Rigellian whispered, "I got the opportunity to take another coil of wire. So I grabbed it in case you wanted more." He slipped it across, saw it vanish into a pocket. "That's all I intend to steal. Don't ask me again. One can tempt fate too often."

"What's the matter? Is it getting risky? Are they suspicious of you?"

"Everything is all right so far." He glanced cautiously around. "If some of the other prisoners learn that I'm pinching wire they'll start taking it too. They'll snatch it in the hope of discovering what I intend to do with it, so that they can use it for the same purpose. Two years in prison is two years of education in unmitigated selfishness. Everybody is always on the watch for some advantage, real or imaginary, that he can grab off somebody else. This lousy life brings out the worst in us as well as the best."

"I see."

"A couple of small coils will never be missed," the other went on. "But once the rush starts the stuff will evaporate in wholesale quantities. And that's when all hell will break loose. I daren't take the chance of creating a general ruckus."

"Meaning you fellows can't afford to risk a detailed search right now?" suggested Leeming pointedly.

The Rigellian shied like a frightened horse. "I didn't say that."

"I can put two and two together as expertly as anyone else." Leeming favored him with a reassuring wink. "I can also keep my mouth shut."

He watched the other mooch away. Then he sought around the yard for more pieces of wood but failed to find any. Oh, well, no matter. At a pinch he could do without. Come to that, he'd darned well have to do without.

The afternoon was given over to linguistic studies on which he was able to concentrate without interruption. That was one advantage of being in the clink, perhaps the only one. A fellow could educate himself. When the light became too poor and the first pale stars showed through the barred opening in the wall he kicked the door until the sound of it thundered all over the block.

Chapter 8

Feet came running and the spyhole opened. It was Marsin again.

"So it's you, faplap," greeted Leeming. He let go a snort of contempt. "You had to blab, of course. You had to curry favor by reporting me to the officer." He drew himself up to full height. "Well, I am sorry for you. I'd fifty times rather be me than you."

"Sorry for me?" Marsin registered confusion. "Why?"

"Because you are going to suffer."

"I am?"

"Yes, you! Not immediately, if that is any consolation. First of all it is necessary for you to undergo the normal period of horrid anticipation. But eventually you are going to suffer. I don't expect you to believe me. All you need do is wait and see."

"It was my duty," explained Marsin semi-apologetically.

"That fact will be considered in mitigation," Leeming assured, "and your agonies will be modified in due proportion."

"I don't understand," complained Marsin, developing a node of worry somewhere within the solid bone.

"You will—some dire day. So also will those stinking faplaps who beat me up in the yard. You can inform them from me that their quota of pain is being arranged."

"I am not supposed to talk to you," said Marsin, dimly perceiving that the longer he stood by the spyhole the bigger the fix he got into. "I shall have to go."

"All right. But I want something."

"What is it?"

"I want my bopamagilvie—that thing the officer took away."

"You cannot have it unless the Commandant gives permission. He is absent today and will not return before tomorrow morning."

"That's no use. I want it now."

"You cannot have it now."

"Forget it." Leeming gave an airy wave of his hand. "I'll create another one."

"It is forbidden," reminded Marsin very feebly.

"Ha-ha!" said Leeming.

After darkness had grown complete he got the wire from under the bench and manufactured a second whatzit to all intents identical with the first one. Twice he was interrupted but not caught.

That job finished, he up-ended the bench and climbed it. Taking the newly received coil of wire from his pocket, he tied one end tightly around the middle bar and hung the coil outside the window-gap. With spit and dust he camouflaged the bright tin surface of the one visible strand, made sure that it could not be seen at farther than nose-tip distance. He slid down, replaced the bench. The window-gap was so high in the wall that all of its ledge and the bottom three inches of its bars were invisible from below.

Going to the door, he listened and at the right time called, "Are you there?"

When the light came on and the spyhole had opened he got the instinctive feeling that a bunch of them were clustered outside the door, also that the eye in the hole was not Marsin's.

Ignoring everything else, he rotated the loop slowly and carefully, meanwhile calling, "Are you there? Are you there?"

After traversing about forty degrees he paused, gave his voice a tone of intense satisfaction and exclaimed, "So you are there at last! Why don't you keep within easy reach so that we can talk without me having to summon you through a loop?"

Going silent, he put on the expression of one who listens intently. The eye in the spyhole widened, got shoved away, was replaced by another.

"Well," said Leeming, settling himself down for a cozy gossip, "I'll point them out to you first chance I get and leave you to deal with them as you think fit. Let's switch to our own language. There are too many big ears around for my liking." Taking a deep breath, he rattled off at tremendous speed and without pause, "Out sprang the web and opened wide the mirror cracked from side to side the curse has come upon me cried the Lady of—"

Out sprang the door and opened wide and two guards almost fell headlong into the cell in their eagerness to make a quick snatch. Two more posed outside with the fairy glowering between them. Marsin mooned fearfully in the background.

A guard grabbed the loop-assembly, yelled, "I've got it!" and rushed out. His companion followed at full gallop. Both seemed hysterical with excitement. There was a pause of ten seconds before the door shut. Leeming exploited the fact. Pointing the two middle fingers of one hand at the group, he made horizontal stabbing motions toward them. Giving 'em the Devil's Horns they'd called it when he was a kid. The classic gesture of donating the evil eye.

"There you are," he declaimed dramatically, talking to something that nobody else could see. "Those are the scaly-skinned bums I've been telling you about. They want trouble. They like it, they love it, they dote on it. Give them all they can take."

The whole bunch managed to look alarmed before the door cut them from sight with a vicious slam. Listening at the spyhole, he heard them tramp away muttering steadily between themselves.

Within ten minutes he had broken a length off the coil hanging from the window-bars, restored the spit and dust disguise of the holding strand. Half an hour later he had another neatly made bopamagilvie. Practice was making him expert in the swift and accurate manufacture of these things.

Lacking wood for a base, he used the loose nail to dig a hole in the dirt between the big stone slabs composing the floor of his cell. He rammed the legs of the loop into the hole, twisted the contraption this way and that to make ceremonial rotation easy. Then he booted the door something cruel.

When the right moment arrived he lay on his belly and commenced reciting through the loop the third paragraph of Rule 27, Section 9, Subsection B, of Space Regulations. He chose it because it was a gem of bureaucratic phraseology, a single sentence one thousand words long meaning something known only to God.

"Where refueling must be carried out as an emergency measure at a station not officially listed as a home-station or definable for special purposes as a home-station under Section *A(5)* amendment A(5)B the said station shall be treated as if it were definable as a home-station under Section *A(5)* amendment A(5)B providing that the emergency falls within the authorized list of technical necessities as given in Section J(29-33) with addenda subsequent thereto as applicable to home-stations where such are—"

The spyhole flipped open and shut. Somebody scooted away at top speed. A minute afterward the corridor shook to what sounded like a massed cavalry charge. The spyhole again opened and shut. The door crashed inward.

This time they reduced him to his bare pelt, searched his clothes, raked the cell from end to end. Their manner was that of those singularly lacking in brotherly love. Turning the bench upside-down, they tapped it, knocked it, kicked it, did everything but run a large magnifying glass over it.

Watching this operation, Leeming encouraged them by emitting a sinister snigger. There had been a time when he could not have produced a sinister snigger even to win a very large bet. But he could do it now. The ways in which a man can rise to the occasion are without limit.

Giving him a look of sudden death and total destruction, a guard went out, staggered back with a heavy ladder, mounted it and suspiciously surveyed the window-gap. As an intelligent examination it was a dead loss because his mind was concerned only with the solidity of the bars. He grasped each bar with both hands and shook vigorously. His fingers did not touch the thread of wire nor did his eyes detect it. Satisfied, he got down and tottered out with the ladder.

The others departed. Leeming dressed himself, listened at the spyhole. Just a very faint hiss of breath and occasional rustle of clothes nearby. He sat on the bench and waited. In short time the lights blazed on and the spyhole popped open.

Stabbing two fingers toward the hole, he declaimed, "Die, faplap!"

The hole snapped shut. Feet moved away, stamping much too loudly. He waited. After half an hour of complete silence the eye offered itself again and for its pains received another two-fingered curse. Five minutes later it had yet another bestowed upon it. If it was the same eye all the time it was a glutton for punishment.

This game continued at erratic intervals for four hours before the eye had had enough. Leeming immediately made another coiled-loop, gabbled through it at the top of his voice and precipitated another raid. They did not strip him and search the cell this time. They contented themselves with confiscating the gadget. And they showed symptoms of aggravation.

There was just enough wire left for one more blood-pressure booster. He decided to keep it against a future need and get some sleep. Inadequate food and not enough slumber were combining to make inroads upon his physical reserves.

Flopping full length on the bench, he sighed and closed red-rimmed eyes. In due time he started snoring fit to saw through the bars. That caused a panic in the passage and brought the gang along in another rush.

Wakened by the uproar, he damned them to perdition. Then he lay down again. He was plain bone-tuckered—but so were they.

He slept solidly until mid-day without a break except for the usual lousy breakfast. Then came the usual lousy dinner. At exercise time they kept him locked in. He hammered and kicked on the door, demanded to know why he wasn't being allowed to walk in the yard, shouted threats of glandular dissection for all and sundry. They took no notice.

So he sat on the bench and thought things over. Perhaps this denial of his only measure of freedom was a form of retaliation for making them hop around like agitated fleas in the middle of the night. Or perhaps the Rigellian was under suspicion and they'd decided to prevent contact.

Anyway, he had got the enemy bothered. He was messing them about single-handed, far behind the lines. That was something. The fact that a combatant is a prisoner doesn't mean he's out of the battle. Even behind thick walls he can still harass the foe, absorbing his time and energy, undermining his morale, pinning down at least a few of his forces.

The next step, he concluded, was to widen and strengthen the curse. He must do it as comprehensively as possible. The more he spread it and the more ambiguous the terms in which he expressed it, the more plausibly he could grab the credit for any and every misfortune that was certain to occur sooner or later.

It was the technique of the gypsy's warning. People tend to attach specific meanings to ambiguities when circumstances arise and shape themselves to give especial meanings. People don't have to be very credulous, either. It is sufficient for them to be made expectant, with a tendency to wonder—after the event.

"In the near future a tall, dark man will cross your path."

After which any male above average height, and not a blond, fits the picture. And any time from five minutes to five years is accepted as the near future.

"Mamma, when the insurance man called he really smiled at me. *Do you remember what the gypsy said?*"

To accomplish anything worth while one must adapt to one's own environment. If the said environment is radically different from everyone else's the method of accommodating to it must be equally different. So far as he knew he, Leeming, was the only Terran in this prison and the only prisoner held in solitary confinement. Therefore his tactics could have nothing in common with any schemes the Rigellians had in mind.

The Rigellians were up to something, no doubt of that. They wouldn't be wary and secretive about nothing. It was almost a dead-sure bet that they were digging a tunnel. Probably a bunch of them were deep in the earth right now, scraping and scratching without tools. Removing dirt and rock a few pounds at a time. Progress at the rate of a pathetic two or three inches per night. A constant, never-ending risk of discovery, entrapment and perhaps some insane shooting. A year-long project that could be terminated in minutes with a shout and a chatter of automatic guns.

But to get out of a strong stone cell in a strong stone jail one doesn't have to make a desperate and spectacular escape. If sufficiently patient, resourceful, glib and cunning, one can talk the foe into opening the doors and pushing one out.

Yes, you can use the wits that God has given you.

By law of probability various things must happen within and without the prison, not all of them pleasing to the enemy. Some officer must get the galloping gripes right under his body-belt. Or a guard must fall down a watchtower ladder and break a leg. Somebody must lose a wad of money or his pants or his senses. Farther afield a bridge must collapse, or a train get derailed, or a spaceship crash at take-off. Or there'd be an explosion in a munitions factory. Or a military leader would drop dead.

He'd be playing a trump card if he could establish his claim as the author of most of this trouble. The essential thing was to stake it in such a way that they could not effectively combat it, neither could they exact retribution in a torture-chamber.

The ideal strategy was to convince the enemy of his malevolence in a way that would equally convince them of their own impotence. If he succeeded—and it was a big if—they would come to the logical conclusion that the only method of getting rid of constant trouble would be to get rid of Leeming, alive and in one piece. If—and it was a big if—he could link cause and effect irrevocably together they'd have to remove the cause in order to dispose of the effect.

The question of how exactly to achieve this fantastic result was a jumbo problem that would have appalled him back home. In fact he'd have declared it impossible despite that the basic lesson of space-conquest is that nothing is impossible. But by now he'd had three lonely months in which to incubate a solution—and the brain becomes wonderfully stimulated by grim necessity. It was a good thing that he had an idea in mind; he had a mere ten minutes before the time came to apply it.

The door opened, a trio of guards scowled at him and one of them rasped, "The Commandant wishes to see you at once. Amash, faplap!"

Leeming walked out saying, "Once and for all, I am not a faplap, see?"

The guard booted him in the buttocks.

The Commandant lolled behind a desk with a lower ranking officer seated on either side. He was a heavily built specimen. His lidless, horn-covered eyes gave him a frigid, unemotional appearance as he studied the prisoner.

Leeming calmly sat himself on a handy chair and the officer on the right immediately bellowed, "Stand to attention in the presence of the Commandant!"

Making a gesture of contradiction, the Commandant said boredly, "Let him sit."

A concession at the start, thought Leeming. Curiously he eyed a wad of papers on the desk. Probably a complete report of his misdeeds, he guessed. Time would show. Anyway, he had one or two weapons with which to counter theirs. It would be a pity, for instance, if he couldn't exploit their ignorance. The Allies knew nothing about the Zangastans. By the same token the Zangastans knew little or nothing about several Allied species, Terrans included. In coping with him they were coping with an unknown quantity.

And from now on it was a quantity doubled by the addition of X.

"I am given to understand that you now speak our language," began the Commandant.

"Not much use denying it," Leeming confessed.

"Very well. You will give us information concerning yourself."

"I have given it already. I gave it to Major Klavith."

"That is no concern of mine. You will answer my questions and your answers had better be truthful." Positioning an official form upon his desk, he held his pen in readiness. "Name of planet of origin?"

"Earth."

The other wrote it phonetically in his own script, then continued, "Name of race?"

"Terran."

"Name of species?"

"Homo nosipaca," said Leeming, keeping his face straight.

Writing it down, the Commandant looked doubtful, asked, "What does that mean?"

"Space-traversing Man," Leeming informed.

"H'm!" The other was impressed despite himself. "Your personal name?"

"John Leeming."

"John Leeming," repeated the Commandant, putting it down.

"And Eustace Phenackertiban," added Leeming airily.

That was written down also, though the Commandant had some difficulty in finding suitable hooks and curlicues to express Phenackertiban. Twice he asked Leeming to repeat the alien cognomen and that worthy obliged.

Studying the result, which resembled a Chinese recipe for rotten egg gumbo, the Commandant said, "Is it your custom to have two sets of names?"

"Most certainly," Leeming assured. "We can't avoid it seeing that there are two of us."

Twitching the eyebrows he didn't possess, the listener showed mild surprise. "You mean that you are always conceived and born in pairs? Two identical males or females every time?"

"No, no, not at all." Leeming adopted the air of one about to state the obvious. "Whenever one of us is born he immediately acquires a Eustace."

"A Eustace?"

"Yes."

The Commandant frowned, picked his teeth, glanced at the other officers. If he was seeking inspiration he was out of luck; they put on the blank expressions of fellows who'd come along merely to keep company.

"What," asked the Commandant at long last, "is a Eustace?"

Gaping at him in open incredulity, Leeming said, "You don't know?"

"I am putting the questions. You will provide the answers. What is a Eustace?"

Leeming informed, "An invisibility that is part of one's self."

Understanding dawned on the Commandant's scaly face. "Ah, you mean a soul? You give your soul a separate name?"

"Nothing of the sort. I have a soul of my own and Eustace has a soul of his own." He added as an afterthought, "At least, I hope we have."

The Commandant lay back in his chair and stared at him. There was quite a long silence during which the side officers continued to play dummies.

Finally the Commandant admitted, "I do not understand."

"In that case," announced Leeming, irritatingly triumphant, "it is evident that you have no alien equivalent of Eustaces yourselves. You're all on your own. Just single-lifers. That's your hard luck."

Slamming a hand on the desk, the Commandant gave his voice a bit more military whoof and demanded, "Exactly what is a Eustace? Explain to me as clearly as possible!"

"I'm in poor position to refuse the information," Leeming conceded with hypocritical reluctance. "Not that it matters much. Even if you gain perfect understanding there is nothing you can do about it."

"That remains to be seen," opined the Commandant, looking bellicose. "Cease evading the issue and tell me all that you know about these Eustaces."

"Every Earthling lives a double life from birth to death," said Leeming. "He exists in close mental association with an entity that always calls himself Eustace something-or-other. Mine happens to be Eustace Phenackertiban."

"You can actually *see* this entity?"

"No, never at any time. I cannot see him, smell him or feel him."

"Then how do you know that this is not a racial delusion?"

"Firstly, because every Terran can hear his own Eustace. I can hold long conversations with mine, providing that he happens to be within reach, and I can hear him speaking clearly and logically within the depths of my mind."

"You cannot hear him with the ears?"

"No, only with the mind. The communication is telepathic, or to be more accurate, quasi-telepathic."

"I can believe that," informed the Commandant with considerable sarcasm. "You have been heard talking out loud, shouting at the top of your voice. Some telepathy, *enk*?"

"When I have to boost my thoughts to get range I can do it better by expressing them in words. People do the same when they sort out a problem by talking to themselves. Haven't you ever talked to yourself?"

"That is no business of yours. What other proof have you that a Eustace is not imaginary?"

Taking a deep breath, Leeming went determinedly on. "He has the power to do many things after which there is visible evidence that those things have been done." He shifted attention to the absorbed officer sitting on the left. "For example, if my Eustace had a grudge against this officer and advised me of his intention to make him fall downstairs, and if before long the officer fell downstairs and broke his neck—"

"It could be mere coincidence," the Commandant scoffed.

"It could," agreed Leeming. "But there can be far too many coincidences. If a Eustace promises that he is going to do forty or fifty things in succession and all of them happen he is either doing them as promised or he is a most astounding prophet. Eustaces don't claim to be prophets. Nobody visible or invisible can foresee the future with such detailed accuracy."

"That is true enough."

"Do you accept the fact that you have a father and mother?"

"Of course," admitted the Commandant.

"You don't consider it strange or abnormal?"

"Certainly not. It is inconceivable that one should be born without parents."

"Similarly we accept the fact that we have Eustaces and we cannot conceive the possibility of existing without them."

The Commandant thought it over, said to the right-hand officer, "This smacks of mutual parasitism. It would be interesting to learn what benefit they derive from each other."

"It's no use asking what my Eustace gets out of me," Leeming chipped in. "I can't tell you because I don't know."

"You expect me to believe that?" asked the Commandant, behaving like nobody's fool. He showed his teeth. "On your own evidence you can talk with him. Why have you never asked him?"

"We Terrans got tired of asking that question long, long ago. The subject has been dropped and the situation accepted."

"Why?"

"The answer is always the same. Eustaces readily admit that we are essential to their existence but cannot explain how because they've no way of making us understand."

"That could be an excuse, a self-preservative evasion," the Commandant offered. "They won't tell you because they don't want you to know."

"Well, what do you suggest we do about it?"

Dodging that one, the Commandant went on, "What benefit do you get out of the association? What good is your Eustace to *you?*"

"He provides company, comfort, information, advice and—"

"And what?"

Bending forward, hands on knees, Leeming practically spat it at him. "If necessary, vengeance!"

That struck home good and hard. The Commandant rocked back, displaying a mixture of ire and skepticism. The two under-officers registered disciplined apprehension. It's a hell of a war when one can be chopped down by a ghost.

Pulling himself together, the Commandant forced a grim smile as he pointed out, "You're a prisoner. You've been under detention a good many days. Your Eustace doesn't seem to have done much about it."

"Not yet," agreed Leeming happily.

"What d'you mean, not yet?"

"As one free to roam at will on an enemy world he had enough top-priority jobs to keep him busy for a piece. He's been doing plenty and he'll do plenty more, in his own time and his own way."

"Is that so? And what does he intend to do?"

"Wait and see," Leeming advised with formidable confidence.

That did not fill them with delight.

"Nobody can imprison more than half a Terran," he went on. "The solid, visible, tangible half. The other half cannot be pinned down by any method whatsoever. It is beyond anyone's control. It wanders loose collecting information of military value, indulging a little sabotage, doing just as it pleases. You've created that situation and you're stuck with it."

"We created it? We didn't invite you to come here. You dumped yourself on us unasked."

"I had no choice about it because I had to make an emergency landing. This could have been a friendly world. It isn't. Who's to blame for that? If you insist on fighting with the Combine against the Allies you must accept the consequences—including whatever a Eustace sees fit to do."

"Not if we kill you," said the Commandant nastily.

Leeming gave a disdainful laugh. "That would make matters fifty times worse."

"In what way?"

"The life-span of a Eustace is longer than that of his Terran partner. When a man dies his Eustace takes seven to ten years to disappear from existence. We have an ancient song to the effect that old Eustaces never die, they only fade away. Our world holds thousands of lonely, disconnected Eustaces gradually fading."

"So ?"

"Kill me and you'll isolate my Eustace here with no man or other Eustace for company. His days will be numbered and he'll know it. He'll have nothing to lose, being no longer restricted by consideration of my safety. Because I've gone for keeps he'll be able to eliminate me from his plans and give his undivided attention to anything he chooses." He eyed the listeners as he finished, "It's a safe bet that he'll run amok and create an orgy of destruction. Remember, you're an alien lifeform to him. He'll have no feelings or compunctions with regard to you."

The Commandant reflected in silence. It was exceedingly difficult to believe all this, and his prime instinct was to reject it lock, stock and barrel. But before space-conquest it had been equally difficult to believe things more fantastic but now accepted as commonplace. He dare not dismiss it as nonsense; the time had long gone by when anyone could afford to be dogmatic. The space adventurings of all the Combine and the Allied species had scarcely scratched one galaxy of an unimaginable number composing the universe, none could say what incredible secrets were yet to be revealed, including, perhaps, such etheric entities as Eustaces.

Yes, the stupid believe things because they are credulous—or they are credulous because stupid. The intelligent do not blindly accept but, being aware of their own ignorance, neither do they reject. Right now the Commandant was acutely aware of general ignorance concerning this life-form known as Terrans. It *could* be that they were dual creations, half-Joe, half-Eustace.

"All this is not impossible," he decided ponderously, "but it appears to me somewhat improbable. There are more than twenty lifeforms associated with us in the Combine. I do not know of one that exists in natural copartnership with another."

"The Lathians do," contradicted Leeming, mentioning the leaders of the opposition, the chief cause of the war.

The Commandant was suitably startled "You mean they have Eustaces too?"

"No, I don't. They have something similar but inferior. Each Lathian is unconsciously controlled by an entity that calls itself Willy something-or-other. They don't know it, of course. We wouldn't know it if our Eustaces hadn't told us."

"How did they find out?"

"As you know, the biggest battles to date have all been fought in the Lathian sector. Both sides have taken prisoners. Our Eustaces told us that each Lathian prisoner had a controlling Willy but was blissfully unaware of it." He grinned, added, "They made it plain that a Eustace doesn't think much of a Willy. Apparently a Willy is a pretty low form of associated life."

Frowning, the Commandant said, "This is something definite, something we should be able to check for ourselves. But how are we going to do it if the Lathians are ignorant of this state of affairs?"

"Easy as pie," Leeming offered. "They are holding a bunch of Terran prisoners. Get someone to ask those prisoners, separately and individually, whether the Lathians have the Willies."

"We'll do just that," snapped the Commandant, his manner that of one about to call a bluff. He turned to the right-hand officer. "Bajashim, beam a signal to our chief liaison officer at Lathian H.Q. and order him to question those prisoners."

"You can double-check while you're at it," interjected Leeming, "just to clinch it. To us, anyone who shares his life with an invisible being is known as a Nut. Ask the prisoners whether all the Lathians are Nuts."

"Take note of that and have it asked as well," ordered the Commandant. He returned attention to Leeming. "Since you could not anticipate your forced landing and capture, and since you have been kept in close confinement, there is no possibility of collusion between you and the Terran prisoners far away."

"That's right."

"Therefore I shall weigh your evidence in the light of what replies come to my signal." He stared hard at the other. "If those replies fail to confirm your statements I'll know that you are a shameless liar in some respects and probably a liar in all respects. Here, we have special and very effective methods of dealing with liars."

"That's to be expected. But if the replies do confirm me you'll know that I've told the truth, won't you?"

"No," said the Commandant savagely.

It was Leeming's turn to be shocked. "Why not?"

Thinning his lips, the Commandant growled, "As I have remarked, there cannot possibly have been any direct communication between you and other Terran prisoners. However, that means nothing. There can have been collusion between your Eustace and their Eustaces."

Bending sidewise, he jerked open a drawer, placed a loop-assembly on the desk. Then another and another. A bunch of them.

"Well," he invited with malicious triumph, "what have you to say to that?"

Chapter 9

Leeming went into something not far off a momentary panic. He could see what the other meant. He could talk to his Eustace, who in turn could talk to other Eustaces. And the other Eustaces could talk to their imprisoned partners.

Get yourself out of that!

He had an agile mind but after three months of semi-starvation it was tending to lose pace. Lack of adequate nourishment was telling on him already; his thoughts plodded at the very time he wanted them to sprint.

The three behind the desk were waiting for him, watching his face, counting the seconds he needed to produce an answer. The longer he took to find one the weaker it would be. The quicker he came up with something good the more plausible it would sound. Cynical satisfaction was creeping into their faces and he was inwardly frantic by the time he saw an opening and grabbed at it.

"You're wrong on two counts."

"State them."

"Firstly, one Eustace cannot communicate with another over a distance so enormous. His mental output just won't reach that far. To talk from world to world he has to have the help of a Terran who, in his turn, has radio equipment available."

"We've only your word for that," the Commandant reminded. "If a Eustace *can* communicate without limit it would be your best policy to conceal the fact. You would be a fool to admit it."

"I cannot do more than give you my word regardless of whether or not you credit it."

"I do not credit it—yet."

"No Terran task force has rushed to my rescue, as would happen had my Eustace told them about me."

"Pfah!" said the Commandant. "It would take them much longer to get here than the time you have spent as a prisoner. Probably twice as long. And then only if by some miracle they managed to avoid being shot to pieces on the way. The absence of a rescue party means nothing." He waited for a response that did not come, finished, "If you have anything else to say it had better be convincing."

"It is," assured Leeming. "And we don't have my word for it. We have yours."

"Nonsense! I made no statements concerning Eustaces."

"On the contrary, you have said that there could be collusion between them."

"What of it?"

"There can be collusion only if Eustaces really exist, in which case my evidence is true. But if my evidence is false, then Eustaces do not exist and there cannot possibly be a conspiracy between non-existent things."

The Commandant sat perfectly still while his face took on a faint shade of purple. He looked and felt like a trapper trapped. The left-hand officer wore an expression of one struggling hard to suppress a disrespectful snicker.

"If," continued Leeming, piling it on for good measure, "you do not believe in Eustaces then you cannot logically believe in conspiracy between them. On the other hand, if you believe in the possibility of collusion then you've got to believe in Eustaces. That is, of course, if you're in bright green breeches and your right mind."

"Guard!" roared the Commandant. He pointed an angry finger. "Take him back to his cell." Obediently they started hustling the prisoner through the door when he changed his mind and bawled, "Halt!" Snatching up a loop-assembly, he waved it at Leeming. "Where did you get the material with which to make this?"

"My Eustace brought it for me. Who else?"

"Get out of my sight!"

"Merse, faplap!" urged the guards, prodding with their guns. "Amash! Amash!"

The rest of that day and all the next one he spent sitting or lying on the bench, reviewing what had taken place, planning his next moves and in lighter moments admiring his own ability as a whacking great liar.

Now and again he wondered how his efforts to battle his way to freedom with his tongue compared with Rigellian attempts to do it with bare hands. Who was making the most progress? Of great importance, who, once out, would stay out? One thing was certain: his method was less tiring to the underfed and weakened body, though more exhausting to the nerves.

Another advantage was that for the time being he had side-tracked their intention of squeezing him for military information. Or had he? Possibly from their viewpoint his revelations concerning the dual nature of Terrans were infinitely more important than details of armaments, which data might be false anyway. All the same, he had avoided for a time what might otherwise have been a rough and painful interrogation. By thus postponing the agony he had added brilliance to the original gem of wisdom, namely, that baloney baffles brains.

Just for the ducks of it he bided his time and, when the spyhole opened, let it catch him in the middle of giving grateful thanks to Eustace for some weird service not specified. As intended, this got the jumpy Marsin to wondering who had arrived at the crossroads and copped some of Eustace's dirty work. Doubtless the sergeant of the guard would speculate about the same matter before long. And in due course so would the officers.

Near midnight, with sleep still evading him, it occurred to him that there was no point in doing things by halves. If a thing is worth doing it is worth doing well—and that applies to lying or to any form of villainy as much as to anything else. Why rest content merely to register a knowing smile whenever the enemy suffered a petty misfortune?

His tactics could be extended much farther than that. No form of life was secure from the vagaries of chance. Good fortune came along as well as bad, in any part of the cosmos. There was no reason why Eustace should not snatch the credit for both. No reason why he, Leeming, should not take unto himself the implied power to reward as well as to punish.

That wasn't the limit, either. Good luck and bad luck are positive phases of existence. He could cross the neutral zone and confiscate the negative phases. Through Eustace he could assign to himself not only the credit for things done, good or bad, but also for things *not* done. In the pauses between staking claims to things that happened he could exploit those that did not happen.

The itch to make a start right now was irresistible. Rolling off the bench, he belted the door from top to bottom. The guard had just been changed, for the eye that peered in was that of Kolum, a character who had bestowed a kick in the rump not so long ago. Kolum was a cut above Marsin, being able to count upon all twelve fingers if given sufficient time to cogitate.

"So it is you!" said Leeming, showing vast relief. "I am very glad of that. I befriended you in the hope that he would lay off you, that he would leave you alone for at least a little while. He is far too impetuous and much too drastic. I can see that you are more intelligent than the other guards and therefore able to change for the better. Indeed, I have pointed out to him that you are obviously too civilized to be a sergeant. He is difficult to convince but I am doing my best for you."

"Huh?" said Kolum, half flattered, half scared.

"So he's left you alone at least for the time being," Leeming said, knowing that the other was in no position to deny it. "He's done nothing to you—yet." He increased the gratification. "I'll do my very best to keep control of him. Only the stupidly brutal deserve slow death."

"That is true," agreed Kolum eagerly. "But what—"

"Now," interrupted Leeming with firmness, "it is up to you to prove that my confidence is justified and thus protect yourself against the fate that is going to visit the slower-witted. Brains were made to be used, weren't they?"

"Yes, but—"

"Those who don't possess brains cannot use what they haven't got, can they?"

"No, they cannot, but—"

"All that is necessary to demonstrate your intelligence is to take a message to the Commandant."

Kolum popped his eyes in horror. "It is impossible. I dare not disturb him at this hour. The sergeant of the guard will not permit it. He will—"

"You are not being asked to take the message to the Commandant immediately. It is to be given to him personally when he awakens in the morning."

"That is different," said Kolum, vastly relieved. "But I must warn you that if he disapproves of the message he will punish you and not me."

"He will not punish me lest I in turn punish him," assured Leeming, as though stating a demonstrable fact. "Write my message down."

Leaning his gun against the corridor's farther wall, Kolum dug pencil and paper out of a pocket. A strained expression came into his eyes as he prepared himself for the formidable task of inscribing a number of words.

"To The Most Exalted Lousy Screw," began Leeming.

"What does 'lousy screw' mean?" asked Kolum as he struggled to put down the strange Terran words phonetically.

"It's a title. It means 'Your Highness.' Man, how high he is!" Leeming pinched his nose while the other pored over the paper. He continued to dictate, going very slowly to keep pace with Kolum's literary talent. "The food is insufficient and very poor in quality. I am physically weak, I have lost much weight and my ribs are beginning to show. My Eustace does not like it. The thinner I get the more threatening he becomes. The time is fast approaching when I shall have to refuse all responsibility for his actions. Therefore I beg Your Most Exalted Lousy Screwship to give serious consideration to this matter."

"There are many words and some of them long ones," complained Kolum, managing to look like a reptilian martyr. "I shall have to rewrite them more readably when I go off duty."

"I know and I appreciate the trouble you are taking on my behalf." Leeming bestowed a beam of fraternal fondness. "That's why I feel sure you'll live long enough to do the job."

"I must live longer than that," insisted Kolum, popping the eyes again. "I have the right to live, haven't I?"

"That is precisely the argument I've been using," said Leeming in the manner of one who has striven all night to establish the irrefutable but cannot yet guarantee success.

"I cannot talk to you any longer," informed Kolum, picking up his gun. "I am not supposed to talk to you at all. If the sergeant of the guard should catch me he will—"

"The sergeant's days are numbered," Leeming told him in judicial tones. "He will not live long enough to know he's dead."

His hand extended in readiness to close the spyhole, Kolum paused, looked as if he'd been slugged with a sockful of wet sand. Then he said, "How can *anyone* live long enough to know that he's dead?"

"It depends on the method of killing," assured Leeming. "There are some you've never heard of and cannot imagine."

At this point Kolum found the conversation distasteful. He closed the spyhole. Leeming returned to the bench, sprawled upon it. The light went out. Seven stars peeped through the window-slot—and they were not unattainable.

In the morning breakfast came an hour late but consisted of one full bowl of lukewarm pap, two thick slices of brown bread heavily smeared with grease and a large cup of warm liquid vaguely resembling paralyzed coffee. He got through the lot with mounting triumph. By contrast with what they had been giving him this feast made the day seem like Christmas. His spirits perked up with the fullness of his belly.

No summons to a second interview came that day or the next. The Commandant made no move for more than a week. Evidently His Lousy Screwship was still awaiting a reply from the Lathian sector and did not feel inclined to take further action before he received it. However, meals remained more substantial, a fact that Leeming viewed as positive evidence that someone was insuring himself against disaster.

Then early one morning the Rigellians acted up. From the cell they could be heard but not seen. Every day at about an hour after dawn the tramp of their two thousand pairs of feet sounded somewhere out of sight and died away toward the workshops. Usually that was all that could be heard, no voices, no desultory conversation, just the weary trudge of feet and an occasional bellow from a guard.

This time they came out singing, their raucous voices holding a distinct touch of defiance. They were bawling in thunderous discord something about Asta Zangasta's a dirty old geezer, got fleas on his chest and sores on his beezer. It should have sounded childish and futile. It didn't. The corporate effort seemed to convey an unspoken threat.

Guards yelled at them. Singing rose higher, the defiance increasing along with the volume. Standing below his window-slot, Leeming listened intently. This was the first mention he'd heard of the much-abused Asta Zangasta, presumably this world's king, emperor or leading hooligan.

The bawling of two thousand voices rose to a crescendo. Guards screamed frenziedly and were drowned within the din. Somewhere a warning shot was fired. In the watchtowers the guards edged their guns around, dipped them as they aimed into the yard.

"Oh, what a basta is Asta Zangasta!" hollered the distant Rigellians as they reached the end of their epic poem.

There followed blows, shots, scuffling sounds, howls of fury. A bunch of twenty fully armed guards raced flat-footed past Leeming's window, headed for the unseeable fracas. The uproar continued for half an hour before gradually it died away. Resulting silence could almost be felt.

At exercise time Leeming had the yard to himself, there being not another prisoner in sight. He mooched around, puzzled and gloomy, until he encountered Marsin on yard-patrol.

"Where are the others? What has happened to them?"

"They misbehaved and wasted a lot of time. They are being detained in the workshops until they have made up the loss in production. It is their own fault. They started work late for the deliberate purpose of slowing down output. We didn't even have time to count them."

Leeming grinned into his face. "And some guards were hurt?"

"Yes," Marsin admitted.

"Not severely," Leeming suggested. "Just enough to give them a taste of what is to come. Think it over!"

"What do you mean?"

"I meant what I said—think it over." Then he added, "But *you* were not injured. Think that over too!"

He ambled away, leaving Marsin uneasy and bewildered. Six times he trudged around the yard while doing some heavy thinking himself. Sudden indiscipline among the Rigellians certainly had stirred up the prison and created enough excitement to last a week. He wondered what had caused it. Probably they'd done it to gain relief from incarceration and despair. Sheer boredom can drive people into performing the craziest tricks.

On the seventh time round he was still pondering when suddenly a remark struck him with force like the blow of a hammer. *"We had not time even to count them."* Holy smoke! *That* must be the motive of this morning's rowdy performance. The choral society had avoided a count. There could be only one reason why they should wish to dodge the regular numbering parade.

Finding Marsin again, he promised, "Tomorrow some of you guards will wish you'd never been born."

"Are you threatening us?"

"No, I am making a prophetic promise. Tell the guard officer what I have said. Tell the Commandant, too. It might help you to escape the consequences."

"I will tell them," said Marsin, mystified but grateful.

The following morning proved that he had been one hundred per cent correct in his supposition that the Rigellians were too shrewd to invite thick ears and black eyes without good reason. It had taken the enemy a full day to arrive at the same conclusion.

At one hour after dawn the Rigellians were marched out dormitory by dormitory, in batches of fifty instead of the usual continuous stream. They were counted in fifties, the easy way. This simple arithmetic became thrown out of kilter when one dormitory produced only twelve prisoners, all of them sick, weak, wounded or otherwise handicapped.

Infuriated guards rushed indoors to drag out the absent thirty-eight. They weren't there. The door was firm and solid, the window-bars intact. Guards did considerable confused galloping around before one of them detected the slight shift of a well-trampled floor-slab. They lugged it up, found underneath a narrow but deep shaft from the bottom of which ran a tunnel. With great unwillingness one of them went down the shaft, crawled into the tunnel and in due time emerged a good distance outside the walls. Needless to say he had found the tunnel empty.

Sirens wailed, guards pounded all over the jail, officers shouted contradictory orders, the entire place began to resemble a madhouse. The Rigellians got it good and hard for spoiling the previous morning's count and thus giving the escapees a full day's lead. Boots and gun-butts were freely used, bodies dragged aside badly battered and unconscious.

The surviving top-ranker of the offending dormitory, a lieutenant with a severe limp, was held responsible for the break, charged, tried, sentenced, put against a wall and shot. Leeming could see nothing of this but did hear the hoarse commands of "Present . . . aim . . . fire!" and the following volley.

He prowled round and round his cell, clenching and unclenching his fists, his stomach writhing like a sack of snakes and swearing mightily to himself. All that he wanted, all that he prayed for was a high-ranking Zangastan throat under his thumbs. The spyhole flipped open but hastily shut before he could spit into somebody's eye.

The upset continued without abate as inflamed guards searched all dormitories one by one, testing doors, bars, walls, floors and even the ceilings. Officers screamed blood-thirsty threats at sullen groups of Rigellians who were slow to respond to orders.

At twilight outside forces dragged in seven tired, bedraggled escapees who'd been caught on the run. Their reception was short and sharp. "Present . . . aim . . . fire!" Frenziedly Leeming battered at his door but the spyhole remained shut and nobody answered. Two hours later he made another coiled loop with the last of his wire. He spent half the night talking into it menacingly and at the top of his voice. Nobody took the slightest notice.

By noon next day a feeling of deep frustration had come over him. He estimated that the Rigellian break-out must have taken most of a year to prepare. Result: eight dead and thirty-one still loose. If they kept together and did not scatter the thirty-one could form a crew large enough to seize a ship of any size up to and including a space-destroyer. But on the basis of his own experiences he thought they had remote chance of making such a theft.

With the whole world alarmed by an escape of this size there'd be a strong military screen at every spaceport and it would be maintained until the last of the thirty-one had been rounded up. The free might stay free for quite a time if they were lucky, but they were planet-bound, doomed to ultimate recapture and subsequent execution.

Meanwhile their fellows were getting it rough in consequence and his own efforts had been messed up. He did not resent the break, not one little bit. Good luck to them. But if only it had taken place two months earlier or later.

Moodily he finished his dinner, when four guards came for him. "The Commandant wants you at once." Their manner was edgy and subdued. One wore a narrow bandage around his scaly pate, another had a badly swollen eye.

Just about the worst moment to choose, thought Leeming. The Commandant would be all set to go up like a rocket at first hint of opposition of any kind. You cannot argue with a brasshat in a purple rage; emotion comes uppermost, words are disregarded, logic is treated with contempt. He was going to have a tough job on his hands.

The four marched him along the corridor, two in front, two behind. Left, right, left, right, thud, thud, thud—it made him think of a ceremonial parade to the guillotine. Around the corner in a little triangular yard there should be waiting a priest, a hanging knife, a wicker basket, a wooden box.

Together they tramped into the same room as before. The Commandant was sitting behind his desk but there were no junior officers in attendance. The only other person present was an elderly civilian occupying a chair on the Commandant's right; he studied the prisoner with a sharp, intent gaze as he entered and took a seat.

"This is Pallam," introduced the Commandant with amiability so unexpected that it dumbfounded the listener. Showing a touch of awe, he added, "He has been sent here by no less a person than Zangasta himself."

"A mental specialist, I presume?" invited Leeming, wary of a trap.

"Nothing like that," said Pallam quietly. "I am especially interested in all aspects of symbiosis."

Leeming's back hairs stirred. He did not like the idea of being cross-examined by an expert. Such characters had penetrating, unmilitary minds and a pernicious habit of destroying a good story by exhibiting its own contradictions. This mild-looking civilian, he decided, was definitely a major menace.

"Pallam wishes to ask you a few questions," informed the Commandant, "but those will come later." He put on a self-satisfied expression. "For a start I wish to say that I am indebted for the information you gave at our previous interview."

"You mean that it has proved useful to you?" asked Leeming, hardly believing his ears.

"Very much so in view of this serious and most stupid mutiny. All the guards responsible for Dormitory Fourteen are to be drafted to battle areas where they will be stationed upon spaceports liable to attack. That is their punishment for gross neglect of duty." He gazed thoughtfully at the other, went on, "My own fate would have been no less had not Zangasta considered the escape a minor matter when compared with the important data I got from you."

Though taken by surprise, Leeming was swift to cash in. "But when I asked, you saw to it personally that I had better food. Surely you expected some reward?"

"Reward?" The Commandant was taken aback. "I did not think of such a thing."

"So much the better," approved Leeming, admiring the other's magnanimity. "A good deed is trebly good when done with no ulterior motive. Eustace will take careful note of that."

"You mean," put in Pallam, "that his code of ethics is identical with your own?"

Damn the fellow! Why did he have to put his spoke in? Be careful now!

"Similar in some respects but not identical."

"What is the most outstanding difference?"

"Well," said Leeming, playing for time, "it's hard to decide." He rubbed his brow while his mind whizzed dizzily. "I'd say in the matter of vengeance."

"Define the difference," ordered Pallam, sniffing along the trail like a hungry bloodhound.

"From my viewpoint," informed Leeming, inwardly cursing the other to hell and perdition, "he is unnecessarily sadistic."

There, that gave needed coverage for any widespread claims it might be desirable to make later on.

"In what way?" persisted Pallam.

"My instinct is to take prompt action, to get things over and done with. His tendency is to prolong the agony."

"Explain further," pressed Pallam, making a thorough nuisance of himself.

"If you and I were mortal enemies, if I had a gun and you had not, I would shoot and kill you. But if Eustace had you marked for death he'd make it slower, more gradual."

"Describe his method."

"First, he'd let you know that you were doomed. Then he'd do nothing about it until eventually you became obsessed with the notion that it was all an illusion and that nothing ever would be done. At that point he'd remind you with a minor blow. When resulting fear and alarm had worn off he'd strike a harder one. And so on and so on with increasing intensity spread over as long a time as necessary."

"Necessary for what?"

"Until your doom became plain and the strain of waiting for it became too much to bear." He thought a moment, added, "No Eustace ever has killed anyone. He uses tactics peculiarly his own. He arranges accidents or he chivvies a victim into dying by his own hand."

"He drives a victim to suicide?"

"Yes, that's what I've said."

"And there is no way of avoiding such a fate?"

"Yes there is," Leeming contradicted. "At any time the victim can gain personal safety and freedom from fear by redressing the wrong he has done to that Eustace's partner."

"Such redress immediately terminates the vendetta?"

"That's right."

"Whether or not you approve personally?"

"Yes. If my grievance ceases to be real and becomes only imaginary, my Eustace refuses to recognize it or do anything about it."

"So what it boils down to" said Pallam pointedly, "is that his method provides motive and opportunity for repentance while yours does not?"

"I suppose so."

"Which means that he has a more balanced sense of justice?"

"He can be darned ruthless," objected Leeming, momentarily unable to think of a retort less feeble.

"That is beside the point," snapped Pallam. He lapsed into meditative silence, then remarked to the Commandant, "It seems that the association is not between equals. The invisible component is also the superior one. In effect, it is the master of a material slave but exercises mastery with such cunning that the slave would be the first to deny his own status."

He shot a provocative glance at Leeming, who set his teeth and said nothing. Crafty old hog, thought Leeming—if he was trying to tempt the prisoner into a heated denial he was going to be disappointed. Let him remain under the delusion that Leeming had been weighed in the balance and found wanting. There is no shame in being defined as inferior to a figment of one's own imagination.

Now positively foxy, Pallam probed, "When your Eustace takes it upon himself to wreak vengeance he does so because circumstances prevent suitable punishment being administered either by yourself or the Terra community? Is that correct?"

"Near enough," admitted Leeming cautiously.

"In other words, he functions only when you and the law are impotent?"

"He takes over when the need arises."

"You are being evasive. We must get this matter straight. If you or your fellows can and do punish someone, does any Eustace also punish him?"

"No," said Leeming, fidgeting uneasily.

"If you or your fellows cannot or do not punish someone does a Eustace then step in and enforce punishment?"

"Only if a living Terran has suffered unjustly."

"The sufferer's Eustace takes action on his partner's behalf?"

"Yes."

"Good!" declared Pallam. He leaned forward, watched the other keen-eyed and managed to make his attitude intimidating. "Now let us suppose that your Eustace finds justifiable reason to punish another Terran—*what does the* victim's *Eustace do about it?*"

Chapter 10

It was a clever trap based upon the knowledge that questions about factual, familiar, everyday things can be answered automatically, almost without thought. Whereas a liar seeking a supporting lie needs time to create consistency. It should have got Leeming completely foozled. That it did not do so was no credit to his own wits.

While his mind still whirled his mouth opened and the words "Not much" popped out of their own accord. For a mad moment he wondered whether Eustace had arrived and joined the party.

"Why not?"

Encouraged by his tongue's mastery of the situation, Leeming gave it free rein. "I have told you before and I am telling you again that no Eustace will concern himself for one moment with a grievance that is wholly imaginary. A Terran who is guilty of a crime has no genuine cause for complaint. He has brought vengeance upon himself and the cure lies in his own hands. If he doesn't enjoy suffering he need only get busy and undo whatever wrong he has done to another."

"Will his Eustace urge or influence him to take action necessary to avoid punishment?"

"Never having been a criminal myself," answered Leeming with great virtue, "I am unable to tell you. I suppose it would be near the truth to say that Terrans behave because association with Eustaces compels them to behave. They have little choice about the matter."

"On the other hand, Terrans have no way of compelling their Eustaces to behave?"

"No compulsion is necessary. A Eustace will always listen to his partner's reason and act within the limits of common justice."

"As I told you," said Pallam in an aside to the Commandant, "the Terran is the lower form of the two." He returned attention to the prisoner. "All that you have told us is acceptable because it is consistent—as far as it goes."

"What d'you mean, as far as it goes?"

"Let me take it to the bitter end," suggested Pallam. "I do not see any rational reason why any criminal's Eustace should allow his partner to be driven to suicide. Since they are mutually independent of others but mutually dependent upon each other, a Eustace's inaction is contrary to the basic law of survival."

"Nobody commits suicide until he has gone off his rocker."

"Until he has done what?"

"Become insane," said Leeming. "An insane person is worthless as a material partner. To a Eustace he is already dead, not worth protecting or avenging. Eustaces associate only with the sane."

Pouncing on that, Pallam said excitedly, "So the benefit they derive is rooted somewhere within Terran minds? It is mental sustenance that they draw from you?"

"I don't know."

"Does your Eustace ever make you feel tired, exhausted, perhaps a little stupefied?"

"Yes," said Leeming with emphasis. How true, brother, how true. Right now he'd find pleasure in choking Eustace to death.

"I would like to pursue this phenomenon for months," Pallam told the Commandant. "It is an absorbing subject. There are no records of symbiotic association among anything higher than the plants and six species of the lower *elames*. To find it among the higher vertebrates, sentient forms, and one of them intangible, is remarkable, truly remarkable."

The Commandant looked impressed without knowing what the other was talking about.

"Give him your report," urged Pallam.

"Our liaison officer, Colonel Shomuth, has replied from the Lathian sector," the Commandant told Leeming. "He is fluent in Cosmoglotta and therefore was able to question many Terran prisoners without the aid of a Lathian interpreter. We sent him a little more information and the result is significant."

"What else did you expect?" Leeming observed, inwardly consumed with curiosity.

Ignoring that, the Commandant went on, "He reported that most of the prisoners refused to make comment or to admit anything. They maintained determined silence. That is understandable because nothing could shake their belief that they were being tempted to surrender information of military value. They resisted all of Colonel Shomuth's persuasions and kept their mouths shut." He sighed at such stubbornness. "But some talked."

"A few are always willing to blab," remarked Leeming.

"Certain officers talked, including Cruiser Captain Tompass . . . Tompus . . . "

"Thomas?"

"Yes, that is the word." Swiveling around in his chair, the Commandant pressed a wall-button. "This is the beamed interview unscrambled and recorded on tape."

A crackling hiss poured out of a perforated grid set in the wall. It grew louder, died down to a background wash. Voices came out of the grid.

Shomuth: "Captain Thomas, I have been ordered to check certain information now in our possession. You have nothing to lose by giving answers, nothing to gain by refusing them. There are no Lathians present, only the two of us. You may speak freely and what you say will be treated in confidence."

Thomas: "Mighty leery about the Lathians all of a sudden, aren't you? You won't fool me with that gambit. Enemies are enemies no matter what their name or shape. Go trundle your hoop—you'll get nothing out of me."

Shomuth, patiently: "I suggest, Captain Thomas, that you hear and consider the questions before you decide whether or not to answer them."

Thomas, boredly: "All right. What d'you want to know?"

Shomuth: "Whether our Lathian allies really are Nuts."

Thomas, after a long pause: "You want the blunt truth?"

Shomuth: "We do."

Thomas, with a trace of sarcasm: "I hate to speak against anyone behind his back, even a lousy Lathian. But there are times when one is compelled to admit that dirt is dirt, sin is sin, and a Lathian is what he is, eh?"

Shomuth: "Please answer my question."

Thomas: "The Lathians are nuts."

Shomuth: "And they have the Willies?"

Thomas: "Say, where did you dig up this information?"

Shomuth: "That is our business. Will you be good enough to give me an answer?"

Thomas, belligerently: "Not only have they got the willies but they'll have a darned sight more of them before we're through."

Shomuth, puzzled: "How can that be? We have learned that each and every Lathian is unconsciously controlled by a Willy. Therefore the total number of Willies must be limited. It cannot be increased except by the birth of more Lathians."

Thomas, quickly: "You've got me wrong. What I meant was that as Lathian casualties mount up the number of unattached Willies will increase. Obviously even the best of Willies cannot control a corpse, can he? There will be lots more Willies loafing around in proportion to the number of Lathian survivors."

Shomuth "Yes, I see what you mean. And it will create a psychic problem of great seriousness." Pause. "Now, Captain Thomas, have you any reason to suppose that a large number of partnerless Willies might be able to seize control of another and different lifeform? Such as my own species for example?"

Thomas, with enough menace to deserve a space-medal: "I wouldn't be surprised."

Shomuth: "You don't know for sure?"

Thomas: "No."

Shomuth "It is true, is it not, that you are aware of the real Lathian nature only because you have been warned of it by your Eustace?"

Thomas, startled: "By my *what?*"

Shomuth: "By your *Eustace.* Why should that surprise you?"

Thomas, recovering swiftly enough to earn a bar to the medal: "I thought you said Useless. Silly of me. Yes, my Eustace. You're dead right there."

Shomuth, in lower tones: "There are more than four hundred Terran prisoners here. That means more than four hundred Eustaces wandering around unchallenged on this planet. Correct?"

Thomas: "I am unable to deny it."

Shomuth: "The Lathian heavy cruiser *Veder* crashed on landing and was a total loss. The Lathians attributed it to an error of judgment on the part of the crew. But that was just three days after you prisoners were brought here. Was it a mere coincidence?"

Thomas, scintillating: "Work it out for yourself."

Shomuth: "You realize that so far as we are concerned your refusal to reply is as good as an answer?"

Thomas: "Construe it any way you like. I will not betray Terran military secrets."

Shomuth: "All right. Let me try you on something else. The biggest fuel dump in this part of the galaxy is located a few degrees south of here. A week ago it blew up to total destruction. The loss was a severe one; it will handicap the Combine fleets for quite a time to come."

Thomas, with enthusiasm: "Cheers!"

Shomuth: "Lathian technicians theorize that a static spark caused a leaking tank to explode and that set off the rest in rapid succession. We can always trust technicians to come up with a glib explanation."

Thomas: "Well, what's wrong with it?"

Shomuth: "That dump has been established for more than four years. No static sparks have caused trouble during that time."

Thomas: "What are you getting at?"

Shomuth, pointedly: "You have admitted yourself that more than four hundred Eustaces are roaming this area, free to do as they please."

Thomas, in tones of stern patriotism: "I am admitting nothing. I refuse to answer any more questions."

Shomuth: "Has your Eustace prompted you to say that?"

Silence.

Shomuth: "If your Eustace is now present, can I question him through you?"

No reply.

Switching off, the Commandant said, "There you are. Eight other Terran officers gave more or less the same evidence. The rest tried to conceal the facts but, as you have heard, they failed. Zangasta himself has listened to the taped records and is deeply concerned about the situation."

"He needn't worry his head about it," Leeming offered.

"Why not?"

"It's all a lot of bunk, a put-up job. There was collusion between my Eustace and theirs."

The Commandant looked sour. "As you emphasized at our last meeting, there cannot be collusion without Eustaces, so it makes no difference either way."

"I'm glad you can see it at last."

"Let it pass," chipped in Pallam impatiently. "It is of no consequence. The confirmatory evidence is adequate no matter how we look at it."

Thus prompted, the Commandant continued, "I have been doing some investigating myself. In two years we've had a long series of small-scale troubles with the Rigellians, none of them really serious. But after you arrived there comes a big break that obviously must have been planned long before you turned up but soon afterward took place in circumstances suggesting outside help. Whence came this assistance?"

"Not telling," said Leeming knowingly.

"At one time or another eight of my guards earned your enmity by assaulting you. Of these, four are now in hospital badly injured, two more are to be drafted to the fighting front. I presume that it is only a matter of time before the remaining two are plunged into trouble?"

"The other two have arbitrated and earned forgiveness. Nothing will happen to them."

"Is that so?" The Commandant registered surprise.

Leeming went on, "I cannot give the same guarantee with respect to the firing squad, the officer in charge of it or the higher-up who ordered that helpless prisoners be shot."

"We *always* execute prisoners who break out of jail. It is an old-established practice and a necessary deterrent."

"We always settle accounts with the executioners," Leeming gave back. "It is an old-established practice and a necessary deterrent."

"By 'we' you mean you and your Eustace?" put in Pallam.

"Yes."

"Why should your Eustace care? The victims were not Terrans. They were merely a bunch of obstreperous Rigellians."

"Rigellians are allies. And allies are friends. I feel bad about the cold-blooded, needless slaughtering of them. Eustace is very sensitive to my emotions."

"But not necessarily obedient to them?"

"No."

"In fact," pressed Pallam, determined to establish the point once and for all, "if there is any question of one being subordinate to the other, it is *you* who serves *him*."

"Most times, anyway," conceded Leeming with the air of having a tooth pulled.

"Well, it confirms what you've already told us." Pallam gave a thin smile. "The chief difference between Terrans and Lathians is that you know you're controlled, whereas the Lathians are ignorant of their own status."

"We are not controlled consciously or subconsciously," Leeming insisted. "We exist in mutual partnership the same as you do with your wife. Sometimes she gives way to you, other times you give way to her. Neither of you bothers to estimate who has given way the most in any specific period and neither of you insists that a perfect balance must be maintained. That's how it is. And it's mastery by neither party."

"I wouldn't know, never having been mated." Pallam turned to the Commandant. "Carry on."

"As probably you are aware by now, this planet has been set aside as the Combine's main penal world," informed the Commandant. "Already we hold a large number of prisoners, mainly Rigellian."

"What of it?"

"There are more to come. Two thousand Centaurians and six hundred Thetans are due to arrive and fill a new jail next week. Combine forces will transfer more enemy lifeforms as soon as we have accommodation ready for them and ships are available." He eyed the other speculatively. "It is only a matter of time before they start dumping Terrans on us as well."

"Is the prospect bothering you?"

"Zangasta has decided that he must refuse to accept Terrans."

"That's up to him," said Leeming, blandly indifferent.

"Zangasta has a clever mind," opined the Commandant, oozing patriotic admiration. "He is of the firm opinion that to assemble a formidable army of mixed prisoners all on one planet, and then add some thousands of Terrans to the mixture, is to create a potentially dangerous situation. He foresees trouble on a scale vaster than we could handle. Indeed, we might lose control of this world, strategically placed in the Combine's rear, and become subject to the violent attacks of our own allies."

"That is quite possible," Leeming agreed. "In fact it's quite probable. In fact it's practically certain. But it's not Zangasta's only worry. It's the one he's seen fit to put out for publication. He's got a private one too."

"And what is that?"

"Zangasta himself originated the order that escaped prisoners be shot. He must have done so—otherwise nobody would dare shoot them. Now he's jumpy because a Eustace may be sitting on his bed and grinning at him every night. He thinks that a few thousand Eustaces will be a proportionately greater menace to him. But he's wrong."

"Why is he wrong?" inquired the Commandant.

"Because it isn't only the repentant who have no cause to fear. The dead haven't either. The arrival on this world of fifty million Eustaces means nothing whatever to a corpse. Zangasta had better countermand that shooting order if he wants to go on living."

"I'll inform him of your remarks. However, such cancellation may not be necessary. As I have told you, he is clever. He has devised a subtle strategy that will put all your evidence to the final, conclusive test and at the same time may solve his problems to his own satisfaction."

Feeling vague alarm, Leeming asked, "Am I permitted to know what he intends to do?"

"He has given instructions that you be told. And already he has swung into action." The Commandant waited for the sake of effect, then finished, "He has beamed the Allies a proposal to exchange prisoners."

Leeming fidgeted around in his seat. Ye gods, the plot was thickening with a vengeance. From the very beginning his sole purpose had been to talk himself out of jail and into some other situation more favorable for sudden departure at high speed. He'd been trying to lift himself over the wall with his tongue. Now they were taking his story and plastering it all over the galaxy. Oh, what a tangled web we weave when first we practice to deceive!

"What is more," the Commandant went on, "the Allies have notified us of their acceptance providing we exchange rank for rank. That is to say, captains for captains, navigators for navigators and so forth."

"That's reasonable."

"Zangasta," said the Commandant, grinning like a hungry wolf, "has agreed in his turn—providing that the Allies take Terran prisoners first and make exchange on a basis of two for one. He is now awaiting their reply."

"Two for one?" echoed Leeming, blinking. "You mean he wants them to release two of their prisoners for every Terran they get back?"

"No, no, of course not." He increased the grin and exposed the roots of his teeth. "They must return two Combine troopers for each Terran and his Eustace that we hand back. That is two for two and perfectly fair, is it not?"

"It's not for me to say." Leeming swallowed hard. "The Allies are the judges."

"Until a reply arrives and mutual agreement has been achieved, Zangasta wishes you to have better treatment. You will be transferred to the officers' quarters outside the walls, you will share their meals and be allowed to go walk in the country.

Temporarily you will be treated as a non-combatant and you'll be very comfortable. It is necessary that you give me your parole not to try to escape."

Holy smoke, this was another stinker. The entire fiction was shaped toward ultimate escape. He couldn't abandon it now. Neither was he willing to give his word of honor with the cynical intention of breaking it.

"Parole refused," he said firmly.

The Commandant was incredulous. "Surely you do not mean that?"

"I do. I have no choice. Terran military law does not permit a prisoner-of-war to give such a promise."

"Why not?"

"Because no Terran can accept responsibility for his Eustace. How can I swear not to get out when half of me cannot be got in? Can a twin take oath on behalf of his brother?"

"Guard!" called the Commandant, visibly disappointed.

He mooched uneasily around his cell for a full twelve days, occasionally chatting with Eustace night-times for the benefit of ears lurking outside the door. Definitely he'd wangled himself into a predicament that was a case of put up or shut up; in order to put up he dared not shut up.

The food remained better in quantity though little could be said for its quality. Guards treated him with that diffidence accorded to captives who somehow are in cahoots with their superiors. Four more recaptured Rigellians were brought back but not shot. All the signs and portents were that he'd still got a grip on the foe.

Though he'd said nothing to them, the other prisoners had got wind of the fact that in some mysterious way he was responsible for the general softening of prison conditions. At exercise time they treated him as a deep and subtle character who could achieve the impossible. From time to time their curiosity got the better of them.

"You know they didn't execute those last four?"

"Yes," Leeming admitted.

"It's being said that you stopped the shooting."

"Who says so?"

"It's just a story going around."

"That's right, it's just a story going around."

"I wonder why they shot the first bunch but not the second. There must be a reason."

"Maybe the Zangastans have developed qualms of conscience even if belatedly," Leeming suggested.

"There's more to it than that."

"Such as what?"

"Somebody has shaken them up."

"Who, for instance?"

"I don't know. There's a strong rumor that you've got the Commandant eating out of your hand."

"That's likely, isn't it?" Leeming countered.

"1 wouldn't think so. But one never knows where one is with the Terrans." The other brooded a bit, asked, "What did you do with that wire I stole for you?"

"I'm knitting it into a pair of socks. Nothing fits better or wears longer than solid wire socks."

Thus he foiled their nosiness and kept silence, not wanting to arouse false hopes. Inwardly he was badly bothered. The Allies in general and Earth in particular knew nothing whatever about Eustaces and therefore were likely to treat a two-for-one proposition with the contempt it deserved. A blank refusal on their part might cause him to be plied with awkward questions impossible to answer.

In that case it would occur to them sooner or later that they were afflicted with the biggest liar in history. They'd then devise tests of fiendish ingenuity. When he flunked them the balloon would go up.

He wasn't inclined to give himself overmuch credit for kidding them along so far. The few books he'd been able to read had shown that Zangastan religion was based upon reverence for ancestral spirits. The Zangastans were also familiar with what is known as poltergeist phenomena. The ground had been prepared for him in advance; he'd merely ploughed it and sown the crop. When a victim already believes in two kinds of invisible beings it isn't hard to persuade him to swallow a third.

But when the Allies beamed Asta Zangasta a curt invitation to make his bed on a railroad track it was possible that the third type of spirit would be regurgitated with violence. Unless by fast, convincing talk he could cram it back down their gullets when it was halfway out. How to do that?

In his cell he was stewing this problem over and over when the guards came for him again. The Commandant was there but Pallam was not. Instead, a dozen civilians eyed him curiously. That made a total of thirteen enemies, a very suitable number to pronounce him ready for the chopper.

Feeling as much the center of attention as a six-tailed wombat at the zoo, he sat down and four civilians immediately started chivvying him, taking it in relays. They were interested in one subject and one only, namely, bopamagilvies. It seemed that they'd been playing for hours with his samples, had achieved nothing except some practice in acting daft, and were not happy about it.

On what principle did a bopamagilvie work? Did it focus telepathic output into a narrow, long-range beam? At what distance did his Eustace get beyond range of straight conversation and have to be summoned with the aid of a gadget? Why was it necessary to make directional search before obtaining a reply? How did he know how to make a coiled-loop in the first place?

"I can't explain. How does a bird know how to make a nest? The knowledge is wholly instinctive. I have known how to call my Eustace ever since I was old enough to shape a piece of wire."

"Could it be that your Eustace implants the necessary knowledge in your mind?"

"Frankly, I've never given that idea a thought. But it is possible."

"Will any kind of wire serve?"

"So long as it is non-ferrous."

"Are all Terran loops of exactly the same construction and dimensions?"

"No, they vary with the individual."

"We've made careful and thorough search of Terran prisoners held by the Lathians. Not one of them owns a similar piece of apparatus. How do you account for that?"

"They don't need one."

"Why not?"

"Because when more than four hundred of them are imprisoned together they can always count on at least a few of their Eustaces being within easy reach at any given time."

Somehow he beat them off, feeling hot in the forehead and cold in the belly. Then the Commandant took over.

"The Allies have flatly refused to accept Terran prisoners ahead of other species, or to exchange them two for one, or to discuss the matter any further. What have you to say to that?"

Steeling himself, Leeming commented, "Look, on your side there are more than twenty lifeforms, of which the Lathians and the Zebs are by far the most powerful. Now if the Allies had wanted to give priority of exchange to one species do you think the Combine would agree? If, for example, the favored species happened to be the Tansites, would the Lathians and Zebs vote for them to get home first?"

A tall, authoritative civilian chipped in. "I am Daverd, personal aide to Zangasta. He is of your own opinion. He believes that the Terrans have been outvoted. Therefore I am commanded to ask you one question."

"What is it?"

"Do your allies know about your Eustaces?"

"No."

"You have succeeded in hiding the facts from them?"

"There's never been any question of concealing anything from them. With friends the facts just don't become apparent. Eustaces take effective action only against enemies and that is something that cannot be concealed forever."

"Very well." Daverd came closer, put on a conspiratorial air. "The Lathians started this war and the Zebs went with them by reason of their military alliance. The rest of us got dragged in for one reason or another. The Lathians are strong and arrogant but, as we now know, they are not responsible for their actions."

"What's this to me?"

"Separately we numerically weaker lifeforms cannot stand against the Lathians or the Zebs. But together we are strong enough to step out of the war and maintain our right to be neutral. So Zangasta has consulted the others."

Lord! Isn't it amazing what can be done with a few yards of copper wire?

"He has received their replies today," Daverd went on. "They are willing to make a common front for the sake of enjoying mutual peace—providing that the Allies are equally willing to recognize their neutrality and exchange prisoners with them."

"Such sudden unanimity among the small fry tells me something pretty good," observed Leeming with malice.

"It tells you what?"

"Allied forces have won a major battle lately. Somebody has been given a hell of a lambasting."

Daverd refused to confirm or deny it. "You are the only Terran we hold on this planet. Zangasta thinks he can make good use of you."

"How?"

"He has decided to send you back to Terra. It will be your task to persuade them to agree to our plans. If you fail, a couple of hundred thousand hostages will suffer—remember that!"

"The prisoners have no say in this matter, no hand in it, no responsibility for it. If you vent your spite upon them a time will surely come when you'll be made to pay—remember that!"

"The Allies will know nothing about it," Daverd retorted. "There will be no Terrans and no Eustaces here to inform them by any underhanded method. Henceforth we are keeping Terrans out. The Allies cannot use knowledge they do not possess."

"No," agreed Leeming. "It's quite impossible to employ something you haven't got."

They provided a light destroyer crewed by ten Zangastans. With one stop for refueling and the fitting of new tubes it took him to a servicing planet right on the fringe of the battle area. This dump was a Lathian outpost, but those worthies showed no interest in what their smaller allies were up to, neither did they realize that the one Terranlike creature really was a Terran. They got to work relining the destroyer's tubes in readiness for its journey home. Meanwhile, Leeming was transferred to an unarmed one-man Lathian scout-ship. The ten Zangastans officiously saluted before they left him.

From this point he was strictly on his own. Take-off was a heller. The seat was far too big and shaped to fit the Lathian backside, which meant that it was humped in the wrong places. The controls were unfamiliar and situated too far apart. The little ship was fast and powerful but responded differently from his own. How he got up he never knew, but he made it.

After that there was the constant risk of being tracked by Allied detector stations and blown apart in full flight. He charged among the stars hoping for the best and left his beam transmitter severely alone; calls on an enemy frequency might make him a dead duck in no time at all.

He arrowed straight for Terra. His sleeps were restless and uneasy. The tubes were not to be trusted despite that flight-duration would be only a third of that done in his own vessel. The strange autopilot was not to be trusted merely because it was of alien design. The ship itself was not to be trusted for the same reason. The forces of his own side were not to be trusted because they'd tend to shoot first and ask questions afterward.

More by good luck than good management he penetrated the Allied front without interception. It was a feat that the foe could accomplish, given the audacity, but had never attempted because the risk of getting into Allied territory was as nothing to the trouble of getting out again.

In due time he came in fast on Terra's night side and plonked the ship down in a field a couple of miles west of the main spaceport. It would have been foolish to take a chance by landing a Lathian vessel bang in the middle of the port. Somebody behind a heavy gun might have stuttered with excitement and let fly.

The moon was shining bright along the Wabash when he approached the front gate afoot and a sentry bawled, "Halt! Who goes there?"

"Lieutenant Leeming and Eustace Phenackertiban."

"Advance and be recognized."

He ambled forward thinking to himself that such an order was manifestly dunderheaded. Be recognized. The sentry had never seen him in his life and wouldn't know him from Myrtle McTurtle. Oh, well, baloney baffles brains.

At the gate a powerful cone of light shone down upon him. Somebody with three chevrons on his sleeve emerged from a nearby hut bearing a scanner on the end of a thin, black cable. He waved the scanner over the arrival from head to foot, concentrating mostly upon the face.

A loudspeaker in the hut ordered, "Bring him into Intelligence H.Q."

They started walking.

The sentry let go an agitated yelp. "Hey, where's the other guy?"

"What guy?" asked the sergeant, stopping and staring around.

"Smell his breath," Leeming advised.

"You gave me *two* names," asserted the sentry, full of resentment.

"Well, if you ask the sergeant nicely he'll give you two more," said Leeming. "Won't you, Sarge?"

"Let's get going," growled the sergeant, displaying liverish impatience.

They reached Intelligence H.Q. The duty officer was Colonel Farmer. He gaped at Leeming and said, "Well!" He said it seven times.

Without preamble, Leeming demanded, "What's all this about us refusing to make a two-for-one swap for Terran prisoners?"

Farmer appeared to haul himself with an effort out of a fantastic dream. "You know of it?"

"How could I ask if I didn't?"

"All right. Why should we accept such a cockeyed proposition? We're in our right minds, you know!"

Bending over the other's desk, hands splayed upon it, Leeming said, "All we need do is agree—upon one condition."

"What condition?"

"That they make a similar agreement with respect to Lathians. Two of our men for one Lathian and one Willy."

"One *what?*"

"One Willy. The Lathians will take it like birds. They have been propagandizing all over the shop that one Lathian is worth two of anything else. They're too conceited to refuse such an offer. They'll advertise it as proof positive that even their enemies know how good they are."

"But—" began Farmer, slightly dazed.

"Their allies will fall over themselves in their haste to agree also. They'll do it from different motives to which the Lathians will wake up when it's too late. Try it for size. Two of our fellows for one Lathian and his Willy."

Farmer stood up, his belly protruding, and roared, "What the blue blazes is a Willy?"

"You can easily find out," assured Leeming. "Consult your Eustace."

Showing alarm, Farmer lowered his tones to a soothing pitch and said as gently as possible, "Your appearance here has been a great shock to me. Many months ago you were reported missing and believed killed."

"I crash-landed and got taken prisoner in the back of beyond. They were a snake-skinned bunch called Zangastans. They slung me into the jug."

"Yes, yes," said Colonel Farmer, making pacifying gestures. "But how on earth did you get away?"

"Farmer, I cannot tell a lie—I hexed them with my bopamagilvie."

"Huh?"

"So I left by rail," informed Leeming, "and there were ten faplaps carrying it." Taking the other unaware, he let go a vicious kick at the desk and made a spurt of ink leap across the blotter. "Now let's see some of the intelligence they're supposed to have in Intelligence. Beam the offer. Two for a cootie-coated Lathian and a Willie Terwilliger." He stared around, a wild look in his eyes. "And find me some-place to sleep—I'm dead beat."

Holding himself in enormous restraint, Farmer said, "Lieutenant, is that the proper way in which to talk to a colonel?"

"One talks in *any* way to anybody. Mayor Snorkum will lay the cake. Go paddle a poodle." Leeming kicked the desk again. "Get busy and tuck me into bed."

SINISTER BARRIER

Introduction by Jack L. Chalker

There is a legend, much believed and repeated, that when Eric Frank Russell submitted *Sinister Barrier* to John W. Campbell at *Astounding* that Campbell was so taken with the bizarre and unusual tale that he talked Street and Smith, publishers of the magazine, into launching a new magazine, *Unknown*, just to showcase it and to have a place for tales that didn't follow conventional *genre* paths. It's a nice story, and even Russell loved hearing it, but it's not true.

What *is* true is that *Barrier* was the first novel in the first issue of *Unknown*. It had indeed been submitted to Campbell for *Astounding Science Fiction*. Campbell was at that time assembling and creating *Unknown* and decided to shift the novel from *Astounding* to the new magazine because it was a perfect length and could fit in either magazine. *None But Lucifer*, by H.L. Gold, which Campbell had given, against Gold's strenuous objections, to L. Sprague DeCamp for a rewrite and polish wasn't back before the debut deadline. He already had a cover originally done for a future ASF, so . . . Thus are legends born.

Russell was a lifelong follower of and admirer of Charles Fort, the collector of odd phenomena like rains of frogs and Saharan ice storms who had written a number of books on the subject and whose followers created a society to compile and collect such reports. The Fortean Society has branches in many countries, and still exists. Fort was a believer in science, but not in scientists; he thought they tended to dismiss or overlook what they found inconvenient, and when pressed on why such bizarre things happened, they often came up with explanations so outlandish they were more unbelievable than magic spells (which Fort didn't particularly believe in, either). Today, this tendency is generally called "the knowledge filter"—when science dismisses evidence as impossible or inconvenient without ever really looking at it.

Russell, who late in life would head the Fortean Society in Britain, looked for an explanation for all those unexplainable things happening, and for all the bizarre nonsense of human behavior as well. In the shadow of Hitler and with World War II only months away, he created a possible science fictional explanation for them. I can't tell you what it is here—they can read our thoughts, you know.

It should be noted that there are two versions of *Sinister Barrier*. The original version as submitted and published in *Unknown* was, Russell later felt, quite limited and dated by the end of the war, as it didn't even factor in atomic weapons and the book was, after all, set in the future. When asked for permission to publish the novel in the U.S. by Lloyd Eshbach of Fantasy Press, he insisted on rewriting and updating the entire book. This was, it must be emphasized, Russell's decision and indeed his demand, *not* the publisher's. It is that "author preferred" rewrite that you will read here, if you dare.

Because, you see, if you read about them you're going to think about them, and then . . . Good luck.

Clipping from a New York daily—
TO BE READ IN A DIM LIGHT, AT NIGHT.

The late Charles Fort, who was a sort of Peter Pan of science and went about picking up whimsies of fact, mostly from the rubbish heaps of astronomy, would have been interested in an incident that occurred Sunday morning on Fifth Avenue between Twenty-ninth and Thirtieth Streets.

Eight starlings in flight suddenly plummeted to the feet of Patrolman Anton Vodrazka, dead. There was no sign of a wound or any other indication of what caused their end. It was at first thought that they might have been poisoned, as were some pigeons at Verdi Square, Seventy-second Street and Broadway, recently.

S.P.C.A. agents said it was most unlikely that eight birds, even if they had been poisoned, would succumb at the same moment in mid-flight. Another report from the same neighborhood a few minutes later didn't help any. A starling, "excited and acting as if pursued by some invisible terror," had flown into a Childs Restaurant on Fifth Avenue, banged into the lights and fallen in the front window.

What killed the eight starlings? What frightened the ninth? Was there some Presence in the sky? . . . We hasten to pass the idea on to the nearest writer of mystery stories.

Chapter 1

"Swift death awaits the first cow that leads a revolt against milking," mused Professor Peder Bjornsen. It was a new slant, and a wicked one, born of dreadful facts. He passed long, slender fingers through prematurely white hair. His eyes, strangely protruding, filled with uncanny light, stared out of his office window which gaped on the third level above traffic swirling through Stockholm's busy Hötorget. But those eyes were not looking at the traffic.

"And there's a swat waiting for the first bee that blats about pilfered honey," he added. Stockholm hummed and roared, a city unconscious of its chains. The professor continued to stare in silent, fearful contemplation. Then suddenly his eyes lifted, widened, flared with apprehension. He drew away from the window, slowly, reluctantly; moving as if forcing himself by sheer willpower to retreat from a horror which beckoned, invisibly beckoned.

Raising his hands, he pushed, pushed futilely at thin air. Those distorted optics of his, still preternaturally cold and hard, yet brilliant with something far beyond fear, followed with dreadful fascination a shapeless, colorless point that crept from window to ceiling. Turning with a tremendous effort, he ran, his mouth open and expelling breath soundlessly.

Halfway to the door he emitted a brief gasp, stumbled, fell. His stricken hand clutched the calendar from his desk, dragged it down to the carpet. He sobbed, hugged hands to his heart, lay still. The spark which had motivated him became extinguished. The calendar's top leaf fluttered in a queer, inexplicable breeze from nowhere. The date was May the seventeenth, 2015.

Bjornsen had been five hours dead when the police got to him. Imperturbably, the medical examiner diagnosed heart disease and left it at that. Snooping restlessly around, Police Lieutenant Baeker found on the professor's desk a note bearing a message from the grave.

"A little knowledge is a dangerous thing. It is humanly impossible to discipline my thoughts every minute of the day, to control my involuntary dreams every hour of the night. It is inevitable that soon I shall be found dead, in which case you must—"

"Must what?" asked Baeker. There was no reply. The voice that could have shocked him with its answer was stilled forever. Baeker heard the medical examiner's report, then burned the note. The professor, he decided, like others of his ilk, had grown eccentric in his old age, being burdened by too much abstruse learning. Heart disease it was, actually and officially.

On May the thirtieth, Doctor Guthrie Sheridan walked with the deliberate, jerky step of an automaton along Charing Cross Road, London. His eyes were shining, frozen lumps, and he kept them focussed on the sky while his legs made their mechanical way. He had the eerie appearance of a blind man following a thoroughly familiar route.

Jim Leacock saw him wending his fascinated way, failed to notice anything abnormal. Dashing up, he yelled, "Hey, Sherry!" all set to administer a hearty slap on the back. He stopped, appalled.

Turning upon him pale, strained features framing eyes that gleamed like icicles seen in bluish twilight, Guthrie seized an arm and chattered, "Jim! By heavens, I'm glad to see you!" His breath was fast, his voice urgent. "Jim, I've got to talk to someone—or go crazy. I've just discovered the most incredible fact in the history of mankind. It is almost beyond belief. Yet it explains a thousand things that we've merely guessed at or completely ignored."

"What is it?" demanded Leacock, skeptically. He studied the other's distorted face.

"Jim, let me tell you that man is not and never has been the master of his fate, nor the captain of his soul. Why, the very beasts of the field—!" He broke off, grabbed at his listener. His voice went two tones higher, held a hysterical note. "I've thought it! I've thought it, I tell you!" His legs bent at the knees. "I'm done for!" He slumped to the pavement.

Hastily, the startled Leacock stooped over him, tore open his shirt, slid a hand down on his chest. No beat was discernable. The once wildly beating heart had packed up—for keeps. Sheridan was dead. Heart disease, apparently.

At the same hour of the same day, Doctor Hans Luther did a very similar thing. Carrying his deceptively plump body at top speed across his laboratory, he raced headlong down the stairs, across the hall. He fled with many fearful glances over one shoulder, and the glances came from eyes like polished agate.

Reaching the telephone, he dialed with shaking finger, got the *Dortmund Zeitung*, shouted for the editor. With his eyes still upon the stairs while the telephone receiver trembled against his ear, he bawled into the mouthpiece, "Vogel, I have for you the most astonishing news since the dawn of time. You must give it space, plenty of space, quickly—before it is too late."

"Let me have the details," suggested Vogel, tolerantly.

"Earth is belted with a warning streamer that says: KEEP OFF THE GRASS!" Luther watched the stairs and sweated.

"Ha-ha!" responded Vogel, without mirth. His heavy face moved in the tiny vision-screen above the telephone, bore the patient expression of one accustomed to the eccentricities of scientists.

"Listen!" yelled Luther. He wiped his forehead with the back of a quivering hand. "You know me. You know that I do not tell lies, I do not joke. I tell you nothing which I cannot prove. So I tell you that now and perhaps for thousands of years past, this troubled world of ours . . . a-ah! . . . *a-a-ah!*"

The receiver swung at the end of its cord, gave forth a reedy shout of "Luther! Luther! What's happened?"

Doctor Hans Luther made no response. Sinking slowly to his knees, he rolled his peculiarly glistening eyes upward, fell on his side. His tongue licked his lips sluggishly, very sluggishly, once, twice. He died in awful silence.

Vogel's face bobbed in the vision-screen. The dangling receiver made agitated noises for ears beyond hearing.

Bill Graham knew nothing about these earlier tragedies, but he knew about Mayo. He was right on the spot when it happened.

He was strolling along West Fourteenth, New York, when for no particular reason he cast a casual glance up the sheer side of the Martin Building, saw a human figure falling past the twelfth floor.

Down came the body, twisting, whirling, spread-eagling, as horribly impotent as a tossed bundle of rags. It smacked the pavement and bounced nine feet. The sound was halfway between a squelch and a crunch. The concrete looked as if it had been slapped by a giant crimson sponge.

Twenty yards ahead of Graham, a fat woman stopped midstep, studied the stain and the bundle while her complexion turned oysterlike. Dropping her handbag, she lay down on the sidewalk, closed her eyes, muttered nonsense. A hundred pedestrians turned themselves into a rapidly shrinking circle with the battered body as its center. They pushed and shoved as they guzzled the sight.

The dead had no face. Its sodden clothes were surmounted by a ghastly mask like one made of scrambled blueberries and cream. Graham felt no qualms as he bent over the corpse. He had seen worse in war.

His strong, brown fingers plucked at the pocket of a sticky vest, drew out a blood-spattered pasteboard. Looking at the card, he permitted himself a low whistle of surprise.

"Professor Walter Mayo! Good grief!"

Swallowing hard, he looked once more at the pathetic remnant sprawled at his feet, then forced his way through the swelling murmuring crowd. The revolving doors of the Martin Building whirled behind him as he sprinted for the pneumatic levitators.

Fumbling the card with unfeeling fingers, Graham strove to assemble his jumbled thoughts while his one-man disk was wafted swiftly up its tube. Mayo, of all people, to pass out like that!

At the sixteenth floor the disk stopped with a rubbery bounce and a sigh of escaping air. Racing along the passage, Graham reached Mayo's laboratory, found its door ajar.

There was nobody in the laboratory. Everything appeared peaceful, orderly, bearing no signs of recent disturbance.

A thirty-foot long table carried a lengthy array of apparatus which he recognized as an assembly for destructive distillation. He felt the retorts. They were cold. Evidently the experiment had not been started.

Counting the flasks, he decided that the setup was arranged to extract the sixteenth product of something which, when he opened the electric roaster, proved to be a quantity of dried leaves. They looked and smelled like some sort of herb.

Papers on an adjacent desk danced in the breeze from a widely opened window. He went to the window, looked out, down, saw the crowd surrounding four blue-coated figures and a crushed form. A death wagon was drawing in to the curb. He frowned.

Leaving the window open, he searched hastily through the papers littering the dead professor's desk, found nothing to satisfy his pointless curiosity. With one last keen glance around, he left the laboratory. His falling disk swept him past two ascending policemen.

A line of phone booths stood in the foyer. Entering one, he spun the dial, saw a girl's clear features glow into the circular visor.

"Give me Mr. Sangster, Hetty."

"Yes, Mr. Graham."

The girl's face dissolved, was replaced by that of a heavy-featured man.

"Mayo's dead," Graham informed, bluntly. "He dropped down the front of the Martin about twenty minutes ago. He dived past sixteen floors, landed almost at my feet. He was unrecognizable except for the scars on his hands."

"Suicide?" The other raised bushy brows inquiringly.

"That's how it looks," Graham admitted, "but I don't think it is."

"Why not?"

"Because I knew Mayo exceedingly well. As a government liaison officer between scientists and the U.S. Department of Special Finance, I have dealt with him personally over a period of ten years. You will remember that I have negotiated four loans for the furtherance of his work."

"Yes, yes." Sangster nodded.

"In general, scientists are an unemotional crowd," Graham continued, "and Mayo was about the most phlegmatic of the lot." He gazed earnestly at the little screen. "Believe me, sir, Mayo was not capable of self-destruction—at least, not while in his right mind."

"I believe you," said Sangster, without hesitation. "What do you wish to have done?"

"The police have every reason to treat this as a simple case of suicide and I cannot interfere because I have no status in such cases. I suggest that all necessary strings be pulled to make sure that the police dismiss this matter only after the most thorough investigation. I want them to sift this to the bottom."

"It shall be as you ask," Sangster assured. His rugged features grew large as they were brought nearer to the distant scanner. "The appropriate department will intervene."

"Thank you, sir," Graham responded.

"Not at all. You hold your position only because we have complete faith in your judgment." His eyes lowered to a desk not visible in the screen. A rustling of papers came over the wires. "Mayo's case has a parallel today."

"What?" ejaculated Graham.

"Doctor Irwin Webb has died. We were in contact with him two years ago. We provided him with sufficient funds to complete some research which resulted in our war department acquiring a self-aligning gunsight operating on magnetic principles."

"I recall it well."

"Webb died an hour ago. The police phoned because they found a letter from us in his wallet." Sangster's face became grim. "The circumstances surrounding his death are very strange. The medical examiner maintains that he died of heart disease—yet he expired while shooting at nothing."

"Shooting at nothing?" echoed Graham, incredulously.

"He had an automatic pistol in his hand, and he had fired two bullets into the wall of his office."

"Ah!"

"From the viewpoint of our country's welfare and scientific progress," continued Sangster, speaking with much deliberation, "the deaths of such able men as Mayo and Webb are too important to be treated lightly, especially when mysterious circumstances intervene. Webb's case seems to be the more peculiar of the two. I want you to look into it. I would like you, personally, to examine any documents he may have left behind. Something of significance may be lying around there."

"But I have no official standing with the police," Graham protested.

"The officer in charge of the case will be notified that you have governmental authority to examine all Webb's papers."

"Very well, sir." Sangster's face faded from the visor as Graham hung up. "Mayo—and now Webb!"

Webb lay on the carpet midway between the door and the window. Flat on his back, with his dead eyes wide open, the pupils were almost hidden where they turned up under the top lids. The cold fingers of his right hand still grasped a dull blue automatic loaded with segmentary bullets. The wall toward which the gun pointed bore eight abrasions; a small group of weals where quarter sections of two split missiles had struck home.

"He shot at something along this line," Lieutenant Wohl said to Graham, stretching a thin cord from the center of the weals to a point four or five feet above the body.

"That's what it looks like," agreed Graham.

"But he wasn't shooting at anything," Wohl asserted. "Half a dozen people were passing along the passage outside when they heard his gun suddenly start blasting. They burst in immediately, found him like this, breathing his last. He strove to say something, to tell them something, but the words wouldn't come. Nobody could have got in or out of his office without being seen. We've checked on the six witnesses and they're all above suspicion. Besides, the medical examiner says it's heart disease."

"Maybe it is," Graham evaded, "and maybe it isn't."

A cold eddy wafted through the room as he spoke those words. A subtle tingling slid up his spine, stirred his back hairs and passed away. His inward self became filled with a vague unease, elusive but strong, like that of a rabbit which suspects the presence of a hawk it cannot see.

"All the same, I'm not satisfied," continued Lieutenant Wohl. "I've got a hunch that this Webb suffered from delusions. Since I've never heard of heart disease causing hallucinations, I reckon he'd taken something that's caused both."

"You mean that he was a drug addict?" Graham queried.

"I mean just that! I'll gamble that the autopsy will show my hunch is correct."

"Let me know if it does," requested Graham.

Opening the doctor's desk, he commenced to search carefully through the neatly arranged files of correspondence. There was nothing to satisfy his interest, nothing to which he could attach special significance. The letters without exception were orthodox, innocent, almost humdrum. His face registered disappointment as he shoved the files back into place.

Closing the desk, he transferred his attention to the huge safe built into the wall. Wohl produced the keys, saying, "They were in his right-hand pocket. I'd have looked through that safe, but was told to hold off for you."

Graham nodded, inserted a key. The cumbersome door swung slowly on its bearings, exposed the interior. Graham and Wohl gave vent to simultaneous exclamations. Facing them hung a large sheet of paper bearing a hasty scrawl: *"Eternal vigilance is the impossible price of liberty. See Bjornsen if I go."*

"Who the deuce is Bjornsen?" snapped Graham, plucking the paper from the safe.

"Don't know. Never heard of him." Wohl gazed in frank puzzlement at the sheet, and said, "Give it to me. It carries marks of writing from a sheet above it. Look, the impressions are fairly deep. We'll get a parallel light beam on it and see if we can throw those imprints into relief. With luck, they'll prove easy to read."

Graham handed him the sheet. Taking it to the door, Wohl passed it outside with a quick utterance of instructions.

They spent the next half-hour making careful inventory of the safe's contents; a task that revealed nothing except that Webb had been a painstaking bookkeeper and had kept close watch on the business side of his activities.

Prowling around, Wohl found a small pile of ash in the grate. It was churned to a fine powder beyond all possibility of reclamation—the dust of potent words now far beyond reach.

"Grates are relics of the twentieth century," declared Wohl. "It looks like he stuck to this one so that he could burn documents in it. Evidently he had something to conceal. What was it? From whom was he hiding it?" The telephone buzzed, and he hastened to answer it, adding, "If this is the station maybe they'll be able to answer those questions for us."

It was the station. The face of a police officer spread across the midget visor while Wohl pressed the amplifier stud so that Graham could listen in.

"We brought out the words on that sheet you gave us," the officer said. "They're pretty incoherent, but maybe they'll mean something to you."

"Read 'em out," Wohl ordered. He listened intently while the distant police officer recited from a typewritten copy.

"Sailors are notoriously susceptible. Must extend the notion and get data showing how seaboard dwellers compare with country folk. Degrees of optical fixation ought to differ. Look into this at first opportunity. Must also persuade Fawcett to get me data on the incidence of goiter in imbeciles, schizophrenics especially. There's wisdom in his madhouse, but it needs digging out."

The reader looked up. "There are two paragraphs, and that's the first."

"Go on! Go on, man!" urged Graham, impatiently. The officer continued while Graham kept eagle eyes upon the visor, and Wohl looked more and more mystified.

"There is a real connection between the most unexpected and ill-assorted things. Oddities have links too surreptitious to have been perceived. Fireballs and howling dogs and second-sighters who are not so simple as we think. Inspiration and emotion and everlasting cussedness. Bells that chime unswung by human hands;

ships that vanish in sunlit calm; lemmings that migrate to the valley of the shadow. Arguments, ferocity, ritualistic rigmarole, and pyramids with unseen peaks. It would seem a nightmarish hodge-podge of surrealists at their worst—if I didn't know Bjornsen was right, terribly right! It is a picture that must be shown the world—if it can be shown without massacre!"

"What did I tell you?" asked Wohl. He tapped his forehead significantly. "A narcotic nut!"

"We'll see about that." Bringing his face closer to the telephone's scanner, Graham said to the distant officer, "File that sheet where it'll be safe. Make two more copies and have them sent to Sangster, care of the U.S. Department of Special Finance at their local office in Bank of Manhattan."

He switched off the amplifier, pronged the receiver. The tiny television screen went blank.

"If you don't mind, I'd like to go with you to the station," he told Wohl.

They went out together; Wohl convinced that here was work for the local narcotic squad; Graham pondering the possibility of the two deaths being natural despite their element of mystery. As they crossed the sidewalk both felt a strange, nervous thrill. Something peered into their minds, grinned and slunk away.

Chapter 2

No new information awaited them at the station. Fingerprint men had returned from Mayo's laboratory as well as from Webb's office, had developed and printed their photographs. There were a mass of prints, some clear, some blurred. Most had been brought out with aluminium powder, a few—on fibrous surfaces—with iodine vapor. The great majority were prints left by the scientists themselves. The others were not recorded on police files.

Experts had gone with complete thoroughness through the dead men's rooms and discovered not the slightest thing to arouse their own suspicions or confirm Graham's. They reported with the faint air of men compelled to waste their time and talents on other people's fads.

"There's nothing left but the autopsy," declared Wohl, finally. "If Webb's a drug addict, the case is cleared up. He died while shooting at some crazy product of his own imagination."

"And Mayo jumped into an imaginary bathtub?" queried Graham.

"Huh?" Wohl looked startled.

"I suggest an autopsy on both—if it's possible to perform one on what's left of Mayo." Graham reached for his hat. His dark gray eyes were steady as they looked into Wohl's blue ones. "Phone Sangster and let him know the results." He hurried out with charactcristic cncrgy.

A pile of wreckage cluttered the corner of Pine and Nassau. Graham got a glimpse over the head of the surging crowd, saw two crumpled gyrocars which appeared to have met in a head-on collision. The crowd thickened rapidly, pushed, stood on tiptoe, murmured with excitement. He could sense their psychopathic tension as he passed. It was like moving through an invisible aura of vibrance. The mob-noumen.

"Disaster is to crowds what sugar is to flies," he commented to himself.

Entering the huge pile of Bank of Manhattan Building, he took a pneumatic levitator to the twenty-fourth floor. Pushing through a gold-lettered door, he said, "Hello, Hetty!" to the honey-blonde at the switchboard, and passed on to a door marked *Mr. Sangster*. He knocked and went in.

While Sangster listened quietly, he made a full report, concluded, "And that's all there is, sir. It leaves us with nothing except my own doubts concerning Mayo, and the peculiar fact of Webb firing a pistol."

"And it leaves us this person Bjornsen," said Sangster, shrewdly.

"Yes. The police haven't been able to get a line on him. They've hardly had sufficient time yet."

"Do the postal authorities hold any mail for Webb, from this Bjornsen?"

"No. We thought of that. Lieutenant Wohl phoned and asked them. Neither the mail carrier nor the sorters remember letters from anyone named Bjornsen. Of course, this unknown—whoever he may be—might not have sent letters or, if he did, they may not have carried the sender's name on the envelop. The only mail for Webb comprises two conventional letters from scientist friends of his college days. Most scientists seem to maintain a wide but erratic correspondence with other scientists, especially fellow experimenters working along parallel lines."

"Which this Bjornsen may have been," Sangster suggested.

"Now there's an idea!" Graham pondered it a moment, then reached for the phone. He got his number, absent-mindedly pressed the amplifier stud, winced when the receiver promptly bellowed into his ear. Resting the receiver on Sangster's desk, he said into the mouthpiece, "Is that the Smithsonian Institute? May I speak to Mr. Harriman?"

Harriman came on, his dark eyes level in the screen. "Hello, Graham. What can I do for you?"

"Walter Mayo is dead," Graham told him, "and Irwin Webb, too. They passed away this morning within an hour of each other." Harriman's face expressed his sorrow while Graham gave him brief details of the tragedies. Graham asked, "D'you happen to know of any scientist bearing the name of Bjornsen?"

"Yes. He died on the seventeenth."

"Died?" Graham and Sangster shot to their feet, and the former said, grimly, "Was there anything unusual about his end?"

"Not that I know of. He was an old man, well past his allotted span. Why do you ask?"

"Never mind. Do you know anything more concerning him?"

"He was a Swedish scientist specializing in optics," replied Harriman, obviously mystified, "and he passed his prime twelve years ago. Some people thought him in his second childhood. His death gained eulogies in a few Swedish papers, but I have noticed no mention of it in the press over here."

"Anything else?" Graham persisted.

"Not much. He was rather obscure. If I remember aright, he commenced his decline when he made himself a laughing-stock with some paper he read to the 2003 International Scientific Convention, at Bergen. It was a lot of gibberish about visual limitations, with plenty of spooks and djinns thrown in. Hans Luther also brought the vials of wrath on his own head by being the only scientist of any prominence to treat Bjornsen seriously."

"And who is this Hans Luther?"

"A German scientist, and a very clever man. He's dead. He died not long after Bjornsen."

"What, another?" Graham and Sangster shouted together.

"What's the matter?" Curiosity was the keynote of Harriman's tones. "You don't expect scientists to live forever. They die just like other people, don't they?"

"When they die just like other people," replied Graham, dourly, "we feel regrets and nurse no suspicions. Do me a favor, Harriman. Get me a complete list of all the internationally known scientists who have died since the first of May, together with every cogent detail you can rake up."

Harriman blinked with surprise. "I'll phone you as soon as I can," he promised, and rung off. Almost at once he came on again with, "I forgot to tell you that Luther is said to have died in his Dortmund laboratory while gabbling some incoherent nonsense to his local paper. He had a heart attack. His death was attributed to dementia and cardiac exhaustion, both brought on by overwork."

He hung on the line, watching for the effect, openly hoping for information. Then he gave it up, repeated, "I'll phone you as soon as I can." He disconnected.

"This thing gets crazier the further we look into it," commented Sangster. He flopped into his chair, tilted it back on its hind legs, frowned his dissatisfaction. "If the deaths of Mayo and Webb weren't natural, they certainly weren't supernatural. Which makes plain, straightforward homicide the only alternative."

"Murder for what?" inquired Graham.

"That's just the hell of it! Where's the motive? There simply isn't any! I can imagine half a dozen countries who might regard the super-swift amputation of America's best brains as a suitable prelude to war, but when Swedish and German scientists get dragged in—with maybe a dozen more nationalities on the list Harriman's compiling—the entire situation becomes complicated to the point where it's absolutely fantastic." Picking up his typewritten copy of Webb's notes, he waved it dismally. "As fantastic as all this stuff." He cocked a speculative eye at the brooding Graham. "Your hunches started us on this hunt after heaven-alone-knows-what. Have you got any ideas to back them up?"

"None," Graham confessed. "Not one. We haven't yet found enough facts to provide the basis for a plausible theory. It's up to me to dig up more details."

"From where?"

"I'm going to see this fellow Fawcett whom Webb mentioned in his jottings. He ought to be able to tell me something interesting."

"Do you know Fawcett?" Sangster registered surprise.

"I've never heard of him. But Doctor Curtis, who is Webb's half-sister, may be able to put me in touch. I know Doctor Curtis well."

A slow smile came on Sangster's heavy face. He said, "How well?"

Graham grinned and replied, "Not as well as I'd like."

"Humph! So that's the way it is! Combining business with pleasure, eh?" He made a negligent gesture. "Oh, well, best of luck! If only you can nail down something more substantial than mere suspicions we can get the Federal Bureau of Investigation on the job."

"I'll see what I can do." The telephone shrilled as Graham reached the door. He hesitated, one hand on the doorknob, while the other grabbed the receiver, laid it on the desk, operated the amplifier.

Wohl's features glowed into the screen. He could not see Graham who was standing outside the scanner's angle of vision. He stared straight at Sangster while he spoke.

"Webb must have had the itch."

"The itch?" echoed Sangster, confusedly. "Why?"

"He'd painted his left arm, from shoulder to elbow, with iodine."

"What the devil for?" Sangster threw an appealing look at the listening Graham.

"Nothing. There wasn't anything the matter with his arm. My theory is either he had the itch or he did it to gratify his artistic instincts." Wohl's tough face cracked into a hard grin. "We've not finished the autopsy yet, but I thought I'd better let you know about this. When you've given it up, I can pose you another just as daffy."

"Out with it, man!" snapped Sangster.

"Mayo had the itch, too."

"Do you mean that he'd painted his arm as well?"

"Yes, with iodine," confirmed Wohl, maliciously enjoying himself. "Left arm, shoulder to elbow."

Staring fascinatedly at the screen, Sangster drew in a long, deep breath, said, "Thanks!" He replaced the receiver, gave Graham a despairing look.

"I'm on my way," said Graham.

Doctor Curtis had a strict, professional air of calm efficiency which Graham liked to ignore. She also had a mop of crisp black curls and a curvaceousness which he liked to admire with frankness she found annoying.

"Irwin had been behaving strangely for more than a month," she told him, unnecessarily eager to keep his attention on the subject about which he had come. "He would not confide in me despite my concern for him, which, I'm afraid, he chose to regard as feminine curiosity. Last Thursday, his peculiar attitude strengthened to a point of such ill-concealed apprehension that I began to wonder if he were on the verge of a nervous breakdown. I advised him to take a rest."

"Did anything occur last Thursday which might have caused him to worry unduly?"

"Nothing," she assured with confidence. "Or nothing that might affect him so seriously as to make him unbalanced. Of course, I must admit that he was extremely upset by the news of the death of Doctor Sheridan, but I don't see why that—"

"Excuse me," Graham interrupted. "Who was Sheridan?"

"An old friend of Irwin's. A British scientist. He died last Thursday, of heart disease, I understand."

"And still they come!" Graham murmured.

"I beg your pardon?" Doctor Curtis opened large, black eyes inquiringly.

"Just a comment," he evaded. Leaning forward, his muscular features intent, he asked, "Did Irwin have a friend or acquaintance named Fawcett?"

Her eyes widened more. "Oh, yes. He is Doctor Fawcett, the resident specialist at the State Asylum. Surely he cannot be involved in Irwin's death?"

"Not at all." He noted the obvious puzzlement which now overlay her normally tranquil pose. He was tempted to take advantage of it and put several more questions he wished to ask, but some queer subconscious quirk, some subtle hint of warning, made him desist. Feeling himself a fool to obey his inward impulses, he went on. "My department has a special interest in your brother's work, and his unfortunate end has left us with several features to clear up."

Apparently satisfied, she gave him her cool hand. "Do let me help you."

He held it until she had to drag it away. "You help by boosting my morale," he chided.

Leaving her, he ran down the steps leading from the twentieth floor surgery, reached the skyway which ran past mighty building-piles at a level three hundred feet above the ground.

A police gyrocar whined along the skyway, stopped before the surgery just in time to meet him as he got to the bottom of the steps. Lieutenant Wohl thrust his head out of its side window.

Wohl said, "Sangster told me you'd be here. I've come to pick you up."

Clambering into the sleek machine, Graham asked, "Has something broken loose? You look like a hound-dog on the scent."

"One of the boys discovered that Webb's and Mayo's last phone calls were both made to some big brain named Professor Dakin." He pressed the accelerator stud, the two-wheeled speedster plunged forward, its encased gyroscope emitting a faint hum. "This Dakin lives on William Street, right near your own hideout. Know him?"

"Like my own hands. You ought to know him, too."

"Me? Why?" Wohl whirled the wheel, took a skyway bend with a cop's official recklessness. The gyrocar kept rigidly upright while its occupants rolled sidewise in their seats. Graham clung to the handrail. Four other drivers on the skyway got the momentary meemies as they bulleted past, glaring after them.

Pulling in some breath, Graham said, "When did the police abandon the moulage method of making casts?"

"Five years back." Wohl aired his knowledge. "We now photograph impressions with stereoscopic cameras. Impressions on fibrous surfaces are recorded in relief with the aid of the parallel light beam."

"I know all that. But why is that method now used?"

"Because it's handier and absolutely accurate."

"Take it on from there," suggested Graham.

"It's been used ever since they found a way to measure stereoscopic depth by means of . . . heck!"—he risked a swift and apologetic glance at his passenger, and concluded—"the Dakin stereoscopic vernier."

"Correct. This fellow is the Dakin who invented it. My department financed his preliminary work. Frequently we get results for our money."

Wohl refrained from further comment while he concentrated on handling his machine. William Street slid rapidly toward them, its skyscrapers resembling oncoming giants.

With a sharp turn which produced a yelp of tormented rubber from the rear wheel, the gyrocar spun off the skyway and onto a descending corkscrew. It whirled down the spirals with giddying effect.

They hit ground level still at top pace, and Wohl straightened out, saying, "Those whirligigs sure give me a kick!"

Graham swallowed a suitable remark, his attention caught by the long, low, streamlined, aluminium-bronze shape of an advancing gyrocar. It flashed toward them along William Street, passed with an audible swish of ripped air, shot up the ramp to the corkscrew from which they'd just emerged. As it flashed by, Graham's sharp eyes registered the pale, haggard face staring fixedly through the machine's plastiglass windshield.

"There he goes!" exclaimed Graham, urgently. "Quick, Wohl—that was Dakin!"

Frantically spinning his wheel, and turning the gyrocar in its own length, Wohl fed current to the powerful dynamo.

The machine leaped forward, hogged a narrow gap between two descending cars and charged madly up the ramp.

"He'll be about six turns above us and near the top," Graham hazarded.

Grunting assent, Wohl muscled his controls as the police speedster spiralled rapidly upward. The fifth twist brought them behind an ancient, four-wheeled automobile holding the center of the chute and laboriously struggling along at a mere thirty.

They gave an impromptu demonstration of the greater mechanical advantage of two wheels with power on both. Cursing violently, Wohl swerved, fed juice, shot around the antiquated obstruction at fifty, leaving its driver jittering in his seat.

Like a monster silver bullet, their vehicle burst from the corkscrew onto the skyway, scattered a flock of private machines, dropped them behind. The speedometer said ninety.

Half a mile ahead, their aluminium-bronze quarry hummed full tilt along the elevated artery and maintained its lead.

Moving his emergency power lever, Wohl grumbled, "This is going to make junk of the batteries."

The gyrocar surged until its speedometer needle trembled over the hundred mark. The gyroscope's casing broadcast the angry sound of a million imprisoned bees. A hundred and ten. The tubular steel supports of the skyway railing zipped past like a solid fence, with no intervals apparent between them. One-twenty.

"The Grand Intersection humpback!" Graham shouted, warningly.

"If he hits it at this crazy pace he'll jump more than a hundred feet," growled Wohl. He narrowed his eyes as he squinted anxiously forward. "His 'scope will give him a square landing, but it won't save his tires. One of them will burst for sure. He's driving like a blithering maniac!"

"That's what makes it so obvious that something is damnably wrong." Centrifugal force held Graham's breath for him as they cut around another decrepit four-wheeler whose driver managed to gesticulate within the split-second available.

"Every jalopy ought to be banned from the skyways," Wohl snarled. He stared ahead. The shining shape of their quarry was whirling headlong around the shallow bend leading to Grand Intersection. "We've gained a bare hundred yards. He's driving all out, and he's got a special sports model at that. You'd think someone was chasing him."

"*We* are," remarked Graham dryly. His eyes sought the rearview mirror while his mind considered the likelihood of Dakin being pursued by someone other than themselves. What was Dakin running from, anyway? What did Mayo take a death-dive to escape? What did Webb shoot at as his dying act of defiance? What wiped out Bjornsen and made Luther expire with a gabble on his lips?

He gave up the fruitless speculation, noted that the road behind was clear of other chasers, raised his eyes as something threw a dark shadow over the gyrocar's transparent roof. It was a police helicopter hanging from spinning vanes, its landing wheels a yard above the hurtling car.

The two machines raced level for a few seconds. Wohl jabbed an authoritative finger at the police car across his vehicle's bonnet, then waved urgently toward the crazy car ahead.

Making a swift gesture of comprehension, the helicopter's pilot gained height and speed. Hopping great roofs, his machine roared through the air in desperate attempt to cut the skyway bend and beat Dakin to the intersection.

Without slackening pace in the slightest, Wohl hit the bend at full one-twenty. Tires shrieked piercingly as they felt the sidewise drag. Graham leaned heavily on the near-side door; Wohl's bulk pressed crushingly on him.

While centrifugal force held them in that attitude, and the tortured gyroscope strove to keep the machine upright, the tires gave up the battle and the car executed a sickening double-eight. It swooped crabwise across the concrete, missed a dawdling phaeton by a hairsbreadth, flashed between two other gyrocars, wiped the fender off a dancing four-wheeler and slammed into the side. Miraculously, the rails held.

Wohl gaped like a goldfish while he dragged in some air. He nodded toward the hump where the skyway curved over another elevated route which swept past it at right angles.

"Holy smoke!" he gasped. "Look at that."

From their vantage point four hundred yards away the crest of the hump appeared to bisect the midget windows of a more distant pile of masonry. Dakin's machine was precisely in the center of the crest with the police helicopter hovering impotently over it.

The fleeing car did not sink in perspective below the crest as it should have done in normal circumstances. It seemed to float slowly into the air until it reached the tops of the bisected windows and exposed a line of panes between its wheels and the crest. There, for one long second, it poised below the helicopter, apparently suspended in defiance of the law of gravity. Then, with still the same uncanny slowness, it sank from sight.

"Mad!" breathed Graham. He dabbed perspiration from his forehead. "Utterly and completely mad!"

He rolled his window downward until a deep dent in its plastiglass prevented it from descending farther. Both men listened intently, apprehensively. From over the crest came a short, sharp sound of rending metal, a few seconds of silence, then a muffled crash.

Without a word they struggled out of their battered gyrocar, sprinted along the skyway, over the long, smooth hump. They found a dozen machines, mostly modern gyrocars, drawn up beside a thirty-foot gap in the rails. White-faced drivers were grasping twisted railposts while they bent over and peered into the chasm beneath.

Shouldering through, Graham and Wohl looked down. Far below, on the side of the street opposite the lower and transverse skyway, a mass of shapeless metal made a tragic heap on the sidewalk. The face of the building that reared itself ten floors from the spot bore deep marks scored by the wreckage on its way down. The ruts of the road to oblivion.

A rubbernecking driver jabbered to nobody in particular, "Terrible! Terrible! He must have been clean out of his mind! He came over like a shell from a monster gun, smacked the side-rails, went right through and into that building. I heard him land down there." He licked dry lips. "Like a bug in a can. What a wallop! Terrible!"

The speaker's emotions were voiced for the rest. Graham could sense their awe, their horror. He could sense the excitement, the sadistic thirst, the corporate soul-stirring of the inevitable mob now gathering three hundred feet below. Mob hysteria is contagious, he thought, as he felt it rising like an invisible and hellish incense. One could get drunk on it. Men who were cold sober individually could be drunk collectively; drunk on mass-emotions. Emotions—the unseen intoxicant!

Another feeling drove away these morbid thoughts as fascinatedly he continued to stare downward: a feeling of guilty fear, like that of a man holding dangerous and punishable opinions in some far country where men are hanged for harboring the wrong thoughts. The sensation was so strong and emphatic that he made a mighty effort to discipline his mind. Dragging his gaze from the scene beneath, he nudged Wohl into attention.

"There's nothing we can do. You've reached the end of Dakin's trail and that's that! Let's get going."

Reluctantly, Wohl backed away from the gap. Noticing the defeated helicopter landing on the skyway, he hastened toward it.

"Wohl, homicide squad," he said, briefly. "Call Center Station on your short-wave, will you, and ask them to have my machine towed in for repairs. Tell them I'll phone a report through shortly."

Returning to the still gaping group of drivers, he questioned them, found one who was bound for William Street. This fellow had an ancient four-wheeler capable of a noisy fifty. Wohl accepted a lift with becoming condescension, climbed in crinkling his nose in disgust.

"Some move with the times, some jump ahead of the moment, and some just stay put." He picked disdainfully at the worn leatherette on which he was sitting. "This hell-buster has stayed put since Tut built the pyramids."

"Tut didn't," Graham contradicted.

"Tut's brother, then. Or his uncle. Or his sub-contractor. Who cares?" His head jerked backward as the driver let in a jumpy clutch and the car creaked forward. He uttered a potent name, looked aggrieved, said to Graham, "I'm letting you tote me around because, being just another wage-slave, I've got to do as I'm told. But I've still no notion of what you're seeking, if anything. Does your department know something special that isn't for publication?"

"We know nothing more than you do. It all started with me having some vague suspicions, and my superiors backing them up." He gazed speculatively at the cracked and yellowish windshield. "I first smelled the skunk. For my pains, I've now got to dig out the stinker—or sing small."

"Well, I've got to hand it to you for getting hunches and having the nerve to play them." He bounced around on his seat, said complainingly, "Look, homicide on the job, in a jalopy! That's where it gets us. Everybody dies, and even we're in a corpse-wagon." He bounced again, hard. "I can see by the way things are shaping that I'll finish up playing with feathers and treacle. But I'm with you as long as I stay sane."

"Thanks," Graham responded, smiling. He studied his companion. "By the way, what's your other name?"

"Art."

"Thanks, Art," he corrected.

Chapter 3

Their careful search of Dakin's place revealed nothing worthy of note; no last, dramatic message, no hidden jottings, no feature that could be considered in any way abnormal. As a route to the solution of their indefinable puzzle, it was somewhat of a dead end.

Discovering the late scientist's original and crude model of his vernier, Wohl amused himself by projecting its standard stereoscopic cube upon a small screen. Twiddling the micrometer focusing screw that controlled the cube's perspective, he made the geometrical skeleton flat enough to appear almost two-dimensional, then deep enough to resemble an apparently endless tunnel.

"Cute!" he murmured.

Graham came out of a back room holding a small, nearly empty vial of iodine in his fingers.

"I looked for this on another hunch. It was in his medicine chest along with enough patent cure-alls to stock a drugstore. Dakin always was something of a hypochondriac." He put the vial on the table, surveyed it morosely. "So that means exactly nothing." His dissatisfied glance went round the room. "We're only losing time in this place. I want to see Doctor Fawcett, at the State Asylum. Can you run me there?"

"I'll phone first." Using Dakin's instrument, he talked to his station, cut off, said to Graham, "There will be no autopsy on Dakin. They can't dissect pulp!" He put away the vernier, pocketed the vial, opened the door. "Come on. Let's have a look at your asylum—some day it may be home, sweet home!"

Darkness was a shroud over the Hudson. A sullen moon scowled down through ragged clouds. Incongruously, a distant neon repeatedly flashed its message in blood-red letters fifty feet high: BEER HERE. Observing it, Wohl subconsciously licked his lips. Fidgeting on the sidewalk, they waited for the gyrocar which Wohl had ordered over the phone.

The machine hummed down the street, its long floodlight blazing. Wohl met it, said to the uniformed driver, "I'll take her myself. We're going to Albany."

Climbing into the seat, he waited until Graham had plumped beside him, eased the machine forward.

Graham said to him, warningly, "We're in a hurry—but not that much."

"What d'you mean?"

"Please, I'd like to get there in one lump. I don't function so well in several parts."

"Nobody functions so well when you get after them. Are you a stockholder in the local graveyard?" Wohl's beefy face quirked. "There's one comfort about hanging around with you."

"What's that?"

"I'll die with my boots on."

Graham smiled, said nothing. The car picked up speed. Twenty minutes later he was hugging the rail as they cornered. Still he said nothing. They pelted northward, reached Albany in hours—good going even for Wohl.

"This is well outside my official stamping-ground," Wohl commented, as they pulled up outside their destination. "So far as I'm concerned, I'm off duty. You've merely brought a friend along."

The new State Asylum sprawled its severe, ultra-modern architecture over a square mile of former parkland. It was very evident that Doctor Fawcett was the leading light in its administration.

He was a skinny little runt, all dome and duck's feet, his top-heavy features triangular as they sloped in toward a pointed goatee beard, his damn-you eyes snapping behind rimless pince-nez.

His small form even smaller behind a desk that looked the size of a field, he sat stiffly upright, wagged Graham's copy of Webb's jottings. When he spoke it was with the assertive air of one whose every wish is a command, whose every opinion is the essence of pure reason.

"A most interesting revelation of my poor friend Webb's mental condition. Very sad, very sad!" Unhooking his pince-nez, he used them to tap the paper and emphasize his pontifications. "I suspected him of having an obsession, but must confess that I did not realize he'd become so completely unbalanced."

"What made you suspicious?" Graham asked.

"I am a chess enthusiast. So was Webb. Our friendship rested solely upon our mutual fondness for the game. We had little else in common. Webb was entirely a physicist whose work had not the slightest relation to mental diseases; nevertheless, he showed a sudden and avid interest in the subject. At his own request, I permitted him to visit this asylum and observe some of our patients."

"Ah!" Graham leaned forward. "Did he give any reason for this sudden interest?"

"He did not offer one, nor did I ask for one," replied Doctor Fawcett, dryly. "The patients who interested him most were those with consistent delusions coupled to a persecution complex. He concentrated particularly upon the schizophrenics."

"And what may those be?" put in Wohl, innocently.

Doctor Fawcett raised his brows. "Persons suffering from schizophrenia, of course."

"I'm still no wiser," Wohl persisted.

With an expression of ineffable patience, Doctor Fawcett said, "They are schizoid egocentrics."

Making a gesture of defeat, Wohl growled, "A nut's a nut whether in fancy dress or otherwise."

Fawcett eyed him with distaste. "I perceive you are a creature of dogmatic preconceptions."

"I'm a cop," Wohl informed, blinking. "And I know when I'm being given the runaround."

"You must pardon our ignorance, doctor," Graham chipped in smoothly. "Could you explain in less technical terms?"

"Schizophrenics," answered Fawcett, speaking as one speaks to a child, "are persons suffering from a special type of mental disease which, a century ago, was known as dementia praecox. They have a split personality the dominant one of which lives in a world of fantasy that seems infinitely more real than the world of reality. While many forms of dementia are characterized by hallucinations which vary both in strength and detail, the fantastic world of the schizophrenic is vivid and unvarying. To put it in as elementary a manner as possible, he always has the same nightmare."

"I see," commenced Graham, doubtfully.

Putting on his glasses with meticulous care, Fawcett stood up. "I will let you see one of the inmates in whom Webb is interested."

Showing them through the door, he conducted them along a series of passages to the asylum's east wing. Here, he reached a group of cells, stopped outside one, gestured.

They peered cautiously through a small, barred opening, saw a naked man. He was standing by his bed, his thin legs braced apart, his unnaturally distended abdomen thrust out. The sufferer's ghastly eyes were fixed upon his own stomach with unwavering and hellish concentration.

Fawcett whispered rapidly, "It is a peculiarity of schizophrenia that the victim often strikes a pose, sometimes obscene, which he can maintain without stirring for a period of time impossible to the normal human being. They have phases when they become living statues, often repulsively. This particular case is a typical poseur. His stricken mind has convinced itself that he has a live dog inside his abdomen, and he spends hours watching for a sign of movement."

"Good heavens!" exclaimed Graham, shocked.

"A characteristic delusion, I assure you," said Fawcett, professionally unmoved. He looked through the bars as if academically considering a pinned moth. "It was Webb's irrational comments about this case that made me think him a little eccentric."

"What was Webb's reaction?" Graham glanced again into the cell, turned his eyes thankfully away. The thought in his mind was the same as that in Wohl's—but for the grace of fate, there go I!

"He was fascinated by this patient, and he said to me 'Fawcett, that poor devil has been prodded around by unseen medical students. He is mutilated trash tossed aside by supervivisectionists.' " Fawcett stroked his beard, registered tolerant amusement. "Melodramatic but completely illogical."

A shudder ran through Graham's muscular frame. Despite iron nerves, he felt sick. Wohl's face, too, was pale, and both sensed the same inward relief when Fawcett led the way back to the office.

"I asked Webb what the deuce he meant," Doctor Fawcett continued, quite unperturbed, "but he only laughed a little unpleasantly and quoted that adage about when ignorance is bliss it is folly to be wise. A week later he phoned me in a state of considerable excitement and asked if I could get him data concerning the incidence of goiter in imbeciles."

"Did you get it?"

"Yes." Fawcett dived down behind his huge desk, slid open a drawer, came up with a paper. "I had it here ready for him. Since he's dead, the information comes too late." He flipped the paper across to Graham.

"Why," Graham exclaimed, looking it over, "this states that there is not one case of goiter among the two thousand inmates of this asylum. Reports from other asylums give it as unknown or exceedingly rare."

"Which doesn't mean anything. It's evidence only of the negative fact that imbeciles are not very susceptible to a disease which isn't common." He glanced at Wohl, his tones slightly acid. "When a disease isn't common, it's because not many people are susceptible to it. Probably the same data applies to any two thousand bus drivers, or paint salesmen—or cops."

"When I catch goiter, I'll tell you," promised Wohl, surlily.

"What causes goiter?" Graham put in.

Fawcett said, promptly, "A deficiency of iodine."

Iodine! Graham and Wohl exchanged startled glances before the former asked, "Has a superfluity of iodine anything to do with imbecility?"

His goatee wagging, Fawcett laughed openly. "If it did, there would be a great proportion of idiots among seafaring folk who eat foods rich in iodine."

A message burned into Graham's mind, red-hot. Wohl's face betrayed the fact that he'd got it also. A message from the illogical dead.

Sailors are notoriously susceptible.

Susceptible to what? To illusions and to maritime superstitions based upon illusions?—the sea serpent, the sirens, the Flying Dutchman, mermaids, and the bleached, bloated, soul-clutching things whose clammy faces bob and wail in the moonlit wake?

Must extend the notion, and get data showing how seaboard dwellers compare with country folk.

Displaying a forced casualness, Graham retrieved Webb's notes from the desk. "Thanks, doctor. You've been a great help."

"Don't hesitate to get in touch with me if I can be of further assistance," Fawcett advised. "If you do eventually arrive at the root cause of poor Webb's condition, I'd appreciate the details." His short laugh was more chilling than apologetic. "Every competent analysis of a delusion is a valuable contribution to knowledge of the whole."

They returned to New York as fast as they had left, their cogitating silence being broken only once when Wohl remarked, "The entire affair suggests an epidemic of temporary insanity among scientists whose brains have been overworked."

Graham grunted, offered no comment.

"Genius is akin to madness," persisted Wohl, determined to bolster his theory. "Besides, knowledge can't go on increasing forever without some of the best minds giving way when they strain to encompass the lot."

"No scientist tries to learn the lot. Knowledge already is far too much for any one mind, and that is why every scientist is a specialist in his own field though he may be an ignoramus about things totally outside the scope of his own work."

It was Wohl's turn to grunt. Concentrating on his driving with no better results at the sharpest corners, he voiced not another word until he arrived at Graham's address. Then he dropped his passenger with a brief, "See you in the morning, Bill," and hummed away.

The morning was bright, symbolic of a new day that brought early developments. Graham was standing before his mirror, his electric shaver whirring busily, when the telephone shrilled. The youth in the visor eyed him and said, "Mr. Graham?"

"Yes, I'm Graham."

"This is the Smithsonian," responded the other. "Mr. Harriman had a message for you late last night but was not able to get in touch with you."

"I was in Albany. What's the message?"

"Mr. Harriman said to tell you he has been to all the news agencies, and finds they've reported the deaths of eighteen scientists within the last five weeks. Seven of them were foreigners, and eleven American. The number is about six times the average, as the news agencies rarely report more than three per month."

"Eighteen!" ejaculated Graham. He studied the face picked up by the faraway scanner. "Have you got their names?"

"Yes." The youth dictated them while Graham copied them down. He gave their respective nationalities. "Anything more, sir?"

"Please convey my thanks to Mr. Harriman and ask him to phone me at the office when convenient."

"Very well, Mr. Graham." The youth disconnected, left him pondering deeply. "Eighteen!"

On the other side of the room the telenews receiver's gong chimed softly. Crossing to it, he raised the lid, exposed the press-replica screen which, in his apparatus, was licensed for the *New York Sun's* transmissions.

The *Sun's* early morning edition began to roll at sedate reading-pace across the screen while he watched it with part of his mind elsewhere. Presently, his eyes sharpened and his concentration returned as another headline appeared.

SCIENTIST'S DEATH DIVE

PROFESSOR SAMUEL C. DAKIN, FIFTY-TWO YEARS OLD, WILLIAM STREET PHYSICIST, TOOK THE GRAND INTERSECTION HUMPBACK IN HIS SPORTS GYROCAR LAST EVENING, AND PLUNGED TO HIS DEATH AT MORE THAN A HUNDRED MILES AN HOUR.

The report continued to half-column length, included a photograph of the wreck, several references to "this departed genius," and stated that the police were looking into the cause of the tragedy. It concluded with a comment to the effect that this was the third successive death of a New York scientist since the previous morning, "those of Professor Walter Mayo and Doctor Irwin Webb having been detailed yesterday in our evening edition."

From the automatic-record locker beneath the screen, Graham extracted his photographic copy of the *Sun's* evening issue. Mayo's and Webb's cases were in juxtaposition; the former headed: MAYO FALLS FROM MARTIN; and the latter: ANOTHER SCIENTIST DIES. Both reports were superficial, revealing nothing more except that "the police are investigating."

Wohl turned up just then. He charged into the apartment, his eyes agleam. He waved the *Sun* aside with a short, "I've seen it."

"What's all the excitement about?"

"My hunch." He sat down, breathed heavily. "You're not the only one who gets hunches." He puffed, grinned apologetically, puffed again. "They've held those autopsies. Mayo and Webb were full of dope."

"They were drugged?" asked Graham, incredulously.

"It was mescal," Wohl went on. "A special and very highly refined form of mescal. Their stomachs contained strong traces of it." A pause while he got his breath. "And their kidneys were rich in methylene blue."

"Methylene blue!" Graham's mind struggled in vain to make something rational of this information.

"The boys followed up these facts pretty fast. They found mescal, methylene blue, and iodine in Mayo's, Webb's and Dakin's laboratories. We'd have found them ourselves if we'd known what to look for."

Graham nodded agreement. "It's fair to assume that an autopsy on Dakin would have produced the same result."

"I would think so," Wohl approved. "The boys also discovered that the junk in the furnace of Mayo's distillation setup was Indian hemp. God knows how he'd smuggled it in, but that's what it was. It looks as if he must have been about to experiment with drugs other than mescal."

"If he was," declared Graham, positively, "it was solely by way of scientific experiment. Mayo was never a drug addict."

"So it seems," said Wohl, dryly.

Graham tossed him the list provided by Harriman. "Take a look at that. According to the Smithsonian, those eighteen have rolled up during the last five weeks. The law of averages suggests that three or maybe four of those deaths were normal and inevitable." He seated himself on a corner of the table, swung one leg to and fro. "That, in turn, suggests that the others were not normal. It also means that we're involved in something a darned sight bigger than first it seemed."

Scanning the list, Wohl commented, "Not only big, but crazy. All drug cases have their crazy aspects. This one's so daffy that it's stuck on my mind since last night." He made a face. "I've kept on picturing that guy we saw in the cell—pregnant with dog."

"Let's forget him for a while."

"I wish I could!"

"What we've got to date," Graham continued, thoughtfully, "poses several questions the answers to which ought to lead us somewhere." He stabbed an indicative forefinger at the list which Wohl was still holding. "We don't know on what basis those news agencies determine their average of three. Is it over the last twelve months, or the last five years, or the last twenty? If it's a long-term average, this month's deaths beat it by six times, what were last month's casualties and last year's? In other words, what are the total deaths since the start?—and what started them?"

"The first suicide began them," Wohl declared. "The rest were imitative." He handed back the list. "Take a look over police files sometime. You'll find time after time when murder and suicide were temporarily contagious. One spectacular and well-publicized crime often induces several others of similar type."

"I've said from the beginning and I still maintain that these weren't suicides. I knew Mayo and Dakin very well indeed. I knew Webb by repute. They just weren't the psychological types likely to indulge in self-destruction, even if full of drugs."

"That's the point," Wohl emphasized, stubbornly. "You knew them sober. You didn't know them snowed-up. A guy hopped to the eyeballs isn't the same individual—he's someone else. He's capable of anything, including shooting at thin air or jumping off a roof."

"I'll give you that much." Graham looked bothered as he folded the list and put it in his pocket. "This mescal feature is a puzzler."

"Not to my mind, it isn't. The drug traffic is spread by personal recommendation. I reckon that some scientist, driven half-nuts by overwork, has found a new-fangled stimulator more dangerous than he knows. He's used it, suggested it to others, and some of them have tried it. Maybe it worked for a while, but, like arsenic, it's accumulative. It piled up inside them until eventually they went gaga one by one." He spread broad hands. "And here we are!"

"I wish it were as simple as that—but something inside me says that it isn't."

"Something inside you," scoffed Wohl. "Another dog!"

Preoccupied, Graham watched the morning *Sun* still crawling across his screen. He opened his mouth to voice a suitable retort, closed it without speaking. The blurred words on the screen suddenly sharpened, became clear. He stood up as Wohl followed his gaze.

NOTED EXPERT'S END

STEPHEN REED, SIXTY, OF FAR ROCKWAY, CREATED A SCENE OUTSIDE THE CENTRAL LIBRARY ON FIFTH AVENUE THIS MORNING AND THEN THREW HIMSELF UNDER AN EXPRESS LOAD-CARRIER. HE WAS KILLED IMMEDIATELY. REED WAS ONE OF THE WORLD'S LEADING AUTHORITIES IN OPTICAL SURGERY.

Graham switched off the receiver, closed down the screen, reached for his hat. "Nineteen!" he said, softly.

"Oh, holy smoke!" Wohl got up, followed him to the door. "Here we go again!"

Chapter 4

As usual, most of the half a hundred witnesses of the last of Stephen Reed had vanished beyond trace. Someone hurriedly had called a cop, the police officer had phoned his station, and a reporter waiting there had passed the news to the *Sun*.

It took two hours to find three onlookers. The first was a pear-shaped man with sweaty jowls.

He said to Graham, "I was passing this guy and not taking much notice. I got enough to worry me, see? He let out an awful yell, did a sort of dance and ran into the traffic."

"And then?"

"I could feel what was coming and looked away."

The next proved to be a bulky blonde. She was edgy. She held a small handkerchief in her hand and nervously nibbled at one corner of it while she talked.

"He gave me a turn. He came along like someone watching for a ghost. I thought he'd seen one. He shouted, waved his arms about, and rushed madly into the road."

"Did you hear *what* he shouted?" Graham asked.

She gnawed the handkerchief again. Her pale blue eyes were scared.

"He upset me so much that I didn't catch it. He bawled loudly and hoarsely, at the top of his voice. Something about, 'No! No! For pity's sake, no!' and a bit of other crazy stuff."

"You didn't see anything that might have caused him to act like that?"

"No—that was the worst of it!" She had another chew, shifted her eyes around as if straining to see the unseeable.

"She'll be consulting clairvoyants before this week is through," commented Wohl, as she departed.

The third witness, a suave, well-groomed man with a cultured voice, said, "I noticed Mr. Reed walking toward me with a most peculiar look in his eyes. They were bright and glassy, as if he'd primed them with belladonna."

"Done what?" put in Wohl, curiously.

"Primed them with belladonna, like we do on the stage."

"Oh." Wohl subsided.

"He was looking alertly all over the place, up and down and around. He had an air of apprehension. I felt that he was seeking something he did not want to find."

"Go on," urged Graham.

"As he came near me his face went white. He seemed stricken with sudden and acute fear. He made desperate gestures, like a man trying to ward off a fatal blow, screamed incoherently and raced into the road." The witness shrugged fatalistically. "A twenty-ton load-carrier hit him. Undoubtedly, he died instantaneously."

"You didn't hear what he said?"

"I'm afraid I didn't."

"There was nothing to indicate the reason for his fear?"

"Not a thing," assured the other, authoritatively. "The incident moved me so much that I sought immediately for a cause. I could not find one. It appeared to me that he must have been overcome by some feature not apparent—a tumor on the brain, for example."

"We are very much obliged to you." Graham watched the suave man go. He brooded silently while Wohl picked up the phone and called the morgue.

What was that subtle, unidentified essence in the human make-up which occasionally caused Malaysians to run amok, foaming at the mouth, kriss in hand, intent on wholesale and unreasoning slaughter? What other essence, similar but not the same, persuaded the entire nation of Japanese to view ceremonial suicide with cold-blooded equanimity? What made fanatical Hindus gladly cast themselves to death before the lumbering juggernaut? Was this present outbreak due to the insidious hold of some new virus, breeding and spreading in places more civilized, perhaps stimulated horrifically by mescal, iodine and methylene blue?

He gave up the speculation as Wohl pronged the phone. Wohl turned to him with the martyred air of one burdened for past sins.

"They won't be carving Reed for a while, but they've found he fits the general pattern in one respect: he'd painted himself with iodine."

"Left arm?"

"No. Evidently he believed in variety, or perhaps he was plain ornery. He did his left leg, hip to knee."

"Then we can add him to our list," decided Graham. "We can say he's another case without being able to define said case."

"Yes, I guess so."

"You know, Art, this drug addict theory of yours may apply to the mescal, but what about the other items being used in association with it? Methylene blue and iodine aren't drugs in the sense that you mean. They're innocuous, they're not habit-forming. They don't make folk go haywire."

"Neither does water, but plenty of people take it with whisky."

Graham made an impatient gesture. "That's beside the point. As I see it, we've two logical steps still to take. The first is to give this Reed's place the once-over. The second is to seek expert advice on what mescal, methylene blue and iodine can do to people when used like all these bodies have been using it."

"Reed's dump is way out," Wohl remarked. "I'll get the car."

The home of the late Stephen Reed was a bachelor's villa run by a middle-aged and motherly housekeeper. Outside of domestic arrangements, she knew nothing and, when told the tragic news, promptly became incapable of telling anything she might have known.

While she retired to her room, they raked expertly through Reed's study. They found a formidable mass of papers through which they searched with frenzied haste.

"The chief will be the next to have a heart attack," Wohl prophesied, grabbing himself another handful of letters.

"Why?"

"The local boys ought to be in on this. The way you make me go rampaging around other people's bailiwicks would give him an apoplectic stroke. You may not know it, but you've got me headed straight for demotion."

Graham grunted derisively, continued with his search. It was some time before he came up with a letter in his hand.

"Listen to this." He read it aloud. "Dear Steve, I'm sorry to learn that Mayo is giving you some of his stuff. I know you're deeply interested, of course, but must tell you frankly that to play with it is a waste of valuable time. My advice is that you throw it in the ashcan and forget it. It will be safer there, as I know only too well." He glanced up. "It bears Webb's address, and it's signed, 'Irwin.' "

"What's the date on it?"

"May twenty-second."

"Not so old."

"A double-link," Graham observed. "Mayo to Webb and Reed. It's being passed from one to another. I expected that."

"So did I." Wohl turned over papers, scanning them rapidly. "Personal recommendation, like I told you. Though it looks like Webb tried to discourage Reed for some reason."

"The reason was that to fool around with it meant death—and Webb knew it even then! On May twenty-second he knew that his days were numbered as surely as I know that I'm standing here in my pants. He wasn't able to do much about it, but he tried to steer Reed away from the grave."

Looking up from his rummaging, Wohl complained, "You say the damnedest things. You'll be suggesting that the finger is put on us next."

"I'm not so sure that it won't—once we really start to get someplace."

The same cold shiver insinuated itself into his back muscles, and he flexed his shoulder-blades in an effort to shake it off. He had a keen sense of psychic frustration, as if his brain were permitted to probe in all directions except one. Whenever it tended that way a warning bell sounded within him and his questing mind obediently withdrew.

Cramming a handful of insignificant papers back into its file, he growled, "Not a thing. All about eyeballs and optic nerves. He slept with 'em and ate 'em."

"Same here," agreed Wohl. "What's conjunctivitis?"

"Eye-trouble."

"I thought it was something to do with railroad switching." He thumbed through the last of his sheets, returned them to their place. "He's got no laboratory or surgery here. He operated at the Eye and Ear Hospital, in Brooklyn. We ought to try there, eh?"

"I'll call the office first. Time I reported." Using Reed's phone, Graham had a long talk with Sangster, finished, said to Wohl, "We're wanted there sooner than immediately. They've been waiting for us since first thing this morning. Sangster's acting like somebody's swallowed an atom bomb."

"*We?*" emphasized Wohl raising his eyebrows.

"Both of us," Graham confirmed. "Something mighty important is in the wind." Rubbing his chin, he surveyed the room in open disappointment. "This place is as fruitful as a vacuum. Whether or not we're wanted urgently, we'd better try that hospital on our way—it's our last chance to get an item out of Reed."

"Let's go."

Doctor Pritchard, a tall, slender and youthful individual, got them after the hospital's secretary had passed them from hand to hand. Welcoming them, he gave them chairs, took off his white coat.

"I suppose you wish to question me about poor Reed?"

"You know he's dead?" Graham shot at him.

Pritchard nodded soberly. "The police informed us. They phoned soon after it happened."

"Whether it was suicide is a moot point," Graham told him. "Maybe he bumped himself deliberately, maybe he didn't, though I don't think he did, myself. Nevertheless, the evidence shows that he was far from normal at the time. Can you explain his condition?"

"I can't."

"Had you noticed him behaving queerly of late?"

"I don't think so. I was his assistant, and I'm sure that I'd have noticed any exceptional peculiarity of his." He thought a moment. "Up to three days ago he was more than usually preoccupied. That is nothing extraordinary in a person of his character and profession."

"Why up to three days ago?" Graham persisted.

"I've not seen him since then. He'd taken a short leave of absence, to complete some work."

"He gave you no indication of the nature of that work?"

"No. He was never communicative about his outside interests."

"Did you know Professor Mayo or Doctor Webb?"

"I've heard of them. I don't know them."

"Did Reed ever mention either of them to you? Or had he spoken of being involved with them in any way?"

"No," said Pritchard, positively.

Graham gave Wohl a look of defeat. "A dead end!" He returned his attention to Pritchard. "Reed was an eminent ophthalmic surgeon, I understand. Would that cause him to take a special interest in drugs?"

"Within certain limits it might."

"Have you anyone here who is an authority on drugs in general?"

Pritchard pondered again. "I reckon Deacon is our best for that—d'you want him?"

"Please."

He rang a bell. To the attendant who responded, he said, "Ask Doctor Deacon if he's free to come here for a minute."

Deacon arrived looking irritated. He was rubber-gloved and had a beam-light strapped over his iron-gray hair.

"This is a devil of a time to—" he began. He saw Graham and Wohl, added, "I beg your pardon."

"Sorry to disturb you, doctor," Graham soothed. "I'll save your time by being brief. Can you tell me what happens to a person who paints himself with iodine and doses himself with mescal and methylene blue?"

"He ends up in an asylum," asserted Deacon, without hesitation.

Wohl uttered a pained, "Youps!" and stared down at his stomach.

"You mean that literally?" pressed Graham. "It would expedite insanity?"

"Nothing of the sort! I mean no more than that he'd be insane to do anything so pointless."

"That isn't what I want, doctor. I'm asking for the physical effects, without regard for the motive."

"Well," said Deacon, more amiably. "I don't pretend to advise you as authoritatively as could certain other specialists, but I'd say the mescal would drive the subject higher than a kite if he absorbed a sufficient dosage. The methylene blue

would cleanse the kidneys and discolor the urine. As for the iodine, it would function as a germicide, stain the skin and, being a halogen, would permeate the whole
system in very short time."

"Do you think the three in association might create another and more positive
effect—say by one assisting the reaction of another, like a catalyst?"

"You've got me there," Deacon confessed. "Multiple interactions are still the
subject of research and will continue to be for many years to come."

Graham stood up, thanked him and Pritchard, then said to Wohl, "Looks as if
Reed was a very late comer in this deadly game. He never had time to say much,
do much. Whatever is behind this can hit quick and hit hard."

"It's harder to hit a moving object," observed Wohl, with grim humor. He followed Graham out. "Back to Sangster now?"

"Yes. We'd better get there fast. He'll be jumpy if we don't reach him soon."

Sangster had with him a tall, middle-aged and dapper individual of military
appearance. Frowning pointedly at the clock as the two arrived, he introduced the
newcomer as Colonel Leamington.

'The entire investigation has been taken out of this department's hands," Sangster
announced, without beating about the bush. Reaching across his desk, he handed
Graham a paper.

The sheet rustled in his fingers as Graham read, "Your application for immediate transfer to the United States Intelligence Service has been approved, and said
transfer is effected as of this date. You will take your commission and accept orders from Colonel John H. Leamington who, until further notice, you will regard
as your departmental superior."

Gulping as he noted the famous signature at the bottom of the letter, he looked
inquiringly at Sangster. "But, sir, I have made no such application."

"You may tear the letter up, if you wish," Sangster remarked.

Colonel Leamington intervened with, "The position, Mr. Graham, is that we
wish you to continue your investigation with better facilities than are accorded
you in your present position."

"Thank you," he answered, somewhat dazed.

"One of our news-agency men reported the questions made by Harriman on
your behalf. It drew our attention to a matter that otherwise might have escaped
us for some time." He stroked his neatly clipped mustache, his face serious, very
serious. "Eleven of these departed scientists were Americans. They were men of
incalculable value to their country. Great as it may be, their loss is as nothing
when compared with the menace of further losses. The Government cannot ignore their sudden and mysterious demise."

"I see."

'Then you accept this commission?" pressed Colonel Leamington.

"Yes, yes, of course!" He studied the letter with concealed pride which was not
lessened by Wohl's open envy. To be one of the Government's most tried and trusted
band, one of Uncle Sam's most privileged operators!

Taking his ring from Leamington, he put it on the right hand, third finger. It
fitted perfectly, and he knew that it must have been prepared in anticipation of

his acceptance. He also knew that upon its super-hard iridium inner surface were delicate inscriptions too small to be seen with the naked eye; microscopic data giving his name, height, weight, Bertillon measurements and fingerprints formulae, as well as his Service number and a faithful though infinitely small copy of his own signature.

This modest ornament was his only badge, his only warrant of authority, its meaning concealed from all but those equipped to read—but it was the open sesame to officialdom everywhere.

As these thoughts passed through his mind there came a faint and eerie sense of overhanging peril; the warning note again, vague, indefinite, but thoroughly disturbing. He looked once more at his ring, knew that it could be regarded from another and ghastlier angle: it might prove the sole means of identifying him in horrible, mangling death—as many others had been so identified.

What was it that Webb had talked about? "Mutilated trash cast aside by super-vivisectionists."

Pushing the memory aside, he said, "One thing, colonel: I would like to have the continued cooperation of Lieutenant Wohl. He's in this as deeply as me—and we need each other."

He evaded Wohl's look of gratification, listened while Leamington replied.

"Har-humph! Somewhat irregular, but I think it can be arranged. I have little doubt that the chief of police can be persuaded to grant Lieutenant Wohl a roving commission until such time as he's seen this job through."

"Thank you, sir," Graham and Wohl chorused.

Sangster's phone yelped for attention, he answered it, passed it to Graham, saying, "Harriman."

"Hello, Harriman," called Graham. "Yes, I got your list. Thanks a lot!" He paused as the second phone on Sangster's desk clamored deafeningly, and Sangster reached to take it. "There's a deuce of a row here. The other phone bawling. What was that you said?" He paused, listened, then said, "Sorry, Harriman, I can't tell you anything just yet. Yes, six times the average is something that calls for an explanation, and that's what I'm out to get—if it can be got!"

He ceased speaking while Sangster put down the other phone and whispered, "Doctor Curtis, for you."

"Listen, Harriman," he continued hurriedly, "all these scientists are people of different nationalities, ages and types. The conclusion is that nothing is being aimed at any one country—unless someone is clever enough and ruthless enough to bump some of his own in order to avert suspicion. I doubt that."

Harriman said, 'There's nothing political about this, any more than there is about a new disease."

"Exactly! Different as they may be, these scientists *must* have shared one thing in common—the thing that directly or indirectly brought about their deaths. I want to find that common denominator. Rake me up every detail you can discover about the persons on your list and any earlier cases you may see fit to add. Phone them to"—he looked inquiringly at Leamington, was given a number, and finished—"to Colonel Leamington at Boro 8-19638."

Ringing off, he took up the other phone, spoke rapidly. The others studied his changing expression as he talked.

Finishing, he told them, "Doctor Curtis has received a long-distance call from Professor Edward Beach. He said that he had just read the accounts of Webb's and Mayo's deaths. He expressed much sorrow, but Doctor Curtis thought him unusually curious about the details of the tragedies."

"Well?" prompted Leamington.

"This Beach is an old friend of Webb's, according to Doctor Curtis. I know him, too. He's the man who designed the stereoscopic owl-eye camera which the police use in conjunction with Dakin's vernier. He is employed by the National Camera Company, at their Silver City plant, in Idaho. Beach is precisely the sort of scientist likely to have valuable information concerning Mayo, Webb and Dakin." He paused a moment, to lend impressiveness to what he was about to say, then added, "Especially since he made a point of asking Doctor Curtis whether she knew if Webb, like Mayo and Dakin, had been working on Bjornsen's formula prior to his end."

"Bjornsen!" ejaculated Sangster.

"You can see the implication," Graham went on. "Beach is linked to these others exactly as *they* were linked to each other—by correspondence based on mutual interests. He's got a place in this death-chain, but death hasn't reached him yet! He's a prospective victim still in condition to talk. I've got to see him and make him talk before he becomes body number twenty." He consulted his watch. "With luck, I can catch the 10:30 stratplane for Boise."

Wohl said, "Do I come, or are you on your own?"

"I'll take this by myself. While I'm on my way, phone Battery Park Stratosphere Station, Art, and book me a seat on the 10:30."

Reaching for the phone, Wohl asked, "And after that, I do what? Give me something to follow—I hate wasting time."

"You can make a cross-check on the data Harriman's getting. See if you can make contact with the police authorities in all the places where these scientists died, ask them for full and complete details of the deaths. Get them to check thoroughly on every item no matter how minute or seemingly unimportant. Bully, cajole or do whatever else you can to persuade them to obtain exhumation orders and conduct autopsies." He looked at Leamington. "Is all this okay with you, Colonel?"

"I'm satisfied to let you run this your own way," Leamington approved. "I'm taking it for granted that the man who starts something is best fitted to finish it."

"We're worrying about quite a lot of people who started something that none of them finished," Graham pointed out. "This thing—whatever it is—has a remarkable aptitude for finishing the starters before they get anywhere." He grinned ruefully. "I'm not immortal, either—but I'll do my best."

Snatching his hat, he was gone, bound for Battery Park, the 10:30 stratplane and the worst disaster in the history of the New World.

Chapter 5

The New York-Boise-Seattle stratosphere express dived down from the atmosphere's upper reaches, cut its oxygen from its pressurized cabin, leveled with a thunderous burst of rockets, swept beneath the undersides of fleecy clouds.

With the little town of Oakley nestling on its banks, Goose Creek rolled under the fleet vessel's bow. Far to port and well to stern gleamed the northern fringes of Utah's Great Salt Lake. About a hundred and fifty miles to go—a mere ten minutes' run!

A cigarette that Graham had lit over Oakley was still only half consumed when the stratplane banked away from the valley of the Snake and curved toward Boise. The turn brought Silver City on the port side where it was easily perceivable in the dry, dustless atmosphere of the locality. Its white and cream-colored buildings glowed in the sun-light. Bobbin-shaped chemical reservoirs of the National Camera plant, slung on huge towers, stood out clearly on the city skyline.

Thrusting his feet at the footrests to resist body-surge caused by the ship's rapid deceleration, Graham took two more drags of his cigarette, cast another glance at the far vista of Silver City. For a moment, it was still there, sharp and clear in detail upon the horizon; the next moment it had gone in a mighty cloud of heaving vapor.

Crushing his cigarette between unnerved fingers, he rose partway in his seat, his eyes staring incredulously at the faraway spectacle. The cloud bloomed hugely, swelled with the primal vigor of an oncoming dust-storm, its bloated crests curling angrily as they gained altitude. Small black specks soared above this upper edge, hung momentarily in mid-air, dropped back into the swirling chaos.

"God in heaven!" breathed Graham. His eyes strained unbelievingly. He knew that for the strange specks to be visible from such a distance they must be big, very big—as large as buildings. In those tense seconds it was as if he were endowed with a front seat at the dropping of a bigger and better atom bomb—with people in the back seats watching seismographs a thousand miles away.

The stratplane's tail swung round, concealed the distant drama. Unaware that anything abnormal was taking place, its pilot brought the vessel down in a long, dexterous curve that dropped Silver City behind intervening spurs of the Rockies. Making a perfect landing, the great machine rushed over the concrete, its rockets blasting spasmodically. With a final swerve, it stopped alongside a tower-topped building that bore in large white letters the word: BOISE.

Graham was first out. Descending the portable steps in a manner that startled its handlers, he hit the concrete, made to run around the ship's tail, but stopped, appalled.

About a hundred civilians and officials were scattered over the stratosphere station's areaway, but none advanced to greet the arrival. They stood stock still at various points around the space, their faces turned to the south, their eyes narrowed as they strove to bring a long range into focus.

In that direction, sixty miles away, yet thrusting high above minor sprawls of the Rockies, was the cloud. It was not mushroom-shaped as other ominous clouds had been. It was twisted and dark and still growing. It had become an awful pillar that reached to the very floors of heaven and sought to thrust through like a gaseous fungus rooted in hell; a great, ghastly erection of swirling, flowing, sullen clouds poised like a visible column of earthly woe and lamentations.

The noise! The noise of that far phenomenon was infinitely terrible even though muted by distance; a sound of tortured, disrupted air; a sound as if something insane and gargantuan were running amok through the cosmos, ripping, tearing, rending everything on which it could lay its mammoth hands. Titan on a bender!

All faces were pale, uncomprehending, while that far column poked its sable finger into the belly of the void, and from the void came an eldritch yammering like stentorian laughter booming through the caverns of beyond. Then, abruptly, the cloud collapsed.

Its gaseous crown continued to soar while its semi-solid base fell back. It dropped from sight with all the shocking suddenness of a condemned felon plunging through a trap. The thing was gone, but its swollen soul still rose and drifted westward, while its hellish rumbles and muffled roars persisted for several seconds before they faded and died away.

The hypnotized hundred stirred, slowly, uncertainly, as in a dream. Five officials moved stupidly toward the idling stratplane, their minds confused by the vision in the south. To one side of the concrete area, a private flyer resumed his walk toward his sports machine. Graham beat him to it.

"Quick! Take me to Silver City—government business!"

"Eh?" The flyer regarded him with a preoccupied air.

"Silver City," repeated Graham, urgently. His powerful fingers gripped the other's shoulder, shook it to emphasize his words. "Get me to Silver City as swiftly as you can."

"Why should I?"

"Dammit!" Graham roared, looking dangerous, "d'you want to argue at a time like this? You can take me—or have your machine confiscated. Which is it to be?"

The note of authority in his voice had its effect. The flier came to life, said hastily, "Yes, sure! I'll take you." He did not ask who Graham was, nor demand his purpose. Clambering hurriedly into his highly streamlined, two-seater, ten-jet job, he waited for his passenger to get in, then blew fire from the tail. The sports model raced along the concrete, lifted, screamed at a sharp angle into the blue.

Their destination lay beneath an obscuring pall of dust that was settling sluggishly as they progressed. It was just as they roared immediately overhead that a vagrant blast of wind cleared away the desiccated murk and bared the site of what had been Silver City.

Looking down, the pilot yelled something which became lost in the bellow of the stern tubes, fought to regain the controls that momentarily had slipped from his grasp. With cherry-red venturis vomiting fire and long streams of vapor, the ship zoomed close to the ground, brought into near view a scene that made Graham's stomach contract sickeningly.

Silver City was gone; the area it once had occupied was now an enormous scar on the face of Idaho, a five-mile-wide wound dotted with wreckage through which crept, crawled and limped a pathetically small number of survivors.

Jittery with shock, the pilot made an impromptu landing. Choosing a smooth stretch of sand on the north fringe of the scar, he brought his machine down, touched, lifted, touched, tilted, dug the starboard wingtip into soft soil. The machine reeled in a semicircle, tore off its wing, fell on its starboard side with the port wing sticking grotesquely into the air. The pair scrambled out unhurt. They stood side by side and studied the scene in complete silence.

Only one hour ago this had been a neat, clean and busy city of some thirty-five thousand souls. Now it was a field torn from the domain of hell, a crater-pitted terrain relieved only by low mounds of shattered bricks, tangles of distorted girders. Pale cobras of smoke still waved and undulated to the tune of distant groans. Here and there, a stone parted raspingly from its neighbor, a girder contracted in iron agony.

There were other things; things from which eyes avert and minds recoil; things photographed, but not for publication. Gaudy gobs and crimson clots inextricably mixed with tatters of wool and shreds of cotton. A jello shape in shredded denims. A parboiled head still exuding steam. A hand stuck to a girder, fingers extended, reaching for what it never got—and giving God the high-sign.

"Worse than the Krakatoa explosion," declared Graham, his voice soft, low. "Even worse than the Mont Pele disaster."

"What a blast! What a blast!" recited the pilot, gesturing in nervous excitement. "This is atomic. Nothing less than an atom bomb could have done it. You know what that means?"

"You tell me."

"It means that every inch of this ground is deadly. We're being sprayed every second we stand here."

"That's too bad." Graham nodded at the wrecked plane. "Maybe you'd better take to the air, eh?" He made his voice more tolerant. "We don't know that it's atomic—and by the time we find out it'll be too late, anyway."

A figure emerged laboriously from behind a pyramid of twisted girders in the middle distance. It limped around craters, side-stepped shapeless but infinitely terrible obstructions, made a lopsided, lurching run toward the waiting pair.

It was a human being, a man whose rags flapped around his raw legs as he progressed. He came up to them showing dirt and blood camouflaging an ashen face that framed a pair of glowing, half-mad optics.

"All gone," announced the newcomer, waving a trembling hand toward the place whence he had come. "All gone." He chuckled crazily. "All but me and the little flock who are worthy in the sight of the Lord." Squatting at their feet, he rolled his red-rimmed eyes upward, mumbled in tones too faint to be understood. Blood seeped through rags dangling on his left hip. "Listen!" he ordered, suddenly. He cupped a quivering hand to his ear. "Gabriel sounded his horn and even the song of the birds was stilled." He giggled again. "No birds. They came down in a dead rain. Out of the sky they fell, all dead." He rocked to and fro on his heels, mumbled again.

The pilot went to his plane, returned with a pocket-flask. Taking the flask, the sitting man gulped potent brandy as if it were water. He gasped, gulped some more. Emptying it, he handed it back, resumed his rocking. Slowly the light of sanity returned to his eyes.

Struggling to his feet, he teetered while he gazed at the others and said, in tone a little more normal, "I had a wife and a couple of kids. I had a real good wife and two damn fine kids. Where are they now?" His eyes blazed anew as they shifted from one to the other, desperately seeking the answer that none could give.

"Don't lose hope," soothed Graham. "Don't lose hope until you know for certain."

"Tell us what happened," suggested the pilot.

"I was fixing a patent no-draft cowl on a chimney on Borah Avenue, and I was just reaching for a piece of wire when the entire universe seemed to go bust. Something grabbed me, threw me all over the sky, then dropped me. When I got up, there wasn't any Silver City anymore." He put his hands over his eyes, held them there a moment. "No streets, no houses. No home, no wife and kids. And dead birds falling all around me."

"Have you any idea of what caused it?" Graham inquired.

"Yes," declared the man, his voice pure venom." It was the National Camera Company, fooling around with something they'd no right to touch. Looking for another ten percent, and damn the consequences. May everybody connected with it be blasted body and soul, now and forever more!"

"You mean that the explosion was located in their plant?" put in Graham, stemming the tirade.

"Sure!" The speaker's orbs mirrored his hate. "Their tanks blew up. They had a battery of cylinders holding a million gallons of silver nitrate solution, and every gallon of it went up at once, and sent everything straight to Hades. Why do they let 'em keep stuff like that in the middle of a city? Where's their right—and who says so? Somebody ought to be swung for that! Somebody ought to be hoisted higher than the city went!" He spat fiercely, rubbed his swollen lips. Death was in the set of his jaw. "Wiped out peaceful homes, and happy families, and—"

"But silver nitrate in solution won't disrupt like that."

"Won't it, mister?" retorted the victim, his tones sheer sarcasm. He gestured all-embracingly. "Look!"

His listeners looked. They found nothing to say.

Cars began to pour along the road from Boise, the van-guard of a veritable cavalcade that was to continue for a week. A plane swooped overhead, another and another. An autogyro bumped to earth half a mile away. Two helicopter ambulances floated inward, prepared to follow suit.

Temporarily disregarding causes, and reckless of consequences, a thousand pairs of feet trod through the graveyard of the West, a thousand pairs of hands pulled cautiously at wreckage, plucked maimed but living creatures from the soil. In his haste to rescue the living, no man thought of tormented atoms spitting invisibly, of hard radiations piercing his own body time and time again.

Ambulances, wheeled and winged, official or rush-converted, raced in, departed only to come again and again. Stretcher-bearers stamped a broad, firm path that later was to become the exact route of Mercy Street. flying journalists hovered in hastily hired helicopters a few hundred feet above, their televisors recording the horror below, broadcasting agony and pathos in extravagant adjectives not one-tenth so moving as the photographic reality depicted on the screens of a hundred million telenews receivers.

Graham and his pilot slaved with the rest, slaved long after dusk had fallen and night had spread its able shroud over the dead that yet remained. A gibbous moon crawled up, spewed its beams over the sights below. The hand on the girder maintained its gesture.

A gore-smeared gyrocar, with silent driver, carried Graham back to Boise. Finding a hotel, he washed, shaved, put a call through to Colonel Leamington.

The news of the disaster had shaken the world, said Leamington. Already the president had received messages of sympathy from fifteen foreign governments as well as from countless individuals.

"We're taking every necessary action to determine as soon and as definitely as possible whether this is another Hiroshima, Black Tom, or Texas City," he continued. "That is to say, whether its cause is attributable to assault, sabotage or accident."

"It's no Hiroshima," Graham told him. "It wasn't an atomic explosion—or not in any sense we understand. It was an ordinary, commonplace bang, a molecular disruption, but on a gigantic scale."

"How d'you know that?"

"They've rushed in Geiger counters from all directions. I questioned a bunch of operators just before I left. They say radiation is not abnormal as far as they've searched. The area seems safe. If anything is radiating, it's something not detectable by the means being employed."

"Humph!" growled Leamington. "I guess we'll get that report here shortly." He was silent for a few seconds, then said, "If it so happens that you come across anything suggesting a connection between this awful disaster and your investigation, you must drop everything forthwith and get in touch with me. In such circumstances, the whole affair would be far too great for one man to handle."

"There is no evidence of such a connection," Graham pointed out.

"Nothing—until you uncover something!" Leamington riposted. "In view of what has gone before, I feel mighty suspicious. Unless he is one of the few survivors, Beach is now the twentieth on the list exactly as you feared. He is a mouth closed before you could reach him precisely as all the others were closed. I don't like it!"

"Maybe, sir, but—"

"Graham, I repeat most emphatically that if you stumble on any sort of a link between this holocaust and the work on which you're engaged, you must give up at once and report to me without delay."

"Very well sir."

"In that event, the best brains in the country must be conscripted to meet the issue." Colonel Leamington's voice trailed off, then came back strongly. "What do you think of the situation yourself?"

Graham hesitated before replying. He knew that he was as far from the truth as he'd been at the start, but he could not force aside the strange, uncanny feeling that had obsessed him since the death of Mayo. It seemed ridiculous to attach importance to sensations which, though strong and persistent, were elusively vague. Was that feeling akin to the hunch which had put him on the track of something yet to be found? Were those psychic warnings somehow related to his investigatory insight? Was it intuition, or empty superstition, or merely jumpy nerves?

Coming to a decision, he spoke slowly and deliberately. "Chief, I've still not the slightest idea of what is behind all this, but I've a notion that there are times when it's dangerous to talk about it." A thought became born in his mind, and he added, "I believe there are times when it's dangerous even to *think* about it."

"Absurd!" scoffed Leamington. "True telepaths don't exist, hypnotism is very much overrated, and there are no known mechanical means of tapping anyone's secret thoughts. Besides, how the devil can any investigation be conducted without thought?"

"That's the hell of it," responded Graham, dryly. "It cannot. Therefore I must take the risk."

"Are you serious, Graham?"

"Never more so! I believe, or rather I feel that there are times when I can stew this affair in my mind, freely and with profit. Just as positively, I feel that there are inexplicable moments when to think would be sticking out my neck with a vengeance. Why I feel that way is something I can't explain. Maybe I'm nuts—but the deeper I get into this case the more I respect my own nuttiness."

"Why?"

"Because," said Graham, "I'm still perpendicular—while the others are horizontal!"

He put down his receiver, a queer light in his eyes. Somehow, he knew that he was right in his estimate of danger. He must take a risk, an awful risk, against odds infinitely terrible because completely unknown. *Eternal vigilance is the impossible price of liberty.* If he, like Webb, must succumb in vain effort to pay that price, well, so be it!

Police Chief Corbett eventually found one in the top ward of the overflowing Center Hospital. According to him, this fellow was the only employee of the National Camera Company among three thousand survivors rescued from what was left of Silver City.

The patient was bandaged from head to feet, his eyes being covered, only his mouth exposed. A strong odor of tannic acid exuded from him, bore mute witness to his extensive burns. Graham sat at one side of the bed, Corbett at the other.

A weary nurse said, "Five minutes—no more! He's very weak but stands a chance if you'll give him one."

Putting his lips close to a bandage-covered ear, Graham asked, "What exploded?"

'The tanks," came a faint whisper.

"Silver nitrate?" inquired Graham, doing his best to convey incredulity in his tones.

"Yes."

"Can you explain it?"

"No." A dry, swollen and discolored tongue licked along cotton fringes over the burned lips.

"What was your job?" Graham put quietly. "Lab worker."

"Research?"

"Yes."

Graham wasted a meaning glance on the listening Corbett, then said to the man on the bed, "On what work were you engaged at the time of the disaster?"

There was no reply. The mouth closed under its wrappings, the breathing became inaudible. Alarmed, Corbett signaled a nurse.

Hurrying up, the girl fussed over the patient. "He's all right. You've got two more minutes." She dashed away, her face pale, lined with long duty.

Graham put his question again, got no answer. With a frown, he signed to Corbett to take over.

"This is Police Chief Corbett, of Boise," declared that official, severely. "Your questioner is a member of the United States Intelligence Service. More than thirty thousand people died in yesterday's blast, and the few remaining are in no better shape than you. The discovery of the cause of this tragedy is more important than your loyalty to your employers. I advise you to speak."

The mouth remained stubbornly closed.

"If you refuse to speak," Corbett continued, "means may be found to—"

Waving him into silence, Graham brought his own lips near the recumbent form, and murmured, "Doctor Beach authorizes you to tell all you know."

"Beach!" exclaimed the man on the bed. "Why, he warned me to say nothing!"

"He warned you?" Graham was thoroughly startled. "He warned you when? Has he seen you *here?*"

"An hour before you came," admitted the other, in a low voice.

With a mighty effort, Graham suppressed a desire to shout, "Then he's alive!" but kept his wits and said, coolly, confidently, "Much may happen in an hour. You can speak without fear."

The other stirred feebly. "We found the new emulsion the day before yesterday," he told them, reluctantly. "Under Beach's supervision, we'd been looking for it for nearly three months. It was an intensive, three-shift, night-and-day job pushed through as if it were costing someone a thousand bucks a second. Beach never let up. It would have taken an individual worker ten years to develop the stuff, but there were sixty of us on the job with all the company's resources at our disposal. Wyman eventually found it Wednesday morning, but we didn't know for certain that he'd actually got it until we tested it a few minutes before the explosion."

"What kind of an emulsion was it, and how did you test it?" Graham encouraged.

"It was a photographic emulsion susceptible to frequencies far into the infra-red, farther than any commercial plates have been able to reach. It touched the ultra-radio band. According to Beach, such an emulsion ought to record things like suns—I don't know why; none of us knew why. We made routine exposures with Wyman's compound and, sure enough, we developed negatives recording things like little suns."

"Go on! Go on!" Graham urged.

"We looked them over curiously and talked about them a lot. These suns were small spheres of invisible radiation, three or four of them, floating above the roof of Number Four Extraction Shed. Somehow—I can't explain how or why—the sight of them made us greatly excited in a sort of horrible, heart-leaping way. Beach was home at the time the test proved positive, so Wyman phoned him, and was in the middle of telling him about it when—*wham!*"

"But Beach definitely knew of the existence of these phenomena before you succeeded in photographing them?"

"Of course! I don't know where he got the information, but he had it all right—from somewhere."

"He never gave you any clue to the nature of these objects?"

"No. He told us only what they ought to look like on a negative. Nothing more. He was tight-mouthed on the subject."

"Thanks!" said Graham. "I guess you've helped me plenty."

Leaving his chair, he paced slowly out of the ward, followed by the deeply puzzled Corbett. Continuing along the curved drive leading to the road, they stopped by the police chief's gyrocar.

In response to some weird impulse, some strange but urgent notion he could not identify or explain, Graham drove his thoughts away from the recent examination and compelled them to concentrate elsewhere. It was difficult to govern his own mind in such dictatorial fashion, and for several seconds he sweated in mental agony while he forced his stubborn thoughts into an innocuous path. He drew a woman from his memory, let his mind enjoy her picture, the curl of her crisp, black hair, the curve of her hips, the tranquil smile which occasionally lit her heart-shaped face. Doctor Curtis, of course. Being male, he had no trouble in considering her unprofessionally. She'd no right to expert status, anyway; not with a form like that!

His memory was still conjuring her calm, serene eyes for him to look into when Corbett got into his car and rumbled, heavily, "Pity that guy couldn't tell us what those sun-things might be."

"Yes," agreed Graham, hardly hearing. He closed the car's door upon the burly chief. "I'll call at your office soon after dinner." He walked hastily away, the vision still firmly held in the grasp of his own peculiarly vivid imagination.

Lowering his plastiglass window, Corbett called after him, "Those little suns need investigating, I reckon. They've got plenty to do with all this—I'll gamble my life on that!" Receiving no comment, the chief cast a disgusted look at Graham's broad back, and proceeded to gamble his life by prodding the starter-switch with a broad forefinger.

The gyrocar whined like an eager dog, slid easily forward, built up speed. Its velocity increased until the machine was screaming along and splitting wind in a way that flapped the sunblinds along the street. Bulleting through a narrow gap in cross traffic, it beat the automatic signals at the intersection, sent shocked pedestrians scuttling in all directions. Madly, it plunged past another block, made a slight curve when crossing the second intersection, plunged head-long into the concrete wall of a corner building. The car crushed itself down to half its normal length, and a two-ton concrete block cracked right through. The sound of the impact was a minor explosion that reverberated time and time again through surrounding streets.

The noise battered imperatively on the eardrums of the self-hypnotized Graham. He fought fearfully, desperately, half-insanely to hold a feminine face before his mental vision, to reject, keep out, beat off the knowledge that yet another had paid the terrible penalty for being curious about little suns.

While crowds—unconsciously protected by their own ignorance—milled and gaped around the distant wreck, Graham, made vulnerable by his own suspicions, threatened by the unseen, battled with himself as he walked steadily away—battled to view a mirage to the complete exclusion of everything else. He paced onward, grimly onward, fighting to camouflage his own betraying mind; and as he fought, he won.

Chapter 6

The path was a crazy snake, mottled in the moonlight, twisting and turning as it crawled upward, ever upward. The few hours that had gone since Corbett became paste now seemed a year. Graham pushed the memory away, ducked into the shadow of a natural obelisk that poised at one side of the track. A bilious moon let its sickly beams fall over sullen corks and brooding pines, illuminating the rough landscape in the pale ghastliness.

The hidden man's feverish eyes searched the pools of shadow that lined and pitted the route he had just traversed; his ears strained to catch sounds different from the sibilant rustling of branches, scrape of boughs, burble of distant waters—sounds he could attribute only to things that invariably were silent. Involuntarily, for no other purpose than to soothe his too-alert soul, he was looking for the unseeable, listening for the unhearable, waiting for that which lets no man wait when his time is due.

For a full five minutes he stood thus, his nerves strained, his muscles taut, his mind and body prepared to meet whatever menace might explode from the silence and the dark.

But there was nothing, nothing—only harsh rocks that thrust ragged outlines toward equally ragged clouds, only sentinel pines standing guard around the camp of night.

Several times had he stopped and stood thus, examining the trail behind, and each time the path remained empty, undisturbed.

Those stalkers in the ebon hours, slinking in his steps, skulking furtively through the gloom, were creatures of his overwrought mind. He had enough self-possession to know that they were fantastic products of his tired and regimented imagination, yet he could not forbear to seek occasional vantage posts and compel his sleep-hungry eyes to seek confirmation of the nightmares haunting his brain.

He stared until he had convinced himself of his own misapprehension, emerged from the black bar of shadow cast by the obelisk, continued up the trail. Stumbling over broad cracks, slipping in deep ruts, tripping over loose stones part-hidden in the inadequate light, he hastened along.

The path curved tortuously around the mountain, ended in a tiny, elevated valley surrounded by towering walls on all sides but one. A building squatted at the farther end of the valley, hugging low to the ground, architecturally cowering. It was no ramshackle erection, but a sturdy conglomeration of concrete and local rock, low-slung, drab, ominous in its complete seclusion.

At the valley's mouth stood an ancient, decrepit finger-post, its faded board bearing in awkward scrawl the words:

MILLIGAN'S STRIKE. He looked at the board, eyes narrowed, peering closely, then glanced back along the trail. Nothing stirred.

Jet shadows cast by surrounding cliffs swallowed his own shadow as he stole through the valley, reached the silent building, surveyed its cold, impassive windows. No light blazed welcome from those glassy squares, no noise of human movement came from within those grim walls. There was no sound save that of a loosened stone rolling somewhere back along the trail. That tiny, distant clatter set him back against the wall, one hand in his pocket. He watched the moonlit mouth for fifteen minutes.

Giving it up, he rapped heavily upon the armorplate door, tried its handle, found it locked. He knocked again, using a large pebble to increase the noise. There was no response. Turning his back to the door, his bloodshot eyes staring through the gloom toward the distant, moonlit fingerpost, he swung a heavy, steel-shod boot at the armorplate, hammering it like a gong until the entire building echoed and re-echoed its urgent clamor.

Horror clawed at his heart while he battered frantically for entry. Perhaps others had gone in before him: others who had not knocked or opened, yet had passed silently and insidiously inside; others at whom it was futile to shoot, from whom it was useless to run.

Fighting off his panic, he gave the door a final, tremendous blow. If there was no response within one minute, he was going to bust a metal guard off a window, using a good, heavy rock for the purpose. At all costs he must get in, even if it were necessary to wreck the place. Putting his ear against the armorplate, he listened intently, heard a faint humming that grew into a low whine.

Frank relief brightened his features as the whine ceased. A short, metallic rattle followed; slow, deliberate feet approached the door. A chain clanged, a battery of bolts creaked aside, the lock snapped back, the door opened a bare six inches.

From the blackness a deep, rich voice demanded, "Well?"

Graham introduced himself in six swift words, then asked, "Are you Professor Beach?"

The door opened wide, and the man hidden in the interior gloom said quickly, "Come in, Graham. We've met before. I could not identify you in this infernal darkness."

Entering, Graham heard the door slam and lock behind him. A hand grasped his arm, steered him across a completely obscured floor, stopped him at the other side. Metal grated and clanged before his face, the floor sank under his feet. An elevator, of all things, in such a place as this!

Light floated upward, the floor ceased its descent. Graham saw the other's face in revealing rays. The scientist was still the same tall, thin-featured, dark-haired personage that he used to be. The burden of time rested lightly upon this man, for Graham could note little difference in the face he had not seen for several years. But there was one difference, a startling one—*the eyes.*

Beach's thin, curved, hawklike nose jutted between a pair of cold, hard optics unearthly in their brilliance. There was a hint of mesmerism in their deliberate, calculating and penetrating stare, something overpowering in their weird glow.

"Why the darkness upstairs?" queried Graham, still fascinated by those uncanny orbs.

"Light attracts nocturnal creatures," replied Beach, evasively. "They can be a nuisance." He studied his visitor. "How did you come to look for me here?"

"The editor of the local sheet in Boise knew that you'd been spending a lot of time in this place. He said he was sending a reporter here in the morning, to see whether you were alive or dead. I beat him to it."

Beach sighed. "I suppose a horde of snoopers is inevitable after what has happened. Oh, well—" He ushered Graham into a small, book-lined room, gave him a chair. Carefully shutting the door, he took a seat opposite. His long, slender fingers built a church and steeple while his odd eyes bored steadily into the other's. "I am indeed sorry that we should meet again in such terrible circumstances. I presume that your visit is connected with the Silver City disaster?"

"It is."

"But since the Department of Special Finance is not involved, it cannot have an interest in the matter?" Beach's dark, finely curved brows lifted questioningly.

"No," agreed Graham. Taking off his ring, he handed it across. "Probably you've heard about those even if you haven't seen one. Its inner surface bears a microscopic inscription which is my warrant as a member of the United States Intelligence Service. You may check it under a microscope, if you wish."

"Ah, the Intelligence Service!" The eyebrows sank into a thoughtful frown. Beach rolled the ring to and fro between his fingers, gave it back without bothering to inspect it. "I'll take your word that it is what it purports to be." His frown deepened. "If you want to know why the silver nitrate exploded, I cannot tell you. In the next few weeks I shall be asked for an explanation by policemen, factory inspectors, industrial chemists, press reporters, time and time again. They'll all be wasting breath. I am totally unable to offer an explanation."

"You lie!" declared Graham, flatly.

With a resigned sigh, the scientist came to his feet, walked slowly to the door through which they had entered. Finding a hooked rod, he used it to drag a large screen down from its slot in the ceiling. Satisfied that the screen completely covered the door, he returned to his seat.

"Why do I lie?"

Back hairs were erect on Graham's neck as he answered, "Because you, and you alone, know that the stuff was mysteriously disrupted by some weird phenomena that you were trying to photograph. Because someone working under your command finally took a forbidden picture—and Silver City died in the counterblast!"

He swallowed hard, feeling certain that in speaking thus he had signed his own death warrant, and was amazed to find that he still lived. Studying Beach for the effect of his words, he noted only the spasmodic tightening of the folded hands, and an almost indiscernible flicker in the burning eyes.

"Whatever wiped out that town," continued Graham, "were the same thing or things that have eliminated an unknown number of the world's best scientists. It is my investigation of the deaths of some of those scientists—American ones—that has led me to you!"

Producing his wallet, he extracted a telegram, passed it to Beach. The latter murmured its words as he read them.

"GRAHAM CARE OF BOISE POLICE: SOLE COMMON DENOMINATOR DASH ALL WERE FRIENDS OF BJORNSEN OR FRIENDS OF HIS FRIENDS STOP HARRIMAN."

"That refers to last month's quota of dead." Graham stabbed an accusing finger at the scientist. *"You* were a friend of Bjornsen's!"

"True," admitted Beach. "True." He looked down at his hands, ruminated awhile. "I was a very old friend of Bjornsen's. I am one of the few such who still remain." He raised his gaze, looking his opponent straight in the face. "I will also confess that I have much information which I intend to keep entirely to myself. What are you going to do about it?"

The other's bold defiance might have beaten individuals less persistent than Graham, but the investigator was not to be so easily defeated. Leaning forward, arms akimbo on broad knees, his muscular face intent, the Intelligence man did his best to convey the impression that he knew far more than the other suspected, more than he was ready to state at that moment.

Earnestly, he said, "Irwin Webb left a concealed message that we deciphered, a message telling much of what he had discovered. He declared that it was a picture which must be shown the world—if it can be shown without massacre."

"Massacre!" Beach's voice was harsh. "Is not the fate of Silver City enough? One man finds the picture, looks at it, *thinks* about it—and in a lightning flash thirty thousand pay the penalty with their earthly bodies and perhaps with their very souls. Why, even now your own thoughts are your most dangerous enemy. Knowing what little you may know, thinking about what you know, pondering it, turning it around in your mind, you invite destruction at any given moment, you tag yourself as a child of perdition, you are doomed by the involuntary activity of your own mind." His gaze slid toward the door. "If that fluorescent screen over the door happens to glow, neither I nor the strength of the civilized world can save you from instant death."

"I am aware of the fact," responded Graham, evenly. "My risk is no greater than your own, and cannot be increased by knowing the things you know. I cannot die *more* by knowing more!" He refrained from looking round at the screen, kept his whole attention upon the brilliant eyes opposite. If anything illuminated that screen, he would see it in those eyes. "Since there has been massacre despite the fact that the truth is not generally known, matters could hardly be worse if the truth were known."

"An assumption," scoffed Beach, "based on the erroneous promise that whatever is bad cannot be worse." He kept his gaze on that screen. "Nothing was worse than the bow and arrow—until gunpowder came. Nothing worse than that—until poison gas appeared. Then bombing planes. Then supersonic missiles. Then atom bombs. Today, mutated germs and viruses. Tomorrow, something else." His laugh was short, sardonic. "Through pain and tears we learn that there's always room for further improvement."

"I'm willing to argue that with you when I'm in possession of all the facts," Graham retorted.

'The facts are beyond belief!"

"Do you believe them?"

"A fair question," Beach conceded, readily. "With me, belief does not enter into the matter. Faith has no relation to what one learns empirically. No, Graham, I don't believe them—I *know* them!" Moodily, he massaged his chin. "The incontrovertible evidence already accumulated leaves no room for doubt in understanding minds."

"Then what are the facts?" demanded Graham, his expression urging the other to speak. "What blotted out Silver City? What cut short the experiments of a clique of scientists, ending their lives in manner calculated to arouse no suspicion? What murdered Police Chief Corbett this afternoon?"

"Corbett? Has he gone too?" With his blazing eyes directed over his listener's shoulder toward the screened door, Beach pondered lengthily. There was silence in the room except where a tiny clock numbered the moments toward the grave. One mind worked hurriedly, while the other waited with phlegmatic grimness. Finally, Beach got up, switched off the lights.

"We can observe that screen more easily in darkness," he commented. "Sit here next to me, keep your eyes on it, and if it glows, force your thoughts elsewhere— or heaven itself won't help you!"

Shifting his chair next to the scientist's, Graham gazed through the gloom. He knew that at last the case was about to break, and his conscience kept nagging him unmercifully.

"You ought to have obeyed orders!" silently screamed the still, small voice within him. "You ought to have made contact with Leamington as you were instructed! If Beach becomes a corpse, and you with him, the world will learn nothing except that you have failed—failed as have all the rest—because you refused to do your duty!"

"Graham," commenced Beach, his voice rasping through the darkness, cutting short the investigator's mental reproaches. "The world has been given a scientific discovery as great, as important, as far-reaching in its implications as the telescope and the microscope."

"What is it?"

"A means of extending the visible portion of the spectrum far into the infrared."

"Ah!"

"Bjornsen discovered it," Beach went on. "Like many other great discoveries, he stumbled across it while seeking something else, had the sense to realize what he'd found, developed it to usability. Like the telescope and the microscope, it has revealed a new and hitherto unsuspected world."

"A revealing angle on the ever-present unknown?" Graham suggested.

"Precisely! When Galileo peered incredulously through his telescope he found data that had stood before millions of uncomprehending eyes for countless centuries; new, revolutionary data which overthrew the officially endorsed but thoroughly famous Copernican system of astronomy."

"It was a wonderful find," agreed Graham.

"The microscope provides a far better analogy, for it disclosed a fact that had been right under the world's nose since the dawn of time, yet never had been suspected—the fact that we share our world, our whole existence, with a veritable multitude of living creatures hidden beyond the limits of our natural sight, hidden in the infinitely small. Think of it," urged Beach, his voice rising in tone "living, active animals swarming around us, above us, below us, within us, fighting, breeding and dying even within our own bloodstreams, yet remaining completely concealed, unguessed-at, until the microscope lent power to our inadequate eyes."

"That, too, was a great discovery," Graham approved.

Despite his interest, his nerves were still jumpy, for he started at the unexpected touch of the other's hand in the gloom.

"Just as all these things evaded us for century after century, some by hiding in the enormously great, some in the exceedingly small, so have others eluded us by skulking in the absolutely colorless." Beach's voice was still vibrant and a little hoarse. "The scale of electro-magnetic vibrations extends over sixty octaves, of which the human eye can see but one. Beyond that sinister barrier of our limitations, outside that poor, ineffective range of vision, bossing every man-jack of us from the cradle to the grave, invisibly preying on us as ruthlessly as any parasite, are our malicious, all-powerful lords and masters—the creatures who really own the Earth!"

"What the devil are they? Don't play around the subject. Tell me, for Pete's sake!" A cold sweat lay over Graham's forehead as his eyes remained fixed in the direction of the warning screen. No glow, no dreadful halo penetrated encompassing darkness, a fact he noted with much relief.

"To eyes equipped to see them with the new vision, they looked like floating spheres of pale-blue luminescence," declared Beach. "Because they resembled globes of living light, Bjornsen bestowed upon them the name of Vitons. Not only are they alive—they are intelligent! They are the Lords of Terra; we, the sheep of their fields. They are cruel and callous sultans of the unseen; we, their mumbling, sweating, half-witted slaves, so indescribably stupid that only now have we become aware of our fetters."

"*You* can see them?"

"I can! Sometimes I wish to God that I had never learned to see!" The scientist's breathing was loud in the confines of the small room. "All who duplicated Bjornsen's final experiment became endowed with the ability to penetrate that barrier of sight. Those who saw the Vitons got excited about it, thought about the discovery and walked into the shadow of death. From within limited distance, the Vitons can read human minds as easily as we could read an open book. Naturally, they take swift action to forestall the broadcasting of news which eventually might lead to our challenging their ages-old predominance. They maintain their mastery as cold-bloodedly as we maintain ours over the animal world—by shooting the opposition. Those of Bjornsen's copyists who failed to hide the knowledge within their minds, or, possibly, were betrayed by dreams while helpless in their slumbers, have had their minds and mouths closed forever." He paused, added, "As ours may yet be closed." Another pause, timed by the steady ticking of the little clock. "There, Graham, is your living purgatory—to know all is to be damned. An exceptionally powerful mind may seek refuge by controlling its daytime thoughts, all the time, every minute, every second, but who can control his dreams? Aye, in slumber lies the deadliest peril. Don't get into that bed—it might be loaded!"

"I suspected something of the sort."

"You did?" Surprise was evident in Beach's tones.

"Ever since I commenced my investigation I've had queer, uncanny moments when I've felt that it was tremendously important to shift my thoughts elsewhere. More than once I've obeyed a crazy but powerful impulse to think of other things, feelings, believing, almost knowing that it was safer to do so."

"It is the only thing that has spared you," Beach asserted. "But for that, you'd have been buried at the start."

"Then is my mental control greater than that of more accomplished men such as Bjornsen, Luther, Mayo and Webb?"

"No, not at all. You were able to exercise control more easily because what you were controlling was merely a vague hunch. Unlike the others, you did not have to suppress a full and horrible knowledge." Ominously, he added, "The real test will lie in how long you last after this!"

"Anyway, thank heavens for my hunches!" murmured Graham, gratefully.

Beach said, "I suspect that you do not have hunches. If those feelings of yours, though vague and unreasoning, were powerful enough to command obedience in defiance of your rational instinct, it is evident that you have extrasensory perception developed to an unusual degree."

"I'd never thought of that," Graham admitted. "I've been too busy to take time off to analyze myself."

"The faculty, though not common, is far from unique." Getting up from his chair, Beach switched on the lights, pulled a drawer from a large filing cabinet. Raking through a mass of press clippings that filled the drawer, he extracted a bunch, looked them over.

"I have data concerning many such cases going back for one hundred fifty years. Michele Lefevre, of St. Ave, near Vannes, in France, was repeatedly tested by French scientists. Her extrasensory perception was estimated as having sixty percent of the efficiency of her normal sight. Juan Eguerola, of Seville, seventy-five percent. Willi Osipenko, of Poznan, ninety percent." He pulled a clipping out of the bunch. "Here's a honey. It's taken from British *Tit Bits* dated March 19, 1938. Ilga Kirps, a Latvian shepherdess, of Riga. She was a young girl of no more than average intelligence, yet a scientific curiosity. A committee of leading European scientists subjected her to a very thorough examination, then stated that she undoubtedly possessed the power of extrasensory perception developed to such an amazing degree that it was superior to her natural eyesight."

"Stronger than mine," commented Graham as the scientist put the clippings back, turned off the light, resumed his seat.

"The power varies. Ilga Kirps was a Viton hybrid. Extrasensory perception is a Viton trait."

"What!" His fingers clawing at the arms of his chair, Graham sat upright.

"It is a Viton faculty," repeated Beach, calmly. "Ilga Kirps was the fairly successful result of a Viton experiment. Your own case was less fruitful, perhaps because your operation was prenatal."

"Prenatal? By God, d'you mean—?"

"I've outgrown the age of saying what I don't mean," Beach assured. "When I say prenatal, I mean just that! Further, I say that had we never been cursed with these luminosities, we should not also be cursed today with most of our complications in childbirth. When someone suffers, it's not the unfortunate accident it's believed to be! Why, Graham, I now accept the possibility of a phenomenon which all my life I've rejected as patently absurd, namely, that of virgin births. I accept that there may have been times when helpless, unsuspecting subjects have been artificially inseminated. The Vitons are continually meddling, experimenting, practicing their super-surgery on their cosmic cattle!"

"But why, why?"

"To see whether it is possible to endow human beings with Viton abilities." There was silence for a moment, then Beach added, dryly, "Why do men teach seals to juggle with balls, teach parrots to curse, monkeys to smoke cigarettes and ride bicycles? Why do they try to breed talking dogs, train elephants to perform absurd tricks?"

"I see the parallel," Graham acknowledged, morbidly.

"I have here a thousand or more clippings telling about people mysteriously endowed with inhuman powers, suffering from abnormal or supernormal defects,

giving birth to atrocious monstrosities which promptly have been strangled or
hidden forever from human sight. Others who have endured inexplicable experiences, unnatural fates. Remember the case of Daniel Dunglass Home, the man
who floated from a first-floor window before the astounded eyes of several prominent and trustworthy witnesses? His was a thoroughly authentic case of a person
possessing the power of levitation—the Viton method of locomotion! You should
read a book called *Hey-Day of a Wizard.* It tells all about Home. He had other
weird powers as well. But he was no wizard. He was a Vitonesque-humanoid!"

"Good heavens!"

"Then there was the case of Kaspar Hauser, the man from nowhere," Beach
went imperturbably on. "Nothing comes out of a vacuum, and Hauser had an
origin unlike anything else. Probably his was in a Viton laboratory. That, too,
may have been the eerie destination of Benjamin Bathurst, British ambassador
extraordinary to Vienna, who, on November 25, 1809, walked around the heads
of a couple of horses—and vanished forever."

"I don't quite see the connection," Graham protested. "Why the devil should
these super-creatures make people disappear?"

Beach's grin was cold and hard in the darkness. "Why do medical students make
stray cats disappear? From what wondering, puzzled pond vanishes the frogs that
later are to be dissected? Who snitches a pauper's body from the morgue when the
viscera runs out a mile farther down the street?"

"Ugh!" said Graham, with frank distaste.

"Disappearances are commonplace. For example, what happened to the crew
of the *Marie Celeste?* Or the crew of the *Rosalie?* Were they suitable frogs snatched
from a convenient pond? What happened to the *Waratah?* Did that man who, at
the last moment, refused to sail on the *Waratah* have extrasensory perception, or
was he instinctively warned off because he was an unsuitable frog? What makes
one man suitable, another not? Does the former live in continual peril; the latter
enjoy lifelong safety? Is it possible that some peculiar, unidentifiable difference in
our mutual make-ups means that I am marked for death while you remain un-
touchable?"

"That's something only time will show."

"Time!" spat Beach, contemptuously. "We've carried the devil on our backs
perhaps a million years and only now are aware that he's there. Homo sapiens—
the man with a load of mischief!" He murmured some underbreath comment to
himself, then went on. "Only this morning I was studying a case to which no
solution had been found in ten years. The details are given in the London *Evening
Standard* of May 16, 1938 and the *British Daily Telegraph* of several dates thereafter. The 5,456-ton vessel *Anglo-Australian* vanished at short notice, without trace.
She was a modern, seaworthy boat plowing through smooth, tranquil waters when
she and her crew of thirty-eight abruptly became as if they had never been. She
disappeared mid-Atlantic, within fifty miles of other ships, shortly after sending a
radio message stating that all was well. Where has she gone? Where are most of
the thousands of people who have been listed and sought for years by the Bureau
of Missing Persons?"

"You tell me." Graham's eyes raked the darkness for the screen, failed to find it. Somewhere in the black it was standing, a silent sentry, waiting, guarding them, yet unable to do more than give them split-second warning of invaders that they alone must resist.

"I don't know," confessed Beach. "Nobody knows. All we can say is that they've been seized by agencies only now within our ken, powers unfamiliar but in no way supernatural. They have been taken for purposes at which we can but guess. They have gone as they have been going since the beginning of history and as they'll keep on going in the future. A few have come back, warped in ways we've not been able to understand. Those we have crucified, or burned at the stake, or shot with silver bullets and buried in garlic, or incarcerated in asylums. Still more have been taken and will continue to be taken."

"Maybe," said Graham, skeptically. "Maybe."

"Only a month ago the New York-Rio stratplane passed behind a cloud over Port of Spain, Trinidad, and didn't reappear. A thousand eyes saw it one moment, not the next. Nothing has been heard of it since. Nine months ago the Soviet's Moscow-Vladivostok new streamliner vanished in a similar way. That's not been heard of, either. There has been a long series of such cases going back for decades, right to the earliest days of aeronautics."

"I can recall some of them."

"What happened to Amelia Earhart and Fred Noonan; to Lieutenant Oskar Omdal, Brice Goldsborough and Mrs. F.W. Grayson; to Captain Terence Tully and Lieutenant James Medcalf; to Nungesser and Coli? Some, perhaps, crashed, but I have little doubt that others did not. They were snatched away, exactly as human beings have been snatched for century after century, singly, in groups, in shiploads."

"The world must be told," swore Graham. "It must be warned."

"Who can tell, can warn—and live?" asked Beach, caustically. "How many would-be tellers lie tongue-tied in their graves? How many thousands more can be silenced as effectively? To talk is to think, and to think is to be betrayed, and to be betrayed is to die. Even we, in this lonely hideout, may eventually be found by some roaming invisible, overheard, and made to pay the penalty of knowing too much; the price of inability to camouflage our knowledge. The Vitons are ruthless, utterly ruthless, and it is ghastly evidence of the fact that they blew Silver City to hell the moment they found that we'd discovered a means of photographing them."

"Nevertheless, the world must be warned," Graham insisted, stubbornly. "Ignorance may be bliss—but knowledge is a weapon. Humanity must know its oppressors to strike off their chains."

"Fine-sounding words," scoffed Professor Beach. "I admire your persistent spirit, Graham, but spirit is not enough. You don't yet know enough to appreciate the impossibility of what you suggest."

'That's why I've come to you," Graham riposted. "To learn enough! If I leave here ill-informed, the blame for my shortcoming will be yours. Give me all you've got—I cannot ask for more."

"And after that?"

"I'll take the responsibility and the risk. What else can I do?"

Silence in the ebon gloom while the two sat by the wall facing the screen, one nervously impatient, the other brooding grimly. Silence pregnant with swift, conjecturing thoughts and timed by slow, deliberate ticks. It was as if the fate of the world was being weighed in the balance of one man's mind.

Suddenly, Beach said, "Come!" Turning up the lights, he opened a door near the still inactive screen, switched on more lights that revealed the neat, orderly length of a compact and well-equipped laboratory.

Darkening the room they were leaving, Beach closed the connecting door, indicated a bell on the laboratory wall, and told the other, "If that screen in the next room glows, a photosensitive cell will operate and cause this bell to ring. If it does ring, you'd better muddle your thoughts swiftly and completely—or prepare for the worst."

"I understand."

"Sit there," ordered Beach. He washed his fingers with a spot of ether, picked up a bottle. "This reaction of Bjornsen's is synergistic. D'you know what that means?"

"It's a purely associative effect."

"Correct! You've your own way of expressing it, but it's as good a definition as I've heard. It's a reaction produced by drugs functioning cooperatively which none can produce separately. You can see what that means—to test the effects of multiples in all possible combinations means a number of experiments running into astronomical figures. Synergy will keep research busy for years. They mightn't have stumbled on this one for fifty years to come. If Peder Bjornsen hadn't had the brains to recognize a stroke of luck when he saw it, we'd all—" He let his voice trail off while he tilted the bottle over a measuring vial, counting the drops with utmost care.

"What makes now?" Graham asked, watching him.

"I'm going to treat you according to Bjornsen's formula. It will blind you for a few minutes, but don't let that scare you—it will only be your rods and cones readjusting themselves. While your sight becomes modified, I'll tell you every detail I've been able to gather."

"Is this treatment permanent in effect, or temporary?"

"It seems permanent, but I wouldn't be dogmatic about that. Nobody's had it long enough to be sure." Putting down the bottle, he came to Graham with the vial in one hand and a small pad of cotton wool in the other. "Here goes," he said, "and listen carefully to what I tell you—my opportunity to repeat it may never come!"

Unconsciously, he was prophetic there!

Chapter 7

There were pale streamers struggling across the lowering moon, a deep, almost solid blackness in the valley. The building squatting in sullen loneliness at one end was completely hidden in the murk of night, and also hidden was the figure that edged through its armorplate door and flitted through the gloom toward the sighing pines.

For a moment, the figure became a man-shaped silhouette in the moonlight by the crumbling fingerpost, then it faded into the less-revealing background of trees. A pebble rattled on the trail, a twig snapped farther on, then there was only the whispering of multimillion leaves, the moan of night breezes among the boughs.

At the other end of the trail a mountain ash spread concealing arms over a narrow, racy cylinder of highly polished metal. Something dodged around the trunk of the ash, merged with the cylinder. Then came the soft click of a well-oiled lock, a low but powerful hum. A startled nightbird squawked its alarm as the cylinder projected itself from the black pool beneath the tree, flashed along the highway, bounded over the farther crest.

The same cylinder stood in the Boise Strat-Station at dawn. On one side, weak stars still twinkled against a back-drop of gradually lightening gray; on the other, the sky mirrored the pink of oncoming day. Morning mists were a gauzy veil on the Rockies.

Yawning, Graham said to Police Lieutenant Kellerher, 'There are very special reasons why Beach and myself are leaving at different times and by different routes. It is absolutely imperative that one of us reaches Washington. I hold you personally responsible for picking up Beach in one hour's time, and seeing him safely on the *Olympian.*"

"He'll be on it, don't you worry!" Kellerher assured.

"Good! I'll leave it to you." With another wide yawn, Graham ignored the lieutenant's fascinated stare at his eyes, climbed into the rear seat of a racy looking army jetplane that was ready to rush him eastward.

The pilot bent forward in his seat, gave his machine the gun. Short plumes of fire and long streams of vapor shot backward from the vessel's tail and from other tubes flushed into the trailing edges of its mirror-polished wings. With a rising howl that soon lost its lead and fell behind them, they dived into the morning sky, their vapor trail stretching and thinning, the lagging noise of their jets bouncing off the mountain peaks.

Whizzing high over jagged points of the Rockies which speared the red dawn, the pilot leveled off. Graham gaped repeatedly as he suppressed more yawns, stared through the plastiglass with eyes whose utter bleariness failed to conceal their underlying luster.

The jets shivered steadily half a mile ahead of their sound. Graham's chin sank slowly onto his chest, his eyelids drooped, fluttered futilely, then closed. Overcome by the rhythmic vibration of the jets, and the swing and sway of the plane, he began to snore.

A bump and a swift rush of wheels along the runway awoke him. Washington! Nudging him gently, the pilot grinned, gestured to his clock. They had made excellent time.

Four figures hurried toward the machine as he got out. He recognized two of them: Colonel Leamington and Lieutenant Wohl. The others were burly individuals who carried themselves with an authoritative air.

"Got your wire, Graham," announced Leamington, his sharp eyes afire with anticipation. He pulled the message from his pocket, read it aloud. "'Case busted wide open. Solution important to peace of world and worthy of Presidential attention. Meet me army special due Washington port two forty.'" He worried his mustache. "Your information must be of terrific consequence?"

"It is!" Graham's gaze turned to the sky, his cold, shining orbs focused on seeming nothingness. "Unless I take the greatest care, I won't live to tell it! You'll have to hear me in some underground place, a well-protected site such as the basement of a government building. I'd like you to have a Blattnerphone running, so that you'll have a record of what I've said if it so happens that—despite my care and good fortune—my story is stopped partway through the telling."

"Stopped?" Leamington eyed him with a puzzled frown.

"I said stopped. Mouths can be and have been stopped, any time, any place, without warning. Mine's liable to be slapped shut quicker than any, knowing what I know. I want someplace safer if only insofar as it's less conspicuous."

"Well, I guess that can be arranged," agreed Leamington.

Ignoring the curious expressions with which the others were listening to his remarks, Graham went on. "I also want you to have somebody take Doctor Beach off the *Olympian* when it reaches Pittsburgh tonight. He can be flown here, and he'll confirm my statements—or complete them."

"Complete them?"

"Yes, if they don't get completed by me."

"You talk very strangely, Graham," opined Leamington, conducting the other toward a waiting gyrocar.

"No more strangely than men have died." Getting into the machine, the rest following, he added, "You'll get the whole story, in plain, understandable terms, pretty soon—and maybe you'll be sorry you ever listened to it!"

Talk he did; to an audience of thirty seated on rows of hard, uncomfortable chairs in a cellar two hundred feet below street-level. A fluorescent screen, obtained at short notice from a government laboratory, covered the only door, its supersensitive coating inert, lifeless, but prepared to emit a warning glow with the passage of invisible intruders. Overhead, a stony barrier between the secret session and the snooping skies, towered the mighty bulk of the War Department Building.

It was a mixed audience, uneasily attentive, expectant and slightly skeptical. There sat Colonel Leamington, with Wohl and the two Federal operatives who had met Graham on his arrival. Left of them fidgeted Senators Carmody and Dean, confidants of the country's chief executive. Willets C. Keithley, supreme head of the United States Intelligence Service, was a broad-shouldered, phlegmatic figure on the right, his personal secretary by his side.

Behind these were a number of scientists, government officials, and advisory psychologists to a total of two dozen. That shrewd face topped with a white mane showed the presence of Professor Jurgens, the world's leading expert on mass-psychology or, as his friends preferred to describe it, 'mob reaction.' The thinner, darker features staring over his shoulder belonged to Kennedy Veitch, leading ray expert. The six sitting on his left represented the thousand brains still striving to produce the wavicle bomb, long-sought-for successor of the atom bomb. The rest were men equally able, each in his own sphere, some unknown, some internationally famous.

The attention of all became fixed exclusively upon the speaker whose glittering eyes, hoarse voice and expressive gestures drove into their receptive minds the full and dreadful import of his subject. In one corner, magnetized wire ran smoothly through the Blattnerphone, recording the revelation with mechanical accuracy.

"Gentlemen," commenced Graham, "some time back the Swedish scientist Peter Bjornsen stumbled on a new line of research which he followed, bringing it to a successful end about six months ago when he found that he was able to extend the range of human vision. He accomplished this feat with the aid of iodine, methylene blue and mescal, and although the manner in which these components react relatively to each other is not fully understood, there is no doubt of their efficiency. A person treated with them in the manner prescribed by Bjornsen can perceive a range of electromagnetic frequencies much wider than that permitted to natural sight."

"How much wider?" inquired a doubting voice.

"The extension is in one direction only," Graham answered. "It is far into the infrared. According to Bjornsen, the limit lies in the ultra-radio band."

"What, seeing heat?" pursued the other.

"Seeing heat—and beyond it!" Graham assured.

He raised his voice above the resulting murmur of astonishment as grimly he carried on. "Exactly how this effect is achieved is something for you scientists to puzzle over. What I am concerned with here, what concerns this country, what concerns the entire world is an astounding fact that this discovery literally has dragged into the light." He paused, then gave it to them straight from the shoulder. "Gentlemen, another higher form of life is master of this world!"

Surprisingly, there was no burst of voices raised in angry protest, no skeptical jeers, not even a buzz of conversation. Something had hold of them, some communal sense of truth, or perhaps a mutual recognition of the speaker's complete sincerity. So they sat there as if glued to their seats, showing him row after row of shocked, speculative and apprehensive eyes, their faces betraying the fact that his statement exceeded their most fantastic expectations.

"I assure you that this is factual and beyond all disproof," declared Graham. "I have seen these creatures myself. I have seen them, pale but queerly glowing balls of blueness, floating through the sky. A pair of them skimmed swiftly, silently, high above me as I slunk along the lonely trail from Beach's isolated laboratory in the mountains between Silver City and Boise. One of them bobbed in the air above Boise Strat-Station shortly before my plane took off to bring me here. There were dozens over Washington when I arrived. There are scores over the city at this very moment, some probably swaying above this building. They favor haunts of humanity; for terrible reasons they cluster thickest where our numbers are greatest."

"What are they?" put in Senator Carmody, his plump features flushed.

"Nobody knows. There has not been sufficient time to study them. Bjornsen himself thought them alien invaders of fairly recent origin, but admitted that this was sheer guesswork as he had no data on which to base an opinion. The late Professor Mayo agreed that they're of extraterrestrial origin, but opined that they have conquered and occupied this planet many thousands of years ago. On the contrary, Doctor Beach thinks they are native to Earth, just as microbes are native. Beach says that the late Hans Luther went further, and on the strength of evidence about our physical shortcomings, suggested that these things are true Terrestrials, while we are the descendants of animals which they've imported from other worlds in cosmic cattle-boats."

"Cattle!—cattle!—cattle!" The word shuttled around the audience. They mouthed it as if it were foul.

"How much *is* known about these creatures?" someone put.

"Very little, I'm afraid. They've not the slightest resemblance to human beings, and, from our point of view, they are so utterly and completely alien that I cannot see how it will ever be possible for us to find a common basis that will permit some sort of understanding. They look like luminescent spheres, about three feet in diameter, their surfaces alive, glowing, blue, but totally devoid of observable features. They don't register on an ordinary infrared film, though Beach has now recorded them with the aid of a new emulsion. They aren't detectable by radar, evidently because they absorb radar pulses instead of reflecting them. Beach asserts that they tend to swarm in the vicinity of radar antenna, like thirsty children around a fountain. He thinks they inspired us to develop radar—and thus provide them with another incomprehensible pleasure at the price of our own sweat."

His listeners' features bore a strange mixture of awe and horror as he continued, saying, "It is known that these weird spheres employ extrasensory perception as a substitute for sight, and that they have this faculty developed to an amazing degree. That is why they have always been able to comprehend us while we've not been able to see them, for sixth-sense mental awareness is independent of electromagnetic frequencies. They also utilize telepathy in lieu of vocal chords and hearing organs—or perhaps it's merely another aspect of this same extrasensory perception. At any rate, they can read and understand human thoughts at short range, but not at long range. Beach gave them the name of Vitons, since obviously they are not flesh, and are composed of energy. They are neither animal, mineral nor vegetable—they are energy."

"Absurd!" ejaculated a scientist, finding at last something within the scope of his training. "Energy cannot hold so compact and balanced a form!"

"What about fireballs?"

"Fireballs?" it caught the critic on one foot. He gazed uncertainly around, subsided. "I've got to admit you have me there. Science has not yet been able to evolve a satisfactory explanation of those phenomena."

Graham said, seriously, "Yet science agrees that fireballs are compact and temporarily balanced forms of energy which cannot be duplicated in any laboratory. They may be dying Vitons. They may be these very creatures, as mortal as us, whatever their life-span, falling in death, dispelling their energy in suddenly visible frequencies." Taking out his wallet, he extracted a couple of clippings. *World-Telegram,* April 17: case of a fireball that bounced through an open window into a house, scorched a rug where it burst. Same day, another hopped erratically two hundred yards down a street and popped into nothingness with a blast of heat. *Chicago Daily News,* April 22: case of a fireball that floated slowly across a meadow, entered a house, tried to rise up a chimney, then exploded, wrecking the chimney."

Replacing the clippings, he smoothed his hair tiredly. "I borrowed those from Beach. He has a huge collection of clippings dating back one hundred fifty years. Nearly two thousand of them deal with fireballs and similar phenomena. When you look through them, knowing what at long last is known, they look different. They're no longer a mere collection of off-trail data. They're a singular collection of cogent, highly significant facts which makes you wonder why we've never suspected what has now been discovered. The terrible picture has been there all along—but we weren't able to get it into proper focus."

"What makes you say that these things, these Vitons, are our masters?" queried Keithley, speaking for the first time.

"Bjornsen deduced it from observation, and his followers came inevitably to the same conclusion. A thinking cow could soon discern the mastery of whoever leads its kind to the slaughterhouse! The Vitons behave as if they own the Earth—which they do! They own you and me and the president and every king or criminal who has been born."

"Like hell they do!" swore a voice at the back.

Nobody looked round. Carmody frowned his displeasure at the interruption, the rest concentrated their attention on Graham.

"Little has been discovered," Graham told them, "but that little means plenty. Beach has satisfied himself that not only are the Vitons composed of energy, but also that they live on energy, feed on it—*our* energy! So far as they're concerned, we exist as energy-producers which kindly nature has provided to satisfy whatever they use for bellies. Thus, they breed us, or incite us to breed. They herd us, drive us, milk us, fattening on the currents generated by our emotions in precisely the same way that we fatten on juice involuntarily surrendered by cattle to whom we have given fodder containing stimulants for lactation. Show me the highly emotional man whose life has been healthy and long, and you show me the Vitons' prize cow, the medal-winner!"

"The devils!" snapped a voice.

"If you ponder this to the full, gentlemen," Graham persisted, "you will realize its awful implications. The nervous energy produced by the act of thinking, also as the reaction to glandular emotions, has long been known to be electrical or quasi-electrical in nature, and it is this output which nourishes our shadowy superiors. They can and do boost the harvest anytime they want, by stimulating rivalries, jealousies, hatreds, and thus rousing emotions. Christians against Moslems, whites against blacks, Communists versus Catholics, all are grist to the Viton mill, all are unwitting feeders of other, unimaginable guts. As we cultivate our food, so do the Vitons cultivate theirs. As we plow our fields, sow and reap, so do they plow and sow and reap. We are fleshly soil, furrowed with Viton-dictated circumstances, sown with controversial ideas, manured with foul rumors, lies and willful misrepresentations, sprinkled with suspicion and jealousy, all that we may raise fine, fat crops of emotional energy to be reaped with knives of trouble. Every time someone screams for war, a Viton is using his vocal chords to order a Viton banquet!"

A man sitting near Veitch stood up and said, "Maybe you know what some of us are doing. We're trying to make atom-splitting behind the times. We're trying to find a way to bring about the complete dissipation of subatomic particles into primal energy. We're trying to make a wavicle bomb. If we ever get it, boy, it'll be some bomb! Even a little one will rock the world." He licked his lips, looked around. "Are you suggesting that we're Viton-inspired?"

"You haven't made such a bomb?"

"Not yet."

"There's your answer," said Graham, dryly. "Maybe you'll never make one. Or if you do, you may never use it. But if you do make one—and drop one—!"

There came a heavy knock on the door, its sudden sound making several start in their seats. A uniformed man entered, whispered briefly to Keithley, then took his departure. Keithley arose, his face pale, his tones vibrant. He looked at Graham, then at the audience, and spoke slowly, earnestly.

"Gentlemen, I regret to inform you that I have just been told that the *Olympian* has been involved in a collision twenty miles west of Pittsburgh." He swallowed hard. His strain was obvious. "Many people have been injured, and one killed. The casualty is Doctor Beach!"

Amid a babble of comment from his horrified listeners, he sat down. For a full minute the audience shifted about, muttered, stared at each other, at the screen, at the feverish eyes of Graham.

"Another informed mind has been tossed into oblivion," Graham commented, bitterly. "The hundredth or the thousandth, for all we know!" He spread dramatic arms. "We eat, but we do not roam haphazardly around seeking wild potatoes. We grow them, and in growing them we improve them according to our notions of what potatoes ought to be. Similarly, our emotional tubers are not enough to fill higher and mightier bellies; they must be grown, stimulated, bred according to the ideas of those who do the surreptitious cultivating."

"That," he shouted, bunching a strong fist and shaking it at his wide-eyed hearers, "is the sole reason why human beings, otherwise rational enough, ingenious enough to amaze themselves with their own cleverness, cannot conduct world affairs in a way that does justice to their intelligence. That is the reason why, in this present day and age, we can build glories greater than history has ever held, yet live among the miserable monuments to our own destructive powers, and cannot build peace, security, tranquility. That is the reason why we advance in science, and all the emotion-producing arts, and all the exciting graces, but not in sociology, which has been hamstrung from the beginning."

Expressly, he rolled wide an imaginary sheet of paper, and said, "If I were showing you a microphotograph of the edge of an ordinary saw, its peaks and valleys would be a perfect graph representing the waves of emotion which have upset this world with damnable regularity. Emotion—the crop! Hysteria—the fruit! Rumors of war, preparations for war, accusations of preparations for war, actual wars, ferocious and bloody; religious revivals, religious riots; financial crises; labor troubles; color rivalries; ideological demonstrations; specious propaganda; murders, massacres, so-called natural disasters, or slaughter in any emotion-arousing form; revolutions and more wars.

His voice was loud, determined as he went on. "Despite the fact that the enormous majority of ordinary men of all colors and every creed instinctively yearn for peace and security above all else, this world of otherwise sane, sensible people cannot satisfy that yearning. *They are no allowed to satisfy it!* Peace, real peace, is a time of famine to those higher than us in the scale of life. There must be emotion, nervous energy, great, worldwide crops of it, brought into being, somehow, anyhow."

"It is atrocious!" swore Carmody.

"When you see this world riddled with suspicion, rotten with conflicting ideas, staggering beneath the burden of preparation for war, you can be certain the harvest time is drawing near—a harvest for others. Not for you, not for you—you are only the poor, bleeding suckers whose lot it is to be pushed around. *The harvest is for others!*"

He bent forward, his jaw jutting aggressively, his eyes burned into theirs. "Gentlemen, I am here to give you Bjornsen's formula that you may test it for yourselves. Maybe there are one or two among you who think I've been no more than making noises. God knows, I really wish that I'm deluded! So, soon, will you!" His grin was hard and completely humorless. "I ask, I demand that the truth be given the world before it becomes too late. Humanity will never know peace, never build a heaven upon earth while its collective soul bears his hideous burden, its collective mind is corrupted from birth. Truth must be a weapon, else these creatures would never have gone to such drastic lengths to prevent it from becoming known. They fear the truth, therefore the world must learn the truth. The world *must* be told!"

Sitting down, he covered his face with his hands. There were things he could not tell them, things he did not want to tell them. Before morning some of them would have gained the ability to test the facts, they would gaze into the dreadful skies—and some of them would die. They would die screaming the guilty knowledge that filled their minds, the fear that stuffed their leaping hearts. They would fight futilely, run uselessly, babble the dying protests of the damned, and expire helplessly.

Dimly, he heard Colonel Leamington addressing the audience, telling the scientists to go their separate ways with care and circumspection, to take with them mimeographed copies of the previous formula, to test it as soon as possible and inform him of the results immediately they were obtained. Above all, they were to exercise mental self-control, keeping well apart so that at worst their minds could betray them only as individuals and not as a group. Leamington, too, appreciated the danger. At least, he was taking no chances.

The governmental experts went out one by one, each accepting his slip of paper from Leamington. All looked at the seated Graham, but none spoke. Their faces were grim, and ominous thoughts already were burgeoning in their minds.

When the last of them had gone, Leamington said, "We've prepared sleeping quarters farther below this level, Graham. We must take good care of you until the facts have been checked, because Beach's death means that you're now the only one with first-hand information."

"I doubt it."

"Eh?" Leamington's jaw dropped in surprise.

"I don't think so," asserted Graham, wearily. "Heaven alone knows how many scientists have had private information about Bjornsen's discovery. Undoubtedly, some dismissed it on sight, as manifestly ridiculous—or so they thought. They never bothered to test it for themselves, and their omission saved their lives. But there may be others who have confirmed Bjornsen's claims and have been fortunate enough to have escaped detection up to the moment. They will be terrified, haunted men, driven half-mad by their own knowledge, afraid to risk ridicule, or precipitate their own end, or even cause a major holocaust by shouting from the housetops. They'll be down, way down somewhere out of sight, skulking silently around, like sewer-rats. You'd have hell's own job finding them!"

"You think that general dissemination of the news will cause trouble?"

"Trouble is putting it mildly," Graham declared. "The word for what will happen isn't in the dictionary. The news will be broadcast only if the Vitons fail in their positive attempts to prevent it. If they deem it necessary, they'll have no compunctions about wiping out half the human race to preserve the blissful ignorance of the other half."

"Supposing that they can do it," Leamington qualified.

"They've organized two world wars and have kept us emoting in suspense for the last twenty years over the possibility of a third and even bigger one." Graham rubbed powerful hands together, felt dampness oozing between the pores. "What they could do before they can do again."

"You're not suggesting that they're so all-powerful that it's futile to struggle against them, are you?"

"Most definitely not! But I don't underestimate the enemy. That's a mistake we've made too many times in the past!" He noted Leamington's wince without commenting upon it. "Their numbers and strength still remain a matter of speculation. Pretty soon they'll be swarming all over the place, looking for ringleaders of mutinies, dealing with them quickly, thoroughly—and finally. If they discover me, and remove me, you'll have to seek some other survivor. Bjornsen told his friends, and there's no telling just how far the news has spread through purely personal channels. Dakin, for instance, got it from Webb, who got it from Beach who got it from Bjornsen. Reed got it from Mayo and back to Bjornsen by another route. Dakin and Reed got it third-hand, or fourth-hand or maybe tenth-hand, but it killed them just the same. There may be a few others who, more by luck than anything else, have managed to keep alive."

"It is to be hoped so," said Leamington, with a touch of gloom.

"Once the news does get out, those of us who know it now will all be safe. The motive for removing us will then have ceased to exist." There was pleased anticipation in his tones, the glee of one who looks forward to ridding himself on an intolerable burden.

"If the results gained by these scientists bear out your statements," interjected Senator Carmody, "I, personally, shall see to it that the President is informed without delay. You can depend upon all the action of which the government is capable."

"Thanks!" Nodding gratefully, Graham arose, went out with Leamington and Wohl. They conducted him to his temporary refuge many levels deeper beneath the War Department Building.

"Say, Bill," spoke Wohl; "I collected a mess of reports from Europe that I've not had a chance to tell you about. There have been autopsies on Sheridan, Bjornsen and Luther, and the results were exactly the same as in the cases of Mayo and Webb."

"It all ties up," remarked Colonel Leamington. He patted Graham on the shoulder, performing the action with an amusing touch of paternal pride. "Your story is one that is going to strain the credulity of the world, but I believe you implicitly."

They left him to the much-needed sleep he knew he would not get. It was impossible to slumber with the crisis so near to hand. Mayo had gone, and he had seen him go. He had seen Dakin flee from a fate that was fast, determined, implacable, and he had anticipated and heard Corbett's similar end. Tonight—Beach! Tomorrow—who?

In the cold, damp hours of early morning, the news burst wide over a startled planet, broke with breathtaking suddenness and with a violence that transcended everything. The whole world howled in horror.

Chapter 8

It was three o'clock in the morning of June the ninth, 2015, and the seldom-mentioned but superbly efficient United States Department of Propaganda was working overtime. Its two huge floors in Home Affairs Building were dark, deserted, but half a mile away, hidden in a two-acre basement comprising a dozen great cellars, slaved the department's complete staff augmented by eighty willing helpers.

One floor above them, held by an immense thickness of concrete and steel, rested the mammoth weights of several old-fashioned presses, clean, bright, oiled, kept for years on constant readiness against the time when there might be a nationwide breakdown in the television news-reproduction system. One thousand feet higher soared the beautifully slender pile that was the home of the semi-official *Washington Post*.

Into the hands of the bustling four hundred, jacketless, perspiring, were being drawn the threads of communication over an entire world. Television, radio and cable systems, stratplane couriers, even the field—signaling sections of the fighting forces were theirs to command.

For all the intense activity, there was no sign of it at ground-level. The Post Building stood apparently lifeless, its mounting rows of windows reflecting a multitude of sallow moons. Unconscious of the frantically active battalion far below him, a patrolling police officer stamped his lonely way along the sidewalk, his eyes on a distant illuminated clock, his mind occupied with nothing more damning than the cup of coffee at the end of the beat. A cat ran daintily across his path, vanished into the shadows.

But down, down, down, far underneath the brooding monoliths, buried amid a million unsuspecting sleepers, the four hundred toiled in preparation for the awful dawn. Morse keys and high-speed autotypers rattled brief, staccato messages or longer, more ominous ones. Teletypers chattered furiously through chapters of information. Telephones shrilled and emitted metallic words while, in one corner, a powerful multi-channel shortwave transmitter forced impulses through its sky-high antenna and out to faraway ears.

News flowed in, was dissected, correlated, filed. Bleeker has completed the test, reports that he is watching two spheres gliding over Delaware Avenue. Okay, tell Bleeker to forget it—*if he can!* Here's Williams on the phone, saying he's made his test and can see luminescent spheres. Tell Williams thanks, and to go bury himself fast! Tollerton on the wire, saying test comes out positive and that he's now observing a string of blue globes moving high across the Potomac. Tell him to go underground and take a sleep.

"That you, Tollerton? Thanks for the information. No, sorry, we're not permitted to tell you whether other tests have produced reports confirming your own. Why? For your own sake, of course! Now stop thinking about it and go bye-bye!"

It was a noisy but systematic hurly-burly in which incoming calls squeezed their way between outgoing messages and every long-distance talker yearned for priority over every other. Here, a man clung desperately to a phone during his twentieth attempt to raise station WRTC in Colorado. Giving it up, he made a contact request to the police department in Denver. Over there, in one corner, a radio operator recited into his microphone in a patient monotone, "Calling aircraft-carrier Arizona. Calling aircraft-carrier Arizona."

In the middle of it all, exactly at the hour of four, two men arrived through the tunnel which for a decade had provided swift means of egress for thousands of still-damp newspapers being rushed to the railroad terminus.

Entering, the first man respectfully held the door open for his companion. The second man was tall, heavily built, with iron-gray hair, light gray eyes that looked calmly, steadily from a muscular confident face.

While this last one stood appraising the scene, his escort said, simply, "Gentlemen, the President!"

There followed a momentary silence while every man came to his feet, looked upon the features they knew so well. Then the chief executive signed them to carry on, permitted himself to be conducted to an enclosed booth. Inside, he adjusted his glasses, arranged some typewritten sheets in his hand, cleared his throat and faced a micro-phone.

The signal lamp flashed. The President spoke, his delivery assured, convincing, his voice impressive. Two blocks away, hidden in another basement, delicate machinery absorbed his voice, commenced to reproduce it two thousand times.

Long after he had departed, the machinery sped on, pouring forth tiny reels of magnetized wire which were snatched up, packed in airtight containers, and rushed away.

The New York-San Francisco stratplane left at five o'clock with a dozen canned reproductions of the President's speech hidden in its cargo. It dropped three of them en route before its pilot lost control of his thoughts—whereupon it disappeared forever.

The four-thirty special for London received the first score of copies, bore them safely across the Atlantic, delivered them at their destination. The pilot and copilot had been told that the sealed cans contained microfilms. They thought they were microfilms, and thus anything—or any things—which may have been interested in their thoughts were successfully deceived into believing the same.

About three-quarters of the reproductions had been received by the time zero hour arrived. Of the missing quarter, a few had suffered natural and unforeseeable delays, while the remainder represented the first casualties in the new and eerie conflict. The speech could have been made quite easily by the President in person, over a nationwide hook-up. And just as easily the speech could have been defeated at utterance of the first sentence, by death lurking at one microphone. Now, in effect, there were fifteen hundred Presidents ready for fifteen hundred microphones so completely scattered that some waited in America consulates and embassies in Europe, Asia and South America, some were ready on solitary islands in the Pacific, several were aboard warships far out at sea, away from human—and Viton—haunts. Ten were located in Arctic wastes where harmless flickers in the sky were the only Vitonesque phenomena.

At seven o'clock in the morning in the eastern states, at noon in Great Britain, and at equivalent times elsewhere, the news splashed over the front pages of old-fashioned papers, glowed into telenews screens, stood out starkly on stereocine screens, blared from loudspeakers, bawled over public address systems, was shouted from the housetops.

A low, incredulous cry of anguish came from the world of mankind, a wail that grew with growing belief and built itself into a shrill, hysterical scream. The voice of humanity expressed its shock, each race according to its emotional trend, each nation to its creed, each man to his glands. In New York, a frightened mob filled Times Square to suffocation point, surging, shouting, shaking fists at sullen skies, driven bellicose by peril in the manner of cornered rats. In Central Park, a seemlier crowd prayed, sang hymns, screamed for Jesus, protested, wept.

Piccadilly, London, was messed with the blood of forty suicides that morning. Trafalgar Square permitted no room for traffic, even its famous lions being concealed beneath a veritable flood of half-crazy human figures, some howling for the august presence of George the Eighth, others bellowing orders at the Lord God Almighty. And while the lions crouched even lower than humanity was crouching, and surrounding white faces were staring sweatily at wages-of-sin-is-death orators, Nelson's Column broke at its base, leaned over, propped itself for one tremendous second against another column of shrieks, fell and crushed three hundred. Emotion welled to the heavens, bright, clear, thirst-quenching emotion!

Mohammedans embraced Christianity that morning, and Christians became Mohammedans, Buddhists, boozers . . . anything. The churches swapped inmates with the bordellos and the asylums eventually gained from both. While many of the sinful made haste to bathe themselves in holy water, the pure did some mind-diverting wallowing in iniquity. Each according to his lights, but all a little unbalanced. Every one a Viton-cow satisfactorily stimulated to over-swollen udders!

But the news was out despite every attempt to prevent it, despite various obstacles to its broadcasting. Not all newspapers had acceded to official requests that their front pages be devoted to the authorized script. Many asserted their journalistic independence—or their proprietors' dimwitted obstinacy—by distorting the copy with which they had been provided, lending in humor or horror according to their individual whims, thus maintaining the time-honored freedom of gross misrepresentation which is the freedom of the press. A few flatly refused to print such obvious balderdash. Some mentioned it editorially as a manifest election stunt for which they were not going to fall. Others loyally tried to comply, and failed.

The New York Times came out with a belated edition stating that its early morning issue had not appeared because "of sudden casualties among our staff." Ten had died in the *Times* office that morning. The *Kansas City Star* came out on time loudly demanding to know what sort of a dollar-snatching gag Washington had cooked up this time. Its staff survived.

In Elmira, the editor of the *Gazette* sat dead at his desk, the television-printed data from Washington still in his cold grasp. His assistant editor had tried to take the sheet, and had slumped on the floor beside him. A third sprawled near the door, a foolhardy reporter who had dropped even as his mind conceived the notion that it was up to him to fulfill the duty for which his superiors had given their lives.

Radio Station WTTZ blew itself to hell at the exact moment that its microphone became energized and its operator opened his mouth to give the news which was to be followed by the presidential speech.

Later in the week, it was estimated that seventeen radio stations in the United States and sixty-four in the entire world had been wrecked mysteriously, by supernormal means, in time to prevent the broadcasting of revelations considered undesirable by others. The press, too, suffered heavily, newspaper offices collapsing at the critical moment, being disrupted by inexplicable explosions, or losing one by one the informed members of their staffs.

Yet the world was told, warned, so well had the propagandists prepared beforehand. Even invisibles could not be everywhere at once. The news was out, and a select few felt safe, but the rest of the world had the jitters.

Bill Graham sat with Lieutenant Wohl and Professor Jurgens in the latter's apartment on Lincoln Parkway. They were looking through the evening editions of every newspaper they'd been able to acquire.

"The reaction is pretty well what one might expect," commented Jurgens. "Some mixture! Look at this!"

He handed over a copy of *The Boston Transcript*. The paper made no mention of powers invisible, but contented itself with a three-column editorial ferociously attacking the government.

"We are not concerned," swore the *Transcript*'s lead writer, "with the question of whether this morning's morbid scoop is true or untrue, but we are concerned with the means by which it was put across. When the government exercises powers that it has never been given by mandate of the people, and practically confiscates the leading pages of every newspaper in the country, we perceive the first step toward a dictatorial regime. We see a leaning toward methods that will never for one moment be tolerated in this free democracy, and that will meet with our uncompromising opposition so long as we retain a voice with which to speak."

"The problem that arises," said Graham, seriously, "is that of whose views this paper represents. We can assume that the person who wrote it did so with complete honesty and in good faith, but are those opinions really his own, or are they notions which cunningly have been insinuated into his mind, notions which he has accepted as his own, believes to be his own?"

"Ah, there lies the peril!" agreed Jurgens.

"Since all our data points to the fact that the Vitons sway opinions any way they want them, subtly guiding the thoughts that best suit their own purposes, it is well-nigh impossible to determine which views are naturally and logically evolved, which implanted."

"It is difficult," Jurgens conceded. "It gives them a tremendous advantage, for they can maintain their hold over humanity by keeping the world divided in spite of all our own attempts to unite it. From now on, every time a troublemaker shoots his trap, we've got to ask ourselves a question of immense significance; who's talking now?" He put a long, delicate finger on the article under discussion. "Here is the first psychological counterstroke, the first blow at intended unity—the crafty encouragement of suspicion that somewhere lurks a threat of dictatorship. The good old smear-technique. Millions fall for it every time. Millions will always fall so long as they would rather believe a lie than doubt a truth."

"Quite." Graham scowled at the sheet while Wohl watched him thoughtfully.

The Cleveland Plain Dealer takes another stand," Jurgens observed. He held up the sheet, showing a two-inch streamer. "A nice example of how journalism serves the public with the facts. This boy fancies himself on satire. He makes sly references to that vodka party in Washington a fortnight ago, and insists on referring to the Vitons as 'Graham's Ghouls.' As for you, he thinks you're selling something, probably sunglasses."

"Damn!" said Graham, annoyedly. He caught Wohl's chuckle, glared him into silence.

"Don't let it worry you," Jurgens went on. 'When you've studied mass psychology as long as I've done you'll cease to be surprised at anything." He tapped the paper. "This was to be expected. From the journalistic viewpoint, truth exists to be raped. The only time facts are respected is when it's expedient to print them. Otherwise, it's smart to feed the public a lot of guff. It makes the journalist feel good; it gives him a sense of superiority over the suckers."

"They won't feel so darned superior when they've got an eyeful."

"No, I guess they won't." Jurgens mused a moment, then said, "I don't wish to seem melodramatic, but would you be good enough to tell me whether any of these Vitons are near us at this moment?"

"There are none," Graham assured him. His wide, glistening eye gazed through the window. "I can see several floating over distant roofs, and there are two poised high above the other end of the road, but there are none near here."

"Thank goodness for that." Jurgens' features relaxed. He used his hand as a comb, passing thin fingers through long, white hair, smiled quietly as he noted that Wohl's face also expressed relief. "What I'm curious about is the problem of what is to be done next. The world now knows the worst, but what is it going to do about the matter—what *can* it do?"

"The world must not only know the worst, but also see it in all its grim and indisputable actuality," said Graham, earnestly. "The government has practically co-opted the big chemical companies in its plan of campaign. The first step will be to put on the. market large and cheap supplies of the materials cited in Bjornsen's formula, so that the general public may see the Vitons for themselves."

"Where does that get us?"

"It gets us a big step toward the inevitable show-down. We must have a united public opinion to back us in the coming fight, and I'm not talking parochially, either. I mean united the world over. All our numerous squabbling cliques, political, religious, or whatever they may be, will have to drop their differences in the face of this greater peril and unitedly support us in future efforts to get rid of it once and for all."

"I guess so," admitted Jurgens, doubtfully, "but—"

Graham went on, "Moreover, we must gather as much information concerning the Vitons as it may be possible to obtain. That is because what we know about them to date is appallingly little. We need more data, we need it in quantities that can be supplied only by thousands, maybe millions of observers. At the earliest possible moment we must counterbalance the Vitons' enormous advantage in having an ages-old understanding of human beings, and gain an equally good comprehension of them. Know thine enemy! It is futile to scheme, or oppose, until we can make an accurate estimate of what we're up against."

"Perfectly sensible," Jurgens conceded. "I see no hope whatever for humanity until it has rid itself of this burden. But you know what opposition means?'

"What?" Graham encouraged.

"Civil war!" His distinguished features grave, the psychologist wagged a finger to emphasize his words. "You will not get a chance to strike one miserable blow at these Vitons unless first you've managed to conquer and subdue half the world. Humanity will be divided against itself—they'll see to that. The half that remains under Viton influence will have to be overcome by the other half, in fact you may have to exterminate them not only to the last man, but also the last woman and child."

"I can't see them being that dopey," Wohl put in.

"So long as people insist on thinking with their glands, their bellies, their wallets or anything but their brains, they'll be dopey enough for anything," declared Jurgens, fiercely. 'They'll fall for a well-organized, persistent and emotional line of propaganda and make suckers of themselves every time. Remember those Japs? Early last century we called them civilized, poetic; we sold them scrap iron and machine tools. A decade later we were calling them dirty yellow bellies. In 1980 we were loving them and kissing them and calling them the only democrats in Asia. By the end of this century, they may be hell's devils again. Same with the Russians, cursed, cheered, cursed, cheered—all according to when the public was ordered to curse or cheer. Any expert liar can stir up the masses and persuade them to love this mob or hate that mob, as suits the convenience of whoever's doing the stirring-up. If ordinary but unscrupulous men can divide and rule, so can Vitons!" He turned from Wohl to Graham. "Mark my words, young man, your first and most formidable obstacle will be provided by millions of emotional dimwits among your fellow beings."

"I fear you may be right," admitted Graham, uneasily.

Jurgens was right, dead right. Bjornsen's formula was marketed a mere seven days, in immense quantities, and the first blow fell early in the morning of the eighth day. It fell with thunderous vim which humanity felt like a psychic blast.

An azure sky splashed with pink by the rising sun spewed two thousand thin streamers of flame from the invisibility of its upper reaches. The streamers curved downward, whitening with condensation. Thickening as they lost altitude, they resolved themselves into mighty back-blasts of strange, yellow stratosphere planes.

Below lay Seattle, a few early citizens on its broad streets, a few wispy columns of smoke rising from stoked furnaces. Many amazed eyes turned to the sky, many still-sleeping heads tossed on their pillows as the aerial armada howled across Puget Sound, swooped over Seattle's roofs.

The bulleting rush brought the howl up in pitch to a shrill scream as the yellow horde rocketed over the rooftops, the badge of a flaming sun showing on the underside of each stubby wing. Black, ominous objects excreted in pairs and waggled downward from sleek, streamlined fuselages, fell for a hushed age, buried themselves in the buildings beneath. The buildings promptly disrupted in a mad, swirling, mêlée of flame, fumes, bricks and splintered timbers.

For six hellish minutes Seattle shuddered and shook to an uninterrupted series of tremendous explosions. Then, like wraiths from the void, the yellow two thousand vanished into the stratosphere whence they had come.

Four hours later, while Seattle's streets still sparkled with shards of glass and her living still moaned amid the rains, the invaders reappeared. Vancouver suffered this time. A dive, six minutes of inferno, then away. Slowly, lackadaisically, their condensing blast-streaks dissipated in the upper regions, while beneath lay pitted avenues, strewn business-blocks, crushed homes around which wandered silent, thin-lipped men, sobbing women, screaming children, some whole, some not. Here and there a voice shrieked and shrieked and shrieked like one of the damned doing his damnedest in a world of the damned. Here and there a sharp report brought quietness and peace to someone urgently in need of both. A little lead pill was welcome medicine to the partly disemboweled.

It was coincidentally with that evening's similar and equally effective attack on San Francisco that the United States government officially identified the aggressors. The markings on the attackers' machines should have been sufficient indication, but this evidence had seemed too unreasonable to credit. Besides, officialdom had not forgotten the days when it had been considered expedient to strike blows under any flag but one's own.

Nevertheless, it was true. The enemy was the Asian Combine, with whom the United States was supposed to be on friendliest terms.

A despairing radio message from the Philippines confirmed the truth. Manila had fallen, the Combine's war vessels, air machines and troops were swarming through the entire archipelago. The Filipino army no longer existed, and the United States Far East carrier fleet—caught on distant maneuvers—was being attacked even as it raced to the rescue.

America leaped to arms while its leaders met to consider this new problem so violently thrust upon them. Playboy financiers made ready to dodge the draft. End-of-the-world cultists took to the hills and waited for Gabriel to come fit them with halos. Among the rest, the mighty masses making ready for sacrifice, a fearful questioning went whispering around.

"Why didn't they use atom bombs? Haven't they got any—or are they wary because we've got more?"

With or without atom bombs, so savage and unprovoked an assault was Viton-inspired, and no doubt about it. But how had the luminosities managed to corrupt and inflame the normally slumbersome Asian Combine?

A fanatical pilot, shot down while attempting a crazy solo raid on Denver, revealed the secret. The time was ripe, he asserted, for his people to enter into their rightful heritage. Powers unseen were on their side, helping them, guiding them toward their divinely appointed destiny. The day of judgment had arrived and the meek were about to inherit the earth.

Have not our sages looked upon these little suns and recognized them as the spirits of our glorious ancestors, he asked with the certitude of one who poses the unanswerable question. Is not the Sun our ancient emblem? Are we not sons of the Sun, fated in death to become little suns ourselves? What is death but a mere transition from the army of abominable flesh to the celestial army of the shining spirit, where much esteem is to be gained in company with one's honorable fathers and one's exalted fathers' fathers?

The path of the Asians is chosen, he yelled insanely, a path sweetened by the heavenly blossoms of the past as well as the unworthy weeds of the present. Kill me, kill me—that I may take my rightful place with ancestors who alone can lend grace to my filthy body!

Thus the mystic rambling of the Asian pilot. His entire continent was afire with this mad dream, cunningly conceived and expertly insinuated within their minds by powers that had mastered the Earth long before the era of Emperor Ming; powers that had the precise measure of the human cow, knew when and where to jerk its dangling udders. The notion of plausibly "explaining" themselves as ancestral spirits did full credit to the infernal ingenuity of the Vitons.

While the Western Hemisphere mobilized as speedily as it could in the face of constant and inexplicable handicaps, and while the Eastern pursued its holy war, the best brains of the Occidental world sought frantically for means by which to refute the insane idea placed in Asian minds, means to bring home to them the perilous truth.

In vain! Had not the Occidentals themselves first discovered the little suns and, therefore, could not dispute their existence? Onward, to victory!

The hordes of the spiritually inflamed poured out of their formally peaceful boundaries, their eyes aglow with ignorance instead of knowledge, their souls dedicated to a divine mission. Los Angeles shriveled in a sudden holocaust that fell upon it from the clouds. The first lone enemy flier to reach Chicago wrecked a skyscraper, minced a thousand bodies with its concrete and steel before a robot-interceptor blew him apart in mid-air.

By August the twentieth, no atom bombs, no radioactive gases, no bacteria had been used by either side. Each feared the retaliation which was the only effective defense. It was a bloody war and yet a phony war.

But Asian troops were in complete possession of the whole of California and the southern half of Oregon. On the first of September, the air-borne and submarine transports cut their increasing losses by reducing their flow across the Pacific. Contenting itself with consolidating and holding the immense foothold it had gained on the American continent, the Asian Combine turned its attention in the opposite direction.

Triumphant troops poured westward, adding maddened Viet Nam, Malaysian and Siamese armies to their strength. Two hundred ton tanks with four-feet treads rumbled through mountain passes, were manhandled when bogged by humanity in the mass. Mechanical moles gnawed broad paths through previously impassable jungles, bulldozers shifted and piled their litter, flamethrowers burned the piles. Overhead, stratplanes dotted the sky. In sheer weight of numbers lay the

Asians' strength. Theirs was the greatest weapon, the weapon possessed by every man . . . that of his own fertility.

Into India they swept, a monstrous conglomeration of men and machines. The ever-mystical and Viton-infested population received them with open arms and three hundred million Hindus became recruits at one swoop. They added themselves to the swarms of the Orient, thus making one quarter of the human race the poor dupes of an Elder People.

But not all bent the knee and bowed the head. With superb cunning the Vitons boosted the emotional crop by inciting the Moslems of Pakistan to oppose. Eighty millions of them stood with their back to Persia and barred the way. The rest of the Moslem world made ready behind them. Frenziedly, they died for Allah, and impartially Allah fattened the Vitons.

The brief breathing space permitted by pressure being transferred elsewhere enabled America to get its wind and recover from the initial shock. The press, once given exclusively to every aspect of the conflict, now saw fit to devote a little space to other matters, especially to Bjornsen's experiments in the past, and news about Vitons' activities both past and present.

Inspired by the resurrection of Beach's collection of press clippings, several papers searched through their own morgues in an effort to discover cogent items which once had been ignored. There was a general hunt for bygone data, some conducting it in the hope of finding support for pet theories, others with the more serious intention of gaining worthwhile knowledge about the Vitons.

Holding the opinion that not all people could see identically the same range of electromagnetic frequencies, *The Herald-Tribune* asserted that some were endowed with wider sight than others. Wide-sighted persons, said *The Herald-Tribune,* had often caught vague, unrecognizable glimpses of Vitons many times in the past, and undoubtedly it was such fleeting sights that had given birth to and maintained various legends of banshees, ghosts, djinns and similar superstitions. This implied that spiritualists were Viton-dupes on an organized basis, but for once *The Herald-Tribune* overlooked religious susceptibilities.

Only a year ago, *The Herald-Tribune* itself had reported strangely colored lights seen floating through the sky over Boston, Massachusetts. Reports of similar lights had been made at various times, and with astonishing frequency, as far back as they could trace. A singular feature of all reports was that they'd been received with a total lack of science's much-vaunted curiosity: every expert had dismissed them as odd phenomena devoid of significance and unworthy of investigation.

For example: February, 1938—Colored light seen sailing high over Douglas, Isle of Man. November, 1937—Fall of a tremendous ball of light frightened inhabitants of Donaghadee, Ireland, other, smaller balls of light being seen floating in the air at the same time. May, 1937—Disastrous end of German transatlantic airship Hindenburg attributed to "St. Elmo's fire." The scientists tied a tag on this mysterious phenomena—and went back to their slumbers. July, 1937—Chatham, Massachusetts, station of the Radiomarine Corporation reported a message from the British freighter *Togimo,* relayed by the American vessel *Scanmail,* saying that mysterious colored lights had been sighted five hundred miles off Cape Race, Newfoundland.

New York Times, January 8, 1937—Scientists, fed up counting sheep, produced a new theory to explain the blue lights and "similar electric phenomena" frequently seen near Khartoum, Sudan, and Kano, Nigeria.

Reynolds News (Britain), May 29,1938—Nine men were injured by a mysterious something that dropped from the sky. One of them, a Mr. J. Hurn, described it as "like a ball of fire." *Daily Telegraph,* February 8, 1938—Glowing spheres were reported to have been seen by many readers during an exceptional display of the Aurora Borealis, itself a rare sight in England. *Western Mail* (Wales), May, 1933—Balls of phosphorescence observed gliding over Lake Bala, mid-Wales. *Los Angeles Examiner,* September 7, 1935—Something described as a "freak lightning bolt" fell in bright sunshine at Centerville, Maryland, hurled a man from a chair and set fire to a table.

Liverpool Echo (Britain), July 14, 1938—What witnesses described as "a big blue light" invaded Number Three Pit, Bold Colliery, St. Helens, Lancashire, contacted lurking gases and caused "a mystery explosion." Blue lights that caused no blips on watching radar scopes caused air-raid sirens to be sounded in Northern Ireland, and fighter-interceptors roared upward, January 17, 1942. No bombs dropped, nothing was shot down. The news was suppressed in the papers and the Germans were suspected of some new devilment. Four months earlier Berlin's guns had blasted at "navigation lights" when no planes were over.

Sydney Herald and Melbourne Leader had made astonishingly lavish reports on glowing spheres, or fireballs, which for unknown reasons had infested Australia throughout, the year 1905, especially in the months of February and November. Eerie conventions had been held in the Antipodes. Veterans of World Slaughter had conferred, sky-high. One such phenomenon, seen by Adelaide Observatory, moved so slowly that it was watched for four minutes before it vanished. *Bulletin of the French Astronomical Society,* October, 1905—Strange, luminous phenomena seen lurking around Calabria, Italy. The same kind of phenomena, in the same area, had been reported in September, 1934, by *Il Popolo d'Italia.*

Someone found an ancient and tattered copy of *The Cruise of the Bacchante* in which King George the Fifth, then a young prince, described a strange string of floating lights, "as if of a phantom vessel all aglow," seen by twelve members of the *Bacchante*'s crew at four o'clock in the morning of June 11, 1881.

Daily Express (Britain), February 15, 1923—Brilliant luminosities were seen in Warwickshire, England. *Literary Digest,* November 17, 1925—Similar luminosities seen in North Carolina. *Field*, January 11, 1908—Luminous "things" in Norfolk, England. *Dagbladet,* January 17, 1936—Will-o'-the-wisps in southern Denmark, hundreds of them. Scientists sought onion blight at twenty thousand feet, but not one pursued a will-o'-the-wisp. It wasn't their fault; like all saints and sinners, they went where Viton-inspired to go. *Peterborough Advertiser* (Britain), March 27, 1909—Queer lights in the sky over Peterborough. Over following dates, the *Daily Mail* confirmed this report, and added others from places farther away.

Something emotional might have been happening in Peterborough in March 1909, but no paper published anything correlative as between human and Viton activities . . . though there are human functions which are not news.

Daily Mail (Britain), December 24, 1912, ran an article by the Earl of Erne describing brilliant luminosities that had appeared "for seven or eight years" near Lough Erne, Ireland. The things that started Belfast's sirens wailing, in 1942, soared from the direction of Lough Erne, Ireland. *Berliner Tageblatt,* March 21, 1880— "A veritable horde," of floating luminosities were seen at Kattenau, Germany. In the same century, glowing spheres were reported from dozens of places as far apart as French Senegal, the Florida Everglades, Carolina, Malaysia, Australia, Italy and England.

Journalistically enjoying itself, *The Herald-Tribune* went to town by issuing a special edition containing twenty thousand references to luminosities and glowing spheres culled from four hundred issues of *Doubt.* For good measure, it added a parallel-beam photographed copy of Webb's jottings, publishing them with the editorial opinion that this scientist had been working along the right lines prior to his death. In the light of recently acquired knowledge, who could say how many schizophrenics were really unbalanced, how many were the victims of Viton meddling, or how many were normal people fortuitously endowed with abnormal vision?

"Were all those second-sighters as simple as we thought?" demanded *The Herald-Tribune,* paraphrasing Webb. "Or was it that they could scan frequencies just beyond the reach of most of us?"

Then followed more quotations resurrected from the past. The case of a goat that pursued nothingness across a field, then dropped dead. The case of a herd of cattle that suddenly went mad with fear, and raced around a meadow obligingly sweating their emotions into empty air. Hysteria on a turkey ranch when eleven thousand gobblers went nuts in ten minutes . . . thus providing unseen travelers with a snack. Forty-five cases of dogs that howled piteously, put their tails between their legs and belly-crawled away—from nothing! Cases of contagious insanity in dogs and cattle, "too numerous to list," but all of them proof—asserted *The Herald-Tribune*—that animal eyes functioned differently from all but those of a minority of human beings.

The public absorbed very word of this, wondered, feared, trembled in the night hours and by day. White-faced, jittery mobs raided the drugstores, snatched up supplies of Bjornsen's formula as fast as they became available. Thousands, millions treated themselves according to instructions, saw the facts in all their hellish actuality, had their few shreds of doubt torn away.

In Preston, England, nobody perceived anything abnormal—until it was found that the local atomic-defence chemical plant had substituted toluidine blue for methylene blue. In Yugoslavia, a Professor Zingerson, of Belgrade University, dutifully treated himself with iodine, methylene blue and mescal, peered myopically at the sky and saw no more than he'd seen since birth. He said as much in a bitingly sarcastic article published in the Italian *Domenica del Corriere.* Two days later a globe-trotting American scientist persuaded the paper to print his letter suggesting that the good professor either take off his lead-glass spectacles or substitute ones with lenses made of fluorite. Nothing more was heard from the absent-minded Yugoslavian.

Meanwhile, in the west of America, monster tanks made tentative thrusts and occasional forays across the fighting line, clashed, blew each other into metal splinters. High-speed stratplanes, gun-spotting helicopters, highly streamlined helldivers and robot bombs criss-crossed the skies of California, Oregon and militarily important points east. Neither side yet made use of atomic explosives, each hesitant about starting a process beyond human power to end. Basically, the war followed the pattern of earlier and equally or less bloody wars; despite improved techniques, automatic and robotic weapons, despite development of armed conflict to a push-button affair, the ordinary soldier, the common foot-slogger remained supreme. The Asians had ten for the other side's one, and were breeding ahead of their losses.

Distance shrank even more after a further month of battle when supersonic rockets joined the fray. High out of sight and far beyond sound, they streaked both ways across the Rockies, mostly missing their intended targets, yet still striking ferociously at tightly packed haunts of humanity. A ten-mile miss at one, two or three thousand miles range was mighty good shooting. All the way from Bermuda to Llasa, any place became liable to erupt skyward at any time, the noise following afterward.

So the skies flamed and glowed and spewed death with dreadful impartiality while men of all creeds and colors moved through their last minutes and final hours protected mentally by hope of survival and lack of knowledge of what awaited them at the next stroke of the clock. Heaven and earth had combined to create hell. The common people bore it with the animal fatalism of the lower orders, seeing with eyes more understanding than of yore, constantly conscious of a menace more invincible, more revolting than anything born of their own shape and form.

Chapter 9

Amid surrounding wreckage, the Samaritan Hospital still stood untouched. New York had suffered enormously since the Asian invasion had commenced, and great rockets continued to arrive from the enemy's faraway mobile launchers. By sheer good fortune, or by virtue of that occasional hiatus in the laws of chance, the hospital remained unharmed.

Scrambling out of his battered gyrocar three hundred yards from the main entrance, Graham gazed at the intervening mound of rubble blocking the street from side to side.

"Vitons!" warned Wohl, leaving the car and casting an anxious eye at the sullen sky.

Nodding silently, Graham nodded that there were a great number of the weird spheres hanging in the air above the tormented city. Every now and then, an underground giant heaved in his earthly blanket, puked a mass of bricks and stones, then roared with pain. Dozens of waiting spheres swooped down, eager to lap his vomit. Born of fire was their food, and well-cooked . . . the feast of human agony.

The fact that the huge majority of human beings were now able to see them made not the slightest difference to these ultra-blue vampires. Aware or unaware, no man could prevent a hungry phantom from seating itself on his spine, inserting into his cringing body strange, thrilling threads of energy through which his nervous currents were greedily sucked.

Many had gone insane when suddenly selected for milking by some prowling sphere; many more had flung themselves to welcome death, or had committed suicide by any means conveniently to hand. Others who still clung desperately to the remnants of their sanity walked, crept or slunk through the alleys and the shadows, their minds in constant fear of sensing that queer, spinal shiver caused by the insinuation of thirsty tentacles. The days of God's own image were long forgotten. Now, it was every man a cow.

That cold, eerie shiver running swiftly from the coccyx to the cervical vertebrae was one of the most common of human sensations long before the Vitons were known or suspected; so common that often a man would shiver and his companions jest about it.

"Somebody's walking over your grave!"

There was revulsion in Graham's lean, muscular features as he clambered hastily over the mass of broken granite and powdered glass, slipping and sliding on outcrops of small, loosely assembled lumps, his heavy boots becoming smothered in fine, white dust. His nostrils were distended as he climbed; he was conscious of that sour, all-pervading blitz-odor, a smell of men and matter crushed together and grown stale. Topping the crest, his wary eyes turned upward, he half-ran, half-jumped down the farther side, Wohl following in a tiny avalanche of dirt.

Hurrying across the cracked and pitted sidewalk, they passed through the gap of the missing entrance gates. As they turned up the curved gravel drive leading to the hospital's front doors, Graham heard a sudden, choking gasp from his companion.

"By heavens, Bill, there's couple of them after us!"

Looking behind, he caught a split-second glimpse of two orbs, blue, glowing, ominous, sweeping toward him in a long, shallow dive. They were three hundred yards away, but approaching with regular acceleration, and the grim silence of their oncoming was a horrifying thing.

Wohl passed him with a breathlessly sobbed, "Come on, Bill!" His legs were moving as they'd never moved before. Graham sprang after him, his heart doing a crazy jig within his ribs.

If one of those things got hold of either of them, and read the victim's mind, it would immediately recognize him as a key man of the opposition. All that had saved them so far had been the Vitons' difficulty in distinguishing one human being from another. Even the vaqueros of the huge King-Kleber Ranch could not be expected to know and recognize every individual beast, and, for the same reason, they had been fortunate enough to escape the attention of these ghastly superherdsmen. But now—!

He ran like hell, knowing full well as he raced along that flight was useless, that the hospital held no hope for the damned, provided no sanctuary, no protection against superior forces such as these—yet feeling impelled to run.

With Wohl one jump in the lead, and the bulleting menaces a bare twelve yards behind, they hit the front door and went through it as if it didn't exist. A startled nurse stared at them wide-eyed as they hammered headlong through the hall, then put a pale hand to her mouth and screamed.

Soundlessly, with terrifying persistence, the pursuing spheres swept past the girl, shot round the farther corner and into the passage taken by their intended prey.

Graham caught an eye-corner vision of the luminosities as he skidded frantically around the next bend. They were seven yards behind and coming on fast. He dodged a white-coated intern, vaulted a long, low trestle being wheeled on doughnut tires from a ward, frightened a group of nurses with his mad pace.

The glossy parquet was treacherous. Wohl's military boots hit the polish, he slipped in mid-flight, fought to retain balance, went down with a thud that shook the walls. Unable to stop, Graham leaped over him, slid along the glossy surface, crashed violently into the facing door. The door creaked, groaned, burst open.

His shoulder muscles taut with expectation, he whirled around to face the inevitable. Surprise filled his glittering eyes. Bending down, he hauled Wohl to his feet, gestured toward the end of the passage.

"By God!" he breathed. "By God!"

"What's up?"

"They came around that corner, then stopped dead. They hung there a moment, went deeper in color, and departed as if the devil himself was after them."

Gasping for wind, Wohl said, "Boy, we're damn lucky!"

"But what made them scram?" persisted Graham, looking puzzled. "It has never been known for them to give up like that. I've never heard of them letting up on a victim once they've got his number. Why did they do it?"

"Don't ask me." Grinning in unashamed relief, Wohl dusted himself vigorously. "Maybe we weren't good enough for them. Maybe they decided we'd make a lousy meal and they could do better elsewhere. I don't know—I'm no fount of wisdom."

"They often depart in a hurry," said a cool, even voice behind them. "It has occurred repeatedly."

Swiveling on one heel, Graham saw her standing by the door with which he had collided. The light from the room behind made a golden frame for her crisp black curls. Her serene eyes looked steadily into his.

"Surgery's sugar-babe," he told Wohl, with unnecessary gusto.

Wohl gave her an appraising up-and-down, and said, "I'll say!"

Miffed, she put a slender hand on the door as if to close it. "When you pay a social call, Mr. Graham, please arrive in seemly manner, and not like a ton of bricks." She tried to freeze him with her glance. "Remember that this is a hospital and not a jungle."

"You'd hardly find a ton of bricks dumped in the jungle," he pointed out. "No, no, please don't close that door. We're coming in." He marched through, followed by Wohl, both ignoring her iciness.

They seated themselves by her desk, and Wohl studied a photograph thereon. Pointing to it, he said, "To Harmony from Pop. Harmony, eh? That's a nice name. Was your pappy a musician?"

The ice broke a little. Taking a chair, Doctor Curtis smiled. "Oh, no. I guess he just liked the name."

"So do I," Graham announced. He threw her the I-spy eye. "I hope it'll suit us."

"Us?" Her finely arched brows rose a trifle.

"Yes," he said, impudently. "Someday."

The temperature of the room sank five degrees. She tucked her silk-clad legs under her chair away from his questing eyes. The whole floor quivered, and a distant roar came down from the sky. All three sobered immediately.

They waited until the roar died away, then Graham began, "Look, Harmony—" He paused, added, "You don't mind if I call you Harmony, do you?" and without waiting for her reply, went on, "What's this you were saying about the Vitons beating it frequently?"

"It is very mysterious," Doctor Curtis admitted. "I don't know of any explanation for it, and so far I've had no time to seek one. All I can tell you is that immediately the hospital's staff became equipped to see these Vitons we discovered that they were frequenting the hospital in fair numbers. They were entering the wards and feeding on pain-racked patients from whom, of course, we carefully kept this knowledge."

"I understand."

"For some reason, they did not bother the staff." She looked questioningly at her listeners. "I don't know why they didn't."

"Because," Graham told her, "unemotional people are just so many useless weeds from their viewpoint, especially in a place containing so much fine, ripe, juicy fruit. Your wards are orchards!"

Her smooth, oval face registered the brutality of his explanation with a look of distaste. She continued, "At certain periods, we have noticed that every luminescent sphere in the hospital has hurried away as rapidly as possible, not returning for some time. It happens three or four times a day. It has happened just now."

"And very probably it saved our lives."

"Possibly," she admitted with calculated disinterest which deceived neither.

"Now, Doctor . . . er . . . Harmony"—he wiped out Wohl's grin with a hard glare—do you know whether each exodus coincided with some consistent feature in hospital routine, such as the administering of certain medicines to patients, or the operating of the X-ray apparatus, or the opening of particular bottles of chemicals?"

She considered awhile, apparently oblivious of her questioner's intent gaze. Finally, she got up, searched through a file, dialed her telephone, consulted somebody in another part of the building. There was satisfaction in her features as she ended the call.

"Really, it was most stupid of me, but I must admit that I did not think of it until your questions brought it into my mind."

"What is it?" Graham urged.

"The short-wave therapy apparatus."

"Hah!" He slapped his knee, bestowed a look of triumph on the interested Wohl. "The artificial fever machine. Isn't it screened?"

"We've never been able to screen it completely. We've tried to do so, because it interfered with the reception of local television receivers, sending checkered patterns racing across their vision plates. But the apparatus is powerful, its short waves are penetrating, it has defied all our efforts, and I understand that the complainants have had to screen their receivers."

"On what wave-length does it operate?" pursued Graham.

"One and a quarter meters."

"Eureka!" He bounced to his feet, alight with the fire of battle. "A weapon at last!"

"What d'you mean, a weapon?" Wohl was not overly impressed.

"The Vitons don't like it. We've seen that for ourselves, haven't we? Heaven alone knows how its emanations appear to their alien senses. Perhaps they feel it as unbearable heat, or sense it as the Viton equivalent of an abominable smell. Whatever the effect may be, we've the satisfaction of knowing they like to get away from it as fast as they can travel. Anything that makes them want to go someplace else is, *ipso facto,* a weapon."

"I reckon maybe you've got something," Wohl conceded.

"If it is a weapon, or a potential one," remarked Doctor Curtis, seriously, "surely the Vitons would have destroyed it? They never hesitate to destroy where they deem it necessary. Why should they leave untouched this threat to their existence—if it is a threat?"

"I can imagine nothing better calculated to draw despairing humanity's attention to the properties of therapy cabinets than to go around destroying them."

"I see." Her large, dark eyes were thoughtful. "Their cunning is indeed great. They think way ahead of us all the time."

"All the time so far," he corrected. "What of yesterday when we've still got tomorrow?" He reached for her telephone. "I must pass this information to Leamington without delay. Maybe it's dynamite. Maybe it is what I hope it is— and God help us if it's not! Besides, it may be enough to permit some of his gadgeteers to throw together an apparatus which will give protection to tonight's meeting."

Leamington's tired, worn features grew into the tiny visor. They relaxed somewhat as he listened to Graham's hasty flow of data. Finishing, Bill Graham turned to Doctor Curtis.

"This meeting is a scientific one to be held at nine o'clock this evening in the basement of National Guarantors Building, on Water Street. I'd like to take you along."

"I'll be ready at eight-thirty," she promised.

Professor Chadwick already was in the middle of his speech when Bill Graham, Harmony Curtis and Art Wohl moved quietly down the center aisle, took their seats. The basement was full, the audience silent, attentive.

At one end of the front row, Colonel Leamington twisted around, attracted Graham's attention, jerked an indicative thumb toward a large cabinet standing guard by the only door. Graham nodded his understanding.

With a rolled newspaper in one hand, the other left free for his frequent gestures, Professor Chadwick was saying. "For a couple of months *The Herald-Tribune* has been exhuming masses of data and still hasn't dug out the half of it. The amount of material is so enormous that one cannot help but marvel at the barefaced manner in which the Vitons were able to operate with complete confidence in humanity's lack of suspicion. To them, we must have seemed witless beyond words."

"Which we were," commented a cynical voice from the rear.

Chadwick sighed hasty agreement and went on, "Their methods of 'explaining' their own errors, omissions, mistakes and oversights by insinuating superstitious notions to 'account' for them, backing up those notions by the performing of so-called miracles when required, and the production of poltergeist and spiritualistic phenomena when asked for, does full credit to the hellish ingenuity of these creatures whom we call Vitons. They have made the confessional box and the seance-room their centers of psychic camouflage; the priest and the medium have been equally their allies in the devilish work of seeing that the blind masses stay blind." He brushed a sardonic hand from left to right. "Thus the wide-sighted always have been able to take their pick: visions of the holy virgins, or saints, or sinners, or the shades of the late lamented. Step up, boys, they're all yours!"

Someone laughed mirthlessly, a cold, grating laugh that jarred on the hearers' nerves.

"The Herald-Tribune's data is, in grim fact, a record of human gullibility, a record of how men in the mass can look facts in the face—and deny them! It is a record of how people can see fish and call them flesh or fowl, according to the conventionalisms of dogmatic tutors as purblind as themselves, according to their personal fears of losing invisible shares in nonexistent heavenly mansions, according to their credulous belief that God may deny them wings if they, in turn, assert that a sight authoritatively declared to be straight from heaven may indeed have come straight from hell." He paused, added in a hearable undertone, "Satan was a liar from the first—they said it!"

"I agree," boomed Leamington, not giving a damn whose personal idiosyncrasies were being kicked around.

"I've discovered a good deal of cogent data, myself," continued Chadwick. "For example, things we now know to be Vitons were frequently in the Fraser River district of British Columbia early in 1938. They got into the papers time and time and time again. A British United Press report dated July 21, 1938, says that the huge forest fires then ravaging the Pacific coast of North America were caused by something described as 'dry lightning,' admitted to be unique phenomena.

"In 1935, in the Madras Presidency of India, was reported an esoteric sect of floating-ball worshippers who, apparently, could see the objects of their devotions which were quite invisible to non-believers. Attempts to photograph what they were worshipping invariably failed, though I know and you know what might have been recorded had the photographers been able to employ Beach's emulsion.

The Los Angeles Examiner of mid-June, 1938, reported a case paralleling that of the late Professor Mayo. Headed: FAMOUS ASTRONOMER LEAPS TO DEATH, it stated that Doctor William Wallace Campbell, president emeritus of the University of California, had met his end by flinging himself from the window of his third-floor flat. His son ascribed his father's act to his fear of going blind. Personally, I feel that while his fear may have had direct connection with his sight, it was not in the manner then believed!"

Disregarding supporting murmurs from his audience, Professor Chadwick said, "Believe it or not, but one man's extrasensory perception, or his wide-sightedness, was so well developed that he was able to paint an excellent picture showing several Vitons floating over a nightmarish landscape and, as if somehow he sensed their predatory character, he included a hawk in the scene. That picture is Mr. Paul Nash's *Landscape of a Dream,* first exhibited in 1938, and now in the Tate Gallery, in England. Nash himself died very suddenly a few years later."

Turning his eyes toward Graham, the speaker declared, "All the evidence we have been able to gather shows beyond doubt that the Vitons are creatures of primal energy held in a form both compact and balanced. They are neither solid, nor liquid nor gas. They are not animal, vegetable or mineral. They represent another, unclassified form of being which they share with fireballs and like phenomena, but they are not matter in the general accepted sense—they're something else which is strange to us but in no way supernatural. Maybe they're a mess of wavicles complex beyond all possibility of analysis by any instrument we have today; we know they're so peculiar that our spectroscopic tests of them have proved worthless. It seems to me that the one possible weapon we can bring against them is something influencing their own strange matter-state, namely, a form of energy such as a radiation having a heterodyning effect, something that might interfere with the Vitons' natural vibrations. The discovery made only today by Mr. Graham, of the Intelligence Service, amply confirms this theory." Raising his hand and beckoning to Graham, he concluded, "So I now ask Mr. Graham to give you the valuable information he has obtained, and I feel sure that he will be able to assist us still further with some useful suggestions."

In a strong, steady voice, Graham recounted his experience of a few hours before. "It is imperative," he told them, "that at once we should undertake intensive research in short waves projected on the radio-beam system, and determine which particular frequencies—if any—are fatal to Vitons. In my opinion, it is desirable that we set up a suitable laboratory in some far away, unfrequented spot distant from war areas, for our evidence is that Vitons congregate where humanity swarms most thickly, and very rarely visit uninhabited regions."

"That is an excellent idea." Leamington stood up, his tall form towering above his seated neighbors. "We have ascertained that the Vitons' numerical strength is somewhere between one twentieth and one thirtieth that of the human race, and it is a safe bet that the majority of them hang around fruitful sources of human and animal energy. A laboratory hidden in the desert, a locality sparse in emotional fodder, might remain unobserved and undisturbed for years."

There came a loud buzz of approval from listeners as Leamington sat down. For the first time since the Bjornsen-precipitated crisis, they felt that humanity was getting somewhere, doing something to rid itself once and for all of the burden of the centuries. As if to remind them that optimism should be modified by caution, the ground quivered, a muted rumble sounded outside, then followed the roar from the sky as lagging sound caught up with its cause.

Already Leamington had in mind a suitable site for the establishment of what he hoped would be the first anti-Viton arsenal. Ignoring outside noises, the Secret Service chief bestowed a fatherly smile on his protégé still standing on the platform. Instinctively, he knew that this plan would go through, and that Graham would play the part best calculated to enhance the reputation of the Service. Leamington had never demanded more of his boys than just their bodies and souls. He had never received less than that.

"It is of little avail," Graham reminded, as outside sounds died away, "to battle the Asians without also attempting to subdue their crafty overlords. To wipe out the luminosities is to remove the source of our enemies' delusions, and bring them back to their senses. They're humans, like us, those Asians—take away their mad dreams and you'll take away their fury. Let's strike a blow by giving our solitary clue to the world."

"Why not organize our native scientists and get them on the job?" inquired a voice.

"We shall do that, you may rest assured. But as we know to our cost, a thousand widely separated experimenters are safer than a thousand in a bunch. Let the entire western world set to work, and nothing—visible or invisible—can prevent our ultimate triumph!"

They roared their agreement as he stared absently at the cabinet still standing guard over the only door. The memory of Beach was a dull pain within his mind which held other and equally tragic memories—the rag-doll appearance of Professor Mayo's broken body; the sheer abandon with which Dakin had plunged to his sickening end; the horrid concentration in the eyes of the sufferer with an imaginary dog in his belly; Corbett's dying *crump* as he smacked into stone; the great black banner of tormented atoms which had been unfurled above Silver City.

Not much use damping their spirits in this rare moment of enthusiasm. All the same, it was as clear as daylight that short-wave research could move in only one of two directions—the right one, or the wrong one. Wrongness meant slavery forever; and the first indication of rightness would be the heartless slaughter of every experimenter within reasonable reach of success.

There was murder in prospect, murder of every valuable intellect in the front-line of the eerie campaign. It was a dreadful certainty that Graham had not the heart to mention. As the audience fell silent, he left the platform. The silence was broken by the now familiar feature of sudden death.

The floor jumped six inches northward, settled slowly back. While the occupants of the basement posed in strained attitudes, the tearing rumble of tottering masonry came to them through the thick walls. Then the vile bellow from the sky as if the Creator were enjoying the agonized writhings of his own creations. A pause, followed by the lower, lighter rumble of vehicles dashing along the street, heading for the new area of wreckage, blood and tears.

Sangster was worried and made no attempt to conceal the fact. He sat behind his desk in the Office of the Department of Special Finance, in Bank of Manhattan, watched Graham, Wohl and Leamington, but spoke to none of them in particular.

"It's twelve days since that international broadcast giving a line to everybody from hams to-radio manufacturers," he argued. "Was there any interference with that general call? There was not! Did one radio station get picked up and tossed around? No, not one! I say that if short-waved research was a menace to the Vitons they'd have played merry hell to prevent it. They'd have listed the radio experts and had a pogrom. There'd have been slaughter all the way from here to there. But the Vitons took no notice. So far as they were concerned, we might have been scheming to wipe them out by muttering a magic word. Ergo, we're on the wrong track. Maybe they avoided therapy sets just to put us on the wrong track. Maybe they're doing the laughs they can't make up the sleeves they haven't got." He tapped his desk nervously. "I don't like it, I don't like it."

"Or maybe they want us to think the same way," Graham put it, easily.

"Eh?" Sangster's jaw dropped with suddenness that brought grins to the others' faces.

"Your views are proof that the Vitons' disinterest ought to be our discouragement." Strolling to the window, Graham regarded the battered vista of New York. "I said 'ought,' mark you! I'm suspicious of their seeming nonchalance. The damned things know more of human psychology than experts of Jurgens' type are likely ever to learn."

"All right, all right!" Mopping his brow, Sangster pawed at some papers on his desk, extracted a sheet, held it up. "Here's a report from the Electra Radio Corporation. Their twenty experts might as well be shooting craps. They say short waves stink. They've thrown at passing luminosities every frequency their plant can concoct, and the spheres merely ducked out as if they'd encountered a bad smell. Bob Treleaven, their leading wiseacre, says he almost believes the cursed things really do sense certain frequencies as their equivalent to odors." He tapped the paper with an accusatory finger. "So where do we go from here?"

"'They also serve who only stand and wait,'" quoted Graham, philosophically.

"Very well. We'll wait." Tilting back in his chair, the bothered Sangster put his feet on the desk and assumed the expression of one whose patience is everlasting.

"I've tremendous faith in you, Bill, but it's my department's money that is being poured into all this research. It would relieve my mind to know what we're waiting for."

"We're waiting for some experimenter to come near frizzling a Viton." Graham's leathery face grew grim. "And although I hate like hell to say it, I think we're waiting for the first of another series of corpses.

"That's what has got me uneasy." Leamington's voice chipped in, his tone low, serious. "These infernal orbs frequently are prying into minds. Some day, Bill, they'll examine yours. They'll realize they've found the ace—and you'll be deader than a slab of granite when *we* find *you*."

"We've all got to take chances," said Graham. "Heck of a one I took when I chose to be born!" He gazed through the window once more. "Look!"

The others jolted him, gazed out. A fat, gray cloud was blooming from the base of the Liberty Building. Sound caught up with sight even as they looked, and there came an awful crash that shook the neighborhood. Then the skyward sound arrived, a terrific yelp that changed pitch with Doppler effect as it descended.

Four seconds later, with the cloud at its fattest, the immense bulk of the pitted and glassless Liberty Building leaned over, slowly, ever so slowly, lowering itself with the mighty reluctance of a stricken mammoth. It reached a crazy angle, hesitated in seeming defiance of the law of gravity, its millions of tons a terrible menace to the area it was about to devastate.

Then, as if an unseen hand had reached forth from the void and administered the final, fateful push, the enormous pile fell faster, its once beautiful column splitting in three places from which girders stuck like rotten teeth. The noise of its landing resembled a bellow from the maw of original chaos.

Ground rumbled and rolled in long, trembling waves of plasmic agitation. A vast, swirling cloud of pulverized silicate crept sluggishly upward.

A veritable horde of spheres, blue, tense, eager, hungry, dropped from immense heights, streaked inward from all directions, their paths direct lines concentrated on this latest fount of agony.

Over the Hudson, another string of spheres ghoulishly were following a flying bomb, clinging to it like a tail of great blue beads. The bomb hammered steadily for Jersey City. Shortly, it would tilt downward and start to scream, and the women beneath it would try to outscream it . . . and the Vitons would enjoy them with the silence of dumb vultures.

"One rocket!" breathed Leamington, still staring at the smoke-obscured wreck of the Liberty Building. "I thought at first they'd started with atom bombs. God, what a size that one must have been."

"Another Viton improvement," opined Graham, bitterly. "Another technical advantage they've given to their Asian dupes."

On Sangster's desk a telephone whirred with suddenness that plucked at their already taut nerves. Sangster answered it, pressed the amplifier button.

"Sangster," rattled the phone, in sharp, metallic accents, "I've just been called by Padilla on the radio-beam from Buenos Aires. He's got something! He says . . . he says . . . Sangster . . . *oh!*"

Alarmed by Sangster's wildly protruding eyes and ghastly complexion, Graham leaped to his side and looked into the hesitant instrument's visor. He was just in time to see a face slide away from the tiny screen. It was a vague face, made indistinctly by a weird, glowing haze, but its shadowy features conveyed a message of ineffable terror before it shrank completely from sight.

"Bob Treleaven," whispered Sangster. "It was Bob." He stood like one stunned. "They got him—and I saw them get him!"

Taking no notice, Graham rattled the telephone, raised the operator. He danced with impatience while the exchange tried to get an answer from the other end. No response could be obtained, not on that line, nor on alternative lines.

"Give me Radiobeam Service," he snapped. "Government business—hurry!" He turned to the white-faced Sangster. "Where's Electra's place?"

"Bridgeport, Connecticut."

"Radiobeam Service?" Graham held his lips close to the mouthpiece. "A recent call has been made from Buenos Aires to Bridgeport, Connecticut, probably relayed through Barranquilla. Trace it and connect me with the caller." Still clinging to the phone, he beckoned Wohl.

"Take that other phone, Art. Call Bridgeport's police headquarters, tell them to get out to the Electra plant, and keep for us whatever they may find. Then beat it down and have the car ready. I'll be one jump behind you."

"Right!" With a grunt of eagerness, Wohl snatched up the other instrument, jabbered into it hurriedly. Then he was gone.

Graham's call got through, he talked for some time, his jaw muscles lumping while he listened to the faraway speaker. Finishing, he made a second and shorter call. He looked moodily disappointed as he shoved the phone aside and spoke to the others.

"Padilla is stiffer than an Egyptian mummy. The relay operator at Barranquilla is also dead. He must have listened in and heard something we're forbidden to know. The knowledge he gained has cost him his life. This is a time when I could do with being in four places at once." He massaged his chin, added, "A million to one Treleaven is as dead as the rest."

"Well, you've got your corpses," commented Leamington, with complete lack of emotion.

His remark came too late. Already Graham was outside the door and dashing down the passage toward the levitator shafts. There was something retributory in his fast lope, and a harder gleam lay behind that other gleam filling his wide-sighted eyes. The rods and cones of his pupils had undergone more than spectroscopic readjustment—they now vibrated with hate.

Air sighed in the bowels of the building as Graham's disk dropped at reckless pace, bearing him toward street level and the waiting gyrocar. Reaching bottom, he sprang out, his nostrils distended like those of a wolf which has found the scent and is racing to the kill.

Chapter 10

The Electra Radio Corporation's small but well equipped laboratory was meticulous in its orderliness, nothing being out of place, nothing to mar its prim tidiness save the body flopped beneath the dangling telephone receiver.

A burly police sergeant said, "It's exactly as we found it. All we've done is make a stereoscopic record of the cadaver."

Bill Graham nodded his approval, bent, turned the body over. He was not repelled by the look of horror which vicious, glowing death had stamped upon the corpse's features. At deft speed he frisked the victim, placed the contents of the pockets on an adjacent table, examined them with shrewd attention.

"Useless," he commented, disgustedly. "They don't tell me a thing worth knowing." He shifted his gaze to a small, dapper man fidgeting miserably beside the police sergeant. "So you were Treleaven's assistant? What can *you* tell me?"

"Bob got a call from Padilla," babbled the small man, his frightened eyes flickering from the questioner to the object on the floor. Nervously, his manicured fingers tugged at his neatly trimmed mustache.

"We know that. Who's Padilla?"

"A valuable business connection and a personal friend of Bob's." He buttoned his jacket, unbuttoned it, then returned to the mustache. He seemed to be afflicted with too many hands. "Padilla is the patentee of the thermostatic amplifier, a self-cooling radio tube which we manufacture under his license."

"Go ahead," Graham encouraged.

"Bob got this call and became very excited, said he'd spread the news around so it couldn't be stopped. He didn't mention the nature of this news, but evidently he thought it red-hot."

"And then?"

"He went straight into the lab to ring up somebody. Five minutes later a gang of luminosities whizzed into the plant. They've been hanging around for days, sort of keeping an eye on us. Everybody ran for dear life excepting three clerks on the top floor."

"Why didn't they run?"

"They've not yet had eye-treatment. They couldn't see and didn't know what was happening."

"I understand."

"We came back after the luminosities had left, and we found Bob dead beneath the phone." Another jittery fumble at the mustache, and another frightened shift of gaze from questioner to corpse.

"You say that the Vitons have been hanging around for days," put in Wohl. "During that time have they snatched any employee and pried into his mind?"

"Four." The small man became more nervous than ever. "They have had a poke at four within the last few days. That made it pretty awful for us. There was no way of telling who they'd pick on next. We couldn't work so well daytimes and we couldn't sleep nights." He gave Wohl a pathetic look, and went on, "They got the last one yesterday afternoon, and he went insane. They dropped him outside the gates and left him a gibbering idiot."

"Well, there weren't any about when we arrived," remarked Wohl.

"Probably they're satisfied that this counterstroke has prevented the plant from becoming a possible source of danger to them for the time being." Graham could not restrain a smile as he noted how the jumpiness of the little man contrasted with the elephantine indifference of the police sergeant. "They'll come back!"

He dismissed the witness and other waiting employees of the radio plant. With Wohl's help, he searched the laboratory for notes, memo-pads or any seemingly insignificant piece of paper that might record a clue, his mind recalling the cryptic messages left behind by other and earlier martyrs.

Their efforts were in vain. One fact and one only was at their disposal—the fact that Bob Treleaven was decidedly dead.

"This is hell!" groaned Wohl, despairingly. "Not a lead. Not one miserable little lead. We're sunk!"

"Use your imagination," Graham chided.

"Don't tell me you've picked up a line?" Wohl's honest eyes popped in surprise. He scanned the laboratory, trying to find something he'd overlooked.

"I haven't." Bill Graham grabbed up his hat. "In this crazy business nobody lives long enough to hand us a useful line, and we've no choice but to spin our own. Come on—let's get back."

It was as they flashed through Stamford that Wohl shifted his thoughtful gaze from the road, glanced at his passenger, and said, "All right, all right—is it a family secret or something?"

"What d'you mean?"

"This line you're spinning."

"There are several. To start with, we've not got enough data concerning Padilla. We'll have to get more, and some of it may prove well worth having. Then again, it seems that Treleaven had about five undisturbed minutes at that phone before he was put out of the running. He was on to Sangster for less than a half a minute, and that was his last call in this sinful world. So unless it took him four and a half minutes to reach Sangster—which is not likely—I reckon maybe he phoned somebody else first. We'll find out whether he did and, if so, whom he called."

"You're a marvel—and I'm dumber than I thought," said Wohl.

Grinning sheepishly, Graham continued, "Lastly, there's an unknown number of radio ham stations operating between Buenos Aires, Barranquilla and Bridgeport. One or two may have snooped the commercial beams while raking the ether. If any one of them happened to be listening in, and caught Padilla's talk, we want him as badly as do the Vitons. We've got to find that guy before it's too late!"

"Hope," recited Wohl, "springs eternal in the human breast." His eyes roamed up to the rear-view mirror, rising casually, then becoming fixed in fearful fascination. "But not in mine!" he added, in choked tones.

Slewing around in his seat, Graham peered through the car's rear window. "Vitons—after us!"

His sharp eyes switched to the front, the sides, taking in the terrain with photographic accuracy. "Step on it!" His thumb found and jabbed the emergency button just as Wohl shoved the accelerator to the limit. The crisis-bank of extra batteries added their power, and with the dynamo screaming its top note, the gyrocar leaped forward.

"No use—they've as good as got us!" gasped Wohl. He manhandled the machine around an acute bend, corrected three successive side-slips, straightened up. The road was a broad ribbon streaming past their wildly whirling wheels. "We couldn't escape at twice this pace."

"The bridge!" Graham warned. Feeling surprised by his own coolness, he nodded toward the bridge rushing nearer at tremendous pace. "Hop the bank and dive into the river. It's a chance."

"A . . . lousy . . . chance!" breathed Wohl.

Offering no comment, Bill Graham again glanced backward, saw their ominously glowing pursuers about two hundred yards behind and gaining rapidly. There were ten of the things speeding through the atmosphere in single file, moving with that apparently effortless but bulletlike pace characteristic of their kind.

The bridge widened in perspective as it shot nearer; the ghostly horde picked up fifty yards. Anxiously, Graham divided his attention between the scenes in front and at rear. This, he could see, was going to prove touch and go. A split second would be the difference between one chance in a million and no chance at all.

"We'll barely do it," he shouted above the dynamo's howl. "When we hit the water, fight out and swim downstream for as long as you can hold breath. Don't come up for more than a quick gulp. Stay down for as long as they're around even if you have to soak for a week. Better that than—" He left the sentence unfinished.

"But—" commenced Wohl, his face registering strain as the oncoming bridge leaped at their front wheel.

"Now!" roared Graham. He didn't wait for Wohl to make up his mind; his powerful fingers clamped upon the wheel, twisted it with irresistible power.

With a protesting screech from the sorely maltreated gyroscope, the slender car went hell-for-leather up the bank. It vaulted the top a bare foot from the bridge's concrete coping, described a spectacular parabola through the air. Like a monster, twenty-foot missile, it struck the water with force that sent shocked drops flying high above roadlevel. A tiny rainbow shimmered momentarily in the shower.

Down, down went the machine amid an upsurging fountain of waggling bubbles. It vanished, leaving on the troubled surface a thin, multicolored film of oil over which ten baffled luminosities skimmed a temporary defeat.

It was fortunate that he'd had the foresight to fling open his door the instant before they struck, Graham realized. Inward pressure of water would otherwise have kept him prisoner for several valuable seconds. Sinuously moving his tough, wiry body, and with a mighty kick of his feet, he got free of the car even as it settled lopsidedly upon the river's bed.

Making fast, powerful strokes, he sped downstream at the utmost pace of which he was capable, his chest full of wind, his eyes straining to find a way through the liquid murk. Wohl, he knew, was out—he had felt the thrust upon the car as the police lieutenant got clear. But he couldn't see Wohl; the muddiness of the river prevented that.

Bubbles trickled from his mouth as his lungs reached point of rebellion. He tried to increase the rate of his strokes, felt his heart palpitating, knew that his eyes were starting from their sockets. A lithe swerve shot him upward, his mouth and nostrils broke surface, he exhaled, drew in a great gasp of fresh air. He went down again, swimming strongly.

Four times he came up with the swiftness of a trout snatching at a floating fly, took a deep, lung-expanding gulp, then slid back into the depths. Finally, he stroked to the shallows, his boots scraped pebbly bottom, his eyes rose cautiously above the surface.

The coruscant ten now were soaring from a point on the bank concealed by the bridge. The hidden watcher followed their ascent with calculating eyes, followed them until they were ten shining pinpoints under the edge of the clouds. As the blue specters changed direction, drifting rapidly eastward, Graham staggered out of the water and stood dripping on the bank.

Silently and undisturbed the river flowed along. The lone man regarded its placid surface with perplexity that quickly changed to open anxiety. He ran upstream, his clothes still shedded water, his mind eager yet fearing to see the other side of the bridge.

Wohl's body grew visible through the concrete arch as the runner came nearer. Moisture squelched dismally in Graham's boots while he pounded along the shred of bank beneath the arch and reached the police lieutenant's quiet form.

Hastily combing wet hair from his forehead, Graham stooped over the other's limp legs, wound his arms around them. His hands gripping the back of Wohl's cold thighs, Graham heaved himself upright, his muscles cracking under the other's weight.

He hugged the body, looking downward at its dangling head. Water drooled from Wohl's gaping mouth and over Graham's boots. Graham shook him with a jerky upward motion, watching resultant drops. When no more came, he laid Wohl face downward, squatted astride him, placed wide, muscular hands over breathless ribs, began to press and relax with determined rhythm.

He was still working with an utterly weary but stubborn rocking motion when the body twitched and a watery rattle came from its throat. Half an hour later, he sat in the back of a hastily stopped gyrocar, his arms supporting Wohl's racked form.

"Got a hell of a crack on the noggin, Bill," wheezed Wohl. He coughed, gasped, let his head loll weakly on the other's shoulder. "Stunned me at the start. Maybe it was the door. It faced upstream, and it slapped back on me. I sank, came up, sank again. I was breathing water." His lungs made faint gurgling noises. "I feel like a month-old floater."

"You'll be all right," Graham comforted.

"Goner . . . thought I was a goner. Said to myself this was the end. Hell of an end . . . just rubbish . . . garbage . . . in the river. Up and down, up and down, amid muck and bubbles, for ever and ever and ever." He leaned forward, dribbling. Graham pulled him back again. "I was up . . . fighting like a maniac . . . lungs full. Broke top . . . and a goddam Viton grabbed me."

"What?" shouted Graham.

"Viton got me," Wohl repeated dully. "Felt its ghoulish fingers . . . feeling around . . . inside my brain . . . searching, probing." He coughed harshly. "All I remember."

"They must have lugged you in to the bank," declared Graham, excitedly. "If they've read your mind they'll anticipate our next moves."

"Feeling around . . . in my brain," murmured Wohl. He closed his eyes, breathed with vibrant, bronchial sounds.

Pursing his lips, Leamington asked, "Why didn't they kill Wohl as they have done the others?"

"I don't know. Perhaps they decided that he knows nothing really dangerous to them." Bill Graham returned his superior's steady stare. "Neither do I, for that matter—so don't take it for granted that I'm apt to die on you every time I go out."

"You don't fool me," Leamington scoffed. "It's a marvel how your luck's held out so far."

Letting it pass, Graham said, "I'll sure miss Art for the next few days." He sighed gently. "Were you able to get me that data on Padilla?"

"We tried." Leamington emitted a grunt of disgust. "Our man down there can discover sweet nothing. The authorities have their hands full and no time to bother with him."

"Why? Have they got the usual attack of *manana?*"

"No, it's not that. Buenos Aires was badly blitzed by the Asians shortly after we cabled. The city's in a bad state."

"Damn!" swore Graham. He bit his lips in vexation. "There goes one possible lead."

"That leaves us the ham stations to check," observed Leamington, dismally. "We're on that job right now. It'll take some time. Those blasted hams have a fondness for hiding themselves on mountain tops and in the depths of jungles. They pick the darnedest places."

"Can't you call them on the air?"

"Oh, yes, we can call them on the air—like I can call the wife when she's someplace else. They listen out when the spirit moves them." Sliding open a drawer, he extracted a sheet of paper, handed it across. "This came in just before you returned. It may mean something, or it may not. Does it convey anything to you?"

"United Press report," read Graham, rapidly scanning the lines of type. "Professor Fergus McAndrew, internationally known atom-splitter, mysteriously disappeared this morning from his home in Kirkintilloch, Scotland." He threw a sharp glance at the impassive Leamington, returned his attention to the sheet. "Vanished while in the middle of enjoying his breakfast, leaving his meal half eaten, his coffee still warm. Mrs. Martha Leslie, his elderly housekeeper, insists that he had been kidnapped by luminosities."

"Well?" asked Leamington.

"Kidnapped—not killed! That's queer!" The investigator frowned as his mind concentrated on this aspect. "It looks as if he could not have known too much, else he'd have been left dead over his meal rather than snatched. Why snatch him if he was no menace?"

"That's what gets me down." For once in his disciplined life, Leamington permitted his feelings to gain the upper hand. He hammered on his desk, said loudly, "From the very beginning of this wacky affair we've been tangled in a mess of strings all of which lead to people who are corpses, or people who aren't anything any longer. Every time we run after something we trip over a fresh cadaver. Every time we make a grab a vacuum. Now they've started hoisting evidence clean out of existence. Not even a body." He snapped his fingers. "Gone—like that! Where's it going to end? *When* is it going to end—if ever it does end?"

"It'll end when the last Viton ceases to be, or the last human being goes under." Graham flourished the United Press report and changed the subject. "This McAndrew, I reckon, must have a mind fairly representative of the world's best talent at this particular time."

"So what?"

"They won't content themselves with probing his mind, as they've been doing up to now. They'll take his entire intellect to pieces and find what makes the wheels go round. I can't see any other reason for making a snatch rather than the usual killing. My guess is that the Vitons have become uneasy, maybe scared, and they've taken him as a suitable subject for their super-surgery." His eyes flamed with intensity that startled his listener. "They're trying to measure an average in order to estimate probabilities. They're losing confidence and want to know what's coming to them. So they'll weigh this McAndrew's brain power, and from that they'll deduce the likelihood of us being able to discover whatever they're afraid of us finding."

"And then?" Leamington hissed the question.

"We suspect that Padilla found something, maybe by design, or perhaps by accident, but we must also allow for the possibility that he was no more than a wild guesser who got wiped out deliberately to mislead us. A South American red herring." Graham stood up, his tall form towering above his chief's desk. He wagged an emphatic finger. "This kidnapping, if I'm right, means two things."

"Those are what?"

"Firstly, that there *is* a lethal weapon waiting to be discovered by us—if we've the ability to find it. The Vitons are vulnerable!" He paused, then said carefully, "Secondly, if their study of McAndrew's mind satisfies them that we have the talent to find and develop this weapon, they'll take every possible action to meet the threat—and damn quick! Hell is going to pop!"

"As if it isn't popping already!" remarked Leamington. He waved an all-embracing hand. "Can you conceive anything more desperate than our present situation?"

"Better the devil you know than the devil you don't," Graham riposted. "We *know* what's popping now. We don't know what they'll start next."

"If they think up any new hellers," said Leamington, "by God, they'll about finish us!"

Graham made no reply. He was buried in thought, deep, worried thought. One, now dead, had credited him with extrasensory perception. Maybe it was that, or perhaps it was second sight—but he knew that a bigger and better hell was on the way.

Darkness, deep, dismal darkness such as can swathe only a city once lurid with light. Apart from firefly flashes of gyrocars hurtling with masked headlamps through New York's glassless and battered canyons, there was nothing but that heavy, depressing, all-pervading gloom.

Here and there circles of wooden posts coated with phosphorescent paint gleamed greenly in the night and warned drivers of immense pits left by blasting rockets. That sour stench of war was stronger than ever, the smell of upheaved earth and fractured mains, broken bricks and torn bodies.

On uptown Sixth a small red flashlight waved to and fro in the darkness, causing Graham to brake his speedster. It slowed, stopped, and he got out.

"What's the idea?"

A young officer emerged from concealing blackness. "Sorry, mister, your machine's wanted." He remained silent while Graham revealed his identification, then declared, "I can't help it, Mr. Graham. My orders are to commandeer every vehicle attempting to pass this point."

"All right, I will not argue the matter." Reaching inside the gyrocar, Graham hauled out his heavy topcoat, writhed into it. "I'll walk."

"I'm really sorry," the officer assured. "There's serious trouble out west and we need every machine on which we can lay our hands." He turned to two of his olive-drab command, barely visible in the dark. "Rush this one to the depot." Then, as the pair clambered in, he pressed the button of his red-lensed flashlight, signaled another approaching gyrocar to stop.

Graham paced hurriedly along the road. There were tottering walls at his side, some temporarily shored with timber braces. On the other side gaunt skeletons of what once had been great business blocks stood in awful solitude.

An anti-aircraft battery occupied the square at the end. He passed it in silence, noting the aura of tension emanating from the quiet, steel-helmeted figures surrounding the sleek, uplifted muzzles. A duty of appalling futility was theirs; the guns, the cunning proximity fuses, the more cunning predictors couldn't beat to the draw a rocket traveling far ahead of its own sound. The most they could hope for was an occasional robot-bomb, or a crazy Asian with ambitions of honorable suicide. Nothing else.

Beyond the square, precariously poised on a shattered roof, was a combined listening-post and radar unit. The quadruple trumpets of the former angled uselessly toward the westward horizon; the hemispherical antenna of the latter rotated dutifully but to little effect. Although he could not see them, he knew that somewhere between the roof-post and the guns were more tensed, silent figures waiting by the Sperry predictor—waiting for that banshee wail announcing the approach of something slow enough to detect and, perhaps, bring down.

A bright pink aurora sparkled for one second over the Palisades, and the bellow of the explosion drifted in eons later. Whatever caused it sent a tidal wave racing up the Hudson. Another sparkle came a moment later, higher up the Jersey side of the river, near Haverstraw. Then silence filled the sky.

But the road was not silent. From the depths immediately beneath came a strange, persistent sound: the sound of a mighty gnawing. That subterranean *scrunch, scrunch, scrunch* was audible all the way along, and accompanied the stealthy walker for a mile.

There, far down below the very foundations of the city, great jaws of beryllium steel were guzzling the bedrock. Mechanical moles were chewing through the substrata, forming the arteries of a new and safer city beyond reach of rockets and bombs.

"When all that's finished," mused Graham, whimsically, "the former subway will be the El!"

Turning left, he saw a blotch of solid darkness in the less material dark. The dim form was on the opposite side of the road, hurrying nearer on steel-shod heels that clanked noisily.

They were almost level, and about to pass, when from a swollen cloud hidden in the general blackness there plunged a ball of cold blue light. Its sudden, ferocious onslaught was irresistible. The vaguely seen human figure sensed imminent peril, whirled around, gave vent to a blood-freezing shriek that ended in a gasp.

While Graham clung close to the deeper shadows, his hard eyes registering the incredibly swift attack, the luminosity bobbed around its victim, illuminating him in pale, sickly light. He saw the fine, brilliant streamers of its tentacles insert themselves in the body. The thing burped a couple of rings like immaterial halos that spread outward and faded away. The next moment, the shining devil soared, bearing the body aloft.

Another was similarly snatched from the vacant lot two hundred yards farther along the road. Passing a skeletal rooming house, Graham saw hunter and hunted crossing the open area. Lit by the former's ghostly glow, the latter's fantastically elongated shadow fled ahead of him.

The prey had all the frantic motion of one fleeing from a product of fundamental hell. His feet hit earth in great, clumping strides, while queer, distorted words jerked from his fear-smitten larynx.

Iridescent blue closed upon him and formed a satanic nimbus behind his head. The blue swelled, engulfed both the runner and his final, despairing scream. The Viton spewed two rings before it took the body skyward.

A third and a fourth were picked from Drexler Avenue. They saw the downward swoop of blue. One ran. The other fell on his knees, bent in dreadful obeisance, covered the nape of his neck with his hands. The runner bellowed hoarsely as he ran, his belly heaving, his bladder out of control, his terror-filled tones a veritable paean of the damned. The kneeler remained kneeling, as if before his personal joss. The joss was as impartial as any other god. They were taken simultaneously, sobbed together, soared together, true believer and heretic alike, both the sinner and the saved. The Vitons displayed no preferences, showed no favors. They dished out death as impartially as munitions-makers or meningococci.

Moisture was lavish on Graham's forehead as he stole up the driveway, passed through the doors of the Samaritan Hospital. He wiped it off before seeing Harmony, decided he would say nothing of these tragedies.

She was as cool and collected as ever, and her richly black eyes surveyed him with what he felt to be a sort of soothing serenity. Nevertheless, they saw into him deeply.

"What has happened?" she asked.

"Happened? What d'you mean?"

"You look bothered. And you've just wiped your forehead."

Pulling out a handkerchief, he mopped it again, said, "How did you know that?"

"It was smeary." The eyes showed alarm. "Were they after you again?"

"No, not me."

"Someone else?"

"What's this?" he demanded. "A quiz?"

"Well, you looked off-balance for once," she defended.

"I'm always off-balance when talking to you." He drove other, deadlier matters out of his thoughts and gave her the springtime look. "I'll be normal when I've got used to you, when I've seen more of you."

"Meaning what?"

"You know what I mean."

"I assure you I've not the remotest notion of what you're trying to suggest," she said, coldly.

"A date," he told her.

"A date!" Her eyes supplicated the ceiling. "In the midst of all this, he comes seeking dates." She sat down behind her desk, picked up her pen. "You must be stark, staring mad. Good day, Mr. Graham."

"It's night time, not day," he reminded. He emitted an exaggerated sigh. "A night for romance."

She sniffed loudly as she commenced writing.

"All right," he gave in. "I know when I'm given the brush-off. I get used to it these days. Let's change the subject. What d'you know?"

She put down the pen. "I was waiting for you to return to your senses. I've been wanting to see you the last few hours."

"Have you, begad!" He stood up delightedly.

"Don't be conceited!" She waved him down. "This is about something serious."

"Oh, lordie, aren't I something serious?" he asked the room.

"I had Professor Farmiloe around to tea."

"What's he got that I haven't?"

"Manners!" she snapped.

He winced, subsided.

"He's an old dear. Do you know him?"

"A bit—though I don't want to now." He put on an exaggerated expression of jealousy and contempt. "Aged party with a white goatee, isn't he? I believe he's Fordham's expert on something or other. Probably takes care of their tropical butterflies."

"He was my godfather." She mentioned this fact as if it explained everything. "He's some kind of a physicist."

"Bill," he prompted.

She took no notice.

"I think he's—"

"Bill," he insisted.

"Oh, all right," she said, impatiently. "Bill, if it pleases you." She tried to keep her face straight, but he caught the underlying hint of a smile and gained considerable satisfaction therefrom. "Bill, I think he's got an idea of some sort. It bothers me. Every time somebody gets an idea, he dies."

"Not necessarily. We don't know how many are still living who've been nursing ideas for months. Besides, I'm alive."

"You're alive because you appear to have only one idea," she observed, tartly. Her legs went under her chair.

"How could you say that?" He registered shock.

"For heavens sake, will you let me keep to the subject on which I wish to talk to you?"

"Okay." He gave her an annoying grin. "What makes you think old Farmiloe is afflicted with a notion?"

"I was talking to him about the luminosities. I wanted him to explain why it's so difficult to find a weapon against them."

"And what did he say?"

"He said that we hadn't yet leaned how to handle forces as familiarly as substances, that we'd advanced sufficiently to discover the Vitons but not enough to develop a means of removing them." Her fine eyes appraised him as she went on. "He said that we could throw energy in all sorts of forms at a Viton, and if nothing happened we just had no way of discovering why nothing had happened. We can't even capture and hold a Viton to find out whether it repels energy or absorbs it and re-radiates it. We can't grab one to discover what it's made of."

"We know they absorb *some* energy," Graham pointed out. "They absorb nervous currents, drinking them like thirsty horses. They absorb radar pulses—radar can't get a blip out of a Viton. As for the mystery of their composition, well, old

Farmiloe's right. We've no idea and no way of getting an idea. That's the hell of it."

"Professor Farmiloe says it's his personal opinion that these luminosities have some sort of electro-dynamic field, that they can modify it at will, that they can bend most forms of energy around them, absorbing only those that are their natural food." Revulsion suffused her features. "Such as those nervous currents you mentioned."

"And we can't reproduce those with any known apparatus," Graham commented. "If we could, we might be able to stuff them until they burst."

Her smile crept back. "I happened to remark that I'd like to have a magic spoon and stir them up like so many blue puddings." Her slender fingers curled around an imaginary spoon, stirred in vigorous ellipses. "For some weird reason, he seemed fascinated when I made this demonstration. He copied me, waving his finger round and round as if it was some new sort of game. It was only my foolishness—but why should he be equally foolish? He knows a lot more about energy problems than I can hope to learn."

"Doesn't make sense to me. D'you think he's in his second childhood?"

"Most decidedly not."

"Then I don't get it." Graham made a defeated motion.

"Not giving any indication of what was on his mind, he looked slightly dazed, said he'd better be going," she continued. "Then he wandered out in that preoccupied manner of his. As he went, he remarked that he'd try to find me that spoon. I know that he really meant something by that: he was not reassuring me with idle words—*he meant something!*" Her smoothly curved brows rose in query. "He meant—what?"

"Nutty!" decided Graham. He made a stirring motion with an invisible spoon. "It's nutty—like everything else has been since this crazy affair began. Probably Farmiloe is stupefied by learning. He'll go home and try to develop a haywire eggbeater, and finish up playing with it while in Fawcett's care. Fawcett's got dozens like that."

"You wouldn't make such remarks if you knew the professor as well as I do," she retorted sharply. "He's the last person who'd become unbalanced. I'd like you to go and see him. He may have something worth getting." She leaned forward. "Or would you rather arrive too late, as usual?"

He winced, said, "Okay, okay, don't hit me when I'm down. I'll go see him right away."

"That's being sensible," she approved. Her eyes changed expression as she watched him stand up and reach for his hat. "Before you go, aren't you going to tell me what has got you worried?"

"Worried?" He turned around slowly. "That's a laugh! Ha-ha! Fancy, me worried!"

"You don't deceive me. All that date-making small-talk of yours didn't fool me, either. I could see you were bothered the moment you came in. You looked ripe for murder." Her hands came together. "Bill, what is it?—something new?—something worse?"

"Oh, darn!" He thought a moment, then said, "You might as well be told, I guess. You'll learn it sooner or later, anyway."

"What is it?"

"They don't seem to be killing them any more. They're snatching them bodily now, and taking them God knows where." He spun his hat round in his hand. "We don't know why they're snatching them, or what for. But we can have our dreams . . . bad dreams!"

She paled.

"It's the latest version of the oldest gag," he added, brutally, "a fate worse than death!" He put the hat on his head. "So for pity's sake, look after yourself and keep out of their way to what extent you can. No ducking out of your dates, even by going skyward, see?"

"I've not made a date."

"Not yet. But someday you will. When all this mess is cleaned up, you're going to be pestered plenty." He grinned. "I'll have nothing else to do, then—and I'm going to spend all my time doing it!"

He closed the door on her faint wisp of a smile. Sneaking through the gates and into the murky road that crawled beneath a sky of jet, he knew that that smile still lingered with the memory of his words. But he couldn't think for long about her smile.

In the distance the hidden clouds dripped great blobs of shining blue; rain from the overhead hell. There was a mutual soaring of ghastly globules a little later. They were too far off for him to see clearly, but he sensed that the phenomena were ascending burdened.

With his mind's eyes, he saw stiff, unmoving human figures rising in the tentacled grasp of repulsive captors, while below their helpless bodies ten thousand guns gaped at the lowering sky, a thousand listening trumpets awaited the advent of another enemy which, at least, was flesh. The pond was being scoured for frogs even while the frogs were battling each other, cannibalistically.

"We shall measure our existence by its frogs."

He wondered how this epidemic of kidnappings would appeal to an observer not yet treated with Bjornsen's sight-widening formula. Undoubtedly, this awful demonstration of superior powers justified the fearful superstitions of the past. Such things had happened before. History and the oldest legends were full of sudden frenzies, levitations, vanishings, and ascensions into the blue mystery of the everlasting sky.

His thoughts jerked away from the subject, switched to the old scientist who had hurried home with a strange idea, and he said to himself, "Bill Graham, I'll lay you a dollar to a cent that Farmiloe either is demented, departed or dead."

Satisfied with this sportingly morbid offer, he turned down Drexler, sneaked cautiously through the deepest shadows, his rubber-soled shoes padding along with minimum of sound, his agate-like, glistening eyes wary of ambush in the night-time clouds. Down, down below his slinking feet the beryllium-steel jaws gnawed and gnawed and gnawed at the hidden ores and secret rocks.

Chapter 11

Professor Farmiloe was dead beyond all possible doubt, and Graham knew it the moment he opened the door. Swiftly, he crossed the gloom-filled room, ran his pencil torch over its windows, made certain that its light-bottling drapes permitted no vagrant gleam to pass outside. Satisfied, he found the wall-switch, flicked current through the center bulb.

A two-hundred watts blaze beat down on the still figure of the scientist, making mocking sparkles in his white hair which was framed by arms bent limply on the desk. Sitting in his chair, Farmiloe looked as if he had fallen asleep, couching his weary head within his arms. But his was not the sleep that is broken by the dawn—it was slumber of another kind, dreamless and never-ending.

Gently, Graham lifted the bowed shoulders, shoved a hand through the shirt-front, felt the cold chest. He studied the aged and kindly face, noted that it was quite devoid of that terrorized expression which had distorted the features of other dead.

He had reached a pretty good age, Farmiloe. Maybe his end was natural. Maybe his clock inevitably had reached its fateful time and tick—and the luminosities had not been involved in the tragedy. At first glance, it didn't look as if they'd been involved; that peaceful expression, plus the fact that he'd died and not been snatched. The hell of it was that if an autopsy showed death to be caused by heart failure it would mean nothing, absolutely nothing.

Weirdly vibrant filaments could absorb quasi-electrical nervous currents with sufficient swiftness and greed to paralyze the heart's muscles. People—old people especially—could die of similar trouble having no connection with supernormal manifestations. Had Farmiloe suffered no more than the natural ending of his allotted span? Or had he died because his wise old brain had harbored a thought capable of being developed into a threat?

Looking lugubriously at the body, Graham cursed himself. " 'Or would you rather arrive too late, as usual?' She was damn prophetic there! Johnny-come-too-late, that's me, every time! Why the heck didn't I take after the old geezer the moment she mentioned him?" Ruefully, he rubbed his head. "Sometimes I think I'll never learn to get a move on." He looked around the room. "All right, Fathead, let's see you make a start!"

In mad haste, he searched the room. It wasn't a laboratory, but rather a combined office and personal library. He treated the place with scant respect, well-nigh tearing it apart in his determination to discover whatever it might hold worth finding. He found nothing, not one solitary item to which he could tie a potent line. The mass of books, documents and papers seemed as devoid of meaning as a politician's speech. There was a touch of despair in his lean features when finally he gave up the search, made to go.

Its balance disturbed by his maneuverings, the body slid gradually in its seat, flopped forward, its arms spreading across the glossy surface of the desk. Putting his hands beneath cold armpits, Graham took the pathetic weight, bore it toward a couch. Something fell to the floor, rolling metallically. Laying the body full length, Graham covered its face, composed its worn, veined hands. Then he sought for the thing that had fallen.

It was an automatic pencil—he spotted its silvery sheen close by one leg of the desk. He picked it up. Obviously it must have dropped from Farmiloe's cold fingers, or from his lap.

The find stimulated him afresh. Memory of others' dying ramblings made the pencil seem highly suggestive. Of course, Farmiloe might well have been struck out of this life and into the next—if he had been thus smitten—at the very moment his mind broadcasted the thought that his pencil was about to record. It was a thoroughly unVitonic principle to give the sucker an even break: their killings came without warning or hesitation, and they killed for keeps.

At that stage, he amazed himself by perceiving an angle he'd overlooked before, namely, that the Vitons could not read. A point so obvious had not occurred to him until that moment. The Vitons had no optical organs, they employed extra-sensory perception in lieu of same. That meant that they passed sentence of death on whoever nursed dangerous ideas, or conceived the notion of recording such ideas in manner not plain to them. Possibly printed patterns on paper, or written ones, meant nothing to their alien senses; they dealt in thoughts, not in pen, pencil or typeface; they were the masters of intangibles rather than the concrete and substantial.

That meant that if Farmiloe had used this pencil it was likely that his record remained, had not been destroyed, exactly as the other messages had not been destroyed. For the second time Graham went through the drawers of the desk, looking for scratch-pads, notes, any kind of hurried scribble that might convey something significant to an understanding mind. Transferring his attention to the top, he satisfied himself that its writing-block and blotter were quite unmarked, looked through two scientific books, examining them leaf by leaf.

No luck. That left only the *Sun*. The late night final lay spread but unopened in the middle of the desk, positioned as if Farmiloe had been about to peruse it when abruptly he lost interest in the world's news. With his photographic eyes poring over the sheet, the intelligence man breathed deeply when he found a penciled mark.

It was a thick, swiftly-scrawled ring; a slashing circle such as a man might make in a moment of frenzy—or in the very last moment of life.

"If they got him," mused Graham, "evidently he did this after they got him. Death isn't coincident with stoppage of the heart; the brain does not lose consciousness until several seconds later. I once saw a dead guy run ten steps before he admitted he was dead."

His tongue licked along dry lips while he tried to decipher this message from the grave. That frantically drawn ring represented Farmiloe's last stand: the fading brain's stubborn effort to leave a clue no matter how crude, hurried or far-fetched.

In a way it was pathetic, for it was the professor's dying tribute to the intelligence and deductive qualities of his own kind. It was also wacky, it could not well have been wackier—for the ring encircled the printed drawing of a bear!

In the advertising columns, depicted against an iceberg background, the animal was standing upright, its right forepaw extended in a persuasive gesture, an irritating smirk of commercial pride upon its face. The subject of its appeal was a large and ornate refrigerator beneath which appeared a few cajoling words:

"I stand for the world's best refrigerator—you'll find me on its door."

"That ad writer doesn't suffer from excess of modesty," grunted Graham. He pored over it defeatedly. "Sleep," he decided. "I'll have to get some sleep, else this'll put me among the knitters of invisible wool!"

Neatly tearing the advertisement from the page, he folded it, placed it in his wallet. Then he switched out the light and departed.

Entering a phone booth in the subway on his route home, he called police headquarters, told them about Farmiloe, gave rapid instructions between repeated yawns. Next, he tried Boro 8-19638, obtained no response, felt sleepily surprised that the intelligence department's office did not answer. He was too far gone in fatigue to query the matter or to develop suspicions and apprehensions. They didn't answer—so to hell with 'em.

Later, he fell into bed, thankfully closed eyes red-rimmed with weariness. One mile away, a high-altitude battery, Sperry predictor, radar early-warning outfit and listening post stood unattended in the dark, their former operators involuntarily removed from their posts. Knowing nothing of this, he tossed uneasily in fantastic dreams that featured a deserted office surrounded by a sea of living, scintillating blue through which strode the gigantic figure of a bear.

The unease he ought to have felt the night before made up for its absence with the morning. He tried to reach the intelligence department's office on the phone, still got no reply, and this time reacted sharply. Something fishy there, bawled his refreshed and active brain—better watch your step.

He watched his step carefully a little later as the approached he building. The place looked innocent enough; it sat there with all the studied indifference of a recently set mousetrap. The nearest Vitons were well to the west, dangling from the undersides of fat clouds and apparently contemplating their navels.

He hung around for a quarter of an hour, sharing his attention between the ominous building and the menacing sky. There seemed no way of discovering what was wrong with Leamington's phone except that of going in and finding out. Boldly, he entered the building, made toward a levitator shaft. A man emerged from the attendant's niche at the side of the levitator bank, made toward him.

This fellow had black eyes and blacker hair stuck on a chalk-white face. He had black clothes, shoes, hat. He was a sartorial dirge.

Sliding across the parquet in easy, pantherish strides, he harshed, "You—!" and fired directly at Graham.

If the intelligence man had been one degree more assured or a fraction less edgy, it would have cost him half his noggin. As it was, he felt the bullet sections whip wickedly above his scalp as he dived to the floor. Going prone, he rolled madly, hoping to cannon against the other's splayed legs before he could fire again, but knowing that he could not make it in time.

His back muscles quirked in agonized anticipation of a split bullet's quadruple impact. There came the expected blast, sharp and hard. Nervous conditioning forced open his mouth in readiness for the yelp his throat did not utter. In that astounding moment of realization that again he had not been hit, he heard a weird gurgling followed by a thud.

A crimson-streaked face fell into the arc of his floor-level vision, a face in which eyes retained an insane glare even as their luster died away. Graham leaped to his feet with the quick suppleness of an acrobat. He gazed down dumbly at his stricken attacker.

A low groan drew his attention to one side. Jumping the body of the man in black, he sprinted to the stairs winding around the bank of pneumatic levitators, bent over the figure sprawling awkwardly at the bottom of them.

Still clinging to a warm automatic, the figure stirred weakly, moved with little, pitiful motions that exposed four blood-soaked holes in the front of its jacket. The other hand dragged itself up, showed Graham a plain, gold ring.

"Don't worry about me, pal." The figure's speech came in forced, bubbling gasps. "I got down this far . . . couldn't make it any farther." Legs twitched spasmodically. The dying man let go his weapon, dropping it with a clatter. "I got the swine, anyway. I got him . . . saved you!"

Holding the ring in his fingers, Graham's glance flashed between the man at his feet and the soberly dressed shape of his assailant. Outside, hell blew off its top and roared its fury, the building swayed, and nearby masonry poured down, but he ignored these sounds. What was a fatally wounded operative doing at the very entrance to the intelligence department? Why hadn't the office answered his calls of last night and this morning?

"Leave me. I'm done!" Feebly, the operative tried to push away Graham's hands as they tore open the gory jacket. "Take a look upstairs then get out fast!" He choked up a bloody froth. "Town's . . . full of nuts! They've opened the asylums and the crazy are . . . on the loose! Get out, brother!"

"God!" Straightening, Graham knew that the man at his feet had slipped way forever. Snatching up the dropped automatic, he dashed into the nearest levitator. Masonry was still tumbling outside, but he didn't hear it. What awaited him upstairs?

"Take a look upstairs then get out fast!"

The segmentary automatic ready in his grip, his glistening eyes gazing up the shaft, he danced with impatience as his disk soared with what seemed to be excruciating slowness.

A horrible queasiness permeated his stomach when he looked into Leamington's New York field office. The place was a shambles. He counted them quickly—seven! Three bodies lay near the window, their cold faces indelibly stamped with the mark of diabolical fate. Their guns were in their jacket-holsters, unused. They'd never had a chance!

The other four were scattered haphazardly around. These had drawn their weapons and used them. One of the quartet was Colonel Leamington, his riddled frame retaining dignity even in death.

"The trio by the window were settled by Vitons," decided Graham, forcing aside his dazed horror, compelling himself as calmly as possible to weigh up the situation. "The rest killed each other."

Momentarily oblivious of the warning to get out fast, he moved nearer the chief's desk, studied positions, attitudes. It was not difficult to reconstruct the series of events. Evidently the pair by the door—the last to arrive—had opened up on Leamington and the other, but had not been quick enough. Leamington and his aide had swapped shots simultaneously with the newcomers. The result was a likely one; these modern segmentary missiles were blatantly murderous compared with old-fashioned, one-piece bullets.

All the bodies were those of former intelligence men; that was what had him puzzled. He roved around the room, the gun still in his fist, his brow deeply creased as he tried to find the solution.

"Looks like the luminosities first got those three by the window, leaving Leamington and another unharmed—or, at any rate, alive." His frown grew more pronounced. "They left two alive. Why in hell should they have done that? Something mighty queer there!" He edged his buttocks onto the desk while he surveyed the bodies. "After that, three more came along, perhaps because Leamington had summoned them. They turned up, and must have realized something was wrong—for right away they started the fireworks. All five got theirs. Four flopped for keeps. The fifth crawled out and got down the stairs." He hefted the gun, feeling its weight. "But there's nothing to show *why* the fireworks started!"

Swallowing hard, he collected the plain, iridium-lined rings from the dead men's fingers, dropped them into his pocket. Regardless of what had occurred, all these men had been fellow operatives, trusted workers in Uncle Sam's most trusted service.

A bell chimed softly in one corner. Crossing to the telenews receiver, he flipped it open, saw the *Times* screen-exhibited first edition. He scanned it carefully.

Asian pressure increasing in the mid-West, yelled the *Times*. Workers' demonstration demands that atom bomb stocks be released forthwith. European situation extremely serious. Thirty enemy stratplanes brought down in southern Kansas during war's biggest stratosphere dogfight. Four-thousand mile lucky-shot blasts Asian dump, devastating one hundred square miles. Bacteriological warfare shortly, says Cornock. Congress outlaws Viton-worshipping cult.

The page crawled off the screen, was followed by local news. Understanding lightened his face as he read. People were running amok! All over New York, in most of the Occidental world's great cities, people were being kidnapped, spirited into the skies, then returned to earth—and were being returned in mental condition much different from their former state.

Supersurgery in the clouds! The grip tightened upon his gun as the terrible significance burst through the haze created by the slaughter in the office. This was the master-stroke! Ultimate victory was to be made infinitely more certain, and—

in the interim—still more emotional honey was to be produced with the aid of helpless recruits conscripted from the very ranks of the anti-Viton armies!

What was it that poor devil downstairs had said? "Town's . . . full of nuts!" That was it! The three by the window had died resisting, or had been killed as unsuitable for super-surgical purposes. Leamington and the other had been snatched, operated upon, and returned. They had returned as mental slaves of their ghastly opponents. The office had become a trap cunningly designed to get the intelligence operatives—the heart of the resistance—singly, in pairs or in groups.

But the last three, arriving together, somehow had realized their peril. With that unflinching devotion to duty typical of their kind they had blasted Leamington and his companion. Sentiment had no place in fast play of this ugly description. Unhesitatingly, the three had wiped out their own chief, blowing him into swift and bloody death because quick-wittedly they knew that he was no longer their chief, he was a mind-warped instrument of the foe.

The field office had been a trap—*possibly was still a trap!* The thought stabbed through Graham's brain, made him jump toward the window. Staring out, he noted that random clouds had drifted away leaving a clear, blue sky in which the morning sun shone brightly.

There might be a hundred, a thousand luminosities swaying around in that azure bowl, some actually drifting nearer, some guarding the trap and now about to swoop. Even Bjornsen's wonderful formula couldn't enable one to pick out glowing ultra-blue from a background of glowing normal-blue. The basic and the hyper shared the same sheen under the early sun, making both confusing.

The knowledge that his anxious stare was accompanied by equally anxious thoughts, and that his broadcast psycho-vibrations might entice adjacent trappers, made him race for the door without further ado. Best to get clear while yet there was time! He hit the levitators, went down with a rush.

Two men were lounging just inside the front door. He spotted them through the transparent tube of his shaft even as his disk made a rubbery bounce and settled at street level.

Without leaving the shaft, he reasoned quickly, "If those guys were normal they'd show some curiosity about those two bodies lying within their sight. They aren't interested, and therefore aren't normal. They are dupes!"

Before his disk quite had ceased its cushioning motion he dropped it farther, his long, athletic form sinking from sight of the waiting pair. They stiffened in surprise, ran toward the shaft. Both had guns.

Five levels below the street, he stopped, was out of the perpendicular tube and across the basement ere hidden compressors ceased their sighing. Ducking beneath the main stairway, he heard feet stamping at the top. Hefting his automatic, he fled through a series of empty corridors, gained an exit at the building's farther end. Coming out through a steel trapdoor, he sniffed fresh air appreciatively. It was a welcome change from that underground odor of fungus and rats. Wearers of the ring were familiar with six such exits, all unknown to and unsuspected by the general public.

The desk sergeant at the precinct station shoved the phone across the polished mahogany, amputated half a wiener, spoke around it. "That's nothing, feller! Police Commissioner Lewthwaite got his around six o'clock. His own bodyguard done it." Another bite. "What's it coming to when big guys get bumped by their bodyguards?"

"Yes, what?" agreed Graham. He rattled the phone angrily. "Looks like they've wrecked the cityphone system as well."

"All through the night," mumbled the sergeant, forcing the words through his gag. He gulped, popped his eyes, yo-yoed his Adam's apple. "Dozens of them, hundreds! We've bopped them, beat them, shot their pants off and burned them down—and still they come! Some of the nuts were our own boys, still in uniform!" His other hand came up, showing a huge police positive. "When Heggarty reports in, I'll be ready for him—in case he ain't Heggarty! You can't ever tell who's next until he starts something!"

"You can't trust your own mother." Suddenly getting his connection, Graham shouted, "Hi, Hetty!" He grinned sourly as he heard the answer, "Hi!" then snapped, "I want Mr. Sangster, pronto!"

A deep rich voice took over. Graham drew a long breath, recounted his experience of half an hour before, pouring out a rapid flow of words as he described the scene in the intelligence department's office.

"I can't get Washington," he concluded. "They say all the lines are down and the beams out of action. For the time being, I'm reporting to you. There's no one else within reach to whom I can report."

"This is terrible news, Graham," came Sangster's grave tone. "From where are you speaking?"

"How the heck do I know?"

"Surely you know where you are at the present moment?" Sangster's voice went two tones higher in surprise.

"Maybe. But you don't—and won't!"

"Meaning that you refuse to tell me? You suspect *me*? You think I may be yet another of the mentally mutilated?" He was silent a while. His listener tried to discern his expression in the phone's tiny television screen, but the thing was out of order, displaying only occasional glimpses between vague whorls of light and shadow. "I suppose I cannot blame you for that," Sangster went on. "Some of their conscripts act like dumb gangsters, but others display extraordinary cunning."

"All I'd like you to do—if you can find a way of doing it—is get my reports to Washington," Graham said. "I'm too much on the hop to seek a way myself. You'll have to help me there."

"I'll try," Sangster promised. "Anything else?"

"Yes. I'd like to secure the name and address of any other Intelligence operatives who may be in or near this city. They won't all have fallen into that trap. Sometimes some of them don't report in for weeks. I reckon a few must still be roaming free. Leamington was the only one here who had the information I want, but Washington can supply it."

"I'll see what can be done." Sangster paused, then came through a little louder. "A couple of Leamington's recent queries were handled by this department."

"Discover anything?" Graham asked, eagerly.

"A reply from Britain says that McAndrew's laboratory and notes showed that he'd been conducting an interesting line of research in the variation of particle-velocities under heat treatment. Apparently he was hunting the secret of sub-atomic binding power. He'd had no success up to the time of his disappearance, and the British have given him up for dead."

"That's a safe bet!" Graham asserted. "He's been analyzed—and the leftovers have been thrown away. He's in some celestial ashcan—a dismembered rabbit!"

"My own imagination can draw all the pictures without you filling in the colors," reproved Sangster. "Leave me alone with my dreams. It's unnecessary to emphasize their horror."

"Sorry!"

"We've found that no radio amateur eavesdropped on Padilla," Sangster continued. "Whatever he told Treleaven is fated to remain a mystery. Data on Padilla's life reveals nothing except that he was a financially successful radio experimenter. He made a big wad out of simplified frequency modulation. He made his own funeral out of something else—but left no record to indicate what it was."

"I'd given up that lead a couple of days ago."

"You say that as if you've found another and better one." Sangster's voice was pregnant with interest. "Have you?"

"I find one almost every morning," declared Graham, glumly, "and it goes rotten on me by night. As a gallivanting gumshoe, I sure picked myself a heller right at the start!" He pursed his lips and sighed. "What are the governmental experts doing?"

"Nothing, as far as I know. There are two groups assembled in lonely places suggested by Leamington. They've discovered that the very loneliness which is their protection is also their handicap. They plan things, design them, make them—then find that there are no adjacent luminosities on which to test them."

"Gosh, I overlooked that," Graham admitted.

"It's not your fault. None of us thought of it." Sangster was now lugubrious. "If we transfer them to Viton-infested pastures, they'll get wiped out. It's an impasse." He snapped his fingers with impatience.

"Probably you're right, sir," said Graham. "I'll report again directly I've turned up something worth reporting."

"Where are you going now?" The question came sharply.

"I'm deaf in this ear," Graham told him. "Funny—I don't seem able to hear you at all."

"Oh, all right." Disappointment trickled through the wires. "I guess you know best. Take care of yourself!" A loud click signaled that he had rung off.

"When in doubt," offered the desk sergeant, darkly, "see who's making money out of it."

"Who's making it now?" Graham asked.

"Morticians." The sergeant frowned at his listener's grin. "Well, ain't they?"

Chapter 12

The bronze plate said: *Freezer Fabricators of America, Inc.* Graham walked in, spent five minutes sparring a stubborn executive before that worthy agreed to conduct him to the golden name on the old oak door.

That name was Thurlow, and its owner was a living mummy. Thurlow looked as if he'd sweated himself dry in lifelong pursuit of percentages.

"We can't do it," complained Thurlow, after Graham had explained the purpose of his visit. His voice rustled like ages-old papyrus. "We couldn't supply a refrigerator to the Sultan of Zanzibar even if he offered to balance its weight with jewels. Our plant has been engaged wholly on government work since the war began, and we haven't turned out a solitary freezer."

"It doesn't matter." Graham dismissed the point without argument. "I want one for the university to pick to pieces. Give me a list of your local customers."

"Nothing doing!" Thurlow's bony hand massaged his bald, yellow pate. "Things won't always be like this. Someday, my prince will come. Fine fool I'll look with my consumer list circulating among competitors."

"Are you insinuating—?" began Graham, angrily.

"I'm insinuating nothing." Thurlow waved him down. "How do I know you are what you represent yourself to be? That trick ring of yours doesn't mean a goddam thing to me. I can't read its inscriptions without a microscope. Why don't the authorities provide you with a microscope?" His cackle was funereal. *"Heh-heh-heh!"*

Keeping his temper, Graham said, "Will you give me a list if I bring you written authority?"

"Well," Thurlow ceased his cackling, looked cunning, "if what you bring satisfies me, I'll give you a list. What you bring had better be convincing. No slick competitor is going to gyp me out of a list just because trade's gone haywire."

"You need not fear that." Graham stood up. "I'll get something in clear writing, or else the police will make application on my behalf." Stopping by the door, he asked one more question. "How long have you been using that bear as a trademark?"

"Ever since we started. More than thirty years." Thurlow waxed pompous. "In the public's mind, the standing bear is associated with a product unrivaled in its sphere, a product which—although I say it myself—is universally accepted as—"

"Thanks!" interrupted Graham, cutting short the eulogy. He went out.

The stubborn one with whom he'd first battled conducted him to the front doors, saying, "Did he oblige?"

"No."

"I thought he wouldn't."

"Why not?"

The other looked troubled. "I shouldn't say it but, frankly, Thurlow wouldn't give milk to a blind kitten."

Regarding him shrewdly, Graham punched his arm. "Why let that worry you? Time's on your side. You'll be in his chair when he's stinking."

"If any of us live long enough to see this through," observed the other, gloomily.

"That's *my* worry," said Graham. "Bye!"

There was a phone booth in the corner drugstore. Graham sized up the four customers and three assistants before turning his back to them and entering the booth.

He was leery of everybody. That warning voice within his mind whispered that he was being sought with grim determination, that at long last it had dawned upon the eerie foe that the source of opposition was not so much the world of science as a small group of investigatory aces—in which he was the ace of trumps.

The Vitons had gained compensation for their inherent inability to distinguish one human being from another, humans who seemed as alike as so many sheep. Other humans had been forcibly enrolled and given the duty of segregating intransigent animals from the flock. The Vitons now were aided by a horde of surgically-created quislings, a hapless, helpless, hopeless but dangerous fifth column.

Short of a prowling luminosity picking on him at random, and reading his mind, he had been safe. Now he was threatened by proxies of his own kind. This brother-kill-brother technique was the newest and deadliest menace.

Dialing his number, he thanked heaven that Wohl's dazed mind had not depicted himself and the locality of his home. Wohl's smothered, disorganized brain helplessly had surrendered its knowledge of the field office, causing wolfish captors contemptuously to leave him upon the bank in their haste to reach the scene of slaughter.

Graham would never tell the burly police lieutenant that he, and he alone, had put the finger on Leamington and the others.

"This is Graham," he said, detecting the lift of a distant receiver.

"Listen, Graham," Sangster's voice came back urgently. "I connected with Washington shortly after you last phoned. We're linked through amateur transmitters—the hams seem to have the only reliable communications system left. Washington wants you right away. You'd better get there fast!"

"D'you know what it's for, sir?"

"I don't. All I've got is that you must see Keithley without delay. There's a captured Asian stratplane waiting for you down at Battery Park."

"Fancy me roaming around in an Asian. Our fighters won't give it five minutes in the air."

"I'm afraid you don't appreciate our true position, Graham. Except for occasional and very risky sorties, our fighters are grounded. If they had only the Asians to meet, they'd soon sweep the skies clear of them. But there are the Vitons, too. That makes a lot of difference. When a Viton can swoop on a pilot, compelling him to land his plane in enemy territory as a free gift from us . . . well . . . we just can't afford to give away men and machines like that. The Asians have gained command of the air. It's a fact that may lose us this war. You take that Asian job—you'll be safer in that."

"I'll do it on the run." Watching the shop through the booth's plastiglass panels, he put his lips nearer the mouthpiece, and went on hurriedly, "I called to ask you to get me a list of local customers from Freezer Fabricators. You may have to get tough with a wizened dummy named Thurlow; the tougher you get the better I'll like it. He's long overdue to have his ears pinned back. I'd also like you to make contact with Harriman, at the Smithsonian, ask him to reach any astronomers who're still active, and find out whether they can conceive any possible connection between the luminosities and the Great Bear."

"The Great Bear?" echoed Sangster, surprisedly.

"Yes. There's a bear hanging around that means something or other. God alone knows what it does mean, but somehow I've got to find out. I've a feeling it's mighty important."

"Important—a bear! It can't be any other animal, eh? It has to be a bear?"

"Nothing but a small bruin," Graham agreed. "I'm pretty sure that the astronomical slant is entirely wrong, but we can't afford to overlook even the remotest chance."

"Refrigerators, wizened dummies, stars and bears!" gabbled Sangster. "Jesus!" He was silent a moment, then moaned, "I think maybe they've got at you, too—but I'll do as you request." Then he said, "Jesus!" again and disconnected.

The trip to Washington was fast and uneventful, but his army pilot sighed with relief as the machine touched tarmac at the destination.

He clambered out, saying to Graham, "It's nice to arrive at where you intended instead of where some blue globe compels you to go."

Graham nodded, got into the waiting car, was whirled away at top pace. Ten minutes later, he was savagely pondering the bureaucratic habit of saving two minutes and wasting ten. He paced the waiting room with hard, restless strides. You wouldn't think there was a war on, the way they let you hang around in Washington.

That couple of scientists, for instance. Heaven only knew whom they were waiting to see, but they'd been there when be arrived, and they acted like they hoped still to be there when finally the rock of ages crumbled into dust. Graham gave them an irritated look over. Talk!—they talked and talked as if worldwide destruction and human slaughter were trifling distractions compared with other and weightier matters.

Arguing about Bjornsen's formula, they were. The little one reckoned that modification of eyesight was caused by molecules of methylene blue transported to the visual purple by iodine as a halogen in affinity, functioning as a carrier.

The fat one thought otherwise. It was the iodine that made the difference. Methylene blue was the catalyst causing fixation of an otherwise degeneratable rectifier. He agreed that mescal served only to stimulate the optic nerves, attuning them to the new vision, but the actual cause was iodine. Look at Webb's schizophrenics, for example. They had iodine, but not methylene blue. They were mutants with natural fixation, requiring no catalyst.

With blissful disregard for other and more urgent matters, the little one started off again, threatening to bring Graham's temper to the boil. The investigator was just asking himself what it mattered how Bjornsen's formula functioned so long as it did function, when he heard his own name called.

Three men occupied the room into which he was ushered. He recognized them all: Tollerton, a local expert; Willetts C. Keithley, supreme head of the Intelligence Service; and finally a square-jawed, gray-eyed figure whose presence brought him stiffly to attention—the President!

"Mr. Graham," said the President, without preamble, "this morning a courier arrived from Europe. He was the fifth they'd dispatched to us within forty-eight hours. His four predecessors died on their way here. He brought bad news."

"Yes, sir," said Graham, respectfully.

"A rocket dropped on Louvain, Belgium. It had an atomic warhead. Europe retaliated with ten. The Asians have sent back twelve more. This morning, the first atomic rocket in this hemisphere arrived on our territory. The news has been suppressed, of course, but we are about to hit back strongly. In brief, the much-feared atomic war has begun." He put his hands behind his back, walked up and down the carpet.

"Our morale is good despite everything. The people have confidence. They feel sure that victory will be ours in the end."

"I'm sure of that, sir," said Graham.

"I wish I were as sure!" The President stopped his pacing and faced him squarely. "The situation now existing is no longer war in the historical sense of the term. If it were, we should win it. But this is something else—it is the suicide of a species! The man who jumps in the river wins nothing but everlasting peace. Neither side can win this battle—except perhaps the Vitons. Humanity, as a whole, must lose. We, as a nation, must also lose, for we are part of humanity. The coolest heads on both sides have realized that from the start, hence the reason why atomic weapons have been held back as long as possible. Now—God forgive us!—the atomic sword has been drawn. Neither side dare take the risk of being the first to sheath it."

"I understand, sir."

"If that were all, it would be bad enough," the President continued, "but it is far from all." He turned to a wall map, pointed to a thick black line broken by a tipsy-vee which speared across most of Nebraska. "The public does not know of this. It represents the area of the enemy's armored penetration within the last two days. It is an Asian salient which we may or may not be able to contain."

"Yes, sir." Graham eyed the map without expression.

"We can make no greater sacrifices. We can hold no stronger foe." The President stepped nearer, his stern eyes looking deep into Graham's. "The courier reported that Europe's situation already is extremely critical, in fact so much so that they can hold out until six o'clock on Monday evening. Until that time, we remain humanity's last hope. After that, Europe's collapse or annihilation. Six o'clock and no later—not one minute later."

"I see, sir." The itelligence man noted the wide-eyed gaze that Tollerton kept upon him, the fixed, keen stare with which Keithley was watching him.

"Frankly, that means there is no way of escape for any of us except by striking an effective blow at the fundamental cause of all this—the Vitons. Either that, or we cease to survive as sentient beings. Either that, or those left of us revert to the status of domestic animals. We have eighty hours in which to find salvation!" The Pesident was grave, very grave. "I don't expect you to find it for us, Mr. Graham. I don't expect miracles of any man. But, knowing your record, knowing that you personally have been involved in all this from the beginning, I wanted to inform you myself; to tell you that any suggestions you can make will be acted upon immediately and with all the power at our command; to tell you that all the authority you require may be had for the asking."

"The President," interjected Keithley, "thinks that if anything can be done by one man, that man is you. You started all this, you've seen it through so far, and you're the likeliest person to finish it—if it can be finished."

"Where have you hidden the experts?" asked Graham, bluntly.

"There's a group of twenty in Florida, and twenty-eight in the interior of Puerto Rico," Keithley replied.

"Give them to me!" Graham's eyes were alight with the fire of battle. "Bring them back and give them to me."

"You shall have them," declared the President. "Anything else, Mr. Graham?"

"Give me absolute authority to commandeer all laboratories, plants and lines of communication that I see fit. Let my requirements for materials be given preference over all else."

"Granted." The President uttered the word with no hesitation.

"One more request." He made it to Keithley, explaining, "His duty will be to watch me. He'll watch me and I'll watch him. Should either of us become a dupe, the other will remove him at once."

"That, too, is granted." Keithley handed over a slip of paper. "Sangster said that you wanted addresses of fellow operatives in New York. There are ten on that list—six locals and four out-of-towners. Two of the local men have not reported for some time, and their fate is unknown."

"I'll try to look them up." Graham pocketed the slip.

"Eighty hours, remember," said the President. "Eighty hours between freedom for the living or slavery for the not-dead." He put a paternal hand on the other's shoulder. "Do the best with the powers we've given you, and may Providence be your guide!"

"Eighty hours," murmured Graham as he raced toward the plane waiting to bear him back to New York.

Down the spine of the New World, a hundred millions were facing three hundred millions. Every hour, every minute thousands were dying, thousands more were being mutilated—while overhead hung the glowing quaffers of the ascending champagne of agony.

The end of the hellish banquet was drawing nigh. The last course was about to be served, an atomic one, in critical masses, served with blood red hands. Then appetites replete with human currents might rest content to wait the further feasts to come, the oldtime, regular guzzlings in humanity's rutting seasons and burying seasons. Eighty hours!

The rush with which he entered his New York apartment took Graham half-way across the floor before he saw the figure dozing in the chair. The center light was cold and dull, but the whole room was aglow with the electric radiator's brilliant flare. Seeing by radiant heat had long lost its novelty to those with the new sight.

"Art!" he shouted, delightedly. "I was about to phone Stamford and ask them to toss you out. I need you badly."

"Well, I'm out," said Wohl, succinctly. "I couldn't stand that hospital any longer. There was an angular ward sister with ambitions. She got me scared. She called me Wohly-Pohly and stole my britches. Ugh!" He shuddered reminiscently. "I bawled for my clothes and they acted like they'd been sold to the junkman. So eventually I beat it without them."

"What—nude?"

"Tut!" Wohl was shocked. His foot nudged a bundle on the floor. "No, in these. The crime wave's awful when even police lieutenants snitch hospital blankets." Standing up, he stretched his arms sidewise, revolved slowly, like a gown model. "How d'you like the suit?"

"Holy smoke, it's one of mine!"

"Sure! I found it in your wardrobe. Bit saggy under the arms, and tight around the fanny, but it'll do."

"Heck of a figure you must have. Too little in front and too much behind," commented Graham. His smile faded as he switched expressions and became serious. He shoved Wohl back into his chair. "Listen, Art. Time's short. I've just got back from Washington, and what I heard there is going to keep me on the jump like a flea on a hot stove. The situation is tougher than I'd imagined." He recounted the march of events since he'd left Wohl in the hospital at Stamford. "So I asked Keithley, and here it is." He handed over a plain, iridium-lined ring. "You've been fired by the police and conscripted by the Intelligence, whether you like it or not. You're now my opposite number."

"So be it." Wohl's studied nonchalance failed to conceal his delight. "How the devil do the authorities manage always to supply rings the correct size?"

"Forget it—we've bigger puzzles to solve." He gave Wohl the clipping he'd taken from Farmiloe's copy of the *Sun*. "We're organizing fast. We've got until Monday evening, by which time it must be conquest or curtains! It doesn't matter whether we starve or die so long as we produce by that deadline." He pointed to the clipping. "That's Farmiloe's dying scrawl. That's our only clue."

"You're certain that it's a clue?"

"Nope! I'm certain of nothing in this precarious existence. But I've a hunch that it is a genuine pointer to something worth knowing—something that cost Farmiloe his life!"

Staring long and hard at the bear posing inanely before an iceberg, Wohl said, "Have you had a refrigerator picked to bits?"

"Sangster dumped one on the university and they took it apart. They went down to the last bolt, screw and piece of wire. There was nothing left for them to do but lick the enamel off the plates."

"It told them nothing?"

"Not a thing. Cold might kill luminosities by slowing down their vibrations, but how're we going to apply it? There's no such thing as a beam of pure cold, nor any likelihood of developing one—it's a theoretical absurdity." Graham glanced anxiously at his watch. "Does that scrawl suggest anything to you?"

"Br-r-r!" replied Wohl, hugging himself.

"Don't act the fool, Art! There's no time for horsing around."

"I always feel the cold," Wohl apologized. He scowled at the taunting advertisement. "I don't like that animal's complacent smirk. It knows we're stuck, and it doesn't care." He returned the clipping to Graham. "All it tells me is what I knew long ago, namely, that you have an astonishing aptitude for digging up the screwiest leads."

"Don't remind me of it!" Graham's voice was an annoyed growl. He transfixed the clipping with an angry finger. "A bear! We've got something here we think is a clue. Maybe it's the master key of our puzzle. Maybe it's salvation in our time if only we can look at it the right way. And it's nothing more than a long, mercenary, self-satisfied looking and probably flea-bitten bear!"

"Yes," Wohl joined in, for lack of anything better to contribute. "A gangling, cockeyed, stinking bear! A lousy polar bear!"

"If only I'd been quicker after Farmiloe, or had met him on his way—" Graham stopped in mid-sentence. A thoroughly startled look sprang into his features. In a voice hushed with sheer surprise, he said, "Hey, you called it a *polar* bear!"

"Sure I did! It's not a giraffe, unless I'm blind."

"A polar bear!" yelled Graham, changing tone with sudden violence that brought Wohl upright. "Polarization! That's it—polarization!" He stirred his finger vigorously in the air. "Circular or elliptical polarization. Hell!—why didn't I see it before? A child ought to have seen it. I'm too dumb to live!"

"Eh?" said Wohl, his mouth agape.

"Polarization, a million dollars to a doughnut!" Graham shouted. His face was deep purple with excitement. It would have looked red to ordinary sight. Grabbing two hats, he slammed one on the startled Wohl's head, where it stuck rakishly. "Out! We're getting out hell-for-leather! We're telling the world before it's too late! Out!"

They fled through the door without bothering to close it behind them. Warily, their eyes watched the heights as they hammered along the sidewalk. Blue dots were glowing in the sky, but none swung low.

"Down here!" puffed Graham. He ducked into a concrete maw whose throat lead to the newer and lower city. Together they went full tilt down the ultra-rapid escalators, hit the levitator banks at first level, descended another four hundred feet.

They were inhaling heavily as they jumped from their disks, found themselves at the junction of six recently made tunnels. Dull rumbles and raucous grinding noises of steadily boring mammoths still spouted from the two newest holes.

Hydrants, telephone booths, public televisors and even a small cigar store already stood in this subterranean area dug only within the last few weeks. Engineers, overseers, surveyors, and laborers were scurrying about laden with tools, materials, instruments and portable lamps. Occasionally, an electric trolley, heavily laden, whirred out of one tunnel and into another. Ominously, workers were fitting radioactive gas detectors to the levitator tubes and the air conditioning vents.

"Vitons rarely find their way down here," Graham observed. "We ought to be able to phone in comparative safety. Take the booth next to mine, Art. Phone every scientific plant, depot and individual you can find listed in the directory. Tell them the secret may be polarization of some sort, probably elliptical. Don't let them argue with you. Tell them to spread it around where they think it'll do the most good—then hang up."

"Right!" Wohl stepped into his booth.

"How long had you been waiting when I arrived?"

"About fifteen minutes." Snatching the directory, Wohl leafed it to page one. "I'd finished dressing only a couple of minutes when you arrived like a guy shot out of a cannon."

Taking the adjoining booth, Graham dialed, got his number. As usual, the visor was out of order, but he recognized the voice at the other end. "Try polarization, Harriman," he said, quickly. "Maybe it's elliptical. Toss it around as fast as you know how—if you want to live!" He disconnected, giving Harriman no chance to comment.

Seven more calls he made, repeating his suggestion with economy of words. Then he rang Stamford Center Hospital, asked what time Wohl had left. The reply made him sigh with relief. The former police officer could not have been snatched and perverted—his time was fully explained.

He had not really suspected the other of being a dupe, particularly since Wohl had shown himself willing to help spread the very information which the enemy was desperately anxious to suppress. But he could not forget Sangster's glum statement that "others display the very essence of cunning." In addition, there was that persistent and sometimes frightening feeling of being the especial object of widespread search. The enemy, he sensed, knew of him—their problem was to find him.

Shrugging, he dialed again, rattled hurriedly through his information, and heard the other say, "Your buddy Wohl's on our spare line right now. He's giving us the same stuff."

"It doesn't matter so long as you've got it," Graham snapped. "Pass it along to as many as you can."

An hour later, he left his booth, opened Wohl's door. "Chuck it, Art. I reckon we've thrown it too far to be stopped."

"I'd got down to the letter P," sighed Wohl. "A gezeeber named Penny was the next." His sigh was deeper, more regretful. "I wanted to ask him if he could spare a dime."

"Never mind the wit." Graham's features registered anxiety as he noted the hands on the huge turret clock over the booths. "Time's flying quicker than zip, and I've got to meet those—"

A faraway roar interrupted him. Ground trembled and shuddered in quick, tormented pulsations, and a tremendous blast of warm, odorous air swept through the area. Things plunged down the transparent levitator shafts, crashed noisily at bottom. Fine powder trickled from the roof. There was the sound of distant shouting.

The uproar spread, came nearer. Shouting, bawling men raced from the tunnels, made a clamorous, gesticulating crowd that packed the subterranean junction. A gargantuan drummer thumped the ground overhead, and more powder streamed down. The drumming ceased; the crowd milled and cursed.

Somebody drove his way through the mob, entered a phone booth, emerged after a minute. He silenced the others by sheer superiority of lung power, gained a hearing. His stentorian tones bounded and rebounded around the junction, fled in dismal wails along the tunnels.

"The exit's blocked! The phone cable is intact, and those on the surface say there's ten thousand tons choking the shaft. Dupes did it!" The crowd howled, flourished fists, looked around for rope and a few victims. "It's all right, boys," roared the speaker. "The cops got 'em! They were dropped on the run." His authoritative eyes roamed over the mass of weary faces. "Get back to Number Four— we've the shortest dig for a bust-through there."

Muttering among themselves, scowling as they went, the workers poured into a tunnel. Before the last one had been swallowed by its gloomy arch, distant thumps and rumbles burst forth with doubled fury. The beryllium-steel jaws resumed their gnawing.

Catching the speaker as he was about to follow, Graham identified himself, asked, "How long?"

"It'll be quickest through Number Four tunnel," replied the other. "There's about ninety feet of solid rock between us and another gang working to meet us. We're joining systems through this hole, and I reckon we can't make it in under three hours."

"Three hours!" Graham had another look at the turret clock and groaned.

Ten of his precious eighty already had drifted away, leaving behind nothing but a shrewd guess yet to be confirmed experimentally. Three more were to be wasted in waiting—waiting for release from earthly depths which, at least, were safer than the perilous surface. Once again a Viton strike had been well-timed . . . or yet again the devil had looked after his own!

It was some small compensation to find that the adjoining system had its exit on West Fourteenth, for it was in the basement of the Martin Building that Graham had arranged to meet the governmental experts along with several others.

Sixty-four of them were fidgeting apprehensively in this deep hideout immediately below the spot where Professor Mayo's crushed body had started the whole series of ghastly events. It was fitting, Graham thought, that the stain of this tragedy should mark the scene of humanity's last boom-or-bust conference.

"You've been tipped about polarization?" he asked. They nodded. One stood up, intending to offer an opinion. Graham waved him down. "No discussions at the moment, gentlemen."

His eagle eyes weighed them individually as he went on, "In spite of their immensely superior powers, we've outwitted our adversaries twice. We've done it with this polarization hint of Farmiloe's, and we did it when first we broadcast news of the enemy's existence. We beat them despite everything they could bring against us. On both those occasions, we succeeded by taking advantage of the Vitons' chief weakness—that they can't be everywhere at once. We're going to use the same tactics again."

"How?" demanded a voice.

"I'm not telling you that in full detail. There may be some among you who are not to be trusted!" His lean, muscular features maintained their grimness as his eyes carefully went over them again. Uneasily, his listeners shifted in their seats, each casting sidelong, wary glances at his neighbors. Their thoughts were readily apparent: what man can I call man—when no man can I call brother? Graham continued, "You're going to be divided into eight groups of eight apiece. You'll be scattered, and no party is going to know the location of any of the other seven. Those who don't know, can't tell!"

More fidgeting, more mutual suspicion. Wohl grinned to himself as he stood at Graham's side. He was enjoying the situation. If among this crowd of reputed bigbrains were a dozen enforced converts of the Vitons, helpless but supremely crafty spies in the human camp, their identity was completely unknown, and there was no ready-made means of detecting them. Any man in this audience might well be sitting between a pair of dreadful proxies.

"I'm taking a group of eight, giving them their instructions in private, and sending them on their way before I deal with the next lot," informed Graham. He selected Kenney Veitch, leading ray expert. "You're in charge of the first group, Mr. Veitch. Please select your seven."

After Veitch had picked his co-workers, Graham led them to another room, told them hurriedly, "You're going to the Acme plant, in Philadelphia. When you get there, you're not merely to carry on with experimentation designed to blot out a few luminosities, for that means—if you happen to be successful—you'll be promptly eliminated by other, nearby globes, and we'll be left wondering why in hell you died. We're sick of wanting to know why guys have died!"

"I don't see how immediate retaliation can be prevented," opined Veitch, his face pale, but his lips firm.

"It cannot—just yet." Graham minced no words, didn't care whether he sounded brutal or not. "You and your men may be blasted to blazes—*but* we're going to know exactly what you've been doing right up to the moment of the blast.

You may be blown to Hades, and we may be impotent to prevent it—but we'll know *why* you've been blown!"

"Ah!" breathed Veitch. His group crowded around him, wide-eyed, possessed of that curious silence of men facing the zero hour.

"You'll have microphones distributed all over your laboratory and they'll be linked through the city's telephone system. You'll also be connected with the police teletype system, and you'll have a police operator in attendance. The army signals corps will provide you with two boys with walkie-talkie sets. There will be fine-definition scanners tied to far-off television receivers. Adjacent buildings will hold observers who'll watch your laboratory continually."

"I see," said Veitch, slowly and doubtfully.

"Every single thing any of you are about to do you're to describe in full detail before you try it. You'll send it through all available channels, the mikes, the teletype, the radios. The scanners will then watch you do it. Distant observers will watch results. If you suffer, we'll know exactly why you suffered."

Veitch offered no remark, and Graham went on, "If you succeed in smearing a luminosity, the technical details of how you accomplished the feat will be known fully and accurately to a large number of people spread over a large area. We'll know the sort of equipment required to repeat the blow, we'll rush it out in quantities, and nothing in heaven, earth or hell will stop us." He studied them steadily. "On your way—and best of luck!"

He turned to Wohl. "Ask Laurie to choose his seven, and bring them in here."

"I didn't like the little runt, the one staring over Veitch's shoulder," remarked Wohl, pausing by the door. "His eyes had hoodlum's heebies."

"And what may those be?"

"A fixed, animal glare. Didn't you notice him? Go have a look through the police art gallery—you'll find dozens with the heebies, usually deranged or hopped-up killers." Wohl looked expectantly at the other. "Not all of them have it, but most do. It depends on the state of their minds at the time they were photographed."

"Yes," agreed Graham, thoughtful. "Come to think of it, I've noticed it in studies of some of those old-time gangsters: Dillinger, Nelson, the Barrow boys, Louie the Lep, and others. Who knows that they weren't sorry instruments of unseen drinkers, human swizzle-sticks used to stir up more emotion—when there weren't enough honeymooners around."

"By cripes!" said Wohl. "Do you suggest that every bridal room is somebody else's soda-fountain?"

"Not every one. Of course not! But some—some!"

"I'd be in a living hell if I had your mind. Why don't you go hang yourself sometime?"

"We are in a living hell, and you know how many cracked up when they discovered it." He made an impatient gesture. "Veitch won't be out of the building yet. Go catch him, Art, and put him wise." He went toward the door. "I'll call Laurie myself."

His frown was still serious, worried, when he got the next group of experts, conducted them to the room.

Chapter 13

The Faraday Electrical Equipment Company's laboratory claimed to be the biggest on the American continent; its size suggested the building of airships rather than the evolving of the more efficient iconoscopes, tubes, and stereo screens.

A battery of enormous Diesel-electrics occupied one end of the hangarlike shed. Mighty transformers reared alongside them; the main switchboard was plenty large enough to serve the chief distributing station of a great city.

Tall, complex tubes of every conceivable type were ranged along one wall, some half finished, many completed but not yet tested. Queer frames formed of bars, rods and tubular loops—experimental models of ultra-short wave beam antennae—were propped against the opposite wall.

No production lines ran through this great hangar; it was the company's playground for the most imaginative of its gadgeteers. A veritable litter of scanners, photo-sensitive cells, partly assembled stereo screens, radio components, wire golliwogs and schematic diagrams marred with doodles lay scattered over tables the size of rooms.

Faraday's thought nothing of pouring a million dollars a year into the wackier channels of research. When the war began, who'd been about to market six-color stereoscopic television-deluxe. Faraday!

Duncan Laurie moodily weighed up the technical junkpile at the disposal of his little band, and said to Graham, "Plane polarization ought not to be overlooked. It should be tried in case Farmiloe was slightly off the mark."

"It's being considered," Graham assured him. "We are letting no chances slide, no matter how remote they seem. Why, we've got one crowd out west investigating a report that the Vitons duck around rainbows, like men portaging past rapids."

"Ye gods!" exclaimed Laurie.

"All the work is properly coordinated. Your gang is to concentrate on hyperbolic polarization."

"Okay." Laurie pulled meditatively at one ear. "These luminosities seem to reflect over a wave-band running from about three million Angstrom units up to four or five. They're damnably difficult to analyze spectroscopically: we can't line an instrument on one long enough to get anywhere. But it's obvious that they're energy in compact and balanced form, and are inertialess."

"Are fish inertialess?" asked Graham.

"Fish?" Laurie was frankly puzzled.

Graham pointed to an overhead skylight. "We've got to forget our conditioning and try looking at things from a novel angle. Up there is the atmospheric ocean which may be infinitely more tangible to the Vitons than it is to us. It's full of blue, shining fish swimming around in their natural habitat, swimming by some propulsive means not given to us creatures crawling around on the bottom."

"But energy—"

"Ordinary light's a form of energy, and has weight," Graham went on. He heard the rattle of the police teletype as he talked. "Being made of prime forces—wavicles or whatnot—I think these Vitons have a sort of substance, though they're not matter as matter is generally understood. We're faced with a fourth and unfamiliar form of matter, a force-form. They have weight, even though it may be minute from our viewpoint. They have inertia, and have to expend energy to overcome it. That's why they suck us like so many lollipops—to renew their tissues." He smiled at Laurie. "Only my own opinions, mind you."

"Possibly you're right," acknowledged Laurie. He favored the skylight with a look of extreme distaste.

"Now," Graham continued, "reports we've collected since we discovered the shoo-fly effects of short-wave therapy cabinets show that the luminosities are susceptible to a radio-band stretching from two centimeters to about one and a half meters. They don't die. They just skedaddle as if stung."

"My guess is that those impulses hamper the whirl of their surface electrons," Laurie opined. "But they don't penetrate."

"Quite! And penetration's what we've got to achieve, not sometime next year, or next month, or next week, but within a few hours! We've chopped at Viton timber and have been smacked in the eye by the splinters. With luck, we're going to bore into their hungry guts by means of polarization. Either that, or we can start mooing, for we revert to what we've always been—just a herd of goddarn cows!" He looked squarely at Laurie. "You've got fifty hours. Start at two centimeters and work up."

"We'll do it!" swore Laurie. He gave sharp orders to his band. The tiny group— dwarfed by the hugeness of place—bustled into activity.

To one side, the teleprinter operator transmitted information as Laurie recited his intentions. Silent but super sensitive microphones also picked up his voice, carried it away in a dozen directions and to varying distances. Scanners fixed to the steel roof trusses recorded the scene from above.

With Wohl at his side, Graham hurried toward the door, and as he reached it the scanners picked up and transmitted a hideous incident that plunged dramatically into the screens of faraway receivers.

All the lights went out simultaneously, the switchboard blew a shower of hot, copper-smelling sparks, and a blaze of vampire blue swelled through an open hopper in the north wall. Elusive gleams of blue reflected the invading Viton from the polished surfaces of jumbled apparatus, shifted and flickered as the apparition arched forward and glided down to floor level.

A human face, fearfully distorted, made leprous by the illumination, sweated directly in the luminosity's path—a homoburger waiting the bite! Hysterical gabbling poured from the face's twitching lips, gabbling that ended a a long hoarse sigh.

Helpless feet dragged on the floor immediately below the glowing devil, scuffled loosely around, rapped on table legs. The brilliant orb bobbed up and down, a limp form dangling beneath it. It made a couple of violent jerks, as if forcing energy-milk from reluctant udders. Glass toppled from an adjacent table, hit the floor, and bounced around horrible imitation of the bobbing globe.

Somebody began noisily to vomit as red flame lanced vividly from the laboratory's west side. Dull, purplish spots appeared momentarily on the invader's scintillating surface. More flame; the sharp, hard crack of the heavy weapon being magnified to deafening proportions.

The luminosity dropped its burden as if discarding an old and empty sack. Vengefully, it shot westward, making a meteoric curve straight into the opposing stream of fire. A voice screamed a terrified obscenity, choked, was silent. The Viton made five savage jerks of guzzlement against the wall.

Swiftness of its departure was breathtaking. Blue whizzed back to the hopper, shone within its open frame, and then was outside. It shrank toward the cloud-wrapped sky. Joe, returning from a bender.

Feet stumbled, voices sounded loudly and querulously in the darkness of a place receiving poor illumination from outside. An unseen hand was quick to close the hopper, making the gloom still deeper. Graham swung wide the door, permitting entry of the afternoon's light.

Away in the farther corner, somebody ran a pencil beam over the switchboard and fuse boxes, worked at them with fingers that trembled uncontrollably.

Power suddenly poured through a multitude of overhead bulbs. Laurie ran down the center aisle, kneeled beside an eye-rolling, arm-jerking form. Sensing Graham at his side, he glanced up at the investigator, his eyes straining in a face like marble.

"He's batty," observed Graham, in cold, matter of fact tones. The prone man gibbered horribly, clutched Laurie hand, moped and mowed. "He gave away nothing. He went nuts as it got him."

"God, this is awful!" breathed Laurie.

"We'll get him away." He looked at the thin ring of fearful onlookers. One of them still was clutching a crucifix. "Back on the job, you men. Don't let this get you." They dispersed, slowly, dazedly. He crossed to the hangar's west side where Wohl was bending over another limp shape.

"Dead as the dodo," announced Wohl, unemotionally.

Stooping, Graham extracted a big police positive from the teletype operator's dead fingers. Placing the weapon on a table, he found a small mirror, reflected light into staring optics. It might have been only his imagination, but he thought he saw that subtle something which is life fade gradually from those upturned eyes.

After searching the victim's form, he straightened, said, "Not a mark! His heart was stopped!"

A siren wailed along the road outside, died away dismally at the open door. Four police officers entered accompanied by one man in plain clothes. Quietly, without comment, they took out the uniformed corpse, came back for the fallen scientist. He was mouthing noiselessly as they bore him away.

Three of the officers got into the car, drove off. The fourth took his seat at the teletype. The man in plain clothes went up to Laurie.

"I'm Ferguson, the replacement."

Laurie stood like one stupefied, his gaze wandering over his companions. Nervously, he tugged at one ear while his face asked his unspoken question.

"Organization," explained Graham. His gesture was a comprehensive sweep indicating the microphones and scanners. "Already your losses have been made good. Go ahead with your task, and let's have some speed—we've got to move quicker than death!"

Dashing out, Graham clambered into a gyrocar, Wohl taking the wheel. He said, "Bet my own speedster is now a wreck somewhere out west."

"Maybe." Wohl tooled out to the middle of the concrete. "Where to?"

"Yonkers. There's an underground laboratory out there. Steve Koenig's in charge." Noting Wohl's curiosity, he added, "There are only two groups in this neighborhood. I'm not revealing where the others are, even to you."

"Meaning I might be grabbed and tapped for information?" Wohl leered at the sky, and pulled a face. "Where do we stand if the victim is *you?* Or do we then sit down and take it?"

"We will stand. Nobody's under the delusion that I'm invincible. There are plenty of other groups beside the sixty-four boys I claimed. I've had nothing whatever to do with the others, and know nothing about them. People in Washington and other places have placed them where they'll do the most good. Moreover, nobody in this country knows where South American and European experts are located, and they know nothing of ours."

"This," decided Wohl, "certainly is one time when it's folly to be wise."

"I'll say!" Graham's expression was thoughtful. "Things have been arranged in such a way that the same applies to me as to everyone else—what I don't know I can't tell."

They swung right, the dynamo whirling powerfully. In a smooth rush, they swept around a huge crater in the road. Above the enormous hole was a quarter-mile gap in the shattered skyway, a break from the ragged ends of which stubby lengths of twisted, rusting girders stuck.

"Some banger!" Wohl let his streamlined machine plummet along in top gear. He covered two miles in a fraction over a minute, slowed at an intersection, turned left.

At that point the sky flashed into several times its normal brilliance, for a split second cast sharp, clear-cut shadows across the street. Then the phenomenon was gone. Wohl braked the car to a stop, waited expectantly. Seconds later, the ground quivered. The weakened, unsupported shell of a nearby building collapsed into the road with an appalling roar, filling it with rubble from side to side. Several Vitons suspended in the sky began to zoom to the west.

"That was atomic," declared Graham. "Some miles out. Probably a rocket."

"If we'd been half an hour ahead—" Wohl left his sentence unfinished.

"We weren't, and that's that. No use going on now. Turn her round, Art. I'll try the Battery."

They raced downtown, away from the distant and giant mushroom which was crackling with death. Bulleting along, they passed Bank of Manhattan.

Graham remarked, "Seems years since I worked from that office." He was silent a moment, then added sharply, "Pull up on this corner, Art."

The gyrocar swung into the curb, stopped. Graham sat hunched in his seat, his eyes on the rearview mirror. Opening the door he writhed out.

"What's up? Can you see that mushroom from here?" Wohl fiddled with his wheel, glanced inquiringly at the other.

"The twenty-fourth floor. Yes, it was the twenty-fourth." Graham's eyes glittered. "Something blue and shining flashed out of an open window on that level just after we passed. I caught sight of it out one corner of my eye. The six middle windows in that row belong to Sangster's dump."

"Meaning?"

"Meaning I'm pretty sure that it was a luminosity." The investigator's features showed ire. "Stick around, Art—I'm going to phone."

Without waiting for Wohl's reply, he entered the nearest building, found a telephone in a deserted and half-wrecked ground level office. In strange contrast with its surroundings, the instrument's visor was intact and functioning perfectly, for a girl's face blossomed in its tiny screen as his call got through.

"Hi, Hetty!" he gave her the usual cheer.

"Hi!" she smiled mechanically.

"Mr. Sangster there?"

"No. He's been out all afternoon. I expect him back before five-thirty." Her voice was peculiarly dull and lifeless, but her smile grew more insistent, more inviting. "Won't you come along and wait for him, Mr. Graham?"

"Sorry, I can't. I—"

"We haven't seen you for such a long time," she pleaded. "What with most of the buildings around us lying flat, and this one almost deserted, it's like living on an island, I'm so lonely, so afraid. Can't you come and chat with me until he arrives?"

"Hetty, I can hardly spare the time." He felt moved by her cajolery even as he stared fascinatedly at the screen, noting the tiniest quirk of her lips, the slightest flicker of her eyelids.

"From where are you speaking?" Again that dull, lifeless, phonographic voice.

His temper started to rise, and there was sweat in the palms of his hands. Evading her question, he said slowly, "I'll come around, Hetty. Expect me about five o'clock."

"That's fine!" Her smile widened, but her eyes held no collaboratory expression. "Be sure to make it. Don't disappoint me, will you?"

"You can depend on me, Hetty."

Disconnecting, he glared a long time at the screen from which her familiar features had faded. His fury was tremendous. He worked his fingers as if itching to strangle someone. Giving vent to a hearty expletive, he hurried back to the waiting gyrocar.

"They've got Hetty," he told Wohl. "She talked and acted as if animated by clockwork. The place is a trap."

"Like the field office was," remarked Wohl. He swallowed hard, tapped his fingers on the steering wheel while he kept watch on the sky.

"Ten to one my own home is also a trap—both Hetty and Sangster know it well." His mounting fury colored his voice. His fists clenched into hard bunches.

"They're creeping nearer and nearer to me every minute. Art, I'm fed up. I can't stand this hunt much longer. I'm going to step up and smack 'em right in the pan—and to hell with 'em!"

"Really?" said Wohl. He propped an elbow on the wheel and his head on one hand. He studied Graham with academic interest. "Just like that, eh? You pull one down from the heavens and you kick into a pulp whatever it uses for a bottom, eh?" Taking his head off his hand, he shouted, "Don't talk like a blithering idiot!"

"What's eating you?"

"Nothing." Wohl showed his iridium-lined ring. "Nothing's going to eat you either, not if I can help it."

"I don't intend to be eaten. That's why I want to smack them with a fast one."

"How're you going to do that?"

"It depends." Climbing into the machine, Graham sat and pondered, keeping wary watch through the transparent roof lest any wandering spheres might drift within telepathic range. "If that trap is toothed with Vitons, then I'm merely talking big, because there's nothing I can do."

"Ah," said Wohl, speaking to the windscreen, "he admits it."

Graham snorted, gave him a look, and added, "But if, as is likely, they've left the dirty work to a bunch of dupes, I'm going in. I'm going to go in and kick out their teeth and walk away with Hetty. Anything wrong with that?"

The other thought it over. "H'm, I guess it could be done if they're relying on dupes. Yeah, you might do it and get away with it, though it's a hell of a risk. I've one objection, though."

"What's that?"

"All this 'I' stuff you use. Who the heck d'you think you are?" He flashed the ring again. "*We* go in and take Hetty!"

"I didn't contemplate trying it single-handed, nor even with you. I'm not all that daft!" Graham had a last look at the Bank of Manhattan. "I found a fellow operative when I returned from Washington, and gave him the chore finding the other nine who're supposed to be functioning hereabouts. If he's managed to trace them, they'll be waiting for me at Center Station. We'll pick them up and see what can be done about this trap. With luck, we may snitch the bait without grabbing the tribulation." He lay back in his seat. "Bank her along, Art—we've got less than one hour."

He looked over the eight of them, noting their clean, square-jawed confident features, and knowing that the remaining pair would never be found. There should have been ten all told. Every one of these young huskies was aware of that fact, and every one knew equally well that soon their number might be lessened still further. But no consciousness of this was evident in their expressions or bearing. These were men of the Intelligence Service, men trained to compensate for losses by doing the work of the missing—and more.

"You know what you're to do?" he asked. They nodded. He jerked a thumb upward, reminding them of the observers twenty floors above, peering across two streets and a wrecked block, and into Sangster's office.

"The boys say there are no luminosities in that office, so it's evident that we have to deal only with dupes. I'm going in. You fellows have got to help me get out."

Again they nodded. None could see any reason why Graham should be so keen to risk his life, but it was enough for them that he intended to do just that; They were prepared to play their part.

"All right, fellows—I'm on my way."

"Me, too," announced Wohl, stepping forward.

"For heaven's sake, keep out of this, Art. We don't know what sort of reactions these proxies have. Hetty was a pal of mine, but she doesn't know you from Adam. If you barge in with me you may ball up the works."

"Oh, damn!" said Wohl.

With a grin for his disappointed companion, Graham hastened out, crossed the intervening space under the watching glasses of his observers above, entered Bank of Manhattan. Five men were lounging around the dusty, neglected foyer. Disregarding them, he walked boldly to the pneumatic levitators, ascended to the twenty-fourth floor.

No more loungers were in sight on this level, but he felt that crazy and somewhat corpselike eyes were watching him as he thrust open the door of the Department of Special Finance.

With a casual, " 'Lo, Hetty!" he closed the door behind him. His keen eyes examined the room, noted the closed door of Sangster's private sanctum, the closed doors of a large cupboard nearby. Sangster himself was not in evidence. Perhaps the girl had told the truth about him.

Outside, a war-worn clock struck twenty in cracked and off-tone chimes. It was precisely five.

Seating himself on a corner of her desk, he swung a nonchalant leg to and fro. "I've been busy, Hetty, as busy as the very devil, else I'd have been in to see you before now. Things are shaping for the showdown—I hope!"

"In what way?" She didn't add, "Bill," as was her habit.

"We're about to produce an anti-Viton weapon at last."

"In short waves?" she asked. Her eyes looked into his, and hair erected on the back of his neck when he saw the emptiness of her formerly lively pupils, a dreadful, soulless emptiness that made her no longer interested in masculine small talk, feminine fripperies or any of her oldtime conversational subjects. Her interests now were different, appallingly different—anti-Viton weapons, and short waves, plus Graham himself as her masters' fall guy.

"Sure!" He stared fascinatedly at her mechanical features. It was hellish to think that this was no longer the vivacious girl once he had known, that this familiar form had become a fleshly robot. "We're searching way down in the centimeters. We've divided a broad band between many groups of experimenters. An army like that can't fail to strike oil."

"That is heartening," she commented in a voice totally devoid of tone. Her pale, blue-veined hands fumbled in her lap, below the edge of her desk, out of his sight. "Do you know where these groups are, and which lines they're trying?"

Triumph mounted within him as she put this childishly apparent question. It was as he'd expected—this poor, warped brain was working obediently along a single track, mechanically following the course on which it had been set. There was cunning here—but no cleverness. Even a moron would have seen through her query.

A twofold duty had been placed upon her: firstly, to bait the trap; secondly, to obtain essential information before giving the death signal. Obviously, the fearful operation to which her protesting mind had been subjected had not endowed her with telepathic powers—if luminosities could so endow their victims. At any rate, she was quite unaware of his shrewd perception.

Hard put to it to conceal his eagerness, he told her, "Although there are a lot of experimental groups, Hetty, I know the location of them all, every one of them." It was a downright, thumping lie, and he told it with no compunction, making it in boastful tones. "You've only got to suggest a wavelength and I can tell you who's about to try it, and where."

The dummy responded by betraying her manipulators; her poor, distorted brain was too automatic for guile. "Point five centimeters," she responded, speaking the words as if they had been engraved upon her tortured mind. Her hands slid forward, reached under her desk. She was making ready for the information—and his reward.

"That's all I wanted to know," Graham growled. He was on his feet and around her desk before she could move.

Putting out his hands to grab her, he saw the door to Sangster's room whip open, and a menacing figure charge toward him. He flung himself forward and down; his automatic was in his hand as he hit the floor. The maniacal invader paused, took sloppy aim, and the sound of his shot was terrific in the confined space.

Things catapulted over Graham's flat back. The cupboard door swung wide. Momentarily ignoring the first attacker, he blasted at the gap in the cupboard, saw splinters fly from the edges, knew that all four bullet sections had gone inside.

A whooping figure bowed low in the opening, bent farther, spewed a bloody froth. It toppled full length, its gory torso a sudden barrier in the path of his crazy fellow.

Profiting by his peril, Hetty lugged out a drawer, snatched something from it. She leaned over her desk toward Graham, her blank, unemotional eyes lined along the sights of a tiny, old-fashioned revolver. Her knuckles whitened. The desk erupted beneath her when with a desperate thrust Graham heaved it over from his side. The little gun spat upward as Hetty toppled in her chair, and its slug went into the ceiling.

Feet were hammering along the passage outside, and someone was bellowing oaths near the levitator shafts. Graham swayed upward with the lithe grace of a striking cobra, fired simultaneously with his first attacker. His left arm jumped involuntarily and went red-hot, but his assailant dropped like a slaughtered steer.

Behind him, the door burst inward, revealed two intelligence operatives, weapons in hand. Hard, explosive noises twanged from the end of the passage. One

missile struck metal, whined shrilly as it went on end over end. Two more thudded into the wooden frame of the door; a third clunked softly into flesh. The
shorter of the two operatives choked, spat, choked again, leaned weakly against
the wall, slid down. He finished in a sitting position, the gun sliding from his
fingers, his head lolling forward.

"Full of them!" swore the other. "The place is crammed with them." Peering
leftward around the weapons, he sent two quick shots down the passage. A volley
of shots from the right went in the same direction, and in the following few seconds of silence, four more operatives slipped into the room.

"Move fast!" urged Graham. "I want this girl out!"

Whirling around with the intention of grabbing Hetty and bearing her away
bodily, he caught a glimpse of distant blue through the open window. "Vitons!"
There were about twenty of the shining spheres, shooting along one behind the
other like a string of immense beads, aiming directly for the room, and nearing
swiftly. The shepherds were coming to the aid of their dogs.

More feet thundered recklessly along the passage. His companions opened fire
as he sprang toward the door. The sitting operative pawed blindly for his gun, fell
on his side, closed his eyes and dribbled blood.

Thumps, groans and mad, pathetic mouthings sounded in the corridor. The
next instant, a swarm of staring dupes were in the room. They made their assault
with complete disregard for personal safety and with the energetic lack of organization of automatons on the loose. They were robots conditioned only to kill,
somehow, anyhow.

A colorless face in which blank eyes goggled ghoulishly came close to Graham's
own. Its lopsided mouth was oozing saliva. He hit it with every ounce he possessed. The face vanished as if snatched into the cosmos. Another replaced it and
he promptly smacked it to the floor.

Somebody lifted a crazy, face-twitching body, hurled it halfway across the room.
A stricken dupe writhed snakishly on the floor, snatched at Graham's left leg. He
used his right to kick the other's schnozzle into something resembling a squashed
strawberry. An operative's gun roared close to his ear, deafening him, and filling
his nostrils with the stink of cordite.

The mad mêleé swept him out of the uproarious office, along the passage to
the levitator shafts. A weight descended crushingly on his shoulder, a thousand
hands seemed to be reaching for him at once.

He saw Sheehan, an operative, shove the muzzle of his gun straight into a slob-
bering mouth and let her blow. Gobs of noggin, slop and goo flew in all directions as the part-headless victim toppled under his stamping feet. Far behind him,
or in front, or in some direction—he didn't know where—a voice was hollering
something about Vitons. He bulled into the horde of dupes, his struggles more
maniacal than their own. Then the whole of existence became an inferno of rag-
ing fire through which he sank and sank and sank until every sound had ceased.

Chapter 14

Easing the bandage around his head, Graham gazed at the distant pile of the Bank of Manhattan, then turned to the others.

"How the devil did we manage to get out of that mess? What happened?"

"Me and my pair had five on our hands in the foyer," explained Wohl. He fondled a damaged knee, winced. "We heard the shenanigans upstairs come echoing down the levitator shafts as the other six went to your aid. A short time later, two of them came down like bats out of hell, bringing you with them. You'd been conked, and I'll say you looked lousy!" He favored the knee again, muttered an oath. "Your stretcher-bearers said they'd got out one jump ahead of visiting luminosities."

"And Hetty?"

"There!" Wohl handed him a pair of field glasses. "She went Mayo's way."

"What, flung herself out?" Wohl's answering nod plunged him into thought.

So the duty imposed upon that poor, warped mind had been a threefold one—she was to end herself with her usefulness.

He was moody as he looked at the tragic bundle on that far sidewalk. In a little while, they'd pick her up and send her to decent repose. Meanwhile, it was fortunate that they'd got out fast and in the nick of time, for once again they were unidentifiable among New York's slinking, wary millions.

Short of sheer chance, or the aid of a dupe, they were as difficult to pick out as individual bees in a mighty swarm. There was good parallelism in an imaginary revolt of the bees. The same elusiveness would protect from superior mankind the few intellectual insects who were seeking a means of replacing formic acid with Black Widow venom. If it came to that, they were bees—bees whose nervous honey was not for others.

He said to Wohl, "Two brought me down? Only *two?*" His inquiring eyes moved to the four disheveled operatives standing near, and two of them fidgeted uneasily, "What of the other four—were they killed?"

"A couple of them were." One of the restless pair waved his hand toward the Bank of Manhattan. "Bathurst and Craig stayed behind."

"Why?"

"Most of the dupes were scattered, wounded or dead, but the Vitons were entering. They were coming in at the top while we were trying to get you out at the bottom. So Bathurst and Craig hung back, and—" His voice trailed off.

"Decoyed them, knowing there could be no escape?" Graham suggested. The other nodded assent.

Two had remained to attract the still invincible but overeager foe; to run and shriek and shriek and die—or become dupes in their turn. They had raced higher in the building, knowing that they would never reach the top, but knowing that by the time their recoiling minds were seized and analyzed, the others would be safely merged in the concealing mass of humanity.

It was a sacrifice made for him. There was no comment Graham could make that would not sound fatuous, and he knew that none was asked or expected. In the tradition of the service, two intelligence operatives had done their duty as they deemed it—and that was that!

Rubbing his throbbing left arm, he lifted the thin bandage beneath the sleeve. A mere flesh wound.

Wohl said, "Let that be a lesson to you: don't rush in where angels fear to tread. It buys you nothing but grief."

"I'm hoping it's bought us salvation," Graham retorted. Taking no notice of Wohl's mystification, he turned to the four operatives.

"You two," he said, selecting a pair, "beat it out to Yonkers. You won't be able to get there direct—there's hard radiation across the route. It may be necessary to take a roundabout road. But you must get there at all costs."

"We'll make it, never worry," assured one.

"Okay. Tell Steve Koenig he's to try point five centimeters sooner than immediately, and that's a hot tip. You'd better split and go different ways if you can: it will double your chances of getting through. Remember—point five centimeters. That's all that Koenig will want to know." He addressed the other couple. "Marconi's have established their underground plant at Queens end of the low-level city. They're fiddling around on their own, without orders from Washington, but they could use the information I've got. So rush along and tell Deacon we've reason to believe that point five centimeters is the critical wavelength."

"Yes, Mr. Graham," answered one.

He spoke to all four. "You'd better say, too, that if either of them gain success they'll have to move fast if they want to stay in business. They'll have to protect their own plant with the first installation they produce, and then the stations from which they draw power. Then—and not until then!—they can supply official demands. Tell them it's absolutely essential that they refuse to be moved by any bureaucratic panic until they've protected their own plants and power stations. D'you understand?"

"Sure, Mr. Graham." They went out, cautiously, yet fast.

Grimness was in the set of his jaws when he remarked to Wohl, "If we discover a way to turn out suitable weapons, we're not going to have them destroyed at the source."

"That's logical," agreed Wohl. He cocked a questioning eye. "You've found something, Bill?"

"Yes, I got the specific detail for which Hetty's mind had been directed to seek. Undoubtedly, the luminosities intended to suck her knowledge as she acquired it and take action accordingly." He ripped a dangling pocket flap from his tattered jacket, scowled at it, flung it away. "If possible, she was to ascertain the location of any experimental group working on or near point five centimeters. Had she been able to identify them, they'd have been smeared around. Probably they'd have smeared other groups simultaneously, just to keep us confused. We'd have had no clue to a potent wavelength—but they'd have put finish to the one they fear."

"Gosh!" Wohl registered a mixture of glee and admiration. "And that's what you dived in to get? The Vitons might just as well have told you themselves!"

"They did," was Graham's succinct reply. "They informed us by proxy. Very kind of them—damn their guts!" He had a look at his watch. "We've to carry on from this point, getting results in a few precious hours. Polarization's the trouble—we're dealing with short radio waves, not ordinary light."

"Never mind," Wohl comforted. "So far you've done fine."

"Me? You mean *we!*"

"I mean you," Wohl persisted. "You've done fine. Every cloud has a silver lining."

"We'll have to see that silver darned quick, else it'll come too—" He stopped, rubbed his pulsing arm, stared at the other. "I seem to remember something about photons changing their double-eights to true spirals when rebounding from polished silver."

"What of it? I spiral off glass—when it holds beer."

"Silver might do it," Graham went on, ignoring him. "The problem's largely one of refraction versus reflection, but silver might do it. There's a good chance that so short a wave might spiral if the beam could be bounced off a silver plate—especially if we use a Bergstrom magnetic field impeller to make the stuff hard and fast by cutting down absorption."

"You bet!" Wohl's grin was apologetic. "It ought to work just like you say. I get the whole idea so clearly I could see it with muffled ears in a dungeon next month."

"The odd chance in a thousand," murmured Graham. "It will be worth trying if Laurie hasn't thought up something better." Ceasing to nurse his injuries, he became suddenly dynamic. "Jump to it, Art—we're going back to Laurie."

A hundred highly skilled craftsmen now toiled and sweated inside the great Faraday shed. They had been commandeered from various local radio and scientific instrument works, and every man knew his stuff so well that Laurie and his little band could concentrate unhampered on their own special jobs.

Valuable hours of non-stop work were represented by the compact but complicated apparatus which glistened and shone in the center of the littered floor. Long, slender tubes sparkled in the assembly's heart: cylindrical screens projected from its turntable framework beneath which were a dozen rubber-tired wheels. From its seat mounted before a small control board the entire setup could be moved and rotated electrically like a crane, drawing power from cables which snaked out of its end couplings and ran across the floor toward the generators.

Here, a worker bent over a true-surfaced peralumin disk and silver-plated it by wire-process metallization. While his electric arc sputtered its rain of minute drops, another worker close by plated another disk with granulated silver by-passed into an exoacetylene flame and thus blast-driven into the preheated surface. Any method would do so long as there was someone capable of doing it with optical accuracy.

Another worker was burnishing a heavily plated disk on a confiscated buffing machine, frequently checking results with a micrometer gauge. Behind him, one of Laurie's experts was completing the assembly of a hemispherical trellis antenna. Two more scientists fussed around a big, cylindrical funnel; one fitting front and rear skeleton-sights to its upper surface, the other making minute adjustments to its complex impeller.

Two hours to go!

Graham came in with an old-fashioned printed paper, rested one foot on the assembly's turntable while he scanned the front page. Iowa threatened by battle for Omaha. Asian armor enters Luxembourg. Madrid obliterated in atom-blast. Scandinavia's last stand today. More atomic rockets flay Britain. It was gloom, gloom, gloom all the way. His eyes found the side column just as Laurie came up. French collapse imminent. He shoved the paper into his pocket.

"Bad news?" inquired Laurie.

"Not so good. There's something else, too. It came from Philly by ham radio. Veitch's nearly completed apparatus was blown to pieces early this morning."

"Ah!" Laurie's bushy brows drew together in a frown. "That suggests he was on the right track. If he was on the right track, then we're on the wrong one."

"Not necessarily. Veitch had a dupe in his crowd. We warned him, and he said he'd kid the fellow along. He didn't want to remove him in case he was replaced by another. Better the devil you know than the devil you don't."

"The dupe did it?"

"Yes—killing himself in the blast. Honorable hara-kari, sort of. A couple of others are wounded." He looked meditative. "I'd have phoned Veitch before now if it hadn't been that all his lines are reserved strictly for outgoing traffic. He ought to have been ready long before anyone else, since he had tons of stuff transported from Florida and it needed only reassembling."

"H'm-m-m! Any other news?"

"Only that Sangster's been located; I was worried about him. They found him in an underground hospital. He was in William Street when that big section of skyway collapsed. He'll recover."

Leaving Laurie, he visited the open space fronting the shed. Here, in the middle of the cleared area, was a ring of giant copper earths, all ready to connect with the multiple condensers of the transmitter's intricate grounding system.

A parade of blue dots, made tiny by distance, wended its way far to the east, somewhere over Long Island. His eyes gleamed as he watched them. Nice fix they were in, he thought, with chronic disregard for his own greater fix. Like hundreds of worried bee-keepers trying to search thousands of hives containing tens of millions of bees. They could go here, and there, and to dozens of other places, but they couldn't be everywhere at one and the same time. That was their weak spot.

His gaze returned to the copper earths, and he wondered whether even this efficient system would absorb the terrific shock imposed upon it by a vengeful enemy. He doubted it. A system ten times the size would not be sufficient to cope with the hell's fury such as had fallen upon Silver City.

The most they could hope for was to destroy one Viton—and let the rest of the world know why Faraday's had been thrown all over the landscape, let it thus know that there still was hope if the struggle could be maintained a little longer. Yes, the end of only one Viton would be enough.

Behind the transmitter's intended site was a wide pit, its six-inch wall of sprayed-on, quick-drying cement diving into the depths like a gigantic pipe. There was a slidepole down its center.

One man was going to operate the transmitter. If he could do it, that man was going to try to save himself from the certain holocaust that success would bring by plunging down the shaft deep, deep into the ebon depths. It was a primitive sanctuary—but the fastest out that could be contrived in the circumstances.

Returning, he asked Laurie, "How long?"

"Fifteen minutes." Laurie mopped his damp and anxious brow. "We'll be all set in fifteen minutes. If it works, we'll have the plant ready for ten more assemblies." He waved a hand to indicate the bustling crowd. "And providing we don't get slaughtered, we'll fling them together in a couple of hours."

"No you won't." Graham's contradiction was flat and authoritative. "You're going to rush those spares away to a safe distance right now. The whole area is liable to be tossed moonward when those Vitons get the rats, and the spares had better be someplace else during the showdown." Finding a microphone, he chattered into it rapidly.

Three minutes later, a line of trucks swung before the doors, each picking up its load and lumbering heavily away. Workers departed in silent, ruminative groups, leaving behind a shop cleared of all but the polarized-wave projector shining in the middle of the floor. A quartet of scientists hurried to complete various connections, make a few last-minute adjustments.

He leaned on the turntable, watching them with a cold patience that surprised himself considering that the testing time was so near. After days of nervous strain, he was suddenly as impassive as a stone Buddha—like a man who finally finds himself in the dental chair after a jumpy hour in the waiting room. His gaze settled on one of the working four, a half pint individual with a tonsure around his balding head.

As this expert completed his task, Graham spoke to him in harsh, deliberate tones. "I don't fancy handling a trick circuit jumping the power line to the impeller switch." The concentrated venom in his voice appalled his hearers.

The runt he had addressed turned on him a wizened, monkeyish face in which pale blue eyes regarded him blankly. Dropping a piece of thin cable, he felt casually in his pocket as if seeking a pair of pliers.

Graham shot him where he poised, the powerful, pointblank blast fairly flinging the fellow backward. While Laurie and the rest looked on white-faced, Art Wohl stepped unconcernedly to the body, felt in its pocket, extracted a small, egg-shaped object.

"Holy smoke, a bomb! He'd have shredded us along with the dingbat!"

"Never mind. Take it away, Art, and dump it in that reservoir out back." He transferred his attention to Laurie. "Unhook that power bypass and check the circuit, Duncan. See if the output is all right. If so, we'll run the thing out and tie it to those earths."

A minute later, Laurie pronounced, "It's ready for action. It'll never function more perfectly even if it achieves nothing."

"Good!" They drove it out, earthed it. Laurie departed with his three men, leaving only Wohl.

Graham sat high up in the assembly, the power, impeller, elevator and turn-table controls within easy reach. A dull, cloudy sky was heavy overhead. He had an argument with Wohl as the smoke and spume of a rocket-shot sprang high in the south.

"Beat it, Art," he ordered. "There are Vitons over there." He indicated a horde of glowing balls roaming in from the northeast. "This is no time to squat here and debate with you. Chase after Duncan and the others—I'll give you half a minute to get clear."

"But—" began Wohl, protestingly!

"Scram!" roared Graham in a frantic voice.

He watched Wohl slouch miserably away, waited until he was out of sight beyond the hangar. Before him as he sat, the cylindrical funnel projected like the barrel of a monster gun. The approaching luminosities were now only a mile distant.

Wide-sighted eyes raked the sky as he gave Wohl time to gain safe distance. The origin of the Vitons would never be known, he decided. Their existence would remain as much a mystery as that of pneumococci, poodles, or any other form of life. But it was his pet theory that they were true natives of Earth, and it was also his hunch that they were about to be wiped off Earth forever—if not by one battling human group, then by some other.

Zero hour had come, the fateful moment had arrived. He swung the great funnel, lined it upon the advancing orbs. The funnel moved lightly on its gimbals, and the entire assembly spun smoothly on its turntable frame. He heard power being made by the whining generators in the hangar, and noted that the time was ninety minutes from Europe's deadline. Snapping a switch, he let the power pour through.

There followed a few seconds' pause while the tubes warmed up. Over there, in strategic posts ten or twelve floors high, distant observers watched through field glasses that trembled in their hands.

The half-centimeter beam fountained into the shaft, polarized, directable. It spiked from the funnel's maw, the axis of its whirling impulses parallel with the skeleton-sights lined upon the Vitons.

This frequency lay beyond even the Bjornsen vision-range, and the beam could not be seen. But its effect was startlingly visible. The leading luminosity of a prowling string of ten stopped in mid-air as if barred by an unseeable obstruction. It turned deeper in color, from bright blue to dark purple, almost instantaneously switched to orange of extreme brilliance, then popped into nothingness. It was gone so utterly and completely that its going shocked the army of hidden observers.

The remaining nine Vitons bobbed around undecidedly, and another stopped, went through the blue-purple-orange-obliteration cycle before the rest scattered at top speed. They bulleted straight upward, into the clouds.

Somebody was bellowing like a mad bull as Graham elevated the funnel and caught a third in full flight. Somebody howled an idiotic remark about it being more sporting to get 'em on the wing.

With the tail of his eye, he saw an enormous gout of yellow-white flame vomit from the general area of Broadway. The noise followed, then the air-blast. It rocked him in his seat. His lips closed firmly, the strange bellowing ceased, and he realized that he had been bawling himself hoarse.

Some sixth sense—probably his extrasensory perception—made him whirl his assembly around. He spun dizzily behind the impeller casing, caught a line of spheres rushing him from the south.

He started yelling again as the leader went deep purple. The following luminosities slowed so suddenly that he fancied they had feet, braced forward, and still skidding. Their velocity was too great for that. They crashed headlong into their stricken fellow at the moment it flared into an eye-searing orange.

"One for Mayo!" he hollered, jigging on his seat. "One for Webb! One for Beach, you dirty, stinking gobs of parasitic lousery! Another for Farmiloe, and the whole damn lot of you for Bjornsen!"

Ceasing his insane howls, he watched the results of the aerial collision. For the space of a single heartbeat, the wildly whirling conglomeration of energy maintained enlarged but spherical form in the astounded heavens. Then it exploded with a terrible roar.

Graham's eardrums bounced against each other. Displaced air almost tore him from his precarious saddle. The entire apparatus wrenched at its fastenings and groaned. While the high-up mess of wavicles went haywire, fierce rays struck him like vicious sunburn, forcing him to close his eyelids to protect his pupils.

But he couldn't keep quiet, he wouldn't keep quiet. This was the end of the trail, this was his lone half hour if never he enjoyed another, and, above all, this was retribution. He whooped like a charging Sioux as deftly he swung the funnel through a ninety degree arc and blasted two scintillating menaces dropping upon him from above.

Now it was clear how they'd set off those tanks in Silver City. A dozen of them, or twenty, or perhaps fifty had committed suicide, plunging into the tanks, merging as they struck. That merging had destroyed their natural balance, collectively converting them into a super-detonator. They had in their ancient lore a secret only recently discovered by their human slaves: the secret of violent disruption when energy-forms—radioactive or Vitonic—exceed critical mass.

That silver nitrate had received the world's worst wallop, a sock in the neck that made the atom bomb look piddling. And that great black finger pointing to where Silver City's souls had gone had been a monstrous column of maddened atoms seeking new unions as they splashed upward.

Whirling his turntable again, he threw a free sample of hell at an oncoming sextet, saw them dispel their energy in visible frequencies and cease to be. These

Vitons could afford to be nonchalant about stuff coming at them along Lissajous' complicated path, for nature had conditioned them to the solar output. They could stand it. Maybe they liked it. But hyperbolic: *that* corkscrewed into their very guts!

There was a tremendous array of luminosities collecting on the extreme limit of the northern horizon. He tried to reach them with his beam, found he was unable to discern any result, concluded that they must be beyond effective range. More man-made volcanoes belched in the east. The air held smells of ozone, burning rubber and wet cement. Voices made indistinct by distance were shouting all around.

He thought of America's grounded air fleet, ten thousand fast, efficient machines that dared not ascend so long as there were luminosities to take control of the pilots' minds and set one against another. That was going to be altered pretty soon. Winged warriors were going to darken the sky, while below them people spoke the sweetest word of any man's war—"Ours!"

So far, he'd wiped out only the reckless, lazy or unwary, but now they knew their danger. A mass attack was about to be made, an onslaught in which the Vitons would demonstrate once and for all the fullness of their united power. They would bullet toward him in companies, battalions, brigades, in numbers far greater than he could slaughter. They were going to blot him off the face of the disputed Earth, and the projector along with him. The end was near, but it had been a great run.

Searching the sky, he saw a squadron of Asian stratplanes zooming eastward with the calm confidence of things in cahoots with God. Puffballs and sparks sprang into being behind and beneath them. He wondered whether their fanatical pilots had witnessed the fate of some of their supposed ancestral spirits, concluded that they had not.

The news ought to have got around by now. It would be all over the New World, and probably Europe had full details. Europe would hold on, knowing that victory was now a matter of time rather than doubt. Maybe one of the other groups also had succeeded. Anyway, it didn't matter—this success at Faraday's was humanity's triumph.

He ceased his pondering when the faraway cohorts soared upward. They made so huge and fantastic an aurora that it became hard to conceive their complete invisibility to ordinary, untreated eyesight. They were a bright blue myriad, a veritable army whose numbers filled the northern sky with a panorama of glowing horror, a heavenly host not born of heaven and long rejected by hell. The speed of their advance was almost incredible.

Even as Graham braced himself for what was coming, a small patch in the enemy's center darkened to purple, went orange, puffed out of existence. It had him puzzled for a moment, then he remembered—Yonkers.

"Good old Steve!" he roared. "He's done it. Give them hell, Steve!"

Shooting power along, he sprayed the rapidly swelling horde. Blue switched to purple and orange, became nixed. An untouched section detached itself from the main body, fell headlong on Yonkers, some changing color as they fell.

The rest shot vengefully toward Graham. He knew what was going to happen, sensed it from the way in which they gradually concentrated themselves as they sped along. Up to the last moment he let them have it hot and strong, canceling them wholesale with furious words and lethal impulses. Then, as they merged suicidally, he reached the pit in four frantic leaps, embraced the pole, let the force of gravity snatch him down.

Ghastly, glowing blue momentarily wavered and undulated over the mouth of the shaft as he dropped at breath-taking speed. The whole sky had become a bowl of glossy azure. Then, abruptly, it flamed unbearably. A brain-searing roar as of the cosmos being ripped to tatters smashed into his already maltreated eardrums. The slide-pole danced like a juggler's wand.

Helplessly, he was flicked off the pole, fell into shaking depths. The shaft quivered from base to mouth, its walls crumbled, earth, stones, lumps of concrete poured after him in a deadly rain. Something bigger and blacker than the rest came unstuck, fell ponderously through general blackness, landed dully on yielding flesh.

Graham emitted a queer sigh. His mind wandered off, a barge of funereal ebony floating in sooty seas.

It was comfortable in bed, so comfortable that the illusion was well worth preserving. Shifting his head contentedly, Graham felt a sharp pain lance through it, opened his eyes.

Yes, he was in bed. He waggled his fingers, felt around. Definitely a bed. Amazedly, he surveyed a white sheet, studied a picture on the opposite wall. It was *A Stag At Bay.* He extended his tongue at it.

A chair creaked at his side; he winced as he turned his head to look, discovered Wohl's broad-shouldered figure.

"Good evening, Rip van Winkle," greeted Wohl, with unctuous politeness. He indicated a clock and a calendar. "It's ten in the evening of Thursday. For three days you've been deaf, dumb, dopey and doubled up. In other words, you've been your natural self."

"Is that so?" Graham's snort was a little less fiery than of yore. He glared toward the stag. "Did you hang that blasted thing? If so, it isn't funny."

Wohl looked at it, endured the pain of thought, then said, "Haw-haw!"

Struggling upward, Graham propped himself on one elbow, ignored his throbbing cranium. "Get me my rags, you ignorant flattie—I'm going places."

"Nothing doing." Wohl's broad hand pressed him gently down. "This is one time when I give orders and you take 'em." He made the declaration with unashamed relish, and went on. "Those luminosities devastated an area a couple of miles in diameter, killed many observers. It took us twelve hours to locate your funk-hole and dig out the lump of catmeat that was you. So lie down and be at peace while Uncle Art tells you some bedtime stories."

Producing a printed newspaper, he opened it, gave a brief sketch of the day's events, reading in a voice that fairly gloated.

"Mayor Sullivan says city now adequately protected. Electra's hundred scores new high for one day's projector output. Two more Asian stratplane squadrons land at Battery Park and surrender." Glancing at his listener, he remarked, "That's merely local stuff. An awful lot has happened while you snored on like a fat hog."

"Humph!" Graham felt peeved. "What about Koenig?"

"He lost two operators when Yonkers took it on the chin. A lot of surrounding observers went west, too. But the rest are all right." Wohl reversed his paper. "Listen to this," he invited. "Nebraska line straightened. Our armor pushes on against weakening opposition. Rebellion spreads through Asian ranks as first transmitters reach front and destroy overhead luminosities. Pacifist Asians seize Chungking and start manufacture of anti-Viton beams. Europe pressing eastward at fast pace. Washington expects Asian offer of armistice and aid in wiping out luminosities." He rolled up the paper, shoved it under Graham's pillow. "The war's as good as over, thanks to you."

"Nuts!" said Graham, sourly. He lifted himself again. "Get me my cover-ups. I'm not a thieving louse like you—I don't snitch blankets."

Wohl came to his feet, stared in mock horror. "By God, Bill, you look awful. You look real bad. I guess you need a doctor." He moved toward the door.

"Don't play the fool," shouted Graham. Hurriedly he sat up, held his head together until it decided not to fall apart. "Fetch me my pants before I get out and paste you one. I'm beating it out of this dump."

"You don't know what's good for you," Wohl reproved from the doorway. "You're in a new underground hospital—it's now the Samaritan."

"Eh?"

"The Samaritan," Wohl repeated. He leered at the stag.

"Ah!" Graham promptly lay flat, produced a hollow groan. "I feel terrible, Art. Maybe I'm dying. Go fetch me a doctor."

"Well!" said Wohl. He struck an attitude, protruding his buttocks and holding an imaginary bow. "Look—Cupid, me!" Then he went out.

She came in presently, sat down, put on her best bedside manner, and inquired, "How're you feeling now?"

"As usual—with my hands." Putting out a hand, he took hold of hers.

She dumped it back firmly. "This is no place for that sort of thing."

"You've never given me the chance anyplace else," he pointed out.

Saying nothing, she stared at the stag without seeing it.

"Hell of a thing," he said.

"I beg your pardon?"

"That." He nodded toward the picture. "Somebody's sarcasm, I guess. Yours?"

"Mine?" She was patently surprised. "Nonsense. If you don't like it, I'll have it moved."

"Please do. It reminds me too much of me. Too much of everybody, if it comes to that."

"Indeed? Why?"

"At bay. We've been at bay back to the dawn of history. First without knowing it, then with full knowledge. It's nice to know that's over. Maybe we'll now have time for fun. You helped with the one, you can help with the other."

"I am not aware of having given any valuable assistance," she said, primly.

"You tipped us about Beach, and therapy cabinets, and Farmiloe. We'd still have been chasing shadows but for you." He sat up, gazing at her. "I'm not chasing any more shadows. I've had enough."

Making no reply, she turned her head sidewise, looked upward meditatively. He drank in the curve of her cheekbone, the sweep of her lashes, and knew she was conscious of his gaze.

"Up there, Harmony, are the stars," he continued. "There may be people out that way, people of flesh and blood like us, friendly people who'd have visited us long ago but for a Viton ban. Hans Luther believed they'd been warned to keep off the grass. Forbidden, forbidden, forbidden—that was Earth." He studied her again. "Every worthwhile thing forbidden, to those folk who'd like to come here, and to us who were imprisoned here. Nothing permitted except that which our masters considered profitable to themselves."

"But not now," she murmured.

"No, not now. We can emote for ourselves now, and not for others. At last our excitements are our own. Two are company, three are none—especially when the third's a Viton. Has it struck you that in the truest sense we're now alone?"

"We—?"

Her face turned toward him, her eyebrows arched.

"Maybe this isn't the place," he observed, "but at least it's the opportunity!" He bent her across his lap, pressed his lips on hers.

She pushed at him, but not too hard. After a while, she changed her mind. Her arm slid around his neck.

Legwork

Astounding, April, 1956

As nearly as an Andromedan thought form can be expressed in print, his name was Harasha Vanash. The formidable thing about him was his conceit. It was redoubtable because justified. His natural power had been tested on fifty hostile worlds and found invincible.

The greatest asset any living creature can possess is a brain capable of imagination. That is its strong point, its power center. But to Vanash an opponent's mind was a weak spot, a chink in the armor, a thing to be exploited.

Even he had his limitations. He could not influence a mind of his own species armed with his own power. He could not do much with a brainless life form except kick it in the rumps. But if an alien could think and imagine, that alien was his meat.

Vanash was a twenty-four carat hypno, jeweled in every hole. Given a thinking mind to work upon at any range up to most of a mile, he could convince it in a split second that black was white, right was wrong, the sun had turned bright green, and the corner cop was King Farouk. Anything he imposed stayed stuck unless he saw fit to unstick it. Even if it outraged common sense, the victim would sign affidavits, swear to it upon the Bible, the Koran or whatever, and then be led away to have his head examined.

There was one terminal restriction that seemed to have the nature of a cosmos-wide law; he could not compel any life form to destroy itself by its own hand. At that point the universal instinct of self-survival became downright mulish and refused to budge.

However, he was well able to do the next best thing. He could do what a snake does to a rabbit, namely, obsess the victim with the idea that it was paralyzed and completely unable to flee from certain death. He could not persuade a Bootean *appolan* to cut its own throat, but he could make it stand still while he performed that service.

Yes, Harasha Vanash had excellent basis for self-esteem. When one has walked into and out of fifty worlds one can afford to be confident about the fifty-first. Experience is a faithful and loving servant, always ready with a long, stimulating draught of ego when required.

So it was with nonchalance that he landed on Earth. The previous day he'd given the planet a look-over and his snooping had set off the usual rumors about flying saucers despite that his ship resembled no such object.

He arrived unseen in the hills, got out, sent the ship up to where its auto mechanisms would swing it into a distant orbit and make it a pinhead-sized moon. Among the rocks he hid the small, compact apparatus that could call it back when wanted.

The vessel was safe from interference up there, high in the sky. The chance of it being observed telescopically was very remote. If the creatures of Earth did succeed in detecting its presence, they could do nothing about it. They hadn't any rocketships. They could do no more than look and wonder and worry.

Yesterday's preliminary investigation had told him practically nothing about the shape and form of the dominant life. He hadn't got near enough for that. All he'd wanted to know was whether this planet was worthy of closer study and whether its highest life form had exploitable minds. It had not taken long to see that he'd discovered an especially juicy plum, a world deserving of eventual confiscation by the Andromedan horde.

The physical attributes of these future slaves did not matter much right now. Though not at all bizarre, he was sufficiently like them to walk around, sufficiently unlike to raise a yelp of alarm on sight. There would be no alarm. In spite of a dozen physical differences they'd be soothed, positively soothed. Because they'd never get a true view of him. Only an imaginary one. He could be a mental mock-up of anything, anybody.

Therefore, the first thing to do was to find a mediocrity who would pass unnoticed in a crowd, get his mental image firmly fixed and impress that on all other minds subsequently encountered until such time as it might be convenient to switch pictures.

Communication was no problem, either. He could read the questions, project the answers, and the other party's own mind could be compelled to supply accompanying camouflage. If they communicated by making noises with their mouths or by dexterous jiggling of their tails, it would work out the same. The other's mastered imagination would get his message while providing the noises and mouth movements or the appropriate tail-jigglings.

Leaving the landing place, he set forth through the hills, heading for a well-used road observed during his descent. A flight of primitive jet-planes arced across the eastward horizon. He paused long enough to watch them with approval. The trouble with prospective servants already discovered elsewhere was that they were a bit too stupid to be efficient. Not here, though.

He continued on his way, bearing no instrument other than a tiny compass needed for eventual return and take-off. No weapon. Not a knife, not a gun. There was no need to burden himself with lethal hardware. By self-evident logic, local weapons were the equals of themselves. Any time he wanted one he could make the nearest sucker hand over his own and feel happy to do it. It was that easy. He'd done it a dozen times before and could do it a dozen times again.

By the roadside stood a small filling station with four pumps. Vanash kept watch upon it from the shelter of thick bushes fifty yards away. Hm-m-m! Bipeds, vaguely like himself but with semi-rigid limbs and a lot more hair. There was one operating a pump, another sitting in a car. He could not get a complete image of the latter because only the face and shoulders were visible. As for the former, the fellow wore a glossy-peaked cap bearing a metal badge and uniformlike overalls with a crimson cipher on the pocket.

Neither example was suitable for mental duplication, he decided. One lacked sufficient detail, the other had far too much. Characters who wore uniforms usually took orders, had fixed duties, were liable to be noted and questioned if seen some place where they shouldn't be. It would be better to pick a subject able to move around at random.

The car pulled away. Peaked Cap wiped his hands on a piece of cotton waste and gazed along the road. Vanash maintained his watch. After a few minutes another car halted. This one had an aerial sticking from its roof and bore two individuals dressed alike; peaked caps, metal buttons and badges. They were heavy-featured, hard-eyed, had an official air about them. They wouldn't do either, thought Vanash. Too conspicuous.

Unconscious of this scrutiny, one of the cops said to the attendant, "Seen anything worth telling, Joe?"

"Not a thing. All quiet."

The police cruiser jerked forward and continued its patrol. Joe went into the station. Taking a flavor-seed from its small pack, Vanash chewed it and meditated while he bided his time. So they were mouth-talkers, nontelepathic, routine-minded and natural puppets for any hypno who cared to dangle them around.

Still, their cars, jet planes and other gadgets proved that they enjoyed occasional flashes of inspiration. In Andromedan theory the rare touch of genius was all that menaced any hypno, since nothing else could sense his existence, follow his operations and pin him down.

It was a logical supposition—in terms of other-world logic. Everything the Andromedan culture possessed had been born one by one of numberless revealing shafts of revelation that through the centuries had sparked out of nothingness in the inexplicable way that such things do. But flashes of inspiration come spontaneously, of their own accord.

They cannot be created to order no matter how great the need. Any species could go nuts for lack of one essential spark and, like everyone else, be compelled to wait its turn.

The trap in any foreign culture lies in the fact that no newcomer can know everything about it, imagine everything, guess everything. For instance, who could guess that the local life form were a bunch of chronic fidgets? Or that, because of it, they'd never had time to wait for genius? Vanash did not know, and could not suspect, that Earth had a tedious, conventional and most times unappreciated substitute for touches of genius. It was slow, grim, determined and unspectacular, but it was usable as and when required and it got results.

Variously it was called making the grade, slogging along, doing it the hard way, or just plain lousy legwork. Whoever heard of such a thing?

Not Vanash, nor any of his kind. So he waited behind the bushes until eventually a nondescript, mousy individual got out of a car, obligingly mooched around offering every detail of his features, mannerisms and attire. This specimen looked the unattached type that are a dime a dozen on any crowded city street. Vanash mentally photographed him from every angle, registered him to perfection and felt satisfied.

Five miles to the north along this road lay a small town, and forty miles beyond it a big city. He'd seen and noted them on the way down, deciding that the town would serve as training-ground before going to the city. Right now he could step boldly from cover and compel his model to drive him where he wanted to go.

The idea was tempting but unwise. Before he was through with this world, its life form would become aware of inexplicable happenings in their midst and it would be safer not to locate the first of such events so near to the rendezvous with the ship. Peaked Cap might talk too loudly and too long about the amazing coincidence of a customer giving a lift to an exact twin. The victim himself might babble bemusedly about picking up somebody who made him feel as though looking into a mirror. Enough items like that, and a flash of revelation could assemble them into a picture of the horrid truth.

He let the customer go and waited for Joe to enter the building. Then he emerged from the bushes, walked half a mile northward, stopped and looked to the south.

The first car that came along was driven by a salesman who never, never, never picked up a hitcher. He'd heard of cases where free riders had bopped the driver and robbed him, and he wasn't going to be rolled if he could help it. So far as he was concerned, thumbers by the wayside could go on thumbing until next Thursday week.

He stopped and gave Vanash a lift and lacked the vaguest notion of why he'd done it. All he knew was that in a moment of mental aberration he'd broken the habit of a lifetime and picked up a thin-faced, sad and silent customer who resembled a middle-aged mortician.

"Going far?" asked the salesman, inwardly bothered by the weakness of his own resolution.

"Next town," said Vanash. Or the other one thought he said it, distinctly heard him saying it and would take a dying oath that it really had been said. Sneaking the town's name from the driver's mind and thrusting it back again, Vanash persuaded him to hear the addition of, "Northwood."

"Any particular part?"

"Doesn't matter. It's a small place. Drop me wherever you find convenient."

The driver grunted assent, offered no more conversation. His thoughts milled around, baffled by his own Samaritanism. Arriving in Northwood, he stopped the car.

"This do?"

"Thanks." Vanash got out. "I appreciate it."

"Think nothing of it," said the salesman, driving away bopless and unrolled. Vanash watched him depart, then had a look around Northwood.

The place was nothing much. It had shops on one long main street and on two short side streets. A railroad depot with a marshaling yard. Four medium-sized industrial plants. Three banks, a post office, a fire station, a couple of municipal buildings. He estimated that Northwood held between four and five thousand Earthlings and that at least a third of them worked on outlying farms.

He ambled along the main street and was ignored by unsuspecting natives while practically rubbing shoulders with them. The experience gave him no great kick; he'd done it so often elsewhere that he now took it for granted and was almost bored by it. At one point a dog saw him, let go a howl of dismay and bolted with its tail between its legs. Nobody took any notice. Neither did he.

First lesson in pre-city education was gained inside a shop. Curious to see how the customers got what they wanted, he entered with a bunch of them. They used a medium of exchange in the form of printed paper and metal disks. That meant he'd save himself considerable trouble and inconvenience if he got hold of a supply of the stuff.

Moving to a crowded supermarket, he soon learned the relative values of money and a fair idea of its purchasing power. Then he helped himself to a small supply and was smart enough to do it by proxy. The technique was several times easier than falling off a log.

Standing unnoticed at one side, he concentrated attention on a plump, motherly shopper of obvious respectability. She responded by picking the purse of a preoccupied woman next to her. Sneaking the loot out of the market, she dropped it unopened on a vacant lot, went home, thought things over and held her head.

The take was forty-two dollars. Vanash counted it carefully, went to a cafeteria, splurged some of it on a square meal. By other methods he could have got the feed for free, but such tactics are self-advertising and can be linked up by a spark of inspiration. To his taste, some of the food was revolting, some passable, but it would do until he'd learned how to pick and choose.

One problem not yet satisfactorily resolved was that of what to do with the night. He needed sleep as much as any inferior life form and had to find some place for it. A snooze in the fields or a barn would be inappropriate; the master does not accept the hay while the servants snore on silk.

It took a little while to find out from observation, mind-pickings and a few questions to passers-by that he could bed down at an hotel or rooming house. The former did not appeal to him. Too public and, therefore, too demanding upon his resources for concealment. In an hotel he'd have less opportunity to let up for a while and be himself, which was a welcome form of relaxation.

But with a room of his own free from constantly intruding servants armed with master-keys, he could revert to a normal, effortless state of mind, get his sleep, work out his plans in peace and privacy.

He found a suitable rooming house without much trouble. A blowzy female with four warts on her florid face showed him his hideout, demanded twelve dollars in advance because he had no luggage. Paying her, he informed her that he was William Jones, here for a week on business, and that he liked to be left alone.

In return, she intimated that her joint was a palace of peace for gentlemen, and that any bum who imported a hussy would be out on his neck. He assured her that he would not dream of such a thing, which was true enough because to him such a dream would have all the makings of a nightmare. Satisfied, she withdrew.

He sat on the edge of the bed and thought things over. It would have been an absurdly simple trick to have paid her in full without handing her a cent. He could have sent her away convinced that she had been paid. But she'd still be short twelve dollars and get riled about the mysterious loss. If he stayed on, he'd have to fool her again and again until at last the very fact that his payments coincided exactly with her losses would be too much even for an idiot.

A way out would be to nick someone for a week's rent, then move and take another boob. That tactic had its drawbacks. If the news got around and a hunt started after the bilker, he would have to change identities.

He wasn't averse to soaking a muttonhead or switching personalities, providing it was necessary. It irked him to have to do it frequently, for petty reasons hardly worth the effort. To let himself be the constant victim of trifling circumstances was to accept that these aliens were imposing conditions upon him. His ego resented such an idea.

All the same, he had to face a self-evident premise and its unavoidable conclusion. On this world one must have money to get around smoothly, without irritating complications. Therefore, he must acquire an adequate supply of the real thing or be continually called upon to create the delusion that he possessed it. No extraordinary intelligence was needed to divine which alternative gave the least trouble.

On other worlds the life forms had proved so sluggish and dull-witted, their civilizations so rudimentary, that it had not taken long to make a shrewd estimate of their worth as future foes and subsequent slaves. Here, the situation was a lot more complicated and required lengthier, more detailed survey. By the looks of it he'd be stalled quite a time. So he must get hold of money in quantities larger than that carried by the average individual And when it ran out, he must get more.

Next day he devoted some time to tracing the flow of money back to a satisfactory source. Having found the source, he spent more time making careful study of it. In underworld jargon, he cased a bank.

The man lumbering along the corridor weighed two-fifty, had a couple of chins and a prominent paunch. At first sight, just a fat slob. First impressions can be very deceptive. At least half a dozen similarly built characters had been world heavyweight wrestling champs. Edward G. Rider was not quite in that category, but on rare occasion he could strew bodies around in a way that would make an onlooking chiseler offer his services as manager.

He stopped at a frosted glass door bearing the legend: UNITED STATES TREASURY—INVESTIGATION. Rattling the glass with a hammerlike knuckle, he entered without waiting for response, took a seat without being invited.

The sharp-faced individual behind the desk registered faint disapproval, said, "Eddie, I've got a smelly one for you."

"Have you ever given me one that wasn't?" Rider rested big hands on big kneecaps. "What's it this time? Another unregistered engraver on the rampage?"

"No. It's a bank robbery."

Rider frowned, twitched heavy eyebrows. "I thought we were interested only in counterfeit currency and illegal transfers of capital. What has a heist to do with us? That's for the police, isn't it?"

"The police are stuck with it."

"Well, if the place was government insured they can call in the Feds."

"It's not insured. We offered to lend a hand. You are the boy who will lend it."

"Why?"

The other drew a deep breath, explained rapidly, "Some smartie took the First Bank of Northwood for approximately twelve thousand—and nobody knows how. Captain Harrison, of the Northwood police, says the puzzle is a stinker. According to him, it looks very much as though at long last somebody has found a technique for committing the perfect crime."

"He would say that if he feels thwarted. How come we're dragged into it?"

"On checking up with the bank Harrison found that the loot included forty one-hundred dollar bills consecutively numbered. Those numbers are known. The others are not. He phoned us to give the data, hoping the bills might turn up and we could back-track on them. Embleton handled the call, chatted a while, got interested in this perfect crime thesis."

"So?"

"He consulted with me. We both agreed that if somebody has learned how to truck lettuce the way he likes, he's as much a menace to the economy as any large-scale counterfeiter."

"I see," said Rider, doubtfully.

"Then I took the matter up at high level. Ballantyne himself decided that we're entitled to chip in, just in case something's started that can go too far. I chose you. The whole office block will sit steadier without your size fourteen boots banging around." He moved some papers to his front, picked up a pen. "Get out to Northwood and give Chief Harrison a boost."

"Now?"

"Any reason why it should be tomorrow or next week?"

"I'm baby-sitting tonight."

"Don't be silly."

"It's not silly," said Rider. "Not with this baby."

"You ought to be ashamed. You're not long married. You've got a sweet and trusting wife."

"She's the baby," Rider informed. "I promised her faithfully and fervently that I'd—"

"And I promised Harrison and Ballantyne that you'd handle this with your usual elephantine efficiency," the other interrupted, scowling. "Do you want to hold down your job or do you want out? Phone your wife and tell her duty comes first."

"Oh, all right." He went out, slammed the door, tramped surlily along the corridor, entered a booth and took twenty-two minutes to do the telling.

Chief Harrison was tall, lean and fed up. He said, "Why should I bother to tell you what happened? Direct evidence is better than secondhand information. We've got the actual witness here. I sent for him when I learned you were coming." He flipped a switch on the desk-box. "Send Ashcroft in."

"Who's he?" Rider asked.

"Head teller of the First Bank, and a worried man." He waited for the witness to enter, made an introduction. "This is Mr. Rider, a special investigator. He wants to hear your story."

Ashcroft sat down, wearily rubbed his forehead. He was a white-haired, dapper man in the early sixties. Rider weighed him up as the precise, somewhat finicky but solid type often described as a pillar of the community.

"So far I've told it about twenty times," Ashcroft complained, "and each time it sounds a little madder. My mind is spinning with the thoughts of it. I just can't find any plausible—"

"Don't worry yourself," advised Rider in soothing tones. "Just give me the facts as far as they go."

"Each week we make up the payroll for the Dakin Glass Company. It varies between ten and fifteen thousand dollars. The day before, the company sends around a messenger with a debit-note calling for the required sum and stating how they want it. We then get it ready in good time for the following morning."

"And then?"

"The company collects. They send around a cashier accompanied by a couple of guards. He always arrives at about eleven o'clock. Never earlier than ten to eleven or later than ten past."

"You know the cashier by sight?"

"There are two of them, Mr. Swain and Mr. Letheren. Either of them might come for the money. One relieves the other from time to time. Or one comes when the other is too busy, or ill, or on vacation. Both have been well-known to me for several years."

"All right, carry on."

"When the cashier arrives he brings a locked leather bag and has the key in a pocket. He unlocks the bag, hands it to me. I fill it in such manner that he can check the quantities, pass it back together with a receipt slip. He locks the bag, puts the key in his pocket, signs the slip and walks out. I file the receipt and that's all there is to it."

"Seems a bit careless to let the same fellow carry both the bag and the key," Rider commented.

Chief Harrison chipped in with, "We've checked on that. A guard carries the key. He gives it to the cashier when they arrive at the bank, takes it back when they leave."

Nervously licking his lips, Ashcroft went on, "Last Friday morning we had twelve thousand one hundred eighty-two dollars ready for the Dakin plant. Mr. Letheren came in with the bag. It was exactly ten-thirty."

"How do you know that?" inquired Richer, sharply. "Did you look at the clock? What impelled you to look at it?"

"I consulted the clock because I was a little surprised. He was ahead of his usual time. I had not expected him for another twenty minutes or so."

"And it was ten-thirty? You're positive of that?"

"I am absolutely certain," said Ashcroft, as though it was the only certainty in the whole affair. "Mr. Letheren came up to the counter and gave me the bag. I greeted him, made a casual remark about him being early."

"What was his reply?"

"I don't recall the precise wording. I'd no reason to take especial note of what he said and I was busy tending the bag." He frowned with effort of thought. "He made some commonplace remark about it being better to be too early than too late."

"What occurred next?"

"I gave him the bag and the slip. He locked the bag, signed the slip and departed."

"Is that all?" Rider asked.

"Not by a long chalk," put in Chief Harrison. He nodded encouragingly at Ashcroft. "Go on, give him the rest of it."

"At five to eleven," continued the witness, his expression slightly befuddled, "Mr. Letheren came back, placed the bag on the counter and looked at me sort of expectantly. So I said, 'Anything wrong, Mr. Letheren?' He answered, 'Nothing so far as I know. Ought there to be?' "

He paused, rubbed his forehead again. Rider advised, "Take your time with it. I want it as accurately as you can give it."

Ashcroft pulled himself together. "I told him there was no reason for anything to be wrong because the money had been checked and rechecked three times. He then displayed some impatience and said he didn't care if it had been checked fifty times so long as I got busy handing it over and let him get back to the plant."

"That knocked you onto your heels, eh?" Rider suggested, with a grim smile.

"I was flabbergasted. At first I thought it was some kind of joke, though he isn't the type to play such tricks. I told him I'd already given him the money, about half an hour before. He asked me if I was cracked. So I called Jackson, a junior teller, and he confirmed my statement. He had seen me loading the bag."

"Did he also see Letheren taking it away?"

"Yes, sir. And he said as much."

"What was Letheren's answer to that?"

"He demanded to see the manager. I showed him into Mr. Olsen's office. A minute later Mr. Olsen called for the receipt slip. I took it out of the file and discovered there was no signature upon it."

"It was blank?"

"Yes. I can't understand it. I watched him sign that receipt myself. Nevertheless there was nothing on it, not a mark of any sort." He sat silent and shaken, then finished, "Mr. Letheren insisted that Mr. Olsen cease questioning me and call the police. I was detained in the manager's office until Mr. Harrison arrived."

Rider stewed it over, then asked, "Did the same pair of guards accompany Letheren both times?"

"I don't know. I did not see his escort on either occasion."

"You mean he came unguarded?"

"They are not always visible to the bank's staff," Harrison put in. "I've chased that lead to a dead end."

"How much did you learn on the way?"

"The guards deliberately vary their routine so as to make their behavior unpredictable to anyone planning a grab. Sometimes both accompany the cashier to the counter and back. Sometimes they wait outside the main door, watching the street. Other times one remains in the car while the other mooches up and down near the bank."

"They are armed, I take it?"

"Of course." He eyed Rider quizzically. "Both guards swear that last Friday morning they escorted Letheren to the bank once and only once. That was at five to eleven."

"But he was there at ten-thirty," Ashcroft protested.

"He denies it," said Harrison. "So do the guards."

"Did the guards say they'd actually entered the bank?" inquired Rider, sniffing around for more contradictory evidence.

"They did not enter on arrival. They hung around outside the front door until Letheren's delay made them take alarm. At that point they went inside with guns half-drawn. Ashcroft couldn't see them because by then he was on the carpet in Olsen's office."

"Well, you can see how it is," commented Rider, staring hard at the unhappy Ashcroft. "You say Letheren got the money at ten-thirty. He says he did not. The statements are mutually opposed. Got any ideas on that?"

"You don't believe me, do you?" said Ashcroft, miserably.

"I don't disbelieve you, either. I'm keeping judgment suspended. We're faced with a flat contradiction of evidence. It doesn't follow that one of the witnesses is a liar and thus a major suspect. Somebody may be talking in good faith but genuinely mistaken."

"Meaning me?"

"Could be. You're not infallible. Nobody is." Rider learned forward, gave emphasis to his tones. "Let's accept the main points at face value. If you've told the truth, the cash was collected at ten-thirty. If Letheren his told the truth, he was not the collector. Add those up and what do you get? Answer: the money was toted away by somebody who was not Letheren. And if that answer happens to be correct, it means that you're badly mistaken."

"I've made no mistake," Ashcroft denied. "I know what I saw. I saw Letheren and nobody else. To say otherwise is to concede that I can't trust the evidence of my own eyes."

"You've conceded it already," Rider pointed out.

"Oh, no I haven't."

"You told us that you watched him sign the receipt slip. With your own two eyes you saw him append his signature." He waited for comment that did not come, ended, "There was nothing on the slip."

Ashcroft brooded in glum silence.

"If you were deluded about the writing, you could be equally deluded about the writer."

"I don't suffer from delusions."

"So it seems," said Rider, dry-voiced. "How do you explain that receipt?"

"I don't have to," declared Ashcroft with sudden spirit. "I've given the facts. It's for you fellows to find the explanation."

"That's right enough," Rider agreed. "We don't resent being reminded. I hope you don't resent being questioned again and again. Thanks for coming along."

"Glad to be of help." He went out, obviously relaxed by the end of the inquisition.

Harrison found a toothpick, chewed it, said, "It's a heller. Another day or two of this and you'll be sorry they sent you to show me how."

Meditatively studying the police chief, Rider informed, "I didn't come to show you how. I came to help because you said you needed help. Two minds are better than one. A hundred minds are better than ten. But if you'd rather I beat it back home—"

"Nuts," said Harrison. "At times like this I sour up on everyone. My position is different from yours. When someone takes a bank, right under my nose, he's made a chump of me. How'd you like to be both a police chief and a chump?"

"I think I'd accept the latter definition when and only when I'd been compelled to admit defeat. Are you admitting it?"

"Not on your life."

"Quit griping then. Let's concentrate on the job in hand. There's something mighty fishy about this business of the receipt. It looks cock-eyed."

"It's plain as pie to me," said Harrison. "Ashcroft was deluded or tricked."

"That isn't the point," Rider told him. "The real puzzle is that of *why* he was outsmarted. Assuming that he and Letheren are both innocent, the loot was grabbed by someone else, by somebody unknown. I don't see any valid reason why the culprit should risk bollixing the entire set-up by handing in a blank receipt that might be challenged on the spot. All he had to do to avoid it was to scrawl Letheren's name. Why didn't he?"

Harrison thought it over. "Maybe he feared Ashcroft would recognize the signature as a forgery, take a closer look at him, and yell bloody murder."

"If he could masquerade as Letheren well enough to get by, he should have been able to imitate a signature well enough to pass scrutiny."

"Well, maybe he didn't sign because he couldn't," Harrison ventured, "not being able to write. I know of several hoodlums who can only because they got taught in the jug."

"You may have something there," Rider conceded. "Anyway, for the moment Ashcroft and Letheren appear to be the chief suspects. They'll have to be eliminated before we start looking elsewhere. I presume you've already checked on both of them?"

"And how!" Harrison used the desk-box. "Send in the First Bank file." When it came, he thumbed through its pages. "Take Ashcroft first. Financially well-fixed, no criminal record, excellent character, no motive for turning bank robber. Jackson, the junior teller, confirms his evidence to a limited extent. Ashcroft could not have hidden the Dakin consignment any place. We searched the bank from top to bottom, during which time Ashcroft did not leave the place for one minute. We found nothing. Subsequent investigation brought out other items in his favor I'll give you the details later on."

"You're satisfied that he is innocent?"

"Almost, but not quite," said Harrison. "He could have handed the money to an accomplice who bears superficial resemblance to Letheren. That tactic would have finagled the stuff clean out of the bank. I wish I could shake down his home in search of his split. One bill with a known number would tie him down but good." His features became disgruntled. "Judge Maxon refused to sign a search warrant on grounds of insufficient justification. Said he's got to be shown better cause for reasonable suspicion. I'm compelled to admit that he's right."

"How about the company's cashier, Letheren?"

"He's a confirmed bachelor in the late fifties. I won't weary you with his full background. There's nothing we can pin on him."

"You're sure of that?"

"Judge for yourself. The company's car remained parked outside the office all morning until ten thirty-five. It was then used to take Letheren and his guards to the bank. It couldn't reach the bank in less than twenty minutes. There just wasn't enough time for Letheren to make the first call in some other car, return to the plant, pick up the guards and make the second call."

"Not to mention hiding the loot in the interim," Rider suggested.

"No, he could not have done it. Furthermore, there are forty people in the Dakin office and between them they were able to account for every minute of Letheren's time from when he started work at nine o'clock up to when he left for the bank at ten thirty-five. No prosecutor could bust an alibi like that!"

"That seems to put him right out of the running."

Harrison scowled and said "It certainly does—but we've since found five witnesses who place him near the bank at ten-thirty."

Meaning they support the statements of Ashcroft and Jackson?"

"Yes, they do. Immediately after the case broke I put every available man onto the job of asking questions the whole length of the street and down the nearest side-streets. The usual lousy legwork. They found three people prepared to swear they'd seen Letheren entering the bank at ten-thirty. They didn't know him by sight, but they were shown Letheren's photograph and identified him."

"Did they notice his car and give its description?"

"They didn't see him using a car. He was on foot at the time and carrying the bag. They noticed and remembered him only because a mutt yelped and went hell-for-leather down the street. They wondered whether he'd kicked it and why."

"Do they say he *did* kick it?"

"No."

Rider thoughtfully rubbed two chins. "Then I wonder why it behaved like that. Dogs don't yelp and bolt for nothing. Something must have hurt or scared it."

"Who cares?" said Harrison having worries enough. "The boys also found a fellow who says he saw Letheren a few minutes later, coming out of the bank and still with the bag. He didn't notice any guards hanging around. He says Letheren started walking along the street as though he hadn't a care in the world but after fifty yards he picked up a prowling taxi and rolled away."

"You traced the driver?"

"We did. He also recognized the photo we showed him. Said he'd taken Letheren to the Cameo Theater on Fourth Street, but did not see him actually enter the place. Just dropped him, got paid and drove off. We questioned the Cameo's staff, searched the house. It got us nowhere. There's a bus terminal nearby. We gave everyone there a rough time and learned nothing."

"And that's as far as you've been able to take it?"

"Not entirely. I've phoned the Treasury, given them the numbers of forty bills. I've put out an eight-state alarm for a suspect answering to Letheren's description. Right now the boys are armed with copies of his pic and are going the rounds of hotels and rooming houses. He must have holed up somewhere and it could have been right in this town. Now I'm stuck. I don't know where to look next."

Rider lay back in his chair which creaked in protest. He mused quite a time while Harrison slowly masticated the toothpick.

Then he said, "Excellent character, financial security and no apparent motive are things less convincing than the support of other witnesses. A man can have a secret motive strong enough to send him right off the rails. He could be in desperate need of ten or twelve thousand in ready cash merely because he's got to produce it a darned sight quicker than he can raise it by legitimate realization of insurance, stocks and bonds. For example, what if he's got twenty-four hours in which to find ransom money?"

Harrison popped his eyes. "You think we should check on Ashcroft's and Letheren's kin and see if any one of them is missing or has been missing of late?"

"Please yourself. Personally, I doubt that it's worth the bother. A kidnaper risks the death penalty. Why should he take a chance like that for a measly twelve thousand when he endangers himself no more by sticking a fatter victim for a far bigger sum? Besides, even if a check did produce a motive it wouldn't tell us how the robbery was pulled or enable us to prove it to the satisfaction of a judge and jury."

"That's right enough," Harrison agreed. "All the same, the check is worth making. It'll cost me nothing. Except for Ashcroft's wife, the relatives of both men live elsewhere. It's just a matter of getting the co-operation of police chiefs."

"Do it if you wish. And while we're making blind passes in the dark, get someone to find out whether Letheren happens to be afflicted with a no-good brother who could exploit a close family likeness. Maybe Letheren is the suffering half of a pair of identical twins."

"If he is," growled Harrison, "he's also an accessory after the fact because he can guess how the job was done and who did it, but he's kept his lips buttoned."

"That's the legal viewpoint. There's a human one as well. If one feels disgrace, one doesn't invite it. If you had a brother with a record as long as your arm, would you advertise it all over town?"

"For the fun of it, no. In the interests of justice, yes."

"All men aren't alike and thank God they're not." Rider made an impatient gesture. "We've gone as far as we can with the two obvious suspects. Let's work out what we can do with a third and unknown one."

Harrison said, "I told you I've sent out an alarm for a fellow answering to Letheren's description."

"Yes, I know. Think it will do any good?"

"It's hard to say. The guy may be a master of make-up. If so, he'll now look a lot different from the way he did when he pulled the job. If the resemblance happens to be real, close and unalterable, the alarm may help nail him."

"That's true. However, unless there's an actual blood relationship—which possibility you're following up anyway—the likeness can hardly be genuine. It would be too much of a coincidence. Let's say it's artificial. What does that tell us?"

"It was good," Harrison responded. "Good enough to fool several witnesses. Far too good for comfort."

"You said it," endorsed Rider. "What's more, an artist so exceptionally accomplished could do it again and again and again, working his way through a series of personalities more or less of his physical build. Therefore he may really look as much like Letheren as I look like a performing seal. We haven't his true description and the lack is a severe handicap. Offhand, I can think of no way of discovering what he looks like right now."

"Me neither," said Harrison, becoming morbid.

"There's one chance we've got though. Ten to one his present appearance is the same as it was before he worked his trick. He'd no reason to disguise himself while casing the job and making his plans. The robbery was so smooth and well-timed that it must have been schemed to perfection. That kind of planning requires plenty of preliminary observation. He could not cotton onto Dakin's collecting habits and Letheren's appearance at one solitary go. Not unless he was a mind reader."

"I don't believe in mind readers," Harrison declared. "Nor astrologers, swamis or any of their ilk."

Ignoring it, Rider ploughed stubbornly on, "So for some time prior to the robbery he had a hideout in this town or fairly close to it. Fifty or more people may have seen him repeatedly and be able to describe him. Your boys won't find him by circling the dives and dumps and showing a photo, because he didn't look like the photo. The problem now is to discover the hideout, learn what he looked like."

"Easier said than done."

"It's hard sledding, chief, but let's keep at it. Eventually we'll get ourselves some-where even if only into a padded cell."

He lapsed into silence, thinking deeply. Harrison concentrated attention on the ceiling. They did not know it, but they were employing Earth's on-the-spot substitute for a rare flash of genius. A couple of times Rider opened his mouth as if about to say something, changed his mind, resumed his meditating.

In the end, Rider said, "To put over so convincingly the gag that he was Letheren he must not only have looked like him but also dressed like him, walked like him, behaved like him, smelled like him."

"He was Letheren to the spit," answered Harrison. "I've questioned Ashcroft until we're both sick of it. Every single detail was Letheren right down to his shoes."

Rider asked, "How about the bag?"

"The bag?" Harrison's lean face assumed startlement followed by self-reproach. "You've got me there. I didn't ask about it. I slipped up."

"Not necessarily. There may be nothing worth learning. We'd better be sure on that point."

"I can find out right now." He picked up the phone, called a number, said, "Mr. Ashcroft, I've another question for you. About that bag you put the money into—was it the actual one always used by the Dakin people?"

The voice came back distinctly, "No, Mr. Harrison, it was a new one."

"What?" Harrison's voice purpled as he bellowed, "Why didn't you say so at the start?"

"You didn't ask me and, therefore, I didn't think of it. Even if I had thought of it of my own accord I wouldn't have considered it of any importance."

"Listen, it's for me and not for you to decide what evidence is, or is not, impor-tant." He fumed a bit, threw the listening Rider a look of martyrdom, went on in tones edged with irritation. "Now, let's get this straight, once and for all. Apart from being new, was the bag identically the same as the one Dakin uses."

"No, sir. But it was very similar. Same type, same brass lock, same general ap-pearance. It was slightly longer and about an inch deeper. I remember that when I was putting the money into it I wondered why they'd bought another bag and concluded that the purpose was to let Mr. Letheren and Mr. Swain have one each."

"Did you notice any distinguishing mark upon it, a price tag, a maker's sticker, initials, code letters, serial number, or anything like that?"

"Nothing at all. It didn't occur to me to look. Not knowing what was to come, I—"

The voice cut off in mid-sentence as Harrison irefully slammed down the phone. He stared hard at Rider who said nothing.

"For your information," Harrison told him, "I can say that there are distinct advantages in taking up the profession of latrine attendant. Sometimes I am sorely tempted." He breathed heavily, switched the desk-box. "Who's loafing around out there?"

Somebody replied, "It's Kastner, chief."

"Send him in."

Detective Kastner entered. He was a neatly attired individual who had the air of knowing how to get around in a sink of iniquity.

"Jim," ordered Harrison, "beat it out to the Dakin plant and borrow their cash-bag. Make certain it's the one they use for weekly collections. Take it to every store selling leather goods and follow up every sale of a similar bag within the last month. If you trace a purchaser, make him prove that he still possesses his bag, get him to say where he was and what he was doing at ten-thirty last Friday morning."

"Right, chief."

"Phone me the details if you latch onto anything significant."

After Kastner had gone, Harrison said, "That bag was bought specifically for the job. Therefore, the purchase is likely to be a recent one and probably made in this town. If we can't trace a sale through local stores, we'll inquire farther afield."

"You do that," Rider agreed. "Meanwhile, I'll take a couple of steps that may help."

"Such as what?"

"We're a scientific species, living in a technological age. We've got extensive, well-integrated communications networks and huge, informative filing systems. Let's use what we've got, eh?"

"What's on your mind?" Harrison asked.

Rider said, "A robbery so smooth, neat and easy is something that begs to be repeated *ad lib*. Maybe he's done it before. There's every likelihood that he'll do it again."

"So—?"

"We have his description, but it isn't worth much." He leaned forward. "We also have full details of his method and those *are* reliable."

"Yes, that's true."

"So let's boil down his description to the unalterable basics of height, weight, build, color of eyes. The rest can be ignored. Let's also condense his technique, reduce it to the bare facts. We can summarize the lot in five hundred words."

"And then?"

"There are six thousand two hundred eighty banks in this country, of which slightly more than six thousand belong to the Bank Association. I'll get Washington to run off enough handbills for the Association to send its entire membership. They'll be put on guard against a similar snatch, asked to rush us full details if any get taken despite the warning or already had been taken before they got it."

"That's a good idea," Harrison approved. "Some other police chief may nurse a couple of items that we lack, while we're holding a couple that he wants. A get-together may find us holding enough to solve both cases."

"There's a slight chance that we can take it farther still," said Rider. "The culprit may have a record. If he has not, we're out of luck. But if he's done it before, and been pinched, we can find his card in no time at all." He pondered reminiscently, added, "That filing system in Washington is really something."

"I know of it, of course, but haven't seen it," Harrison commented.

"Friend of mine down there, a postal inspector, found it handy not long ago. He was hunting a fellow selling fake oil stock through the mails. This character had taken at least fifty suckers by means of some classy print-work including official looking reserve reports, certificates and other worthless documents. There was no description of him. Not a victim had seen him in the flesh."

"That's not much to go on."

"No. but it was enough. Attempts by postal authorities to trap him had failed. He was a wily bird and that in itself was a clue. Obviously he was a swindler sufficiently experienced to have a record. So this friend took what little he'd got to the F.B.I."

"What happened?"

"A *modus operandi* expert coded the data and fed it into the high-speed extractor, like giving the scent to a hound. Electronic fingers raced over slots and punch holes in a million cards a darned sight faster than you could blow your nose. Rejecting muggers, heistmen and various toughies, the fingers dug out maybe four thousand confidence tricksters. From those they then extracted perhaps six hundred bond-pushers. And from those they picked a hundred who specialized in phony oil stocks. And from those they took twelve who kept out of sight by operating through the mails."

"That narrowed it down," Harrison conceded.

"The machine ejected twelve cards," Rider continued. "An extra datum might have enabled it to throw out one and only one. But that was as far as it could go; it couldn't use what it hadn't been given. Not that it mattered. A quick check of other records showed that four of the twelve were dead and six more were languishing in the clink. Of the remaining two, one was picked up, proved himself in the clear. That left the last fellow. The postal authorities now had his name, mug-shot, prints, habits, associates and everything but his mother's wedding certificate. They grabbed him within three weeks."

"Nice work. Only thing I don't understand is why they keep dead men's cards on file."

"That's because evidence comes up—sometimes years later—proving them responsible for old, unsolved crimes. The evil that men do lives after them; the good, if any, is interred with their bones." He eyed the other, ended, "The slaves of the filing system don't like cases left open and unfinished. They like to mark them closed even if it takes half a lifetime. They're tidy-minded, see?"

"Yes, I see." Harrison thought a while, remarked, "You'd think a criminal would go honest once on the files, or at least have the sense not to repeat."

"They always repeat. They get in a rut and can't jack themselves out of it. I never heard of a counterfeiter who turned gunman or bicycle thief. This fellow we're after will pull the same stunt again by substantially the same method. You wait and see." He sighed to the phone. "Mind if I make a couple of long-distance calls?"

"Help yourself. I don't pay for them."

"In that case I'll have three. The little woman is entitled to some vocal fondling."

"Go right ahead." Registering disgust, Harrison heaved himself erect, went to the door. "I'll get busy some place else. If one thing turns my stomach, it's the spectacle of a big man cooing a lot of slop."

Grinning to himself, Rider picked up the phone. "Get me the United States Treasury, Washington, Extension 417, Mr. O'Keefe."

Over the next twenty-four hours the steady, tiresome but determined pressure of Earth technique was maintained. Patrolmen asked questions of store owners, local gossips, tavern keepers, parolees, stool pigeons, any and every character who by remote chance might give with a crumb of worthwhile information. Plain-clothes detectives knocked on doors, cross-examined all who responded, checked back later on any who'd failed to answer. State troopers shook down outlying motels and trailer parks, quizzed owners, managers, assistants. Sheriffs and deputies visited farms known to take occasional roomers.

In Washington, six thousand leaflets poured from a press while not far away another machine addressed six thousand envelopes. Also nearby, electronic fingers sought a specific array of holes and slots among a million variously punched cards. Police of half a dozen towns and cities loped around, checked on certain people, phoned their findings to Northwood, then carried on with their own work.

As usual, first results were represented by a stack of negative information. None of Ashcroft's relatives were missing or had been of late. There was no black sheep in Letheren's family, he had no twin, his only brother was ten years younger, was highly respected, bore no striking likeness and, in any case, had an unbreakable alibi.

No other bank had yet reported being soaked by an expert masquerader. Rooming houses, hotels amid other possible hideouts failed to produce a clue to anyone resembling Letheren's photograph.

The silent searcher through the filing system found forty-one bank swindlers, living and dead. But not one with the same *modus operandi* or anything closely similar. Regretfully it flashed a light meaning, "No record."

However, from the deductive viewpoint enough negatives can make a few positives. Harrison and Rider stewed the latest news, came to the same conclusions. Ashcroft and Letheren were well-nigh in the clear. The unknown culprit was a newcomer to crime and his first success would induce him to do it again. Such a master of make-up had previously concealed himself under some identity other than that now being sought.

First break came in the late afternoon. Kastner walked in, tipped his hat onto the back of his head and said, "I may have something."

"Such as what?" asked Harrison, his features alert.

"There's no great demand for that particular kind of bag and only one store sells them in this town. Within the last month they've got rid of three."

"Paid for by check?"

"Cash on the nail," Kastner responded with a grim smile to the other's look of disappointment, went on, "But two of the buyers were local folk, recognized and known. Both made their purchases about three weeks ago. I chased them up. They've still got their bags and can account for their time last Friday morning. I've checked their stories and they hold good and tight."

"How about the third buyer?"

"That's what I'm coming to, chief. He looks good to me. He bought his bag the afternoon before the robbery. Nobody knows him."

"A stranger?"

"Not quite. I got a detailed description of him from Hilda Cassidy, the dame who waited on him. She says he was a middle-aged, thin-faced, meek sort of character with a miserable expression. Looked like an unhappy embalmer."

"Then what makes you say he's not quite a stranger?"

"Because, chief, there are eleven stores selling leather goods of one kind or another. I've lived here quite a piece, but I had to hunt around to find the one handling this kind of bag. So I figured that this miserable guy would have had to do some going the rounds, too. I tried all the stores a second time, giving them this new description."

"And—?"

"Three of them remembered this fellow looking for what they don't stock. All confirmed the description." He paused, added, "Sol Bergman, of the Travel Mart, says the guy's face was slightly familiar. Doesn't know who he is and can't make a useful guess. But he's sure he's seen him two or three times before."

"Maybe an occasional visitor from somewhere a good way out."

"That's how it looks to me, chief."

"A good way out means anywhere within a hundred-mile radius," growled Harrison. "Perhaps even farther." He eyed Kastner sourly. "Who got the longest and closest look at him?"

"The Cassidy girl."

"You'd better bring her in, and fast."

"I did bring her. She's waiting outside."

"Good work, Jim," approved Harrison, brightening. "Let's see her."

Kastner went out and brought her in. She was a tall, slender, intelligent person in her early twenties. Cool and composed, she sat with hands folded in her lap, answered Harrison's questions while he got the suspect's description in as complete detail as she was able to supply.

"More darned legwork," Harrison complained as she finished. "Now the boys will have to make all the rounds again looking for a lead on *this* guy."

Rider chipped in, "If he's an out-of-towner, you'll need the co-operation of all surrounding authorities."

"Yes, of course."

"Maybe we can make it lots easier for them." He glanced inquiringly across the desk toward the girl. "That is, if Miss Cassidy will help."

"I'll do anything I can," she assured.

"What's on your mind?" Harrison asked.

"We'll get Roger King to lend a hand."

"Who's he?"

"A staff artist. Does cartoon work on the side. He's good, very good." He switched attention to the girl. "Can you come round early and spend the morning here?"

"If the boss will let me."

"He will," put in Harrison. "I'll see to that."

"All right," said Rider to the girl. "You come round. Mr. King will show you a number of photographs. Look through them carefully and pick out distinguishing features that correspond with those of the guy who bought that bag. A chin here, a mouth there, a nose somewhere else. Mr. King will make a composite drawing from them and will keep altering it in accordance with your instructions until he's got it right. Think you can do that?"

"Oh, sure," she said.

"We can do better," Kastner announced. "Sol Bergman is the eager-beaver type. He'll be tickled to death to assist."

"Then get him to come along too."

Kastner and the girl departed as Rider said to Harrison, "Know a local printer who can run off a batch of copies within a few hours?"

"You bet I do."

"Good!" He gestured to the phone. "Can I hoist the bill another notch?"

"For all I care you can make the mayor faint at the sight of it," said Harrison. "But if you intend to pour primitive passion through the line, say so and let me get out."

"Not this time. She may be pining somewhat, but duty comes first." He took up the instrument. "Treasury Headquarters, Washington, Extension 338. I want Roger King."

Copies of the King sketch were mailed out along with a description and pick-up request. They had not been delivered more than a few minutes when the phone whirred and Harrison grabbed it: "Northwood police."

"This is the State Police Barracks, Sergeant Wilkins speaking. We just got that 'Wanted' notice of yours. I know that fellow. He lives right on my beat."

"Who is he?"

"Name of William Jones. Runs a twenty-acre nursery on Route Four, a couple of hours away from your town. He's a slightly surly type, but there's nothing known against him. My impression is that he's pessimistic but dead straight. You want us to pick him up?"

"Look, are you sure he's the fellow?"

"It's his face on that drawing of yours and that's as far as I go. I've been in the business as long as you, and I don't make mistakes about faces."

"Of course not, sergeant. We'd appreciate it if you'd bring him in for questioning."

"I'll do that."

He cut off. Harrison lay back, absently studied his desk while his mind juggled around with this latest news.

After a while, he said, "I could understand it better if this Jones was described as a one-time vaudeville actor such as a quick-change impressionist. A fellow operating a nursery out in the wilds sounds a bit of a hick to me. Somehow I can't imagine him doing a bank job as slick as this one."

"He might be just an accomplice. He got the bag beforehand, hid the cash afterward, perhaps acted as lookout man while the robbery was taking place."

Harrison nodded. "We'll find out once he's here. He'll be in trouble if he can't prove he made an innocent purchase."

"What if he does prove it?"

"Then we'll be right back where we started." Harrison gloomed at the thought of it. The phone called for attention and he snatched it up. "Northwood police."

"Patrolman Clinton here, chief. I just showed that drawing to Mrs. Bastico. She has a rooming house at 157 Stevens. She swears that guy is William Jones who roomed with her ten days. He came without luggage but later got a new bag like the Dakin one. Saturday morning he cleared out, taking the bag. He'd overpaid by four days' rent, but he beat it without a word and hasn't come back."

"You stay there, Clinton. We'll be right out." He licked anticipatory lips, said to Rider, "Come on, let's, get going."

Piling into a cruiser, they raced to 157 Stevens. It was a dilapidated brownstone with well-worn steps.

Mrs. Bastico, a heavy featured female with several warts, declaimed in self-righteous tones, "I've never had the cops in this house. Not once in twenty years."

"You've got 'em now," informed Harrison. "And it gives the place a touch of respectability. Now, what d'you know about this Jones fellow?"

"Nothing much," she answered, still miffed. "He kept to himself. I don't bother roomers who behave."

"Did he say anything about where he'd come from, or where he was going to, or anything like that?"

"No. He paid in advance, told me his name, said he was on local business, and that was that. He went out each morning, came back at a decent hour each night, kept sober and interfered with nobody."

"Did he have any visitors?" He extracted Letheren's photograph. "Someone like this, for example?"

"Officer Clinton showed me that picture yesterday. I don't know him. I never saw Mr. Jones talking to another person."

"Hm-m-m!" Harrison registered disappointment. "We'd like a look at his room. Mind if we see it?"

Begrudgingly she led them upstairs, unlocked the door, departed and left them to rake through it at will. Her air was that of one allergic to police.

They searched the room thoroughly, stripping bedclothes, shifting furniture, lifting carpets, even unbolting and emptying the washbasin waste-trap. It was Patrolman Clinton who dug out of a narrow gap between floorboards a small, pink, transparent wrapper, also two peculiar seeds resembling elongated almonds and exuding a strong, aromatic scent.

Satisfied that there was nothing else to be found, they carted these petty clues back to the station, mailed them to the State Criminological Laboratory for analysis and report.

Three hours afterward William Jones walked in. He ignored Rider, glowered at the uniformed Harrison, demanded. "What's the idea of having me dragged here? I've done nothing."

"Then what have you got to worry about?" Harrison assumed his best tough expression. "Where were you last Friday morning?"

"That's an easy one," said Jones, with a touch of spite. "I was in Smoky Falls getting spares for a cultivator."

"That's eighty miles from here."

"So what? It's a lot less from where I live. And I can't get those spares anyplace nearer. If there's an agent in Northwood, you find him for me."

"Never mind about that. How long were you there?"

"I arrived about ten in the morning, left in the mid-afternoon."

"So it took you about five hours to buy a few spares?"

"I ambled around a piece. Bought groceries as well. Had a meal there, and a few drinks."

"Then there ought to be plenty of folk willing to vouch for your presence there?"

"Sure are," agreed Jones with disconcerting positiveness.

Harrison switched his desk-box, said to someone, "Bring in Mrs. Bastico, the Cassidy girl and Sol Bergman." He returned attention to Jones. "Tell me exactly where you went from time of arrival to departure, and who saw you in each place." He scribbled rapidly as the other recited the tale of his Friday morning shopping trip. When the story ended, he called the Smoky Falls police, briefed them swiftly, gave them the data, asked for a complete check-up.

Listening to this last, Jones showed no visible alarm or apprehension. "Can I go now? I got work to do."

"So have I," Harrison retorted. "Where have you stashed that leather cash-bag?"

"What bag?"

"The new one you bought Thursday afternoon."

Eying him incredulously, Jones said, "Hey, what are you trying to pin on me? I bought no bag. Why should I? I don't need a new bag."

"You'll be telling me next that you didn't hole-up in a rooming house on Stevens."

"I didn't. I don't know of any place on Stevens. And if I did, I wouldn't be seen dead there."

They argued about it for twenty minutes. Jones maintained with mulish stubbornness that he'd been working on his nursery the whole of Thursday and had been there most of the time he was alleged to be at the rooming house. He'd never heard of Mrs. Bastico and didn't want to. He'd never bought a Dakin-type bag. They could search his place and welcome—if they found such a bag it'd be because they'd planted it on him.

A patrolman stuck his head through the doorway and announced, "They're here, chief."

"All right. Get a line-up ready."

After another ten minutes Harrison led William Jones into a back room, stood him in a row consisting of four detectives and half a dozen nondescripts enlisted from the street. Sol Bergman, Hilda Cassidy and Mrs. Bastico appeared, looked at the parade, pointed simultaneously and in the same direction.

"That's him," said Mrs. Bastico.

"He's the man," indorsed the Cassidy girl.

"Nobody else but," Sol Bergman continued.

"They're nuts," declared Jones, showing no idea of what it was all about.

Taking the three witnesses back to his office, Harrison queried them for a possible mistake in identity. They insisted they were not mistaken, that they could not be more positive. William Jones was the man, definitely and absolutely.

He let them go, held Jones on suspicion pending a report from Smoky Falls. Near the end of the twenty-four hours legal holding limit the result of the check came through. No less than thirty-two people accounted fully for the suspect's time all the way from ten to three-thirty. Road-checks had also traced him all the way to that town and all the way back. Other witnesses had placed him at the nursery at several times when he was said to have been at Mrs. Bastico's. State troopers had search the Jones property. No bag. No money identifiable as loot.

"That's torn it," growled Harrison. "I've no choice but to release him with abject apologies. What sort of a lousy, stinking case is this, when everybody mistakes everybody for everybody else?"

Rider massaged two chins, suggested, "maybe we ought to try checking on that as well. Let's have another word with Jones before let him loose."

Slouching in, Jones looked considerably subdued and only too willing to help with anything likely to get him home.

"Sorry to inconvenience you so much, Mr. Jones," Rider soothed. "It couldn't be avoided in the circumstances. We're up against a mighty tough problem." Bending forward, he fixed the other with an imperative gaze. "It might do us a lot of good if you'd think back carefully and tell us if there's anytime you've been mistaken for somebody else."

Jones opened his mouth, shut it, opened it again. "Jeepers, that very thing happened about a fortnight ago.

"Give us the story," invited Rider, a glint in his eyes.

"I drove through here nonstop and went straight on to the city. Been there about an hour when a fellow yelled at me from across the street. I didn't know him, thought at first he was calling someone else. He meant me all right."

"Go on," urged Harrison, impatient as the other paused.

"He asked me in a sort of dumbfounded way how I'd got there. I said I'd come in my car. He didn't want to believe it,'

"Why not?"

"He said I'd been on foot and thumbing a hitch. He knew it because he'd picked me up and run me to Northwood. What's more, he said, after dropping me in Northwood he'd driven straight to the city, going so fast that nothing had overtaken him on the way. Then he'd parked his car, started down the street, and the first thing he'd seen was me strolling on the other side."

"What did you tell him?"

"I said it couldn't possibly have been me and that his own story proved it."

"That fazed him somewhat, eh?"

"He got sort of completely baffled. He led me right up to his parked car, said, 'Mean to say you didn't take a ride in that?' and, of course, I denied it. I walked away. First I thought it might be some kind of gag. Next, I wondered if he was touched in the head."

"Now," put in Rider carefully, "we must trace this fellow. Give us all you've got on him."

Thinking deeply, Jones said, "He was in his late thirties, well-dressed, smooth talker, the salesman type. Had a lot of pamphlets, color charts and paint cans in the back of his car."

"You mean in the trunk compartment? You got a look inside there?"

"No. They were lying on the rear seat, as though he was in the habit of grabbing them out in a hurry and slinging them in again."

"How about the car itself?"

"It was the latest model *Flash,* duotone green, white sidewalls, a radio. Didn't notice the tag number."

They spent another ten minutes digging more details regarding appearance, mannerisms and attire. Then Harrison called the city police, asked for a trace.

"The paint stores are your best bet. He's got all the looks of a drummer making his rounds. They should be able to tell you who called on them that day."

City police promised immediate action. Jones went home, disgruntled, but also vastly relieved. Within two hours this latest lead had been extended. A call came from the city.

"Took only four visits to learn what you want. That character is well known to the paint trade. He's Burge Kimmelman, area representative of Acme Paint & Varnish Company of Marion, Illinois. Present whereabouts unknown. His employers should be able to find him for you."

"Thanks a million!" Harrison disconnected, put through a call to Acme Paint. He yapped a while, dumped the phone, said to Rider, "He's somewhere along a route a couple of hundred miles south. They'll reach him at his hotel this evening. He'll get here tomorrow."

"Good."

"Or is it?" asked Harrison, showing a trace of bitterness. "We're sweating ourselves to death tracing people and being led from one personality to another. That sort of thing can continue to the crack of doom."

"And it can continue until something else cracks," Rider riposted. "The mills of *man* grind slowly, but they grind exceeding small."

Elsewhere, seven hundred miles westward, was another legworker. Organized effort can be very formidable but becomes doubly so when it takes to itself the results of individual effort.

This character was thin-faced, sharp-nosed, lived in an attic, ate in an automat, had fingers dyed with nicotine and for twenty years had nursed the notion of writing the Great American Novel but somehow had never gotten around to it.

Name of Arthur Pilchard and, therefore, referred to as Fish—a press reporter. What is worse, a reporter on a harum-scarum tabloid. He was wandering past a desk when somebody with ulcers and a sour face shoved a slip of paper at him.

"Here, Fish. Another saucer nut. Get moving!"

Hustling out with poor grace, he reached the address given on the slip, knocked on the door. It was answered by an intelligent young fellow in his late teens or early twenties.

"You George Lamothe?"

"That's me," agreed the other.

"I'm from the *Call*. You told them you'd got some dope on a saucer. That right?"

Lamothe looked pained. "It's not a saucer and I didn't describe it as such. It's a spherical object and it's not a natural phenomenon."

"I'll take your word for it. When and where did you see it?"

"Last night and the night before. Up in the sky."

"Right over this town?"

"No, but it is visible from here."

"I've not seen it. So far as I know, you're the only one who has. How d'you explain that?"

"It's extremely difficult to see with the naked eye. I own an eight-inch telescope."

"Built it yourself?"

"Yes."

"That takes some doing," commented Art Pilchard admiringly. "How about showing it to me?"

Lamothe hesitated, said, "All right," led him upstairs. Sure enough a real, genuine telescope was there, its inquisitive snout tilted toward a movable roof-trap.

"You've actually seen the object through that?"

"Two successive nights," Lamothe confirmed. "I hope to observe it tonight as well."

"Any idea what it is?"

"That's a matter of guesswork," evaded the other, becoming wary. "All I'm willing to say is that it's located in a satellite orbit, it's perfectly spherical and appears to be an artificial construction of metal."

"Got a picture of it?"

"Sorry, I lack the equipment."

"Maybe one of our cameraman could help you there."

"If he has suitable apparatus," Lamothe agreed.

Pilchard asked twenty more questions, finished doubtfully, "What you can see anyone else with a telescope could see. The world's full of telescopes, some of them big enough to drive a locomotive through. How come nobody yet has shouted the news? Got any ideas on that?"

With a faint smile, Lamothe said, "Everyone with a telescope isn't staring through it twenty-four hours per day. And even when he is using it he's likely to be studying a specific area within the starfield. Moreover, if news gets out it's got to start somewhere. That's why I phoned the *Call*."

"Dead right!" agreed Pilchard, enjoying the savory odor of a minor scoop.

"Besides," Lamothe went on, "others *have* seen it. I phoned three astronomical friends last night. They looked and saw it. A couple of them said they were going to ring up nearby observatories and draw attention to it. I mailed a full report to an observatory today, and another to a scientific magazine."

"Hells bells!" said Pilchard, getting itchy feet. "I'd better rush this before it breaks in some other rag." A fragment of suspicion came into his face. "Not having seen this spherical contraption myself, I'll have to check on it with another source. By that, I don't mean I think you're a liar. I have to check stories or find another job. Can you give me the name and address of one of these astronomical friends of yours?"

Lamothe obliged, showed him to the door. As Pilchard hastened down the street toward a telephone booth, a police cruiser raced up on the other side. It braked outside Lamothe's house. Pilchard recognized the uniformed cop who was driving but not the pair of burly men in plainclothes riding with him. That was strange because as a reporter of long standing he knew all the local detectives and called them by their first names. While he watched from a distance, the two unknowns got out of the cruiser, went to Lamothe's door, rang the bell.

Bolting rotund the corner, Pilchard entered the booth, called long distance, rammed coins into the box.

"Alan Reed? My name's Pilchard. I write up astronomical stuff. I believe you've seen a strange metal object in the sky. Hey?" He frowned. "Don't give me that! Your friend George Lamothe has seen it, too. He told me himself that he phoned you about it last night." He paused, glowered at the earpiece. "Where's the sense of repeating, 'No comment,' like a parrot? Look, either you've seen it or you haven't—and so far you've not denied seeing it." Another pause, then in leery tones, "Mr. Reed, has someone ordered you to keep shut?"

He racked the phone, shot a wary glance toward the corner, inserted more coins, said to somebody, "Art here. If you want to feature this, you'll have to move damn fast. You'll run it only if you're too quick to be stopped." He listened for the click of the tape being linked in, recited rapidly for five minutes. Finishing, he returned to the corner, looked along the street. The cruiser was still there.

In a short time a flood of *Calls* hit the streets. Simultaneously a long chain of small-town papers took the same news off their wire service, broke into a rash of two-inch head-lines.

Space Platform In Sky.
Ours or Theirs?

Late in the following morning Harrison ploughed doggedly through routine work. At one side of his office Rider sat with columnar legs stretched straight out and read slowly and carefully through a wad of typed sheets.

The wad was the fruit of legwork done by many men. It traced, with a few gaps, the hour by hour movements of one William Jones known to be not the real William Jones. He'd been seen wandering around Northwood like a rubbernecking tourist. He'd been seen repeatedly on the main street and examining its shops. He'd been seen in a supermarket around the time a customer's purse had been stolen. He'd eaten meals in cafes and restaurants, drunk beer in bars and taverns.

Ashcroft, Jackson and another teller remembered a Joneslike stranger making idle inquiries in the bank the week preceding the robbery. Letheren and his guards recalled the mirror-image of William Jones hanging around when they made the previous collection. Altogether, the tediously gathered report covered most of the suspect's time in Northwood, a period amounting to days.

Finishing his perusal, Rider closed his eyes, mulled the details over and over while his mind sought a lead. While he was doing this a muted radio sat on a ledge yammered steadily, squirting across the office the reduced voice of an indignant commentator.

"The whole world now knows that someone has succeeded in establishing an artificial satellite up in the sky. Anyone with a telescope or good binoculars can see it for himself at midnight. Why, then, does authority insist on pretending the thing doesn't exist? If potential enemies are responsible, let us be told as much—the enemies already know it, anyway. If we are responsible, if this is our doing, let us be told as much—the enemies already are grimly aware of it. Why must we be denied information possessed by possible foes? Does somebody think we're a bunch of irresponsible children? Who are these brasshats who assign to themselves the right to decide what we may be told or not told? Away with them! Let the government speak!"

"Yeah," commented Harrison, glancing up from his work, "I'm with him there. Why don't they say outright whether it's ours or theirs? Some of those guys down your way have a grossly exaggerated idea of their own importance. A hearty kick in the pants would do them a lot—-" He shut up, grabbed the phone. "Northwood police." A weird series of expressions crossed his lean features as he listened. Then he racked the phone, said, "It gets nuttier every minute."

"What's it this time?"

"Those seeds. The laboratory can't identify them."

"Doesn't surprise me. They can't be expected to know absolutely everything."

"They know enough to know when they're stuck," Harrison gave back. "So they sent them to some firm in New York where they know everything knowable about seeds. They've just got a reply."

"Saying what?"

"Same thing—not identifiable. New York went so far as to squeeze out the essential oils and subject remaining solids to destructive distillation. Result: the seeds just aren't known." He emitted a loud sniff, added, "They want us to send them another dozen so they can make them germinate. They want to see what comes up."

"Forget it," advised Rider. "We don't have any more seeds and we don't know where to find 'em."

"But we do have something darned peculiar,' Harrison persisted. "With those seeds we sent a pink, transparent wrapper, remember? At the time I thought it was just a piece of colored cellophane. The lab say's it isn't. They say it's organic, cellular and veined, and appears a subsection of the skin of an unknown fruit."

"... *A tactic long theorized and believed to be in secret development,*" droned the radio. "*Whoever achieves it first thereby gains a strategic advantage from the military viewpoint.*"

"Sometimes," said Harrison, "I wonder what's the use of getting born."

His desk-box squawked and announced, "Fellow named Burge Kimmelman waiting for you, chief."

"Send him in."

Kimmelman entered. He was dapper, self-assured, seemed to regard his rush to the aid of the law as a welcome change from the daily routine. He sat, crossed his legs, made himself at home and told his story.

"It was the craziest thing, captain. For a start. I never give rides to strangers. But I stopped and picked up this fellow and still can't make out why I did it."

"*Where* did you pick him up?" asked Rider.

"About half a mile this side of Seeger's filling station. He was waiting by the roadside and first thing I knew I'd stopped and let him get in. I took him into Northwood, dropped him, pushed straight on to the city. I was in a hurry and moved good and fast. When I got there I walked out the car park and darned if he wasn't right there on the other side of the street." He eyed them, seeking comment.

"Go on," Rider urged.

"I picked on him then and there, wanting to know how he'd beaten me to it. He acted like he didn't know what I was talking about." He made a gesture of bafflement. "I've thought it over a dozen times since and can take it no further. I *know* I gave a lift to that guy or his twin brother. And it wasn't his twin brother because if he'd had one he'd have guessed my mistake and said so. But he said nothing. Just behaved offishly polite like you do when faced with a lunatic."

"When you were giving him this ride," asked Harrison, "did he make any informative remarks? Did he mention his family, his occupation, destination, or anything like that? Did he tell you where he'd come from?"

"Not a word worth a cent. So far as I know he dropped straight out of the sky."

"So did everything else concerned with this case," remarked Harrison, feeling sour again. "Unidentifiable seeds and unknown fruit-skins and—" He stopped, let his mouth hang open, popped his eyes.

"... *A vantage-point from which every quarter of the world would be within effective range,*" gabbled the radio. "*With such a base for guided missiles it would be possible for one nation to implement its policies in a manner that—*"

Getting to his feet, Rider crossed the room, switched off the radio, said, "Mind waiting outside, Mr. Kimmelman?" When the other had gone, he continued with Harrison, "Well, make up your mind whether or not you're going to have a stroke."

Harrison shut his mouth, opened it again, but no sound came out. His eyes appeared to have protruded too far to retract. His right hand made a couple of meaningless gestures and temporarily that was the most he could manage.

Resorting to the phone, Rider got his call through, said, "O'Keefe, how's the artificial satellite business down there?"

"You called just to ask that? I was about to phone you myself."

"What about?"

"Eleven of those bills have come in. The first nine came from two cities. The last pair were passed in New York. Your man is moving around. Bet you ten to one in coconuts that if he takes another bank it'll be in the New York area."

"That's likely enough. Forget him for a moment. I asked you about this satellite rumpus. What's the reaction from where you're sitting?"

"The place is buzzing like a disturbed beehive. Rumor is rife that professional astronomers saw and reported the thing nearly a week before the news broke. If that's true, somebody in authority must have tried to suppress the information."

"Why?"

"Don't ask me," shouted O'Keefe. "How do I know why others do things that make neither rhyme nor reason?"

"You think they should say whether it's ours or theirs seeing that the truth is bound to emerge sooner or later?"

"Of course. Why are you harping on this subject, Eddie? What's it got to do with you, anyway?"

"I've been made vocal by an idea that has had the reverse effect on Harrison. He's struck dumb."

"What idea?"

"That this artificial satellite may not be an artificial satellite. Also that authority has said nothing because experts are unwilling to commit themselves one way or the other. They can't say something unless they've something to say, can they?"

"I've got something to say," O'Keefe declared. "And that's to advise you to tend your own business. If you've finished helping Harrison, quit lazing around and come back."

"Listen, I don't call long-distance for the fun of it. There's a thing up in the sky and nobody knows what it is. *At the same time* another thing is down here loping around and imitating people, robbing banks, dropping debris of alien origin, and nobody knows what that is, either. Two plus two makes four. Add it up for yourself."

"Eddie, are you cracked?"

"I'll give you the full details and leave you to judge." He recited them swiftly, ended, "Use all your Treasury pull to get the right people interested. This case is far too big to be handled by us alone. You've got to find the ones with enough power and influence to cope. You've got to kick 'em awake."

He cut off, glanced at Harrison who promptly got his voice back and said, "I can't believe it. It's too farfetched for words. The day I tell the mayor a Martian did it will be the day Northwood gets a new chief. He'll take me away to have my head examined."

"Got a better theory?"

"No. That's the hell of it."

Shrugging expressively, Rider took the phone again, made a call to Acme Paint Company. That done, he summoned Kimmelman.

"There's a good chance that you'll be wanted here tomorrow and perhaps for two or three days. I've just consulted your employers and they say you're to stay with us."

"Suits me," agreed Kimmelman, not averse to taking time off with official approval. "I'd better go book in at an hotel."

"Just one question first. This character you picked up—was he carrying any luggage?"

"No."

"Not even a small bag or a parcel?"

"He'd nothing except what was in his pockets," said Kimmelman, positively.

A gleam showed in Rider's eyes. "Well, that may help."

The mob that invaded Northwood at noon next day came in a dozen cars by devious routes and successfully avoided the attention of the press. They crammed Harrison's office to capacity.

Among them was a Treasury top-ranker, a general, an admiral, a Secret Service chief, a Military Intelligence brasshat, three area directors of the F.B.I., a boss of the Counter Espionage Service, all their aides, secretaries and technical advisers, plus a bunch of assorted scientists including two astronomers, one radar expert, one guided missiles expert and a slightly bewildered gentleman who was an authority on ants.

They listened in silence, some interested, some skeptical, while Harrison read them a complete report of the case. He finished, sat down, waited for comment.

A gray-haired, distinguished individual took the lead, said, "Personally, I'm in favor of your theory that you're chasing somebody not of this world. I don't presume to speak for others who may think differently. However, it seems to me futile to waste any time debating the matter. It can be settled one way or the other by catching the culprit. That, therefore, is our only problem. How are we going to lay hands on him?"

"That won't be done by the usual methods," said an F.B.I. director. "A guy who can double as anyone, and do it well enough to convince even at close range, isn't going to be caught easily. We can hunt down a particular identity if given enough time. I don't see how we can go after somebody who might have *any* identity."

"Even an alien from another world wouldn't bother to steal money unless he had a real need for it," put in a sharp-eyed individual. "The stuff's no use elsewhere in the cosmos. So it's safe to accept that he did have need of it. But money doesn't last forever no matter who is spending it. When he has splurged it all, he'll need some more. He'll try robbing another bank. If every bank in this country were turned into a trap, surely one of them would snap down on him."

"How're you going to trap somebody who so far as you know is your best and biggest customer?" asked the F.B.I. director. He put on a shy grin, added, "Come to that, how do you know that the fellow in question isn't *me?*"

Nobody liked this last suggestion. They fidgeted uneasily, went quiet as their minds desperately sought a solution some place.

Rider spoke up. "Frankly, I think it a waste of time to search the world for somebody who has proved his ability to adopt two successive personalities and by the same token can adopt two dozen or two hundred. I've thought about this until I've gone dizzy and I can't devise any method of pursuing and grabbing him. He's far too elusive."

"It might help if we could learn precisely how he does it," interjected a scientist. "Have you any evidence indicative of his technique?"

"No, sir."

"It looks like hypnosis to me," said the scientist.

"You may be right," Richer admitted. "But so far we've no proof of it." He hesitated, went on, "As I see it, there's only one way to catch him."

"How?"

"It's extremely unlikely that he's come here for keeps. Besides, there's that thing in the sky. What's it waiting for? My guess is that it's waiting to take him back whenever he's ready to go."

"So—?" someone prompted.

"To take him back that sphere has got to swing in from several thousands of miles out. That means it has to be summoned when wanted. He's got to talk to its crew, if it has a crew. Or, if crewless, he's got to pull it in by remote control. Either way, he must have some kind of transmitter."

"If transmission-time is too brief to enable us to tune in, take cross-bearings and get there—" began an objector.

Rider waved him down. "I'm not thinking of that. We know he came to Northwood without luggage. Kimmelman says so. Mrs. Bastico says so. Numerous witnesses saw him at various times but he was never seen to carry anything other than the cash-bag. Even if an alien civilization can produce electronic equipment one-tenth the size and weight of anything we can turn out, a long-range transmitter would still be far too bulky to be hidden in a pocket."

"You think he's concealed it somewhere?" asked the sharp-eyed man.

"I think it highly probable. If he has hidden it, well, he has thereby limited his freedom of action. He can't take off from anywhere in this world. He's got to return to wherever he has stashed his transmitter."

"But that could be any place. It leaves us no better off than before."

"On the contrary!" He picked up Harrison's report, read selected passages with added emphasis. "I may be wrong. I hope I'm right. There's one thing he could not conceal no matter what personality he assumed. He could not conceal his behavior. If he'd chosen to masquerade as an elephant and then become curious, he'd have been a very plausible elephant—but still obviously curious."

"What are you getting at?" demanded a four-star general.

"He was too green to have been around long. If he'd had only a couple of days in some other town or village, he'd have been a lot more sophisticated when in Northwood. Consider the reports on the way he nosed around. He was raw. He behaved liked somebody to whom everything is new. If I'm right about this, Northwood was his first port of call. And that in turn means his landing place—*which is also his intended take-off point*—must be fairly near, and probably nearer still to where Kimmelman picked him up."

They debated it for half an hour, reached a decision. The result was legwork on a scale that only high authority can command. Kimmelman drove nearly five miles out, showed the exact spot and that became the center of operations.

Attendants at Seeger's filling station were queried extensively and without result. Motorists known to be regular users of the road, bus drivers, truckers and many others to whom it was a well-used route, were traced and questioned. Dirt-farmers, drifters, recluses, hoboes and everyone else who lurked in the thinly populated hills were found and quizzed at length.

Four days hard work and numberless questionings over a circle ten miles in diameter produced three people who nursed the vague idea that they'd seen something fall from or rise into the sky about three weeks ago. A farmer thought he'd seen a distant saucer but had kept quiet for fear of ridicule. Another believed he had glimpsed a strange gleam of light which soared from the hills and vanished. A trucker had spotted an indefinable object out the corner of an eye but when he looked direct it had gone.

These three were made to take up their respective points of observation, sight through theodolites and line the cross-hairs as nearly as they could on the portions of skyline cogent to their visions. All pleaded inability to be accurate but were willing to do their best.

The bearings produced an elongated triangle that stretched across most of a square mile. This at once became the second focus of attention. A new area two miles in radius was drawn from the triangle's center. Forthwith police, deputies, troopers, agents and others commenced to search the target foot by foot. They numbered a small army and some of them bore mine-detectors and other metal-finding instruments.

One hour before dusk a shout drew Rider, Harrison and several bigwigs to a place where searchers were cloistering excitedly. Somebody had followed the faint *tick-tick* of his detector, lugged a boulder aside, found a gadget hidden in the hollow behind it.

The thing was a brown metal box twelve inches by ten by eight. It had a dozen silver rings set concentrically in its top, these presumably being the sky-beam antenna. Also four dials ready set in various positions. Also a small press-stud.

Experts knew exactly what to do, having come prepared for it. They color-photographed the box from every angle, measured it, weighed it, placed it back in its original position and restored the boulder to its former place.

Sharpshooters with night-glasses and high-velocity rifles were posted in concealed positions at extreme range. While data on the superficial appearance of the transmitter was being rushed to the city, ground-microphones were placed between the hiding place and the road, their hidden wires led back to where ambushers awaited stealthy footsteps in the dark.

Before dawn, four searchlight teams and half a dozen antiaircraft batteries had taken up positions in the hills and camouflaged themselves. A command post had been established in a lonely farmhouse and a ground-to-air radio unit had been shoved out of sight in its barn.

For anyone else a roadblock set up by tough cops would have served. Not for this character who could be anyone at all. He might, for all they knew, appear in the dignified guise of the Bishop of Miff. But if he made for that transmitter and laid hands on it—

A couple of days later a truck came from the city, picked up the transmitter, replaced it with a perfect mock-up incapable of calling anything out of the sky. This game of imitation was one at which two could play.

Nobody got itchy fingers and pressed the stud on the real instrument. The time wasn't yet. So long as the ship remained in the sky, so long would its baffling passenger enjoy a sense of false security and, sooner or later, enter the trap.

Earth was willing to wait. It was just as well. The biding-time lasted four months.

A bank on Long Island got taken for eighteen thousand dollars. The same technique; walk in, collect, walk out, vanish. A high-ranking officer made a tour of the Brooklyn Navy Yard at a time when he was also attending a conference at Newport News. An official inspected television studios on the twentieth to twenty-fifth floors of a skyscraper while simultaneously tending to office work on the tenth floor. The invader had now learned enough to become impudent.

Blueprints were pored over, vaults were entered, laboratories were examined. Steelworks and armaments plants got a careful, unhurried look-over. A big machine-tool factory actually had its works manager conduct a phony visitor around the plant and provide technical explanations as required.

It wasn't all plain sailing even for someone well-nigh invincible. The cleverest can make mistakes. Harasha Vanash blundered when he flashed a fat roll in a tavern, got followed to his hide-out. Next day he went out without being tailed and while he was busily sneaking some more of Earth's knowledge, somebody was briskly plundering his room. He returned to find the proceeds of his last robbery had vanished. That meant he had to take time off from espionage to soak a third bank.

By August 21st he had finished. He had concentrated his attention on the most highly developed area in the world and it was doubtful whether anything to be learned elsewhere was sufficiently weighty to be worth the seeking. Anyway, what he'd got was enough for the purposes of the Andromedans. Armed with all this information, the hypnos of a two-hundred-planet empire could step in and take-over another with no trouble at all.

Near Seeger's station he stepped out of a car, politely thanked the driver who was wondering why he'd gone so far out of his way to oblige a character who meant nothing to him. He stood by the roadside, watched the car vanish into the distance. It rocked along at top pace, as though its driver was mad at himself.

Holding a small case stuffed with notes and sketches, he studied the landscape, saw everything as it had been originally. To anyone within the sphere of his mental influence he was no more than a portly and somewhat pompous business man idly surveying the hills. To anyone beyond that range he was made vague by distance and sufficiently humanlike to the naked eye to pass muster.

But to anyone watching through telescopes and binoculars from most of a mile away he could be seen for what he really was—just a thing. A thing not of this world. They could have made a snatch at him then and there. However, in view of the preparations they'd made for him there was, they thought, no need to bother. Softly, softly, catchee monkey.

Tightly gripping the case, he hurried away from the road, made straight for the transmitter's hiding place. All he had to do was press the stud, beat it back to Northwood, enjoy a few quiet drinks in a tavern, have a night's sleep and come back tomorrow. The ship would come in along the transmitter's beam, landing here and nowhere else, but it would take exactly eighteen hours and twenty minutes to arrive.

Reaching the boulder he had a final wary glance around. Nobody in sight, not a sound. He moved the rock, felt mild relief when he saw the instrument lying undisturbed. Bending over it, he pressed the stud.

The result was a violent *poof!* and a cloud of noxious gas. That was their mistake; they'd felt sure it would lay him out for twenty-four hours. It did not. His metabolism was thoroughly alien and had its own peculiar reaction. All he did was retch and run like blazes.

Four men appeared from behind a rock six hundred yards away. They pointed guns, yelled to him to halt. Ten more sprang out of the ground on his left, bawled similar commands. He grinned at them, showing them the teeth he did not possess.

He couldn't make them blow off their own heads. But he could make them do it for each other. Still going fast, he changed direction to escape the line of fire. The four obligingly waited for him to run clear, then opened up on the ten. At the same time the ten started slinging head at the four.

At top speed he kept going. He could have lounged on a rock, in complete command of the situation, and remained until everyone had bumped everyone else—given that there was no effective force located outside his hypnotic range. He could not be sure of just how far the trap extended.

The obviously sensible thing to do was to get right out of reach as swiftly as possible, curve back to the road, confiscate a passing car and disappear once more among Earth's teeming millions. How to contact the ship was a problem that must be shelved until he could ponder it in a safe place. It wasn't unsolvable; not to one who could be the President himself.

His immediate fear was well-founded. At twelve-hundred yards there happened to be a beefy gentleman named Hank who found that a brazen escape during an outbreak of civil war was too much to be endured. Hank had a quick temper, also a heavy machine-gun. Seeing differently from those nearer the prey, and being given no orders to the contrary, Hank uttered an unseemly word, swung the gun, scowled through its sights, rammed his thumbs out its button. The gun went *br-r-r-r* while its ammo-belt jumped and rattled.

Despite the range his aim was perfect. Harasha Vanash was flung sidewise in full flight, went down and didn't get up. His supine body jerked around under the impact of more bullets. He was very decidedly dead.

Harrison got on the phone to pass the news, and O'Keefe said, "He's not here. It's his day off."

"Where'll I find him then?"

"At home and no place else. I'll give you his number. He might answer if he's not busy baby-sitting."

Trying again, Harrison got through. "They killed him . . . or it . . . just under an hour ago."

"Hm-m-m! Pity they didn't take him alive."

"Easier said than done. Anyway, how can you retain a firm hold on someone who can make you remove his manacles and get into them yourself?"

"That," said Rider, "is the problem of our Security boys in general and our police in particular. I work for the Treasury."

Replacing the phone, Harrison frowned at the wall. Beyond the wall, several hundreds of miles to the south, a group of men walked onto the dispersal-point of an airport, placed a strange box on the ground, pressed its stud. Then they watched the sky and waited.

The hordes of Andromeda were very, very old. That was why they'd progressed as far as they had done. Flashes of inspiration had piled up through the numberless centuries until sheer weight of accumulated genius had given them the key to the cosmos.

Like many very old people, they had contempt for the young and eager. But their contempt would have switched to horror if they could have seen the methodical way in which a bunch of specialist legworkers started pulling their metal sphere apart.

Or the way in which Earth commenced planning a vast armada of similar ships.

A good deal bigger.

With several improvements.

MANA

Astounding, December 1937

Lazy waters lapped and gurgled across the silver sand. An orange sun crawled high in the heavens, poured its rays through this atmosphere, and etched the higher portion of the beach with a delicate dado of shadow palms.

Omega, the last man on earth, stood naked in the coolness beneath a feathered frond.

He sighed, turned, and strode lithely into a paradise of plants.

Six thousand years, the long, extended years of the final era, had passed over Omega's head. But he was not old as beasts and plants grow old. His age was purely mental, and represented the measure of his satiation.

His body remained young, would always be young. Thousands had died within the sixty centuries of his memory, but he could recall none who had succumbed with physical decay. Men had explored with intellectual satisfaction, the exhausting of curiosity, the desire for mental rest—even as some of the esoteric ones of primeval days had willed their passing because they had lost the urge to live.

Omega was the last, solely because he was not yet satisfied. There was one thing still to be done—if it could be done.

He had lived through and tasted every experience within reach of mankind. He had even exercised his monofecundity and produced a child. But his son refused further issue, lived fast and soon was satisfied.

Thus the flesh of his flesh, with the companions of his past, had slipped like figments of a summer's dream. Men of the latter day knew the difference between what there was to learn and what it was possible to learn. Even human ingenuity could not encompass the cosmos. So each had quaffed his little cup and crept away to sleep. He, Omega, the unsatisfied one, lived on, determined to do that which had been declared impossible.

His feet sped swiftly up a wooded slope; he mounted the crest and saw the towers and minarets of Ultima gleaming through a golden haze that lay along the valley. Exercise had tired his muscles; he called upon will power molded by a million years of evolution; his body rose into the air, floated over the treetops and across the valley. He landed lightly upon a marble battlement.

Calf muscles ached their protest against his fondness for walking. Omega rubbed them into submission, sat and rest awhile, then stepped off the battlement and floated to the silent boulevard beneath.

Eerily, like the central figure of an allegorical picture, his form drifted across the dusty, unmarked highway, his feet swinging restfully twenty inches above the surface.

No other forms were levitated, and none walked through the peaceful avenues of that once-mighty city. Silent spires spiked to the azure vault above. Idle battlement reproduced the skyline of ancient Tintagel. Flying buttresses arched boldly to walls that knew no secrets to conceal.

Omega moved toward a dull metal door set in the opposite wall.

The door opened, Omega floated through it, along a corridor and into his laboratory. His feet felt the cold kiss of stone; he stepped to a glass-topped case and peered into it with eyes that shone as brightly as eyes that found the world still new.

"Mana," he murmured. His voice sighed softly, like the wind that quivers in the reeds along the water's marge. *"Mana."* He often talked to himself. The habit was his only concession to loneliness. He pressed a stud that caused a dull, warm glow to spread through the interior of the case.

"Nothing," they said, "could perpetuate mankind forever," he proclaimed. "Nothing.

"Nothing that man could make, or produce could make, or produce, or build, or give, could endure as long as Nature endures. The valleys shall be raised, and the hills shall be made low. All that humanity has made, all that humanity can leave, shall crumble into the dust; and the empire that once was, and soon is not shall, shall be given over to the birds of the air, the beast of the field, the trees, the shrubs, and the creeping growths."

His fingers rapped on the case; he noted resulting movements below the glass.

"Patience," he told himself. "The thousandth failure may but precede the first success."

Eagerly he strode to a complicated chair that stood with tilted back against a maze of instruments. Suspended above the seat by simple counterweights was a great metal hood.

"It must be photons," declared Omega, standing before the chair. "A thousand experiments have shown that either cosmic rays or photons perform the function of carriers of *mana*. And I still maintain that it cannot be cosmic rays. If it were, there could be no *mana*, upon the ozone-wrapped Perdel, in Alpha Centauri."

Seating himself in the chair, he continued to reason.

"Therefore, by simple elimination, it must be photons. And upon this planet only we bipeds were really susceptible to their natural intensity, other life being less affected. But if I can increase the strength, passing an abnormal load along a beam of photons, a positive reaction should be hereditary. It would, I think, be handed from generation to generation, and—"

His lips snapped shut: he raised an arm and pulled down the hood until it covered his head completely A contact on the armrest closed beneath his firm fingers and the apparatus woke to life.

There was no noise, nothing to indicate action save a swift turn and steady trembling of needles within three dials, and a mighty, angling leap of a concentrated beam of cold light.

Omega sat limply, the machine behind him driving a double cone of pyschowaves through the back of his head. The cones narrowed through his brain, emerged from his eyes, passed through lenses set in the front of the hood, and entered the wave trap that gleamed mirrorlike at the base of the light transmission tube. In effect, the trap was the focal point of Omega's mind.

The beam of cold light was a thin column of intense brilliance as it poured up the tube, angled across to the case, and again angled into the interior. The glow from the case was vanquished by the new and mightier illumination.

For fifteen minutes the last man sat half concealed beneath the metal sheath. Then his damp fingers opened the contact; his hand raised the hood and exposed a face strained with fatigue.

He crossed the case, stared through its glass top.

"Mechanistic behaviorism may serve as a crutch—but never as a ladder," he told the unheedful subjects of his experiment.

A small heap of rotten wood lay in one corner of the case. In the center, between two highways swarming with pedestrians, stood a midget box mounted upon microscopic wheels. Near it rested a Lilliputian bow with a bundle of tiny arrows.

Raising the lid of the case, Omega inserted a hand and moved the little cart with a touch of slender fingers. Delicately, he shot an arrow from the miniature bow, and saw ants scuttle in all directions. Patiently, he rubbed two shreds of wood into flame, and let them burn at a safe distance from the rest of the heap.

"I feel one degree more stupid after each attempt. The light must be transporting it somewhere."

He watched the agitated ants as he stood and mused awhile. Then he sighed, closed the lid, and floated from the room.

Timeless day and immeasurable night upon a world that rolled in sluggish mourning for glories long departed. Omega stood upon a battlement and turned his face to the fiery ring that split the midnight sky from horizon to horizon. Incredibly ancient scrawlings upon records long since perished had described the beauty of the satellite from which this ring was born. Omega doubted whether the serene loveliness of the Moon had exceeded the glory of the remnants.

The light of the lees of Luna served to reveal the triumph upon the face of the last man, and the case of ants clasped firmly in his arms, With a frown for his sensation of mental weakness, but a contrasting smile upon his lips, he stepped off the battlement and glided like a phantom above the leafy cohorts that pressed eagerly upon the marble outskirts of Ultima. His figure floated onward, far above the treetops where wooden arms were raised in worship of the ring.

Over a tiny glade he ceased his forward progress, wavered in the slight, cool breeze, descended slowly, and felt his feet sink into a dewy cushion of earth. He placed the case upon the grass, opened its lid, tilted it, and watched the ants depart.

Satisfaction shone upon his features while he studied a group of insects laboriously surging out of the midget cart. They pushed, and pulled, twisted its wheels this way and that, and finally trundled it into the secret path of grassy jungle, He watched it disappear with its load of splinters of rotten wood, the bow and arrows resting on top. He stretched his form, and raised a glowing face to the heavens.

"When the first hairy biped rode the waters on a log, that was *mana,*" he proclaimed. "When fire was found, and made, and used, that was *mana.* Whenever men struggled one step higher up the ladder of life, it was *mana.*" He swung an arm in a sweep embracing the entire cosmos. "Even as it was given to us by those whom we could never know, I give it to those who can never know men. I give it as our everlasting monument."

His nerves grew taut as he summoned his weakened will. He floated upward, faster, faster, toward the elegiac ring. He was bound for space, where eternal sleep came easily and was undisturbed. There were no regrets within his soul, and he uttered no farewell. He cast one glance downward at aimless billows surging on a printless shore. His eyes passed thence to the woodland glade, caught the first flicker of a tiny fire, and he was satisfied.

Omega, the last man, had presented the ants with fire, the wheel and the bow. Best of all, he had given them what both the first man and the last had called *mana—intelligence.*

Mechanical Mice

Astounding, January 1941

It's asking for trouble to fool around with the unknown. Burman did it! Now there are quite a lot of people who hate like the very devil anything that clicks, ticks, emits whirring sounds, or generally behaves like an asthmatic alarm clock. They've got mechanophobia. Dan Burman gave it to them.

Who hasn't heard of the Burman Bullfrog Battery? The same chap! He puzzled it out from first to last and topped it with his now world-famous slogan: "Power in Your Pocket." It was no mean feat to concoct a thing the size of a cigarette packet that would pour out a hundred times as much energy as its most efficient competitor. Burman differed from everyone else in thinking it a mean feat.

Burman looked me over very carefully, then said, "When that technical journal sent you around to see me twelve years ago, you listened sympathetically. You didn't treat me as if I were an idle dreamer or a congenital idiot. You gave me a decent write-up, and started all the publicity that eventually made me much money."

"Not because I loved you," I assured him, "but because I was honestly convinced that your battery was good."

"Maybe." He studied me in a way that conveyed he was anxious to get something off his chest. "We've been pretty pally since that time. We've filled in some idle hours together, and I feel that you're the one of my few friends to whom I can make a seemingly silly confession."

"Go ahead," I encouraged. We had been pretty pally, as he'd said. It was merely that we liked each other, found each other congenial. He was a clever chap, Burman, but there was nothing of the pedantic professor about him. Fortyish, normal, neat, he might have been a fashionable dentist to judge by appearances.

"Bill," he said, very seriously, "I didn't invent that damn battery."

"No?"

"No!" he confirmed. "I pinched the idea. What makes it madder is that I wasn't quite sure of what I was stealing and, crazier still, I don't know from whence I stole it."

"Which is as plain as a pikestaff," I commented.

"That's nothing. After twelve years of careful, exacting work I've built some-thing else. It must be the most complicated thing in creation." He banged a fist on his knee, and his voice rose complainingly. "And now that I've done it, I don't know what I've done."

"Surely when an inventor experiments he knows what he's doing?"

"Not me!" Burman was amusingly lugubrious. "I've invented only one thing in my life, and that was more by accident than by good judgment." He perked up. "But that one thing was the key to a million notions. It gave me the battery. It has nearly given me things of greater importance. On several occasions it has nearly, but not quite, placed within my inadequate hands and half-understanding mind plans that would alter this world far beyond your conception." Leaning forward to lend emphasis to his speech, he said, "Now it has given me a mystery that has cost me twelve years of work and a nice sum of money. I finished it last night. I don't know what the devil it is."

"Perhaps if I had a look at it—"

"Just what I'd like you to do." He switched rapidly to mounting enthusiasm. "It's a beautiful job of work, even though I say so myself. Bet you that you can't say what it is, or what it's supposed to do."

"Assuming it can do something," I put in.

"Yes," he agreed. "But I'm positive it has a function of some sort." Getting up, he opened a door. "Come along."

It was a stunner. The thing was a metal box with a glossy, rhodium-plated sur-face. In general size and shape it bore a faint resemblance an upended coffin, and had the same, brooding, ominous air of a casket waiting for its owner to give up the ghost.

There were a couple of small glass windows in its front through which could be seen a multitude of wheels as beautifully finished as those in a first-class watch. Elsewhere, several tiny lenses stared with sphinx-like indifference. There were three small trapdoors in one side, two in the other, and a large one in the front. From the top, knobbed rods of metal stuck up like goat's horns, adding a satanic touch to the thing's vague air of yearning for midnight burial.

"It's an automatic layer-outer," I suggested, regarding the contraption with frank dislike. I pointed to one of the trapdoors. "You shove the shroud in there, and the corpse comes out the other side reverently composed and ready wrapped."

"So you don't like its air, either," Burman commented. He lugged open a drawer in a nearby tier, hauled out a mass of drawings. "These are its innards. It has an electric circuit, valves, condensers, and something that I can't quite understand, but which I suspect to be a extremely efficient electric furnace. It has parts I rec-ognize as cutters and pinion-shapers. It embodies several small-scale multiple stampers, apparently for dealing with sheet metal. There are vague suggestions of an assembly line ending in that large compartment shielded by the door in front. Have a look at the drawings yourself. You can see it's an extremely complicated device for manufacturing something only little less complicated."

The drawings showed him to be right. But they didn't show everything. An efficient machine designer could correctly have deduced the gadget's function if given complete details. Burman admitted this, saying that some parts he had made "on the spur of the moment," while others he had been "impelled to draw." Short of pulling the machine to pieces, there was enough data to whet the curiosity, but not enough to satisfy it.

"Start the damn thing and see what it does."

"I've tried," said Burman. "It won't start. There's no starting handle, nothing to suggest how it can be started. I tried everything I could think of, without result. The electric circuit ends in those antennae at the top, and I even sent current through those, but nothing happened."

"Maybe it's a self-starter," I ventured. Staring at it, a thought struck me. "Timed," I added.

"Eh?"

"Set for an especial time. When the dread hour strikes, it'll go of its own accord, like a bomb."

"Don't be so melodramatic," said Burman, uneasily.

Bending down, he peered into one of the tiny lenses.

"*Bz-z-z!*" murmured the contraption in a faint undertone that was almost inaudible.

Burman jumped a foot. Then he backed away, eyed the thing warily, turned his glance at me.

"Did you hear that?"

"Sure!" Getting the drawings, I mauled them around. That little lens took some finding, but it was there all right. It has a selenium cell behind it. "An eye," I said. "It saw you, and reacted. So it isn't dead even if it does just stand there seeing no evil, hearing no evil, speaking no evil." I put a white handkerchief against the lens.

"*Bz-z-z!*" repeated the coffin, emphatically.

Taking the handkerchief, Burman put it against the other lenses. Nothing happened. Not a sound was heard, not a funeral note. Just nothing.

"It beats me," he confessed.

I'd got pretty fed up by this time. If the crazy article had performed, I'd have written it up and maybe I'd have started another financial snowball rolling for Burman's benefit. But you can't do anything with a box that buzzes whenever it feels temperamental. Firm treatment was required, I decided.

"You've been all nice and mysterious about how you got hold of this brain wave," I said. "Why can't you go to the same source for information about what it's supposed to be?"

"I'll tell you—or, rather, I'll show you."

From his safe, Burman dragged out a box, and from the box he produced a gadget. This one was far simpler than the useless mass of works over by the wall. It looked just like one of those old-fashioned crystal sets, except that the crystal was very big, very shiny, and was set in a horizontal vacuum tube. There was the same single dial, the same cat's whisker. Attached to the lot by a length of flex was what might have been a pair of headphones, except in place of the phones were a pair of polished, smoothly rounded copper circles shaped to fit outside the ears and close against the skull.

"My one and only invention," said Burman, not without a justifiable touch of pride.

"What is it?"

"A time-traveling device."

"Ha, ha!" My laugh was very sour. I'd read about such things. In fact, I'd written about them. They were buncombe. Nobody could travel through time, either backward or forward. "Let me see you grow hazy and vanish into the future."

"I'll show you something very soon." Burman said it with assurance I didn't like. He said it with the positive air of a man who knows darned well that he can do something that everybody else knows darned well can't be done. He pointed to the crystal set. "It wasn't discovered at the first attempt. Thousands must have tried and failed. I was the lucky one. I must have picked a peculiarly individualistic crystal; I still don't know how it does what it does; I've never been able to repeat its performance even with a crystal apparently identical."

"And it enables you to travel in time?"

"Only forward. It won't take me backward, not even as much as one day. But it can carry me forward an immense distance, perhaps to the very crack of doom, perhaps everlastingly through infinity."

I had him now! I'd got him firmly entangled in his own absurdities. My loud chuckle was something I couldn't control.

"You can travel forward, but not backward, not even one day back. Then how the devil can you return to the present once you've gone into the future?"

"Because I never leave the present," he replied, evenly. "I don't partake of the future. I merely survey it from the vantage point of the present. All the same, it is time-traveling in the correct sense of the term." He seated himself. "Look here, Bill, what are you?"

"Who, me?"

"Yes, what are you." He went on to provide the answer. "Your name is Bill. You're a body and a mind. Which of them is Bill?"

"Both," I said, positively.

"True—but they're different parts of you. They're not the same even though they go around like Siamese twins." His voice grew serious. "Your body moves always in the present, the dividing line between the past and the future. But your mind is more free. It can think, and is in the present. It can remember, and at once is in the past. It can imagine, and at once is in the future, in its own choice of all the possible futures. Your mind can travel through time!"

He'd outwitted me. I could find points to pick upon and argue about, but I knew that fundamentally he was right. I'd not looked at it from this angle before, but he was correct in saying that anyone could travel through time within the limits of his own memory and imagination. At that very moment I could go back twelve years and see him in my mind's eye as a younger man, paler, thinner, more excitable, not so cool and self-possessed. The picture was as perfect as my memory was excellent. For that brief spell I was twelve years back in all but the flesh.

"I call this thing a psychophone," Burman went on. "When you imagine what the future will be like, you make a characteristic choice of all the logical possibilities, you pick your favorite from a multitude of likely futures. The psychophone, somehow—the Lord alone knows how—tunes you into future reality. It makes you depict within your mind the future as it will be shaped in actuality, eliminating all the alternatives that will not occur."

"An imagination-stimulator, a dream-machine," I scoffed, not feeling as sure of myself as I sounded. "How do you know it's giving you the McCoy?"

"Consistency," he answered, gravely. "It repeats the same features and the same trends far too often for the phenomena to be explained as mere coincidence. Besides," he waved a persuasive hand, "I got the battery from the future. It works, doesn't it?"

"It does," I agreed, reluctantly. I pointed to his psychophone. "I, too, may travel in time. How about letting me have a try? Maybe I'll solve your mystery for you."

"You can try if you wish," he replied, quite willingly. He pulled a chair into position. "Sit here, and I'll let you peer into the future."

Clipping the headband over my cranium, and fitting the copper rings against my skull where it sprouted ears, Burman connected his psychophone to the mains, switched it on; or rather he did some twiddling that I assumed was a mode of switching on.

"All you have to do," he said, "is to close your eyes, compose yourself, then try and permit your imagination to wander into the future."

He meddled with the cat's whisker. A couple of times he said, "Ah!" And each time he said it I got a peculiar dithery feeling around my unfortunate ears. After a few seconds of this, he drew it out to, "A-a-ah!" I played unfair, and peeped beneath lowered lids. The crystal was glowing like rats' eyes in a forgotten cellar. A furtive crimson.

Closing my own optics, I let my mind wander. Something was flowing between those copper electrodes, a queer, indescribable thing that felt with stealthy fingers at some secret portion of my brain. I got the asinine notion that they were the dexterous digits of a yet-to-be-born magician who was going to shout, "Presto!" and pull my abused lump of think-meat out of a thirtieth century hat—assuming they'd wear hats in the thirtieth century.

What was it like, or, rather, what would it be like in the thirtieth century? Would there be retrogression? Would humanity again be composed of scowling, fur-kilted creatures lurking in caves? Or had progress continued—perhaps even to the development of men like gods?

Then it happened! I swear it! I pictured, quite voluntarily, a savage and then a huge-domed individual with glittering eyes—the latter being my version of the ugliness we hope to attain. Right in the middle of this erratic dreaming, those weird fingers warped my brain, dissolved my phantoms, and replaced them with a dictated picture which I witnessed with all the helplessness and clarity of a nightmare.

I saw a fat man spouting. He was quite an ordinary man as far as looks went. In fact, he was so normal that he looked henpecked. But he was attired in a Roman toga, and he wore a small, black box where his laurel wreath ought to have been. His audience was similarly dressed, and all were balancing their boxes like a convention of fish porters. What Fatty was orating sounded gabble to me, but he said his piece as if he meant it.

The crowd was in the open air, with great, curved rows of seats visible in the background. Presumably an outside auditorium of some sort. Judging by the distance of the back rows, it must have been a devil of a size. Far behind its sweeping ridge a great edifice jutted into the sky, a cubical erection with walls of glossy squares, like an immense glasshouse.

"F'wot?" bellowed Fatty, with obvious heat. "Wuk, wuk. wuk, mor, noon' n'ni'! Bok onned, ord this, ord that." He stuck an indignant finger against the mysterious object on his cranium. "Bok onned, wuk, wuk, wuk. F'wot?" he glared around. "F'nix!" The crowd murmured approval somewhat timidly. But it was enough for Fatty. Making up his mind, he flourished a plump fist and shouted, "Th'ell wit'm!" Then he tore his box from his pate.

Nobody said anything, nobody moved. Dumb and wide-eyed. The crowd just stood and stared as if paralyzed by the sight of a human being sans box. Something with a long, slender streamlined body and broad wings soared gracefully upward in the distance, swooped over the auditorium, but still the crowd neither moved nor uttered a sound.

A smile of triumph upon his broad face, Fatty bawled, "Lem see'm make wuk now! Lem see'm—"

He got no further. With a rush of mistiness from its tail, but in perfect silence, the soaring thing hovered and sent down a spear of faint, silvery light. The light touched Fatty. He rotted where he stood, like a victim of ultra-rapid leprosy. He rotted, collapsed, crumbled within his sagging clothes, became dust as once he had been dust. It was horrible.

The watchers did not flee in utter panic; not one expression of fear, hatred or disgust came from their tightly closed lips. In perfect silence they stood there, staring, just staring, like a horde of wooden soldiers. The thing in the sky circled to survey its handiwork, then dived low over the mob, a stubby antenna in its prow sparking furiously. As one man, the crowd turned left. As one man it commenced to march, left, right, left, right.

Tearing off the headband, I told Burman what I'd seen, or what his contraption had persuaded me to think that I'd seen. "What the deuce did it mean?"

"Automatons," he murmured. "Glasshouses and reaction ships." He thumbed through a big diary filled with notations in his own hands. "Ah, yes, looks like you were very early in the thirtieth century. Unrest was persistent for twenty years prior to the Antibox Rebellion."

"What rebellion?"

"The Antibox—the revolt of the automatons against the thirty-first century Technocrats. Jackson-Dkj-99717, a successful and cunning schemer with a warped box, secretly warped hundreds of other boxes, and eventually led the rebels to victory in 3047. His great-grandson, a greedy, thick-headed individual, caused the rebellion of the Boxless Freemen against his own clique of Jacksocrats."

I gaped at this recital, then said, "The way you tell it makes it sound like history."

"Of course it's history," he asserted. "History that is yet to be." He was pensive for a while. "Studying the future will seem a weird process to you, but it appears quite a normal procedure to me. I've done it for years, and maybe familiarity has bred contempt. Trouble is though, that selectivity is poor. You can pick on some especial period twenty times in succession, but you'll never find yourself in the same month, or even the same year. In fact, you're fortunate if you strike twice in the same decade. Result is that my data is very erratic."

"I can imagine that," I told him. "A good guesser can guess the correct time to within a minute or two, but never to within ten or even fifty seconds."

"Quite!" he responded. "So the hell of it has been that mine was the privilege of watching the panorama of the future, but in a manner so sketchy that I could not grasp its prizes. Once I was lucky enough to watch a twenty-fifth century power pack assembled from first to last. I got every detail before I lost the scene which I've never managed to hit upon again. But I made that power pack—and you know the result."

"So that's how you concocted your famous battery!"

"It is! But mine, good as it may be, isn't as good as the one I saw. Some slight factor is missing." His voice was suddenly tight when he added, "I missed something because I had to miss it!"

"Why?" I asked, completely puzzled.

"Because history, past or future, permits no glaring paradox. Because, having snatched this battery from the twenty-fifth century, I am recorded in that age as the twentieth-century inventor of the thing. They've made a mild improvement to it in those five centuries, but that improvement was automatically withheld from me. Future history is as fixed and unalterable by those of the present time as is the history of the past."

"Then," I demanded, "explain to me that complicated contraption which does nothing but say *bz-z-z.*"

"Damn it!" he said, with open ire, "that's just what's making me crazy! It can't be a paradox, it just can't." Then, more carefully, "So it must be a seeming paradox."

"O. K. You tell me how to market a seeming paradox, and the commercial uses thereof, and I'll give it a first-class write-up."

Ignoring my sarcasm, he went on, "I tried to probe the future as far as human minds can probe. I saw nothing, nothing but the vastness of a sterile floor upon which sat a queer machine, gleaming there in silent, solitary majesty. Somehow, it seemed aware of my scrutiny across the gulf of countless ages. It held my attention with a power almost hypnotic. For more than a day, for a full thirty hours, I kept that vision without losing it—the longest time I have ever kept a future scene."

"Well?"

"I drew it. I made complete drawings of it, performing the task with all the easy confidence of a trained machine draughtsman. Its insides could not be seen, but somehow they came to me, somehow I knew them. I lost the scene at four o'clock in the morning, finding myself with masses of very complicated drawings, a thumping head, heavy-lidded eyes, and a half-scared feeling in my heart." He was silent for a short time. "A year later I plucked up courage and started to build the thing I had drawn. It cost me a hell of a lot of time and a hell of a lot of money. But I did it—it's finished."

"And all it does is buzz," I remarked, with genuine sympathy.

"Yes," he sighed, doubtfully.

There was nothing more to be said. Burman gazed moodily at the wall, his mind far, far away. I fiddled aimlessly with the copper ear-pieces of the psychophone. My imagination, I reckoned, was as good as anyone's, but for the life of me I could neither imagine nor suggest a profitable market for a metal coffin filled with watchmaker's junk. No, not even if it did make odd noises.

A faint, smooth whir came from the coffin. It was a new sound that swung us round to face it pop-eyed. *Whir-r-rl* it went again. I saw finely machined wheels spin behind the window in its front.

"Good heavens!" said Burman.

Bz-z-z! Whir-r! Click! The whole affair suddenly slid sidewise on its hidden castors.

The devil you know isn't half so frightening as the devil you don't. I don't mean that this sudden demonstration of life and motion got us scared, but it certainly made us leery, and our hearts put in an extra dozen bumps a minute. This coffin-thing was, or might be, a devil we didn't know. So we stood there, side by side, gazing at it fascinatedly, feeling apprehensive of we knew not what.

Motion ceased after the thing had slid two feet. It stood there, silent, imperturbable, its front lenses eyeing us with glassy lack of expression. Then it slid another two feet. Another stop. More meaningless contemplation. After that, a swifter and farther slide that brought it right up to the laboratory table. At that point it ceased moving, began to emit varied but synchronized ticks like those of a couple of sympathetic grandfather clocks.

Burman said, quietly, "Something's going to happen!"

If the machine could have spoken it would have taken the words right out of his mouth. He'd hardly uttered the sentence when a trapdoor in the machine's side fell open, a jointed, metallic arm snaked cautiously through the opening and reached for a marine chronometer standing on the table.

With a surprised oath, Burman dashed forward to rescue the chronometer. He was too late. The arm grabbed it, whisked it into the machine, the trapdoor shut with a hard snap, like the vicious clash of a sprung bear trap. Simultaneously, another trapdoor in the front flipped open, another jointed arm shot out and in again, spearing with ultra-rapid motion too fast to follow. That trapdoor also snapped shut, leaving Burman gaping down at his torn clothing from which his expensive watch and equally expensive gold chain had been ripped away.

"Good heavens!" said Burman, backing from the machine.

We stood looking at it a while. It didn't move again, just posed there ticking steadily as if ruminating upon its welcome meal. Its lenses looked at us with all the tranquil lack of interest of a well-fed cow. I got the idiotic notion that it was happily digesting a mess of cogs, pinions and wheels.

Because its subtle air of menace seemed to have faded away, or maybe because we sensed its entire preoccupation with the task in hand, we made an effort to rescue Burman's valuable timepiece. Burman tugged mightily at the trapdoor through which his watch had gone, but failed to move it. I tugged with him, without result. The thing was sealed as solidly as if welded in. A large screwdriver failed to pry it open. A crowbar, or a good jimmy would have done the job, but at that point Burman decided that he didn't want to damage the machine which had cost him more than the watch.

Tick-tick-tick! went the coffin, stolidly. We were back where we'd started, playing with our fingers, and no wiser than before. There was nothing to be done, and I felt that the accursed contraption knew it. So it stood there, gaping through its lenses, and jeered *tick-tick-tick*. From its belly, or where its belly would have been if it'd had one, a slow warmth radiated. According to Burman's drawings, that was the location of the tiny electric furnace.

The thing was functioning; there could be no doubt about that! If Burman felt the same way as I did, he must have been pretty mad. There we stood, like a couple of prize boobs, not knowing what the machine was supposed to do, and all the time it was doing under our very eyes whatever it was designed to do.

From where was it drawing its power? Were those antennae sticking like horns from its head busily sucking current from the atmosphere? Or was it, perhaps, absorbing radio power? Or did it have internal energy of its own? All the evidence suggested that it was making something, giving birth to something, but giving birth to what?

Tick-tick-tick! was the only reply.

Our questions were still unanswered, our curiosity was still unsatisfied, and the machine was still ticking industriously at the hour of midnight. We surrendered the problem until next morning. Burman locked and double-locked his laboratory before we left.

Police officer Burke's job was a very simple one. All he had to do was walk round and round the block, keeping a wary eye on the stores in general and the big jewel depot in particular, phoning headquarters once per hour from the post at the corner.

Night work suited Burke's taciturn disposition. He could wander along, communing with himself, with nothing to bother him or divert him from his inward ruminations. In that particular section nothing ever happened at night, nothing.

Stopping outside the gem-bedecked window, he gazed through the glass and the heavy grille behind it to where a low-power bulb shed light over the massive safe. There was a rajah's ransom in there. The guard, the grille, the automatic alarms and sundry ingenious traps preserved it from the adventurous fingers of anyone who wanted to ransom a rajah. Nobody had made the brash attempt in twenty years. Nobody had even made a try for the contents of the grille-protected window.

He glanced upward at a faintly luminescent path of cloud behind which lay the hidden moon. Turning, he strolled on. A cat sneaked past him, treading cautiously, silently, and hugging the angle of the wall. His sharp eyes detected its slinking shape even in the nighttime gloom, but he ignored it and progressed to the corner.

Back of him, the cat came below the window through which he just had stared. It stopped, one forefoot half-raised, its ears cocked forward. Then it flattened belly-low against the concrete, its burning orbs wide, alert, intent. Its tail waved slowly from side to side.

Something small and bright came skittering toward it, moving with mouselike speed and agility close in the angle of the wall. The cat tensed as the object came nearer. Suddenly, the thing was within range, and the cat pounced with lithe eagerness. Hungry paws dug at a surface that was not soft and furry, but hard, bright and slippery. The thing darted around like a clockwork toy as the cat vainly tried to hold it. Finally, with an angry snarl, the cat swiped it viciously, knocking it a couple of yards where it rolled onto its back and emitted softly protesting clicks and tiny, urgent impulses that its feline attacker could not sense.

Gaining the gutter with a single leap, the cat crouched again. Something else was coming. The cat muscled, its eyes glowed. Another object slightly similar to the curious thing it had just captured, but a little bit bigger, a fraction noisier, and much different in shape. It resembled a small, gold-plated cylinder with a conical front from which projected a slender blade, and it slid along swiftly on invisible wheels.

Again the cat leaped. Down on the corner, Burke heard its brief shriek and following gurgle. The sound didn't bother Burke—he'd heard cats and rats and other vermin make all sorts of queer noises in the night. Phlegmatically, he continued on his beat.

Three quarters of an hour later, Police Officer Burke had worked his way around to the fatal spot. Putting his flash on the body, he rolled the supine animal over with his foot. Its throat was cut. Its throat had been cut with an utter savagery that had half-severed its head from its body. Burke scowled down at it. He was no lover of cats himself, but he found difficulty in imagining anyone hating like that!

"Somebody," he muttered, "wants flaying alive."

His big foot shoved the dead cat back into the gutter where street cleaners could cart it away in the morning. He turned his attention to the window, saw the light still glowing upon the untouched safe. His mind was still on the cat while his eyes looked in and said that something was wrong. Then he dragged his attention back to business, realized what was wrong, and sweated at every pore. It wasn't the safe, it was the window.

In front of the window the serried trays of valuable rings still gleamed undisturbed. To the right, the silverware still shone untouched. But on the left had been a small display of delicate and extremely expensive watches. They were no longer there, not one of them. He remembered that right in front had rested a neat, beautiful calendar-chronometer priced at a year's salary. That, too, was gone.

The beam of his flash trembled as he tried the gate, found it fast, secure. The door behind it was firmly locked. The transom was closed, its heavy wire guard still securely fixed. He went over the window, eventually found a small, neat hole, about two inches in diameter, down in the corner on the side nearest the missing display.

Burke's curse was explosive as he turned and ran to the corner. His hand shook with indignation while it grabbed the telephone from its box. Getting headquarters, he recited his story. He thought he'd a good idea of what had happened, fancied he'd read once of a similar stunt being pulled elsewhere.

"Looks like they cut a disk with a rotary diamond, lifted it out with a suction cup, then fished through the hole with a telescopic rod." He listened a moment, then said, "Yes, yes. That's just what gets me—the rings are worth ten times as much."

His still-startled eyes looked down the street while he paid attention to the voice at the other end of the line. The eyes wandered slowly, descended, found the gutter, remained fixed on the dim shape lying therein. Another dead cat! Still clinging to his phone, Burke moved out as far as the cord would allow, extended a boot, rolled the cat away from the curb. The flash settled on it. Just like the other—ear to ear!

"And listen," he shouted into the phone, "some maniac's wandering around slaughtering cats."

Replacing the phone, he hurried back to the maltreated window, stood guard in front of it until the police car rolled up. Four piled out.

The first said, "Cats! I'll say somebody's got it in for cats! We passed two a couple of blocks away. They were bang in the middle of the street, flat in the headlights, and had been damn near guillotined. Their bodies were still warm."

The second grunted, approached the window, stared at the small, neat hole, and said, "The mob that did this would be too cute to leave a print."

"They weren't too cute to leave the rings," growled Burke.

"Maybe you've got something there," conceded the other. "If they've left the one, they might have left the other. We'll test for prints, anyway."

A taxi swung into the dark street, pulled up behind the police car. An elegantly dressed, fussy, and very agitated individual got out, rushed up to the waiting group. Keys jangled in his pale, moist hand.

"Maley, the manager—you phoned me," he explained, breathlessly. "Gentlemen, this is terrible, terrible! The window show is worth thousands, thousands! What a loss, what a loss!"

"How about letting us in?" asked one of the policemen, calmly.

"Of course, of course."

Jerkily, he opened the gate, unlocked the door, using about six keys for the job. They walked inside. Maley switched on the lights, stuck his head between the plate glass shelves, surveyed the depleted window.

"My watches, my watches," he groaned.

"It's awful, it's awful!" said one of the policemen, speaking with beautiful solemnity. He favored his companions with a sly wink.

Maley leaned farther over, the better to inspect an empty corner, "All gone, all gone," he moaned, "all my show of the finest makes in—Yeeouw!" His yelp made them jump. Maley bucked as he tried to force himself through the obstructing shelves toward the grille and the window beyond it. "My watch! My own watch!"

The others tiptoed, stared over his shoulders, saw the gold buckle of a black velvet fob go through the hole in the window. Burke was the first outside, his ready flash searching the concrete. Then he spotted the watch. It was moving rapidly along, hugging the angle of the wall, but it stopped dead as his beam settled upon it. He fancied he saw something else, equally bright and metallic, scoot swiftly into the darkness beyond the circle of his beam.

Picking up the watch, Burke stood and listened. The noises of the others coming out prevented him from hearing clearly, but he could have sworn he'd heard a tiny whirring noise, and a swift, juicy ticking that was not coming from the instrument in his hand. Must have been only his worried fancy. Frowning deeply, he returned to his companions.

"There was nobody," he asserted. "It must have dropped out of your pocket and rolled."

Damn it, he thought, could a watch roll that far? What the devil was happening this night? Far up the street, something screeched, then it bubbled. Burke shuddered—he could make a shrewd guess at that! He looked at the others, but apparently they hadn't heard the noise.

The papers gave it space in the morning. The total was sixty watches and eight cats, also some oddments from the small stock of a local scientific instrument maker. I read about it on my way down to Burman's place. The details were fairly lavish, but not complete. I got them completely at a later time when we discovered the true significance of what had occurred.

Burman was waiting for me when I arrived. He appeared both annoyed and bothered. Over in the corner, the coffin was ticking away steadily, its noise much louder than it had been the previous day. The thing sounded a veritable hive of industry.

"Well?" I asked.

"It's moved around a lot during the night," said Burman. "It's smashed a couple of thermometers and taken the mercury out of them. I found some drawers and cupboards shut, some open, but I've an uneasy feeling that it's made a thorough search through the lot. A packet of nickel foil has vanished, a coil of copper wire has gone with it." He pointed an angry finger at the bottom of the door through which I'd just entered. "And I blame it for gnawing rat holes in that. They weren't there yesterday."

Sure enough, there were a couple of holes in the bottom of that door. But no rat made those—they were neat and smooth and round, almost as if a carpenter had cut them with a keyhole saw.

"Where's the sense in it making those?" I questioned. "It can't crawl through apertures that size."

"Where's the sense in the whole affair?" Burman countered. He glowered at the busy machine which stared back at him with its expressionless lenses and churned steadily on. *Tick-tick-tick!* persisted the confounded thing. Then, *whir-thump-click!*

I opened my mouth intending to voice a nice, sarcastic comment at the machine's expense when there came a very tiny, very subtle and extremely high-pitched whine. Something small, metallic, glittering shot through one of the rat holes, fled across the floor toward the churning monstrosity. A trapdoor opened and swallowed it with such swiftness that it had disappeared before I realized what I'd seen. The thing had been a cylindrical, polished object resembling the shuttle of a sewing machine, but about four times the size. And it had been dragging something also small and metallic.

Burman stared at me; I stared at Burman. Then he foraged around the laboratory, found a three-foot length of half-inch steel pipe. Dragging a chair to the door, he seated himself, gripped the pipe like a bludgeon, and watched the rat holes. Imperturbably, the machine watched him and continued to *tick-tick-tick.*

Ten minutes later, there came a sudden click and another tiny whine. Nothing darted inward though the holes, but the curious object we'd already seen—or another one exactly like it—dropped out of the trap, scooted to the door by which we were waiting. It caught Burman by surprise. He made a mad swipe with the steel as the thing skittered elusively past his feet and through a hole. It had gone even as the weapon walloped the floor.

"Damn!" said Burman, heartily. He held the pipe loosely in his grip while he glared at the industrious coffin. "I'd smash it to bit except that I'd like to catch one of these small gadgets first."

"Look out!" I yelled.

He was too late. He ripped his attention away from the coffin toward the holes, swinging up the heavy length of pipe, a startled look on his face. But his reaction was far too slow. Three of the little mysteries were through the holes and halfway across the floor before his weapon was ready to swing. The coffin swallowed them with the crash of a trapdoor.

The invading trio had rushed through in single file, and I'd got a better picture of them this time. The first two were golden shuttles, much like the one we'd already seen. The third was bigger, speedier, and gave me the notion that it could dodge around more dexterously. It had a long, sharp projection in front, a wicked, ominous thing like a surgeon's scalpel. Sheer speed deprived me of a good look at it, but I fancied that the tip of the scalpel had been tinged with red. My spine exuded perspiration.

Came an irritated scratching upon the outside of the door and a white-tipped paw poked tentatively through one of the holes. The cat backed to a safe distance when Burman opened the door, but looked lingeringly toward the laboratory. Its presence needed no explaining—the alert animal must have caught a glimpse of those infernal little whizzers. The same thought struck both of us; cats are quick on the pounce, very quick. Given a chance, maybe this one could make a catch for us.

We enticed it in with fair words and soothing noises. Its eagerness overcame its normal caution toward strangers, and it entered. We closed the door behind it; Burman got his length of pipe, sat by the door, tried to keep one eye on the holes and the other on the cat. He couldn't do both, but he tried. The cat sniffed and prowled around, mewed defeatedly. Its behavior suggested that it was seeking by sight rather than scent. There wasn't any scent.

With feline persistence, the animal searched the whole laboratory. It passed the buzzing coffin several times, but ignored it completely. In the end, the cat gave it up, sat on the corner of the laboratory table and started to wash its face.

Tick-tick-tick! went the big machine. Then *whir-thump!* A trap popped open, a shuttle fell out and raced for the door. A second one followed it. The first was too fast even for the cat, too fast for the surprised Burman as well. *Bang!* The length of steel tube came down viciously as the leading shuttle bulleted triumphantly through a hole.

But the cat got the second one. With a mighty leap, paws extended, claws out, it caught its victim one foot from the door. It tried to handle the slippery thing, failed, lost it for an instant. The shuttle whisked around in a crazy loop. The cat got it again, lost it again, emitted an angry snarl, batted it against the skirting board. The shuttle lay there, upside down, four midget wheels in its underside spinning madly with a high, almost inaudible whine.

Eyes alight with excitement, Burman put down his weapon, went to pick up the shuttle. At the same time, the cat slunk toward it ready to play with it. The shuttle lay there, helplessly functioning upon its back, before either could reach it the big machine across the room went *clunk!,* opened a trap and ejected another gadget.

With astounding swiftness, the cat turned and pounced upon the newcomer. Then followed pandemonium. Its prey swerved agilely with a fitful gleam of gold; the cat swerved with it, cursed and spat. Black-and-white fur whirled around in a fighting haze in which gold occasionally glowed; the cat's hissings and spittings overlayed a persistent whine that swelled and sank in the manner of accelerating or decelerating gears.

A peculiar gasp came from the cat, and blood spotted the floor. The animal clawed wildly, emitted another gasp followed by a gurgle. It shivered and flopped, a stream of crimson pouring from the great gash in its gullet.

We'd hardly time to appreciate the full significance of the ghastly scene when the victor made for Burman. He was standing by the skirting board, the still-buzzing shuttle in his hand. His eyes were sticking out with utter horror, but he retained enough presence of mind to make a frantic jump a second before the bulleting menace reached his feet.

He landed behind the thing, but it reversed in its own length and came for him again. I saw the mirrorlike sheen of its scalpel as it banked at terrific speed, and the sheen was drowned in sticky crimson two inches along the blade. Burman jumped over it again, reached the lab table, got up on that.

"Lord!" he breathed.

By this time I'd got the piece of pipe which he'd discarded. I hefted it, feeling its comforting weight, then did my best to bat the buzzing lump of wickedness through the window and over the roofs. It was too agile for me. it whirled, accelerated, dodged the very tip of the descending steel, and flashed twice around the table upon which Burman had taken refuge. It ignored me completely. Somehow, I felt that was responding entirely to some mysterious call from the shuttle Burman had captured.

I swiped desperately, missed it again, though I swear I missed by no more than a millimeter. Something whipped through the holes in the door, fled past me into the big machine. Dimly, I heard traps opening and closing, and beyond all other sounds that steady, persistent *tick-tick-tick*. Another furious blow that accomplished no more than to dent the floor and jar my arm to the shoulder.

Unexpectedly, unbelievably, the golden curse ceased its insane gyrations on the floor and around the table. With a hard click, and a whir much louder than before, it raced easily up one leg of the table and reached the top.

Burman left his sanctuary in one jump. He was still clinging to the shuttle. I'd never seen his face so white.

"The machine!" he said, hoarsely. "Bash it to hell!"

Thunk! went the machine. A trap gaped, released another demon with a scalpel. *Tzz-z-z!* a third shot in through the holes in the door. Four shuttles skimmed through behind it, made for the machine, reached it safely. A fifth came through more slowly. It was dragging an automobile valve spring. I kicked the thing against the wall even as I struck a vain blow at one with a scalpel.

With another jump, Burman cleared an attacker. A second sheared off the toe of his right shoe as he landed. Again he reached the table from which his first toe had departed. All three things with scalpels made for the table with a reckless vim that was frightening.

"Drop that damned shuttle," I yelled.

He didn't drop it. As the fighting trio whirred up the legs, he flung the shuttle with all his might at the coffin that had given it birth. It struck, dented the casing, fell to the floor. Burman was off the table again. The thrown shuttle lay battered and noiseless, its small motive wheels stilled.

The armed contraptions scooting a round the table seemed to change their purpose coincidently with the captured shuttle's smashing. Together, they dived off the table, sped through the holes in the door. A fourth came out of the machine, escorting two shuttles, and those too vanished beyond the door. A second or two later, a new thing, different from the rest, came in through one of the holes. It was long, round-bodied, snub-nosed, about half the length of a policeman's nightstick, had six wheels beneath, and a double row of peculiar serrations in front. It almost sauntered across the room while we watched it fascinatedly. I saw the serrations jerk and shift when it climbed the lowered trap into the machine. They were midget caterpillar tracks!

Burman had had enough. He made up his mind. Finding the steel pipe, he gripped it firmly, approached the coffin. Its lenses seemed to leer at him as he stood before it. Twelve years of intensive work to be destroyed at a blow. Endless days and nights of effort to be undone at one stroke. But Burman was past caring. With a ferocious swing he demolished the glass, with a fierce thrust he shattered the assembly of wheels and cogs behind.

The coffin shuddered and slid beneath his increasingly angry blows. Trapdoors dropped open, spilled out lifeless samples of the thing's metallic brood. Grindings and raspings came from the accursed object while Burman battered it to pieces. Then it was silent, stilled, a shapeless, useless mass of twisted and broken parts.

I picked up the dented shape of the object that had sauntered in. It was heavy, astonishingly heavy, and even after partial destruction its workmanship looked wonderful. It had a tiny, almost unnoticeable eye in front, but the miniature lens was cracked. Had it returned for repairs and overhaul?

"That," said Burman, breathing audibly, "is that!"

I opened the door to see if the noise had attracted attention. It hadn't. There was a lifeless shuttle outside the door, a second a yard behind it. The first had a short length of brass chain attached to a tiny hook projecting from its rear. The nose cap of the second had opened fanwise, like an iris diaphragm, and a pair of jointed metal arms were folded inside, hugging a medium-sized diamond. It looked as if they'd been about to enter when Burman destroyed the big machine.

Picking them up, I brought them in. Their complete inactivity, though they were undamaged, suggested that they had been controlled by the big machine and had drawn their motive power from it. If so, then we'd solved our problem simply, and by destroying the one had destroyed the lot.

Burman got his breath back and began to talk.

He said, "The Robot Mother! That's what I made—a duplicate of the Robot Mother. I didn't realize it, but I was patiently building the most dangerous thing in creation, a thing that is a terrible menace because it shares with mankind the ability to propagate. Thank Heaven we stopped it in time!"

"So," I remarked, remembering that he claimed to have got it from the extreme future, "that's the eventual master, or mistress, of Earth. A dismal prospect for humanity, eh?"

"Not necessarily. I don't know just how far I got, but I've an idea it was so tremendously distant in the future that Earth had become sterile from humanity's viewpoint. Maybe we'd emigrated to somewhere else in the cosmos, leaving our semi-intelligent slave machines to fight for existence or die. They fought—and survived."

"And then wangle things to try and alter the past in their favor," I suggested.

"No, I don't think so." Burman had become much calmer by now. "I don't think it was a dastardly attempt so much as an interesting experiment. The whole affair was damned in advance because success would have meant an impossible paradox. There are no robots in the next century, nor any knowledge of them. Therefore the intruders in this time must have been wiped out and forgotten."

"Which means," I pointed out, "that you must not only have destroyed the machine, but also all your drawings, all your notes, as well as the psychophone, leaving nothing but a few strange events and a story for me to tell."

"Exactly—I shall destroy everything. I've been thinking over the whole affair, and it's not until now I've understood that the psychophone can never be of the slightest use to me. It permits me to discover or invent only those things that history has decreed I shall invent, and which, therefore, I shall find with or without the contraption. I can't play tricks with history, past or future."

"Humph!" I couldn't find any flaw in his reasoning. "Did you notice," I went on, "the touch of bee-psychology in our antagonists? You built the hive, and from it emerged workers, warriors, and"—I indicated the dead saunterer—"one drone."

"Yes," he said, lugubriously. "And I'm thinking of the honey—eighty watches! Not to mention any other items the late papers may report, plus any claims for slaughtered cats. Good thing I'm wealthy."

"Nobody knows you've anything to do with those incidents. You can pay secretly if you wish."

"I shall," he declared.

"Well," I went on, cheerfully, "all's well that ends well. Thank goodness we've got rid of what we brought upon ourselves."

With a sigh of relief, I strolled toward the door. A high whine of midget motors drew my startled attention downward. While Burman and I stared aghast, a golden shuttle slid easily through one of the rat holes, sensed the death of the Robot Mother and scooted back through the other hole before I could stop it.

If Burman had been shaken before, he was doubly so now. He came over to the door, stared incredulously at the little exit just used by the shuttle, then at the couple of other undamaged but lifeless shuttles lying about the room.

"Bill," he mouthed, "your bee analogy was perfect. Don't you understand? There's another swarm! A queen got loose!"

There was another swarm all right. For the next forty-eight hours it played merry hell. Burman spent the whole time down at headquarters trying to convince them that his evidence wasn't just a fantastic story, but what helped him to persuade the police of his veracity was the equally fantastic reports that came rolling in.

To start with, old Gildersome heard a crash in his shop at midnight, thought of his valuable stock of cameras and miniature movie projectors, pulled on his pants and rushed downstairs. A razor-share instrument stabbed him through the right instep when halfway down, and he fell the rest of the way. He lay there, badly bruised and partly stunned, while things clicked, ticked and whirred in the darkness and the gloom. One by one, all the contents of his box of expensive lenses.

went through a hole in the door. A quantity of projector cogs and wheels went with them.

Ten people complained of being robbed in the night of watches and alarm clocks. Two were hysterical. One swore that the bandit was "a six-inch cockroach" which purred like a toy dynamo. Getting out of bed, he'd put his foot upon it and felt its cold hardness wriggle away from beneath him. Filled with revulsion, he'd whipped his foot back into bed "just as another cockroach scuttled toward him." Burman did not tell that agitated complainant how near he had come to losing his foot.

Thirty more reports rolled in next day. A score of houses had been entered and four shops robbed by things that had the agility and furtiveness of rats—except that they emitted tiny ticks and buzzing noises. One was seen racing along the road by a homing railway worker. He tried to pick it up, lost his forefinger and thumb, stood nursing the stumps until an ambulance rushed him away.

Rare metals and fine parts were the prey of these ticking marauders. I couldn't see how Burman or anyone else could wipe them out once and for all, but he did it. He did it by baiting them like rats. I went around with him, helping him on the job, while he consulted a map.

"Every report," said Burman, "leads to this street. An alarm clock that suddenly sounded was abandoned near here. Two automobiles were robbed of small parts near here. Shuttles have been seen going to or from this area. Five cats were dealt with practically on this spot. Every other incident has taken place within easy reach."

"Which means," I guessed, "that the queen is somewhere near this point?"

"Yes." He stared up and down the quiet empty street over which the crescent moon shed a sickly light. It was two o'clock in the morning. "We'll settle this matter pretty soon!"

He attached the end of a reel of firm cotton to a small piece of silver chain, nailed the reel to the wall, dropped the chain on the concrete. I did the same with the movement of a broken watch. We distributed several small cogs, a few clock wheels, several camera fitments, some small, tangled bunches of copper wire, and other attractive oddments.

Three hours later, we returned accompanied by the police. They had mallets and hammers with them. All of us were wearing steel leg-and-foot shields knocked up at short notice by a handy sheet-metal worker.

The bait had been taken! Several cotton strands had broken after being unreeled a short distance, but others were intact. All of them either led to or pointed to a steel grating leading to a cellar below an abandoned warehouse. Looking down, we could see a few telltale strands running through the window frame beneath.

Burman said, "Now!" and we went in with a rush. Rusty locks snapped, rotten doors collapsed, we poured through the warehouse and into the cellar.

There was a small, coffin-shaped thing against one wall, a thing that ticked steadily away while its lenses stared at us with ghastly lack of emotion. It was very similar to the Robot Mother, but only a quarter of the size. In the light of a police torch, it was a brooding, ominous thing of dreadful significance. Around it, an active clan swarmed over the floor, buzzing and ticking in metallic fury.

Amid angry whirs and the crack of snapping scalpels on steel, we waded headlong through the lot. Burman reached the coffin first, crushing it with one mighty blow of his twelve-pound hammer, then bashing it to utter rain with a rapid succession of blows. He finished exhausted. The daughter of the Robot Mother was no more, nor did her alien tribe move or stir.

Sitting down on a rickety wooden case, Burman mopped his brow and said, "Thank heavens that's done!"

Tick-tick-tick!

He shot up, snatched his hammer, a wild look in his eyes.

"Only my watch," apologized one of the policemen. "It's a cheap one, and it makes a hell of a noise." He pulled it out to show the worried Burman.

"Tick! tick!" said the watch, with mechanical aplomb.

Acknowledgments

The following people helped produce this book that you are reading.

Technical help was provided by Mark L. Olson, Tony Lewis, Tim Szczesuil, Deb Geisler, Mike Benveniste, Mark Hertel, Ted Atwood, Dave Anderson, and Alice Lewis.

Proofreading was done by Ann Broomhead, Tim Szczesuil, Mark L. Olson, Dave Anderson, Tony Lewis, Bonnie Atwood, Joe Rico, Mark Hertel, George Flynn, Pam Fremon, Lisa Hertel, Mark Hertel, Suford Lewis, Priscilla Olson, Kelly S. Persons, and Sharon Sbarsky.

The dust jacket design was created by Alice Lewis.

Final copy editing of various portions of the book were done by the following people: George Flynn, Ann Broomhead, Tim Szczesuil, Mark L. Olson and Priscilla Olson.

A very special thanks to Dick Spelman who donated the Del Rey editions that were sacrificed to help produce this book.

The book was set in Adobe Garamond using Adobe Pagemaker and printed by Sheridan Books of Ann Arbor, Michigan, on acid- free paper.

Rick Katze
July, 2001

The following people helped produce the second printing.

Proofreading was done by the following NESFAns: Bonnie Atwood, Gay Ellen Dennett, Pam Fremon, Tony Lewis, Mark L. Olson, Sharon Sbarsky and Tim Szczesuil.

Special thanks to Dave Cortesi who sent in a very useful list of typos from the first printing.

Technical support came from Deb Geisler, Geri Sullivan, Mark L. Olson, Tony Lewis, Mike Benveniste, Dave Anderson and Ted Atwood.

Rick Katze
August 2, 2007

Superlative SF Available
from the NESFA Press

Major Ingredients by Eric Frank Russell..$29

Borders of Infinity by Lois McMaster Bujold $25

From These Ashes by Fredric Brown $29

*A New Dawn: The Don A. Stuart Stories
of John W. Campbell, Jr.* $26

Years in the Making by L. Sprague de Camp $25

The Mathematics of Magic
by L. Sprague de Camp & Fletcher Pratt...$26

First Contacts: The Essential Murray Leinster $25

Here Comes Civilization by William Tenn $29

Immodest Proposals: The Short SF of William Tenn...........................$29

Transfinite: The Essential A. E. van Vogt $29

All titles are hardback unless otherwise noted, and printed on long-life acid-free paper. NESFA Press accepts payment by mail, check, money order, MasterCard, or Visa. Please add $5 postage ($10 for multiple books) for each order. Massachusetts residents please add 5% sales tax. Fax orders (Visa/MC only): (617) 776-3243. Write for our free catalog, or check out our online catalog by directing your Internet web browser to: www.nesfapress.com.

NESFA Press
P.O. Box 809
Framingham, MA 01701
Email: sales@nesfa.org